110638900

RADIANT DAYS,
HAUNTED NIGHTS

RADIANT DAYS,
HAUNTED NIGHTS

GREAT TALES FROM THE TREASURY
OF YIDDISH FOLK LITERATURE

Translated, compiled, and introduced by

JOACHIM NEUGROSCHEL

OVERLOOK DUCKWORTH
NEW YORK • WOODSTOCK • LONDON

First published in 2005 by
Overlook Duckworth, Peter Mayer Publishers, Inc.
Woodstock & New York

NEW YORK:
141 Wooster Street
New York, NY 10012

WOODSTOCK:
One Overlook Drive
Woodstock, NY 12498
www.overlookpress.com

LONDON:
Gerald Duckworth & Co. Ltd.
Greenhill House
90-93 Cowcross Street
London EC1M 6BF

[for individual orders, bulk and special sales, contact our Woodstock office]

Copyright © 2005 by Joachim Neugroschel

All Rights Reserved. No part of this publication may be reproduced or
transmitted in any form or by any means, electronic or mechanical,
including photocopy, recording, or any information storage and
retrieval system now known or to be invented without permission in
writing from the publisher, except by a reviewer who wishes to quote
brief passages in connection with a review written for
inclusion in a magazine, newspaper, or broadcast.

Cataloging-in-Publication Data is available from the Library of Congress

Book design and type formatting by Bernard Schleifer
Manufactured in the United States of America
ISBN 1-58567-731-0 (hc)   ISBN 0-7156-3417-8 (UK hc)
ISBN 1-58567-789-2 (pb)   ISBN 0-7156-3556-5 (UK pb)
1 3 5 7 9 8 6 4 2

CONTENTS

The translator is grateful to Yeshaye Metal (YIVO)
and Aaron Runinstein (National Yiddish Book Center)

INTRODUCTION:
Yiddish Literary Folklore

Folklore, fakelore, folktale, fairy tale, legend, fantasy, saga, fable, myth, mythology, mayse (Yiddish for story, fairy tale, Hasidic wonder tale), Märchen and Hausmärchen and Kindermärchen and Volksmärchen (German for folktale, fairy tale, legend, children's fairy tale), Kunstmärchen (German for artificial fairy tale), midrash (post-Talmudic Biblical exegesis, pronounced medresh in Yiddish), conte de fée (French for fairy tale)—the list seems almost endless, whereby the various terms may overlap and even contradict one another. Furthermore, while I've included some Gentile material that connects with Yiddish material, I've had to exclude Sephardic lore, which barely grazes the Ashkenazi world.

Now, some observers feel that folklore has to be orally transmitted in order to qualify as folklore. The solution seems quite simple: read a story out loud and you've got instant folk literature! Some Old Yiddish stories were meant to be recited or sung to a non-literate audience—for instance, *The Book of Samuel* (Italy, 15th century). But don't forget that, on the other hand, the Yiddish animal fable is more of a written than an oral genre.

Then too, quasi-identical terms mean different things in different cultures:

"The tales of the Grimm Brothers, unlike, say, Andersen's tales, are not individual creations; they are variations of folk stories, of the English term 'folktales' (Erika Timm: *Frau Holle, Frau Percht und verwandte Gestalten*, 2003, p.4)." Studying a folktale means gathering as many versions of it as possible. Erika Timm uses the English term "folktale" in order to avoid the mystical and romantic associations of the German word "Volksmärchen." "It is not 'the' (or 'a') folk that is creative so much as a normally first narrator (who is lost in the mists of time) plus a throng of variation finders. Thus the Volksmärchen, like all Volksliteratur, is a literature that lives in variants."

As described, these concepts may vary in goal and substance. The discovery and/or invention of folkore is often a discovery and/or invention of a nation's real or imagined past. The Yiddish writer S. Ansky—like so many others—feverishly collected folk wares and folktales in an effort to give Yiddish and Jewish culture a tradition that was not limited to the millennia of religious material.

On the other hand, some observers claim that Jewish folklore began with the Jewish Bible. While this may disturb religious fundamentalists (Jewish and Gentile), it does create a national tradition—much as the fundamentalists have done. Take Susan Niditch (*Underdogs and Tricksters. A Prelude to Biblical Folklkore,* 1987, p. xi):

"The Hebrew Bible is rich in underdog tales. . . . The trickster is a subtype of the underdog. A fascinating and universal folk hero, the trickster brings about change . . . via trickery. . . . The underdog and the trickster are traditional characters in a broad, cross-cultural literary corpus. . . . Throughout its history Israel has had a peculiar self-image as the underdog and the trickster."

There are many other features that distinguish Jewish and then Yiddish folklore. S. Ansky, for instance, claims that Jewish folk heroes are more spiritual, Gentile folk heroes more physical. This may certainly be true in many modern Yiddish folk tales, but it misses the mark in Old Yiddish epics like *The Bovo Book.* The title character, Bovo, can be terribly cruel and ferocious—as are the Jewish protagonists of other stories going back to the Bible and surviving in late medieval Yiddish adaptations.

Yiddish, some people say, is a pop language. And this may apply despite the sophistication of Yiddish language and literature—even today. Yiddish Modernism partially implies the very use of Yiddish itself as a "folk" vernacular, as an effort to give Yiddish the stature of modern European and American culture.

The fact remains that so many Yiddish realists have inserted a folktale, a fantasy, a myth into their otherwise realistic fiction. And by the same token, Yiddish translators have produced Yiddish versions of tales from the Bible, the Talmud, and the Midrash. These versions, handed down and even poeticized in rhymes and meters, have become a staple of Yiddish literature. They form part of the efforts to reach women and some men, who do not know Hebrew and Aramaic. As such, they can be treated as bridges between the Holy Tongues and the Yiddish vernacular—translating and popularizing.

My overall aim in this collection is to show the enormous breadth and depth of mostly identified Yiddish "folk" literature from its roots to its full modern blossoming—however "folk" may be defined. I've deliberately used a few stories that may not always lend themselves to treatment as folk material, but that someone, somewhere, will accept as folk substance. I've also arranged these works in such a manner that each piece should define itself and help to define or challenge the other works.

All in all, I've ignored material that I employed in my earlier anthologies, and I've tried as far as possible to include authors that I've not utilized elsewhere.

You may or may not accept most of these stories as folklore or as works containing folklore—but I hope you'll at least enjoy them either way.

Belle Harbor, February 2004

ANONYMOUS

In Genesis (22:1–13), we are told that, in order to test Abraham's loyalty, God commands him to sacrifice his beloved son Isaac. The father complies and is about to slaughter his son when God, seeing that Abraham does indeed fear Him, sends an angel to stop the father, who then offers up a ram instead.

"The Binding of Isaac" has been often dealt with in religious texts as well as in Jewish folklore. However, a very different outcome is described in the Hebrew Midrash (post-Talmudic legend) titled "Vayosha" (Rescue), a twelfth-century homiletic text that has been the basis of several Yiddish adaptations.

For a thorough scholarly treatment that includes a Romanization of two texts about Abraham's sacrifice, see Wulf-Otto Dreessen: *Akedass Jizhak* (in German).

THE SONG OF ISAAC
(1510/11)
(Mantua and Brescia, Italy)

IT IS WRITTEN:

Abraham got up in the morning and saddled his donkey, then set out with two boys as well as his son Isaac.

Isaac said to his father: "Where are we going?"

His father replied: "Dear son, we are going to make a burnt offering."

Isaac then said to his father: "We have the fire and the wood, but where is the lamb for the sacrifice?"

Isaac instantly realized what his father had in mind: he wanted to slaughter his son. So Isaac said: "Since the Creator Blessed Be His Name has chosen me, I will do His will."

As they were walking along, Satan, disguised as an old man, came up to Abraham and said: "Abraham, where are you going?"

Abraham said: "I am going to pray."

Satan then said: "Why are you carrying the fire and the wood and the slaughtering knife?"

Abraham replied: "We may be traveling for a day or two, so we will slaughter and roast and eat."

Satan responded: "Ah, you poor old fool. Why do you want to doom such a beautiful child, a boy whom the Creator Blessed Be His Name gave you when you were a hundred years old?"

Abraham replied: "I am acting according to His will."

When Satan saw that he was getting nowhere with Abraham, he transformed himself into a young boy, then went over to Isaac and said: "Tell me, you young and beautiful child, where do you want to go?"

Isaac replied: "I want to go and study the Torah."

Satan replied: "My dear boy, I feel sorry for you because your father wants to destroy you."

Isaac said: "I have given my life to the Creator Blessed Be His name, let Him do with it whatever he wishes."

When Satan saw that he was getting nowhere with Isaac either, he went to Sarah and said to her: "Where are Abraham, your husband, and your son, Isaac?"

Sarah said to him: "They have gone to study the Torah."

Satan said to her: "Oh, you poor old fool. Abraham, your husband, has gone to slaughter your only son, Isaac!"

But she refused to believe him.

When Satan saw that he was getting nowhere with any of them, he transformed himself into a large brook, which Abraham had to cross.

Abraham came to the water and he said to his son Isaac: "Wait till I see whether the water is deep or not." Abraham went halfway across the brook, and the water was only up to his knees. So he told his son Isaac: "Follow me and don't be afraid."

Isaac obeyed. But when he walked through the water, it came up to his neck.

When Abraham saw this, he shouted: "Dear Lord God, You should know that I wanted to do Your will, and now we are going to drown. Who shall declare that You are One in this world?"

Thereupon, the Creator Blessed Be His Name shouted at Satan and made the brook run dry [. . .]

Abraham went to the sacrificial place and built an altar, and Isaac himself arranged the rocks and the wood. He then said: "Dear Father, bind my hands and my feet, for I am a young boy of thirty, and you are old. And once I [see] the slaughtering knife, I might not easily lie still. And make sure that you burn me up and reduce me to ashes. And bring the ashes to Sarah, my mother." Isaac then went on: "Dear Father! Once you have slaughtered me and burned me up and you go to my mother, how will you explain my absence? And what will you do in your old age?"

Abraham said: "Dear son! We know that we won't live much longer than you. The same [God] Who has comforted us since you were born, He will continue to comfort us."

Now Abraham took Isaac and threw him on the altar and pressed his knee into Isaac's chest and took hold of the slaughtering knife. When Isaac saw this, he shouted: "Who will go and tell my mother Sarah that my father has slaughtered me?"

At this point, the angels began to weep, and their tears dropped on the knife, so that Abraham was unable to slaughter his son.

But then he placed the knife on Isaac's throat—Isaac's soul promptly left him, and he died.

Now the Creator Blessed Be His Name said to the archangel Michael: "Go and bring him back to life!"

[. . .] Praised be our Lord God, who brings the dead back to life.

That same moment, Abraham raised his eyes and saw a ram with beautiful horns. He took it and sacrificed it in place of his son. And when he had slaughtered it and offered it up, Abraham said: "Instead of my son! Instead of my son!" Then Abraham went on: "Dear Lord God! If ever my children are in difficulty, then think about the sufferings that I and my son have endured! That should be as I stand before You. Amen selah!"

GLIKL BAS YUDA LEIB
(1645-1724)

In her untitled and uncategorized memoirs (1691–1719), Glikl, one of the earliest women writers in Yiddish, weaves in some two dozen narratives—stories, fables, parables, fairy tales—from a variety of often unidentified sources. The main goal of these narratives, like that of the overall text, is to both edify and entertain and particularly to drive home a moral point that Glikl discusses both before and after telling the story. For a detailed study of the author and her time, see *The Hamburg Businesswoman Glikl* (in German; Christians Verlag, Hamburg 2001). This scholarly collection includes Erika Timm's exciting analysis of Glikl's language and Chava Turniansky's fascinating study of Glikl's opus within contemporary Yiddish literature. Turniansky has also penned a Yiddish examination of Glikl's literary sources (*Studies in Jewish Culture in Honour of Chone Shmeruk*, pp. 153–177).

My collection here offers all of Glikl's stories except for "The Pious Jew" (included in *No Star Too Beautiful: A Treasury of Yiddish Stories*) and the second and identical version of "The Philosopher on the Roof."

Glikl's sources and quotations, often not identified, are hard to track down. The first story, brief as it is, requires an explanation that becomes longer than the piece itself.

KING DAVID AND THE TRIO

*E*VERYTHING THAT GOD HAS CREATED He has created solely for His own glory, and [according to the rabbis] "the world will be built with mercy." We know that God—Blessed Be His Name—has created and done everything purely out of grace and mercy, Because God—Blessed Be His Name—does not need a single one of His creatures. But since God Blessed Be He has indeed created so many different things, they all exist only for His glory; and He has created them out of grace and mercy so that they may be useful to us sinful human beings. For everything that has been created is useful to us human beings even though we cannot grasp it or grapple with it.

King David (may he rest in peace) once asked: "Why were a fool and a wasp and a spider created?" He wondered to whom this trio could be useful. But in the end, he realized that these three creatures were useful to him because God used them to keep King David alive, as is described in the Book of Kings. If you wish to know this, you can read about it in the twenty-four books of the Bible. We all know how much grief, misery, and anxiety we sinful human beings endure in this transitory world.

[Editor's note: According to *Otzar ha-Midrashim* (a post-Talmudic collection of Biblical exegeses), David was asking God to whom a fool, a wasp, and a spider might be useful. Along came a fool clutching a stick, with which he then killed a wasp and a spider. When David was being pursued by King Saul, he hid in a cave, where a spider then wove a web across the entrance; the web fooled Saul into thinking that nobody could be hidden there. One night later, David stole into Saul's tent to cut off a lock of the king's hair so that he might subsequently show Saul that he, David, had spared the king's life. But when David tried to leave the tent, the entrance was now blocked by a gigantic general. However, a wasp flew over and stung the sleeping giant, whose now relaxed legs enabled David to escape.]

A SHIP AT SEA

MY DEAR CHILDREN, we have our holy Torah, which can help us understand everything that is useful to us. . . . Let me explain:

A ship was once carrying people across the ocean. One passenger went to the side of the ship and bent deep over the railing and tumbled into the water. He could have drowned. But the skipper spotted the man. He threw him a lot of rope and told him that if he held tight to the rope, he wouldn't drown. And that is our situation, the situation of us sinful human beings, in this world: it is exactly as if we were floating at sea. We are not certain for even a second that we will not drown. Still, God the Almighty created us with grace and mercy so that we may be completely without sin. However, when Adam sinned, the Evil Spirit defeated us. So God created a huge number of armies and angels to carry out His will; and they have no Evil Spirit, they do only good. That is why God created cattle, beasts, and fowl, and all kinds of other creatures, which have only the Evil Spirit and know nothing about doing good.

Now God created human beings in His own image, and, like the angels, they have the power to reason. However, we human beings are given a choice; we can do as we wish: evil, God preserve us, or good. But our great, gracious, kind God, in His mercy, has thrown out rope for us to hold tight to. This rope is our holy Torah, which guides all of us so that we may not drown. And it tells us how great our power is to do as we wish.

THE PHYSICIAN AND THE SEVEN HERBS

*E*VERYTHING WE HAVE IS A GIFT of God's vast grace and mercy. Lucky the man whom God punishes in this world, and we should accept His punishment with love. You can learn that in this tale of a physician, a tale I found in a book by the gaon Rabbi Abraham son of Sabbatai Levi.

There was once a king who had a court physician. The physician was very learned and he was held in very high esteem by the king. But then one day, the physician did something wrong against him. The king was furious and he ordered his men to punish the physician and torture him with irons on his neck and his feet, to strip off his fine garments and put him in coarse, prickly clothes, and to feed him only a piece of barley bread and a little water. The king stationed his men around the prison and told them to pay strict attention to whatever the physician said. After several days, they were to repeat to the king whatever the prisoner uttered.

When the guards then reported to the king, they said: "We've heard nothing from the physician because he hasn't said a word. All this while, we've only sensed that he is very learned."

After keeping the physician in prison for a long time, the king sent for the physician's relatives. When they arrived, they were greatly frightened and trembling because they were worried about the physician and they believed that the king planned to notify them about the physician's death. But when they appeared before the king, he ordered them to go to the prison, to their relative, the physician, and talk to him: perhaps his words would appeal to the king and pass into his ears.

So the relatives went to the physician in the prison and they started talking to him:

"Our lord and kinsman, we are very upset to see your body suffering in this prison and to see them punishing and torturing you with irons on your neck and feet, and instead of various fine dishes that you used to eat, you are merely fed a piece of barley bread, and instead of the best wines that you used to drink, you receive merely a little water. Our lord and kinsman always used to wear silk and satin, and today we see that he is wearing nothing but coarse, prickly woolens. But what truly astounds us is that despite all these afflictions, our lord's face hasn't changed, the flesh on his body hasn't diminished, and he is as strong as ever. Just as our lord and kinsman looked in his good times, that is how we find him now. We beg our lord to tell us how he can endure his great sorrows and all these afflictions, which haven't damaged him or haven't indicated any damage."

The physician replied:

"My dear kinsmen! When I arrived in prison, I brought along seven kinds of herbs, which I mixed together and ground down, and I made them into a potion. I have a sip or two of this potion every day, and that helps to prevent my appearance from changing, my flesh from diminishing, my strength from fading, and it helps me endure my afflictions and keep me content."

His relatives then said to the physician:

"Our lord and kinsman! We beg you: please tell us which herbs you have put into your potion. Some day, one of us may have to endure the terrible afflictions that you are suffering. If that occurs, we would like to make that potion in hopes that we won't die from those terrible afflictions and sufferings."

The physician replied:

"My dear kinsmen, I will tell you!

"The first herb is my faith that God will protect me against all my afflictions and sufferings, no matter how terrible they are, and He will also shield me against the king's hand. For the king's heart is in God's hand. The king has to carry out what God Blessed Be His Name wishes.

"The second herb is the hope and the good advice that I give myself to help me put up with everything and endure all my sufferings. And that is good advice for me, so that I won't get lost in my sorrows.

"The third herb is my knowledge that I have sinned and that I have been imprisoned and suffer my great afflictions and torments all because of my sins, so that I alone bear the guilt. Why should I be impatient or lament? After all, the Bible says: 'Your sins have separated you from your God.' And our sages have also said that no afflictions come upon a man unless he has sinned.

"The fourth herb is as follows. If I did lose my patience and refuse to endure my afflictions and sufferings, and if I were discontent with them, what could I say or do? Would that change matters any? Things could be much worse. If the king ordered his men to kill me, then I would die before my time and I would lose everything, just as King Solomon says: 'Better a live dog than a dead lion.'

"The fifth herb is the knowledge that God is punishing me for my own good with harsh and heavy afflictions, expecting me to free myself from my sins in this world so that I will be worthy of the next world, as the Bible says: 'Fortunate the man whom God punishes with afflictions.' So I delight in my sufferings, and with this delight, I bring a great goodness into the world. As we are told: 'Any man who delights in his afflictions brings redemption into the world.'

"The sixth herb is my delight in my share, and I thank and praise God for that. After all, I could suffer even greater pains with iron bands, and they could beat me and whip me with sticks and rods, and cause other pains that could be worse than death. I now eat barley bread. But if the king wished, they could give me nothing to eat—no barley bread and no wheat bread. Now the king lets me have a little water. If the king wished, they could give me nothing to drink. Now my clothes are made of coarse, prickly wool. If the king wished, I could go about stark naked in summer and winter. And they could even inflict such great sufferings on me that when it was day I could wish for night and when it was night I could wish for day. That's why I put up with these afflictions.

"The seventh herb indicates that 'God's help can come at any moment,' because God is merciful and gracious and He knows what bad things He inflicts on a human being and He thinks about them before sending them to a human being. And God can draw a person out of his misery and He can heal his pains and sufferings.

"And so, dear kinsmen, I've found the seven herbs and I've been using them. They have preserved my appearance and my strength. And that is why every God-fearing person should accept God's punishment willingly and joyfully. For these sufferings are a redemption for his body and they bring him the right to enjoy the everlasting next world, and they assure him that God will give him all good things because he relies on his Creator."

And that is what we can learn from this tale.

THE BIRD FATHER AND HIS CHILDREN

IN HIS MERCY, GREAT AND KINDLY God has parents love their children and help them on the right path. And when their children see their parents guiding them, they do the same for their own children. Here is a parable about that.

Once there was a bird, and he had three young birds. And they were on the edge of the sea. All at once, the old bird saw a great wind rising, and the ocean grew stormier and stormier, and the waves washed across the beach. The father bird then said to his children:

"If we don't instantly fly to the other shore, we'll be doomed."

But the young birds couldn't fly as yet. So the father held one young bird between his feet and flew over the ocean. Halfway across the ocean, the father said to his son:

"My child, what anguish have I suffered for you, and now I'm risking my life for your sake! When I grow old, will you do good for me and take care of me in my old age?"

"My dearest father, get me across the water. When you are old, I'll do anything you ask of me!"

After hearing those words, the old bird threw his son into the ocean, and the young bird drowned. The father said:

"That's what we do to a liar like yourself!"

Next the old bird flew back and took hold of the second little bird. And when they were halfway across the ocean, the old bird asked his son the same thing he had asked his first child. And the son likewise told him that he would do everything in the world for him, just as the first little bird had told his father. And the father likewise threw this second child into the ocean:

"You're a liar too!"

And he flew back to the shore and took hold of the third child, and when he was halfway across the ocean with his third son, he likewise said to him:

"My child, you know how greatly I've suffered for you and risked my whole life for your sake. Now when I get old and can't move, will you also do good for me and take care of me in my old age just as I've taken care of you in your childhood?"

The young bird answered his father:

"My dear father, everything you say is true—you've suffered great misery and anguish because of me, and it's my duty to pay you back if possible. But I can't promise this for certain. When I have children of my own some day, I will take care of them just as you have been taking care of me."

The father replied:

"You're saying the right thing and you're intelligent too. I'll carry you all the way across the water and allow you to live."

From this we can see clearly that even though God has created birds without minds, He has inspired them to bring up their children correctly. And we also see how great the efforts that parents make for their children and raise them with utmost care. But if the children had all that anguish and misery from their parents, they would quickly grow tired of all that.

THE MOUNTAIN OF SAND

İF YOU HAVE OTHER PEOPLE'S MONEY or goods in your hands, you have to guard them even more carefully than your own so that you won't do someone else an injustice—God forbid! For that is the first question you are asked in the afterlife: Were you honest in your business dealings and did you work hard rather than—God forbid—rob and steal a great deal of money so that you could give your children large dowries and leave them large inheritances?

Unhappy the wicked who, for the wealth of their children, lose out on the afterlife, since these parents do not know whether such robbed and stolen money will endure with their children; and even if it should, it can last only for a time but not forever. And why should a man sell this life for the next? If people try to flatten a huge mountain of sand by removing only a few grains every day, they nevertheless hope that they will eventually remove the entire mountain. But—God forbid—to lose eternity, that is, the afterlife—this must be thoroughly pondered and lamented if we are not careful.

ALEXANDER THE GREAT AND THE EASILY SATISFIED SAGES

WHO OF US WOULD WANT TO LIVE the kind of life that is described in the stories about Alexander the Great? Men who were considered great sages lived in a certain country. They themselves spurned the entire world; they ate only what was grown by nature and they drank only water. They never fought or hated one another and they wore no garments.

Alexander the Great, who, as we know, conquered the entire world, heard a great deal about those people, about their lifestyle and their wisdom. So he sent out his envoys, summoning those people to appear before him and to ask their lord and king for grace. If they refused, he would wipe them all out.

And these people told the envoys:

"We come nowhere and we go nowhere. We do not leave our land. We do not yearn for silver and gold. We are content with what God gives us and what nature brings forth. If your king wants to come here because we refuse to leave, and if he wishes to kill us all, then let him do so. For that, he needs no weapons since we will not resist him and we are not concerned about our lives, for we do not live until we are dead. But if your king wishes to come here in peace and hear about our customs and our wisdom, we would be very glad."

Alexander's envoys returned to him and told him everything. The king, together with his finest nobles, prepared for the trip, set out, and arrived in that land. He spent several days there, listening to those sages and learning great wisdom. And he became friends with them and wanted to give them great gifts. But they didn't want anything and they said:

"We don't need any money, any silver, any gold. Nature gives us all we require."

King Alexander replied:

"Tell me what you would like to have, and I'll give you anything."

They all cried out:

"Your majesty, give us eternal life."

The king replied:

"How can I give you eternal life? If I could give that, I would give it to myself!"

The sages then said:

"Now, Your Majesty, think it over carefully, for you know that everything the king does, all his straining and striving, to wipe out so many people and countries—he can hold on to them for only a short while but not for all eternity. What good does it do the king? Why did he do all those things?"

The king was at a loss for words. But then he said:

"That was how I found the world and that is how I have to leave it. A king's heart must engage in warfare."

I, Glikl, am not saying that this is a true story. For all I know, it may be an idolatrous fable. I have written it down here to entertain myself and also to show that there are people in the world who do not care about wealth and who always rely on their Creator.

THE PHILOSOPHER ON THE ROOF

W E HAVE NO ONE TO RELY ON but our Father in Heaven, and every person thinks that his own troubles are the worst.

A philosopher once went out into the street. There he ran into a friend, who loudly complained about the troubles and hardships he had to endure. The philosopher then said:

"Come with me and let's go up to the roof back here."

They went up, and from the roof they could see all the houses in the city. The philosopher then said to his friend:

"Come here, my friend! I want to show you the insides of all the houses in the city. They are filled with troubles and hardships. This house has misery and suffering, and that one has trouble and hardship. My friend, take all your troubles and hardships and throw them among all these houses and pick out any house. . . ."

In short, the philosopher showed his friend that all the houses in the city were filled with misery and suffering.

The friend observed and studied everything and he saw that all the houses had as much as if not more agony and sorrow, and that he would do best to stick to his own misery. And that is what the well-known proverb says:

> The world is full of misery,
> Each man finds his own agony.
> Well, what should we do? If we call upon God with all our hearts . . .
> He will soon send us our just Redeemer. . . . Amen. God's will be done.

EMPRESS IRENE OF CONSTANTINOPLE AND CHARLEMAGNE

AT THIS POINT I WOULD LIKE TO TELL you a lovely story about what happened to an empress and how she patiently endured her suffering.

Emperor Charlemagne was a powerful emperor, as is written in all the German books. He had no wife. So he and his advisors decided that he ought to marry Empress Irene of the Orient: she had no husband and she ruled the entire Oriental empire all by herself.

Emperor Charlemagne sent the empress quite a sizeable delegation, asking for her hand in marriage. He hoped that the Oriental empire and the German empire would thereby live in love, friendship, and unity. So his ambassadors were sent to the empress in Constantinople, requesting that she become Charlemagne's wife and that there should be lasting peace between their two lands. The empress was not against the proposal. She told the delegation that she would respond in several days. The emperor's envoys were delighted and they looked forward to bringing the emperor a huge treasure very soon and enjoying a great celebration in the city of Constantinople, which would welcome them with open arms. So they waited for the empress's final answer.

But—my God!—what a profound change the pious empress suffered during those few short days! Instead of what the envoys expected to hear very soon about the proposed marriage, they had to see a dismal event with their own eyes: in their presence, Empress Irene was expelled from her imperial throne and no longer permitted to rule. For a Constantinople patrician named Nikiphoros had built up a large following and now he declared himself emperor. He was joined by all the imperial servants and he quickly got himself crowned. Right after his coronation, he tried to sweet-talk Empress Irene with lovely words that came from a false heart. He apologized profusely, claiming that everything had happened against his will, and that nothing could be dearer to him than to return to his lower status and continue serving her as befits a servant. But the highest aristocrats had wanted her to retire and to be relieved of the heavy burden of ruling as empress over the entire land and the entire population. So they had resolved to place upon him the heavy yoke of ruling the empire. And even though he felt unworthy of that title, he had finally agreed to abide by their decision and he had taken the crown in order to prevent great misery and all sorts of ill-fated agony. He hoped that this would not cause her any distress and that she would not obscure any imperial secrets or conceal any imperial treasures. He also refused to allow anyone to do her the slightest harm or injury. On the contrary: he would rule in such a way as to make her popular and beloved.

Empress Irene replied:

"Dear Nikiphoros! God, Who rules over all human kingdoms and empires, allotting them as He sees fit and enthroning or dethroning whomever He wishes, placed me, His unworthy and completely undeserving servant, on this supreme and honorable rank, graciously keeping me here. But now, because of my many sins and misdeeds, He has suddenly deprived me of the empire and all my power, yet I must still praise His Name forever. As a righteous woman, I have to repeat what Job said in his suffering: 'The Lord God giveth, the Lord taketh away, blessed be the name of the Lord!'

"Now if you have attained this high rank in an honest way, then you alone are responsible for this and you will eventually have to account to God. As for what has happened to me on several occasions, I know that best. Nor did I lack the means to resist your aristocrats in due time and to treat you like so many others who have dared to make the same effort. Nevertheless, because of my mildness, I alone have caused this transformation and I have helped to bring about what I see with my own eyes and what can no longer be changed. I therefore beg you with all my heart to spare me and to grant me the right to spend the rest of my days in peace and quiet, within this palace, which I myself had built."

Nikiphoros declared that he was willing to grant her wishes if she would swear a sacred oath that she would show him all the imperial treasures, hand them over to him, and conceal nothing from him. But after she swore an oath and handed him all the imperial treasures, Nikiphoros, in the presence of Charlemagne's envoys, banished her to a life of misery on the isle of Lesbos, where she died of grief several years later.

This story teaches us that if such misfortune was inflicted on an empress, who endured all her sorrows with patience, then every human being should be patient in a terrible plight and he should patiently endure everything that God sends him, as I have written earlier.

RABBI YOKHANAN AND HIS CHILD

*E*VERYTHING THAT OUR GREAT GOD does is just. . . .

As I have said a few times and our sages—Blessed Be their memory—have written: Rabbi Yokhanan was a great Tanait [Talmudic scholar]. However, during his lifetime, nine of his sons passed away, and in the rabbi's old age only a three-year-old boy was left.

Now one day, his servants, who were doing the laundry, put a cauldron filled with water over a fire, and the water began to seethe and bubble and it boiled over. Next to the cauldron there was a bench on which the servants were to place the laundry. They sat the child on the bench and forgot all about him. The boy then stood up on the bench and tried to peer into the cauldron as a child will do. But the bench tilted over, and the child tumbled into the boiling water. The child screamed and yammered, so that all the terrified servants and the father dashed over to the cauldron. The father wanted to pull out the child, but all that remained was a finger, for the child was boiled through and through. The father smashed his head against the wall, then he raced over to the study house and yelled at his students:

"Grieve for my destiny, which has brought me so much sorrow! This is the bone of my dead child, whom I have sacrificed to God!"

From then on, Rabbi Yokhanan wore the child's finger on his neck as a keepsake, and whenever he was visited by an unknown Talmudist, he would show him the bone very calmly as if showing him his child.

And now, my dear children, if that happened to that pious and decent man, what can happen to someone else? For Rabbi Yokhanan was a great sage. He studied the Bible and the Talmud; and he also understood the Cabala and the essence of Creation, and he could summon angels and devils. He was a great Cabalist. . . . Despite all that, he was afflicted with misery, yet he remained pious until his death.

THE JOYS OF THE BODY

*G*RIEF WEAKENS THE BODY. But why grieve? It does no good. We sicken our bodies, and if our bodies are sad, we cannot serve God properly. For the holy divine spirit does not rest on a sad body. Long ago, when the prophets wanted the holy spirit to rest on them, they had all sorts of musicians play for them so that their bodies would be joyful. These things are described in our sacred books.

KING DAVID AND HIS CHILD

DURING YOUR FATHER'S LIFETIME, I, your mother, lost a barely three-year-old child, who, as I have written, was without his equal. I am not intelligent enough to have recalled our pious King David: his first child with Bathsheba fell ill, and during the boy's illness, the king showed his grief with fasts, prayers, and charity. Nevertheless, God took the child. The king's servants held their tongues and kept the death a secret, for they said:

"The king was profoundly anguished when the child lay ill and there was some hope of recovery. But what will the king do now when he learns that the child is dead and that there is not the faintest hope of recovery?"

So none of them wanted to tell him the tragic news. However, because of their silence, the pious king realized that the child was dead. He then asked his servants whether the child had died. No one replied. So he understood that his darling child was dead. The king stood up from his ashes, demanded water, and ordered his servants to bring him food and drink, and he then ate and drank. His servants were dumbfounded. Finally, one of them took heart and said:

"Your Majesty, when your child was alive, you were filled with anguish, you didn't eat or drink, and you sat in ashes day and night. But as soon as you heard that your son had died, you accepted the judgment as just, as it should be, you said: 'Blessed is the True Judge. The Lord giveth and the Lord taketh away, Blessed Be the Name of the Lord.' Then you instantly stood up and called for food and drink, as if the child were still alive."

The king said to them:

"Let me tell you, my loyal servants, that when the child was ill and still had his soul, I did everything—I wept and wailed, I repented, I prayed, I gave alms. I thought to myself: Maybe God will take pity and make my child recover. But now that everything has failed, and God has taken back what He put in my care, what good is weeping and wailing? My child will not come back to us. We have to go to him."

You can see how pious King David acted. We can learn from him and we can leave everything up to our dear God, for it is certain that we have committed great sins.

HILLEL, JOSEPH, ELIEZER

GOD HUMBLES ONE MAN and raises another. That is why everyone should be careful, especially people with money: they should not eternally devote themselves to their business day and night, they should study the holy texts and not forget our sacred Torah. As it is written: "Many thoughts are in the human heart, but only God's care—it is eternal. Now "hye," the Hebrew word for "it," is made up of the initial letters of the names Hillel, Joseph, and Eliezer. And I have heard an interpretation of those three letters.

When the Redeemer of the Jewish people comes, God will sit in judgment over all poor people and ask them why they haven't studied the Torah in this world.

And a poor man will reply:

"Lord of the Universe, you know very well that I was poor and that I had to strain to keep my wife and children alive."

And the Lord of the Universe will say:

"Were you poorer than Hillel? After all, it is written that all those who wanted to study in the study house had to give the beadle a penny every day. One Friday, good Hillel wished to go to synagogue, but he didn't have the penny for the beadle. So he climbed up and clung to the window, waiting to hear the Talmudic passage. Meanwhile, a thick snow began falling and it completely covered Hillel, alas. The Sabbath was coming, and the worshipers couldn't understand why it had gotten so dark. So they went out into the street to have a look. There they saw good Hillel, alas, totally buried in snow. He was frozen. So they told the beadle to start a fire quickly and put Hillel next to it so that he might regain consciousness.

"But it's Sabbath!"

To which the sages replied:

"Hillel is worth breaking the Sabbath for."

And Hillel regained consciousness.

That is why the Celestial Court condemns paupers who fail to study the Torah or fail to do good deeds. Hillel was so poor that he didn't even have a penny for the beadle; nevertheless, he did not fail to study the Torah. Indeed, Hillel was so fine a scholar that, had he wanted to profit from his studies in this world by receiving gifts from people, they would have filled his home with gold and silver, for, as we know, he was one of the greatest Talmudists. But all he desired was to study the Torah. He put up with his poverty and totally relied on God. That is why the poor can be held responsible for their failings.

Next, the Celestial Court will judge the wicked, who had a good time in this world, chasing after harlots, preening themselves for these loose women, and committing all kinds of sins. They too will be brought before the Celestial Court and asked:

"Why did you do so many evil things and chase after harlots?"

One sinner will reply:

"God! I was a handsome man, and so the Evil Spirit led me astray, women lusted after me, and I had to give in to their lust."

He will then be told:

"Were you any handsomer than Virtuous Joseph? Were you more attractive than Joseph? He lived in the house of his master's wife, and, at every dusk and every dawn, she sent him a white shirt and a gold comb for combing his hair; and she sent him many other fine inducements to excite him with words. But Virtuous Joseph refused her, he subdued his Evil Spirit because he did not want to defile himself, for it is written [Gen. 39:10]: 'He hearkened not unto her, to lie by her, or to be with her.' This means that he refused to lie with her in this world so that he would not be with her in the next world. And that is why Joseph was, alas, so wretchedly thrown into prison. He might even have lost his life. But he refused to submit to his Evil Spirit. This teaches us that the wicked are responsible for their sins."

Why should I keep writing and writing? After all, our sages recorded these things long ago in their books of ethics.

After the sinners, the Celestial Court will judge the big, fat, rich men, who spent their entire lives eating well and drinking well, but ignoring God and His commandments. And when the court will ask them why they never studied the Torah and never did a good deed, they will reply that because of their wealth and business, they had no time for those things. The court will then ask them:

"Were you wealthier than the high priest, Eliezer the son of Charsom? He had so many inland towns and coastal towns, and so many ships plying the sea. Yet his wealth never prevented him from studying the Torah."

This means that the wealthy are responsible for their actions. And we can clearly see that our excuses will be of little use to us in the afterlife. It is best to follow the precept: "Thou must cleave entirely to the Lord Thy God."

CROESUS AND SOLON

LET NO MAN SAY HE IS HAPPY until his death. In regard to that, let me tell you a story.

Once there was a mighty king named Croesus, who kept a philosopher named Solon in his court. The king greatly esteemed this philosopher, who was truly a great sage.

Now one day, when King Croesus had a great celebration, he put on his royal garments and ordered his entire court to pay him homage in the finest clothes. He then opened his treasuries and brought out his most precious jewels, after which he summoned the philosopher. When Solon entered the court, he bowed and knelt before King Croesus, as was appropriate.

The king said to the philosopher: "My dear Solon! You've had a good look at our wealth, our honors, and our splendors. Have you ever in your life seen a happier man than I?"

"Your Gracious Majesty, I've viewed and pondered everything, but I cannot say that you are happier than a certain man who was a citizen of Athens. This citizen had ten children, whom he raised properly. He was very rich, and he honorably turned his children into great men. They were loyal to their country and loyal to him. And not only was the citizen held in high regard, but he also found the same splendor and riches and honor in his children until he reached old age. And thus he also died happily. I feel that that man was happier than Your Royal Majesty. It is true that you have vast riches and splendor and honor, but Your Majesty is still a young king, and there is no telling what will happen to you in the end. It may even happen that another king or another prince will fight a war with you, he may conquer you and drive you away from your wealth, drive you from your country and your men and perhaps even kill you. What do you know of happiness if your end, God forbid, is miserable and unhappy?"

King Croesus said:

"Solon, what's gotten into you—comparing an ordinary mortal with Our Majesty?"

"Your Royal Majesty! I've done so because that man died happily, and no man should boast of being happy until he has witnessed the end. Perhaps—and I wish it—the king will remain happy until his death. But then again, perhaps what I've said to Your Majesty may come to pass."

The king was furious! He grabbed his gold staff, hit Solon, and ordered him never to enter his court again.

So good Solon went away.

A few years later, King Croesus was still living in his splendor and happiness and he never thought about his good, wise philosopher. But after a time, a border dispute arose [with a neighboring kingdom], and it wasn't long before it developed into a bloody war that dragged on for several years. In the end, Croesus lost the final battle and was defeated. The enemy king captured him, conquered and occupied the entire country, and took Croesus back to the enemy's land.

There, his advisors had to come up with a way of killing the prisoner. Eventually they unanimously condemned him to be burned at the stake. Everything was prepared, and lots of people came from far and wide to watch mighty King Croesus get burned at the stake. A huge pile of wood was set up, and next to it there were all sorts of balsam oils and other fragrant things that were meant to be burned along with King Croesus, so that he would perish in a royal manner.

The king who had defeated Croesus was lying at his window, watching Croesus being led to the stake.

But as they were leading him, he remembered his wise and loyal philosopher and what he had said to the king: "No man should boast of being happy until he has died." Croesus began shouting and yelling bitterly:

"You spoke the truth when you said that no man should consider himself happy until his death!"

When the king, who had prepared the "warm bath without water" for Croesus, was lying at his window, he heard Croesus talking and yelling bitterly, and so he ordered his servants, who were standing near him, to rush to Croesus and bring him back to the king. His order was instantly carried out. Croesus was brought before his conqueror and he knelt in front of him. The king told Croesus to stand up: there was something he wanted to discuss with him, and he asked him:

"My Croesus. You were being led to your death. What were you saying and yelling so bitterly?"

After repeating everything that Solon, his philosopher, had told him, Croesus explained that he had ignored those words and had remained arrogant and had kept doing his evil deeds.

"When I saw death before me, I remembered what my wise and loyal philosopher had told me, namely that no man should consider himself happy until his death. And in my great fear of death, I called out to Solon."

The king, listening to those words graciously and mercifully, thought to himself:

"Croesus too was once a great king, but God put him in my hands. And I haven't died yet either. . . . Who knows? Could the same thing happen to me some day?"

He pardoned King Croesus and gave him back his life, his land, and his people.

That is why, if we human beings are well off, we should nevertheless avoid pride and always remember that we do not know what the end is or will be. That is what we have read in this story.

THE PRINCE AND HIS FALSE FRIENDS

My DEAR CHILDREN! . . . You should never rely on a friend. For as long as you don't need them, everyone wants to be your friend. But when you do need a friend, the same will happen to you as happened in this story, which I want to tell you so as to while away the time.

Once there was a king, who sent his son to a distant land to study all kinds of wisdom. The son remained there for thirteen years. The king then wrote him that it was high time he came home. So the son headed back to his father. The king dispatched a lot of men to greet him and he welcomed his son joyfully. He gave a great banquet for his son, and everyone was quite merry.

After the banquet, the king asked him:

"Did you have a lot of friends in the city where you were studying?"

The son replied:

"My lord, king, and father! The whole city was friends with me."

The king said:

"My son, how did they become your friends?"

The son replied:

"I gave banquets every day, and my friends were all boon companions, and I always served them good wine. So they were all my friends."

The king heard out his son, sighed, and shook his head. Then he went on:

"I thought you had mastered a great deal of wisdom. But your words aren't wise. You regard your fellow boozers as friends, and that's a mistake. For your boon companions are drunkards. You mustn't trust them and you mustn't believe them. While they're drinking, there are no better friends in the world—as if they were born of the same mother. But once the banquet is finished, they wipe their mouths and leave and think to themselves:

"'If you invite me again, I won't take offense. But if you don't invite me, then I have no further use for you!'

"And they will forget all about your brotherhood."

The son answered the king:

"Then, my lord and father, tell me what a friend is, a friend I can rely on."

The king said:

"You should never regard someone as your friend without testing him first."

The son asked the king:

"How should I test him so I can read his mind and his intention and be certain of his friendship?"

The king then said to his son:

"Take a calf, slaughter it secretly, and put it in a sack. Take the sack on your shoulders at night and carry it to the home of your controller, your valet, and your scribe. Summon each man and say to him:

"'Something awful has happened to me! I drank all day, and in my drunken state, I got furious at my father's controller because he spoke harshly to me, and I couldn't stomach it. Without giving it a second thought, I grabbed my sword and killed him. Now I'm scared that my father will find out. He's got a bad temper, he might want to avenge the death. So, as you can see, I put the corpse in a sack and I want you to help me bury it this night.'

"Then," said the father, "you'll instantly see what kind of friend he is."

The son left and then did what his father had told him to do. Lugging the calf's carcass in a sack, he trudged over to the controller's home and knocked on the door. The controller looked through the window and asked:

"Who's knocking at my door so late at night?"

"It's me," the prince replied, "the son of your lord, of your king."

The controller opened the door and came running out:

"Damn it, what is my lord doing here so late at night?"

The prince told him everything and then said:

"Since you're my loyal controller, help me to bury the corpse before daylight."

Upon hearing this, the controller said:

"Get away from me with such things!"

The prince begged the controller to help him bury the corpse. But the controller angrily yelled:

"I won't have anything to do with a big drunkard and murderer! And if you don't want me to stay on as your controller, there are enough other masters!"

And he slammed the door and left the prince standing there.

Next, the prince went to his scribe's home, but his scribe responded just as the controller had done.

The prince then went to his valet's home, told him the same story, and begged him to help him bury the corpse. The valet replied:

"It's true that it's my duty to serve you because you are my lord. But it's not my duty to help you bury a corpse. Nevertheless, I would like to help you, but I'm terrified of your father and his foul temper. If he found out what happened, he'd kill both of us. You'll have to bury the corpse yourself in the nearby cemetery while I stand guard. That way I can warn you in case anyone happens to come along."

And that's what they did. The prince buried the calf in the cemetery, then each man went to his respective home.

The next morning, the controller, the scribe, and the valet got together, and the controller told the other two about the calamity inflicted on the prince, who had wanted the controller to help him bury the murdered corpse, but the controller had refused. Thereupon, the scribe and the valet said:

"He came to us too. We also refused to help him, and so he buried the corpse all alone in the cemetery."

The three men agreed that they mustn't conceal this whole business from the king, they must tell him everything, so he wouldn't blame it on them. And if he killed the poorly brought-up prince, the king would consider them loyal servants.

And that was what they did. They told the king the whole story.

The king then said:

"I swear by my crown that if my son did all that, he will have to pay with his life."

The king summoned the prince and reproached him. But the son refused to confess. So they said to him:

"You put the corpse in a sack and buried it in the cemetery!"

Upon hearing this, the king said:

"I'll send my servants over there, and you'll accompany them and show them the grave."

And that was what they did. They brought the king the sack, which his son had sealed with a seal.

"What do you say now?" the king asked his son.

The son replied:

"Dear lord and father! I made the calf sacred as a false sacrifice. When I slaughtered it, I saw that the calf was wrong and so I refused to accept it for sacrifice. But it would have also been wrong to throw it out in the street, since I had already made the calf sacred. So I buried it in this sack."

The king ordered his servants to open the sack and pour out all its contents. The servants did so and they shook a dead calf out of the sack. The three courtiers were deeply embarrassed in front of the prince, and the king ordered them to be put in prison. And that was what happened. Then the king said to his son:

"Now you can see for yourself whether you should regard someone as your friend before testing him."

The son replied:

"I've now truly understood more than I learned during all those thirteen years. Among my servants, I've found only a half-friend, and that was the valet who stood guard for me. And now, my dear lord and father, give me some good advice. What should I do with my three servants?"

The king said:

"The only advice I can give you is to kill all your servants, so that your valet at least won't learn disloyalty from them."

The son replied:

"How can I kill so many people just because of one person?"

The king said:

"If a sage were imprisoned by a thousand fools, and no one could figure out how to rescue him, I would offer the following advice: Kill all thousand fools in order to rescue the sage. That's why you would do better to kill all your disloyal servants, so that your valet, who is a half-friend, can become a whole friend."

And that was what the prince did. And the valet became his whole friend. And the king's son was now convinced that one shouldn't trust a friend before testing him.

That is why, my dear children, we should not trust any human friend, we should rely only on God. . . . Your Heavenly Father will not abandon you if you serve Him loyally and call to Him. And if ever you are punished, you alone are to blame, for you have been punished because of your misdeeds.

THE KING OF SPAIN

A KING OF SPAIN ONCE ASKED a Jewish scholar to translate a Biblical verse from the Holy Tongue. The scholar did so [and he said that the meaning was as follows].

"He who guardeth Israel neither sleepeth nor slumbereth."

"No, that's not the meaning!" said the king. "I think it means: 'The God who guardeth Israel lets no one sleep or slumber.' If I had slept normally last night, when you Jews would have been falsely accused of killing a Gentile child, you would have all been doomed. But God, who is your guardian, kept me awake. And so I could see them planting a Gentile child's corpse in a Jewish house. If I hadn't seen that, all the Jews would have been killed."

DANILA, EMUNISH, AVDON

WELL, MY DEAR CHILDREN! I can only assume that my misfortunes are due to my terrible sins. Just read the following story, which is certainly true and which certainly happened. Let what happened to the pious king happen truly to me. And if you are wise and think about it, you too will have to admit that this story is true. I have translated it from the Holy Tongue in order to show you that pious and decent people can also suffer and that God Praised Be He can also help them. May He also help us and the whole Jewish people and "Make us glad according to the days wherein Thou hast afflicted us" [Psalms, 90:15]. Amen, Amen!

This is the story of a king who lived in the Arabian lands. He was a powerful king, and his name was Jedidiah. He had many wives, as was customary in the Oriental countries. He also had a lot of children with his wives. He loved all his children and he had them raised as princes and princesses. Now one of his sons was the handsomest of all his offspring. The king loved him more than any of the others, and that was why he overlooked the boy's nasty and wicked actions, as you will hear. This son's name was Avdon.

Now Avdon had a sister who was also very beautiful, and she was called Beautiful Danila. The king also had a son named Emunish, and Emunish fell in love with Danila. But he couldn't overpower her, nor did he confide in anyone, for he feared the king's anger; even though the king also loved him dearly and granted him high positions. But Emunish didn't dare reveal anything about his love for Danila. A great deal of time wore by, and Emunish concealed his feelings so deeply that he grew skinny and scraggy. One of his friends and companions noticed this and said:

"My lord and dear friend! For a long while now, I've been noticing that you've lost all joy in life and that you've been avoiding other people's company. You seek out only isolated places. You've become very emaciated and you look completely different. What is wrong with Prince Emunish? You do have enough wealth and honor, after all! Please tell me, my friend, what's the cause of your distress? Perhaps there is a way for you to lighten your heart and perhaps I can help you?"

"My friend!" Emunish replied. "You've told the truth and you've spoken very wisely. But in regard to what's wrong with me, no one can help me—only a bitter death can free me from my sufferings. And I can't reveal the cause to anybody. However, before dying, I can entrust you, my loyal friend, with my secret, even though I know that you can't help me in my great misery."

Emunish then went on:

"Listen, my loyal friend, let me tell you about the bizarre and outrageous illness and sorrow that afflict me. These are my sickness and my suffering: I've absorbed the poison of beauty from Beautiful Danila. Those are my sickness and my suffering. I've done everything I can to recover from my condition. But God have mercy! The more I think I can get away from Beautiful Danila, the sicker I get from my love. And now my friend, if you can't help me with loyal advice, then I'm totally doomed."

His friend replied:

"Do what I say, and if you follow my advice, then I hope you'll recover immediately. Do this: go to bed and act sick. Your face looks sick anyhow. Don't let anyone into your bedroom aside from your most loyal servants, who know about your hidden disease. And let no other doctor in except for your trusted personal physician. Tell him to spread the news that you are dangerously ill. There is no doubt that the king will then come to you and ask you what you are suffering from. You must, my dear friend, now pretend to be a lot sicker and weaker than you really are, and you must tell the king in a feeble voice that you can't sleep and that you've lost your appetite. Tell him that you've ordered food cooked in various places, but it's disgusted you, and you can't eat.

"Say to your father: 'I've had an idea. There are several ways to keep me alive. If it please the king, let him graciously order his daughter Danila to come here to my chamber and prepare some food for me. Perhaps God will grant that I find the food tasty, so that it will keep me alive.'

"I'm sure that the king won't refuse and he'll send you Beautiful Danila. Once she comes to your room, you should send everyone away because you want to see if the food tastes better when you are alone with me and Danila. Then, my friend Emunish, you will get your pleasure by fair means or foul. What happens next cannot be changed. Your mother, who has captured the king's heart, will know how to soothe his anger."

"My dear friend!" said Emunish. "You've given me such good advice that I already feel better. I have to follow your advice even if it kills me!"

Emunish went to his chamber and got into bed as if he were very sick. He was attended by his loyal personal physician, who spread the news about the illness everywhere, and that was how the king found out. He promptly went to visit the patient. The king conversed amiably with his son and asked him what was wrong. Emunish replied in a feeble voice, saying what his friend had advised him to say—as you have already read. The king then said to Emunish:

"Be comforted, my dear son. Nothing should be refused you anywhere in my kingdom. I'll send you your sister and I hope that the food she cooks will be so tasty and wholesome that you'll fully regain your health and your strength."

The king amiably took his leave of Emunish. He promptly sent for his daughter and told her to hurry to her brother and prepare good food. Perhaps the patient would eat it. Beautiful Danila gladly obeyed her father; she went to Emunish's home and asked the maid what ingredients to use for good food. When Emunish saw that the food was ready, he ordered everyone to leave the room. And when he was alone with his sister, he said:

"My dear sister, bring the food over to my bed so that you can feed me with your hands. Perhaps that will make it tastier."

When Beautiful Danila brought the food over, he grabbed her and said:

"My dear sister, you have to lie with me! Otherwise I'll die!"

Danila was terrified and she said:

"My dear brother! Don't do such outrageous and dishonorable things! Ask the king, and I'm sure he'll let you have me."

But talking and begging didn't help her. Emunish pulled her in and lay with her. He had once loved her so deeply, but now, after carrying out his evil desire, he hated her so thoroughly that he pushed her away and told her to leave.

Danila screamed miserably:

"It's not enough that he's shamed me, he also wants to send me away!"

But her weeping and wailing left Emunish unmoved. He called for his servants and ordered them to throw Danila out of his house. And so, weeping and wailing, Danila left her brother's house. Out in the street, she encountered her brother Avdon. When he saw that she was wailing and that her royal garments were tattered, he said:

"My sister, something awful must have happened to you in my brother's house. Stop shouting and stay in my home until I get even with your brother."

And so, after telling her brother Avdon everything, she had to leave in great shame. When the king heard what had happened, he was furious! But as soon as he saw the queen, Emunish's mother, he forgave his son because the king loved the queen so much. However, Prince Avdon couldn't forget what had occurred.

Sometime later, Avdon organized a great hunt, inviting all the royal princes, including Emunish. That evening, when the hunt was finished, Avdon hosted a grand banquet. And when they all sat there, eating and drinking, he signaled his servants. They surrounded Emunish and killed him. The royal princes were horrified! They mounted their horses and galloped off. One prince went to the king and told him that Avdon had murdered all the royal children. The king was terror-stricken and he burst into a loud lament. This occurred in the presence of Emunish's friend, the bad advisor, who said to the king:

"My lord and king, don't be terrified! Not all the royal children have been killed. I believe that only Emunish has died, for Avdon must have avenged his sister's honor."

No sooner had he spoken, than all the king's children came riding up. But the king was still furious at Avdon and he ordered him never to show his face here again. Avdon couldn't endure the thought of living in exile and he figured that after the king's death, he, Avdon, would inherit the throne even though the king had declared that he was leaving his kingdom to another son.

Using persuasive words, Avdon rallied more and more people to his side until he had gathered the entire populace for an uprising against his father. Few old servants remained loyal to the king. Avdon rode out against his father, occupied the city, and cruelly drove out his father's wives. The king and his loyal servants managed to escape in time. A few servants who had remained with the king, but had then joined Avdon, now hurled stones at the king, berating him and cursing him soundly. The king's loyal servants said to him:

"Rather than watching these bastards disgrace and dishonor the king, we ought to attack them even if they tear us to shreds."

But the pious king wouldn't hear of it and he said to his loyal servants:

"If these terrible things are done by my son, who came from my flesh and is after my life, why shouldn't others do the same? It's all because of my sins."

The battle finally grew too fierce for the king, and he together with his soldiers should have retreated into the forest. Instead, he entered a fortified town and told his men to ride out to his son Avdon in a calm and chivalrous manner:

"For if Avdon invades this fortress, we will all be doomed!"

All the soldiers approved of this advice, and so the king prepared to ride out at the head of his people. However, his loyal generals disagreed, they wouldn't hear of it. They said:

"The king can see very well that this entire struggle is about the king himself. Avdon only wants to kill the king. Then he'll get the kingdom. That's why the king should remain in this fortress and pray to God to put the enemy in our hands."

The king replied:

"Go in peace and may God be with you."

All the soldiers left the town, and the king ordered his marshals to spare Avdon's life. The soldiers went out against Avdon in high spirits and relied on God and on their righteous cause, even though their army was only half the size of Avdon's army. And God sent great confusion to Avdon's men, killing them or driving them away. Avdon's men were terrified, they were confused by their fear of God and His vengeance. Avdon himself fled into a desert, trying to save his life and limb. But the king's men caught up with him and speared him to death. And so the battle ended. But no man wanted to inform the king that his son had been killed.

The king asked:

"Is Avdon still alive?"

But no one wanted to answer the king. They all stole away as if they had lost the battle. The king's loyal marshals noticed this and they came before the king:

"What is the king doing? Is he abandoning all his men, who so chivalrously risked their lives for him and his entire family? Now we see that if only Avdon had survived, the king wouldn't have minded if the rest of us had all been killed. We swear to you: If the king doesn't stand at the gates and speak cheerfully to his people, he will face more troubles than he has endured in his entire life."

The king went along with his marshals' advice. He stood at the gates and spoke cheerfully with each and every person. All his friends and foes came to him, and the king forgave all of them for what they had done to him. And then, shouting jubilantly, beating drums, and blasting rams' horns, all his friends and foes were led back into his kingdom; and the pious king ordered his messengers to proclaim throughout the land that all the subjects who had fled and now feared the king's displeasure should return. They would be welcomed with grace. And the king then said:

"It's as if I'd been first crowned today. So everyone should enjoy my grace!"

And the king ruled securely over his land in peace and honor until his death; and while the king was still alive, his son Frid [Peace] was lovingly anointed and crowned as king.

From this story, we can see that God's punishment comes slowly, but it does come in the end, and God pays back for everything.

ALEXANDER AND THE EYE FROM THE GARDEN OF EDEN

MY SON-IN-LAW WAS FAR too money-hungry, and perhaps it can be said of him: "There are people who care more for money than for their own bodies." And they are insatiable, as we can see from this story about Alexander the Great.

As we know, Alexander traveled all over the earth and conquered the entire world. He then thought to himself: "I'm a powerful man and I've come so far—I must be near the Garden of Eden." And when he reached the Gihon River, one of the four rivers flowing around the Garden of Eden, he had his men construct huge, strong ships. He and his men then boarded these ships, and because of his great intelligence, he reached the entrance of the Garden of Eden. But as he came close, an enormous fire burned up all his ships except for the one he was on, and all his men except for those that were on his ship.

When King Alexander saw that only his ship and its men survived, he began to beg that he be allowed to enter the Garden of Eden. He wanted to see its wonders and tell the whole world about them. But a voice then reached him, telling him to leave because he couldn't enter the Garden of Eden. And the voice said in the Holy Tongue that this entrance was only for the righteous. Alexander begged even harder: If he couldn't enter the Garden of Eden, then at least could something be thrown out to him, something that he could show the whole world as proof that he had been so close to the Garden of Eden. So an eye was thrown out to him.

Upon taking hold of the eye, he didn't know what to do with it. So he was told to place all his silver and gold and all his precious objects on one scale of a balance and the eye on the other scale, and the eye would outweigh them all because the eye was heavier than all those things. King Alexander, who, as we know, was a great sage and philosopher, had learned all his wisdom from his mentor Aristotle, and he wanted to acquire all knowledge. Now he wished to know how such a small eye could possibly outweigh so much silver and gold and other valuables. So he started testing. He got a huge and powerful balance and he placed the eye on one scale and hundreds of pounds of silver and gold on the other scale. But no matter how much he added, it wasn't enough, the eye was still heavier. Alexander was amazed and he begged the voice to explain to him how such a small eye could outweigh so much silver and gold and other things; what could he do to satiate the eye and make it less heavy? The voice replied that Alexander should throw just a little soil on the eye—and that tiny bit would weaken the eye. Alexander did so. He threw a wee bit of soil on the eye, and now even the tiniest object could outweigh the eye. Upon seeing that, Alexander was even more amazed and he asked what this meant. The voice replied:

"Listen, Alexander! You must know that as long as the human eye lives, it cannot be satiated, it never has enough. And the more a man possesses, the more he wants, and he never has enough. That is why the eye outweighs all silver and gold. But the instant a man passes away and soil is thrown upon his eyes, he has enough. That is why as soon as you threw soil on the eye, a tiny object could outweigh it. And look, Alexander! You can see that in yourself. Your empire isn't enough, and the whole world, which you have conquered, isn't enough. You also wanted to come here, to God's children and servants. While you live, nothing is enough for you. You don't want to rest, you want to keep owning more and more. You will die, I tell you, in a foreign land, and your death is not that far off, and they will pour soil upon you. Oh, by then you will have enough with four cubits of earth—you, for whom the whole world was too small! And you, Alexander, will be told not to speak and not to ask, for no one will answer you. And you will be told to hurry away from this place if you do not wish to suffer the same fate as your other ships and your other men."

So the king boarded his ship and sailed to the land of Haudu, and a short time later, he suffered a dreadful, horrible death. For he was poisoned, as we can read in the meticulous description written by his mentor, Aristotle.

As has been said: There are many people who are so greedy for money that they remain insatiable, which is why they often suffer terribly.

THE ANGEL OF DEATH IN LUS

I ENDURED MANY STORMS, and when I attempted to avoid them, I suffered the same fate as the man who tried to elude the Angel of Death by taking refuge in Lus, "because people never die there until they grow very old."

When that man reached the gate at a very old age, the Angel of Death said to him:

"You've come right into my hands so that I can kill you! This is the only place where I have power over you."

KING DAVID AND ABSALOM

MY SON LEIB—MAY HE REST IN PEACE—died at the age of twenty-seven. Even though I endured a lot of heartache and misery because of him, I felt awful about his death—which is natural for parents. One can learn that from the pious King David—may he rest in peace.

The king's son, Absalom, caused his father a lot of distress. But when the king went to war against his son, he ordered his men to spare Absalom's life. And when he learned that his son was dead, the father shrieked and lamented! And he cried out seven times: "Absalom, my son!" By doing so, he brought his son through the Seven Gates of Hell and sent him to Paradise.

And so I forgive my son for all the unhappiness he caused me.

THE EAGLE AND HIS CHILDREN

WHEN I SUFFERED BECAUSE OF MY CHILDREN, I remembered the eagle who took his children upon his wings and said:

"It is better that the hunter shoots at me than at my children."

Anonymous Arthurian Legend
(1789)

The stories about King Arthur's Court, Celtic in origin and widespread in medieval European culture, made their way into Yiddish literature chiefly via German, whereby the German texts might have been recited or chanted to the Yiddish authors, who could not necessarily read the Latin alphabet. In any event, the magic and derring-do of the celebrated king and his knights provided the most widely read literary entertainment among Ashkenazi Jews, far outdoing even the wildly popular Bovo Book. King Arthur is called Artus in German and Artis or Artur in Yiddish.

In 1912, Leo Landau published three Yiddish Arthurian texts, two in verse and one in prose. He Romanized them into Gothic letters—in keeping with their medieval substance—and he supplied a thorough introduction (*Arthurian Legends*, Leipzig, 1912).

A HISTORY
or
A Moral Tale
ABOUT
WONDROUS EVENTS IN THE LIFE OF A YOUNG KNIGHT
SIR GAWAIN
WHOSE TALE REVEALS THE WORKINGS OF DIVINE PROVIDENCE

PART ONE

THE ANCIENT CHRONICLERS HAVE RECORDED, among other stories, a beautiful tale that actually occurred in King Arthur's court. This king reigned over very many lands. His residence was a very mighty and beautiful city, which he had built on the shores of the sea. And that was why he named it Arthurstown. His table was very large, and many princes and counts dined there.

Here, at this royal court, there was a very ancient law, which, under corporal pain, decreed that no one, no servant or vassal, and not even the king and the queen, could eat or drink anything until guests were received. There was never any lack of guests, for the court was so large that newcomers arrived every day. But then one day, it happened that there were no guests. And so everyone at court had to go to bed without eating or drinking anything whatsoever.

The queen, who was starving, got up very early and peered at the sky, praying that they would be fortunate enough to have guests. And finally, in the distance, she spotted a splendid knight riding along. His shield and his helmet sparkled with gold and diamonds, his steed was covered with a golden caparison, and his harness was made of silver and studded with precious stones.

This knight came trotting into the castle garden, where the queen was standing, and he asked someone who this lady might be. "The queen" was the answer. Thereupon he leaped down from his horse and knelt at the queen's feet. She told him to stand up and she asked him what he was seeking.

"Your Gracious Majesty," he said, "I wish to be allowed to honor Your Majesty with a rich girdle, which is set with such gorgeous stones that I would like to think that you have never seen anything like it before. And even though King Arthur collects many harbor excises, I still believe that this girdle cannot be unpleasant for you. Here it is. Please show it to the king and to all courtiers. I will remain here until I hear your gracious decision tomorrow."

The queen, who was overjoyed at being freed from her hunger pangs by this guest, welcomed him very graciously, especially because he had brought her a beautiful present. She amiably accepted it on condition that it be approved at court.

At the table, where the king and all his men were gathered, the queen told the king: "This is a rare and beautiful girdle that an unknown knight wishes to present to me. My acceptance depends on whether Your Royal Majesty has anything against it. It is up to Your Royal Majesty to decide and to graciously apprise me of his decision."

The king showed the girdle to all his knights, who were at the table. And, while showing it, he said that each man should express his opinion. Except for one knight, whose name was Sir Gawain, each man in turn approved of the gift. Some knights said: "This present is very valuable, and we can see no reason to reject it." Others added: "This girdle reveals that its owner must be a very powerful ruler and that this present is meant to show that he is a good friend of Your Royal Majesty even though he does not indicate who he is. Nevertheless, you will learn his identity in due time."

But Sir Gawain protested. "I may be the youngest here," he said. "And that is why I am so deeply embarrassed to voice my assessment. Still, I cannot go along indifferently with the advice given by the entire council. In any given case, it is the duty of each one of us to advise our king according to our own consideration. This sense of duty makes me so bold as to advise Your Royal Majesty, on the basis of my belief, not to accept this present. However valuable this girdle may be, it will in no way honor the king, and much less the queen, if they accept gifts from a lord who is a total stranger. However, if he reveals who he is, and if he proves to be a real king or emperor, then his present should not be rejected."

Sir Gawain's advice appealed to the king, who said he would return the girdle the next day, unless the stranger told them who he was. Since the unknown knight still refused to reveal his identity to the queen, the girdle was handed back to him.

"You are shaming me," he told the queen. "And I believe that the scoundrels sitting at your royal table have advised Your Majesty against accepting my gift. So let them engage in a duel with me if they wish to behave in a chivalrous manner. Tell the king that I challenge his knights to a duel right here in the square. And if they refuse, then I will have my revenge on His Royal Majesty, King Arthur." The knight beat his chest. "I am a man who thinks highly of himself even if you do not know who I am."

Among the knights, there was not a single one who was willing to accept the challenge at the king's request. "If Your Majesty had taken our advice," was their response, "this would not have happened. You preferred Sir Gawain's advice. So let him settle the matter."

Sir Gawain was summoned by King Arthur. "My loyal knight," said the monarch, "I swear to you by my crown and my scepter that you shall enjoy my supreme grace if you defend my honor now. The unknown knight, who wanted to honor the queen with that girdle, is very angry that his gift was rejected. And that is why he has challenged my best knight to a duel. Make sure you win the duel, otherwise he will shame me and my entire court."

"I will serve Your Majesty with my last drop of blood," said Sir Gawain, "and I will do so right away."

The noble knight, Sir Gawain, saddled his horse, girded himself with his weapons and his sword, and, heroic and undaunted, he attacked the unknown knight. The duel lasted for several hours before they made any headway against one another. And finally, in a bloody fight, Sir Gawain was wounded so badly that he was forced to submit to capture by the unknown knight. The king wanted to redeem Sir Gawain for a high sum, but the unknown knight did not care for any money. "I don't need money," he told the king. "My honor is worth far more to me than your entire kingdom."

How very miserable the king felt when he saw Sir Gawain riding off behind the unknown knight as his prisoner. The king's final words were: "God be gracious to you, God be with you."

The unknown knight rode away, followed by Sir Gawain. They traveled very far, through many lands, and eventually, in the sixth month, they reached Cathay. This country, which is surrounded by a wall four cubits thick and thirty cubits high, is very beautiful. Sir Gawain was astonished. He had never before seen such beauty. After a brief ride, they reached a splendid and beautiful town. In the distance, they could see a beautiful castle shining: its roof was covered with excellent gold and decorated with carbuncle buds. Sir Gawain could not get his fill of astonishment—he had never seen such wealth before.

Here, for the first time, the unknown knight spoke to Sir Gawain in a friendly manner. Half a league from that residence, the unknown knight halted in a lovely and fragrant meadow. The two knights dismounted and they let their horses do a little grazing.

"Well, my dear son," said the unknown knight, "how do you like this country and the castle standing there before us?"

"They are very beautiful, my lord. I don't believe there is anything more beautiful in the world."

"My dear son," said the unknown knight, "you will see far more beautiful things in my home. I should finally let you know who I am. I am the emperor of this land, that castle is my citadel. I am Kaduks X, emperor of Cathay." He unbuttoned his over-garment and showed Sir Gawain the imperial Chinese star. "Don't be afraid, be cheerful. There is a lot we have to discuss. I have no son, but almighty and all-knowing God gave me an only daughter in my later years. She is very beautiful, you will have never seen a more beautiful person in all your life. She has more wisdom and intelligence than thousands of others of her sex. She is famous far and wide, that is why she is called the beautiful and intelligent Princess Sharteene. Many high kings and princes have courted her, but I've found none of them satisfactory. I have resolved to give her to no one but a heroic knight. I've got enough of a land and a population, and my successor on the throne won't need more than I have. I have been told that you are the heroic knight whom I demand. That was why I sought you out in King Arthur's court. I admit that you made a wonderful impression on me in our duel, you were very bold and swift. I will be satisfied with you in the future as well. Would you like to marry my Sharteene? Tell me. But she shouldn't be forced on you. If you don't like her, then I will allow you to return to your home. You should also be reimbursed for your travel expenses."

Sir Gawain was frightened. "Ah, gracious lord, you are making fun of me. I think you can offer your daughter a better husband than a captive knight."

"No!" said the emperor. "I'm not making fun of you, I'm not asking for a better man. You've made a wonderful impression on me, and Heaven wishes it too. Fine! We will head for the castle so that you can have a first look at my daughter."

Emperor Kaduks galloped off on the right side with his glittering imperial star, after ordering Sir Gawain to ride on the emperor's left side. As soon as they reached the castle, cannons all around the town were fired, and, in between the booms, musicians blew shawms and trumpets and beat kettle drums. The streets were illuminated and decorated with brass gates, the burghers wore their finest clothes, and, from the castle, a lot of money was thrown out to the paupers. Princess Sharteene welcomed her father. Sir Gawain looked at Sharteene and he was enchanted with her beauty.

In less than a quarter hour, the castle was filled with cabinet ministers as well as counts and princes, who were all in the residence to welcome the emperor. The emperor thanked them and also pointed to Sir Gawain: "I recommend this knight to you, so that you may show him great respect. God willing, he is to marry my Sharteene and be my successor to the throne."

Sir Gawain fell to the emperor's feet and he was raised up by the emperor himself. "Sit down here, next to me, my dear son," said the emperor, offering him a red velvet chair with gold trimming. Sir Gawain bowed, and all the members of the court bowed humbly to their emperor and to Sir Gawain.

"My dear son," said the emperor to Sir Gawain, "do you still believe I'm making fun of you?"

"No!" replied Sir Gawain. "I am convinced of your imperial grace. Your Imperial Majesty must forgive me—I couldn't believe I could be so fortunate."

"How do you like my Sharteene? Have you seen her?"

"Yes, Your Imperial Majesty, I like her tremendously, and I'm very happy! Oh, Heaven, who can fathom your works? How wonderfully you've taken me from that event to the supreme summit of happiness! Yes, Your Imperial Majesty! These events are ordained by the Almighty. I must thank Him first and then Your Imperial Majesty. Thank You, Almighty, for making me so happy through this gracious emperor. I will proclaim Your deeds forever. Your help and Your grace shall be in my loving hymns constantly. And you, Your Imperial Majesty, you are an angel of the Almighty, I will serve you in all events with my last drop of blood, and your Sharteen shall rule my heart and be its queen."

The emperor took Sir Gawain's hand, and they strolled over to Princess Sharteene's chamber. She fell in love with Sir Gawain and welcomed him very courteously. Finally, when the emperor sensed that they were content with one another, he asked Sharteene whether she wished to marry Sir Gawain:

"I'm very favorably disposed to him, and if you love him, then he should be my successor to the throne."

Sharteene blushed and couldn't respond right away. Finally, she confessed her feelings to her father: "My dear and gracious father, if you love someone, then I too love him with all my heart."

Sir Gawain and Sharteene were betrothed, and the wedding was to take place in two months. At the end of the second month, their marriage was celebrated in the castle, in the presence of the entire imperial aristocracy. They all beamed with delight and blessed the bride and groom, expressing their wish that the couple might live in the light of happiness for the rest of their lives. And prior to the ceremony, Emperor Kaduks had Sir Gawain crowned as successor to the throne of Cathay.

At this point, we must recall the prayer that Sir Gawain spoke an hour before the nuptials:

"Oh, Heaven—Almighty, Infinite, and All-knowing Creator, Lord of all hosts and King of all kings! You have raised me from a low station. I thank You. It is Your desire that I marry Princess Sharteene, the daughter of the emperor of Cathay. Our bond is Your doing, Supreme Creator. So grant us Your grace and mercy, forgive us for our ignorant misdeeds that we have committed since childhood, lead us and guide us in Your ways, give us pure hearts to help the poor, to raise up the oppressed, to help widows and orphans.

"Oh, Heaven! I shudder to recall the days when I believed that I would remain a slave all my life! A clap of thunder struck my heart when I had to leave my parents almost in despair. Their sole hope that I would be their support in their old age was gone. I believed that they would be robbed of me forever, and that I would never again see the light that shone on them. Great Ruler, I may have welcomed Your scourge, but the weeping and wailing of my poor parents, who were losing their only son, was like bitter death for me. But since You encouraged my soul to see You as just in everything, my soul did not sink, and You, All-Kindly Lord, after that rain, You let Your sun shine upon me. Fate, which I believed would destroy me, is now the instrument that will make me and my parents happy forever. But sadly, my parents will not be fortunate enough to see me on this happiest day. Lord of all joys, let a feeling of joy flow into their souls, let them dream about this bond, have it proclaimed by an angel. Your power is limitless, grant me Your grace, let me visit them in person this very year, so I can tell them about my wellbeing. I swear that, with Your help, I will visit them this very year and bring them back to my new home, so that they may peacefully enjoy their final years here with me and my wife, and. . . ."

But now Sir Gawain was summoned to the wedding, and so he had to cut off his ardent prayer. He wiped away his tears and again he looked like the golden sun.

The wedding was performed according to the custom of Cathay, and then everyone sat down for the banquet. The tables were silver, the chairs gold, and everything was beautiful and magnificent—the likes of which had never been seen before with any other emperor.

Several months went by, and Sharteene became pregnant, and her husband, Sir Gawain, remembered the oath he had sworn on that holy day of their nuptials. He therefore had to visit his parents. He revealed this to his wife and his father-in-law. "We don't like seeing you take such a long journey," they replied. "You can write letters to your parents. But we do not want you to dishonor your oath. Go with God and let us know when you arrive."

Sir Gawain said good-bye to them and also to the entire aristocracy and left Cathay with ten horsemen and a great sum of money.

Unfortunately, Sir Gawain and his escort were attacked by a gang of highwaymen. His men were too weak to fight them off and they were all killed. Only Sir Gawain was lucky enough to escape their murderous hands by dashing on foot into a forest. Here he wandered some four days before he met another human being. He started to pray: "Oh, Heaven! Kind Father! Do not let me die in this wild forest. Let my poor parents weep before You. Grant my wish, let me embrace them. Let me set eyes again on my poor Sharteene, whom I have left pregnant. I will then gladly sacrifice my life to You, I will joyfully stand before Your throne and render my account."

Boom! Boom! Cannon were fired in back of him. Trembling with fear, he threw himself on the ground. But finally, he mustered his courage. "Who can have fired cannon here?" he wondered. "It must be an endangered ship on a nearby sea signaling for help!"

Sir Gawain then followed the smell of gunpowder and arrived unscathed on a seashore right next to the forest. He found a ship, which had run aground on a sandbar not far from the coast. He took the risk of swimming there and he rescued two people, who were piteously yelling for him to help them. Then the ship sank with all the rest of the travelers.

To judge by their appearance, the two people rescued by Sir Gawain were of a high station. They thanked the noble knight for saving them and they asked him who he was.

"I am Sir Gawain, and who might you be, Milord and Milady?"

"We cannot tell you who we are for we are traveling to Canata. But you should know that you have rescued a king and a queen. If you remain with us until we are fortunate enough to find a ship that can carry us home, you shall have our elder princess as your wife—her name is Anna."

"Thank you, Your Majesty," Sir Gawain replied, "but I am already married. My wife is the only daughter of Emperor Kaduks of Cathay. Not far from here, it was my destiny that my escort of ten dragoons and my servants were attacked and murdered by a gang of highwaymen. All my possessions fell into their hands. Alas! With my own eyes, I saw the killers murder them, and Divine Providence let me escape on foot into this forest. I have spent four days here without eating even a crumb of food. How wonderful are the works of the Almighty! They are unfathomable. His foresight is unending. I already believed that I would become the prey of wild beasts, but now I have had the good fortune to rescue a king and a queen. Who in Cathay could have predicted to what end I would be attacked by highwaymen on my way through this area? I now have the comfort of knowing that the All-Kindly had his reasons for leading me here."

The king and queen were delighted with this story. In the middle of the story, an Arthurian ship and an English ship sailed past them. Sir Gawain and his companions called out to the vessels. Their skippers each sent them a small rowboat. Sir Gawain boarded the Arthurian ship and he was happy to be heading for his fatherland. His companions boarded the English ship.

Regrettably, the Arthurian ship suffered numerous mishaps and was stranded in Greenland for eighteen years.

Meanwhile, Sharteene happily gave birth to a son. He was named Vidvilt Gawain. He had all his father's skills and he outdid his father in strength and beauty. He was the sole comfort of his mother, who moaned for her dear husband every day. "Ah!" she often said to Vidvilt. "What good are all these things? Your father! Your father! He is bound to my heart. It pounds incessantly. I cannot get any rest for even a quarter hour, I cannot sleep. He has been gone for so long, and we still have heard nothing from him. God knows what has happened to him. And you, my dear and beautiful Vidvilt, you have lost a great teacher of virtue. I hope to God that both of us will have the good fortune to embrace him again."

She could not utter those words without tears rolling down her cheeks. Vidvilt wiped away those hot tears with his tender hands. "Don't worry, Mother," he said. "When I grow up, I will find Father."

PART TWO

Vidvilt was in his seventeenth year when he decided that he could no longer stand his mother's wailing. He felt a deep desire to find his father, Sir Gawain. He said to his grandfather: "It is my duty, I owe it to my father, and it should not abandon me even when I draw my last breath. And I hope that Heaven will grant me the good fortune to liberate my despairing mother."

"Go with God, my dear grandchild," said his grandfather. "I hope that you are fortunate enough to find your father and bring new joy to me and your mother."

The old man then said to his Sharteene: "I am glad that young Vidvilt is brave enough to go on a long journey. I have dreamt that he will be happy."

"May your dream come true," Sharteene replied.

Vidvilt had them saddle a good horse, and he took two good loaded pistols and a thick sword. "Farewell, Mama, farewell, Grandpapa."

Emperor Kaduks said: "Farewell, come back safely, and bring along your father."

Sharteene kissed her son again. "God be with you. Come back soon, I wish you every success!"

Vidvilt galloped off without even a servant. After fourteen weeks, he found himself three leagues from Sardinia. Suddenly, he was attacked by six murderers. The young hero not only fought them off, he also wounded them so severely that he managed to deliver them to the residents of Sardinia during his first week there.

This strange tale reached the ears of the king of Sardinia. He instantly summoned this hero and had him recite the entire story. He also asked the hero who he was and to where he was traveling. Vidvilt told the king that he was the grandson of the emperor of Cathay and that he wanted to find his father, Sir Gawain, at King Arthur's court. "It has been eighteen years since he left my mother, and she has heard nothing from him in all that time."

"Sir Gawain!" The king clapped his hands. "And he has been gone for eighteen years?"

"Yes, Your Royal Majesty, do you have any news of him?"

"Perhaps, my dear son. Please excuse me for a moment." The king promptly sent for his queen. She came, and the king received her with great joy. "My loyal wife, I have summoned you so that you might hear a wonderful story. This boy bravely fought off six murderers and brought them to our courts of law. But there is more that I have to tell you. He is a son of Sir Gawain, who saved our lives seventeen years and a few months ago!"

"Thank God," the queen cried, "that we can now show our gratitude to his son."

"Yes, my dear," said the king. "You are right."

Sir Vidvilt was taken aback. "What? My father saved your lives seventeen years ago, and you wish to reward me for his deed? Does that mean he is no longer alive? Is he dead? Oh, my poor mother! Ah!"

"God forbid," said the king and the queen. "Don't be so afraid! We can give you some news about him."

Vidvilt replied: "I can hardly wait. Let me hear what happened to my father and Your Majesty and what news of him you can give me."

"That you will hear, my dear son," said the king. "I and my wife traveled through Canata to Russia. On the way back, our ship, which was not far from the Albanian border, ran aground on a sand bar. We fired our cannon several times but received no response. Then something wondrous happened to us and your father. Your father, who was riding through Albania with a great sum of money and an escort of ten horsemen, was attacked by a gang of highwaymen not far from the coast. All his men were murdered, but your father was lucky enough to escape. He fled into a dense forest right near the sea, where our ship was in the worst predicament. This good hero, the only person to hear our cannon, swam over to our ship, took me and my wife on his back, and swam to shore. Barely two minutes later, the ship went down with all travelers.

"We wanted him to remain with us and marry our elder daughter, but he said that he was married to the daughter of the emperor of Cathay and that he was going to visit his parents in King Arthur's land. He also told us about what had happened to him in the meantime. In the middle of his tale, we were fortunate enough to see two ships sailing by, one bound for Arthur's land, the other for London. We boarded the English ship and sailed to London, then to Sardinia. But your father boarded the Arthurian ship.

"Well, dear Vidvilt, we went to a great deal of effort to locate your father, but, unfortunately, we had no news of him. Next we wrote to King Arthur, and we were told that the Arthurian ship had endured great misfortunes for seventeen years. Yet the skipper was said to be an excellent mariner, on whom we could pin our hopes. Here is the letter than I received just six weeks ago from King Arthur. You can read it for yourself, it does not say much.

"If you wish to follow our advice, stay with us. We will be receiving King Arthur and his entire court within four weeks. He will be marrying our elder daughter. Perhaps your father has reached Arthur safely since the letter was sent, so that you can hear the news directly from the king and his men. We especially want you to marry our younger princess, our intelligent Lorel. She is quite beautiful, virtuous, and her mind possesses twice what a qualified person can promise. It is certainly Divine Providence that has brought you to this area, so that we can show you the gratitude we owe your father. There is no greater honor we can pay you than the hand of Princess Lorel, who is to inherit our entire kingdom."

Vidvilt replied: "Your Royal Majesty, I am amazed at this wondrous tale, which you tell like an angel. God willing, let me hear more about my father. With my father's permission, I will promptly marry Princess Lorel. But so long as I have no news from him, I can enjoy no happiness. For I think about my mother, I think about my tender father, who may be in constant danger every minute of the day. Yes! I will stay with you in this residence until King Arthur arrives, and I can at least participate in your day of jubilation, as is my duty because of your fascinating tale."

"He told me he was searching King Arthur's court for a certain Sir Gawain, who is his father. His mother, he said, is the daughter of Emperor Kaduks."

"And my father has been away from my mother for some eighteen years. I was still in her womb when he said farewell to my mother and my grand-papa and rode off to visit his parents in Arthur's land. Since then we have had no news of him."

"Imagine what joy we would have to see a son of yours. We advise him to stay here until King Arthur arrives."

Vidvilt took this advice very amiably and remained. The adjoining room was opened, and there he sat.

At that point, someone shouted: "The emperor of Cathay together with his daughter has arrived. Their carriage is standing outside the castle!"

Sir Gawain and Vidvilt lost no time, they instantly rushed down to the carriage.

"Ah! Most loyal and gracious father-in-law!" shouted Sir Gawain.

"Happy mother and grandpapa!" shouted Vidvilt.

No greater joy could be wished for. Sir Gawain and Sharteene embraced each other, and Vidvilt kept kissing his father and his mother. Finally, King Arthur and the King of Sardinia led them up to the chamber where the queen of Sardinia and her two princesses were waiting. Amidst the joy of these arrivals, the queen of Sardinia reminded them that Vidvilt had promised to marry Princess Lorel once he found his father. "He is so happy to embrace both his father and his mother joyfully. So if it please you, do not go back on your word."

"This comes from God!" was their answer. "We are content!"

King Arthur took the elder princess and rode away. Vidvilt took the younger princess and was crowned the successor to the throne of Sardinia and he remained there. And, together with his wife and the emperor, Sir Gawain, escorted by the bodyguards of the king of Sardinia and accompanied by his parents, happily set out for Cathay, and there they all lived in peace.

THE DUBNO PREACHER
(DUBNER MAGGID)
(1740-1804)

For religious Jews, sermons, especially the parables narrated by preachers, are crucial to their spiritual life. The best-known Ashkenazi preacher was probably Yankev Krants, the Dubno Preacher, whose oral sermons were set down by his followers and eventually published, first in Hebrew then in Yiddish. Tradition, focusing on the parables rather than on the whole sermon, has spread these tales throughout the Yiddish world. Provided with a moral, but nevertheless entertaining, they were spiritual in content and simple, often one-dimensional, in form and diction. Though an anti-Hasid who was close to the Vilna Gaon, the chief foe of Hasidism, Krants also narrated legends that sounded like Hasidic tales. On the other hand, since a few stories about him described his feats in the third person, they read like traditional rabbinical hagiography. Next, when the Jewish Enlightenment made its inroads in Eastern Europe, Krants assailed it full-force.

PARABLES

For Whose Esteem

A WEALTHY MAN HAD TWO SONS who lived far away from him. One son was very rich and the other very poor. Many years wore by without their seeing their father. One day, a letter arrived from him, summoning them to the wedding of their younger brother.

In his letter, which was addressed to the rich son, the father wrote: "Come, my son, we will all have a wonderful time together—and bring along your poor brother too. I promise that for all the expenses you incur for my esteem, I will repay you and add a nice gift."

Upon reading the letter, the rich son promptly headed for the dry-goods store, where he bought the most expensive fabrics for himself, his wife, and his children, and ordered the finest garments to be made for them. In preparation for the wedding, they got all dressed up in that luxurious attire. When they were about to leave, and the wagon was ready, and the horses were harnessed, the rich man suddenly remembered his brother and he shouted at his servants: "Hurry up, summon my brother! Get him here as fast as you can! Tell him I need him badly!"

The servants brought the poor brother, dragging him by his collar. The poor brother was surprised and he asked his rich brother: "What do you need me for and what do you want from me? Normally, you won't have anything to do with me!"

"Don't ask any questions!" the rich brother yelled. "Climb into the wagon and come along! When I tell you to come along, you come along!"

By the time they reached the father's town, he had already learned that the dear, exalted guests would be arriving. All the in-laws went out to welcome them with great joy. And when the wagon stopped outside the home of the wealthy father, the rich brother was the first to climb down: He was dressed like a count. Next came his wife and children, who were also dressed like aristocrats.

People stood there, gaping and asking: "Who are these nobles?"

And their friends replied: "That's the son of our wealthy man, and his son is likewise very rich."

After that, they saw a pauper, ragged and tattered, and they asked: "And who is that?"

The friends replied: "He's from the same town."

And people wondered: "Could he be a brother or some other relative?"

No one answered.

Meanwhile the in-laws and the guests went indoors, and the klezmers started playing. The party became lively, merry. In a blessed moment, the ceremony took place under the wedding canopy, and everyone danced and caroused as is the custom.

The rich son stayed with his father for two weeks. He then said: "Dear Father! You can see that I obeyed you and I came to have a good time with you at the wedding. But you know I'm a merchant, and my time is very valuable. How can I remain here any longer?"

"Do as you see fit, my son," the father answered. "Who's keeping you here? You can go on home."

The son heard his father's response, and his heart burned like fire. After all, his father had written him that he would cover all their wedding expenses and also give him a beautiful gift. Yet now the father was acting as if he'd forgotten his promise. His hand didn't stir.

The rich son couldn't hold back any longer. He handed his father an itemized bill: his clothes had cost him this, his wife's clothes had cost him that, his children's clothes had cost him this, the trip, including the inns, had cost him that.

"You ordered new clothes," the father replied. "Wear them in good health—you, your wife, and your children. And you should live to order new clothes again."

"But father," the son argued, "you promised you'd repay me all the expenses I incurred for the wedding."

"That's not true," replied the father. "I never promised you that."

The son thereupon produced the father's letter and showed him: "Look, father! You wrote it down in your own hand!"

The father took the letter and read it aloud: "I promise you that for all the expenses you incur for my esteem, I will repay you and add a nice gift."

"Well?" said the son.

"Well, nothing!" the father replied. "I wrote you that I would cover all the expenses you incur for my esteem. If you really wanted to show me your esteem, you would have felt sorry for your poor brother and not brought him here naked and barefoot. You should have also ordered new clothes and new shoes for him as well. That would have meant great esteem for me and great pride and pleasure. But the clothes you ordered were purely for your own esteem, and I never promised to cover those expenses. So what are you complaining about?"

MORAL

When a Jew who celebrates the Sabbath or a holy day invites a poor man to a meal, he is preparing the table for God's esteem, and God will repay him a hundred times over. But if the Jew eats the delicious holiday treats alone, he has prepared the table for his own esteem, and for that he deserves no reward.

Inviting Poverty

A WEALTHY MAN GAVE HIS SON a large amount of money to start his own business and become an independent merchant. The son launched his commerce, but he did badly. He lost money and grew poorer and poorer until he was barely making enough to keep body and soul together.

One day, when the son was in desperate straits, he complained to his father because he assumed that his father would help him out. But instead, his father shouted: "What do you want from me? I gave you a large enough sum. You should have been a good businessman and not have lost money.

Live as well as you can, and be content with what you've got. I'll help you only when I see that you've spent your final kopek and have nothing left."

A while later, a fire broke out in the town, and the flames reached the shop where the wealthy man's son had his bit of merchandise. Friends came rushing over to save the shop. But the son said: "Please—leave my shop alone! Let it burn! It's better for me to be a total pauper. My father will help me. That way I won't have to suffer as a partial pauper."

MORAL

It's better to keep a person from falling than help him to keep standing when he is already falling.

A Souvenir of a Souvenir

A RICH MAN IN A LARGE TOWN had a daughter, for whom he sought a husband with all the virtues. But he was unable to find the right man until he lodged in a village; and there, in a pauper's home, he found a boy, handsome, intelligent, and a good student of the holy texts. The rich man couldn't have wished for a better match. He then brought his wife and his daughter, and both women truly liked the boy. The father was so excited about the prospective marriage that he wanted to sign the engagement contract on the spot and then promptly celebrate the wedding.

However, the pauper protested: "You should at least give me time to prepare a wedding banquet worthy of your esteem. All I've got in the house are crude black bread and sour milk."

"It doesn't matter," replied the rich man. "We all like your son so much that we will enjoy your black bread and sour milk as if they were the most luxurious delicacies. Let's celebrate the wedding!"

From his luggage the rich man produced expensive clothes and shoes, which he brought the groom. He told his servant to remove the boy's old garments and dress him in the new garments. And the wedding took place that evening.

After the wedding, the rich man told his servant to pack up the groom's old clothes and take them home. And even though the rich man spoke very softly, almost secretly, the groom caught his words. During the banquet, when everyone sat there, eating the crude rustic bread, the groom stole away with a piece of bread, hiding it in a pocket of his old clothes, which his father-in-law had ordered his servant to pack. Needless to say, the rich man didn't notice a thing.

When the rich man, his servant, and his son-in-law came home in the large city, the rich man told his servant to lock away the old clothes.

A while later, when the son-in-law had an argument with his father-in-law and disrespected him, the rich man told his servant to bring out the package of old clothes, and he opened it up right in front of the boy, to remind him what his life had been like with his own father. . . . But when the rich man unwrapped the old, tattered clothes, a piece of dry, black rustic bread fell out of a pocket.

Whereupon the son-in-law said: "It's true that when I lived with my father, I went around in rags. But look in what a hurry you were to have me marry your daughter: you didn't mind serving black bread at the wedding banquet! So I can certainly put on airs in regard to you."

MORAL

At the Passover seder, the Lord ordered us to eat bitter herbs so as to remind us of our bitter sufferings under Pharaoh. He also commanded us to eat kharoyses, the brown paste served at the seder to remind us of the clay we kneaded to make bricks when we were slaves in Egypt. God doesn't want us to put on airs and forget our ancient condition. However, we also eat matzos at the seder to remember how quickly the Good Lord wanted us to be His free children—so quickly that He didn't wait for our dough to rise. So we left Egypt with unleavened bread, "the bread of affliction."

The Spiced Dishes

*T*WO MERCHANTS WERE TRAVELING. One was an elderly and experienced man, well-versed in all secular matters. The other was a young man who had just started making his way in the world. His companion was teaching him everything, instructing him on how to conduct himself. However, the younger man was extremely stubborn, and he considered himself smarter than anyone else, so that he often did the opposite of what the elderly man told him to do.

Once, when they came to an inn, they were served two kinds of fish and meat. One kind was cooked simply, the way it is cooked by an ordinary housewife; while the other kind was sharply spiced and peppered, with all sorts of herbs, which emitted a delightful fragrance. The elderly, experienced man ate the ordinary food, while the young man pounced on the spiced dishes, because they keenly whetted his appetite.

Toward midnight, the young merchant woke up and screamed in pain—he had the worst cramps. Now he realized that the spiced and peppered fish and meat he had eaten were old and spoiled, and the innkeeper had spiced and peppered them in order to hide the fact that they were putrid.

MORAL

All the passions a man has are useful because they support not only him but all humanity. However, there are fine and ugly passions. The passion to eat and drink is a good one, the passion for wealth and the passion for women are bad. But just as food and drink are necessary for preserving an individual's life, those other passions are crucial for the existence of the whole world, for if there were no evil lust, people wouldn't build houses, they wouldn't take wives, and the world would be waste and wild. That is why the ugly passions are heavily spiced and peppered—stimulating and appealing, so that people won't shake them off.

An Example of Love

*F*OR MANY YEARS, A RENOWNED SCHOLAR was a rabbi in a large town. When he grew old, he wanted to retire to a smaller town, a shtetl, in order to lead a quiet life, free from the numerous community affairs that he was forced to deal with in the larger town. As is customary, the rabbi first asked the members of the congregation. He summoned them and told them: "I'm old and tired, I want to spend my golden years tranquilly, and so I've decided it would be best for me if I found a small shtetl where I can live with peace of mind. But I won't move without your consent."

The householders saw that the position of rabbi in their town had indeed become too difficult for him, and so they gave him the go-ahead to become a rabbi in a smaller town. The rabbi didn't wait for long, he promptly wrote to a nearby congregation that happened to be in need of a rabbi, and he said he was ready to take on the task of leading the smaller community, for his top priority now was to enjoy a quiet life.

When the letter arrived in the small shtetl, the community rejoiced—this was no trivial matter! The world-famous scholar of the large town wanted to be the rabbi of the shtetl! So the congregation had a meeting, and the finest householders were sent out with carriages to transport the rabbi and his entire family. But when the messengers and the carriages arrived in the large town, people clustered around them, shouting that they wouldn't let their beloved rabbi leave.

The rabbi retorted: "What's wrong with you people? I asked for your permission, and you said I could leave! Why have you changed your minds?"

"You're right, rabbi," they said, and they let the carriages pass.

A bit later, when the shtetl congregants were about to drive back in the carriages, the residents of the large town attacked them—they beat them and bruised them and injured them and yelled: "You've come to snatch our dear rabbi—huh? You're wasting your time—we won't let him go!"

So the shtetl congregants went and complained to the rabbi that their coachmen had been beaten. The rabbi then went to the attackers and asked them: "You did say—didn't you?—that you would let me leave? So why have you changed your minds again? And why do the coachmen deserve to be beaten?"

"Rabbi," the attackers answered, "we didn't mean to harm them, we were trying to act in your best interest! We were concerned that some day those shtetl Jews might think you left us because we no longer wanted you, so that they would no longer respect you properly. We wanted to show them that you are so precious to us that we wouldn't allow you to leave."

MORAL

And that was also what the angels in heaven did when God gave Jews the Torah: the angels protested and strongly opposed His action of taking the Torah from heaven and bringing it to the earth. The angels didn't want the Jews to think that the Good Lord had given the Jews the Torah because it was no longer wanted in heaven.

Respect Is Expensive

*T*HE MAYOR OF A LARGE TOWN picked three householders as administrators of the town. Each administrator was to rule one district. Now one citizen greatly yearned for the respect given an administrator and he was greatly annoyed that the mayor hadn't selected him. So this citizen, who was very rich, went to the king and, through money and influence, he got the king to write the mayor and order him to dismiss one of the three administrators and replace him with the wealthy citizen.

The citizen went home, and his heart was cheerful because he had gotten his way and because he had gotten even with the mayor. Meanwhile it turned out that the town was behind in its tax payments; and according to the old custom, the administrators were responsible for the town. So the mayor had the three administrators imprisoned. Then the rich man arrived with a royal letter ordering the mayor to appoint him as an administrator. So what did the mayor do? He released one of the old administrators and imprisoned the new administrator in his stead.

MORAL

If a man seeks respect, he should be ready to pay for it.

The Fool and His Watch

A FOOL ONCE FOUND A WATCH, but he was so stupid that he didn't know that a timepiece had to be wound up so that the spring would move the hammer, the hammer the small gears, and the small gears the bigger gears. What did the fool do? Whenever he encountered someone in the street, the fool would ask him the time and then set his watch accordingly by pushing the hands. He thought that the whole point of a watch was for the owner to push the hands.

One day, an intelligent man saw the fool standing by the town clock and pushing the hands of his own clock. "You fool!" the wise man cried. "You think that the watchmaker wasted his time making that wonderful clockwork with all its gears, which all work together in a fine order, with one purpose and toward one goal. And so you push the hands yourself and you haven't the foggiest notion of what you're doing!"

MORAL

The evil man, who cares only about himself, doesn't realize the world is arranged in such a way that all people help one another, whereby each person does his bit for the entire community. The evil man lives only for himself, for his own benefit, and, like that fool, he pushes the hands of his watch himself.

A Glutton's Punishment

O NCE THERE WAS A RICH JEW who was a firm believer in hospitality, especially on the Sabbath and on holy days. He enjoyed having guests, both local and foreign, to dinner. Toward that end, he had a special house, where guests could eat as much as they wanted; and he served each guest particular dishes from the diner's homeland. Whenever a guest arrived, the host could tell at first glance where to seat him and what to serve him.

One day, a fine gentleman arrived in respectable attire. The moment the host laid eyes on him, he concluded that this was a decent, noble person, and he seated him at the head of the table, among the finest guests. The gentleman was served roast chicken and saffron rice. And as he ate, he noticed that farther down at the table, the guests were eating beans cooked in bone marrow; these were less noble guests. And farther away still, the gentleman saw paupers, the kind that go begging, and they were eating potatoes and herring.

As the gentleman stared at these paupers, who were eating with gusto, his palate yearned for the coarse fare. Leaning across the length of the table, he held out his fork, thrust it into the bowl of potatoes and herring, and, smacking his lips, he also ate with gusto.

When the host saw this, he grabbed the fine gentleman by the collar, pulled him up, and dragged him over to the paupers at the edge of the table, and he said:

"I mistook you for a decent gentleman, so I sat you at the head of the table, among fine and noble people, and you were served my finest food. But since you prefer coarse dishes, just sit among the beggars. That is your proper place!"

MORAL

The same applies to us Jews. The Good Lord sat us in a beautiful land and gave us the Torah and the temple. But we yearned for idolatry and all sorts of coarse sins. So God drove us from our land and He said: "You want to serve idols, then live among the pagans. That is your proper place!"

The Princely Garments

A GREAT RULER ONCE GOT FURIOUS at his son and expelled him to another land, an enemy nation who deeply hated the inhabitants of the ruler's land. The ruler sent his son there because he wanted him to suffer even more persecution and exile. The father swore that he would feel no pity for his son, and he let him suffer in the enemy land. The son suffered there for a long time, and the inhabitants hounded him and harassed him.

One day, the ruler learned that his son's garments had become worn out and tattered, and he was practically naked and barefoot. The father then instantly sent his son new and lovely garments, as were befitting for a prince. So people asked the ruler:

"Why are you sending him new clothes if you swore you would feel no pity for him?"

The ruler replied: "I sent him new clothes in order to punish him severely. If I hadn't sent him new clothes, someone in that country might have felt sorry for him and given him new clothes, the kind worn by people in that country, and nobody would now realize that my son is a foreigner there. Eventually he would have settled in and become like one of them and forgotten that he was in exile. That's why I sent him princely garments such as he used to wear at home—so that everyone who saw him would remember that he is a foreigner, and they will continue harassing him and giving him no peace."

M O R A L

We Jews have been expelled among non-Jews, and our princely clothing, the Torah, makes others realize that we are a foreign nation. And when
the Good Lord notices that we are even slightly neglecting the Torah, He
sends us to rabbis and sages, who interpret the Law more harshly and add
restrictions. They strengthen the Torah in order to make us adhere to our
Jewish faith, so that Gentiles may recall that we are Jews.

The King's Presents

A GREAT KING USED TO GIVE beautiful presents to all his family members,
his servants, as well as his ministers and advisors, every month, every holy
day, and for every celebration. The king also had physicians, great special-
ists, who cured him and his family members whenever they fell ill. However,
the king gave those doctors no presents. But sometimes, when a physician
was in great trouble or in need of money, the king would help him out.

So the doctors got together and submitted a grievance to the king:

"Please tell us, your majesty, in what respect are we worse than your servants. You give them presents every month, every holy day, at every celebration, but you always leave us out."

"Let me explain," the king replied. "Those people are always with me,
they serve me constantly, regularly. So I give them presents regularly. But you
doctors serve me only irregularly, by chance, in times of misfortune, when
one of us falls ill. So I also pay you by chance, when you happen to be in
trouble or in need of money."

M O R A L

This parable applies to those Jews who go to synagogue every day and
serve the Good Lord at all times, and to those Jews who go to synagogue only
on the Days of Awe or when they are in trouble. The Good Lord is with those
constant Jews all the time, but with the latter Jews only when they are in need.

The Spoiled Only Son

A KING HAD AN ONLY SON who was very weak. The father kept special
doctors, who observed the boy's state of health, and special servants who
served him. The doctors were the finest and most learned in the country. The
servants were the finest and most honest—all of them strong and handsome
like heroes, and also well-versed in all rules of court etiquette, as is fitting for
the servants of a crown prince.

The doctors prescribed what the prince could and could not eat, and the servants made sure that the prince ate accordingly and that he did not eat forbidden foods.

The prince constantly went along with the doctors and the servants. But one day, he suddenly grew wild and did the opposite of what the doctors prescribed and the servants carried out. He started consuming the forbidden food and drink. The doctors and the servants warned him and scolded him, but the prince refused to listen. As a result, he became very sick. His body was covered with sores, because the forbidden foods were like poison for him.

When the king found out, he realized that his doctors and servants weren't good enough, because they knew the boy and the king and they felt sorry for the boy and were unable to be too strict with him. So the king sent the boy far, far away, to a doctor who was strict and mean—a nasty man, who didn't know the king. This doctor was to treat the prince and cut his body, removing all the sores and proud flesh and thereby cleansing his body.

MORAL

We Jews are the prince. Our father, the king of the universe, saw that we were not obeying the doctors and servants—the priests, the levites, and the teachers. So He sent us into exile, among the non-Jews, who do not know the Good Lord, and these Gentiles are supposed to cure us with harsh hands.

The Right Remedy Will Come

A CERTAIN MAN WAS VERY SICK, and he was also very nervous. So he went to a great physician for treatment. It was autumn, a period in which it is very hard to cure the kind of disease that this man was suffering from. The doctor, seeing that his patient was anxious and very jittery, thought to himself: If I tell him to wait until spring, he'll die of terror and impatience. So perhaps I should do something now to alleviate his pain.

"Listen," the doctor said to the sick man, "I'll cure you, but only on condition that you take the medicine I prescribe and that you put yourself entirely in my hands."

The doctor dissolved a little sugar in some water and added a drop of dye to make it look like medicine. "Open your mouth," cried the doctor, "and swallow the spoonful of medicine in one gulp!" The patient plucked up his courage and did so. He imagined that the medicine was very sharp and bitter, which was the reason why the doctor had told him to swallow it in one gulp.

The patient now visited the doctor several times a week until he eventually did feel better—that's how powerful the human imagination can be.

The man decided that he was cured, but when spring came, the doctor sent for him and said: "You should know that you are still deathly sick, and you should start taking remedies. Until now, I've been deceiving you and not giving you the right medicine."

"But I took sharp and bitter medicaments!" the patient argued.

"That was just your imagination," the doctor explained. "Only now will you have the real taste of my remedies, and you'll see the difference between that 'medicine' and the kind I'm going to give you."

MORAL

When we Jews were redeemed from Egypt, we assumed that this was our ultimate salvation, that our sufferings in the desert were the right medicine, and that we were totally cured when we reached the Land of Israel. But after we were driven from our own land, we feel that that medicine was sugar water compared with what we suffer now in exile. However, we can take comfort in the fact that we are getting the right medicine and that we will be truly cured and attain everlasting salvation.

The Mirror

A MAN WAS ANGRY at his only son for committing a great sin toward his father. So the father drove the son away. The son traveled very far, homeless, naked, and starving. Meanwhile his father missed him terribly and he agonized over the boy's sufferings in a foreign land. Nevertheless, the father restrained himself, dug in his heels, and refused to call his son back so that the boy would endure the full measure of the punishment he deserved.

One day, a friend of the father's came to the town where the boy was staying, and the friend saw how miserable the boy was, how sick and gaunt. So he told the son:

"If you do as I say, I'll give you some good advice. You should know that even though your father is at home and lacks nothing, he misses you so deeply that he's become thoroughly bitter and emaciated. Buy a mirror and take it to your father, and when you arrive, hang the mirror on your chest, so that your father can view his own image. You should then cry and plead: 'Just see, dear father, what you look like. Your face is no longer radiant. So please forgive me, dear father, and let me come home again—if not for my sake then for yours.'"

MORAL

Ever since we were driven into exile, our Father in Heaven misses us terribly, and the shekhinah [the divine radiance] no longer shines as it once did. That is why we pray to God, asking for His forgiveness—if not for our sake, then for His.

Rabbi Nakhman
of Braslev
(1772–1810)

A TALE OF A KING WHO
FORCED THE JEWS TO CONVERT
(p. 1815)

ONCE THERE WAS a king. The king issued an edict forcing the Jews to convert. Any Jew who remained in the land had to be baptized. Otherwise he would be driven from the land.

Some Jews were willing to sacrifice their wealth and property and they left the land as paupers, so long as they could keep their faith and remain Jews.

Some Jews were more concerned about their wealth and so they stayed on and were forced to convert. In secret—that is, in private—they followed the Jewish religion, but in public—that is, among people—they dared not behave as Jews.

Then the king died, and his son became king. And he began to rule the land in a very severe fashion. He conquered many lands and became a great sage. And because he treated the lords of the realm in a very severe fashion, they plotted to overthrow him and kill him and all his children.

Now one of the lords was a secret Jew, and he thought to himself: "Why did I convert? Because I cared about my wealth and my property. When they kill the king, and the land will be without a king, people will devour one another alive, for a land cannot possibly be without a king."

That was why he decided to tell the king in secret. He went and told him about the plot. The king then tested the news to see if what the lord had told him was true. And the king saw that it was true.

The king stationed guards the night of the revolt, and they captured the rebels. And each lord was judged and sentenced.

The king then said to the lord who was a secret Jew: "Tell me, what sort of honor can I give you for saving me and my children? Should I make you a lord?

You already have a lordship. Should I give you money? You already have money. Tell me what sort of honor you want, and I will certainly give it to you."

The secret Jew responded: "Will you grant me my wish?"

The king said: "Yes, I will certainly grant you your wish."

The secret Jew said: "Swear to me by your crown and your kingdom."

The king swore.

The secret Jew then said: "My wish is that I be allowed to be a Jew in public, that I be allowed to wear my prayer shawl and my prayer thongs in public."

The king was very annoyed, for no Jews were allowed to live in his kingdom, but he had no choice because he had sworn an oath.

In the morning the secret Jew went and put on his prayer shawl and his prayer thongs in public.

After that the king died, and his son became king.

The new king ruled his land in a very kindly fashion, for he had seen that the lords wanted to overthrow his father. And he conquered many lands and became a very great sage.

The king then summoned all the stargazers so that they could tell him how his offspring might be cut off, so that he could protect them.

And the stargazers told him that his offspring would not be cut off, but that he should beware of a bull and a lamb. And their response was recorded in the royal chronicle.

The king told his children that they should rule the land as he did, in a kindly fashion.

After that he died, and his son became king.

The new king began ruling in a very severe fashion, just like his grandfather.

He conquered many lands and he then hit on an idea: he issued a proclamation saying that no bull and no sheep were to be found in his country, so that his offspring could not be cut off.

After the proclamation he felt that he was not afraid of anyone.

And he ruled the country in a very severe fashion and he became a very great sage.

And he hit on an idea: he would conquer the whole world but without a war. For there were seven parts in the world since the world was divided into seven parts. And there were seven planets—that is, seven stars for the seven days of the week, and each star shone over one part of the seven parts of the world. And there were seven kinds of metals: that is, gold and silver and copper and tin and the rest. And each star of the seven planets shone upon a special kind of metal.

The king then went and gathered all the seven metals and ordered his servants to bring him all the golden portraits of all the kings—the portraits hanging in their palaces—and he made them into a human being. The head was gold, the body silver, and the other limbs were made from the other metals. This man was made of all seven metals.

And the king placed the man on a mountain. And all the seven planets—that is, all the seven stars—shone upon the man.

And whenever a person needed a bit of advice or a counsel about business and didn't know whether to go ahead or not, he would come and face the limb made of the metal pertaining to his part of the world. The person couldn't decide what to do. And if the person *should* do it, then the limb would light up and shine; but if the person should *not* do it, then the limb would darken.

And the king did all that. This was how he had conquered the whole world and had assembled a great deal of money. And the man that the king had made from the seven metals was unable to do anything until the king humbled the exalted from their grandeur and exalted the humble.

The king then went and issued ukazes to all generals and other lords who had great titles—that is, occupied high royal positions. And they all came, and the king annulled their ranks and removed these men from their high positions, even if these positions had come down to them from their great-grandfathers. And the king exalted the humble, putting them in those high positions.

And one of the lords whom the king had humbled was the secret Jew, and the king asked him: "What is your position?"

"My position," he answered, "is only my right to be a Jew in public, a right I was given for what I did for your grandfather."

But the king revoked that right so that this man became a secret Jew again.

One night the king lay down to sleep, and he dreamt that the sky was clear. And he saw all twelve constellations in the sky and he saw that the Bull and the Lamb, which were among the twelve constellations, were laughing at him.

He woke up in a rage and sent for the royal chronicle, and he saw that the chronicle said that his offspring would be cut off by a bull and a lamb. The king was terrified, his heart was pounding furiously.

And the king told the queen about his dream. And she and their children were also terrified. The king was deeply frightened and he summoned all the dream diviners, the readers of dreams, and each one analyzed the dream on his own. But their interpretations did not go into the king's ears.

A sage then came to him and said he had heard from his father that the sun had three hundred sixty-five courses and that there was a place where all three hundred sixty-five courses shone at the same time. And in that place an iron rod was growing. And if the king was terrified, he should go to that iron rod, and his terror would be gone.

The king was glad to hear the sage's words and, together with his wife, his children, his entire family, he went to that place. And the sage went with them. Halfway along the road leading to the rod there is an angel, and this angel is the custodian of anger, for anger creates an angel of destruction, and this angel is the custodian of all destruction. And the traveler must ask this angel, ask him which road to take. For there is a road here, and it is good for a person to take that road. And there is a road that is full of holes, and there is a road that is full of clay, and there are so many other roads. And on one road there is a fire, and if you come within four leagues of that fire you will burn up.

They asked the angel which road to take, and he told them to take the road with the fire. And the king with all his offspring and the sage walked along. And the sage kept looking for the fire, for his father had told him about the fire. And he saw people in the fire, kings and Jews in prayer shawls and prayer thongs. And that was because these kings let Jews live in their lands, that was why they could go through the fire.

The sage then said to the king: "Since I was told that people burn up within four leagues of the fire, I don't want to go any further. If you wish to go further, then go."

And the king and his offspring went. And they were caught by the fire. And the king and all his offspring were burned, they were all swept away.

When the sage returned home, it was a miracle for the lords that the king and his offspring had been cut off. After all, he had been wary of a bull and a lamb, so why had he and his offspring been cut off?

The secret Jew now said: "It was because of me that he was cut off. You see, the stargazers who saw that his offspring would be cut off by a bull and a lamb did not grasp what they saw. The hide of a bull is used for making prayer thongs, and the wool of a lamb is used for making the tassels of the prayer shawl. That is why the king and his offspring were swept away. In those lands where Jews are allowed to live and wear prayer shawls and prayer thongs, the kings were not harmed in the least when they went into the fire. But this king did not allow Jews to live in his land and wear prayer shawls and prayer thongs, and that is why he and his offspring were swept away.

"And that is why the Bull and the Lamb among the constellations laughed at him. The stargazers saw but did not grasp what they saw.

"And that was why the king and his offspring were cut off. Amen. 'So let all Thy foes perish, O Lord!' [Judges, 5:31]."

(The Hebrew version has additional material)

"Why do the nations rage? (Psalm 2:1)"

"Thou shalt break them with an iron rod (Psalm 2:9)." That is the iron rod in the tale.

"Let us break their straps and throw away their strings (Psalm 2:9)." This refers to the prayer-thong and tassel ceremony.

The entire tale is alluded to in the ninth Psalm. Fortunate is the man who has some inkling of these tales, which are very deep mysteries of the Torah.

Yankl Morgenshtern
(1820-1890)

This narrative is an excellent example of how belles lettres can be deliberately transformed into fakelore (see Seth L. Wolitz: "Simkhe Plakhte: From 'Folklore' to Literary Artifact," *Polin*, 2003). According to Wolitz, who points out both anti-Maskilic and anti-Hasidic barbs in this tale: "The character drawn from the shtetl underclass . . . not only subverts the established social order of the traditional Jewish world, but also earns respect from the Gentile ruling class of the Polish Respublica."

Eventually, after many pseudo-folklore treatments, including a stage version as well as deliberately anonymous reprints posing as folklore, the tale was adapted into an episodic fakelore novel by Y. Y. Trunk (1887–1961).

Morgenshtern's tale offers (and suffers from) a widespread moral—as revealed in the final paragraphs.

SIMKHE PLAKHTE OR
THE UNIVERSAL SWINDLER
(1870s or early 1880s)

EVERY PERSON WHO READS this story will derive great pleasure from it—young and old, rich and poor will all enjoy it. This story will work its wit, and every reader will laugh at it.

In the land of Otz there was a small and very pious Jewish shtetl named Narkovve. And a rebbe lived there, an old man, a Hasidic rebbe. The rebbe wore a white smock, and on Friday nights he prayed in his prayer shawl and prayer thongs, and sometimes he provided remedies and sometimes he also charged a fee, and he was truly a great and honest man and also a great pauper, alas!

There was also an orphan girl in the shtetl, a girl who had no father or mother. So the rebbe's wife, feeling sorry for the orphan, took her in and brought her up. In her twenties, she was awfully gorgeous: an awful nose and a face like a gorge, eyes as big as a Hungarian calf, a pair of bulging lips like the jaw of a Russian ox, and fingers like the feet of an elephant. And she was as smart as an old donkey, but—knock on wood—she ate like a horse. And to top it all off, she went barefoot and practically naked. For who should have bought or made something for the poor thing? After all, she had no parents, the rebbe was dirt-poor, and there was no one who really liked her. For if you so much as glanced at her, your bile would burst. You see, her beauty, as depicted, had no peer. No marriages were offered her, no blind man presented himself, and no man who could see desired her. And by now, she was in her thirties.

The rebbe's wife was sitting in the women's section of the synagogue and she heard the women talking about her, chiding her for not providing a marriage for the orphan. And a wealthy, pious, and virtuous lady loudly exclaimed: "If any other household had a girl in her thirties, you and your husband would shout that it's a big sin, a desecration! But for your home, it's not even a peccadillo!" And the other saintly ladies joined in the hollering.

The rebbe's wife went home and told her husband what had happened. And he said: "They're absolutely right! It's truly a great sin."

To which his wife replied: "So what should we do?"

And the rebbe said: "I'm gonna tell you something, and you have to obey me! Take the silver knob of my cane and the silver bits of my prayer thongs and take my fox coat and your gold candlestick and the two bead necklaces and pawn all those things. With the money, the first thing we'll do is dress the girl up, for she's no beauty and also no sage, and she goes around barefoot and practically naked. So who'd marry her? But if she's dressed very beautifully, she'll look different, and a proposal will come very quickly."

The rebbe's wife went and pawned those items for one hundred fifty ducats. The rebbe then said that the girl should be dressed from head to foot in splendid clothes costing no more than fifty ducats, and she would also have a large dowry: "I'll give her a dowry of one hundred ducats so she won't feel ashamed among the wealthy girls of our shtetl. That way, someone is bound to ask for her hand."

So that's what they did. They bought some expensive batiste, a few blouses, a pair of shoes, a red kerchief, and an apron. In short, they dressed her to the nines: so she looked like a nanny goat in her fanny coat.

And once she was splendidly attired, the rebbe said: "Praised be the Lord, she's all gussied up, and her big dowry is ready. Now let's think of a match for her. Even if the bridegroom isn't the cream of the crop, we can still get them hitched."

The rebbe and his wife sat down together with the court beadle, the synagogue beadle, the prayer summoner, the abecedarian, the bath house proprietor, the reliable owner of the kosher butcher shop, and several more such great sages, and they pondered and debated a match for the nanny goat. But they didn't reach any conclusion. For any marriage broker they approached got cold feet at the sight of her face—scared as he was that a possible bridegroom might chop him to smithereens.

Now in that same shtetl there lived a youth named Shimen, but he was nicknamed Simkhe (joy, celebration) and Plakhte (coarse cloth) because he was barefoot and almost naked and that was all he wore. So people shouted at him, "Simkhe Plakhte." And the whole town knew him, for he was a water carrier. All he owned was a few poles and a few buckets and the piece of cloth he was wrapped up in. Those things constituted his entire property. He was neither a great sage nor a great fool. He didn't have a mindset for anything except lugging water and eating. He would carry six buckets for a crust of bread. And everyone knew him—old and young, big and little. And this was his custom: every Thursday night and every eve of a holy day, he would bring water and sand to the maids and help them polish the candlesticks and the silverware. And for that, he would receive a scrap. All year long, he lugged water and chopped wood for a baker, who let him sleep in a niche behind the oven. And for every wedding and every banquet, Simkhe Plakhte would drudge like a horse, lugging water and chopping wood. For that, they let him lick the plates clean. He went barefoot and naked all summer and winter, wrapped only in his piece of coarse cloth. And people only called him Simkhe Plakhte.

Now as the rebbe and the others were musing and mulling about a possible bridegroom for the beautiful nanny goat, the beadle had a flash of inspiration: Simkhe Plakhte was the perfect match! At first, everyone guffawed. But then they decided that it would be a wonderful deed! For Simkhe was already forty years old and he went about barefoot and almost naked—poor thing! What other girl would take him? And no other man would take her! And so everyone agreed on the match. But they were too scared to approach Simkhe with the news! So the rebbe told his beadle: "Go and bring me Simkhe. And mum's the word."

The beadle went and told Simkhe: "The rebbe wants to see you."

Meanwhile the rebbe told his wife to dress the bride-to-be in the splendid clothes they had made for her. By the time Simkhe arrived, she'd be all dolled up from head to foot. They dressed her, and when Simkhe Plakhte arrived in his piece of coarse cloth, balancing his pole and his buckets on his shoulders, he trudged into the vestibule and tried to see the rebbe. But the rebbe's wife told him to leave the pole and the buckets in the vestibule, for it wouldn't do to bring them to the rebbe. Simkhe refused, saying, "This is my entire property! I can't leave it unguarded." And he lugged the pole and the buckets into the rebbe's study.

The rebbe welcomed him enthusiastically and said: "Listen, my dear Simkhe! How come you don't get married? What kind of person remains single? Every Jew needs to get hitched."

Simkhe replied in his coarse peasant voice: "Rebbe, rebbe! I thought you were smart because you're a rebbe! But you've turned out to be a moron! You talk like a mindless teacher! Listen! You tell me to get hitched. Well, who'd wanna marry me?" And he removed the piece of cloth and showed the rebbe that he was naked underneath. Then he went on: "Look! I'm naked. All I own is this cloth and my pole and my buckets. I ain't got a penny to my name. And I can't recite prayers because when my parents died, I was still a child, so I never learned how to pray. So who'd want me?"

The rebbe replied: "Listen, Simkhe. I've got a rich and beautiful girl for you with lots of money!" The rebbe then nodded at his wife, and she brought in the rich bride, who was wrapped in a red shawl like a turkey. The rebbe pointed out her elegant figure and said: "Just look at how beautiful she is. She's one in a million. Just check her out. Look at her wonderful clothes. And she's got a fortune of her own!" The rebbe opened a drawer filled with cash—the hundred ducats' dowry. "Look, our aristocrat, the count who owns our shtetl, doesn't have this much money."

When Simkhe saw the rich girl and the huge amount of cash, he leaped over to the rebbe and shouted: "Rebbe! Rebbe! Okay! Okay! I'll marry her." And he said to the girl: "I love you!"

The rebbe then said: "My boy, let's take an oath. And I'll give you some clothes. And then we can sign the engagement contract. After that, you can marry her, and she'll become your wife."

But Simkhe said: "No, rebbe. First make her my wife, and then we'll draw up the contract some other time."

The rebbe sent for the cantor and for guests. And they found some old clothes for Simkhe—a shirt, trousers, a pair of shoes and stockings, a cap, a belt—and they dressed him from head to foot. Next they drew up the engagement contract. And the rebbe handed Simkhe two ducats to give the bride the groom's traditional gift after the signing of the engagement contract. And the rebbe handed the bride twelve ells of cotton cloth so she could make a Sabbath outfit for the groom. And the engagement party was very merry. And they scheduled the wedding very soon, and she used the cloth to make the groom a wedding outfit.

Several days before the wedding, the rebbe's wife and several other pious ladies made the rounds of the homes and they collected a few shirts and blouses and other clothing for the groom and the bride. And every woman donated some feathers and a couple of women contributed an old feather bed or an old pillowcase until there was enough bedding for the bride and groom.

On the Saturday before the wedding, the rebbe announced that every-one was invited to the ceremony. And so it happened. All the shtetl Jews—big and little, rich and poor—arrived. Some came for a good laugh, some as a pious deed. In short, not even a tot was left at home—all the Jews attended the wedding.

For the wedding present, guests supplied a measure of peas or potatoes or millet or buckwheat or butter. All told, there was enough food for six months. And one man even offered free rent for that period. The pious women also gathered an old cabinet, a bucket, a little dishware for meat and a little dishware for dairy food. Nothing was lacking. Even the guests who had come to laugh brought decent presents. For no Jew ever refrains from performing an act of kindness. In short, it was a very merry wedding, and they all did their best to treat the young couple generously.

The rebbe gave an order that no one was to make Simkhe carry water for free or get a crust of bread for lugging six buckets. Rather, each house-holder should pay Simkhe a kopek for each bucket, for the water carrier now had a wife to support. In short, the rebbe and the rest of the shtetl did what they could to provide an income for the two orphans.

The next morning, the rebbe hosted a breakfast for the young newly-weds, who were then led into their own home. The pious women acquired everything possible for their household. And on each day of the wedding week, a different congregant threw a banquet. At the end of that week, the rebbe told Simkhe that he should treat his spouse decently, and the rebbe's wife, together with other pious ladies, told Simkhe's wife that she should conduct herself properly both in religious matters and with her husband. She should manage a good house and keep the dowry—one hundred ducats—locked up in a cashbox.

Mr. Simkhe Plakhte and his madame were now happier than Rothschild, for they had enough food to last them several months plus free rent for half a year and as much cash as a banker. And they told one another: "Now we can finally live to our hearts' content."

So Mr. Simkhe got down to brass tacks and he said to his madame: "My dear wife, I like everything except for one thing. I have to tell you that I don't like the pots and dishes. They're good for little children but not for us. So go to the market and bring back the finest pots and dishes and earthen vessels as are fitting for us."

Madame Plakhte didn't wait to be asked twice. She went and brought back double-decker pots and dishes, vessels like deep bowls and plates like tubs. And the couple cooked two or three things at once and didn't overeat. And as soon as they had polished off the meal, they didn't wait, they thought about cooking more goodies, and they didn't pause for long. For who was as cheery as Mr. Plakhte and his madame? In short, the household was run like that for several weeks. Until Madame Plakhte saw that things were going downhill. So she said to Simkhe:

"My dear husband, take the pole and the buckets and go carry water in the shtetl. If you earn something, we'll have ready cash. Then, when we're out of food and money, we'll use the fresh cash to stock up. But if you don't earn anything, and we run out of what little we have, we'll starve."

Simkhe heard her out and then he said:

"My dear wife, did I get married in order to lug water? I lugged enough water from my childhood till my wedding! My shoulders can no longer stand the pole and the buckets! I figured that once I got hitched, I wouldn't have to drudge so hard. If I'd known the truth, I wouldn't of gotten hitched in the first place."

Madame replied: "No, my dear husband, every person has to work. If he doesn't work, he doesn't eat."

Simkhe retorted: "The rebbe you lived with doesn't do a stitch of work, yet he's got food."

The wife said: "He's a rabbi, and a Hasidic rebbe at that. And you're no rabbi and no rebbe!"

The husband said: "You were raised in his home, so you know his rites and his habits. Tell me what they are and I'll imitate them. That way, we'll also have work. And I won't need to lug water."

The wife said: "First of all, he wears a white smock and a sash that's made out of a long, white towel, and he sports a high fur hat on his head, and he holds a huge cane with a white knob. I don't know what it is, but I'm sure it's made of tin. And he sits over a big, long, Daily Prayer Book and he rocks back and forth and hollers. And when he prays, he scurries to and fro and he claps his hands, and he makes so much noise that he can be heard from far away. Jews come in and give him money, so he doesn't have to work."

Upon hearing that, Simkhe said: "It's simple, my dear wife. Just do what I say, and I won't have to lug any water either. And we'll eat and drink better than the rebbe. Because I can outdo him in the things you've mentioned. I can clap my hands better than he can. And I can scurry back and forth faster than he can. And I can holler so loud that they'll hear me from one end of town to the other. The only thing I can't do is read the long Daily Prayer Book. But so what! Clapping my hands, scurrying back and forth, and hollering and rocking—that's all I need to do! It's simple, my wife, we'll live a good life. Just do what I say: go and have a white smock made for me. And get me copies of everything the rebbe has. And it will all be fine and dandy."

The wise madame did as she was told. She procured white cloth and had a long smock made with very long sleeves, brass hooks, and a long white towel as a sash. She also knew there was an ancient fur hat in the rebbe's attic, and she went and took the hat. Next, she took the pole from the slop buckets and had a tinsmith add a white tin knob on top of the pole.

When Simkhe tried on the clothes, he said to his wife: "Well, what do you think? Aren't I a genuine rebbe?"

She said, "Yes."

Simkhe went on: "All that's missing is a big, long Daily Prayer Book. Go to the rebbe. He must have a huge shelf filled with prayer books. Bring me a long prayer book—just make sure it's very thick."

She went to the rebbe's home and stole an enormous Talmud volume and she told her husband: "I've brought you a huge Daily Prayer Book. Now you're not missing anything."

Her husband said: "Fine, fine, my wife. Now cook some goodies in several big pots as if they were meant for a rebbe."

But there was little food left, enough for only a few more days. And this was after Shevuoth, the late-summer holiday celebrating the first fruits and the giving of the Torah to the Jews. So for six times a day, they cooked in their biggest pots. But even a well can run dry. Still, Simkhe's wife kept cooking in the big pots, for her husband had become a rebbe, and she was certain that they would not be lacking an income. She cooked, and they stuffed themselves like there was no tomorrow.

Now Simkhe put on the white garment and the cloudburst fur hat. And he clutched the slop-bucket pole and he sat down at the table by the window and he opened the big prayer book and he rocked as if he had the shakes. Then he sent his wife out into the street to see if anyone was coming with money. She stood outside, while he rocked for all he was worth! He kept rocking for several days, but not even a dog showed up. And their supper consisted of the last remaining groats, and a teensy portion of potatoes for tomorrow's breakfast.

When Simkhe and his wife were finishing their supper, she said: "What are we gonna do now? Tomorrow morning we'll eat the few leftover potatoes and then we'll starve. You keep rocking and rocking, but no one comes along."

Simkhe said: "People don't yet know that I'm a rebbe. Nobody's seen me in rabbinical clothes. I'll go pray in synagogue tomorrow. Once people see me, they'll start coming. But while I'm praying, make sure you don't devour the potatoes."

She said: "Don't worry. I'll cook them and save them for you. But if you're away for a long time, I'll get hungry and eat them up. We've got almost no food, and I can't stand the shortage."

The next morning, when Simkhe got up, he put on his big fur hat, his long, white smock with sleeves as wide as stockings and a long, white towel as his sash, and with a slop-bucket pole in his hand. He held his prayer thong and prayer shawl under his arm. And he again told his wife not to eat up their breakfast—God forbid! And away he went.

When he reached the marketplace, he caused a big turmoil and a terrible hullabaloo. People thought he was a devil. And when they saw that it was Simkhe Plakhte, they shouted and they laughed their heads off. The whole town, young and old, came dashing over. He couldn't get away from them, he barely escaped with his life. Eventually, he wound up in the synagogue.

When the students and the worshipers caught sight of him, you can imagine what happened. They hurled a rag, an old hat, a slipper, a house shoe at his head. He barely managed to escape with his life. Out in the street, a whole army of urchins—young and old—was waiting for him. The laughter and the violence were dreadful. He tried to pray. But he couldn't. So he rushed out of the town. They chased him for a while. He eventually raced into the distant forest, which was three miles away. The urchins and hunters started back.

Simkhe went deep into the forest, and there he donned his prayer thongs and buried his head in his prayer shawl, while the white smock sparkled. He stood under a huge tree and he rocked and prayed.

Now the owner of the town was a great count, who owned many towns and villages. And he also served as minister when the monarch asked him to judge a competition. The count lived several miles from the forest and he loved to go hunting—that is, riding through the forest and shooting wild beasts. And he had a steed that was the apple of his eye.

That day, he tied his steed to a tree and strode into the forest with his gun. When he came back, ready to gallop home, his horse was gone. The count was miserable. He rushed into the forest, looking for his steed. He was very warm because of the hot day. While seeking his horse, the count spotted a man in a prayer shawl and in white clothes. The man was rocking intensely. Now since the count was very educated, he knew from his books and from the Bible that the greatest ancient worshipers had prayed and studied in forests. Moses (of blessed memory) had studied in the forest. King David (of blessed memory), the prophet Elijah, and other great men, Hasidic administrators, sages, Talmudists—all of them had prayed and studied in forests. And when the count saw a man wrapped in a prayer shawl, sporting prayer thongs, and dressed in white, he knew that this must be a very great man, a secret Jewish saint, or a prophet.

The count waited until the man had recited the Eighteen Benedictions. Then the count bowed and he asked the man who he was.

Simkhe said: "I am the assistant rebbe of Narkovve."

The count said: "I believe that you are from Narkovve, but not that you are the assistant rebbe. I know the head rebbe, and he isn't fit to be anything but your servant. My dear assistant: I know very well that if you come to pray in the forest, you must be a great man even if you are only the rebbe's assistant. But that's only among other people, so they won't realize how great you are. I have a request for you. Today, I lost my horse, and I'd rather lose a village than lose my steed. Please tell me: where is my horse?"

Simkhe trembled from head to foot. He was scared that his wife might eat up the final potatoes, and so he wanted to dash home and therefore get rid of the count as fast as possible.

So Simkhe said to the count: "Run very quickly to the other end of the forest. Your horse is standing there by a tree. Two wolves are about to tear it to shreds. But it is fending them off. Still, it's very tired. Dash over there with your gun and shoot one wolf. The other wolf will run away."

The count ran to the other end of the forest. Meanwhile, Simkhe raced home more dead than alive. Upon reaching his house, he hid under the bed and he said to his wife: "Don't tell anybody I'm hiding here, the count will soon be dispatching someone to kill me because I deceived him."

In olden times, a count was like a monarch in his town. He did anything he wanted to.

Simkhe's wife said to Simkhe: "You moron! Get out from under the bed and sit down at the table! First of all: maybe nobody'll come here! And if somebody does come—God forbid—they'll easily find you under the bed."

In short, his wife barely managed to get him out from under the bed. Simkhe sat down at the table, and she served him a bowl of potatoes. But he felt worse than a corpse, he couldn't eat, his heart was bitter, and his belly was locked.

Let's leave Simkhe Plakhte at the table and let's return to the count.

The count ran to the other end of the forest and there he found everything as Simkhe had described it. The steed was standing with his head against a tree, while two wolves stood there, about to tear the horse to shreds, whereby the horse was fending them off with its hind legs. But by now, the horse was so exhausted that it was foaming at the mouth. Upon spotting this, the count swiftly shot one wolf dead. The other wolf ran away. The count then mounted his steed, but rather than heading home, he galloped off to the shtetl.

En route, he told himself: "That's no assistant, that man works directly with God. He's no ordinary human being, he's an angel. Lucky for me that he lives in my town. And how fortunate for me that I had the privilege of seeing him and conversing with him—a privilege that's not enjoyed by millions of people!"

And the count, in his hunting clothes, galloped swiftly to his town. There, he headed straight to the rebbe's house. The rebbe bowed, for he knew him, because the count had given him several measures of wheat or wood on a number of occasions.

While the rebbe was bowing and scraping, the count said: "Please stop bowing. And please send for your assistant, have him come immediately."

The poor messenger hurried off and got the real assistant, an elderly scholar. Upon seeing him, the count said in Polish: "That's not him! Go and bring me the real assistant."

They swore that this was the real assistant. The count blew up and he said: "I demand that you bring me the real assistant! You know very well who I mean!"

The rebbe quickly sent his beadle to get the important men and the synagogue wardens. They came dashing over and they bowed to the count.

The count said to them: "I graciously demand that you bring me the real assistant! If not, you'll be sorry!"

They brought a scholar, a teacher, and a Hasid. But the count said about each man: "That's not him!"

So they asked the count: "Your Lordship, what does the assistant look like?"

The count replied: "You aren't worthy of his visit! You aren't worthy of polishing his boots! He is a great man! And compared with him, you are animals! He doesn't even care to pray with you! He prays and studies in the forest. And if you don't take me to him, I'll destroy you the way God destroyed Sodom!"

The Jews were miserable. They didn't know what to do. And the only scholar in the shtetl was here. But the count kept saying: "That's not him!"

However, since the count said that the assistant prayed in the forest, the beadle whispered to the others: "Maybe he means Simkhe Plakhte. Because today I saw the students chase him out of the synagogue. People said that he had run into the forest."

So the rebbe said to the wardens: "Go and send for him!"

The wardens said to the count: "There's one other possible man in town, and we are sending for him! He may be the one you mean."

So the messenger went to Simkhe and told him to come to the rebbe. The count of the shtetl was there and he had asked for Simkhe. But Simkhe wouldn't hear of it! When the messenger returned and explained that Simkhe refused to come, the wardens told the count: "We sent for him, and the messenger told him that you were here. But he refused to come."

The count said: "If it's the man I'm looking for, he's right about not wanting to come. For I am not worthy of his visit. You Jews just don't know who he is. But I know! So lead me to him!"

The town worthies, the wardens, and the rebbe led the count to Mr. Simkhe Plakhte's home. Mr. Plahkte was sitting in his white smock and Turkish fur hat and with the slop-bucket pole on the big prayer book, and he seemed to be having the shakes. And he was so terrified that he turned as white as a ghost. The count opened the door, and the others followed.

Upon seeing him, the count promptly doffed his hat, bowed his head, and fell to his knees as if before the king. Taking this in, the Jews were frightened and astonished. When the count saw Simkhe's pale face and his dark home and his dismal household, he was furious at the Jews and he angrily said: "You are thieves, killers, and swindlers! And you've been all those things for a long time! If a man is no thief and no swindler, if he's an honest-to-goodness servant of God—then you kill him! Our helper was also killed by somebody! The prophet Jeremiah was thrown into a lime pit, the prophet Zechariah was killed in the temple, the prophet Isaiah had his mouth sliced open—and you want to do the same thing to him. May you all rot in hell! You all live in mansions, but you make him live in a pigsty! I'm going to make you pay for that!"

When Madame Plakhte heard the count, she opened her mouth like Balaam's ass and she spoke. (She didn't know any blessings or morning prayers, but she did know Polish!) In the presence of the other Jews, she said to the count: "Not only are we tormented by hunger and poverty, but they don't pity us at all! So my husband is taking his life into his hands when he ventures out into the street. They throw rocks at him! Today they wanted to kill him at the synagogue!"

Next she showed the count the tiny measure of cold potatoes. And she said: "That's the only food we've got in the house! But he can't eat because they tortured him so horribly today!"

Upon hearing that, the count grew as furious as a tiger and he ground his teeth at all the Jews and he said: "I'm riding home now, but I'll be returning here soon with a bunch of peasants, and any of you who's harmed him will get a hundred lashes in the marketplace. That'll teach you!"

And from a pouch he produced a big silk sack of pure gold ducats and he handed it to Simkhe's wife and he said to her: "You should buy food immediately and not worry about tomorrow. Because tomorrow, and maybe even today, I'll take care of everything. You will lack nothing. And please make a list of all the people who tortured your husband, and I'll skin them alive."

And the count bowed and knelt down in front of Mr. Simkhe and with great servility he said good-bye and left. But before leaving, he told Mr. Simkhe: "You won't be living here for long. I'll be giving you wonderful mansions, which you deserve."

When all the Jews were outside, the count said to them: "Didn't I tell you that you weren't worthy of his visit? For he is a divine spirit. And since you tortured him, I will torture you."

And he furiously galloped off.

The Jews were awfully ashamed and frightened, for they were as scared of the count as if he were the angel of death. And they couldn't figure out what was going on with Mr. Simkhe Plakhte.

So they consulted the rebbe about going to see Simkhe and his wife. The Jews would plead with them to ask the count to let them go. For the count could wipe them out along with their children. But when they entered Simkhe's home, they were unable to speak with the couple, for Madame Plakhte was already busy cooking. She had put up twelve triple-decker pots containing meat, derma, potatoes, and barley. The fireplace was sizzling and crackling for all it was worth. And Simkhe was virtually a book of memories—he reminded them of what else they needed to buy for the gobble machine. When he looked at the fireplace, his heart surged in sheer delight. No sooner were the town worthies allowed to speak than they begged him to intercede for them with the count. Balaam's ass blared out: "Yeah, yeah! Don't let him go through the streets, and just keep punishing him, so he'll go into the forest!"

They swore to Simkhe that nobody would say anything nasty to him anymore and that they would respect him. Simkhe then promised to intercede for them, and the worthies said good-bye reverentially and left. The rebbe and the town worthies exchanged glances and wondered if they were dreaming or waking. For they were well acquainted with Simkhe and his wife and they also knew that the count was wise and learned as well as being a nobleman. They were at a loss to grasp what was happening. And they were scared that Simkhe might harm them in some way.

When the count returned home, he was very cheerful, his face was radiant with joy. The countess and their children respectfully asked him where he had been for such a long time. He must have had a wonderful hunt—that is, shot a lot of animals.

The count said: "My dear wife and my dear children, I had great luck on my hunt today. It's dearer to me than all my wealth and riches. I'm the happiest man in the world. And you all may also consider yourselves lucky because of what I found while hunting in the forest. I came upon a treasure that will make us happy forever. I met a man who is a man of God. He knows many things just like the Good Lord himself. He is the greatest sage and the greatest scholar of all the Jews. And he knows what's happening on the earth and in the heavens."

And the count told the countess and their children the whole story about the horse and the wolves.

And when they heard it, they said: "Why didn't you ask him where he could be found? You might need him some day."

The count said: "I spent all day tracking him down. It was an arduous task. And I conversed with him and his wife. The Jews refused to help me out. Maybe they don't realize who he is. But tomorrow, I'll take you to meet him so that you get to know him yourself."

When the countess and the children heard that, they were overjoyed, and they eagerly looked forward to the daytime, so they could go and visit that man of God and his wife. They just couldn't wait.

Early the next morning, they had breakfast, and the count ordered his men to harness four horses to a splendid, brightly decorated coach. The count and the countess sat in that coach, while their married children sat in a second coach, and their unmarried children in a third coach. These coaches were accompanied by several big wagons containing wheat, chickens, calves, and many other things, all sorts of fruit, and many peasants. And the marvelous train halted outside Mr. Simkhe Plakhte's cottage.

The whole town saw the coaches and they recognized them as belonging to the count. And they all saw the count's destination. The coaches stood outside Simkhe's door, and the count and his sons went inside, clutching their hats in great respect. And each person bowed and kissed the hand of the holy rabbinical assistant. Next, the count obtained permission to bring in his wife and his daughters, who all kissed Madame Plakhte's hand.

The count then told Mr. Simkhe to choose any building in town that he wanted. Now a three-story house stood in the middle of the marketplace— it was the finest and biggest mansion in the shtetl. And that was the building that Mr. Simkhe desired. So the count bought it, went to the notary public, and registered the property as belonging to Mr. Simkhe in perpetuity. Next, they purchased wonderful furniture and they furnished six rooms and a marvelous kitchen. And Mr. Simkhe and his wife were led into the mansion.

The count sent for his court tailor and told him to clothe Mr. Simkhe from head to foot in the most splendid silks—five or six suits and a silk dressing gown as well as a genuine white satin smock and a white silk belt, plus some expensive furs. The countess took Madame Plakhte by the hand and led her to her court tailor for ladies and also to a shop, where they bought all sorts of splendid clothing as well as marvelous linen and bedding. And they also went to a goldsmith and bought all kinds of ornaments, and they decked out Madame Simkhe like a princess. And they gave her a pouch containing several hundred ducats.

And the count and his wife said to Mr. Simkhe and his wife: "Don't save the money, buy whatever your heart desires. You won't lack cash, we'll send you more every week."

And they left two peasants to serve Mr. Simkhe and his wife and take care of the household. The two peasants were given a room to live in at the top of the mansion. And the count also gave Mr. Simkhe his gold watch. And the countess left many presents for Madame Simkhe. And the count and the countess said good-bye very respectfully to Mr. Simkhe and his wife and they told the two peasants to be very loyal and the count and his wife went home.

Upon reaching his home, the count was so overjoyed that he threw a grand ball. And he summoned all the servants and messengers and told them about the rabbinical assistant. They were all surprised and delighted.

Our Mr. Simkhe and his wife started procuring new utensils. They put aside the old utensils, which were already too small, and they bought pots the size of water cans and bowls the size of tubs. And they spent entire days doing nothing but watching and watching over the food. A whole troupe of peasants couldn't have devoured all the chow that this couple gobbled up every day. And they received food from the count every week, flour, calves, chickens, plus wood and a pouch full of money.

The countess also sent a few good milk cows and cowhands to milk them and churn butter, so that Madame Plakhte could have enough milk and butter for her needs.

In short, Mr. Simkhe Plakhte lived splendidly in several luxuriously appointed rooms, where he was served by a few male and female domestics in a household resembling an aristocratic court. He wore only silk, while his old fur hat was put out of sight. He now wore a sable hat worth a hundred rubles, while his long, white smock and his white belt were pure satin. He also carried a genuine bamboo cane with a solid silver knob weighing half a pound.

Madame Plakhte was dressed like a countess. And they also had two Jewish servants in the kitchen. The townsfolk looked at this household and some laughed and some exploded. But they were forced to be respectful, lest someone report them to the authorities.

Mr. Simkhe was dressed like a great Hasidic leader. After giving it some thought, he hired a man who was well-versed in the customs of such hypocrites and could brag about swindling with the holy rebbe's help and claiming he ate nothing. And, with signs and wonders, he proved that he could conjure up angels.

That man was also his personal assistant, and this assistant taught him how to pray a little. And his wife also hired an old woman who could pray and read properly and could teach Madame Plakhte how to do these things. And, like a real rebbe's wife, she made a grand entrance in the synagogue, carrying the women's Yiddish prayer book. And Rebbe Simkhe's assistant became the manager of his affairs. And he lived on a sumptuous scale for there was never any lack of money. He built a ritual bath in his court and a large study house with several books, plus a special room with sacred books for the holy rebbe. And Rebbe Simkhe declared that his house should be open to poor people. Anyone who came hungry left with a full stomach. Both Rebbe Simkhe and his wife gave lots of charity, and his private study was beautifully painted and furnished, and there were many candlesticks and lamps. And by the door, there was a huge ritual washstand with a huge basin, both made of copper, and there were two large towels, and there was a big mezuzah on a silver doorpost. The place looked as if it belonged to a genuine rebbe. Rebbe Simkhe sat in his private study and day and night he gobbled food like a hog.

Every week, the count sent more money than Rebbe Simkhe and his wife needed, and the count and the countess and their entire household considered it a great privilege to have such a godly man in their town, for they erroneously believed that he would save them from the worst distress or disease. And the godly man's name spread far and wide to all the aristocrats and peasants in all the surrounding villages, for the count and the countess sang his praises among all the nobles. And all the great nobles sent huge gifts to the godly man. In short, Rebbe Simkhe and his wife lived very happy and joyful lives such as no rich man could lead. They had all the good things, and there was no lack of money. And they didn't worry about the future, all they cared about was the food they prepared in huge pots and bowls and plates. And that was how they spent the next few restful years.

One day, something happened to the count. Among all the chambers in his palace, there was one small room that no one else ever entered. The door was constantly locked, and the window faced a backyard, and the backyard was surrounded by a high wall. This room contained all the count's wealth and property. A huge chest stood there, and inside it there was a small, artistically worked chest of pure gold, and the small chest contained diamonds and brilliants worth millions. And that wasn't even the most important treasure, for the chest also contained a big parchment sheet. In gold letters, the parchment described the count's entire family tree, indicating that he was a count by birth and of royal seed. And the document was dearer to him than all the diamonds and brilliants. And he went to that room every day and looked at the small chest and was overjoyed.

Now one day he entered the room and he was horror-stricken because the large chest had been forced open and the small chest was gone. He promptly ran out and raised a hullabaloo! His men searched, they suspected a lot of people, they beat them, they tortured them. But it was no use, they couldn't find even the slightest trace of the vanished chest. So the count went to the court of law. He conferred with great forensic sages, and he announced that the man who uncovered the theft would be given a whole village. But that didn't help either. So he went to consult old priests who solved mysteries. It cost the count a great deal of money, but these old priests didn't help either.

The count didn't want to go to Rebbe Simkhe because he thought: "Maybe I'll get to the bottom of this with other people's help. That way, I won't have to bother that godly man."

But when six months passed without a solution to the mystery, and the count had spent a whole lot of money and had become sick and crazy, he did have to bother that godly man after all.

Our Rebbe Simkhe didn't anticipate this at all as he sat there in royal attire, gobbling and guzzling like two fat slobs. Suddenly, a splendid coach drawn by four horses and fit for a count came rolling up. And the count's young son as well as coachmen and lackeys stood in front of Simkhe Plakhte's mansion, and the young count stepped inside very respectfully with his hat under his arm and he said to Rebbe Simkhe:

"Mr. Prophet, I bring you best greetings from my father and my mother and our entire household, and we all kneel before you. You see, my father has a problem, a very weighty problem, which he didn't wish to bother you with. But since nobody has managed to help him, he is forced to bother you. He has therefore ordered me to be so good as to bring you to his palace, for he's convinced that you are certain to help him."

When Simkhe heard those words, his heart turned bitter. He then went to his wife with his bitter heart and he said to her: "My dear wife, you'd better prepare my pole and my buckets. Who knows if I'll even be privileged to use them again? I may get killed, for the blister will be punctured once the count realizes that I'm just a crude and simple ignoramus. He'll figure out that I was just guessing about his horse and the wolves and he'll be mortified because he spent so much on me. He'll be so embarrassed that he made such a fool of himself and he'll get even with me."

To make a long story short: willing or not, off he drove. When he arrived at the palace, the count welcomed him very respectfully and begged his pardon for bothering him and he said to Simkhe: "I did everything I could to avoid bothering you. But since no one can help me, I'm forced to bother you. For this whole business must be a trifle for you. "

And the count told Simkhe the whole story from A to Z. Rebbe Simkhe heard him out and his eyes darkened and his heart grew bitter. And he thought to himself: "I'd be better off being a water carrier."

So he said to the count: "I must tell you that this is no trifle. This is a very big thing. This can't be solved as quickly as you think. I'll need three days. And I'll have to be all alone until I hit on a solution, for this is a heavenly matter."

In the village, there was a Jewish tavern keeper with a huge tavern and a small room to live in. The windows of that room faced a field. When the count heard that Simkhe needed three days, he sent for the Jewish tavern keeper and said to him: "Empty out your small room and clean it up. And you and your household will live in the big tavern. And this godly man will live in the small room for three days, and you should treat this great man as if he were I. And you must go to town and buy him food and drink worthy of a count. I'll pay for everything. For your reward, you can rent the tavern scot-free for a year. But if I hear that you haven't treated him well, then I'll kick you out of my village."

And the count very respectfully took the godly man and personally led him to the tavern, where everything was ready for him. The count said good-bye to Rebbe Simkhe, who then sat down all alone in the small room and felt totally miserable.

All the peasants and farmhands from the village knew that the godly man was there. The ones who had been wrongfully suspected were now delighted that the truth would come out, showing that they were honest people. And the count's palace was likewise very cheerful, for the people there expected the theft to be cleared up. And for the three days, the count summoned all the neighboring counts. And peasants came hurrying from other villages when they heard that the godly man was there, and they were delighted. But, alas! Rebbe Simkhe's heart was bitter and sour.

When the count had left, the tavern keeper and his wife laughed their heads off at Simkhe, for they knew him. But then the tavern keeper drove to town with good poultry to be slaughtered, and he bought all sorts of goodies and fruits, plus good wine and other good beverages and coffee and sugar and all the things that are needed for a great man. And the tavern keeper's wife cooked and roasted, and they brought Simkhe several large bowls and plates filled with fish and meat and all sorts of delicacies. For they knew that he didn't indulge in regular fasts.

To make a long story short: They covered the tables with enough food for a wedding. But Rebbe Simkhe couldn't eat, his heart was as bitter as death. His belly was closed, and his heart had turned to stone. He couldn't get even a smidgen down his throat. His throat was shut. All he could do was pace back and forth, and his life was bitter. A few hours later, the tavern keeper and his wife brought in fresh food. How amazed they were upon seeing that Simkhe hadn't touched a thing. That evening, they brought in his dinner. But they had to take back those vessels and the food exactly as they had brought them.

Nor could Simkhe sleep a wink. He practically fell out of bed when he thought about how bitter his end would be. At the crack of dawn, he put on his prayer shawl and prayer thongs, and he prayed to the extent that he knew how to pray.

When the tavern keeper and his wife brought him his breakfast, and they saw that he hadn't touched last night's dinner, and they found him standing in the large prayer shawl, they were surprised and terrified. And they said to one another: "It's not gratuitous after all. Who knows what hidden saint or Hasidic leader he is and who knows what punishment we'll have to endure for laughing at him?"

The fireplace and the kitchen were piled high with pots, plates, and platters, all of them filled with food. For Simkhe hadn't eaten even a crumb, but the tavern keeper had to prove to the count that he had prepared meals for the visitor.

During the second night, which would usher in the third day, Simkhe lay there in a miserable state. He didn't sleep a wink. Meanwhile, the door was shut, the moon shone through the window, and as Simkhe lay there, lost in thought, he heard a loud voice coming through the window: "Mr. Prophet! Mr. Prophet!"

At first, Simkhe was scared. But when those words were shouted several times, and the stranger begged him to open the window, even though a normal rebbe wouldn't open the window or talk with a nocturnal stranger no matter what, our Rebbe Simkhe didn't make a fuss, he stood up. I don't know if he washed his hands first. At any rate, he opened the window and shouted: "Who's there? Who's there?"

The stranger replied: "Please lower your voice. I have to talk to you about an important matter, and nobody must hear. My name is Stepan. I've got the small chest containing the diamonds and everything else. Nothing is missing, and the chest is hidden in a place that nobody knows, and nobody has touched it. I know very well that you are a man of God. And you know the whole story, but if I tell the count, he'll kill me. I only got married six months ago and I love my wife very much. If the count finds out that I know where the chest is, he'll have us both killed. I beg you— please have pity on me, take the chest and hand it back to the count in a wise manner and make sure he doesn't know the truth. And I'll reward you generously."

Simkhe replied: "What are you talking about? Don't I know how lucky you are that you've come to me? Where did you conceal the chest?"

Stepan answered: "From there to the forest, the road is flanked by trees, and I counted off twelve trees. I dug a hole under the thirteenth tree and buried the chest there."

Simkhe then asked: "Are you sure nobody else knows about it?"

Stepan said: "Not even my wife knows about it. Come with me and I'll show you the hiding place. And you can take the chest. But remember God, and don't tell anyone that I'm the thief."

Even though it was night, Rebbe Simkhe climbed out the window and accompanied Stepan. And Stepan grabbed a spade and dug up the hole. And they found the chest. It lay there just as Stepan had said.

Simkhe told Stepan to leave the chest where it was. They should cover it well and pour lots of soil over it. Simkhe then told Stepan: "Go home and go to bed and don't tell anyone about this, don't say a word. Otherwise you'll die on the spot."

Stepan doffed his cap and fell to his knees and he said: "My lips are sealed." And he left.

Rebbe Simkhe felt cheerful and he went back to the tavern. He silently climbed in through the window of his small room and closed the window. Then he stood at the window and stared at the spot where the small chest was buried. For he was scared that Stepan might change his mind and dig up the chest. Rebbe Simkhe stood there until dawn. Then he put on a white silk jacket as well as prayer thongs and a prayer shawl and he stood at the window and rocked to and fro.

When it was broad daylight, the count arrived together with many aristocrats and important men. They had all come to see and delight in the man of God and witness his grand miracles. They halted outside. Only the count set foot in the tavern. The door to the small room was still locked.

The count asked the tavern keeper whether he had treated the rebbe decently. To which the tavern keeper replied: "My Lord, I treated him like a count. However, he didn't eat or drink the whole time he was here." And the tavern keeper showed the count the pots and pans and plates that were filled with food—fish and meat, cooked and roasted, and with good wine.

The count was astonished and he said: "I'm so sorry that I took advantage of him and tormented him." And the count went out and summoned all the aristocrats and showed them the food and explained that the saintly man had been fasting for three days now.

The count tiptoed very softly to the door and peered through the crack and he saw the saint standing there, wrapped in his holy garments and rocking to and fro. The count then summoned all the aristocrats, and they all saw it for themselves and were amazed.

But Simkhe sensed the count's presence, he recognized his voice. So he began to play his tricks. He clapped his hands and stamped his feet and he suddenly opened the door. The count and all the aristocrats quickly doffed their hats and fell to their knees at Simkhe's feet.

And Simkhe told the count: "You will have your property back today. Summon all the people who live in your village and have them line up with men on one side and women on the other. The same applies to the aristocrats and their wives and daughters. And the same also applies to all the Jews here: the Jewish tavern keeper, the mothers-in-law, the wives, and even their grown daughters should stand on one side. And once they have fallen in, they will all stand ready. Next, you should come over to me, and everyone else should stand under the trees."

The count and the other aristocrats hurried over, for they were very eager to witness the great wonder. To make a long story short: it wasn't long before they were all lined up in accordance with what Simkhe had told them to do. And the count came over to Simkhe, and the two of them went over to the people lined up there with great respect as if paying homage to a monarch. And Simkhe and the count walked together.

Now Simkhe said to the count: "Come with me and watch what I do and hear what I say, but keep silent."

Rebbe Simkhe went along the entire line of women from start to finish and placed his hand upon each woman's heart, and as he removed his hand, he shook his head and yelled very loudly: "No! No! She's pure! She knows nothing about the theft!"

When he was done with the women, he went to the men. And he did the same thing from start to finish as he had done with the women. However, when he placed his hand on Stepan's heart, he felt it pounding like a bell, but he said nothing. Instead, he yelled out in front of every man: "No! No! He is innocent of the theft!"

And because none of these people knew the truth, they regarded Rebbe Simkhe as a real man of God. And they all liked him very much.

When Rebbe Simkhe was done with the men, he turned to the count and said loudly so that everybody would hear him: "You must know that you have suspected all these people for no reason. They are all honest. But you have to have your chest today because I gave you my word."

Rebbe Simkhe wrapped himself in his prayer shawl, pulled down his big fur hat, clutched his bamboo cane, and he rocked to and fro and pointed at the four corners of the sky. And he drew the prayer shawl over his head and covered his face and his hat. And he shook his cane like a red fir branch at the Feast of Tabernacles. Then for several minutes he remained as mute as a corpse. And suddenly he shouted angrily at the count: "No! No! Nobody took your chest! It is a celestial matter. You will have it soon."

And all the people, including the Jews, heard and witnessed everything, and they were astonished. Simkhe handed the count his bamboo cane and, together with the count and the entire populace, Simkhe went over to the first tree. There he told the count to loudly hit the tree three times. The count did so. And Simkhe then asked the count: "Did you hear what the tree said?"

The count replied: "No."

Simkhe then said: "The tree said that it doesn't have the chest."

And they did the same thing with the second tree, and the third, until they reached the right tree. And when the count hit the tree three times, Simkhe jumped for joy and clapped his hands and shouted at the count: "What are you waiting for? Didn't you hear the tree holler that the chest is buried here? It was brought here from heaven. Now hurry up and bring me a spade. Only you alone must go!"

The count dashed away and came back with a spade. Simkhe then told him to dig a hole two spades deep. And the count did so. How terrified the count and all the aristocrats were when they saw the chest. The count took hold of the chest and showed it to everyone who was there. The aristocrats and the villagers all doffed their hats and knelt at Simkhe's feet as if he were a god. And the peasants and the peasant women knelt down and shouted: "This is God's right hand!"

The reader can now see the great awe and respect that were paid to Rebbe Simkhe Plakhte. And the tavern keeper and his wife couldn't endure the fact that they had laughed at Rebbe Simkhe. They now said: "Who knows what will happen to us for laughing at such an angel!?"

To make a long story short: Simkhe was taken to the count. But they couldn't keep him for long, since the count and the other aristocrats knew that he had been fasting for three days. And he was showered with great and lavish presents and lots of money. Each aristocrat gave Simkhe his gold watch and all his signet rings. The result was a mound of money and jewelry. It was then placed in a small chest, and the count himself gave Simkhe a small chest full of cash and gold and silver and jewelry. In short, it all equaled the treasures of Corah, the rich man who rebelled against Moses.

They honored Simkhe by harnessing the splendid coach and four. And the countess and her children and the aristocrats with their wives and children rode in a huge number of coaches. For each person considered it a privilege to escort the rebbe, and every peasant who had a wagon and one horse loaded as much as he could—a good calf and good chickens and a honeycomb, and they brought peasants for Simkhe. In short, a whole throng accompanied the rebbe's coach. And the count asked Simkhe's permission to join him in the coach. Rebbe Simkhe gave him permission. And so the two of them sat in the same coach. When the throng entered the town, the inhabitants were astonished to see so many people and they wondered where the throng was heading. And how amazed they were to see all the coaches drawing up at Rebbe Simkhe Plakhte's home. And they all virtually exploded upon seeing him climb out of the coach. And the aristocrats all stood there with bare heads as if facing a monarch. And Simkhe led the way into his home.

And the countess greeted Madame Simkhe and hugged and kissed her and gave her lavish presents and she said: "How lucky you are to be married to such a sacred man!"

And the aristocrats had a huge parade in the town. And each one said to Rebbe Simkhe: "I'll send you good things every week."

And the peasants said the same thing.

And they all took their leave with great reverence and drove away. And they all kept their word to Rebbe Simkhe.

The townsfolk couldn't stand it and they didn't have a clue as to what was happening. So they asked the Jewish tavern keeper who lived in the village. And he told them the whole story. And he said to the townsfolk: "The count and the other aristocrats aren't crazy. Rebbe Simkhe is truly a divine angel. If I hadn't seen the great wonders myself, I wouldn't have believed it. And you should know that you are committing a grave sin if you make fun of him and laugh at him."

And the townsfolk were astonished. And they wondered: "Maybe he *is* a hidden saint." And they saw that he behaved in a very Jewish fashion, and his house was open to paupers. And he supported poor Talmud students.

In short, he acquired a great reputation in the world. And many people consulted him for remedies. And the rebbe's manager taught him all sorts of phony remedies: take palm branches and cook them in bathhouse water; recite Psalm 100 seven times; recite Psalm 7 twenty times; put white chicken feathers on your belly and you will give birth to a boy; get soil from a grave and carry it in a white pouch on your neck to ward off the evil eye—God forbid; place three times eighteen unripe fruits under your pillow, and in the morning place the money in the rebbe's charity box secretly, so that no one can see it. That is a remedy for hemorrhoids. Liver salt with rose honey cooked in buttermilk is a remedy for eye complaints. And a lot more of that nonsense. The rebbe was a fast learner, for he was very good at playing tricks. In short, he was renowned throughout the land.

Men and women came to consult him from all over the world and each one told wonders and miracles about the hidden saint. And the rebbe and his wife devoted themselves to food just like horses. And everyone who visited them considered it a great honor to shake the holy rebbe's hand. In short, he grew as high as the heavens. The whole world came to him.

There were also genuine Hasids and rebbes and scholars and they paid him great respect. And when the visiting Hasids and scholars secretly talked with the rebbe's assistant, they asked him why the rebbe—long may he live— never divulged his learning at a meal. The assistant replied: "Who among you will grasp the rebbe's learning? The rebbe also studies the cabala and the great mysteries. His learning is beyond human comprehension."

The thief likewise wanted the rebbe to show his learning at the table. He sat with the glutton and the guzzler day and night and recited all the stories from the Bible and he made sure that the rebbe was well-versed in all those stories.

One Sabbath, there were many scholars and Hasids in the rebbe's home and they begged him to discuss a Biblical passage. The assistant promised them that he would plead with the rebbe to recite something. "But what will come of it? You won't understand a word. For his learning consists of hidden mysteries."

After the meal, the rebbe opened his lips, gaped and gawked, and recited. He managed to imitate the conduct that his assistant had taught him, but he couldn't recall the stories. "Ha, ha, ha, ni, ni, ni, oy, oy, oy! When Noah waged war against the Philistines in the desert and he lost, it was decreed that Isaac should be bound and sacrificed. And the sacrifice led to the long Jewish Exile. Oy, oy, oy, ha, ha, ha, ni, ni, ni. Wash your hands and pray. And let the light be scattered for the saint."

After prayers, one Hasid said to another: "Are you an expert in the Bible?"

The other Hasid replied: "Ha, ha! And do you fancy yourself an expert in the Bible? That's Cabala."

A third Hasid said: "That's very profound. That's the deepest mystery."

The rebbe's assistant replied: "I told you that his learning was meant for the angels, and not for mere humans."

When the visitors headed home, they spread the word that the rebbe could recite hidden secrets. "The Torah," it is said, "is beyond measure and beyond expression."

Hasids and scholars and very minor rebbes gathered from many towns, and they came to hear the rebbe discuss the mysteries of the Torah. At the table the rebbe again played his tricks and he said: "When King Nimrod fought a war against King Saul, Daniel interpreted the dream of the seven cows that Pharaoh saw by the Jordan. And because the Jordan was filled with blood, it didn't rain in the Holy Land, and when they atone for the sin of killing Jonah in the Temple, Goshen will be reborn, and it will rain again."

The rebbe divulged this and other wisdom and he told about how King Agag waged war against Nebuchadnezzar. "And after the war, Joseph was sold into Egyptian slavery with his brothers, and they had no rest until Corah built an ark to survive the flood. And that was an allusion to the first Temple." And the rebbe revealed all sorts of other hidden secrets that only a great Cabalist might comprehend.

The Jews exchanged glances and they were all too embarrassed to admit that they didn't grasp a single word. Instead, each Jew said: "I fully understand it all. It involves profound secrets that are worth traveling a thousand leagues to hear." And every Jew said the same thing because they were embarrassed in one another's presence. There were some among them who were true sages and scholars and who realized that Simkhe was a phony rebbe, a simpleminded guzzler and glutton who deserved to have his arms and legs broken. But they had to hold their tongues. And they had to say that they hadn't heard such wisdom in all their lives and that they had to come here. For if anyone had contradicted the rebbe, God forbid, he would be labeled a heretic and he'd be taking his life in his hands.

The simple Jews and the peasants believed that he was a divine man, and his fame spread far and wide. In short, people came from the four corners of the world. And they poured money over him like sand. And they each felt privileged to be paying the rebbe's fee.

And every week, both aristocrats and peasants, especially his own count, sent him all sorts of delights. In short, Rebbe Simkhe enjoyed universal glory and gorged himself like a glutton and a guzzler. And he sat peacefully for a long time.

Many years later, when Rebbe Simkhe had been living peacefully and in great pleasure, and his fame had spread far and wide, a major problem occurred for the monarch, and no remedy was found. So they sent for all the ministers to come and ponder and try to hit on a solution. And Simkhe was also summoned for he was a minister too. The monarch sat on his throne for several days, but no one came up with a remedy. He then remembered Rebbe Simkhe.

The count and the monarch were well-acquainted for they had gone to school together and they had remained close friends since childhood. The count said to the monarch: "Your Majesty, we have found help. We don't have to cudgel our brains for a solution. I have a special man living in my town—a pure angel. He knows everything, just like God Himself. Send for him, he'll help us instantly."

However, the king was a great sage, he didn't believe in such foolish old wives' tales. And he burst out laughing! He said to the count: "If I didn't know that you were a great sage, I wouldn't be surprised. But since I know that you are a great sage, I'm surprised that you're mouthing such foolish things."

The count replied: "Your Majesty, you've known me since childhood and you know very well that I'm a lot more skeptical about such matters than you. And I wouldn't believe it even if a thousand people told me they believed it. But I saw it with my own two eyes, so why shouldn't I believe it?" And the count told the monarch all about his horse and all about his chest, and everyone was very surprised.

And several ministers said: "We've heard that this is truly a great and learned man." But the king refused to believe them.

They all discussed the king's comment and they said: "What harm will it do to send for him? We won't ask him anyway for the advice that we need. For we can't have a Jew, an ordinary civilian, know our secrets. But we will determine whether he truly knows anything."

The king then said: "Write him that he is to get here as fast as possible!"

The count said: "Do you think he is a normal person like us? You have to send him your royal coach with a band and several generals. And I'll join him. I'll plead with him to come back with me."

And that's what happened. Several marvelous coaches containing the greatest generals were dispatched. And the king's son and the count sat in the royal coach and they arrived in the town.

When the townsfolk saw the royal coach and the lesser coaches and all the highest persons, they wondered where this procession was heading. And how astonished they were when all the coaches halted at Rebbe Simkhe's door. And all the generals and the king's son and the count stepped into Rebbe Simkhe's home. The townsfolk laughed and they also burst with envy, and no one dared say a word.

When the guests entered with great reverence, the count said to his divine man: "Do you see how loyal I am to you? I want to make you a lot happier than I am myself, but that's not within my power, for I'm only a mere count. However, I did build you up to the king. And if you can guess the answers to their questions, the king will make you happy. And it is to show you deep respect that they've sent you the royal coach and all the supreme generals."

When Simkhe heard that, his heart grew bitter. He thought to himself: "If only the king were sick or if only the devil would take him before he built me up to the king!" And Simkhe said to his wife: "God only knows if I won't need my pole and my buckets again. Or maybe I won't have to use them, for if you cheat a king even very slightly, you are risking your life. It's as bitter as death. There's nothing you can do whether you want to or not. You have to have a heart of stone. And I have to go back with the escort."

In short, they rode back to the king. When they arrived, Simkhe was welcomed very reverentially, and they put him up at a Jewish inn. And the highest personages were told to treat him at the king's expense for the rebbe couldn't eat at the royal court. They prepared a splendid lunch for him, a meal fit for a king. But he couldn't eat a crumb. His mouth and his heart were closed. For he pictured the dark fate awaiting him here. Still, they urged and pleaded, so he forced himself to eat a morsel.

While he ate, the senate and all the ministers wondered what they should ask him. But they couldn't hit on anything very quickly. So they advised Simkhe to spend three days at the inn. And during those three days, they would figure out what to ask him.

That afternoon, they summoned the rebbe to the royal court. And the king and the entire senate very respectfully said to him: "Dear holy man, we ask you very reverentially to spend three days at the inn. You will be summoned on the third day, and if you manage to answer the hidden question that we will ask you, you will be happy forever, and so will your children and your children's children."

Simkhe said: "Fine."

They very respectfully led him into the inn and they stated the royal order: the innkeeper was to treat the guest like a king and give him anything he desired. The king would foot the bill.

The innkeeper obeyed. He put the guest up in a splendid room and prepared a meal fit for a king. But Simkhe's gall was bursting—poor man! For he was truly the master of all gorging and guzzling and he was the most famous of all famous gluttons.

But now his heart was shut. And he felt bitter and sour upon thinking about the third day, when he would be summoned by the king. His mortal dread was worse than it had been in regard to the count's chest, for a count is not as great as a king, but the king could swiftly take Simkhe's life when he discovered that the rebbe was just a simple glutton, who had made a fool of the king and the entire senate.

In short, Simkhe neither ate nor drank nor slept. He merely paced to and fro in his splendid room. Meanwhile, the monarch kept summoning the innkeeper and asking him whether he was treating the guest well. So the innkeeper told him the whole truth: he had prepared meals fit for a king, but the guest hadn't eaten even a crumb. Instead, he was fasting—he didn't eat, he didn't drink, he didn't sleep.

When they heard this, and the count said that Simkhe hadn't eaten or drunk for three days and three nights in regard to the chest, the royal court began to feel that Simkhe might be a saintly man after all. And he would certainly be able to answer their question. Now they began wondering what to ask him, so they would know he was truly a celestial spirit.

The most noble of all the ministers was chosen to ponder and to figure out a question, and he was selected because he was truly a great sage. And he said: "In regard to our royal mystery, we shouldn't ask him any question. For an issue concerning the state should not be revealed to any human being. Make up your minds. If he's a simple, ordinary man, then he certainly won't be able to help us. But if he's really a great sage, then it won't do for a commoner to know our deepest secrets. So we mustn't ask him anything regarding our problem or say even a word about it. We should ask him something in an entirely different area, so we can find out what he's capable of."

This advice appealed to the king and the entire senate.

Now they still had to figure out what to ask him. So the same minister, the sage, said: "You should know that if he's truly a sage, then he will hit on the most difficult solution. For a real sage can display the greatest wisdom. But he never comes up with any stupidity. And a fool can reveal no wisdom, only sheer stupidity. Now wisdom comes in two forms. One form consists of what a man has worked out of himself: natural wisdom. While the other form consists of divine wisdom. Just as it is written: 'The Lord gave wisdom unto King Solomon (may he rest in peace).' That was divine wisdom. If the sage is naturally wise, he can reveal his wisdom but never any foolishness. However, if he is given divine wisdom, he can display anything, both wisdom and foolishness—it's all the same to him. For Heaven reveals everything to him—whatever he wants and whatever he needs.

"So let's ask him a foolish question that he won't expect. And if he's able to reply, then we'll know that he's a genuine sage with celestial wisdom, a truly divine man who is completely great in heaven. And when it turns out that he is truly a divine sage, then we should pay him great reverence and give him great presents. For he can help us overcome the worst adversity and shield us against all evil."

The king and the entire senate agreed with the minister. Now they had to figure out what to ask the rebbe—an unexpected question. Everyone had a different suggestion, which appealed to nobody.

In the king's chamber, where the ministers were sitting and pondering, the wall had a rectangular niche with a small, lovely door. And not far from the niche, there was a cage containing a bird. So the ministers decided to put two days' worth of food and drink for the bird in the cage and to release the bird and place it in the niche and lock the door to the niche and remove the cage from the chamber and thereby conceal any trace of the bird. And they would ask the rebbe what had happened there. "And if he answers correctly, we'll know that his wisdom is divine and that he is very great."

Everyone liked this advice and they followed it. They removed the bird from the cage and placed it in the niche. And when they were about to close the door to the niche, the bird flew out. They chased it until they caught it and they placed it in the niche a second time, and it flew out a second time. And they chased it again until they caught it. The third time they caught it, the king himself held it tight, so it couldn't fly away. And the bird was locked in the niche. And all the ministers had to swear that the whole business was to be kept top secret.

And now, my dear reader, we will go and see what Rebbe Simkhe is up to. The poor man was in the throes of misery, unable to eat, unable to drink, unable to sleep. And his dull mind was dried out from pondering too much. On the third night, which was to be followed by the Day of Reckoning, Simkhe felt the presence of death.

Then he made up his mind: "I'll tell them the whole truth. The first two times, I was lucky. But the third time, in front of the king, I wasn't so lucky. I'll come out with the entire truth. I'll admit that I'm a simple, uneducated man. After all, they won't kill me for the sake of truth. My count will take back everything he gave me, and I'll go back to lugging water. But at least I'll survive. And if I don't tell the truth, if I put on a heavenly face and pretend to be a rebbe, and they find out that I don't know beans, that I'm a liar, then my life won't be worth a plugged kopek." Simkhe was delighted with his decision, for he truly saw no other possibility.

At the crack of dawn, he reeled off his prayers, kept on the prayer shawl and prayer thongs, and donned his white jacket and his fur hat (like a cloudburst on his head). He looked like an angelic rebel.

Suddenly, the king's great men entered the room. When they saw Simkhe in his attire, they were as scared as if they were facing the angel of death. They waited until he took off the shawl and the thongs. Then they reverentially asked him to accompany them. He did so, and he pretended that he was eager to go. He looked eager on the outside, but his innards were bursting with fear.

When they reached the palace, the king and all the ministers were already seated and were waiting for him. Simkhe didn't wait to be questioned. Instead, he began to tell the whole truth: "Your Highness and you gentlemen, you don't need to ask me anything. The first time, the bird managed to fly freely. And it also managed the second time. But the third time, the king caught the bird and held it tight, and the bird couldn't manage."

However, the king and all the ministers didn't have a clue as to what the fool was saying or getting at. Upon hearing him speak, they figured he had guessed their secret. And before he was even finished, there was a loud clapping and shouting. "Hurray! Hurray!" And they were all astonished and they all dropped to their knees in front of God's sage. For they believed that he got his wisdom from God—just like King Solomon, may he rest in peace.

Upon seeing and hearing everything, Simkhe had a brainstorm, and he didn't say another word. He was as silent as a wall. The others were overjoyed and dumbfounded, for they didn't know how reverentially to treat him. And since they knew that he hadn't had any food or drink for several days, they didn't wish to hold him up. They reverentially accompanied him back to the inn and they sent for the royal orchestra, and it played for the divine man. And they lit great illuminations throughout the town. And lamps and candles shone in all the streets and all the windows—everything in honor of the heavenly man. And the count was aggrandized to the very heavens.

The king and all the ministers hugged and kissed the count, for he had made it possible for them to meet the divine man and witness the great wonders. The queen also heard everything. And she asked her husband to invite the holy man back to the royal palace, so that she might have the privilege of seeing him and paying him great respect. The king was afraid he might say the wrong thing to the angel. But the count asked him, and when the count returned to the queen with the glad tiding that the holy man would accept the invitation, the queen and all the courtesans dressed in splendid garments to welcome the guest. And they scattered roses all along the way and greeted the rebbe with very rich and splendid presents.

Rebbe Simkhe made a point of going to the synagogue and he was accompanied by the king and all the important people. And Simkhe had a special prayer recited for the king. All the Jews gathered here in honor of the king. And the king greeted the Jews in a very lovely fashion and he made a huge donation to the synagogue and to the poor. Then they reverentially went back to the royal palace. And all the Jews respectfully escorted them.

And they all shouted: "Long live our king and our queen and all their children and may they all be happy!"

When they drew up at the palace, they found lots of harnessed coaches, and the royal coach was prepared for Rebbe Simkhe, and it was loaded with gold, and silver, and money, and lots of very expensive gifts. And the king and the queen accompanied him for a stretch and wished him bon voyage. And before saying good-bye, the king said to Rebbe Simkhe: "What I've given you is only temporary. Very shortly I'll send you enough for your children and children's children, and I'll take care of you like a father with his own offspring."

Many Jews also came and they tossed notes and fees into the coach, and Rebbe Simkhe gathered them together, and any Jew he nodded at felt as if he were in seventh heaven.

The count and the king's son and Rebbe Simkhe sat in the royal coach, and they were accompanied by other V.I.P.s in many other coaches. And when they were a league or two from the town, the harbingers and the music-makers galloped on ahead. And they lined up at the entrance to Simkhe's home and played their music in honor of Madame Simkhe and they informed her that her beloved husband was arriving, and they brought a friendly greeting from the queen and all the great ladies and a friendly letter from the queen. Madame Simkhe opened the letter, which was all Greek to her, and she offered her profuse thanks. And when all the coaches arrived, including the royal coach, the whole town came and watched as the count and the king's son and several generals escorted Simkhe and stood servilely. And all these great men remained in the town for several days, and they celebrated every day and enjoyed themselves thoroughly, and they left great presents and celebrated with the rebbe and his wife. And then the visitors took off.

Within a few days, the king issued a statement saying that the whole world should know that no holier man with divine wisdom existed than the great genius Simkhe Plakhte, and that no one should sully or do anything against his sacred reputation—God forbid!—on pain of death.

And every week and every month, the royal court sent the rebbe gifts and money galore, and his fame spread from one end of the world to the other, among both Jews and Gentiles. People arrived here every day from all corners of the earth. And out of every hundred sick people ninety-nine perished and only one survived. Those who died were forgotten, but not the one who survived. And the news traveled all over the world: the rebbe had saved a life. And so the whole world was deceived by that ignoramus. And even sages and scholars were bamboozled and they traveled to see him and they believed in this glutton and guzzler as if he were a real prophet (please excuse me for mentioning them in the same breath). And the swindler bedazzled the entire world. And visitors had to wait and wait at his door before enjoying the privilege of admission. And the news spread that he fasted from one Sabbath to the next, because no one had ever seen him eating. And indeed he never ate, he simply chowed down like a blind horse. But he was very sly about it, and only his wife knew the truth, and she sneaked the food into the house so that no one would catch on. And she publicly lamented that her husband refused to eat even a crumb.

And important people also showed up, rabbis, rebbes (including rebbes like this one), and scholars (even those who knew he was a swindler). For in every town that had a Hasidic prayer house there was a Hasid prayer house named the Holy House of the Saintly Simon.

And the Cabalists secretly claimed that Simkhe Plakhte was the reincarnation of the Saintly Simon (may he rest in peace), because the name "Plakhte" is numerologically identical with the name "Plakhte."

And anyone who didn't visit him, who didn't travel to meet him, was not considered a decent person. And so sages and scholars had to consult him against their will. And if a sage saw through the swindle, he shouted the whole truth, shouted that the world was crazy for visiting this glutton and guzzler, this ignoramus who deceived God and the world. And people believed in this thief and liar who couldn't tell his ass from his elbow, who didn't—as we Jews say—know the difference between cursing Haman and blessing Mordecai.

However, the rebbe's followers all hollered: "This intruder is a heretic! He'll never go to heaven because he lacks the faith of the sages!"

Another sage said to this Hasid: "Listen, brother! I can see through the swindle and the lunacy of the world as well as you can, for I've pondered it thoroughly. When a lucid and intelligent man comes among lunatics, he doesn't dare call them lunatics, he has to say that whatever they do is very correct. For if he calls them crazy, they will holler that *he* is the crazy one. And sometimes he won't even be certain of his life. So, my dear friend, keep calm and let everyone stick to his folly, for we can't turn the whole world upside down."

The other sage replied: "You are right, my dear friend."

So the two sages conferred secretly and they also stepped into the Hasidic prayer house and joined the late-afternoon Sabbath meal. And they grabbed a herring's tail from the plate and some of the rebbe's leftovers and they toasted him: "Long live the rebbe!" And they also told of his great wonders, which they had neither seen nor heard. And Simkhe revealed even deeper teachings.

One Sabbath, loads of Hasids arrived, and the rebbe's assistant had spent all that week instructing the rebbe on interpreting a Biblical passage on the Sabbath. But Simkhe Plakhte had the memory of an old cat. When it came time for him to reveal his interpretation, all the Hasids stood there very quietly, to enjoy the privilege of hearing the profound teachings from those holy lips. The rebbe began very ecstatically, for the flames of aquavit blazed inside him, and he gobbled down practically all the meat and all the fish that he was served and he left scraps for his followers. The Hasids exchanged glances, and each one assumed that the rebbe was harboring a profound secret. And they all thirsted to hear the sacred words. And so the rebbe opened his mouth like Balaam's donkey and he said:

"When Ham murdered his brother Cain, Potiphar built the Ark. And the Ark contained Balaam the Evil and Nebuchadnezzar, and Jonah, Jonah, Jonah, Jonah. The dove flew away and it carried Balaam the Evil on its right wing and Nebuchadnezzar on its left wing. Meanwhile war was being fought between King Ahasuerus and Balak, son of Zippor. And because in Shushan the Israelites partook of the banquet of Balak, son of Zippor, Ahasuerus dashed into the desert to scold the Israelites. When the dove saw that the king wanted to scold the holy Jews, it spread one wing, as is written, and a hard donkey fell from that wing, as it is written, and Balaam jumped down and straddled the donkey, as is written, and killed Ahasuerus. Next came Samuel, and he killed Balaam, because he had destroyed the First Temple, and the result was the birth of Haman, who hanged King Nebuchadnezzar in the land of Egypt. And when Corah made peace with Haman in regard to Sarah's tomb, which Jacob had bought from Sechem. And then an oracular voice was heard. As it is written, no wisdom will help you. Or any strength. As is written in the Holy Talmud: 'As you make your bed, so must you lie in it.' Then again you find that King David (may he rest in peace) said in the Book of Esther: 'If you don't comb your hair, you'll develop elflocks.' And it is also written: 'You pay each person according to what he earns.' Because Corah shamed the two saintly men and refused to kowtow to them. But Haman greatly respected Mordecai and fulfilled his every wish. For it is written: 'Spit the root and spill the child.' And may all my Hasids likewise reach such a grand privilege. So everyone should say 'Amen.'"

And everyone shouted: "Amen! Amen! Amen!"

The horrible Biblical interpretation was in deadly danger. The ignoramuses were so terrified that they practically kicked the bucket. And the sages and scholars almost exploded with laughter, which they had to squelch. Otherwise they would have been uncertain of their lives. And the real sages said to one another: "There's truth in the old adage: 'Where ignorance is bliss, 'tis folly to be wise.'"

Simkhe and his wife lived very well and had large treasures. And they bamboozled the whole world. And they had children who were likewise gluttons and guzzlers. And important people wanted to join their families through marriage. And Simkhe and his wife died amid great respect and esteem. And their children inherited a huge legacy. But their treasures were soon frittered away, for these offspring were used to gobbling and guzzling like their parents, the holy gobblers. And the calves and the poultry and the money and all the good stuff sent to them by the nobility—everything soon stopped. The aristocrats now refused to send even a crumb. So Simkhe's children were left high and dry. They gobbled as long as they had something to gobble. But then they were at a loss as to what came next. For usually, such people are raised like wild oxen—to gobble, to guzzle, to dance and prance and loaf around. And they always shout at an old man: "Now listen! Who the hell are you? You think you're a Hasid too?"

These people know such things. But that's all they know. They have no learning, no wisdom, no knowledge, no vocation. When their uncles, the Hasids, pass away, these offspring go a-begging through all the lands. They are put up in the Hasidic prayer houses. Sometimes they steal, sometimes they mooch. At a wedding or a holiday banquet, they stuff their guts. For after all, they are the children of saints. But their wives suffer at home. And their children are also brought up like wild beasts.

Simkhe's offspring likewise wished to run things that way. But only a single one was a sage and not a total moron. He had a little knowledge and was actually quite smart. And he knew that the whole business about his father's renown was swindle and theft. So he summoned his brothers and he said to them:

"Dear brothers! Do as I tell you, and everything will come out right. We have to learn a trade. And we will earn our livelihood honorably with our ten fingers and not deceitfully like our father. Just as our father bamboozled the whole world and stole money from every single person. We see that our father's wealth suffered scorn and derision and melted like snow. For such gains cannot endure, they are ill-gotten. Our father couldn't do otherwise, alas, he couldn't help it, he was already quite old when he began and he had no knowledge of the Scriptures. How do we know that we can be as lucky as he was? For theft also requires luck. And we can't rely on having the same luck as our father, who was totally bewildered in his Biblical interpretations, he confused parsley with pepper and buttermilk—as the saying goes. Yet everyone claimed he was totally right because luck was on his side. But you can't always count on luck. Now the man who has a trade can truly hope for luck and he too can grow wealthy. Still, even if doesn't have luck, he can at least bank on having his daily bread."

His brothers obeyed him and each learned a craft. One became a tailor, the other a lace maker, and they did quite well. They made a lot of money and became rich merchants. And they deeply loved their brother for giving them such good advice. And they had their children learn properly and they found excellent spouses for them. And their children also became merchants and they knew reading and writing and arithmetic. And they led peaceful lives with their children and children's children and they found favor in the eyes of God and man.

This story is meant to show the blindness of the world. And the intelligent man should not be dazzled by the vanity of vanities, he should seek only the truth.

SONYA THE WISE WOMAN

In 1916–1917, A. Litvin (pseudonym for S. Hurwitz) published a four-volume ethnographic opus entitled *Yídishe Neshómes* (*Jewish Souls*). Appearing in New York City during World War I, Litvin's collection ran the gamut of Eastern European Jewish life—a society greatly disrupted and partly destroyed by the war.

One of Litvin's informants was a stocking maker known as Sonya the Wise Woman (Sonya Khakhome), who told Litvin several folktales, some deriving from the Jewish religious tradition, some from the international folklore repertoire. Aside from "A Tale of a 'Baal-Shem' and a 'Dybbuk'" (included in *The Dybbuk and The Yiddish Imagination*), these are all of Sonya's stories that Litvin published (Vol. 3, inconsistent pagination).

INTRODUCTION
Sonya the Wise Woman and Her Tales

IN THE PROVINCE OF MOLLIVE, there is an old woman who is known for her shtetl wisdom, her old sayings, and her folktales. I met her quite by chance. Her name is Sonya Naimark. She's roughly eighty. She's "near her time," she says when talking about her age. Nevertheless, she is in such good shape, looks so lively, healthy, and cheerful, that it's a true delight to converse with her. I spent several hours with her, which wasn't easy for me. She comes from an important family and is proud of her family tree. Initially, I had a hard time getting to her, but then I managed to gain her trust. She got quite *haymish* (familiar) with me and she talked quite spontaneously. And then she began reciting proverbs and stories.

Sonya Naimark tells her tales like a true artist. Her language is very colorful and inventive, it's sharp and flavorful. She often weaves in a rhyme, a Biblical verse, and even a Talmudic quote. But she in no way resembles a *zogerin* (a woman who reads prayers for the other women to repeat in the women's section of the synagogue). She was the one who taught me that there used to be female wedding jesters. Such a jester, she said, once paid her three rubles for a tale that she taught her, and that the female jester then recited at weddings. Sonya herself is far removed from being a jester. She is, as I have said, proud and also dignified. That's why you have to treat her with reverence. Old and young, whomever she admits, enjoy conversing with her and are delighted with her sayings and her stories.

I wrote down some of them directly from her lips, I tried to record them verbatim as she told them. Let me transmit "A Tale of Abraham and Nimrod," as recited by Sonya Naimark.

A TALE OF ABRAHAM AND NIMROD

*E*MPEROR NIMROD WANTED to become a God. And he convinced everyone that he was divine. But only Abraham stood in his way and rebelled against him.

What was Nimrod to do with him?

Nimrod seized him and threw him into the limekiln. Threw him into the flames and went away cheerfully. People realized that Abraham was strolling about in the limekiln as if he were in a vineyard. Not a hair on his head was singed!

Things got worse. . . . Nimrod summoned his advisors. What should he do with that Jew-boy? . . . They all agreed that Nimrod was a god, but he, Abraham, refused to go along with it.

They decided to drive him away to the ends of the earth, they banished him to Haran.

When Abraham arrived in Haran, he built a cottage with a door on each of its four sides. He was very hospitable. As it is written: "Whoever wishes, enter and eat!"

Nimrod heard about it and he was extremely annoyed! How could that be? Nimrod had meant to drive him away, maybe turn him into a poor Jew. But Abraham had become filthy rich.

So Nimrod ordered his servants to harness some horses. He wanted to see what was happening with Abraham. Was what people were saying about him true? Riding into Abraham's courtyard, Nimrod was welcomed as a fine guest: the horses were promptly fed hay and oats, and he himself, Nimrod, was served food and drink, the finest and the best.

Nimrod stayed on for a couple of days. He saw that everything he'd been told was true. He couldn't take it. He wanted to leave. He started harnessing the horses. Abraham's assistant came over to Nimrod and said: "The boss wants you to come and settle accounts with him."

Nimrod figured that Abraham bore him a grudge, and that was why he wanted to get money from Nimrod. He said to the assistant: "He should tell me how much I owe him, and I'll pay him. I won't go to him, I don't want to see his face. . . ."

So the assistant went back to Abraham and transmitted the message. Abraham replied: "Let him come here. I've got a large account to settle with him."

Nimrod got angry and he said: "Tell him to let me know what I owe him. A thousand ducats is a thousand ducats! So long as I don't have to see his mug!"

So the assistant went back to Abraham and repeated those words. Well, when Abraham heard that, he ordered his assistant to close the gates: "He has to come to me, he's not an emperor here!"

Nimrod saw he was getting nowhere, so he took heart and went to Abraham. Abraham offered him a chair. But Nimrod didn't want to sit, didn't want to talk to Abraham. "Tell me how much I owe you!" he snapped. "And I'll cough it up!"

"I can't just tell you in the twinkling of an eye," said Abraham. "You've got a big account to settle."

Nimrod was at the end of his rope! "What kind of account? I only spent two days here. Let it be a thousand rubles! I'll pay you right away. I don't want to owe you anything!"

"Two days?" Abraham was startled. "You're mistaken. It's been forty years since you expelled me. Throughout these forty years I've given everyone food and drink. Anyone who rides by or rides away says to me: 'God will repay you.' Today you came here and you said that you were God. So pay up, brother! For everybody, for the past forty years."

Nimrod had a heavy heart. Where could he dig up all that money? He dithered. He couldn't come up with anything. "Where can I dig up all that money?" he asked Abraham. "I don't have it!"

"What do you mean you don't have it?" said Abraham. "You're a god, you have to support the world. Otherwise, you are not a god! You should give me a signed document saying that you are no longer a god!"

Nimrod saw that things were going badly for him, he was outfoxed. So he handed Abraham a signed document stating that he, Nimrod, was not a god.

Ever since then, we know that God is in heaven, and that Abraham achieved his goal.

A TALE ABOUT HOW A SMART PAUPER
CHEATED A WEALTHY MISER
OUT OF TWO THOUSAND RUBLES

ONCE THERE WAS A very rich but very bad man—as the supporters of democracy put it: a bourgeois! He would have given all his teeth for a kopek! Across the road from him there lived a pauper. And he was a cheerful guy despite his poverty. He was annoyed because the miser was such an awful person that you couldn't get a kopek out of him. So the pauper figured out a way of getting the miser's cash.

He started dashing around the marketplace as if he were engrossed in something, he ran past his home and right across from the miser's shop. He ran back and forth, preoccupied, as if mulling over goodness knows what kind of business.

When the miser saw him, he wondered: What kind of business was his neighbor absorbed in? For no matter how rich the miser was, he always envied the pauper and he was annoyed that the pauper might be doing better business than he, the miser.

So the miser stopped his neighbor and asked him: "Tell me, Avreml, how come you're so absorbed? If you've got some kind of great deal cooking, let's be partners."

"A wonderful deal! Really, a wonderful deal!" replied the pauper. "What do you think? A man runs around for nothing? . . . But why should you care? Don't you have your own dealings? Aren't you rich as it is? Are you bothered if someone else makes money?'

"God forbid!" said the miser. "I'm not bothered! May God help you! I was just being curious!"

"Well," said the poor neighbor, "since you're so curious, I'll tell you. I just received a letter from Novozibkov—a Russian is selling tobacco, twenty loads. . . . A net profit of eight thousand rubles. . . . From hand to hand. . . . I'm setting out immediately!"

"Eight thousand rubles? What are you talking about?" The miser was thrilled. "Do you need a couple of thousand for the deal? I'll put up the cash, and we can be partners!"

"Take your money?" The pauper waved him off. "C'mon! It won't work. Asking for money before we even work out the principle. You'll keep badgering me: 'What's happening? What's the news?' Nope, I'm gonna find me another partner, someone better than you."

The rich miser swore on a stack of Bibles, on the heads of his wife and kids, that he wouldn't badger his neighbor, he'd be patient until everything was sold and accounts were drawn up.

"Well, if you really mean it," said the pauper, "then fork over the two thousand rubles, and we'll be partners, half and half. Four thousand rubles! May the Good Lord give us luck! But remember what we agreed on!"

"Of course! Of course! What do you think? Certainly!"

The miser blissfully forked over the two thousand rubles, and the neighbor was to instantly head for Novozibkov to buy the two hundred loads of tobacco, while the miser sat and waited for the four thousand silver rubles.

The pauper set out, but he didn't head for Novozibkov, he went to a nearby shtetl. And there he lived it up! He wrote letters to his wife, saying that the deal was fabulous. It had turned out that there was twice the profit they had expected. The wife showed the letters to the miser, and he read them in sheer delight. He rubbed his belly and he simply couldn't wait for the money.

Eventually, Avreml left the shtetl and came home. He rode in a coach, as suits a rich man. His wife was very glad to see him. She prepared a fine lunch. After finishing the delicious lunch, he lay down for a nap, as is customary for rich people.

The rich miser had already seen the "merchant" drive past his shop. He paid no heed and he concealed himself in his home, pretending that he was in no hurry. But because of the silver rubles, he was at the end of his rope. He couldn't wait to see his money! It wouldn't do though: a promise is a promise.

The rich miser waited for one hour, two hours, three. He was on pins and needles. So he sent over a servant to find out what was happening. The answer was: "Shush! He's napping. He's resting up after his long trip. . . . Such a harsh journey! . . ."

Another hour wore by—two hours. The miser couldn't stand it any longer. . . . He went over to greet the pauper. What could happen? He'd avoid talking business. He'd wait till his neighbor broached the subject.

He arrived at his neighbor's home. There he ran into the pauper's wife. He turned on his charm:

"My best to your husband!"

"Our best to you!"

"Has he come back safe and sound? How is he? What's he up to?"

"He's taking a nap, he's resting up. . . . What a difficult trip! All the way to Novozibkov and back. . . ."

Suddenly, the miser heard someone coughing. Avreml was waking up, scratching himself. The miser waited a bit. The door opened. Avreml appeared in a fine dressing gown and elegant slippers. He performed the ritual of washing his hands slowly, comfortably.

"Good day to you, Sir!" said the miser.

"Good day to you! Have a seat. Cough, cough! The samovar!"

Avreml's wife set out the samovar. He poured a glass for himself and a glass for his guest, who was waiting for his money. They drank their tea. The miser sipped his tea with a quaking heart.

"You really want to know about the business, huh?" said Avreml, and he kept glancing slyly at his partner.

"If you want to tell me," the miser stammered, "then it's fine with me. Tell me. . . ."

"Well," said Avreml, "this is what happened. I arrived in Novozibkov and I had a look at the merchandise. Money galore! I bought a hundred loads of tobacco, hitched up the horses, and off we went! After three or four miles, we saw a black cloud spreading across the sky. It was frightening! Pitch-black! Suddenly: Boom, boom! Thunder and lightning! A storm! A flood! The horses reared. You could have killed them—but they dug in their heels. The Gentiles accompanying me yelled: '*Mi starem!*' Which means: 'Let's stop!' We stopped. We were so scared that we all hid under the tobacco. A lightning bolt struck the wagons, and they burned up. A thunderbolt roared, and it devoured us! We lay under the wagons. A horrible mess! We thought it was the end of the world!

"Lightning flashed again. The sky split apart, and a man came down. He was as big as the entire earth and he shouted in Russian: 'Good morning, guys! Can we smoke a pipe?'

"'We can!' we replied, with our teeth chattering.

"He pulled a pipe from inside his shirt—a pipe the size of the city! He grabbed a load of tobacco and stuffed it into his pipe. . . . A whole wagonload! Into his pipe! A whole wagonload! One after another. . . ."

"Oh, oh, oh! All of it!" The miser reeled and he wrung his hands and he stammered: "Oh, oh, oh! A pipe!"

"You bastard!" Avreml shouted. "You're upset because of the tobacco! Because of your money! What if the giant had stuffed me into his pipe?! I've got eight little kids, you know! You bastard! You don't have a heart!"

The miser sat down, almost fainting, as pale as the wall, with gaping eyes.

"C'mon! Don't faint!" said Avreml. "When you come later, I'll give you the leftover wool!"

"When later?" the miser asked, glad to get something. . . . Better than nothing. . . .

"Come by in the evening."

The miser came back that evening. He and the pauper went across the field. The pauper led him across gardens and over fences.

"Where are you taking me?" asked the rich man.

"We'll reach the wool soon," said Avreml. "Over there. Can you see it? Between the two fences, through the narrow alley. A herd of sheep is coming from the field. They'll scratch their backs on this side of the fence, you see, and there'll be wool on the other side of the fence. And you can take the wool for yourself."

Despite his aching heart, the rich man burst out laughing.

"Don't laugh!" said Avreml. "You won't take that either."

A TALE OF TWO PARTNERS WITH PARADISE AND GEHENNA

INTRODUCTION

Most of Sonya Naimark's stories (like the songs of Munye the beadle's son) are a part of cultural history—especially Jewish life in Russia during the past few centuries. They are slices of life—experience, faith, and superstition. They reflect social conditions and economic circumstances. Let me focus on another two or three of her tales.

"A Tale of Two Partners" takes place in modern times, at the start of the Haskala (Jewish Enlightenment), when boys and girls started dancing together. Jews began drinking tea from the Sabbath samovar and smoking a Sabbath cigar. Jews were no longer ruled by Jewish community leaders and by their fear of prison sentences ordained by those leaders. The rulers could do nothing against the heretics and the libertines in this world. But just as the libertines didn't believe in an old-fashioned Gehenna and its iron rods and burning pans, they nevertheless came up with a modern Gehenna for modern sins.

"A Tale of Two Partners" colorfully depicts such a Gehenna. Here is the story:

*T*WO PARTNERS—Borekh son of Zorekh and Beryl son of Shmerl—had business dealings in St. Petersburg and they lived together like two brothers. But one day, one partner had to move to Moscow, and the two friends had to split apart. However, they took a solemn oath, with heaven and earth as their witnesses, that whichever friend died first would visit the other friend and tell him what was going on in the afterlife.

Now one day, the partner in St. Petersburg went out and he spotted a horseman galloping past. Beryl recognized his friend Borekh and he shouted: "Stop! Stop! C'mon!"

But the friend had already vanished. So Beryl jumped into a coach and told the driver to follow the horseman. But it was useless—he was gone.

Beryl felt that something was wrong. So he sent a wire to Moscow asking for news about Borekh. The response was that Borekh had died, and the funeral had taken place at the very moment that Borekh had appeared to Beryl. So Beryl now waited for news about the afterlife. He waited one year, two years, three, but nothing came!

One day, Beryl was standing on the boulevard in St. Petersburg. Suddenly, Borekh came over, took Beryl's hand, and led him along. "Damn it, brother," said Beryl. "Tell me what's been happening with you, and let me go home!"

But Borekh led him through fields and forests, until they reached a desert. Borekh then said: "You'll find a cave here. You should go ten cubits down and ten cubits up. That's where you'll find Paradise. And that's where I am." And he vanished.

So Beryl followed his friend's instructions and he reached Paradise. Paradise was a hunched shack. Inside the shack, Jews were standing and praying. It was raining, and water was running inside the roof: slick, dark, dirty water.

Beryl thought to himself: "Who'd a thunk? What a Paradise!" He asked: "Where is Borekh son of Zorekh?"

They replied: "Further on, in the next room."

Beryl walked into the next room. There, Jews were sitting on wobbly benches amid shaky stands and poring over holy books. In the third room, Hasids were sitting with a broken bottle of liquor, crooning in ecstasy. Beryl asked: "Is Borekh son of Zorekh here?"

They replied: "He's in Gehenna."

"Well," he thought to himself. "Your Paradise isn't exactly my idea of fun." He then said aloud: "Where is Gehenna?"

They told him to go to a different cave: ten cubits down, ten cubits up. So in he crawled—what choice did he have?

Creeping out, Beryl looked and he saw a building forty cubits long and forty cubits wide—a palace, the size of the circus arena in Mohilev. At the entrance there was a sentry in a fine uniform and with a fine rifle.

"Is this Gehenna?"

"Yep."

Beryl went inside: he found a hall decorated with the most expensive things. Musicians were playing, and boys and girls were dancing together and living it up. Beryl asked: "Where is Borekh son of Zorekh?"

They answered: "In the next room."

So he went into the next room. A bunch of people were sitting round a table, playing cards and drinking cognac. Borekh wasn't there. "He's in the third room," they said. So Beryl went into the third room and looked. There he saw his partner, Borekh son of Zorekh, sitting in an armchair, like a king in his army, like a dog in a manger, holding a glass of tea in one hand and a cigar in the other. A sip of tea, a puff of smoke. . . .

"Oy!" shouted Beryl. "This is Gehenna? Damn it if this isn't Paradise! How come, brother? How come you didn't tell me? You could've told me, you know. Why did you lead me through all that murk?"

Borekh replied: "I'm well off, you say? Oh, brother! Just look at my lips, my palate—can you see how burned they are? Do you remember the Sabbath? The way we set up the samovar and drank Sabbath tea? And smoked a Sabbath cigar? Well, when I died, they set up a boiling samovar and stuck a cigar in my mouth, and I have to keep drinking and smoking, nonstop, with no end in sight!"

"Well, but what about the ones over there—dancing, playing cards, sipping cognac?"

"It's the same with them! Play, brother, and drink! Play and drink! Dance, brother, dance! If a dancer gets exhausted, the evil angel of punishment whips him and yells in Russian: 'Dance, brother! Dance, dance! Don't stop!'"

Naturally, this tale was meant to teach Beryl that he should listen to Borekh and stop drinking Sabbath tea.

A TALE OF A DIRTY ROLL

IN THE AFTERLIFE, the punishment fits the sin, measure for measure.

Once there was a very rich, but very tightfisted man, who had never in his life given alms to a single pauper. One day he was traveling with rolls in his travel bag. One roll fell out and landed in the mud. A pauper came running up. He shouted that he hadn't eaten for three days. He begged for charity to keep his body and soul together. The rich man threw him the dirty roll. That was the first and last time that the rich man felt any pity for another human being.

So what do you think happened?

Right after his death, he was granted Paradise in the True World of the afterlife, for he had saved a Jew from starving to death. But he wasn't given a place with all the other virtuous Jews. He had to sit by himself at a broken table, where they had put the filthy roll that he had thrown the pauper.

A TALE OF A TEACHER AND THREE WISEDOMS

INTRODUCTION

This tale is very different from the other stories and more interesting. (A *melámmed* is a teacher in an elementary religious school.)

A MELÁMMED WAS IN HIS HOME, and he was so starved that his belly was swollen up. So he went out in search of a teaching job. After a while, he decided to write a letter home. But he figured that being broke wasn't much fun. So he managed to earn a few rubles. But whenever he was about to write the letter, he'd run out of cash.

Month after month went by, year after year, and by now it was a total of seven years. At last, he struck it rich. God found him enough work, and the teacher made three thousand rubles. With all that money why not go home? He'd never written his wife.

En route, he stopped off at the county fair in Nizhniy. He had cash inside his shirt and he reeked of success! So he looked at merchandise, he looked at shops, tables, benches full of great stuff. And at the dead center of the market, he found a big store. The store was empty, the shelves were empty, and an old Jew with a white beard was sitting at the table. The teacher walked past the store every day and he saw the same man in the store, which had no merchandise.

Finally, the teacher stepped inside and asked: "Sir, where is your merchandise?"

"My merchandise?" the Jew responded. "It's inside my shirt."

The teacher figured the man would show him pearls, brilliants, diamonds. So he asked him: "Just where is your merchandise?"

The Jew replied: "I deal in wisdom."

The teacher asked: "How much does a wisdom cost?"

"A thousand rubles," said the Jew.

The teacher really enjoyed the situation. He did have money and he was looking for a business deal. So he took out a thousand-ruble bill and put it on the table.

The old Jew said: "When you see a straight path through the woods, a rough and filthy path, and, next to it, a twisting path, a dry path, you should only take the filthy path, the straight path."

"That's the wisdom?" the teacher asked. "What else can you tell me?"

"Another wisdom costs another thousand rubles."

So the teacher plunked down another thousand rubles, and the old Jew said: "You should stop off at an inn, where the innkeeper and his wife are alike."

The teacher was awfully annoyed that he had spent two thousand rubles. But with a bitter heart, he pulled out the third thousand-ruble bill and asked for another wisdom.

"When you lose your temper," said the Jew, "you should delay your anger until tomorrow."

The teacher was out of money, so he walked away. At his side, a line of wagons was rolling, and it contained Gentiles. So he tried to test the obvious truth of all three wisdoms. For instance: when he took the straight path, he crept up to his knees in water. But the Gentiles took the dry, twisting path. En route, they were attacked by highwaymen and killed, while the teacher wasn't harmed because he was on the straight path.

Eventually, he halted outside an inn, but the innkeeper and his wife were not alike. The husband was old, and the woman was very young, a beauty. So the teacher went to the inn across the road, where the innkeeper and his wife were alike. That night, the teacher saw a young priest climb in through the window in the first inn and kill the innkeeper. After a while, the teacher saw the young priest jump back out through the same window. So the teacher jumped down without being noticed, he grabbed an axe and chopped off four of the priest's fingers.

The next day, there was a big ruckus. The police came, and they questioned five Christian aristocrats who'd spent the night at the inn. The aristocrats were in danger of doing hard labor. But the teacher, who knew the truth, saved them by revealing the real culprit, the priest. That was why each aristocratic rewarded the teacher with a thousand rubles. So the wisdoms made him not only wise but wealthy. Finally, the third wisdom should demonstrate its validity.

The teacher arrived home in his shtetl. He asked about his wife. Did anyone know where she was? He was told: "She's running an inn not far from here. Her husband abandoned her! She's been a grass widow for seventeen years already."

The teacher went to the inn but didn't reveal himself. At night, he saw a boy come over, the boy sat down on the woman's bed and spent time with her. The teacher was furious: he wanted to grab a pistol and shoot them both. Then he remembered the third piece of advice—to delay his anger until tomorrow.

Early the next morning, the teacher went to the innkeeper, his wife, who didn't recognize him, and he said: "I had a dream, I saw a boy enter your room around midnight, sit down on your bed, and the two of you had such a lovely time together. . . . How can a virtuous Jewish woman do such a thing?"

The woman explained that the boy was her son, who'd been born seventeen years ago. Her husband had abandoned her. The boy was a good student of the holy books, he spent all his days and nights at the synagogue. But at midnight, he would come to her and converse a little.

Now the teacher revealed himself. Everyone was joyful, and delighted and they saw the truth of the old saying: "Wisdom is the best merchandise."

I must point out that when I retold Sonya Naimark's tales, I couldn't stick to the original texts, that is, I tried not to add to or subtract from her style. These published tales are simply weak reflections of what I heard from her lips. The movements are missing, the gestures, the motions, the naïve enthusiasm of her performance, the sound of her voice, her artistic sincerity, which cannot be rendered with mere words. You have to listen to her directly so that these tales may have the impact they make when she tells them.

—A. Litvin

A. LITVIN
(COLLECTOR)

For information about A. Litvin, see the introduction to Sonya the Wise Woman. The following stories are included in Litvin's collection *Yídishe Neshómes* (*Jewish Souls*), 1917, vol. 5, pagination inconsistent.

HOW ROTHSCHILD MADE HIS FORTUNE

(A Legend Recounted in the Jewish Town Registry of Czortkow)

THE CZORTKOW REGISTRY IS one of the most interesting that have, luckily, survived. I held the registry in my hand. Access to it was difficult. It is in the possession of the current rebbe of Czortkow. I had to pull a lot of strings, but I was helped by people in high places, including the rebbe's own daughter, Khave, who persuaded him to let me see the registry.

I found a lot of interesting things in it, but, unfortunately, several important pages had been torn out.

The missing portions included the tale about how Rothschild had become so wealthy. Still, this legend survives on the lips of thousands of Czortkow Hasids, who tell it on behalf of the old Rebbe of Czortkow (of blessed memory) and his son, the current Rebbe of Czortkow, Srulniu (long may he live). Both of them, in turn, the old rebbe and his son, the current rebbe, cite the town registry as their source. There is no reason whatsoever to assume that the registry did not contain this story, for the registry was in their possession and can still be found in the library of the rebbe, who treasures it like the apple of his eye. The torn-out pages may have served as material for the sacred books that Hasidic story gatherers have published about the famous Rebbe of Czortkow, Hershele, and his even more famous son, Shmelke. Upon consulting this tome, I found several items taken from, but no longer contained in, the Czortkow registry. I have no doubts at all that the missing pages were torn from the registry by the authors of that work, which includes the story of Rothschild's wealth—though casual and shortened. I am offering a fusion of the two sources, the written and the oral one—the latter as told to me by reliable informants on behalf of the two rebbes of Czortkow. This is what the legend tells us:

Mayer Anshel, the founder of the Rothschild clan, was a Jew from Czortkow. In his youth, he was named simply Mayer Anshel and he worked as a servant for Rabbi Hershele, the Hasidic rebbe of the town.

After that, Mayer Anshel got married in Snyatin, a small shtetl near Czortkow. He may have been fed up with his job as a domestic or perhaps he received a dowry of several ducats. In any case, he left the rebbe and opened a store in Snyatin. Evidently, Mayer Anshel was a better shopkeeper than an assistant to the rebbe. For in a short time, it was rumored in Czortkow that the store was doing well.

Then, on the day before Passover, Rabbi Hershele suffered a horrible setback. He'd been going around with the wooden spoon and the feathers, throwing out the leavened dough or bread from all corners, as stipulated by Jewish law and custom on the eve of Passover. Next, after cleaning out every open or hidden nook and cranny, every crack and hole, he checked the drawer of his table, where he normally sat, poring over the sacred tomes. To his great joy, the drawer was clean and pure, it didn't have a single crumb of leavened matter. Unfortunately, to his great anger and amazement, he couldn't find the pouch containing the five hundred ducats that he kept there.

Had the cash been his, the rebbe wouldn't have been so distressed. For he was the kind of rebbe who, by his very nature, didn't care about money. However, this money belonged to someone else: it had been deposited with the rebbe in regard to an arbitration. The ducats had also been saved up by poor Jews, the dowries of orphans, for whom the rebbe's drawer had always been the safest place, an iron cashbox. All that money, the hope and comfort of dozens, perhaps hundreds of people, had disappeared. What would become of all the paupers in Czortkow? What would he say to all the people who had entrusted him, their rebbe, with their property?

And that was why Rabbi Hershele was so distressed upon finding the drawer empty.

A hubbub ensued in the rebbe's home. They thought hard: Who could've taken the money? Whom could they suspect?

After a lot of thinking, they recalled that Mayer Anshel, after leaving town six months ago as a poor messenger, had opened a shop, and people said that he was doing well and had money.

While Mayer Anshel had been the rebbe's messenger, people scarcely gave him a second thought. Why bother thinking about a messenger? When he'd left, they'd simply hired a new messenger. Was there any shortage of poor boys in the shtetl? No rebbe ever remained without a messenger for long. Was Mayer Anshel an honest man or not? The question was pointless. What messenger would steal from a rebbe? Especially a rebbe like Hershele, a tsadik who was famous not only in Czortkow but much farther away— famous as a miracle worker and a saintly man. Besides, what could you steal from the rebbe aside from his old caftan, the wooden spoons, and the pewter dishes?

In short, there was no reason to think about Mayer Anshel, think good or bad. Now when the rebbe and his wife heard that God had made their former messenger prosper in his trade, they were simply delighted. For when God wishes it, He can always give, and the person He gives to probably deserves it.

But now, they were suddenly faced with a tough question. How had Mayer Anshel obtained so much money and success? The rebbe realized that he hadn't opened his drawer since Mayer Anshel had left the rebbe's home. Since that time, no one had brought the rebbe any money to hold.

And the suspicion about the former messenger grew and grew. It deeply pained the rebbe to suspect another Jew. But no one else had ever had access to the rebbe's study. There was no other likely suspect. Had it been the rebbe's own money, he certainly wouldn't have suspected a Jew. After all, it says in the Book of Job: "The Lord hath given and the Lord hath taken away." But how could the rebbe endure the tears and sorrows of poor Jews, of widows and orphans?

And with a very heavy heart, the rebbe went to Snyatin, the nearby shtetl where Mayer Anshel lived. The rebbe had said nothing to anyone. Until he could convince himself that Mayer Anshel was the thief, the rebbe refused to slander a Jew—God forbid!

Mayer Anshel was quite surprised when the rebbe showed up. He couldn't believe his eyes: how did he deserve this honor? He didn't know what to do.

However, his joy was quickly shattered when he noticed that the rebbe's face and his words were extremely nervous. Little by little, he came to understand what had brought the rebbe to Mayer Anshel, the messenger.

For an instant, Mayer Anshel blanched and didn't respond. He asked the rebbe to sit a while. He'd be back soon. The rebbe shouldn't feel distressed, Mayer Anshel would hand over the money. . . .

Rabbi Hershele had to wait for several hours. But finally, Mayer Anshel returned.

"Rebbe," he said, "here's two hundred ducats for now. But don't worry, you'll be getting the rest of the money. I'll be sending it to you in installments."

Rabbi Hershele left, greatly relieved. A Jew remains a Jew, after all. . . . It had been an awful time. . . . Mayer Anshel had done something foolish!

But no tsadik can stand where penitents stand. The shopkeeper would certainly return the remaining sum. And the rebbe was happy for the sake of the widows and orphans.

Mayer Anshel kept his word. He sent the remaining three hundred ducats in installments.

A year or two passed, and the entire matter was almost forgotten. Suddenly, one beautiful or ordinary morning, a government horseman drew up at Rabbi Hershele's home and ordered the rebbe to come back with him to the governor, who required his presence.

The rebbe was terrified. And the whole shtetl was extremely worried. Perhaps an expulsion was in the offing, or someone had started a blood libel. But there was nothing the Jews could do. When the governor summons you, you have to obey. The congregation hired a wagon for the rebbe and accompanied him with blessings: "May God shield you and all Israel from evil."

Rabbi Hershele drove to the governor's estate, escorted by the horseman. And the Jews sat in the synagogues and recited Psalms.

Contrary to Rabbi Hershele's expectation, the governor received him amiably. But the rebbe was even more terrified when the governor asked him: Hadn't five hundred ducats been stolen from the rebbe some time ago? How did he, a poor rabbi, amass that much gold?

The rebbe told him the story—though not fully. The money had belonged to the shtetl, some of it had been deposited with him in regard to an arbitration, some had been the savings of poor Jews, and so forth. It had been stolen, but no one knew who the thief was.

The rebbe didn't want to expose Mayer Anshel to the governor. Why ruin a Jew's reputation? Especially since the culprit had repaid every last bit.

The governor stepped out of the room for a while and then came back. He was holding a pouch containing five hundred gold ducats, which he placed on the table right in front of the rebbe.

The rebbe was amazed. That was his pouch with his ducats. What was going on? How had the pouch come into the governor's possession? And the ducats? And what about Mayer Anshel?

"This is your pouch, Rebbe," said the governor. "Do you recognize it? Well, take your ducats. . . . The mystery has been solved. The thief had time only to spend three ducats before he was caught. The remaining four hundred ninety-seven are here. Take the cash and go home."

Rabbi Hershele was dumbfounded. The money remained on the table. He didn't move toward it. Several minutes later, upon regaining his composure, he stammered: "What kind of riddle is this?"

The governor summoned a peasant and his wife. When she saw the rebbe, she tearfully threw herself at his feet and begged him to forgive her, and her husband did the same.

The matter was promptly cleared up.

The peasant's wife had been hired to clean the rebbe's home on the day before that Passover, when the money had vanished. While cleaning the rebbe's study, she had found the table drawer open and, inside it, the pouch with the ducats. She lived in a neighboring village and she brought the money to her husband. He kept it hidden for a long time. Eventually, he couldn't stand it any more. He took one ducat to the village tavern keeper and spent it on liquor. He said he had found the ducat. Several days later, he spent a second ducat at the tavern. Then, when he showed up with a third ducat, he aroused suspicion. He was interrogated and brought to the governor. After a sound whipping, the peasant confessed and told him where the pouch with the money was.

The story quickly spread through the entire shtetl. Now Rabbi Hershele no longer considered it necessary to hide the truth. He went to Mayer Anshel in Snyatin, handed him the five hundred ducats, and asked him why he had taken the guilt upon himself and where he had obtained the funds to repay the ducats that someone else had stolen.

"I saw," said Mayer Anshel, "that the rebbe was greatly distressed, and I felt sorry for the paupers. . . . So I sold or pawned my entire household and I borrowed wherever I could in the shtetl until I had gathered the two hundred ducats. Next, I tightened my belt, and the Good Lord helped me— I was able to repay the remaining sum. . . ."

"Mayer Anshel!" Rabbi Hershele exclaimed, saying good-bye to his former messenger, heartily and ardently. "Mayer Anshel! You are a rare Jew! Good-bye! May the Good Lord bless you and let you thrive in everything you do! You and your children and your children's children. . . .

And Rabbi Hershele's blessing came true. . . .

THE TREASURE

*T*HESE EVENTS TOOK PLACE some fifteen years ago, and while the Treasure disappeared, the Jews of Czortkow can't forget. They talk about it with regret and annoyance, but no anger.

The Treasure's disappearance was so sudden, so mysterious. After "it" first arrived, the dream lasted some four or five months—the golden dream whose magic glow lit up the entire shtetl: everyone, literally everyone, young and old, rich and poor. From Hershel Rapaport, the rebbe's first assistant, to Yosel the drayman; from Shuya, the rebbe's cantor, to Dobbe, the nail cutter and bathhouse attendant.

Actually, the Treasure was no "it"—it was a "she." A pale, skinny woman with the pensive and saintly face of a rebbe's wife. People guessed she was some fifty years old. She turned up at the cantor's door. No one knew where she came from or who she was. But who cared what she was, if you knew what she could do, and what she had brought along?

Her conduct was very bizarre, very surprising. She was always surrounded by a whole throng of women. Her personal servant, who also acted as her interpreter, was a woman named Rokhl Shtekel (may she rest in peace). But even Rokhl could communicate with her only through the door, no one ever dared enter that woman's private room.

She took her meals with the rebbe's assistant, who considered her presence a rare honor, which gladdened his heart. Furthermore, she slept in the same bed as his wife. As for her wardrobe, she wore silk and velvet, and she changed her clothes every day. She freely gave alms to the poor. She also traveled in the finest carriages. The drivers fought over her and refused to take her money. She visited a bathhouse every day. The attendant provided her with all the comforts. Tailors sewed her frocks gratis. Shopkeepers sent her the finest and most expensive wares—as many as she wanted.

Her Sabbath began at twelve noon on Friday. She'd lock herself in her cottage and, until after Havdolah, the ceremony marking the end of Sabbath, she'd practice what the Hasids call "seclusion and meditation." If she stepped out for a minute because she needed something from her servants, from her bodyguards, she spoke just a few words and only Hebrew.

On a dark night, she and her throng of women would leave the shtetl, and there, in a mysterious conversation, she would suddenly raise her shawl. The women then spotted two radiant diamonds in her hand. Each diamond was the size of a challah. . . .

Sometimes, her hand would release a clay cup and shatter it loudly. She would then fling herself on the ground and mysteriously pick up some kind of circular, glittering object that seemed to have caused the loud noise. She would pick up the object and pocket it quickly, though giving the women enough time to see that the object was a gold ducat.

Sometimes, from some unknown source, she would produce a whole packet of ducats and break them each in turn. The members of her "suite" gaped and gawked in surprise. But none of them dared to ask her for even half a ducat or even just a piece.

And so little by little, it became "clear" *who* she was and *what* this was all about. At first, people whispered, then they spoke more and more precisely: in the homes, in the streets, in the synagogues, and—if you'll excuse my mentioning them in the same breath—the secular and the religious bathhouses. Everyone knew that she was a "Treasure," a hidden saintly woman, whom God had sent to Czortkow.

Sometimes, on a Sabbath, the admiring Jews saw her disappear in the room that Shaye the cantor had turned over to her, and there she practiced her meditation. At some point, an old and esteemed Jew, with bushy eyebrows and a long, wide, gray beard, would come by and spend the day with her. Then he would leave as quietly and as unobserved as he had come and he would vanish in the night.

Next, she would emerge and speak to the women:

"Did you see who visited me?"

"Yes, who is he? . . ."

"The prophet Elijah."

"The prophet Elijah? Really?"

And the entire shtetl tried to find him. To at least catch a glimpse of him—but it was no use.

The prophet Elijah had disappeared.

From the very start, the modern Jews in the town had sneered at the Treasure just as they sneered at all the Hasidic superstition and foolishness. But one of them, Shaye the watchmaker, was a *Shapirnik* (a follower of the enlightened rabbi, Shaye Mayer Shapiro). Now Shaye was a mordant satirist, whom the entire shtetl dreaded like fire, and from time to time, he shot his darts at the "Treasure's" Hasids and their women—for instance: He said that the "diamond challahs" were pieces of rotten wood; that the "broken ducats" were paper buttons. But more venomous than his critique was his sneer. Whenever he ran into one of the "Treasureniks," he would sneer and snap out a flippant remark, and the Hasid would jump away! The remark would bore and drill and chew into the victim's brain day and night—that's how powerful the watchmaker's remark was.

Gradually, the other Shapirniks switched from silent scorn to sharp criticism. The shtetl grew more and more riled up with every passing day, and the simple, ordinary Jews, the drivers, started grumbling among themselves.

"The ducats are there, and Elijah has also revealed himself, so how much longer do we have to wait?"

The Treasure noticed that people were whispering, and that the drivers who drove her to the bathhouse every day were getting less servile. So *she* started handing out more charity.

Zorekh the bathhouse attendant—a new bath! Yosel the driver—six horses like lions and his own cottage. Leybish the dry-goods dealer—two brick houses. Henekh the tailor—a cottage.

Since these were highly explicit actions, the Jews great calmer. But just for a while. Soon, an outright revolution exploded!

The Jews were at the end of their tether! It was no use "her" asking them to wait a bit longer, that the time hadn't come, that people weren't deserving as yet. It didn't help. The shopkeeper checked the Treasure's account— it was close to five hundred ducats. The tailor certainly couldn't wait any longer. People started asking her for money, dunning her from all sides.

However, the longest person to hold out was Hershel Rapoport, the rebbe's assistant. He covered her debt to the shopkeeper. And so she promised to repay him a thousand ducats for every single ducat he had put up. . . .

Now one dark and muddy night, Yosel was driving her, when suddenly, in the midst of the mire, he turned off into a side street, halted, and announced tersely:

"For the Treasure! Otherwise, knock!"

The day and the hour were drawing near, and people deserved to have the Treasure show herself.

But not everyone merited it, and not every place was worthy. . . .

Behind the old cemetery, there is a pit; and beyond the pit, a stone; and beyond the stone, three stumps. And the Treasure was supposed to reveal herself on the middle stump.

She would be brought there by three women and her bodyguard—people who had more faith in her and served her more loyally.

The day and the hour had come. It was Friday. The entire shtetl was bogged down in suspense, impatience, and heart-pounding expectation. But no one, except for the two fortunate women, had the nerve to show up, either at her cottage or along the route that the Treasure would take.

This was the first time that the women were allowed to enter the Treasure's private room, see the Treasure with their own eyes, touch her with their own hands, carry her. . . .

She lifted the pillow and told the women to take her by the head of the bed. This was a small chest with a handle, a very ordinary chest wrapped up in a shawl.

"Take both at once," she ordered them. "While you carry me, nobody should look hard at the chest."

The trembling women grabbed the handle and lifted the chest together, groaning: "Heavy!"

But their faces were wreathed in happy smiles. They knew that gold was heavy. . . .

Soon. . . . Soon. . . .

Prior to leaving the cottage, she announced earnestly and solemnly:

"Until we arrive, you must not stop, you must not say a word, you must not let go of the chest. If it falls and touches the ground, the gold will turn into stones."

They were already outside the shtetl, creeping through gardens, climbing over fences, and they finally reached the hill.

Where was she leading them?

But they didn't dare speak, they didn't dare stop. They were sweating hard. They were straining their final strength, clutching the handle with their fingers, terrified that they might drop the chest, shaking and dragging on and on. . . .

Now they felt that their strength had ebbed. One woman tried to draw a breath and she collapsed. The other woman likewise. . . .

The chest banged down on the rocky hillside and shattered.

There was no treasure inside, only a bunch of stones.

By the time the women came to, she was gone.

Several weeks later, she was arrested in Czernowitz.

And—a bizarre thing! Either Austria didn't have a precise law to cover this matter; or else the Christian judges were more amused by the profound ignorance and stupidity of the Czortkow Jews than angry at the con artist; or else the victims were too embarrassed to tell the whole truth. Whatever the reason, the defendant got off scot-free.

As a result, the modern Jews in Czortkow attacked the Hasids more fiercely, and whenever one of the victims spotted Shaye the watchmaker in the distance, he would take a detour of three streets to avoid running into him.

Once, however, in a narrow alley, Shaye bumped face to face into Hershel Rapoport, the rebbe's assistant, who, for a time, had served the Treasure food and drink and let her sleep in the same bed as his wife. There was no room for Hershel to escape Shaye. And the venomous jokester remarked with his usual sarcasm:

"It's a weird thing, Mr. Hershel, do you know what people are saying? They claim that the Treasure was a man and not a woman."

Shaye the watchmaker has grown quite old, but he's still the same mordant comedian as ever.

H. LEIVICK
(1888-1962)

Famous for his poems and plays, especially *The Golem* (1920), H. Leivick, pen name for Leivick Halper, wrote a number of verse narratives, some of which deal with folklore motifs. His works, starkly influenced by European Expressionism, were scarred by the horrors he experienced during his imprisonment in Siberia. And while he managed to settle in New York in 1913, he was shattered by the reports of anti-Jewish violence during World War I, especially in the Russian-occupied territories, then during the interwar period, and finally the Nazi genocide of Jews.

The theme of transformation into an animal is common throughout world literature and not just folklore. Leivick may have been influenced by a story in *The Mayse Book* (1602), "The Rabbi Who Was Turned into a Werewolf" (*Great Tales of Jewish Fantasy and the Occult*). This tale was similar to "Le Bisclavret" (The Werewolf) by Marie de France (twelfth century), who, however, wrote about a nobleman transformed into a wolf.

THE WOLF
A CHRONICLE
(1920)

1

It was on the third morning,
When the sun was rising in the east,
And no trace was left of the town

And the sun rose higher and higher,
Until it reached the zenith of the sky,
And the sun's rays encountered the rabbi's eyes.

And the rabbi was lying on a mound of stones and ashes
With a squeezed mouth and bulging pupils,
And his soul was dark and silent and that was all.

And when his eyes felt the hot rays,
They opened wide and they gazed and gazed,
Until his body began to stir and awaken.

And when the rabbi stood up and he saw
That he was the sole survivor of a murdered town
Without synagogues and without Jews and without his wife and children—
The rabbi didn't know what to do.

He stood there and he mulled and was amazed
That he had been spared and left to survive.

And he strained his eyes and his ears:
To see if someone might be crawling out of the ruins,
To hear a shot perhaps, so that he might go over.

But it was no use straining his eyes and his ears,
For no one emerged from under the ruins,
And no shot resounded from anywhere.

And he strained his eyes even harder and tried
To catch a glimpse of any of the victors.
But even the victors were nowhere in sight:
Heaps of ashes, chimneys, smoldering flames,
Silence—and that was all.

So he stood there, and the situation was awful,
And he didn't know what to do at all.

The rabbi then tore himself away and he started
Seeking and thrusting his hands in the heaps,
Trying to find at least the limbs of the victims
And burying them according to the Jewish tradition.

But it was no use seeking and digging through the heaps,
For no trace of a grave was to be found,
For everything was coal and ashes, and that was all.

The rabbi sat down on a toppled chimney
And he took off his shoes to recite the Lamentations,
But then it turned out that he'd forgotten the words.

And when he felt that he'd forgotten all the words,
A stream surged up from the pit of his stomach;
And since the stream couldn't reach his eyes,
It stopped in his tight, grieving heart—
And the rabbi didn't know what to do at all.

When the night came and covered
The ruin-laden town with vast darkness,
The rabbi got up from his chimney,
Which he'd been sitting on,
He turned his face toward the west
And he started out in his stocking feet,
Trudging along the broad road
That led into the forest.

The broad road was strewn with all sorts of things,
With rifles and caps and shattered wheels,
And the soil was crushed and smashed
By bullets and grenades,
By horses' hooves and soldiers' feet,
And around the dirt road and over the dirt road—
Darkness and silence, and that was all.

And when the rabbi had trudged for several miles,
An icy wind came blasting from the north,
And the rabbi felt a great fatigue in his body
And coldness in all his bones.

So the rabbi sat down on the ground to rest,
And then he lay down on the middle of the road,
His open eyes peering at the sky.
And the sky was high and deep and spangled
With myriads and myriads of stars.

And when the rabbi looked with his open eyes,
The myriads and myriads of stars
Began to pull away from their places and whirl
And cut and strike one another

And split one another,
Until they were devoured by the darkness.

And when the rabbi saw the stars fading out,
It didn't bother him, he kept on looking.
And when one star, the last, an obstinate star,
Refused to be snuffed out,
The rabbi held out his right hand
And pointed one finger until that star
Turned green and red and yellow
And still refused to be snuffed out.

So the rabbi lowered his right hand
And placed it on both his eyes
Because he was no longer bothered by the last star.
And his hand lay on his eyes
Until it slipped down to the ground
Because he started nodding off.

And just as he was on the verge of dozing,
It suddenly struck him that he hadn't prayed,
He hadn't recited his afternoon and evening prayers
And he hadn't recited his nightly prayers:
And he sat up and wanted to pray—
But he had forgotten the melodies.

And when he saw that he had also forgotten how to pray,
A second stream spurted up from the pit of his stomach,
And when the stream was again unable to reach his eyes
And it stuck in the middle of his throat—
The rabbi couldn't stand it anymore,
And he jumped up and started running,
Further and further on the broad road.

The laps of his rabbinical coat
Fluttered apart like two black wings,
And the wind tore his rabbinical hat from his head,
And the sand pulled the stockings from his legs,
And so, bareheaded and barefoot,
He suddenly slammed into the darkness
Of the deep and enormous forest.
And suddenly his brain was ignited

And it opened into two gates,
And a vast brightness poured into his eyes,
And he saw the deep and enormous forest
Through and through, from end to end.

And when he saw the forest through and through,
His eyes could no longer endure
The huge light of the enormous space,
And his breathing pounded the final strokes,
And because of its sorrow his body was drawn to the ground.
And for the first time that day,
His choking throat emitted
A hoarse moan, the vestige of a sound,
And a moment later—so he thought—
The real scream would come.

And he collapsed with his forehead on a tree
And pummeled his bare chest with both his hands,
And pounded and tore from his innards
The unscreamed screams of his sorrow.

And he ran deeper into the forest,
And the moment he crossed the border,
He felt his legs being grabbed
And entangled by dense barbed wires.
And he had no time to free his legs,
When the nets engulfed his entire body
And knocked him down on all fours
And pulled him and dragged him and rolled him
Up and down, over pits and exposed roots,
And tore off pieces from his clothes,
And then, with his clothes all torn off,
The nets ripped patches of skin from his naked flesh.

And when the rabbi saw that he was buck-naked,
His face lit up with a strange smirk,
And a sharpness drew across his teeth,
And a salty dribble across his tongue,
And his lower lip began to droop.

And when he started spitting out the salty dribble,
Fine hairs began to bristle from under his skin,

To stick out and grow.
And lie in rows, lie in rows,
Smooth and fallen in one place,
Standing and bristling in another place.

And when the rabbi in his dread
Wanted to cover his eyes with his hands—
He saw that his fingers were joined together
And unrolling and sharpening,
With long, hard, bent nails;
And he felt as if someone were putting a hoop on his back
And forging together the back of his neck
And his fallen shoulders.

And his ears started pulling away and dropping.
And the tongue in his maw started whipping out from under his palate
And clustering and pressing between his teeth
And slipping and thrusting longer and longer,
And his eyes started bulging
And turning under his brows like round wheels
And igniting in green and frosty fires.

And again he saw the vast forest
Through and through, from end to end,
And his breathing started pounding
New and seething newborn strokes,
And he sprang up on all fours
With a sharpened and disheveled back,
And his eyes devoured the darkness.

And as if all his innards wanted to rip from his belly,
A third stream spurted up to his throat
And it didn't want to stick in his gullet,
And a wild roaring burst through the forest,
A louder and louder howling,
And the roaring was followed by a nimble leap—
A leap that looked like an arch.

And the forest heard the wild howling
And the nimble leap of a beast—
For an instant his stormy breathing stopped;
And an instant later, the forest

Swung the storm further apart
And pulled it in deeper and deeper
And tore and hurtled the pieces,
And kept absorbing and concealing
The wild roaring and howling.

And there was storm and darkness and nothing else

2

And Jews driven out from other areas
Began arriving in the town
And started rebuilding the ruined houses,
And, before anything else, the great synagogue,
Because half-walls of the great synagogue had survived,
And because the Jews were still few in number,
They didn't need more than one synagogue.

And when the synagogue was rebuilt with windows and doors,
They placed the Torah scroll in the Holy Ark,
The single scroll they had rescued and carried
From their own areas.

And after evening prayers, they stayed on in the synagogue
Till late at night and they rejoiced.
And their joy was mixed with sorrow,
Because they had no rabbi of their own,
And their sorrow was even greater
Because no member of the local congregation
Had come home again.

And in the midst of their rejoicing,
The Jews all suddenly started trembling
Because they thought they were hearing
A bizarre and distant weeping from somewhere.

And when they fell silent and pricked up their ears,
Their terror worsened and worsened,
Because they truly heard, from far, far away,
The drawn-out howling of a beast,
A howling that reached the synagogue.

At first, a nasty roaring, as if a beast were being torn to shreds,
Then the howling grew faint and desperate, like the lament
Of a dog that opens its heart to the moon,
And then the howling grew softer and softer,
A sobbing that sounded like human weeping.

And when the Jews dashed out of the synagogue,
And listened to the semi-nocturnal darkness,
They heard nothing more
Except the pounding of their own hearts
And the rustling of the scorched trees,
Which stuck out from among the ruins,
Pouring out their final leaves in the night,
For autumn had come to the earth.

And the Jews trudged silently to their houses.
And they felt that whoever had howled so loudly
Lay hidden under a wall or a chimney,
And he was silent because he was lying in wait
Ready to leap out and pounce....

And when the Jews suddenly saw the moon creep out
In the sky as if from a cellar,
Exposing all the vastness beyond the ruins,
As far as the circular wall of the enclosed woods,
Which surrounded the town on all sides—
The Jews again felt the nakedness of the streets
And they knew that the ruins were not theirs,
And that they, these Jews, were strangers here.

And when they were inside their houses,
They stood in the darkness for a long time
And peered in terror through the panes
And watched the white shine of the moon grow whiter and whiter,
And all the cracks in the ruins were opened.

And then, in their terror, they fell asleep.

And the moon turned its face away from the town
And closed up all the cracks in the ruins;
And the chimneys and the heaps of ashes
Became chimneys and heaps of ashes again.

And the shadows that had started emerging
And craning their necks and reaching for the heights
Fell back upon the cracks of the ruins
And lay there the way the dead ought to lie.

Because the moon was far across the forest,
Sieving through the branches and peering
Into the green eyes of the wolf,
Who lay there, tormented by his howling.
And the eyes of the wolf beat back with their greenness
And peered into the very heart of the moon,
And tangled moonbeams dangled from the trees and branches,
Blood dripping down from white and green.

And the moon left its dead beams
Dangling from the branches
And glided far beyond the forest.
And the beams dangled there until
They started tearing off from their gallows
And dropping one by one upon the wolf's nape
And cutting through his hide down to his marrow,
Reminding him of something pleasant and radiant.
And the wolf half-closed his eyes and rounded his body
Like a hoop, holding his head on his back legs
And nestling his hide and smirking to himself.

And the forest was thick and opaque,
And only the tree tops were billowing above
And darkening the low inkyness even more.

And suddenly the forest leaped up,
Its eyes facing west,
Because the western wind brought fragrances to his nostrils—
The same fragrances that he had smelled at nightfall,
That had made him dizzy at nightfall,
Because the storm had fused all the winds.

And the wolf's nostrils trembled with sharpness,
And joy swept over his moustache,
And his teeth ground and bit into one another
All the way into the gums—

And the stillness awoke
And, ring after ring, it rolled through the forest, from end to end,
Until all the veins in the trees had burst
And exploded in all directions—
The wolf's triumphant roar.

And the leaves and the roots and the forest trails
Were whirled and plucked under the claws
Of the wolf's hasty stride.

3

And it was in the morning, when the Jews
Were leaving the synagogue after praying,
And when their hearts were still echoing
With the blasts of the autumnal ram's horn,
And when their eyes were still peering with last night's fear,
They spotted a Jew hurrying from the broad road
And heading towards the synagogue,
And they all welcomed him here.

And when they saw that the stranger was wearing
A silk coat and a rabbinical fur hat,
Their joy was boundless,
And they each held out his hand and wished him peace.

And when the stranger didn't respond to their greeting,
And he kept striding toward the synagogue,
And he didn't halt for even a second,
And he didn't utter a single word,
The Jews all noticed that there were no shoes on the stranger's feet,
Only a pair of tattered socks,
And the fur cap was filthy and threadbare,
And the coat was ripped and shredded,
And his hairy, blood-stained chest was visible,
And his entire face seemed sunken
In the clumps of a bizarre and disheveled beard;
And the Jews felt the grief in the stranger,
And they remembered that they too were mourners, like him,
And they exchanged glances but didn't utter a single word,
And in their curiosity, they followed the stranger

To the synagogue courtyard,
And they hoped that he would soon speak of his own accord,
And that they would hear his dismal but honored words.

The stranger kept averting his eyes from the Jews,
And so, looking at no one, he approached the synagogue entrance
And pulled out the door and stepped inside
And he settled on a seat bv the eastern wall,
Right by the Holy Ark,
And he still didn't open his lips to utter a word.

And the Jews stood around him, and with every passing moment
They grew more and more frightened of his silence,
For only now did they see the color of his eyes
And hear the heavy breathing of his naked chest.
And in the presence of his silence, the entire synagogue
Exposed its cold discomfort to his eyes:
And when the Jews were about to lower their heads,
Ashamed to look at the naked walls,
At the small, plain cabinet that served as a Holy Ark.
And all at once, the stranger stood up and said, he said:
"What do you want? Go away! It's my place
On the eastern wall—the rabbi's place."

And the Jews understood that he wasn't all there,
And they exchanged glances and didn't know what to do.

And the stranger caught them exchanging glances,
And he tore off his coat and started pounding
Both his fists upon his heart,
And wheezing words tore through his teeth:
"Who told you to rebuild the ruins?
Whatever is ruined should remain ruined.
And who told you to become my heirs?
Go get an axe or a knife and give me a decent burial—
A decent burial, Jews, I beg you."

And the dizzy stranger collapsed on the bench,
Because he hadn't uttered a human word for weeks,
And he himself didn't know where the words were coming from,
And he felt as if something inside him had torn off
And had dropped into a grave and had dragged him along.

And the Jews thought that he had fainted,
And they grabbed his hands and tried to revive him:
And the stranger soon came to and he started talking
With a sobbing voice as if he were crying:
"I beg you, Jews, give me my due, a decent burial—
I deserve death, death from a stranger;
I would cut my throat myself
And thrust a thorn into each eye
And chop off my hands and throw them to the dogs—
But I can't do that myself! Someone else has to do it for me!
I beg you, bring an axe and give me my due."

And as he talked, he collapsed on the floor
And clung to the feet of the Jews—
Until his weeping suddenly stopped,
And his throat choked up with other sounds.

And the Jews didn't hear the other sounds,
And they bent over him and tried to lift him up,
But the stranger lay there, heavy and sunken,
And no one could move him from the spot.

And suddenly one of the Jews sprang up
And dashed across the synagogue, shouting wildly
Because the stranger had dug all his teeth into the Jew's hand.

And when the Jews saw the bitten hand,
They rushed from the synagogue, one by one,
Leaving the fallen stranger all alone.

And the stranger lay there for a long time, with his face down,
His legs twisting, and his arms stretched out,
And his eyes were open, and his ears were pricked up,
And his shoulders were twitching silently and more silently,
And the smirk of his bite was resting on his lips.

And then, when the smirk had faded,
His shoulders stopped twitching,
And his body rolled over, face up,
And he lay there, stretched out, with his face up,
Until around noon.

And in the afternoon, when the sun was sinking toward evening,
Shining its cold shine through the western windows,
The stranger got up from the floor and settled
In the same place as before, next to the Holy Ark.
And he sat and peered at the western windows,
And at all the walls and all the benches,
As if he were seeing them for the first time.

And he sat there and sat there until his face
Hinted at a pale glint of a thought,
And the pale glint grew clearer and clearer,
Emerging from his eyes like a solid decision.
And he got up and started walking, trudging across the synagogue,
Every so often grabbing benches and lecterns,
Because his knees kept buckling,
And his body kept getting pulled down toward the floor;
And he kept trudging with half-closed eyes,
And he felt a wild joy when he knocked over a lectern,
And the crash kept echoing in all the corners
And swirling a column of dust in the western rays,
And the rays kept growing turbid and swaying like dead cobwebs.

And when the crash of the first lectern had faded,
The stranger knocked over a second lectern
And then the rest, quickly, vehemently, one by one, until the synagogue
Was filled with a thick, dark cloud of dust.

And his quick vehemence grew stronger in him,
And he danced in a circle on the platform.
He leaped across the tumbled benches and he stamped his feet
And hurled his arms around, and kept driving the columns of dust
Harder and harder, in turbid, swirling circles,
And not a single sound tore from his maw,
Because the sounds choked inside him, waiting for later.

And his head started turning and dangling,
And his palate tightened in the heat and dryness,
So he got down on all fours and he crept and crawled
And rolled over on his back
And he banged his forehead on the walls and the floor.
And then he slunk upon the platform,
And then upon the small table on the platform,

And he stretched out full-length,
And his head dangled with his shoulders.

And his eyes twisted to the side,
And they rebounded from the Holy Ark,
And the glint of a distant memory flickered across them;
And when that glint was snuffed,
His eyes still couldn't turn away from the curtain of the Ark
And they stuck like needles deep into his marrows.
And the stranger got up and he heavily forced himself
To clamber down from the table and then from the platform,
And with buckling legs he dragged himself over
To the steps of the Holy Ark.

And he stood by the steps for several moments and then
Clambered to the top with his face toward the curtain,
And he stood and he stood there, frozen solid.
And he felt a prickling in his temples, and that was all,
Because he was all frozen on the inside as well.
And little by little, the prickling covered his entire body,
And his arms circled the Holy Ark like two rings,
And his head started digging and drilling in
And wrapping itself in the folds of the curtain;
And with the top of his brain, like the horns of an ox,
He pierced and gored the small doors,
Till the skin of his brain was blotched and blistered,
And his entire face had burst and bloodied.
And when his nostrils smelled his own blood,
The yells concealed in his innards
Tore and rolled into his gullet.

And when he felt the yells coming, his limbs
Began to dance for joy,
And with his final vehemence, his head poked holes
In the small doors until they burst
With all their holes, through and through,
And his eyes flashed with the glow of the wooden handles of the scroll
And the internal darkness beyond the Torah.

And the instant he saw the internal darkness,
His eyes twisted of their own accord,
And they started bulging and creeping out of their sockets,

As if they wanted to bore into the very heart of the darkness.

And suddenly his eyes pulled back,
And his head turned around,
And his neck cracked as if broken,
And his entire body rolled like a rock
And tumbled down the steps to the floor,
And a sharp shout remained stuck between his teeth.

And he didn't lie on the floor for more than a moment,
He sprang back with new vehemence—
And the roars of his gullet
Rolled to all the walls and corners of the synagogue.

And after he bounded out of the synagogue,
The impetuous storm of his bellowing
Burst across the overturned benches and lecterns.

4

And it was time for afternoon prayers when the stranger
Dashed from the synagogue to the road leading into the forest.
And when the congregants entered the synagogue
And saw all the devastation
And the shattered doors of the Holy Ark
And the bloody and shredded curtain of the Ark,
They all burst into tears.

And when they saw the stranger's coat on the floor,
And he was gone—the men couldn't grasp what was going on,
And their hearts were filled with misery.
And they recited their afternoon and evening prayers
And they went home, and once at home
They were terrified of talking about those events
So as not to terrify their wives and children.

And at midnight, when everyone was asleep,
A light autumn rain was drizzling from the sky,
And through the gloom the surrounding woods
Drew closer to the darkened cottages—
And in their sleep, the Jews suddenly heard from below their windows
The same howling they had heard the previous day.

And when a few minutes had passed,
And the howling grew bigger and stronger and closer,
They realized that an actual beast was howling,
And not somewhere in the forest but right here in the town,
And everyone thought that the danger lurked under his own windows,
And they tried to curtain and shutter the panes.
And the mothers nestled their children
So that the beast wouldn't hear their voices.
For they all figured that the beast was dashing
From street to street, from yard to yard.
And with bated breath, they listened carefully
To hear the beast's treading through the silence.

And nobody heard the beast's treading.
Because the beast wasn't dashing through the yards,
He was standing in the middle of the market,
On the rim of the well,
Pulling the bizarre howling from his innards,
Baying with a slashed throat at the darkened cottages.

And there was no rest and no pause in the howling.
Hour after hour, the whole second half of the night,
The tireless and clumsy yelling
Rolled across the town, through rain and through wind.

And it was a mixture of baying and bellowing
And a drawn-out screeching and a stormy roaring,
And in every change in the howling, a challenge was hidden,
An appeal and, more than anything, a prayer.
And more than anything, the prayer terrified all hearts,
Because it recalled a human weeping.

And the Jews who had windows facing the market
Tried to stick out their heads to see what was happening,
And then they instantly pulled their heads back in,
Because through the darkness
They felt the green fire of two wolfish eyes.

And when the wolf saw those heads,
His entire body shuddered,
And his neck drew out further
In a convulsion of rattling lamenting.

And the lament dragged on until daylight.
And when the dawn started creeping
Out from its hiding place, blind and trembling,
And the wolf with his howling heart
Couldn't wait for someone to come and receive him—
And so he lapsed into silence and leaped from the well
And dashed swiftly through the ruins.

5

And the new community went through unhappy days
And even unhappier nights.
Because night after night, when midnight struck,
The wolf seemed to grow out of the ground,
Take his place in the middle of the market,
And keep howling till dawn.
And whatever the Jews did to drive him away,
Their efforts made him even more obstinate,
And his visits grew even more punctual.

And one night, the Jews set several fires
Around the well and in all the corners of the market,
And they secretly watched through their windows,
For they knew that wolves are scared of fire.
And how amazed they were when they saw
That instead of fearing the fires, the wolf
Leaped into the flames, and his paws hurled out
Pieces of burning wood in all directions,
And he whirled and spun in a dance,
Shrouded in billows of smoke and ashes:
And then, sated with dancing, he leaped up
To his constant place and started howling.
And the Jews understood better than before
That something was wrong. Their fear of the wolf
Had changed into a fear of themselves.
And the wolf's baying had taken root in their hearts,
Digging underneath their new hopes and dreams,
And resounding in prickly, icy echoes.

All kinds of stories circulated from person to person,
Spreading all over the area,

Preventing the growth of the new congregation.

And, most surprising of all for the Jews,
The wolf never approached their cottages
And never once appeared in the streets,
And they saw clearly that he hadn't come
To pounce or tear to shreds,
He had come for something else.

And they were even more surprised one day,
When several Jews, the boldest ones, girded themselves
With axes and rifles and headed toward the market, and,
Hiding behind a ruin, they fired their rifles.
And instead of jumping off the rim of the well
And dashing away or attacking them,
The wolf remained standing on the rim,
And all at once, breaking off all his roaring,
He craned his neck toward the lurkers and waited.

And the instant the lurkers saw his eyes
And, in their glow, his waiting throat,
They trembled so hard that their arms and legs were paralyzed,
And breathlessly they barely made it home.

And terror ate so deep into their hearts
That they couldn't come to for days on end.

And now they all sensed that something was happening for their sake,
And they stopped looking for a way to drive the beast away,
And they received the nightly terrors
With agonizing patience and distress and with obedient grief.
And for whole days and whole nights,
They prayed and recited psalms and wept,
And they spent the Ten Days of Repentance
Praying and fasting until the Day of Atonement.

6

And on the night of the Day of Atonement, after Kol Nidre,
The worshippers did not go home.
And they spent all night in the synagogue,

And, clad in white smocks and surrounded by candles,
They stood there and they prayed to God.

And when the twelfth hour was drawing near,
Their weeping grew louder and stronger,
And their hearts pounded with impatient waiting,
Because every minute dragged on—an eternity.
And they sensed (and they didn't know why)
That this night would bring the solution of the mystery,
And that something extraordinary would happen to them.
And they wrapped themselves deeper in their prayer shawls
As if trying to conceal themselves.

And when the first strokes of midnight struck,
Their weeping became a genuine storm,
As if they were trying to drive the howling away,
To keep it from approaching the synagogue.
And, buried in their prayer shawls and glowing with waxen light,
They themselves looked like pieces of ignited wax—
Ready to splutter and about to melt.
And suddenly, they all lapsed into silence,
And with their heads emerging from their prayer shawls,
They thrust their eyes deep into the hush
That shrouded the synagogue's walls and its ceiling.

And when a minute had passed and two and three—and the hush
Was not disrupted by anything or anyone,
A stream of joy swept over all the heads:
And they stood there as if they'd been aroused from a bad dream
And still didn't believe their own ears.

But the hands of the clock were way, way past twelve,
And the howling of the beast still didn't start.

And they mustered their courage and stepped into the courtyard,
And from far away they saw that the well was deserted,
And the entire area was dipped in moonlight silver,
And they raised their eyes to the heavens and, enchanted
And imbued with soft, bright sorrow,
They heard the fluttering and saw the protective wings
Of the Lord of the Universe.

And their hearts were filled with pity,
Pity for themselves and for their wives and children,
And for their renounced and rebuilt houses,
And for the ruins that weren't covered,
And that, in their shame and fallen state,
Wept, like sinners, to the Lord of the Universe,
Wept for rebuilding and restoring.

And the heavens were deep and wide open,
And in the wide-open depths, hurrying and trembling stars
Were racing and fading and igniting again
On their agonizing paths; and those whose fate
Was calm and everlasting openness gazed down
At the world more open and more calmly,
Gazed down with their clear and penetrating eyes.

7

And the next day, the fasting passed quickly and easily
For the Jews, virtually unnoticed.
And when it was time for Neila,
The final prayer on the Day of Atonement,
And the evening shadows shrouded the synagogue
In a deep and joyful darkness,
The Jews felt light and purged,
And their faces looked like mirror images:
And they recited their Neila prayers with fresh strength.

And it never occurred to anyone
That the wolf was standing behind the synagogue door,
Scratching with his claws and ready to jump inside,
Because not a single eye saw the wolf
Running from the forest and through the streets,
And reaching the synagogue porch and stretching out full-length
By the door and waiting.

And when the blower of the ram's horn lifted it to his lips
And blew the blasts for Neila,
The door of the synagogue burst open,
And a long and flimsy howling
Blended with the hearts of the blasts.

And before the Jews had time to look around,
The wolf was already standing on the steps to the platform,
His big and burning eyes boring into the crowd,
And the crowd, like a herd of sheep, flocked around the pulpit,
Where the prayer leader was standing,
And he couldn't scream because he was speechless
And he couldn't stir a single limb to escape.
And the wolf stood there silently and waited.
And suddenly, he tore away from the steps
And jumped across the heads of the congregants,
Jumped upon the prayer leader
And grabbed his throat with his front paws
And hurled him to the floor and started strangling him.

And the terrified crowd made a dash for the door
And nearly abandoned the prayer leader
To a certain death inflicted by the wolf—
But then one Jew grabbed a lectern
And with its sharp edge he smashed it into the wolf's head
And split his brain apart.
And the wolf rolled away from his victim
And drenched with blood he collapsed on the floor.

And the entire congregation, in turmoil and torment,
Grasped everything that had occurred in secret,
And they beat the wolf's neck and his back
And kicked him in his belly and his knees.

And suddenly, a shout emerged from under the earth,
And everyone's hands, stopping their torment,
Remained in midair as if paralyzed
Because the patch of darkness had suddenly begun to stir,
And rolled upward with an open face.
And two human eyes shone through the darkness
And enveloped all the Jews, calmly and brightly.
And the crowd burst into a loud weeping,
Because no wolf was lying, tortured, in a pool of blood—
It was a Jew in a rabbinical fur hat,
And they all recognized the guest, the stranger.

And the tortured man gathered his final strength

And began to move his dying lips.
And all the Jews heard his comforting words:
"I'm fine now, very fine—don't cry, Jews."

And he breathed his last.

Hersh Dovid Nomberg
(1876-1927)

Perhaps the first conscious aesthete in Yiddish literature, Nomberg wrote a great number of polished and realistic tales about dreamers, artists, intellectuals, and also the poor, as well as haunting poems. In his later years, he concentrated on essays, travelogues, and other forms of journalism. Despite his realism, Nomberg—so typically of Yiddish realists—penned a few lyrical stories based on folk motifs.

RAYA-MANO
(pub. 1922)

I

THE LAND OF THE FIVE RIVERS, where the sun burns so hot overhead, and the lotus blooms, was blessed with prophets, who were given to the people. They were meant to teach the people and to help them and guide them along the thorny roads of life and through the dark gates of death. The hearts of the people trustingly beat to the words of the prophets, who were famous throughout the land, and there was a blessing for every mother: "May God let you give birth to a prophet."

Amid the hurly-burly of life, the population, particularly every tribe that lived on the shores of the sacred Ganges River, did not forget its ancient pedigree, which was passed down from father to son, from generation to generation. The ancient tradition told about a noble and sublime race that was descended from the gods themselves and had been sent down to the dismal earth to atone for the sins of that race. That was why a note of sadness constantly resounded in the souls of the people, and their hearts remained open and alert to intellect and matters of intellect. They didn't care for labor, and their lives could not fill out what a man does to maintain his life; they loved leisure, idleness, thinking, and dreaming, lying on grass for a long time, gazing wistfully into the depth of the sky and into the abyss of their own souls. In those days, they didn't know about opium, which intoxicates and weaves cheerful and magical fantasies. That was why people turned to the living words on the lips of prophets, the words that woke them and elevated them.

There were two kinds of prophets, prophets of sadness and prophets of laughter, and both kinds taught the same teachings:

"The world is a blazing fire, every yearning of your heart is like straw on the fire, and every craving is a new and consuming flame. For every yearning gives birth to a new yearning and every craving a new craving, and the blazing fire is vast and endless. Why does a man struggle to fill his heart, which never becomes full, and the intellect is never sated? The will to live is a tiny spark in your hearts, and you have blown up that spark, and now look! That spark has burst into flame, and you all stand in the midst of those flames, and you haven't brought any water to put out the fire, you've simply added straw and wood."

That was what the prophets taught, and the population obeyed and took those words to heart.

When a prophet of sadness spoke, his voice was soft and tremulous and it flowed with a great deal of mercy, and just as the notes of a harp flow through the dark night from somewhere far, far away, the words of the prophet were absorbed into all hearts and were soothing and healing. People heard, and their hearts thought about their fate, their neverending struggle.

And when the prophet of laughter spoke, his voice was clear, pure, and transparent, as pure as the voice of a silver chime. He didn't reprove, he merely laughed at the sinful foolishness of the world. Thread by thread, he undid the net that fantasy had woven around the human intellect, he unraveled that net in order to catch and entangle the human intellect with variety, with effort and concern.

Each prophet was destined for his sacred mission right upon emerging from his mother's womb. In fact, the good news was announced to the mother the instant she conceived. And when the baby left the womb, he got to his feet, took seven paces forward, then turned around, took three more paces, and bowed to the gathering. And if a crease appeared on his forehead, it was a sign that he would grow up to be a prophet of sadness; but if a smile appeared on his lips, they knew that he was a prophet of laughter.

In those days, an old building stood on the shore of the Ganges: it housed the temples of the god of sadness and the god of laughter. You reached the temple of sadness across dry land. If you had sanctified your soul and your body according to the law, the priests would lead you inside and remove the veil from the holy image of the god of sadness, and you saw a sad face—anxious eyes, and a forehead covered by a heavy cloud of purified hardship.

On the other hand, you reached the temple of the god of laughter across water. First, all alone, you boarded a small boat and moved through waves that hastily smacked against that place. You had to display a contempt toward death; and once you had completed the route safe and sound, you were privileged to see the holy image of the god of laughter with his deep, good eyes, with the two creases flanking his lips, and, on his forehead, the many creases that told about past sadness, about life and hardship that had been overcome, about mountains that had been flattened, and about abysses that were filled with the ashes of a heart that had consumed itself.

When a prophet of sadness became an adult, his path led to his god; while a prophet of laughter had to resist the powerful temptation until he was sanctified for the god of laughter.

But woe to the prophet of laughter who saw the god of sadness once in his lifetime, and woe to the prophet of sadness to whom the face of the foreign god was revealed. Great was his sin against his own intellect, and that sin could never be wiped away. He was homeless on the earth and cursed and cast out from all worlds.

Everyone knew that.

II

And when Raya-Mano's mother, a pious and virtuous woman, conceived him, a divine man appeared to her and announced the news that she had a prophet in her womb.

And the divine man said: "I see a tiny cloudlet rising in your clear sky, and I see a black spot marring your happiness, you pious and virtuous woman. But I don't know of any solution."

And the woman gave birth to a son, and the boy took seven paces forward and three back and he bowed, and a crease appeared on his forehead. So everyone knew that a prophet of sadness had been born.

Yet they were all surprised. The child's lips simultaneously showed a faint, faint smile, barely discernable.

When the child was weaned, his mother brought him to the god of sadness and made offerings according to the law, and the boy, Raya-Mano, was raised by the priests and prophets to become a prophet of sadness.

In time, however, they recognized wild signs in the child. He sometimes knelt before the holy image of his god, and his eyes were open to absorb the sadness pouring from the god's eyes, and a holiness rested on the child's face. But suddenly, his lips quivered and something like the shadow of a smile flashed across them.

Nothing like that had ever happened before, nor was anything like that set down in the holy books.

So they sent for the boy's mother and asked her:

"You pious and virtuous woman, you mother of a prophet! Tell us! Weren't you in the temple of the god of laughter on this side of the river? You see, we don't know what the matter is with your son: Will he bring great happiness or great unhappiness to the children of the earth?"

And the mother replied:

"No, I wasn't in the temple of the god. But a divine man brought me the news that I would bear a prophet, and the man said: 'I see a black spot marring your happiness.'"

The priests heard her out, shook their heads, and peered anxiously at the growing prophet.

They didn't let him go outside, they told everyone who talked to the child not to mention the name of the god of laughter in front of the child, and the child was not to know about the divine image that stood facing the rushing waves.

And so that was how the child was raised, concealed and isolated from the world, alone with the holy books. And the child raised his heart with the pain of all worlds, with the great sadness that infuses all living things and all dead things, and his voice grew purer and purer day by day and it poured out, quivering, like the notes of a harp, notes that floated through a dark night from far, far away.

Yet he found no rest, the young prophet. And he grew absorbed in his thoughts and he was conquered by the great sadness of the world, and his soul poured out in soft, white notes, and the shekhinah—the divine presence—of sadness began resting on him and shone down from his purified face. Then suddenly, a bizarre string quivered in his heart. It was as if he had seen laughing eyes somewhere, a scornful face and some kind of strange and unfamiliar world. Where had he seen those eyes? When had he lived in that world? And what did the foreboding of his heart signify? And what was he doing here, and what was he seeking?

He mused briefly, but the restfulness had left his heart for entire days and nights.

And on some nights, a huge terror suddenly disrupted his sleep, and his heart pounded swiftly. He dreamed about the god of laughter and he was frightened by the face, and yet his heart was drawn to him and his soul yearned for him.

And then one night, when he awoke in his great terror, he woke up the eldest of the priests and opened his heart to him:

"When I was absorbed in thoughts of great sadness, I fell asleep and then I dreamed about an old, gray man. He was so calm, scornful, and so full of laughter. . . . And he fixed his eyes on me. . . ."

"What kind of eyes were they?" asked the old servant of god.

"Good eyes, deep eyes, full of peace and calm. . . . And scorn, a great scorn, lay in them. . . . And laughter on his lips. . . . The kind of laughter that pierces a human being. . . . I'm terrified, holy man! An evil spirit is plaguing me, help me, godly man."

The old man stood up from his bed in the middle of the night, he led the boy to the fire he had lit and he stared and stared at the boy's face until he made out two small, faint laughter creases on either corner of his lips.

"Terrible!" the old man mused in his heart; but he said nothing to the boy. He neither comforted him nor did he try to subdue the boy's fear.

III

One day, Raya-Mano was inside the four empty walls of the temple and he pricked up his ears to listen to the waves rushing outside. Something important seemed to be happening there. Boats were coming and going, and the hubbub sounded like the rowing of many vessels and the treading of many people springing ashore on hard marble. The old teacher was in a mournful mood that day and he gazed anxiously at the boy.

"Today something's going to happen," the teacher mused, but he said nothing to the young man and asked him nothing. As of that night, their hearts grew apart. The young prophet no longer poured out his soul to the old man, and the old man no longer conversed so intimately with him. He no longer kissed the young prophet and he no longer smoothed the boy's curls with his old and trembling hand. And today, they stood even more alien to one another, even wider apart.

And that night, Raya-Mano's sleep drifted far away and he strained his ears to catch every sound, every last rustle from the outside. Throughout his long upbringing, when he was alone with the four walls, with his own intellect and with the holy books, his ears had become so refined as to catch the slightest distant echo, even though the walls were thick and solid. And he sensed that the populace was celebrating a service to a god whom the youngster didn't know. And toward midnight, the hubbub faded, and Raya-Mano seemed to see a huge throng kneeling down and praying a silent prayer. And after that stillness, the notes of holy chants began quivering in the air. Once a year, this worship occurred here as well, an adoration of the god of sadness, and these worshipers likewise knelt until midnight, and then chants broke the stillness. But these chants were quite different. They flowed from different sources and they poured into different seas, they weren't those chants with their drawn-out notes, stiff and straight notes, which were virtually frozen inside their borders. Now they romped and frolicked and they chased one another, and they got tangled and disentangled in a reveling dance, and one star beckoned to another star, and the sun laughed at the moon in the new melodies.

And the young prophet pressed his ear to the wall, and his intellect thirstily drank the new chants, which were intoxicating, and their intoxication drove away the great sadness and seeped into his intellect, into every last cell of his soul, and shattered it and corrupted it. But the poison was sweet! It brought the echoes of new worlds, and a comfort and a thorough scrubbing for the destruction it had caused. And Raya-Mano stood there all night long and listened endlessly.

And toward dawn, just as the eastern sky turned pale, the chanting stopped, and a heavy stillness settled all around. Now the boy was deeply alarmed. And he remained alone with his ravaged and shattered soul, and he burst into a loud weeping, and his pain was so sharp that he tore out his beautiful curls.

"What's wrong?" asked the frightened old man.

"I heard, I listened," he stammered, "all night long. A holy day was celebrated out there, a holy day for a god I'm not acquainted with. My heart is ravaged, my soul is shattered. Tell me, old man, tell me: what does it mean, what did I hear? My fear is great and it will be the death of me."

"What did you hear?" the old man asked..

"I heard chants, hymns to an alien god. . . ."

"What kind of chants?"

"They laughed, they poked fun. They frolicked and they got entangled in a wild dance, and they pierced the depths of my soul in order to destroy it and rebuild it, and I listened, I listened all night long, and their magic captured me. and it was as if whole throngs of white doves and whole throngs of black crows were flying and wheeling overhead, all night long, until dawn. . . . I feel awful, miserable, lonesome—please don't leave me, my father!"

The old man didn't respond, he didn't comfort the boy and he didn't talk to his heart to soften his fear. Instead, he kept silent and shook his gray-haired head.

And Raya-Mano fell to the old man's feet and kissed the dust in front of the old man and wept and begged:

"Please don't leave me, old man. Look: my young heart cannot endure the great burden of yearning. Look: my fear devours me day after day, and you have stopped comforting me, and your dry lips haven't kissed me for weeks now, and your skinny fingers haven't smoothed my hair for a long time now, and my pain is deep, and I can't escape. And out there, on the outside, there is a different world, there are different chants. Why do you conceal that new world from me? What secret, old man, are you hiding in your heart from me? Help me, holy father, help! Tell me!"

The old man silently heard him out, then placed his arms across his chest and replied:

"I can tell you nothing, my child. A great danger is hovering over your young head, and I can't help you."

IV

And the time came when Raya-Mano could no longer subdue his yearning heart. One night, he silently left the four walls and stole outside, as stealthy as a thief or a criminal. Filling his lungs, he inhaled the fresh air, and he gazed up at the deep blueness of the sky, at the scores of large and small stars, and at the foggy splotches on the Milky Way, and he saw them, but his intellect couldn't absorb them, and he didn't weave them into the web of his soul. Once the worm of skepticism started gnawing at his heart, everything in the world became alien, isolated, and unattached. All night long, he walked to and fro along the banks of the holy Ganges River. And those alien chants resounded in his soul. And at the first glimmer of dawn, he saw the temple, with its gates open and facing the water, and he realized that this was the home of the alien god.

And the following night, he took off in a small boat across the rushing waves and he reached the temple safe and sound. With a trembling hand, he removed the veil from the holy image, and the god of laughter revealed himself to the boy's eyes, and the god of laughter stood there calmly and peered at the child with his laughing eyes. A great ecstasy took hold of the young prophet, and he knelt down and hugged the legs of the holy god. This was what he had been seeking for such a long time—the image had appeared to him in dreams! And so, like a man from whose eyes a membrane has been torn so that he may view the radiant world, Raya-Mano now saw a new radiance in a new world. The holy face, the creases in his forehead, had gathered all the suffering in the world, they contained the great sadness, but it had been transformed into laughter. The suffering of the world laughed out of the god's eyes, the great suffering and the great sadness. The entire world, with its network of variety, had been transformed into laughter. And Raya-Mano stood there all night long, thirstily drinking the laughter that flowed from the godly eyes and transformed the boy's heart.

And the boy came here every night to serve his new god alone, to drink from his deep source, and his intellect was never sated no matter how much he drank.

But then one night, something dreadful occurred:

Raya-Mano was kneeling before his god, praising and chanting, and his flesh and his soul clung to his god and were drawn to him like iron to a magnet, and the boy kissed and hugged the holy image, and now his arms sensed that the image was the same on the other side. Slowly he walked around to the other side and halted, and he saw the familiar image of the god of sadness. It was a horrible sight: a body with two faces, and the two faces were identical: one exterior, one image; but this face was laughing and that face was grieving.

And Raya-Mano saw what no prophet and no saint had ever seen: he saw the twofold intellect, the double form—one laughing and one grieving, both flowing from the source of a single god.

From then on, Raya-Mano started wandering through the world, and his intellect knew no rest.

He was a prophet and he had been sanctified as a prophet in his mother's belly; but the populace didn't know him, didn't respect him, and didn't draw from his intellect.

Raya-Mano might be preaching to the populace, his face laughing, and his skillful tongue belittling and ridiculing all the hardship suffered in all times by men and gods. And his voice sounded like the tinkling of a silver chime, and pain laughed, and sorrow laughed. Yet in the midst of that laughter, you could catch the echo of great sadness, and his soul abruptly came pouring out as soft words of yearning. . . . The populace listened but didn't know what this meant.

At other times, Raya-Mano might be reproving and awakening hearts and lamenting the torture of human beings and all other living things; and like the sounds of a harp, notes drifting from far, far away in the night, his voice trembled; and the great sadness came pouring from his intellect; and suddenly, his intellect was transformed, his expression was altered, and the roar of laughter covered the sadness. . . . The populace heard it and was angry because the beautiful melody had been disrupted, it was angry at the prophet who could only split minds.

"He ain't no prophet, he's a lunatic," the populace cried.

And when he raised his voice to speak, the children poked fun at him and threw dirt at him.

So the prophet fled the settled areas, and he lived with the ascetics in the desert and, like them, he tortured and purified his body, and he spent whole days peering into the burning sun so that his eyes would hurt, so that he could learn to endure all pain silently and patiently, just as the ascetics teach. But he did not become a saint. In the midst of his asceticism, he was attacked by the god of laughter; and peering into the sun, his painful eyes laughed at pain, at the world, at asceticism.

And so he went to the prophets of laughter, but it didn't help. For in the midst of his laughter, he was attacked by the spirit of sadness, and his voice started trembling and yearning.

And that was how Raya-Mano spent his years, unattached, without a friend or a beloved, lonesome and lonely, chased and cursed by the youngsters in the street.

He saw the double image, and his entire life atoned for his sin.

And when he died, his death wasn't lamented, and he wasn't buried among the prophets, and his name wasn't mentioned for any good. But there was one intelligent man in the country, and he had traveled to many lands and had seen many nations and had gathered wisdom, and he said:

"Pay respect to the name of Raya-Mano. He bore the greatest pain of the intellect."

HAPPINESS
(A Fairy Tale)
(pub. 1909)

*I*N THE ENDLESS UNIVERSE, through the tremendous cosmos, an angel was flying.

He hadn't folded his wings for many, many years. And he had been flying and flying nonstop for many, many years. Here a sun and there a star and there an errant comet, and the angel halted and asked:

"Can you tell me, please: where is Earth located?"

And no sooner had he heard the reply, "I don't know," than he flew away.

Every minute was precious, every second.

Many, many years ago, the angel had heard about the plight of the unhappy people on Earth, their harsh and bitter lives—and his angelic heart filled with pity. He threw himself down before the Throne of Glory and begged God to grant happiness to human beings, and God answered his prayer and he promptly handed happiness to the angel, who was to bring it to the unhappy people on Earth.

And this angel descended from Seventh Heaven, and he has been wandering ever since, among suns, stars, and comets, and he is looking for Earth.

His right hand is clutching happiness, and his white wings stir lightly in the thin ether. A thousand years have worn by, he has flown through millions of solar systems—but no one knows the location of Earth with its unhappy people.

Sometimes a tear rolls down from the angel's eye. Ah! Who can say whether his radiant wings are carrying him away from Earth?

But still—he *is* an angel after all.

His tear rolls down—not on his long wandering, but on poor humans who thirst and strive for happiness, which he, the angel, carries in his right hand.

"Can you please tell me the location of Earth with its unhappy people?"

"No."

And the angel then flies on, inspired by his ideals.

Meanwhile the world grows old and new. People change, and ideals and religions change—and unhappiness rules everywhere!

"Where do we find happiness?!" the unhappy humans sigh.

Once, an old stargazer, an astronomer, peered up at a wandering comet. For a long time, he kept his eye glued to his telescope, following the comet wherever it turned. He didn't stop even when eating or sleeping. He would then have his young son replace him, and—he no sooner finished eating than he returned to his telescope.

The comet was very angry:

"What does that old wizard want from me? What's he after? Am I a thief? Is that why he stalks me?"

The comet got even angrier.

Suddenly, the angel caught up with the comet and asked him in his sad and gentle voice:

"Mr. Comet, do you happen to know the location of Earth with its unhappy people?"

"People on Earth?" the comet angrily replied. "Those are only old wizards and young killers. . . ."

"Ah, poor people," the angel sighed. "All because of their great unhappiness—alas! No, Mr. Comet, you mustn't get angry, hatred is a sin!"

And the happiness in his right hand shone and gleamed so strongly that even the comet's eyes, upon seeing it, grew radiant, and his dismal, misanthropic soul grew lighter.

"Where is Earth?"

With a long, thick beam, the comet pointed at the location of Earth.

"Ah, how far from Heaven has Earth wandered!" the angel sighed softly. "And all because of great unhappiness."

And the angel then continued his journey.

Meanwhile, on Earth, the astronomer noticed the angel and, through the telescope, he saw something glowing in the angel's right hand. And just like a prophet prophesizing for a long time that an angel is flying with happiness, the stargazer assumed that the angel was now bringing happiness to human beings. . . .

And the newspapers then brought the news to the entire world.

"An angel is flying with happiness. . . ." people said wherever there were human tongues.

All stargazers focused their telescopes and clearly saw the angel coming closer and closer to Earth.

They started calculating and they calculated that the angel would reach Earth on such and such day, at such and such an hour, at such and such a minute, and on such and such a degree.

And the scheduled day arrived, and people from all over the world gathered at the scheduled place.

The crowd became very dense. People started crushing, fighting, punching. . . . They even began stabbing and killing one another.

Rivers of human blood were flowing there, and the moaning and yammering of the dying rose all the way up to the sky. . . .

From far away, the angel saw people shoving and pressing one another, and with his final bit of strength, the angel started shouting from on high:

"Stop fighting! I've got happiness for everyone!" But they didn't hear him.

When the angel flew nearer to Earth, when his radiant eyes saw the slashed-up victims, when his ears heard the moaning and groaning, a tear rolled down from his radiant eyes and fell upon happiness.

From then on, radiant happiness has been stained.

People say that the angel, who was worn and weary because of his long journey and because of what he saw on Earth, fainted dead away, and happiness dropped from his right hand.

S. ANSKY
(SHLOYME-ZANVL RAPOPORT)
(1863-1920)

Today, Ansky is most famous for his play *The Dybbuk*. However, writing first in Hebrew, then in Russian and in Yiddish, Ansky, at a certain point, strove to assimilate to Russian culture, but ultimately returned to the Jewish fold. Aside from his prolific oeuvre of verse, plays, stories, memoirs, essays, and translations, he tried to imitate the Russian return to the "folk" by gathering Yiddish folklore as the source of the Jewish soul. From 1912 to 1914, he headed the Ethnographic Expedition, which combed Eastern Europe for folk material—until the eruption of World War I. Ansky died in 1920 just a few months before the premiere of *The Dybbuk*.

The two selections translated below express the variety of themes and styles in Ansky's treatments of folk traditions.

A SACK OF FLOUR
(1912)

1

In the ancient days before
The destruction of the Temple,
When the Jewish state was grand and
Mighty, and the Jews were ruled
By the wisest and most famous
Monarch—by King Solomon,
In a corner of Jerusalem,
An old crone, a bitter widow,
Lived in a dilapidated
Hovel, amid want and hunger.

With her pay for arduous labor,
The old crone went to the market,
Where she bought a bit of grain.
And she ground it by herself
In her neighbor's quern—the hand mill.
Next, the widow baked three rolls
To sustain her for a week.
But just as she took the rolls
From the oven, a pale man
Turned up at the threshold and
Tearfully he said to her:
"Please take pity on me, Madam,
Pity on a wretched man.
I've come from the land of Ophir.
And I carried merchandise,
Ships filled up with massive cargoes—
Spices, olive oil, purple wool.
Suddenly a horrible tempest
Roiled and churned across the sea.
All my ships with all my cargoes
And with all my many servants
Were devoured by the deep.
I alone was swept ashore
By a billow of the ocean.
For the past three days, I've wandered,
Starving, feeble, miserable.
Give me bread to still my hunger."
And the crone felt sorry for the
Merchant from the land of Ophir,
And she handed him a roll. . . .
Scarcely had he left her shack,
When another man appeared
At the threshold, sick and feeble,
Wearing only rags and tatters.
And the man cried in despair:
"Bread! I'm weak and faint with hunger
I escaped a bloody war
By some unknown miracle. . . .
Once I lived a quiet life
By the lofty mountains of
Gilead, serving God in Heaven,
Cultivating my own vineyard.

All at once, like savage beasts,
Philistine invaders came,
Burning, trampling everything,
Slashing everyone with their swords,
Slaughtering my wife and children.
For a long time I was lying
In the field. . . . When I came to, I
Dashed away from death and graves. . . .
For the past three days, I've wandered,
Starving, feeble, miserable.
Give me bread to still my hunger!"
The crone looked at him and, not
Hesitating for a moment,
Handed him the second roll.
A short while wore by, and then
The door of the hovel opened
Slowly, and an old blind beggar
Turned up at the threshold and,
Softly, tearfully, fearfully,
He explained to the old widow:
"Trouble, old age, need, and hunger
Have devoured all the strength
Of my body and my soul.
I'm blind from my mother's womb,
And I live on charity.
In the past, my only daughter
Led me by my hand to guide me.
But now she is paralyzed,
And I'm left in misery.
In the darkness, with no guide,
I trip often on a stone.
But I very seldom, seldom
Trip over a crust of bread.
I knock on a door, it opens,
And I step into a cottage,
And I don't know who's inside.
Who are you? A man? A woman?
Are you young or full of years?
But I sense a human being.
Brother, brother, please take pity,
Pity on an old, blind beggar,
Still my hunger with your bread."

Filled with pity, the old widow
Handed him her final roll.

2

Later, when the fear of starving
Took hold of the poor old widow,
She combed every nook and cranny
Of her wretched hovel, looking
For at least a crust of bread.
But she couldn't find a crumb.
So she went to see a neighbor,
A rich merchant, a grain dealer,
To beg him for just a bit
Of grain or a bit of flour.
But her neighbor answered her:
"I will not lend grain or flour—
Specially to a nearby neighbor.
In the end, what's done is done!
And we'll end up in a fight! I
Want to live in peace and quiet
And in harmony with my neighbors.
But I do feel sorry for you.
Go into my empty granary
(Yesterday I sent my grain
To the distant land of Egypt).
In the cracks you're sure to find
Lots and lots of seeds of wheat—
If they haven't rotted yet.
Gather them—a gift for you,
Which I give with all my heart.
Pray, just pray to God for me."
And the widow stepped into the
Empty granary and gathered
Seeds of wheat from all the holes,
Seeds half-rotten, and she ground them,
Filling up a teensy sack,
Which she took back to her hovel.
Now the world grew very silent,
And the sky grew clear and pure.
But then suddenly, a savage
Storm came churning, and it grabbed
The old woman's teensy sack
And it swept it out to sea.

The old widow halted there,
Stood there bitter and confused.
Stretching her arms toward the sky,
She began to rant and rail:
"God, I just don't understand!
When I gave my last few crumbs
To three starvelings at my door,
I was carrying out Your will.
So why must you punish me
With Your dreadful storm and wind?
But perhaps I'm sinning now. . . .
Maybe it occurred without
God's will and without His knowledge.
Winds are great big mischief-makers,
Fighting them is totally useless.
They make rackets every night,
Yelling, laughing, weeping, shrieking,
Rattling all the doors and windows. . . .
It appears that they no longer
Follow God's commandments now. . . ."
And the crone was furious
About God's dishonored will.
She trudged home and then, forgetting
All about her hunger, she
Went to bed and fell asleep.

3

The old widow had a dream:
She dreamed that an old and wizened
Man appeared to her and said:
"You should know that our great ruler,
Our good King Solomon,
Cannot suffer an injustice.
Go to his grand palace, tell him
What the wind has done to you.
And he'll discipline the wind,
Punish it severely then."
The old woman now awoke
And recalled the dream she'd dreamed.
Then she promptly started out
To King Solomon's royal palace.
There she bowed and told the monarch

Everything that had occurred,
Everything that had happened to her.
Solomon, the most famous ruler,
Listened patiently and then
Gently answered the old woman:
"Do not grieve because the wind
Robbed you of your sack of flour
With no sacred will of God.
I will punish it so harshly.
And you'll be rewarded for
Your entire loss and sorrow."
Well, no sooner had he finished
Than three unknown men came in.
They approached the royal throne
And fell prostrate on their faces.
Next, the eldest of the three
Launched into an explanation:
"We are three merchants from Sidon,
And we deal in spices, ointments,
Ivory, and rubber too.
We had our goods on a ship,
As we usually do,
Sailing to your country's shore.
All at once, a tempest burst,
Turning waves into huge mountains,
Digging valleys in the sea.
And the tempest tossed our vessel
Like a splinter all around.
Then our vessel crashed into a
Rock, a sharp and jagged rock,
Smashed a deep hole in the deck.
And the sea came rushing through,
Hastily and endlessly,
And the boat began to sink
Just like lead into the deep,
Into the profound abyss.
When we saw death hovering
Right before our eyes, we knelt
Or we bowed or stretched out prostrate,
Worshiping your God in Heaven,
And we swore an oath to Him:
If He shielded us from death,

If He rescued our vessel,
We'd bring an entire third
Of our goods and assets here,
To deliver to the poor.
Scarcely had we sworn our oath
When the tempest did subside,
And our vessel glided quickly
To the beaches of your kingdom.
When we sprang ashore, we first
Made a sacrifice to God.
Then we made an inventory
Of the cargo in our vessel.
And the figure was correct:
Thirty thousand silver shekels.
We subtracted an entire
Third, ten thousand silver shekels,
And we brought that total here
To deliver it to you. . . ."
And the eldest of the merchants
Handed Solomon the gift: a
Sack of shekels for the king.

4

After listening silently
To the merchants, Solomon,
Wisest of all kings on earth,
Started asking them some questions:
"I would truly wish to know
How the leak was fixed, and how the
Sea stopped pouring through the hole
That the rock smashed in your vessel."
"Oh, Your Majesty!" replied
One of the three Sidon merchants.
"It seems that the vessel's hole
Was plugged fully with a small
Sack of flour—which I've brought here."
And he handed Solomon
A small sack of sodden flour.
And the king signaled the widow,
Summoned her, showed her the sack.
"Isn't this the very sack
That the wild wind grabbed from you?"

"Yes, indeed, that sack is mine!"
The old woman answered him.
"But the flour's soaked and rotten—
Of no use to anybody."
"Very true!" the monarch smiled.
"So, dear lady, I will give you
Personally another sack. . . ."
And instead of flour, the monarch
Handed her the sack of shekels.
But the poor old widow didn't
Take the sack of silver shekels.
She then murmured to the king:
"Dearest monarch! Keep your silver!
I've already been rewarded!"

THE REBBE OF APTE AND TSAR NICHOLAS I

NICHOLAS I WAS A BITTER ENEMY not so much of Jews but of Judaism. All his life, he looked for ways of rooting out the Jewish religion and getting Jews—God help us—to convert to Christianity. That was why he planned to issue three anti-Jewish edicts. First of all, he ordered the burning of the Talmud and all the other sacred Jewish books. Secondly, Jews would no longer be permitted to celebrate the Sabbath. And thirdly, Jews had to cut off their beards and sidelocks and wear short garments. The tsar penned all three edicts with his own hands, but he had not as yet sealed the documents with his imperial seal.

That same night, the rebbe of Apte dreamed about the terrible misfortune that was being inflicted on Jews.

The next morning, the rebbe assembled all his Hasids. But instead of telling them about his dream, he asked his followers for the date and time of their births. It turned out that one man had been born on the same day and at the same hour as Nicholas I. The rebbe then ordered that they make royal garments—just like the kind worn by the tsar (though of plain cloth, to keep down the cost, and, according to Jewish law, without mixing wool and linen). The rebbe also asked them to make an imperial crown of paper, get hold of a big sword, build an imperial throne, and place the throne on the platform in the synagogue. Next, the rebbe wrote out the texts of Nicholas's edicts on three sheets of paper.

When everything was completed, the rebbe summoned the man who was born on the same day and at the same time as the tsar. The rebbe ordered the Hasid to don the "imperial" garments, gird his loins with the sword, and sit down on the throne, which was flanked by two Hasids dressed as Russian soldiers and clutching naked swords. Next to the throne, there was a table, on which the rebbe placed the three documents. As for the other Hasids, the rebbe told them that no matter what they saw or heard, they were strictly prohibited from uttering a word or making a gesture. Otherwise they would be in great danger.

When everything was ready, and the Hasid in imperial garments was sitting on the throne, the Rebbe of Apte, wearing his Sabbath smock, entered the synagogue, halted at a distance from the throne, bowed deeply to the pseudo-tsar, and, coming closer, he shouted: "Long live our emperor, Tsar Nicholas I! May his glory be enhanced!"

He then signaled to his followers to do the same, and they all shouted: "Long live our emperor, Tsar Nicholas I! May his glory be enhanced!"

The pseudo-tsar glared at the rebbe and angrily snapped: "Who are you?"

The rebbe bowed even deeper and answered with great servility: "Your Majesty! I am your servant, Yeshue Heshel, the Rebbe of Apte."

Upon hearing those words, the pseudo-tsar jumped up and, with savage wrath, he screamed: "You slimy worm! You filthy, disgusting yid! How dare you approach my imperial throne!"

When the other Hasids heard their friend cursing their rebbe, they were terror-stricken and they started pulling his coattails. But the pseudo-sentries flanking the imperial throne pounced on them, brandishing their naked swords, and they would have injured the Hasids if they hadn't scurried away and hidden in the corners.

The rebbe bowed again and replied: "Your Majesty! I dare to approach your imperial throne because a whole nation has sent me to kneel at your feet."

The pseudo-tsar shouted: "Talk!"

And the rebbe began: "Your Majesty! My prayer is for my soul, and my request is for my people. You have penned a decree to burn our Talmud and all our sacred books. By doing so, you will hurl Jews into an abyss of fear and sorrow. Take pity on us and rip up the decree!"

The pseudo-tsar furiously hollered: "I am determined to root out the Jewish faith—and I will do so!"

The rebbe retorted: "You will *not* do so! Before you, powerful kings, rulers over the entire world, lifted their hands against the Jewish faith. But they failed to vanquish it. Instead, they aroused the wrath of the Almighty and they were severely punished."

Spreading out both arms, the rebbe tearfully added: "Your Majesty! Almighty God has entrusted you with the sheep of the House of Jacob, and you will have to answer to Him for them! Just look at the fear and sorrow of the people of Israel! Its temple is in ruins, its land was stolen by foreigners, and now it roams the world, abandoned and driven among the nations. It has no leaders and protectors of its own. All that remains of its former grandeur is its holy Torah, which is dearer to a Jew than life itself. If you now reach out and deprive him of his holy Torah, then remember, Your Majesty, what the prophet Nathan told King David about the spiteful rich man who took a pauper's only sheep. . . ."

The pseudo-tsar sat there, silent and with his head drooping. Suddenly he raised his head and spoke: "You are right, old man! I will destroy the order!"

And he took the first order from the table and ripped it to shreds.

The rebbe took one step closer to the imperial throne, bowed deeply, and said with great servility: "Your Majesty! Once you have imbued yourself with grace toward the people of Israel, and you have allowed the Jews to keep their holy books, do not interfere with their carrying out their commandment. You have written an order prohibiting the Jews from celebrating the Sabbath. Yet the fourth commandment of our Decalogue states: 'Remember the Sabbath day to keep it holy.'"

The pseudo-tsar glared angrily at the rebbe, but held his tongue. He took the second order and ripped it to shreds.

Now the rebbe took one more step toward the imperial throne and he said: "Your Majesty! You also penned a decree ordering Jews to cut off their beards and sidelocks and wear short garments. Show your deep grace and rip up this order too!"

The rebbe hadn't even finished speaking when the pseudo-tsar yelled furiously: "I'm fed up with your requests—you dirty, insolent yid!"

And leaping up from his imperial throne, he pounced on the rebbe, slapped him twice, then grabbed his smock and threw the rebbe out into the street. Meanwhile the crown came tumbling off the pseudo-tsar's head. The instant it fell, the pseudo-tsar halted in the middle of the synagogue like a man who doesn't understand what's happened to him. The other Hasids pounced on him and started cursing him for lifting his hand against the rebbe. But the man swore that he remembered nothing, and upon hearing that he had cursed and struck the rebbe, he burst into bitter tears.

Now the rebbe, with a bloody face, came back into the synagogue. He went over to the pseudo-tsar, placed his hand on the man's back, and said cheerfully: "Don't cry and don't grieve, my son! The two of us have pulled off a difficult piece of work. Too bad the crown fell off too soon."

During the time that the Rebbe of Apte had been standing in front of the pseudo-tsar, the real Nicholas I had been sitting on his imperial throne, reading the three orders and preparing to place his seal upon them. As he sat there, his mind teemed with everything the Rebbe of Apte had said to the pseudo-tsar, and Nicholas decided not to issue the first two orders; instead, he ripped them up. But then he placed his seal on the third edict. And when the order was issued, and Jews were forced to cut off their beards and side-locks and wear short garments, Jews wept and fasted and created a sensation. But no one realized that two more horrible edicts had almost been issued, and that they had been annulled thanks to the the Rebbe of Apte.

Later on, when the rebbe was talking about Nicholas I, he said: "He's nowhere as bad as I thought."

Moyshe Leib Halpern
(1886-1932)

Born in Galicia, Halpern moved to New York in 1908. A prolific and celebrated poet, he wrote little prose and seldom dealt with folk motifs such as he treated in these texts.

BANGDIL, KIRLIKI, AND THE STREETWALKER

ONE EVENING, WHEN BANGDIL was sitting on the hill, gazing upward and playing two or three pieces on his bagpipe, his friend Kirliki, the gray-haired dwarf, said to him:

"Don't be sad, old friend, just because you can't fly. The tearful brightness that stretches out to you when you play two or three pieces on your bagpipe isn't very far or very high; it is down below, in the town. And if you want to go there, I'll show you the way."

And so Bangdil stood up and followed his friend.

When they entered the forest, Kirliki became very cold. So Bangdil played two or three pieces on his bagpipe. Then a wild beast stripped off its hide and gave it to Kirliki to wear. And Kirliki really liked that.

Eventually, Kirliki ran out of the bread that he had brought along, for he was a big eater. So Bangdil again played two or three pieces on his bagpipe, and field mice came dancing over and they brought food for Kirliki. And again, Kirliki really liked that.

However, when they reached the town, and Kirliki was supposed to lead Bangdil to the tearful brightness, he pointed to a young woman who was standing by a streetlight at the foot of the tower, but he refused to let his friend approach her.

"First of all," said Kirliki, "she's not crying, and that's a sign that she isn't yours. And secondly, I met her before you did."

"Then why did you bring me here?" asked Bangdil.

Kirliki replied that he'd brought him here to play two or three pieces on his bagpipe—so that the woman wouldn't ask Kirliki for anything, since he had nothing.

All at once, Bangdil reached the very top of the tower, but he himself couldn't tell how he'd gotten there. It was only up there, as if he were on the peak of the hill at home, that he remembered what his friend Kirliki was waiting for down below.

But this time, no sooner had Bangdil picked up his bagpipe and played two or three pieces than the young woman below stretched out her arms and grew up to him miraculously.

And since the tower could no longer block the light of the setting sun for her, she actually became very bright. And then, when Bangdil played two or three pieces on his bagpipe, the woman likewise cried—and so intensely that even a blind man down below could have seen her tears if he had only lifted his head.

"Have you seen my friend Kirliki, young woman?"

"He's down below, circling the hem of my long red dress, like a tiny fly, and he's looking for his friend Bangdil in order to have him play two or three pieces on his bagpipe for him."

THE RED HORSEMEN AND
THE PRINCE—THE DOG

AT DAWN, A PACK OF DOGS had gathered at the cemetery and, turning their muzzles toward the east, they started howling at the red patch of sky, as if trying to drive the day back into its hiding place.

All at once, the female dog, who was standing next to an old headstone, emitted a staccato shriek and began thrashing about. She emitted another staccato shriek, but was unable to extricate herself.

And horrible as this may look, it is nevertheless true. A man with a blue, swollen face was clutching the dog with his skinny arms around her belly and, with an open mouth, he was creeping under her udders.

However, like all dogs, this one was used to human beings, and she sensed that the man meant her no harm; so she calmed down: and with her eyes fixed on the red sky, she wept mutely.

It was as if she were telling the sun: "Just look at man—the god of the earth also under my belly!"

The dog thought neither about the gold buttons on the man's jacket nor about his collar and his epaulettes, for there is a limit to the thoughts of beasts; just as they go about clad in their own fur, they have no concept of what goes on among humans in regard to their clothing.

That's why the dog didn't care where that man had come from. It was enough for he that he was lying under her udders, which were empty.

She was only scared—and you could tell by her eyes—that he might draw the blood from her body, for she could feel that he was hungry.

Now all the dogs stopped howling and, craning their necks and pricking up their ears, they faced west.

There, on the hillock between earth and sky, two horsemen emerged from the darkness, as if by magic.

At first, they sat there, holding their hands over their eyes, like people gazing into the distance.

Perhaps if the morning sun hadn't illuminated them, they wouldn't have been seen at all. But now, with their horses and their lances, they looked, from afar, like sheer fire.

We cannot say for certain that the riders spotted the dogs before the dogs started howling again—perhaps they had, perhaps they hadn't. But when they lunged forward with their heads and their lances, two huge fiery birds seemed to be charging through the air, forcing the dogs to flee. And the female dog likewise tore away—indeed, as she had previously feared, with a bloody udder.

"Are you the prince whose corpse we have to bring back?" the riders asked the man cowering silently on the ground, his face blue and swollen, his eyes gaping up, his maw gawking, his nuzzle splattered with blood. One of the riders, the one with tiny eyes like slits, marked with red chalk, asked:

"Cat got your tongue, you dog?"

The dog on the ground opened his maw more fearfully, focused his glassy eyes, struggled to stand up, remained on all fours, and began hopping. A lance was about to be hurled—the man knelt down and bowed to the ground and, with arms outstretched like front paws and his gullet upward, he sat like that. Again he was asked by the mounted rider, and he started howling again, softly at first, then louder and even louder. A doggish weeping resounded from another part of the cemetery, and some more doggish weeping from another part, until they were surrounded by howling, and the dogs bounded off in all directions. But the man with the swollen face didn't see the lance that was pointed at him. Instead he howled at the small patch of red sky, where the sun was rising; and his howling was so long and drawn-out and so filled with fear, as if an entire forest had awoken after a thousand years.

Now the cheekbones convulsed, the cheekbones of the rider with red slits instead of eyes; and his fist, clutching his lance aloft, clenched. The lance would flash like lightning and skewer the howling gullet and crucify the kneeling man.

But now the other rider raised his hand, and with his eyes, which were so big and bright that they looked like two weeping stars at night—he stared at the rider with the raised lance, stared at his brother, and very slowly, its movement barely visible to the naked eye, that arm sank. The breath was still fire—you could tell by the breastbones, the way they rose and sank, and the upper teeth pressed like iron on the lower teeth, as shown by the nuzzle, but the lance together with the head sank slowly, very slowly. He battled with himself as with a wild bull whose horns he clutched.

A great and wondrous singing of silence could be heard in that battle with himself. And the radiant eyes won out and not the fist with the lance.

"You are right, my brother," said the victor, bowing to him. "Let the pleading of a weeping nation be sacred for us. We were sent out for the blood of the men with the gold collars—and not the blood of a starving dog."

And step by step, as if a single heart had completed the dream, a heart hallowed by pain and the purity of generations—both horsemen trotted off on the path, toward the red patch of sky, and behind them he came leaping on all fours, the man with the blue, swollen face, and he howled so lamentably that all the dogs who had scurried away now turned around and joined him in howling after the two riders, until they, with bowed heads, had ridden into the sun.

SHMUEL BASTOMSKI
(EDITOR)
(1891–1942)

꒰ꕥ꒱

Bastomski, a folklorist, educator, and Yiddishist, gathered Yiddish folktales, including some that had been printed in small pamphlets, so-called storybooks (*mayse-bikhlekh*). To preserve their feel, I've translated an entire chapbook, which Bastomski himself, according to his preface, had discovered in two identical editions (1890 and 1910). Aside from adding punctuation, modernizing the spelling, and supplying a title for each piece, he reprinted the text as is in 1927. The motif of a mystical Prague was current in Jewish folklore, especially in connection with the golem—who, however, does not appear in this pamphlet, despite the constant presence of Rabbi Gur Aryeh (Lion's Roar), the nickname of Rabbi Leyb (Lion, 1525–1609), the traditional creator of the golem. On the other hand, these stories contain elements that derive from a number of diverse Jewish and non-Jewish sources, including *The Odyssey* and the hegemonic tales of the Baal-Shem-Tov, the founder of Hasidism, as well as the international folklore treasury.

YIDDISH FOLKTALES AND LEGENDS: LEGENDS OF OLD PRAGUE
(Vilna, 1927)

THE KIDNAPPED RABBI

IN A SMALL SHTETL not far from Prague, there lived a very poor rabbi. This rabbi often visited Great Rabbi Gur Aryeh in Prague and complained to him about his dire poverty. But Rabbi Gur Aryeh did not reply. He merely told him to study the holy books diligently and to render a true judgment.

One day, when the shtetl rabbi was visiting Rabbi Gur Aryeh, he again lamented his terrible poverty for he had to marry off his children. But Rabbi Gur Aryeh did not reply. He merely said:

"God Blessed Be He should help you to avoid desecrating the Sabbath."

The rabbi did not understand. So he said:

"I most likely won't desecrate the Sabbath. . . . But what about my request? I have to marry off my children."

The Grand Rabbi repeated: "God should help you to avoid desecrating the Sabbath."

The visitor went home very sadly because Rabbi Gur Aryeh hadn't replied to his request and because he had predicted that the visitor would desecrate the Sabbath. The visitor just couldn't understand.

A short while later, on a Friday, two great merchants arrived in the shtetl and they wished to see the rabbi. They were asked:

"What do you want from the rabbi?"

The merchants answered:

"We want to celebrate the Sabbath with the rabbi."

The townsfolk told the merchants:

"The rabbi is very poor. He can't provide food."

The merchants said:

"That's no problem. We'll pay him as much money as he likes. But we want to celebrate the Sabbath with him."

They were then taken to the rabbi. He welcomed them very grandly, and they gave his wife money to provide a marvelous Sabbath and serve a lot of liquor.

The rabbi was delighted to have such fine guests.

During the meal on Friday evening, the merchants asked the rabbi:

"How come you're so poor?"

He answered:

"The shtetl is very tiny, and the congregants are very poor. That's why they can't afford to pay me."

The merchants then asked:

"Why don't you move to a large town?"

The rabbi answered:

"I can't find one. Every town probably has a rabbi already. But I can be a rabbi in the biggest town, for I'm a great scholar. I'm thoroughly versed in the Talmud."

The merchants then asked him:

"But if you found a larger town, would you move there?"

The rabbi said:

"Yes."

The merchants said:

"We want to tell you the whole truth. Our country is very rich, but there is little learning there. That is: Few people know how to study the holy texts. If we want a rabbi, we need to take him from a foreign land. Today our rabbi passed away. So we are looking for a new rabbi. We've been told that you are a great scholar and also very poor. So you certainly would like to come back with us. You can say farewell on Sunday, and we'll pay you a lot of money so you can buy elegant clothes. We'll also leave a lot of money with your wife and your children, and we'll have you join us in our carriage. And once you've spent a few weeks in our country and you've been accepted, we'll send carriages to bring your family in great honor."

The rabbi asked them:

"How many leagues is it to your country?"

They replied:

"One hundred leagues. And our country is a rich country, with all kinds of food."

The rabbi then said:

"I'll have to confer with my wife during Sabbath, and I'll give you an answer after the Sabbath."

The guests asked the rabbi to reveal some of his wisdom. He did so, and they were overjoyed. They ordered a lot more liquor and they kept urging the rabbi to leave with them.

After dinner, the rabbi told his wife the whole story. She too kept urging him and she said:

"We've already got grown-up children. Do we have to become homeless and move away from our family just to marry them off? Also: if you prosper, you can sit and study the holy books and serve the Good Lord, for poverty overcomes religion."

To make a long story short, the rabbi decided to accept the offer. On Sunday, he told the merchants that he was ready. The merchants were delighted. They signed the rabbinical contract and paid the rabbi two hundred ducats, saying:

"You should leave one hundred ducats with your wife, and for one hundred ducats, you should buy elegant garments, for it wouldn't look good if you entered our country in shabby clothes."

The merchants remained for several days, waiting for him to acquire his elegant garments. He then said good-bye to the entire shtetl. The Jews wept and wailed, for they already missed the rabbi, who was a great scholar and a great sage. Such men are rare.

The rabbi left with the merchants. They honored him greatly until they arrived in their country. However, upon arriving, they chained his feet together and said:

"You thought you'd come here as a rabbi, but you're here to get killed."

The rabbi wept and lamented:

"What do you have against me? Let me go and I'll return to my home!"

But they laughed at him and said:

"We've tricked you! You'll never escape us! You're going to get killed!"

To make a long story short, they hauled him into their town, left him inside a big palace, locked the door, and went away.

The rabbi saw that the palace was very large and he was terrified inside the chambers. That evening, his captors brought him food, put it down, and then locked the door. In the morning, they brought him food again, putting it down and promptly relocking the door. The rabbi kept moving every day and he kept seeing new rooms every day. But when it was time to eat, he would return to his chamber, so nobody would know that he kept leaving it. The instant the door was locked, however, he went through all the rooms, looking for some kind of door or hole that would enable him to escape.

One day, he reached a room where he spotted a door. He dashed over to the door, but when he reached it, he found a huge abyss. The abyss was too wide for him to jump across, and there was no place where he could reach the door. He tried to figure out what to do next. Then, in a corner, he saw a locked closet. He broke the lock and opened the closet. Inside, he found a small glass case that contained a human head. The terrified rabbi said:

"What are you doing here?" He was about to grab the head.

The head replied:

"Don't touch me! If anyone touches me, I have to shout, and people will come racing over. You ought to know: I'm the head of a Jew. I was beheaded, and they inserted the name of Satan under my tongue. The country serves me, and whatever question they ask me, I respond with the strength of the name of Satan. I've been serving here for seven years. And after seven years, a new head is needed. That's why you've been brought here. For my seven years will soon be up. Then they'll remove the name of Satan from under my tongue, they'll kill you and insert the name of Satan under your tongue, and then you'll be uttering prophesies for them."

The rabbi was amazed at those words and he told the head:

"Can't they find another Jew instead of me? How come they traveled so far to find me?"

The head replied:

"Let me explain. The man whose head they serve, and which tells us everything they ask, has to be a first-born son, and his father has to be a first-born, and his father's father has to be a first-born, and that must be the case for the last seven generations. . . . Now when the seven years were coming to an end, the people asked me: 'Where can we find such a man?' I told them to locate you, for you and your fathers have been first-borns for seven generations. That was why they tricked you into coming here."

The rabbi asked:

"Is there any way I can escape here?"

The head replied

"When they find out you've escaped, they'll ask me where you are, and I'll have to answer them, for, because of the name of Satan under my tongue, I have to respond truthfully to anything they ask me."

"Then why don't you advise me what to do?"

"If you obey me, you will succeed. Just swear that you'll obey me." The rabbi swore to obey the head. And the head then told him: "You ought to know that the abyss you see in front of the door is not an abyss, it's a magical illusion. Remove the name of Satan from under my tongue, take [me] along, go through the door at night, and escape. When you reach the open fields, you should bury me according to Jewish law. And from there you can escape to your own country."

The rabbi did as the head had told him. He waited until nightfall, then he took the head, went through the door, and escaped, and he buried the head according to Jewish law. Next, he walked two days and two nights until he reached a town. He was starving. He found a court, stepped into the kitchen, and asked for a piece of bread. The people there felt sorry for him, so they gave him a piece of bread, but he couldn't talk to them because he didn't understand their language. So they communicated by using signs. To make a long story short, he began serving them, bringing them wood and water, and they would give him a piece of bread.

He spent several days there and he was greatly esteemed by the chef, whom the rabbi served very loyally. The rabbi had already learned a few words in their language. Now the chef was employed by the monarch. The rabbi grew very close to the chef. He would mainly watch the cooking, and the chef relied greatly on him.

One day, the chef went out, and the rabbi put on the foods, which were ready to cook, but the chef was late. Meanwhile the food was ready, and when the chef returned and saw that the meal had been prepared, he was delighted, for it was dinnertime. If the king wished to eat and the meal wasn't ready, the chef would be sentenced to death. That was why the chef thanked the rabbi profusely and he said:

"Sit with me. I'll give you food and drink, and you'll help me cook."

The rabbi despaired of ever returning home, he was afraid to reveal that he was Jewish, and he didn't know the route.

It was time for the meal, and so the chef carried it to the king. And when the king tasted the food, he summoned the chef:

"Tell me the truth immediately! Who prepared this food?"

The chef was so terrified that he couldn't reply. When the king saw how terrified he was, he said to the chef:

"Why are you afraid? This is the best food I've ever eaten. Why is today's meal so different from past meals? Someone else must have cooked it."

So the chef told him the whole story:

"Some time ago, a stranger came here, a beggar. He's been employed in my kitchen, and he serves me in exchange for a piece of bread. Today I went out and I was a bit late. Meanwhile, the stranger put on the food and cooked it himself."

The king then said to the chef:

"Send me that man. I want to see him."

The chef dashed away and summoned the rabbi for the king. The king said to the rabbi:

"Did you cook this meal?"

The rabbi was terrified, but the king said:

"Don't be afraid, tell me the truth."

The rabbi said:

"Yes, I cooked it."

The king said to him:

"Who are you?"

The rabbi said:

"I come from a distant land, but I've lost my way. I was traveling by sea, and the sea brought me here."

The king thereupon said to him:

"From now on, you will be the chef. I'll make you rich, and I'll make you a great aristocrat."

So the rabbi became chef, and the king esteemed him more and more until he became prime minister. The rabbi remained very pious and he ate only kosher food. One day, he went to the royal library, and there he found a copy of a cabbalistic text, the Zohar, and he opened it. The rabbi remembered that he had often recited passages from the Zohar, and he burst into tears, which made him forget that he was in a foreign country. His bitter weeping was heard by the princes of the realm. They stepped into the library and saw him clutching a sacred tome and weeping bitterly. They were very envious of him. So they went to the king and said:

"Your prime minister is sitting in the library, clutching a sacred tome and weeping loudly and bitterly. It's obvious that he's lost his mind."

The king was horrified, for he deeply loved his prime minister, who was the king's advisor in all matters. The king had won many wars because of his advice, for the prime minister was a great sage, and God was with him. The king sent for his prime minister and took him into a private room and said:

"Tell me the truth! Why were you crying so bitterly and clutching a sacred tome?"

The terrified rabbi said:

"I'll tell you the truth. You ought to know that I am Jewish and that I've been away from my country for a long time. Today I found a sacred Jewish tome that I used to study constantly. When I started reading it, I recalled my homeland and I know that I'll never reach it again. I left my wife and my children there. And that's why I cried so bitterly."

Upon hearing this, the king was frightened and he said:

"I don't know what I should do with you, for we have a law that anyone who harbors a Jew must be executed—even if it's the king himself! When people find out that you're a Jew, they'll kill us both. If I kill you, I'll deeply regret it, for I truly love you. But if I allow you to live, someone might find out the truth. For the time being, stay here until nightfall, and I'll try to figure out what to do with you."

The rabbi remained in the room, not daring to leave. He sat there, weeping. For he had been saved from one death but would face another in the morning. He prayed to God, begging to be rescued.

In the middle of the night, the king came to the rabbi and said:

"I've finally figured out what to do with you. I can't kill you. Down in the town there is an empty brick house surrounded by a large fort that no one has been able to take. Lots of kings have tried to take it, and countless armies have been killed there, but no one has managed to take the fort. For when you approach it, the fort hurls enormous rocks and kills a lot of men. Nobody knows what that is. However, there is a tiny door in the fort. I'll go there with you, have you enter, and lock you in. You'll be killed, but I won't have to watch."

The king took him and went with him. The rabbi wept bitterly, for he might not be buried according to the Jewish law.

To make a long story short, the king made the rabbi enter through the tiny door, locked him in, and returned to his castle. And no one found out.

When the rabbi approached the fort, no one bothered him. He then stepped inside the brick house to see what was there. After passing through the tiny door, he felt as if he were walking across human corpses. Terrified, he took refuge in a corner, standing there and waiting until daybreak so he could see what there was. (When the king had taken him here, he had given the rabbi a piece of bread to eat before dying.)

At daybreak, the rabbi saw that the entire brick house was crammed with dead people lying side by side. When the morning was bright, all the dead came alive, somebody washed their hands, and then they prayed raucously to the Good Lord. The rabbi nearly died of fright. But they didn't bother him. After finishing their prayers, they collapsed on the floor and were dead again. The rabbi was very sorry that he hadn't asked them to show him a way out, to a road that would take him home. But it was too late. The rabbi prayed, then he ate the piece of bread. He thereupon waited till morning, hoping to talk to the corpses.

The next day, the rabbi was ready to see them awake and have their hands washed. Weeping loudly, he began to speak:

"Gentlemen, I'm a Jew and I've lost my way, I'm far from home. Can you show me a road that will take me home again?"

These people replied that after prayers they would lend him their beadle, who washed their hands, and the beadle would show the rabbi the way home. The rabbi was to obey the beadle no matter what he said.

The rabbi asked them:

"Gentlemen, who are you?"

And they answered:

"We are the great followers of the Zohar. One day, we bogged down in a crucial argument. So we assembled here and we agreed that we wouldn't leave until we had settled the matter. Otherwise we would die here. And so we yelled out our prayers. And we sacrificed ourselves by actually dying. Now since our deaths were premature, we received an award for our self-sacrifice: no living creature in the world can come here, so that we can lie here peacefully and arise every morning to pray to the Good Lord. But don't ask us anything else."

And that was what happened. After prayers, they told the beadle to guide the rabbi. The beadle took the rabbi's hand and led him and he told the rabbi that he was not to address or answer anyone until he entered his home. It was Friday. And the beadle guided him until nightfall. The rabbi now saw that he was standing outside his home, and his wife was coming out to light a Sabbath candle. The moment he spotted her, he was so happy that he greeted her: "Hello!"

That same instant, he found himself standing far from the town. The beadle had vanished, for the rabbi had broken his promise. And now it was night. The rabbi was terrified of celebrating the Sabbath out in the fields beyond the town. But he couldn't have reached the town in time. Still, he was so frightened that he desecrated the Sabbath by walking to the town and to his home. When his wife and his children saw him, they were ecstatic, for a long time had passed since he had left them. And they asked him:

"What happened to you? And why are you back? You went with the merchants to be a rabbi in their country, didn't you?"

And he told them the whole story from start to finish. The shtetl had a wonderful celebration, for the rabbi's life had been saved in so many ways.

When Rabbi Leyb saw the rabbi, he welcomed him and said:

"I prophesized everything: The Good Lord would save you from desecrating the Sabbath. But how would you desecrate it? If you hadn't done so, your sufferings would have cleansed you of your sins, and you would have become a great hero in the afterlife. But you have committed the sin of desecrating the Sabbath."

However, Rabbi Leyb granted the rabbi repentance.

THE KING WHO WAS CREATED FOR A DAY

*T*HE FOLLOWING STORY really occurred.

One night, Rabbi Gur Arye was blessing the new moon with his congregation, when he saw a man flying through the air and falling next to him. After the completion of the ceremony, the rabbi summoned the man to his home and he asked him:

"Who are you and how do you manage to fly through the air?"

The man replied: "Rabbi, let me tell you the whole story."

The Stranger's Story

I'M A RESIDENT OF ANOTHER TOWN and I was sailing across the sea with a cargo of merchandise. Unfortunately, the boat was shattered and it sank with all my goods and all hands and passengers. But the Good Lord worked a miracle: I managed to cling to a plank, and a Turk grabbed hold of the same plank. We floated on the seawater, until the waves carried us to a small island. We went ashore and roamed the island for two days without food. We were looking for a settlement, but we couldn't find one. We were feeble with hunger and fatigue. Then, in the distance, we spotted a herd of sheep and we were ecstatic. We went toward them. The shepherd was very tall and had only one eye in the middle of his forehead. We were terrified, for we saw that he was a savage and an ogre, and we tried to flee. But he wouldn't let us escape, he sat us next to him until nightfall. And when it grew dark, he began driving the sheep into a huge fold.

He forced us into the fold as well and locked the gate. Then the ogre lit a fire and sat down to eat. In the midst of his meal, he came over, groped my whole body, and saw that I was very skinny. He let me go and then he groped the Turk, who was very fat. The ogre grabbed a spit, plunged it into the Turk's belly, and placed him over the fire. He roasted him to a turn and then gobbled him up. There was a bottle of wine next to him. The ogre guzzled down the wine and fell asleep.

I was terrified, for I knew that the ogre would eventually eat me too. When he fell asleep, and the fire kept burning next to him, I thought to myself:

"I'm doomed anyway, so I'll try to kill him. For he gobbled a lot and he guzzled down a whole bottle of wine. He must be sound asleep."

I stole over to the fire, took hold of the spit, and heated it in the flames. Then I thrust the spit into the ogre's single eye and I hid among the sheep. The ogre woke up, screaming, and he groped his way all over the courtyard, hunting for me. But he didn't find me because he was blind. Then he opened the gate and stood there to prevent me from getting through the gate, for the fence was very high, and he knew there was no other way out.

He let out the sheep one by one, groping each sheep to make sure I wasn't on it. But the sheep were very tall. So I held on to a sheep's belly hair and I passed through the gate, even though the ogre groped that sheep. The Good Lord rescued me from the groping ogre. I had taken along a piece of bread that had been lying next to him, and I dashed away with all my strength so that he wouldn't grab me. Then I ate a piece of bread and I thoroughly relished it for I hadn't eaten in several days.

After that, I trudged on until I saw a huge palace in the distance. I headed toward it, but when I arrived, the palace was totally deserted. I was terrified, because there were thieves here: they were out in the countryside during the day and back in the palace during the night. I was at a loss as to what I should do. I was scared to remain but I didn't know where to flee, to escape the thieves.

Suddenly, I noticed a stove with a tiny door and I hid inside, so that I could observe what went on during the night. At nightfall, I heard the din of a large army. The band played on in sheer delight, and somebody yelled:

"The king is coming here!"

I was very scared.

Meanwhile, the king arrived, and a lot of candles were lit. The king sat down on a golden throne and he said:

"Anyone with a grievance or a judgment can appear before me, and I will respond to all of them."

A great many people appeared before him with their grievances, and he judged each one very aptly. They liked his verdicts and they held him in high esteem.

This went on until twelve midnight. After twelve, two men came dashing over to him. They dragged him off the throne ferociously and tore him to shreds. None of the men remained. I waited until daybreak, and when the day came, I was deathly afraid. I didn't know what to say and I didn't know what had happened.

I came out of the stove and I walked around, looking for food, but I didn't find anything to eat. All the rooms were deserted.

That night, the same thing occurred as on the previous night. The king sat on a golden throne, and litigants appeared before him. His verdicts were very intelligent, and everyone liked them and held him in high esteem, and the band played very beautifully.

But when twelve midnight came, two men dashed over to him and tore him to bits, and nobody remained. I then figured that I ought to wait until the following night, when the king would be there, and people would approach him with grievances. I too would approach him with a grievance: my desire to go home. Perhaps he could do me a favor, for so long as he was king, people obeyed him, and perhaps he could order them to get me home. And if he told them to kill me, what would I lose? I was already doomed to starve to death.

And that's what I did. I waited until nightfall. Then the king arrived and sat down on his throne and said:

"If anybody has a grievance or needs a judgment, let him appear before me."

I climbed out of the stove and walked over to the king and fell to my knees and wept and I said:

"Your Majesty, I've lost my way here because my ship went down. I clung to a plank, and the waves carried me to this small island. And today I don't know where I am, and I haven't eaten for several days. So, Your Majesty, I beg you to take pity on me and to order your servants to get me home."

I found grace with the king, and he said to me:

"Your request is granted."

And he immediately told a servant:

"Take this man to his home and do not harm him and start out now, for he is hungry."

The guide promptly took my hand, led me outside, and started running with me. On the way, I asked him:

"My Lord, please tell me: What is that whole business with the king? He's a king every night and in command, and everyone holds him in high esteem. And then he is torn to shreds?"

My guide answered me:

"That man is Nero, the slaughterer. He's been dead for many years. But during his lifetime, he murdered a lot of people, and he wanted to conquer the entire world and be the emperor of the entire world. That is why he is re-created every night and crowned as monarch, and he rules until twelve midnight. Then he receives his just deserts, he is torn to shreds just as he tore so many victims to shreds. The Good Lord pays measure for measure."

The Jew told Rabbi Gur Aryeh this entire story. Rabbi Gur Aryeh was amazed and he said:

"Praised be the Good Lord, who rescued you from the sea, from the one-eyed ogre, and from the harm done to the king."

YOUNG RABBI LEYB'S VERDICT

*T*HIS IS WHAT HAPPENED: When Rabbi Leyb was still a child, the following incident occurred.

In the city of Prague, there were two shops side by side. A Jew sat in one shop and a German Christian in the other. One day, the Jew was counting money in his shop, while the German, inside his own shop, observed the Jew through a crack in the thin dividing wall. The Jew was counting his various coins. The German then went to the king of the city and said to him:

"A large sum of money was stolen from my shop." And he reeled off the numbers of coins that he had seen the Jew counting. "Please give me men to find the thief."

The king gave him some men, and the German searched a few shops but came up with nothing. Next, he entered the Jew's shop. He searched it and found the Jew's money, which matched the German's figures, so that the coins and the Jew were taken to the police station. However, a lot of people testified in the Jew's favor, calling him an honest man and not a thief. The Jew cried out and said:

"The German is next door to me. He must have seen me counting my money in my shop. That's why he knows how many coins I have of each sort."

Well, there is no mistaking the truth. The police felt that the Jew was right, but they couldn't return his money, because the German was also crying out, and his figures matched the coins. The police simply didn't know what to do. The case came before the king, and the king said he would sleep on it and issue a verdict tomorrow.

That evening, the king went strolling in his vineyard. Next to his vineyard there was a large square, a playground for the children of the city. The king saw that a lot of Jewish children were sitting and playing there. The children said:

"Let one of us be a rabbi, and we'll bring him a lawsuit."

The children agreed, and they chose the future Rabbi Leyb as the judge. They sat him on a huge rock so that people would know he was the rabbi. They all stood in front of him, and he sat high above them like a rabbi. And two boys went up to him and said:

"Rabbi, we are engaged in a lawsuit."

And one boy pretended to be the Jew who was falsely accused of theft, and the other boy played the German who had falsely accused the Jew. And they presented the same arguments as the real-life litigants had presented to the police. They argued very insistently in front of the "rabbi," and he listened to both sides. He asked the German:

"What do you deal in?"

The German said:

"Pork and olive oil—greasy things."

Then the "rabbi" asked the Jew:

"What do you deal in?"

The Jew said:

"Kosher things, dry things—sugar and all sorts of pharmaceuticals."

The "rabbi" then said to the boys acting as his assistants:

"Put on a pot and boil some water, then throw the coins into the boiling water. If we see grease collecting on the surface, we'll know that the money belongs to the German. For if he constantly handles greasy things, the grease will stick to his coins. But if there is no grease, then the money belongs to the Jew."

The king of Prague heard everything and he asked:

"Who is that boy whom they've made into a rabbi?"

The king was told that the boy was Gur Arye, a great sage and a great scholar, who was growing into a divine man.

The king sent for him and kissed the boy and said:

"You have the wisdom of Solomon in you."

From then on, the boy was held in great esteem by the king.

That evening, the king went home, and the next day, he sent for the two shopkeepers. The king asked the Jew:

"What do you deal in?"

The Jew replied:

"Kosher things, dry things—sugar and all sorts of pharmaceuticals, and a lot of dry merchandise."

The king ordered his men to boil a pot of water and to throw the coins into the boiling water and see whether any grease collected on the surface. If the money belonged to the German, it would have to be greasy, for he constantly handled greasy things. They boiled the water and dropped in the coins, but no grease collected on the surface. The king promptly ordered his men to hand the money to the Jew and to punish the German horribly. The king said to the German:

"You falsely accused a man, but it did you no good."

And the king ordered his men to torture the German until he confessed that he had been peering through a crack in the wall and watching the Jew count his money. And the German had felt a great lust for those coins. The king ordered him to be hanged, and they gave the Jew the German's possessions—the culprit was punished measure for measure. And everyone who witnessed the king's wisdom and his verdict thanked him heartily and they all said:

"Let the king live forever, as Bathsheba said about a dying King David. For as of today, no one will bring a false accusation. And praised be the Good Lord, for the truth will out. God should help us to walk in the ways of truth."

RABBI LEYB SAVES THE JEWS OF PRAGUE FROM EVIL DECREES

RABBI LEYB, KNOWN AS THE GUR ARYEH, was on excellent terms with the ruler of Prague. The king held him in high esteem, and the rabbi served as his advisor. He visited the king every day, and the king would go strolling with him. He regarded the rabbi as a great sage and an honest man. He nicknamed him Leybl, Lion's Cub. And thanks to his dear friend, the king was favorable to Jews and greatly liked them. Indeed, the king told his guards that the rabbi could visit the king whenever he wanted.

One day, the rabbi appeared before the king, who had just finished his meal. The rabbi saw that the king was very sad, and he asked him:

"Your Majesty, why are you so sad?"

The king replied:

"Let me tell you the whole truth. My ministers have sent me documents for me to seal. And these documents contain very evil decrees against your Jews."

The rabbi said to the king:

"Have you sealed them already?"

The king said:

"No, but I have to seal them, for I've had to cope with them about Jews for some time now. They want to expel all Jews from our country, but I refuse to go along with that, and we've been arguing about it. But they've argued so vehemently that I've said I would seal the evil decrees against Jews."

The rabbi asked him:

"Where are the documents?"

The king said:

"They are in my small case together with my seal."

The rabbi begged the king to rip up the documents. But the ruler said:

"I can't, I've already given my word."

However, the rabbi kept pleading until the ruler became very sad, and he said to the rabbi:

"Let's stroll a bit in my garden."

And the two of them went strolling, and they kept discussing the evil decrees. But the king grew very tired and he said:

"Let's sit down a bit."

They sat down. And the king was so weary that he dozed off after saying to the rabbi:

"I'm going to lie down a bit. Wait until I get up again."

So the rabbi sat there while the king slept. The king dreamed that a small king of a small country, which was under his control and paid him a tribute, now rebelled and refused to pay him. A letter arrived from the king of that country and the letter said:

"You know that I now refuse to pay you a tribute, for I used to be afraid of you, but today I've become very strong and I'm no longer afraid of you. And if you want to fight a war, then come here. I'm no longer afraid of you."

When the ruler read the letter, he hit the ceiling. He then ordered an aristocrat to lead two thousand men and march to the small country and shatter the fortification and terrify the rebellious king so that he'd stop rebelling and that he'd know that he *should* be afraid of the king of Prague. He should humble himself and continue paying the tribute.

The aristocrat obeyed and led his army to the small country. But the small king defeated the aristocrat and wiped out his army. The shamed aristocrat appeared before the king of Prague and told him about the outcome of the battle. He said that the rebel's hand was very strong today and had wiped out the aristocrat's entire army and that he alone had escaped. The king was furious and he said to the aristocrat:

"Take ten thousand men and attack him and wreak vengeance on him and his entire country. Kill the men and torture the women and children in prison and bring the ruler back to me alive."

The aristocrat marched off with his entire army and he fought the small king for two years. Then the king of Prague received a letter from the aristocrat, and the letter said:

"Your Majesty, I led the entire army to the rebellious country and I attacked it with all our strength. But the king and his army outfought us and killed a lot of our men, and a lot of our men starved to death, for the enemy wouldn't let us get supplies. And they attacked us more and more powerfully. I was left with very few men. That is why I advise you to gather your own army and take your soldiers into battle yourself, for the enemy is very powerful today. When you arrive there, you will believe me, for you suspect that I am not loyal to you. Believe me when I say that I have fought loyally, but the enemy is very powerful."

When the king of Prague read the letter, he grew very angry. For not only had the enemy rebelled and refused to pay their tribute, but they had also killed a lot of his soldiers. So the king gathered his entire army and furiously marched to the rebellious country and said:

"I won't allow anyone to survive. I will burn all the towns, and all memory of that country will be wiped from the face of the earth. No one will know that that country ever existed."

And the king and his army arrived at the rebellious country, launched into a great battle, and the battle dragged on for two years. And the small king defeated the king of Prague, killing lots of men and then capturing him alive and imprisoning him. The small king brought the king of Prague back to his town and locked him in a room so tiny that the prisoner couldn't lie down or sit, he could only stand. High up there was a tiny window, through which he was given bread and water. And he spent eleven years there. Sometimes he would peer out through the tiny window, and one day he spotted Rabbi Leyb. He shouted at the rabbi:

"Oh, Leybl! Save me and get me out of here! You used to help me in my troubles, and I've already been here for eleven years. I'm all skin and bones, and my hair and my nails have grown very long."

The rabbi went over to him and said:

"What will happen if I get you out of there and take you home and set you on your throne again, so that you rule again?"

The king laughed and said:

"You say something that I don't demand of you. All I ask is that you get me out of prison and bring me home. I will then be your servant, so long as I don't have to rot in this awful prison."

The rabbi said to him:

"If I get you out of there, will you rip up the evil decrees that you issued against the Jews while you were in power?"

The king said to him:

"You're a sage but you talk a lot of nonsense! I've been imprisoned any number of years. And where are the edicts? By now, there's a new ruler in Prague. I'll say it again: If you get me out of this prison, you can be my ruler, and I'll be your servant!"

The Gur Aryeh said to him:

"You know that everything I tell you is the truth. I'll get you out of there and take you home and seat you on your royal throne, and you will be king again. But remember: When you sealed evil decrees against the Jews, I asked you to rip up those documents, but you said you couldn't, they were signed and sealed in your case. If you like, give me your seal, I'll go into your private study and tear up the seal and take out the edicts and rip them up and reseal them with your seal."

The king took out his seal, which he still had, and he gave it to Rabbi Gur Aryeh. And the rabbi went into the king's study and tore open the king's seal on his case and took out all the documents and ripped them up and resealed them with the king's seal. And even though the entire business was merely the king's dream, the king did give the rabbi his seal while he was still sleeping. And the rabbi had really taken out the documents and ripped them up and resealed the case.

The rabbi came back to the king in the vineyard, and the king was still asleep. And the rabbi handed back the royal seal. And the king took it and slipped it into his pocket. And the king dreamed that the rabbi took him from his prison through the tiny window and brought the king back to his vineyard. And the king awoke in a wonderful mood and he saw that he was sitting in his vineyard. He threw his arms around the Gur Aryeh and kissed him and said to him:

"I'm very thankful to you, Leybl, because you got me out of a horrible prison and brought me to such a radiant place. And if you wish, you can be king, and I will be your servant."

The Gur Aryeh said:

"Your Majesty, think where you have been. Remember when we went on a stroll."

The king said:

"Yes, I remember. But a lot of years have passed."

The Gur Aryeh said:

"No, it was today."

The king checked his watch. A mere hour had gone by. And now the king realized that it had all been a dream. And he said to the rabbi:

"Good for you, Leybl! Now I see that I did good by not sealing the evil decrees against the Jews, and I see that Jews are very honest. From now on, I will no longer believe any libels against the Jews. For I see that my advisors are not loyal and that they act out of hatred for the Jews. That's why my advisors urge me to take such awful steps. And praised be God for preventing me from issuing the evil decrees."

And the king held the rabbi in a lot greater esteem and he always asked his advice about everything. The rabbi was as dear to him as his own life and he never did anything without first consulting the rabbi. And the king always did what the rabbi advised him to do. And it was very good for the king.

THE WONDROUS BALL

THE GUR ARYEH WAS A CLOSE ADVISOR to the king of Prague. Now one of the king's ministers was terribly envious of the rabbi because of his higher position. That's why the minister kept saying wicked things about him to the king. But the king refused to listen for he knew that the minister was simply envious. Meanwhile, the Gur Aryeh kept gaining more and more prestige with the king, who couldn't let a day pass without seeing him. For the king knew that the rabbi was a great saint and an honest and loyal advisor.

One day, the minister said to the king:

"Why do all your advisors and dignitaries invite you to their balls, but the rabbi, your loyal advisor, never invites you to a ball? That's why I think he should invite all of us to a ball in his home."

The minister knew that the rabbi was a pauper and couldn't invite the king to a ball. The rabbi would refuse the king's request, and that would lower him in the king's esteem. When the rabbi appeared before the king, the king said to him:

"How come you never invite us to a ball in your home? You are one of my dignitaries. That's why I want you to invite me and the other dignitaries to a ball in your home."

The Gur Aryeh said:

"You are right. Give me a month, and I'll throw a ball in your honor, with all pleasures, finer than any ball that's ever been thrown in your honor."

The king said:

"Good! I'll give you one month. But you mustn't shame me, and the royal dignitaries shouldn't have to avenge me."

The king then told the minister, who was the rabbi's enemy, that the rabbi had said he would throw a grand ball for the king and all his dignitaries. The minister laughed and said to the king:

"He's laughing at you, for how could he afford to throw a ball in your honor? He's a poor man, a rabbi, he earns a weekly salary. He's not rich and he's not a merchant."

The king said:

"You'll see that he'll truly carry it out, for he never tells lies."

But the minister didn't believe it. It couldn't happen. And he checked on the rabbi daily to see if he was preparing for the banquet. However, the rabbi kept sitting with his students and studying the holy texts. The minister was delighted. Then came the day before the ball. The minister again checked to see what the Gur Aryeh was doing. And the minister was told that the rabbi was sitting and studying. He was not thinking about a banquet and he had no place to throw a ball in the king's honor. The minister was delighted.

Now the time for the banquet was approaching, and the rabbi went to the king and invited him, together with all his dignitaries, to come to the ball. The king was amazed, for the minister had told him that he had checked on the rabbi every day to see whether he was preparing for the ball. And the minister had been told each time that the rabbi was studying and not making any preparations. Nevertheless, the king promptly called for his dignitaries and went to see the rabbi, for the king knew perfectly well that the Gur Aryeh was a godly man. That's why it came as no surprise that he had made no preparations, for the king knew perfectly well that the rabbi wouldn't shame him. So the king and all his dignitaries went to the rabbi's home. And the minister again sent someone to check on the rabbi and see whether he had prepared the ball. But he was told that the Gur Aryeh was sitting in a small room and he wasn't preparing any ball. The minister was delighted.

However, the rabbi took them to the river running through Prague, for the air was very good there. And there they saw a huge and luxurious palace. And the rabbi led them into the palace. And they saw that tables were set with all kinds of gold, silver, and diamond utensils. There were also many servants waiting on the king and all the dignitaries.

The king was astonished at the beauty of the palace with all the precious utensils and the many servants, for only a king could throw such a costly ball. The king said nothing and he sat down at one of the tables, and so did all his greatest dignitaries. And the servants placed a knife and fork and spoon and a diamond salt shaker in front of the king. The king was more astonished at the salt shaker than anything else, for he had no diamond salt shaker among his treasures.

The Gur Aryeh said to them:

"Please don't take along any of these utensils. You can use them but do not remove them."

The banquet was very lavish, with many expensive wines and many delicacies and a lot of fruit and all the pleasures. After the banquet, the rabbi took his guests strolling in a luxurious garden, which had a lot of expensive fruit that didn't grow in that country. The guests were amazed at all these things, for this was a royal ball.

They all said good-bye to the rabbi and left. But the minister couldn't leave, for when he reached the door, he couldn't move. The guests were all surprised and they informed the king. The king went to have a look and he saw that the minister couldn't move. So the king said to him:

"Ask the Gur Aryeh, and you'll be able to leave. He is probably behind this."

The minister asked the rabbi, and the rabbi said to the king:

"He certainly won't be able to leave, for I announced that nobody should take any utensils from the table. But he took the diamond salt shaker, and that's why he can't leave. Only the king has the right to remove anything at all. If he borrows something for a time and then returns it, I will lend it to him, but not to anybody else."

The minister had to confess that he had taken the salt shaker, for never in his life had he set eyes on such a precious and beautiful object. And now he handed the salt shaker to the rabbi and then left. Next, the king asked the rabbi whether he could borrow the salt shaker for a brief time so he could make a replica. And the king said to the rabbi:

"Could you possibly sell it to me? I'll pay you any price you ask."

The Gur Aryeh said:

"I can't sell it, for I've borrowed it myself. But take it, and return it once you are asked to do so."

And the king was delighted with the salt shaker, for he would be making a replica.

And he and all the dignitaries left very cheerfully. On the way back, the king said to the minister, who hated the rabbi:

"Today I and all my dignitaries realize that you are my enemy, for we see that the rabbi is my best friend, and you want to keep getting even with him, you want to kill him. That is a sign that you are my enemy. For if you want to get even with my friend, that's the same as getting even with me. So as of today, you may no longer see my face."

The king was surprised by everything at the ball. How had the rabbi managed to do it? Only a monarch could afford to throw such a ball. Several weeks later, the king received word that the ruler of another country had been preparing a grand ball and had already invited great monarchs. Suddenly, everything had vanished—the royal court, the servants, and all the wines and delicacies. No one was able to tell what had become of everything. Then, several days later, the palace arrived together with the utensils, the servants, and the precious garden. But there were no wines. However, nothing troubled the monarch more than the disappearance of the diamond salt shaker. The loss upset him more than anything else. If anyone knew its whereabouts, he should tell the monarch. He was so ashamed in front of the rulers, whom he had invited to a ball. And when they had arrived, the palace had vanished, and all the delicacies, which had cost endless sums of money. Nevertheless, the loss of the salt shaker upset the monarch more than anything else, for such a utensil was very rare.

The king of Prague told the story to the rabbi, who told the king to send the salt shaker to the bereaved monarch and to describe the rabbi's ball. The rabbi, he said, was a Jew and served him as his advisor, and he was an honest and truthful man. He had transferred the entire palace for the ball, which he had promised to throw for the king of Prague and his dignitaries. The rabbi had told his guests not to remove any utensil, for he had borrowed everything and would have to return everything. Only the king wished to borrow the salt shaker, so he could find whose palace it was and whose utensils they were, for he knew they wouldn't lose the salt shaker for good.

And from that moment on, the rabbi rose even higher in the king's esteem.

THE BLOOD LIBEL

It was the year 5329 (Christian year 1569). A rich Jew lived in Prague and he was so pious that he never did business himself. His wife handled all his dealings, while he sat and studied the holy texts. The merchant had an only son, a wonderful boy. The boy also sat and studied the holy texts and he was very pious, too. And that was how the rich man conducted himself every day. He sat and studied while his wife ran the business with its many employees. And when his time to die came, he called for his dear son and said to him:

"My son, I am leaving you a lot of money, but you have to behave as I taught you—that is, you must always sit and study and never get involved in any sort of commerce. Only your wife should engage in business and have lots of employees, and the Good Lord will certainly help you."

The son promised to obey his father, and when the father died, the son kept his word and he sat and studied and was very pious. His wife was a woman of great valor and she ran the entire business. And the Good Lord made them very successful.

But then one day, the business started going downhill. The wife lost a lot of money and the business started failing. So she said to her husband:

"My dear husband, until now you have obeyed your father's last will and you haven't gotten involved in any commerce. But things are different today, my business is going downhill. I'm scared of losing other people's money, God forbid! So you have to disobey your father's last will and get involved in commerce if only for two hours a day. The Good Lord will take pity on us, so we won't lose other people's money."

The husband didn't want to take her advice. But he was scared of losing other people's money. So he visited his father's grave, where he wept bitterly, and he said:

"My dear father, I certainly do wish to obey your last will. But what should I do? The Good Lord has punished me by making me lose a lot of money, and I'm scared that I might lose other people's money, God forbid. That's why I have to disobey your last will and look in on our business for two hours a day. Perhaps the Good Lord will help me."

He wept very bitterly and he went home very angrily.

That night he dreamed that his father appeared to him and said:

"My dear son, I authorize you to look in on the business for two hours a day, but no longer than that. For you should continue to sit and study and to serve the Good Lord, and He will help you."

And so the son got involved in the business for two hours a day and he checked all their accounts.

One day, upon checking an account, he realized that his business was rapidly going downhill, for he had lost quite a lot of money. So he summoned his wife and he said to her:

"My dear wife, I saw in an account that we've lost a lot of money. We have to sell off all our merchandise as well as our home and our shops so that we can pay our debts. And with whatever's left we'll move to a small shtetl. We can't remain in Prague, for we've led a very wealthy and charitable life here. Our expenses were very high, so we can't be stingy now. But we can economize in a small shtetl. We'll lead a quiet life and we'll give alms as best we can."

His wife then said to him:

"I'll go along with whatever you like."

For she was a virtuous and obedient wife. And he did as he had planned. He sold off all his merchandise, paid off all his creditors, and he still had a lot of money left. Next he rented several wagons and, together with his wife and his children, he left Prague in search of a small shtetl.

He found one toward the Sabbath, which he planned to celebrate at an inn. Friday evening, he went to synagogue. Upon entering the synagogue, he saw that everyone was extremely poor, for they were wearing dirty and ragged clothes. When he returned to the inn, he said to his wife:

"The people in this shtetl are very poor, so I think we ought to settle here."

She asked him:

"Why should we live here?"

He said:

"I see that they all wear ragged clothes. There's not a rich man among them. If we settle here, we'll be rich by contrast, and no one will damage our business."

So they settled here. Then, on Sunday, he summoned a few inhabitants and he asked them:

"What kind of work do you do, how come you're so poor, and why isn't there a lovely house anywhere in this shtetl?"

They said to him:

"We don't have a single rich Jew in our shtetl. And normally, a rich man's home is surrounded by lots of other homes. But since we're all paupers, we have to go to the forest to earn our livelihood. For there's a huge forest near our shtetl, and big merchants use the forest and make tar there. We go there every Sunday and we make tar all week long. And we earn a meager living and then we go home for the Sabbath. That's why the clothes we wear are smeared with tar, for we can't afford a special Sabbath wardrobe. Nor can we afford to improve our homes. That's why they're all so ramshackle."

The rich man said to them:

"I wish to settle here, for I am very rich. I want to build a large home and a large shop. I want to hire many of you and make some of you my agents in my shops, and some of you will be my servants, and I will lend money to some of you, so you can start your own businesses—whatever you're good at. And with God's help, you'll have decent lives and good livelihoods. I'll build huge stores, for many people will come shopping here. And gradually the shtetl will develop into a major commercial center."

The rich man then hired lots of people to bring him lumber from the forest and rocks to build large homes and shops. He also hired a lot of people to supervise the construction. And he built large homes and expensive stores. And he sent employees to Prague and he bought merchandise and he built a huge store. And he made a big profit, for his shtetl did better than all the surrounding shtetls.

The shtetl kept growing bigger and lovelier, for lots of inhabitants improved their homes and established inns, and the rich man earned a lot of money. He also gave them fabrics to make fine clothes and to pay their installments gradually. In short, he gave them decent lives. And many people came to this shtetl to do business and to buy goods. The shtetl inhabitants loved him and respected him deeply, for he had brought them all decent lives.

One day, the shtetl commissioner needed some merchandise, but he wasn't in the shtetl, he resided in a village. He said to his servant:

"Hitch up the wagon. We're going to a large town to do some shopping."

The servant said to him:

"Sir, why don't you shop in your own shtetl?"

The commissioner said:

"There's never any merchandise in my shtetl, so I have to shop in a bigger town. My inhabitants are very poor. There's not a rich man among them. I'd rather not see their poverty."

The servant said:

"Sir, recently a rich and fine man settled there, a very wise and pious man. He built a huge palace and huge stores, and he carries all sorts of merchandise. And all the surrounding shtetls get their merchandise from him, and he provides a livelihood for all the people in his shtetl. Many people have already improved their homes. You should go to the shtetl, you won't recognize it, the shtetl has been totally overhauled."

Upon hearing this, the commissioner said to his servant:

"Hurry, go and hitch up. We'll drive to our shtetl, and I'll have a look."

The commissioner drove right into the shtetl, and his servant took him to see the rich man.

When the commissioner entered the store and saw lots of merchandise, he asked the lady of the house:

"Who are you?"

He told her that he was the shtetl commissioner. She then started conversing with him very intelligently. He was surprised at her fine mind, her beauty, and her ornaments. For he had never been able to converse with the people in the shtetl. Their poverty had dulled their minds. The rule is: He who does business is smart, for he constantly converses with merchants. However, they had always been in the forest. That's why their minds had dulled.

The commissioner was delighted and he asked her:

"Where is your husband?"

She said:

"My husband constantly sits and studies the holy texts and he serves the Good Lord. He gets involved in business only two hours every day. If you wish to wait for him, you can see him and talk to him."

And the commissioner waited in the store until the husband arrived.

And when the commissioner saw the husband, he was very surprised. For the husband was very appealing and dignified, while the other shtetl dwellers were very unattractive. And the commissioner started conversing with him. The husband spoke with great respect and great intelligence. The commissioner was astonished at the man's wisdom and elocution and he said:

"I've never met such a sage in all my life."

For in conversing with him, the commissioner saw that the husband was well-versed in all wisdoms. And he hugged and kissed him and he said:

"I'm very thankful to you, for you've turned the townlet into a town and you've provided decent lives for the inhabitants. And so, my friend, you ought to know that the duke of our town resides in Prague, for Prague belongs to him. That's why the local court is always empty, while I reside in a village, on other estates. But today I'm going to write the duke a letter and tell him about how you've settled here, how you've turned the townlet into a town and how you've provided a decent life for the inhabitants. He's bound to visit you in order to thank you and give you presents."

And the commissioner said good-bye to the merchant, he hugged him very warmly, thanked him very warmly, and left. And upon arriving home, he wrote a letter to the duke and told him the whole story; he explained that the shtetl was very fine today, and the inhabitants no longer had to make tar. Now they were merchants and agents of the rich man. He lent them money to do business with, and he had many employees in his home and in his stores, and there were many lovely homes, and many merchants came to do business there. And the commissioner asked the duke to specifically visit the town and the rich man. The duke would derive a lot of pleasure from the shtetl, for he would see that his town had a different appearance, and he would see the great wisdom of the rich man and his wife.

And when the letter came, and the duke read it, he ordered his servants to quickly prepare his carriage and immediately drive him to the commissioner's home, and the two of them now drove to the shtetl. And when the duke arrived there, he saw that there were lots of lovely houses, and the people were well dressed, and he was delighted. Next he drove to the rich man's shop. The duke was welcomed very honorably and respectfully by the lady of the house, for she understood that he was the duke of the town—she had seen the commissioner show him great deference. And the duke asked her:

"Where is your husband?"

She dashed off to find her husband and she told him that the duke of the town was in the shop:

"He's come specifically to see us, because the commissioner told him that we've made the shtetl a decent town, and the duke wants to thank us. He also wants to see you in private, so come right away."

The rich man and his wife went to the store. And when the duke saw him, he hugged him warmly and thanked him warmly for making the shtetl a decent place, and the duke said to him:

"I'd never been able to come here because of the poverty and the tar making. But today, I can speak with the inhabitants."

The duke conversed with the rich man and he saw how learned he was, and they conversed for several hours. The rich man invited the duke into his home and he served him expensive delicacies. And the duke said to the rich man:

"My heart adheres to yours in love. I just can't leave you."

And the duke went to spend the night in his court, and the next morning he went back to the rich man and conversed with him for several hours. On the third day, he summoned the rich man to the ducal court. To make a long story short, the rich man stayed there for a month, and he had to converse with the duke every day, for the duke couldn't live without him, he loved the rich man like his own life.

After four weeks, the duke said to him:

"I can't leave here without you, for I can't live without you. So put your employees in charge of your shops and your dealings, and you and your wife will come back to Prague with me, and I'll put all my estates in your hands, so you can supervise them, and you will handle all the accounts of my commissioners. And no bit of grain will be sold without your knowledge, so you can profit as a broker. And I'll cover all your expenses—all sorts. And I'll give you a home with wood, water, and light. And you'll put aside whatever you earn, and you'll open a large wine shop, and I and all my servants will buy our wine there. But you've got to pay attention to my possessions; for I own the city of Prague and all the surrounding villages, and I see that you are a great sage and a great saint. So you will be honest and loyal in regard to my business."

And that's what was decided. The rich man put his agents in charge of his shops, and he and his wife returned to Prague with the duke. And the duke gave him a document stating that the rich man was in charge of all the duke's estates. The rich man was the top commissioner and he was to receive accounts from all the commissioners. And the duke bought him a large palace and he sent him lots of grain to eat and lots of money to cover his expenses.

And the rich man was greatly esteemed by the duke. And he opened a wine shop and took in a great profit, for the duke and all his servants bought wine there. And he was greatly esteemed by the entire city. And he constantly sat in synagogue and studied the holy texts. But for two hours a day he got involved in business and paid heed to the ducal accounts and did everything very honestly.

One day, the agent of the wine shop came and said to him:

"Sir, I'm missing a thousand ducats, but I swear I didn't steal anything. In checking an account, I saw that the money was missing. I don't understand it."

The rich man said:

"Does anyone owe you that sum?"

The agent said:

"I don't remember that anyone owes me a thousand ducats for wine. It can't be."

The rich man was very angry at the agent and very surprised that so much money was missing, for he knew that the agent was an honest man. He certainly hadn't stolen anything. So the rich man said:

"Check your account again, for this can't be."

And the agent left furiously.

Meanwhile, a note arrived from the bishop of Prague, and he wrote the agent:

"Since I owe you a thousand ducats for wine, and I'm throwing a grand ball tomorrow, please supply me more wine, and I'll pay you everything in a little while."

Upon reading the note, the agent joyfully hurried over to his employer and said to him:

"The thousand ducats are accounted for—I forgot the bishop's debt."

And he showed the note to his employer. The rich man was very angry and he said:

"Don't give him any more wine. Once he pays us the thousand ducats he can borrow again."

The agent then said to the bishop's messenger:

"Go and tell you employer that my boss has told me not to give the bishop any more wine until he pays the thousand ducats he owes him."

And the messenger went and told the bishop. The bishop was furious at the wine dealer for shaming him in front of many people. The rich man refused to give him the wine on credit, and the bishop was supposed to throw a ball tomorrow, but he had no money.

So he went to the town commissioner and told him the whole story and begged him to get even with the wine dealer for deliberately shaming him. The commissioner instantly sent for the wine dealer. The messenger said to him:

"The commissioner is very angry and wants to see you!"

The wine dealer was very angry at the commissioner and he said to the messenger:

"Go and tell the commissioner that I refuse to see him. If he wants to talk to me, let him come here!"

The messenger brought that message to the commissioner. And the commissioner was furious at the wine dealer and he said to a few servants:

"Force him to come here, and I'll clap him in chains, for he cursed at me."

When the servants came to the wine dealer, he laughed at the commissioner and he said to the servants:

"Go and tell the commissioner to come here immediately. I have to check his account in regard to the estate he's in charge of. I've got a document from the duke, it gives me the right to check the accounts of all the commissioners."

When the servants went and told the commissioner, he shuddered and he hurried over to see the wine dealer, and he pleaded with him and he said:

"Forgive me, I didn't realize you had such a high position with our duke. That's why I said such nasty things about you."

And the commissioner went home in disgrace and he said to the bishop:

"I can't do anything to him, I'm scared of him."

The bishop now told a Christian to hide a small, stabbed, Christian corpse in the wine dealer's cellar. They would then search his home and find the corpse. They would claim that the Jew had stabbed him to death because he needed blood to bake matzos for Passover.

"That way we'll get even with him, and you'll enjoy the afterlife."

And the Christian obeyed the bishop and went home. There he had a sick child. He promptly stabbed him and concealed him in the wine dealer's open cellar.

And when the first night of Passover came, and the Jews were having their seder, the wine dealer, as head of the household, was reclining very cheerfully on the traditional Passover pillows. Suddenly, the bishop walked in with lots of people and began to search for the murdered Christian, and they found the corpse in the cellar. The bishop wanted to clap the wine dealer in irons right away. But the duke found out and he sent the bishop a message that he was to do absolutely nothing to the wine dealer. The duke would vouch for him and deliver him for the trial. And he would be tried by no one except the king and the pope.

The bishop didn't put the Jew in prison. But he did put sentries outside the Jew's home to make sure he didn't run away. Next, they called for the king and the pope and asked them to come and try the Jew. And the whole city prayed for the rich man. And the Gur Aryeh, the rabbi of Prague, suffered greatly and prayed to the Good Lord to help the rich man fight the blood libel.

One night, the Gur Aryeh went to bed. And his sleep was very tormented. Then he was informed in the middle of the night:

"Stop fasting and go to the town. Find a man named Leybele the Stocking-Maker. He can help the accused. No one else can help him."

But they laughed at the rabbi and they said:

"What use is Leybele the Stocking-Maker? Do you want to buy stockings from him?"

The rabbi said to them:

"Why do you care that I need him? Just show me where he lives."

They showed him. Leybele lived in a tiny cottage outside Prague, and he was very poor.

The Gur Aryeh entered the cottage, and Leybele greeted him, and he said:

"What can I do for you?"

And the Gur Aryeh said:

"I need something from you."

Leybele said to the rabbi:

"Do you want to buy a pair of stockings?"

The rabbi said:

"No."

And he told Leybele the whole story. And Leybele laughed very hard and he said to the rabbi:

"All I can do is make stockings. How can I talk to a king and a pope?"

But the rabbi said to Leybele:

"Don't worry, you will save the life of a great saint. And if you refuse, I'll issue an evil decree against you, for I am the Gur Aryeh, the rabbi of Prague."

Leybele said to him:

"Rabbi, you go home, and I'll go on foot, for the trial is taking place on Shevuoth (when we Jews celebrate the gathering of the first fruits and the giving of the Torah). I'll be in Prague, and with God's help the Jew will be pure."

The Gur Aryeh then said good-bye to Leybele, drove home, and announced that the Jew would be rescued with God's help.

On the eve of Shevuoth, Leybele left his home and headed toward Prague. On the way, he encountered the pope, who was going to Prague for the trial. When the pope saw the pauper, he stopped and asked him:

"Who are you and where are you going?"

Leybele replied:

"I'm a Jew and I'm going to Prague for Shevuoth."

The pope said to him:

"Climb aboard and you'll reach Prague a lot sooner. For according to tradition, a pope is a humble and compassionate man."

Leybele, the pauper, climbed in and sat next to the pope. Along the way, they conversed. And the pope asked the pauper:

"Why do you have to go to Prague?"

Leybele said:

"I need a trifle."

And the pauper asked the pope:

"Why are you going to Prague? What business do you have there?"

And the pope said:

"I'm going there in regard to a problem that the bishop has with a Jew. The Jew killed a Christian before Passover and drew out his blood for Passover, and the bishop found out. Together with the king, I have to pass judgment on the Jew."

The pauper said to the pope:

"I'm also going there because of the blood libel."

The pauper begged the pope not to go to the court without him.

And at court the bishop yelled at the judges:

"Just because the duke holds the Jew in high esteem, does that give the Jew the right to kill a Christian? He should therefore be killed himself!"

The pope turned to the pauper and said:

"What do you say?"

The pauper said to the pope:

"I want to prove to you that the Jew didn't kill anyone. The bishop ordered the murder."

And the pauper led them, and many people went to see the wonders. And the pauper led them to the grave of the murdered child, and the pauper ordered them to remove the corpse from the coffin and he told the child to sit down, and the pauper said:

"Do you see who is standing next to you? Sit up."

The child sat up, and the pauper said:

"Why are you holding your tongue? Tell us who stabbed you!"

The child began to tell what had happened to him. The bishop had come to the child's father and had said to him:

"I promise that you will enjoy the afterlife if you stab your child and conceal the corpse in the wine dealer's cellar. For he shamed me, and your child will die anyhow, for he's very sick."

"And after urging and urging him, he finally talked my father into going along with his plan. I started to weep and yell: 'What do you want to do to me? What do you want of me?' But it was no use. He sharpened a knife and came to me with the knife and stabbed me. After that, I don't know what else happened."

Leybele said to him:

"Go and lie down again."

And Leybele said to the king and the pope:

"Now what do you have to say about the bishop? Not only did he tell the father to kill the child, he also wanted to murder the Jew."

The king and the pope immediately ordered their men to hang the bishop and the child's father on the gallows that had been set up for the Jew.

And everyone was amazed at what Leybele had done. Eventually he was held in high esteem by the king, and he was shown great respect.

ANGELS FLY
(A Folktale about Rabbi Jonathan of Prague)

In PRAGUE, THERE LIVED A RABBI named Jonathan. And there was also an emperor. Rabbi Jonathan was an advisor at the imperial court and he was greatly beloved by the emperor.

One day, the emperor asked him:

"The whole world believes in Jesus, but not you Jews. Why is that?"

What should the rabbi have replied? So for now, he didn't answer.

Across from the palace where the emperor resided, there was a church with a high spire.

Several days after that conversation, Rabbi Jonathan was taking a walk and he halted in front of the church and gazed up at the spire. He gazed, and people gazed. The people didn't know what he was gazing at, but he knew what he was gazing at. And now a huge crowd gathered there. Finally, a bold man in the crowd went and asked Jonathan:

"Rabbi, what are you gazing at up there?"

The rabbi replied: "Don't you see? Angels are flying up there."

Each gazer passed it on and they all kept gazing: "Where?"

"There! There!"

Until everyone believed it.

Now when everyone saw the angels, the crowd grew bigger and bigger. The emperor, peering through his window, saw the huge crowd, and all the people were gazing upward. So the emperor asked: "What's up there?"

They replied: "The Jewish rabbi sees angels flying up there."

The emperor found that very "interesting," and he went out. He wanted to see for himself.

They made way for the emperor, and he reached the rabbi. And he said to him: "Jonathan, you see angels flying up there? Show me where."

Jonathan replied: "You don't see them? There! There!"

Now since the rabbi showed so much certainty, and all the gazers said they saw the angels, the emperor likewise replied that he could see them.

They all gazed for a while. Then the emperor took the rabbi's arm, and they went to the imperial court. From there, the emperor led Jonathan to an orchard, where they would be alone. And the emperor said: "Listen, Jonathan, tell me the truth. Did you really see flying angels? An old emperor can't be fooled!"

Jonathan asked: "What? You didn't see them?"

"I have to tell you the truth. I can't say that I saw them."

In short, the emperor asked him over and over whether he had seen the angels, and Jonathan kept saying that he had seen them.

"Do you get my point?" Jonathan finally asked him. "That is the answer to the question you asked me: Why do all nations believe in Jesus, but not the Jews? You see? All nations have been talked into believing in him, and I can likewise talk a nation into believing, just as I talked a crowd of people into believing that angels were flying over the church."

A MAN DOESN'T KNOW WHERE HE IS GOING

(A Folktale about Rabbi Jonathan of Prague)

One morning, Rabbi Jonathan of Prague was walking past the imperial palace, where the emperor was standing on the balcony.

And the emperor asked him: "Jonathan, where are you going?"

Jonathan said: "I don't know."

This angered the emperor, and he had the rabbi arrested for a couple of hours. He kept him for two or three hours, then he released him and he asked him: "Now will you tell me where you were going?"

Jonathan replied: "I was planning to go and pray. I didn't know that you'd arrest me. So what should I have answered? You can see for yourself that a man doesn't know where he's going."

(Narrated by Mariashe Rapoport-Khaimson
Written down by S. Bastomski, Vilna, 1923)

SHLOYME BASTOMSKI
(EDITOR)
(1891-1941)

In his introduction to his anthology of Yiddish folk riddles, Bastomski bewails the lack of printed Yiddish folklore. Here is virtually the entire text of his *Yiddish Folk Riddles* (*Yidishe Folksretenishn*, second edition, Vilna, 1923). Many of the riddles are in verse, most in prose.

YIDDISH FOLK RIDDLES

Spread white, sown black, whoever sees it, understands it. (A book)

Spread white, sown black, wherever you send it, there it goes. (A letter)

Smooth as silk, white as snow. You look into it, and you see double. (A mirror)

Not a shirt, and yet sewn. Not a tree, and yet full of leaves. Not a person, and yet it talks to the point. (A book)

As high as a wall, as thick as a peasant. Sweet as sugar, bitter as gall. (A tree with fruit and leaves.)

It grows in the woods, it hangs in the shop, you touch it—and it weeps. (A violin)

Everyone uses it, everyone needs it, the emperor doffs his hat in front of it, the world has named it a "comb." (This is the kind of riddle that contains its own solution)

A guard, a sentry, burned and forged, it doesn't take alone, it doesn't give to another. (A lock)

A black Tartar, it's got nails, wherever you send it, there it goes. (A shoe)

An iron horse with a flaxen tail; wherever you push it, there it goes. (A needle and thread)

It sews for everyone, it dresses everyone, but it goes naked itself. (A needle)

It flies without wings, it builds without bricks, it lies down like a lord, and it stands up like a fool. (Snow)

He goes up and he takes out, he goes down and shakes off. (A chimney sweep)

A living man strikes a dead thing, the dead thing yells, and it's heard far away. (A man ringing a bell)

A white wall and a yellow wall. If you want to reach the yellow, you have to break the white. (An egg)

A sheet spread out, peas sown, a plate in the midst. (The sky with stars and moon)

I don't go on the ground, I don't look at the sky, I don't count the stars. (A fish)

My father's son, but not my brother. Who am I? (Myself)

The father has money—and he can't count over. The mother has a quilt—and she can't cover herself. The sister has hair—and she can't comb it. The brother has an apple—and he can't eat it. (The stars, the sky, the sunbeams, the moon)

A fat mother, a red father, a tall son, a crazy daughter. (A fireplace, a fire, smoke, the wind)

As green as grass—but not that. As red as blood, but not good as yet. As black as coal. Ah, that's right. (A cherry)

A two-footer sits on a three-footer and holds a one-footer. Along comes a four-footer and grabs the one-footer. The two-footer chases after the four-footer, while the three-footer tumbles over. (A cobbler sits on a three-legged stool and holds a shoe. A dog grabs the shoe, and the cobbler chases after it, while the stool tumbles over.)

Four rabbis sit in a room, all the same age, all can study together. Somebody wants to come in—whose hand should he shake first? (The door latch)

Two brothers, one is my uncle, the other isn't. Who is he? (My father)

Two brothers sit in a tree but don't see one another. (Two eyes)

Four brothers wear one hat. (A table)

A hundred brothers without a mother are all tied together. (A broom)

Four young ladies chase one another but can't reach one another. (Four wheels)

A young lady sits on the roof and smokes a pipe. (A smoking chimney)

A bluish plate filled with peas. (The starry sky)

A patch on a patch but without a seam. (A head of cabbage)

A head without hair, milk without udders. (A herring)

A white mouth, and black as coal. (A pan)

A new tool full of holes. (A sieve)

A leprous hand hangs on the wall. (A sieve)

A lot of goats scamper on a twisted tree. (People on a staircase)

White tools hang on a red string. (The teeth)

A board lies in water but doesn't rot. (The tongue)

A keg rolls down a narrow alley but it doesn't shatter. (An eye)

You climb over it, and it stands calmly. (A ladder)

It sleeps in the daytime, it lives in the night. (A lamp)

In summer it puts on its fur, in winter it takes off its fur. (A tree)

For six months, people walk over me; for six months, they ride over me. (A river)

It runs and runs and it doesn't budge. (A clock)

It runs with a load, it stops with a load. (A wall clock)

It runs and runs, counts days and years, not born of humans. (A clock)

I have no feet and yet I run, I have hands and they strike. (A clock)

It has ears but it doesn't hear, it has a mouth but it doesn't eat, it has no feet but it stands. (A pail)

A dead man has this. If a living man had it, he would die on the spot. (Death)

Adam—of earth; Abraham—of the limekiln; Joseph—burned up. What is it? (A clay pot)

The father hasn't yet gone out in the world, and the son is already on the roof. (Fire and smoke)

Turned and turned and then put away in the corner. (A broom)

On a rich man's table, it has four feet, touch it—and it pours. (A samovar)

If you throw this down, it can't be lifted. (Spit)

The more you take of this, the bigger it gets. (A pit)

It is born of water, it gets lost in water. (Salt)

It is born of fire, it is lost in fire. (Coal)

It comes in through one door, it goes out through two doors. (Wood in the stove; the ashes come out through the door, the smoke through the chimney)

It comes out of the earth, it goes into the earth. (Water)

Alone I am poor, and I make another rich. (A zero)

I can't talk so long as I don't have a drink. (A pen)

A young lady sits on the roof, she cooks fish and tastes—what is missing? (What she tastes is missing)

Everything goes into this—what is it? (The mind)

What does the emperor see rarely, the shepherd constantly, and God—never? (His equal.)

What is the hardest thing in the world? (Recognizing your own faults)

What is the easiest thing in the world? (To give advice); (For a mother: carrying her child in her hands)

What is the fastest thing in the world? (A thought)

What is it that nothing can do without? (A name)

What is tomorrow, what will yesterday be? (Today)

What is higher than thought for a rabbi? (A skullcap)

What grows without rain? (Interest)

What does a billy goat become after seven years? (Eight)

What is under a featherbed? (Warmth)

Which is heavier? A pound of iron or a pound of down? (They're equal)

What can you see but not take on? (Your shadow)

In what sort of vessel can you not pour water? (A full vessel)

Why are Jews so poor? (Because their God lives forever, and they can't become his heirs)

Why isn't a Jew afraid of death? (When death is here, it's not here; and when death isn't here, it's here)

Why does a rooster move with closed eyes? (Because he knows his wisdom by heart)

Why can't a tinsmith and a chimney sweep be cited as witnesses? (Because they risk their lives for money)

Who wasn't born but did die? (Adam)

Who is a creditor of your head? (The fur hat maker)

For what does a Christian priest buy a cane with a big knob? (For money)

Who knows what someone is missing? (A thief)

Who is turned down before he even asks? (A pauper)

Who has never told a lie? (A mute)

Who always comes too early? (Death)

Who always comes too late? (Intelligence)

Which girl mustn't get a fiancé? (A girl who's already got one)

Who is more useful dead than alive? (A cheapskate)

Which load is heavier the more people carry it? (Trouble)

Which food is first parve, then non-kosher, then a meat dish? (An egg: non-kosher when it lies under the hen, and a meat dish after it hatches)

Which Jew wears the biggest hat? (The Jew with the biggest head)

On which holiday do you eat well and sleep badly? (The Feast of Tabernacles—because Jews sleep in makeshift huts)

What sack holds water even though it's full of holes? (A sponge)

Which war killed one fourth of the world's population? (When Cain killed Abel)

Whose death was mourned by the entire world? (Abel's)

How many bagels can you eat on an empty stomach? (Only one bagel; after that, your stomach is no longer empty)

Where is it very dark when it's light, warm when it's cold, cold when it's warm? (In a cellar)

When are dumplings tasty? (When you eat them)

When is glass thrown but not broken? (When you shower people with wedding gifts)

When do you hit without hurting? (When you hit on a plan)

When is a merchant in a shirt? (He's always in a shirt, never in two)

When can a pauper live like an emperor? (In a dream)

A deaf man heard a mute talking, and a bind man saw a hare dashing; a cripple chased the hare, a naked man put it in his pocket and took it home? What was it? (A dream)

Once a guess entered a tavern, and there he found a young girl. He asked her:

"Where is your father?"

She replied: "My father is throwing living things on dead things."

The merchant asked: "Where is your mother?"

The girl replied: "My mother is sick with pride."

The merchant asked: "Where are your brothers?"

The girl replied: "They're looking for what they haven't lost."

The merchant didn't understand and he then asked: "What should I do with my horses?"

The girl replied: "Marry your horse with the summer or the winter."

The merchant still didn't understand. How should we grasp her answers? (The father was sowing seeds, the mother was giving birth, the brothers were picking berries, the horse should be hitched to a wagon or a sleigh)

One day, a Jew had to ferry a goat, a wolf, and a head of cabbage across a river. The boat could only hold two of them. The Jew didn't dare leave the wolf alone with the goat, for the wolf might eat it up. Nor could he leave the goat with the cabbage, for the goat might eat it up. How did the Jew manage to ferry all three across the river? (First he ferried the goat across, leaving the wolf with the cabbage, for the wolf didn't eat cabbage; next, the Jew ferried the cabbage across and brought back the goat; then he ferried the wolf across, left it with the cabbage, went back for the goat, and ferried it across)

As swift as a rooster, as small as a poppy seed, as heavy as a stone. (A spark)

It strikes without hands, it hangs on the wall, it runs without feet, it can stand on a table? (A clock)

You stuff it and stuff it, but it doesn't get full? (A sack with holes)

When it goes, it lies? (A shadow)

It walks during the day, it stands during the night? (A shoe)

Built high, kept low, sweet as sugar, bitter as gall? (The sky, the earth, life, death)

You get me for free, yet you give up your life for me? (Death)

A young girl is cooking fish: the more she gets, the less she has? (The more she eats of it)

Red cows are standing in a stable; a black ox comes in and drives out the cows? (Red coals are in an oven; a hearth broom comes in and sweeps out the coals)

A broad mother, a tall father, a blind daughter, a crazy son-in-law? (The earth, the sky, the night, the wind, the lightning)

A dense forest, a bare field, two lanterns, one bell, two walls, two ropes with laundry, the man of the house is taking a bath? (The hair on the head, the face, the eyes, the nose, the cheeks, the teeth, the tongue)

How does a cat get across a stream? (Wet)

When do you put the teeth on a shelf? (When you put a comb on a shelf)

Who is the haughtiest man? (A drayman , because he keeps everyone in back of him).

Where does a person encounter his best friend? (In a mirror)

When does a tailor not get angry at his work? (When he's sewing a shroud)

Who is safe from dying young? (An old man)

Who is never not good? (Death)

Who is never not bad? (A mother)

What is born flying, lives lying down, and dies running? (Snow)

Whom are you afraid of in front, whom in back, and whom from both sides? (A buck, a horse, a fool [or a bad person])

What roars louder than a mill? (Two mills)

Who are these three people? One is higher than anyone else; people doff their hats to the second man; if I weren't for the third one, the town would have no rabbi's wife? (A chimneysweep, a barber, a rabbi)

A man dreams that he is sailing in a boat with his father and his mother. The boat starts sinking, and the man can save only himself and one other person. He can save either his mother or his father—what does he do? (He wakes up)

Three merchants and three thieves were supposed to ferry across a river, and there was only one skiff, and it could hold only two people. Each merchant was afraid to remain on a shore with two thieves. So how did they get across the river safely? (First two thieves went across and one thief returned and ferried the third thief across; then one thief brought back the skiff and remained alone on the riverbank; now two merchants went across; one thief and one merchant returned; the thief stepped ashore, and the two merchants ferried across the river; finally, the last two thieves sailed across the river.

I am black, black is my face, I am burned in fire, I am boiled in water, ladies and gentlemen consume me. (Coffee)

Higher than a house, smaller than a mouse, sweet as sugar, bitter as gall. (A bee)

Clad white, sewn black, wherever you send it, it speaks. (A letter)

I stand high and emit smoke. (A chimney)

It's slippery and pointed and it circles a string. (A candle)

In a dark alley, something rolls, yellow inside, white outside. (An egg)

I was walking along a path, I found a body without a soul, it talked without a mouth, a donkey boasted about a horse. (An egg)

I come from far away, fire and water color me, I have a foe, if I don't see him, I am red, if I see him, I am dead. (A fiddle)

A keg fell down and shattered; no cooper can repair it. (An egg)

Narrow on top, wide on the bottom, thoroughly sweet, in a white shirt, in a blue dress. (A sugar cone)

Two mothers have five children each, and every child has the same name. (The fingers)

Everyone desires it, but is unhappy when he has it. (A long life)

You've enjoyed it, it's cost money, and in the end it's washed away in water. (The bread tossed into the river during the ceremony of Tashlikh, symbolizing the sins washed away for the new year.)

Dough in the daytime, a cake at night. (A bed with bedding)

It goes during the day, it stands at night. (A broom)

A circle in the daytime, a snake at night. (A belt)

Two poles are standing, on the poles there is a kneading trough, on the trough a pitcher, on the pitcher a loaf of bread, grass grows on the bread, sheep graze on the grass. (The legs, the belly, the neck, the head, the hair)

A white bottle, a red cork, if you don't drink it, you won't live. (The mother's breast)

Nine rooms, eight windows, two sources, and one drinker. (Nine months of pregnancy, eight days of lying in, two breasts, one child)

Can rain fall for two days? (No, because the first day is followed by the night)

A child says to a father: "You are my father but I am not your son." How can that be? (The child is a daughter)

When is the best time to eat? (When a rich man wants food, when a pauper has food)

When does a blind man see? (In his dreams)

When doesn't a town need a rabbi? (When it's got a dog to eat non-kosher meat and when it's got a potter to make a new pot)

What is the equal of half a cake? (The other half)

What belongs to you and yet is used by others more than by you? (Your name)

What sings better than a fiddle? What digs deeper than a spade? (Good luck, bad luck)

What is a pauper always certain of? (Death)

Why is a Jew better off than one who's been baptized? (The Jew can still convert)

Who has never told a lie? (The person who was born a mute)

Who was never born but did die? (Adam)

Who can never curse you? (A mute)

Which is the greater pauper? The one who wears a weekday coat on the Sabbath or the one who wears a holiday coat on weekdays? (The one who wears a holiday coat on weekdays)

Who is more useful after he dies? (A skinflint)

Why are there more questions than answers in the world? (Because a fool can also ask questions)

Why shouldn't we pray for an end to our troubles? (Because an end to our troubles is an end to our lives)

HOW DID HE SAVE HIMSELF FROM DEATH?

ONCE THERE WAS A GREAT EMPEROR, a nasty anti-Semite. He couldn't endure having any Jews in his capital. So he issued an edict stating that any Jew who set foot in the capital had to say something. If it was a lie, he would be hanged, and if it was the truth, he would be shot. One day, a Jew entered the city and said something that stunned the emperor's servants and prevented them from doing anything to him. What did the Jew say? (He said: "Today you are going to hang me." Now if they hanged him, it would mean that he'd told the truth, so he'd have had to be shot. But if he were shot, it would mean that he'd told a lie, and so he'd have had to be hanged.)

TASHRAK
(PSEUDONYM FOR YISROEL-YOYSEF ZEVIN)
(1872-1926)

Raised in a Hasidic household, Zevin migrated to New York in 1889. Here, he eventually devoted himself full-time to journalism and literature, providing Yiddish adaptations of Talmudic, aggadic, and even Buddhist tales (Mayselekh far Kinder, 1928). Unfortunately, Tashrak (an acronym for the blasts of the ram's horn at Rosh ha-Shona) doesn't indicate the sources of these Buddhist parables.

FIVE STORIES ABOUT BUDDHA, THE INDIAN PROPHET

What is Light?

*T*HERE ONCE LIVED A GREAT SCHOLAR who was thoroughly versed in the holy books. Now this scholar loved arguing with everyone and splitting hairs, and he called everyone a fool and an ignoramus!

He thought the world of himself—the world.

Now one day, this great scholar went out in the street, carrying a lantern in broad daylight. Since it was a bright and sunny day, people were surprised that the scholar was carrying a lantern. But no one dared ask him, for they knew that nobody could bring hjm around, and that if anyone asked him, he would call that person: "Ignoramus! Moron!"

However, there was one man, a very simple man, who was not intimidated, for everyone knew anyway that he was uneducated, but he was decent and intelligent by nature. This man gathered his courage and asked the scholar:

"Could you please explain to me, an ignorant man, why you carry a lantern in broad daylight?"

"I do so because the world is dark, you idiot!" the scholar shouted. "And I'm looking for light!"

"I feel really sorry," said the ignorant but intelligent man. "I feel really sorry for a great scholar like yourself who can't see the radiant sun which shines on all of us equally."

"Where is the sun?" the scholar asked.

And the ignorant man replied: "Your arrogance has blinded you to the light of the world. You should know that this sun which I see shines not only in the sky but also in the hearts of all people who love one another and regard one another as brothers."

The Prophet's Farm Work

Radvaja, a wealthy farmer, was once celebrating the harvest festival, and he was delighted with the bumper crops of his fields.

During the celebration, the prophet Buddha arrived, holding his beggar's bowl in his hand.

"You'd do better," said the farmer, "if you worked for a living rather than begging. Look, I plow and I sow, and that's why I've got food. Do the same, and you'll have food too."

And the prophet replied:

"Well, my lord, I also plow and sow, and that's how I obtain food."

"Are you a farmer?" asked the farmer. "Where are your oxen? Where are your seed and your hook plow?"

"Faith is the seed that I sow," the prophet replied. "Good deeds are the rain that makes my seed grow. Wisdom and humility are the hook plow, my intelligence is the handle and the reins, and my constant striving is the ox that pulls my hook plow. The fruits of my fields are the afterlife."

The wealthy farmer then filled a golden bowl with rice and milk and handed it to the prophet, saying: "May the teacher of people eat his fill, for his hook plow yields fruits that live forever."

The Burning Palace

A RICH MAN LIVED IN A PALACE. The palace was very large but also very old. The walls and the columns were rotted and the roof was very dry. One day, while sitting there, the rich man smelled smoke. He dashed outdoors and saw that the entire building was ablaze. The man then remembered that his children were playing inside the palace, and he shuddered.

The terrified father stood there, not knowing what to do. He heard his children running about indoors and jumping and shouting merrily and cheerfully. He knew that if he told them the palace was on fire, they wouldn't believe him. They'd think he wanted them to play outdoors. And if he dashed into the building and grabbed just one child at a time, he'd be unable to save the others, who'd scoot away from him and be lost in the flames.

Suddenly the father had a wonderful idea. "My children love toys," he mused. "If I promise them some beautiful playthings, they'll obey me."

He now yelled: "C'mon children! Look at the lovely presents your father has brought you! Why, you've never seen such wonderful toys in all your lives! Come out as fast as you can!"

And lo and behold! Children came running from all parts of the burning palace. They were mesmerized by the word "toys," and their good father had bought them some marvelous playthings. But the children then ignored their presents, they gaped at the fire and they realized what great danger they had been in. They thanked their intelligent and loving father, who had saved them from certain death.

The prophet is well acquainted with human children, and he tells them that if they are good, they will receive good things, and that is how he saves them from evil.

And there are times when the children see the great danger that the prophet has saved them from, and they praise his name.

The Blind Man

A MAN WHO'D BEEN BLIND SINCE BIRTH and had never seen the light of the world once said:

"I don't believe there are such things as light and colors, I don't believe that there are white people and black people. I don't believe that grass is green and that there are white flowers and yellow and red and blue flowers. No one has proven their existence to me, and if there's something no one can prove, I am not obligated to believe it exists."

A friend began arguing with the blind man and getting him to grasp what eyesight means.

"You've simply talked yourself into believing those things," said the man who'd been blind since birth. "If day and night existed, I'd be able to touch them with my hands."

A Luxurious Life

WHEN BUDDHA WENT INTO THE WORLD, teaching people to be decent and just, he eventually reached a town where the citizens came out to welcome him and bow to him.

However, there was a rich man who did not bow, and he said to the prophet: "The prophet must forgive me. I'm too fat and I can barely move on my feet."

"Would you like to know why that is?" Buddha asked.

"Yes," said the rich man. "And perhaps the prophet can teach me how to find a cure."

"There are five things that lead to a condition like yours," the prophet explained. "Too much food, too much sleep, too much pleasure-seeking, too little work, and too little thought. Control your appetite for food and everything else, and you'll become a normal human being."

A few years later, Buddha arrived in the same town, and the rich man came out to welcome him like everyone else, bowed like everyone else, and said:

"Great prophet! You healed my body. Now advise me how to heal my mind, so that I can think and grasp everything like all wise and learned men."

And the prophet replied:

"So long as you keep your body healthy, your mind will also remain healthy. For a healthy mind can exist only in a body that is properly cared for and never flouts the laws of nature."

BEN MORDKHE
(?-1946)

Some of the most popular Yiddish folk stories concern the fools of Khelm, the Yiddish Gotham. Khelm itself goes back to Schildburg (1598), the German Gotham, tales about which were translated into Yiddish during the eighteenth century. Eventually, the Yiddish versions, either written or oral, were thoroughly Judaized—to such an extent that very few Yiddish speakers are aware of the German origins. In the modern era, tales and even poems about the Khelmites have been produced by a host of Yiddish authors including Y. Y. Trunk, Yankev Glatshtein, Mani Leib, Yosl Lerner, and M. Kipnis (see *No Star Too Beautiful: A Treasury of Yiddish Literature*).

THE FOOLS OF KHELM
(1928)

The Beadle of Khelm

WHEN KHELM WAS FINALLY DONE with everything a Jewish town should have, when its beautiful synagogue was completed, as well as its graveyard and its bathhouse (if you'll forgive my mentioning them in the same breath), the inhabitants decided to hire a beadle. This beadle would serve the town and knock on the window shutters when it was time to call out the congregants for special prayers.

Well, they found a very fine man and they hired him as their beadle. When the beadle viewed everything in the synagogue, he saw that the stove was very beautiful. And he thought to himself: "This is no good. Some day, thieves will come and carry it off."

What did the beadle do? He took a piece of chalk and wrote out a Hebrew sentence on the stove: "This stove belongs to the great synagogue of Khelm." This calmed the beadle down, and he stopped worrying about thieves.

When the Khelmites saw what their beadle had done, they were delighted and they praised him to the skies. One said to the other: "Now that's what I call a loyal beadle!" And all they talked about was the beadle's loyalty. But they didn't know how to reward him.

Finally, however, an opportunity presented itself.

When the beadle grew old and feeble and could no longer go and knock on the shutters, the Khelmites took down all the shutters in town and brought them to the synagogue.

"Just look, our loyal beadle," they said to him. "Knock on the shutters right here, and that will save you the trouble of trudging through the snow on your feeble legs."

The Rabbi of Khelm

KHELM HAD A GREAT RABBI. He was truly a learned sage, as is fitting for such a fine congregation. But there was one thing wrong: no Khelmite knew whether or not the rabbi had a head.

What was the cause of this ignorance?

It was quite simple. The rabbi had once vanished from the town, and no one could tell what had become of him. So the Khelmites set out to find him. They looked high and low until they found a headless man lying in a field. So they put on their thinking caps:

If the rabbi had a head, then this man wasn't the rabbi. But if the rabbi had no head, then this man must be their rabbi. The Khelmites mulled and mulled but they reached no conclusion.

So they went to ask the beadle, who had always served the rabbi.

And the beadle replied:

"To tell you the truth, I'm not sure whether or not he had a head (may he rest in peace!). He was always wrapped up in his prayer shawl, and I could see only what was below it."

So the Khelmites went to ask the bathhouse owner.

And the bathhouse owner replied:

"Frankly, I lashed him with switches every Friday. But he used to lie on the top bench, which was filled with thick steam, and all I could see was his feet."

So they went to ask the rabbi's wife.

And she replied:

"All I know is that my husband (may he swell in paradise!) had a nose. For on the eve of Sabbath, he would always prepare some snuff. But I don't know whether or not he had a head."

And even today, the Khelmites still don't know whether or not their rabbi had a head.

The Scribe of Khelm

*K*HELM ALSO HAD A SCRIBE. And he was smart and successful like all the clerics and congregants of Khelm. One day they found him writing a note in huge letters. So they asked him:

"Why are you writing in such huge letters?"

The scribe replied:

"Well, you see. I'm writing to my uncle, and the poor man (Heaven help us) is deaf in both ears."

The Preacher of Khelm

1

*O*NCE THERE WAS A PREACHER, and he gave sermons every Sabbath and on holy days and often during the week. And his sermons were as sweet as honey. The Khelmites were delighted. And the preacher himself was strong and healthy (knock on wood), and the whole town was happy.

But one day, the preacher got sick and went to bed. So much for his preaching. Gone were his honey-sweet sermons.

The Khelmites were down in the dumps. They couldn't understand what was wrong with their beloved preacher. Nor did they know what medicine to give him.

So the congregants had a meeting. And they met and mulled for seven days and seven nights. One man said the preacher had an ague. Another man said he had a bad heart. A third man said something else. A fourth man said something different. To make a long story short: they decided to take the patient to a big city and consult a great physician.

No sooner said than done. They rented a wagon and put the preacher inside it. They also sent along the beadle to serve the preacher and talk to the great doctor.

They arrived at the doctor's office, and the beadle explained: "Our preacher was strong and healthy. He gave sermons on the Sabbath and on holy days and during the week. Everything was good. But then suddenly he fell sick, and no one knows what's wrong with him."

The doctor examined the beadle and said:

"It's nothing. He should go to the country, get some fresh air, and stroll through the grass and the fields. That will cure him."

2

When the patient and the beadle returned to Khelm, the Khelmites all had a meeting to hear what the beadle had to say.

And he explained: "The preacher has to be among trees and fields and grasses."

The Khelmites were astonished: "Well, we know that castor oil is good for a tummy ache, exorcising an evil eye is good for a headache. But what kind of remedies are fields and grasses? And what kind of disease can be cured with fields and grasses? Go know!"

So the Khelmites met and mulled for seven days and seven nights. One man said: "The disease." Another man said: "Another disease." They mulled and they mulled but they reached no conclusion. Suddenly, the teacher at the Jewish elementary school sat up and he banged on the table and shouted: "Listen! I know what that's all about! Fields and grasses are a remedy for a calf that's still in its mother's womb. I remember that when my black cow was about to give birth, I was advised to send her out to the countryside, where there's fine grass and pastures. That means that our preacher is about to give birth to a calf."

The Khelmites were stunned by their teacher's great wisdom, and they were also delighted that their beloved preacher was about to give birth to a calf.

So they met for another seven days and seven nights, wondering what to do. At last, they decided that all the boys should attend only this teacher's elementary school so as to acquire his wisdom. And as for the preacher, he was to move in with the village Jew out in the countryside. There the preacher would be in the open fields and fine pastures until he bore his calf.

After reaching that decision, Khelm simply danced for joy.

3

So they rented a wagon. Then they put in the preacher and the beadle, so that the beadle could serve the patient until the happy moment when the calf would be born—oh, happy day! Once the happy moment arrived, the beadle was to bring the glad tidings to Khelm.

The preacher and the beadle arrived in the countryside. The beadle and the villager agreed on a price for the preacher's room and board, and the preacher started living in the fresh air, the fat pastures, and he ate with a hearty appetite. The preacher grew fatter and rounder. His face grew fuller and shinier, and his belly grew bigger and bulkier. The beadle watched this growth and was proud of the preacher and grew more and more impatient for the coming happy moment.

And finally the happy moment arrived.

One fine morning, the beadle woke up and looked in on the preacher, who was sound asleep on another bed. The beadle looked again. Aha! A red calf with a white spot on its forehead was lying on the clay floor next to the preacher's bed. The calf had just seen the light of day. It squinted, unfamiliar as it was with the light. Its temples quivered—a sign that the calf could not yet endure the cool air.

The beadle instantly realized what had occurred. He jumped off his bed, quickly pulled on the *arbe-kanfes*, an undergarment worn by Orthodox Jews, leaped into his trousers, and clutched his shoes because he didn't want to waste time slipping into them. Full speed ahead, he carried the glad tidings to Khelm.

"Mazel-tov!" the beadle yelled at the top of his lungs as he dashed through the streets, waving his shoes like a flag. "Mazel-tov! Our preacher has born a calf! Mazel-tov!"

The news soon spread all over Khelm, and all the homes and streets were filled with great joy. The teachers let their charges leave early. Housewives started preparing expensive holiday meals, and all the respectable congregants visited their beadles and rabbi to wish them "Mazel-tov!"

The Khelmites instantly gathered for a meeting in the congregation's meeting hall, and they raised their glasses in honor of this great holy day and wished the preacher and his calf "Le-Khaim!"

Then they earnestly pondered what to do next. However, there was no time to ponder for long, and the congregants decided: Since the preacher had survived everything safe and sane, they would throw a huge banquet for the entire town, and the rabbi and his trustees and the worthy congregants were to lead the preacher and his calf into the town with great pomp and circumstance, with singing and dancing and music, and take the preacher and his calf to the huge banquet.

4

The rabbi, his trustees, and the worthy congregants put on their Sabbath best and, accompanied by the town klezmers, they set out into the countryside.

When they reached the villager's home, they found the preacher strong and healthy. His face was glowing, his eyes were shining. As for the calf: well, it had gotten stronger throughout the day and more and more used to the world. It stood very solidly on its little legs, nicely wagging its tail and springing about like a full-grown calf.

Upon seeing this, the Khelmites were delighted. They toasted the preacher —"Le-Khaim!"—they shouted "Le-Khaim" again, and there was no end to their joy. Next, they headed back to town. But first they gathered the preacher's things and put them in the wagon. The preacher sat down on his belongings, and the Khelmites tied the calf's legs together and placed it next to the preacher.

The rabbi and the trustees likewise settled in the wagon, while the rest of the Khelmites clustered around the klezmers, who led the procession with their flutes and drums and fiddles.

"Forward march!" the rabbi commanded them.

The wagon lurched off. Bu then suddenly, the villager came dashing out of his cottage.

"You robbers! What are you doing?! Why are you stealing my calf?"

The Khelmites burst out laughing. They figured that the villager was either crazy or dead-drunk from the toasts. But he dug in his heels: he demanded the return of the calf.

So the rabbi earnestly asked him: "You gross peasant! Where do you see your calf?"

The villager retorted: "What do you mean? The calf that's tied up in your wagon!"

The congregants couldn't contain themselves: "Our preacher—long may he live!—gave birth to this calf!"

The villager tried to prove that he was right. But the Khelmites had lost patience and they yelled at the driver: "Hey! Whip your horse and let's go!"

5

The villager saw that he was in trouble. So he grabbed hold of a wagon wheel and shouted for his wife to come to his rescue. She came out, saw what was happening, grabbed hold of another wheel, and yelled for her daughters to come and rescue them. So the daughters dashed over. They saw what was happening and each daughter grabbed hold of another wheel and they hollered at the tops of their lungs.

The Khelmites were terrified! Pulling up their coattails, they scurried away! The only people remaining were the passengers in the wagon: the preacher, the rabbi, the trustees, and the calf.

The rabbi realized that they had to come to terms with the villager. And he said:

"Listen, villager, what do you want from us?"

And the villager replied:

"I don' want nothin' from you! Give me my calf and then leave for all I care."

"What right do you have to a calf that was born to our preacher?"

The villager replied:

"No, no! Not the preacher! My piebald cow gave birth to this calf!"

A new riot ensued. The villager and his family argued that their cow had given birth to the calf, and the Khelmites argued that their preacher had given birth to the calf.

They argued and argued, but they couldn't come to terms. Finally, they hit on a plan: they were to find two arbitrators, and the litigants would abide by their decision.

They brought in two arbitrators: they were from the countryside but they were also the grandsons of Khelmites and therefore, needless to say, great sages.

The arbitrators said:

"Everyone knows that a calf is drawn to its mother. We'll put the piebald cow on one side of the courtyard and the preacher on the other. The calf will stand off at a distance. If the calf runs over to the cow, it will mean that the cow is the mother. But if the calf runs over to the preacher, it will mean that he gave birth to the calf."

The rabbi and the trustees liked this decision, and they were utterly astonished at the wisdom of the arbitrators.

6

Their advice was carried out. They took the preacher down from the wagon and had him stand to the right. Then they had the cow stand to the left and the calf on the far side of the courtyard. They whipped the calf. The calf sprang and ran over to where the preacher of Khelm was standing.

This convinced everyone that the calf belonged to the preacher. Even the villager and his wife and daughters had to admit that their argument was entirely unjust. What could they do?

They also got into the wagon with the preacher and the rabbi and the trustees and the calf, and the wagon rolled off to the town. They arrived at the huge banquet, and everyone had a wonderful time. They ate and drank all night long, and they praised and lauded the wonderful wisdom of the Khelmites, and they couldn't get enough of the good fortune of their preacher, who had given birth to a calf.

ANONYMOUS

❧

In 1930, the prolific Yiddish folklorist Y. L. Kahan spent two days in the Austrian province of Burgenland, visiting the Jewish communities there and recording Yiddish folk songs and folktales. This material was then published the following year (*Yivo Bleter*, Vol. II, 1931, Vilna). Here are stories he gathered, mainly from teenagers, in these outposts of Western Yiddish. Some narratives are specifically Jewish, some derive from the international folklore repertoire, some are a blend of both sources.

These communities were doomed: In 1938, Nazi Germany invaded Austria.

FOLKTALES FROM BURGENLAND, AUSTRIA
(1930)

A Tale about an Old Woman with Lots of Children

*T*HERE WAS ONCE AN OLD WOMAN who had lots and lots of children. One day she said to them: "Children, behave. I'm going into town and I'm going to bring you something lovely."

When the old woman had left, the children locked themselves in the house. The wolf instantly came by and crooned: "Children, children, open up!" The children were frightened and they kept silent. The wolf crooned a second time: "Children, children, open up!"

The children hid themselves: one under the table and one under the bed, one behind the chest and one behind the stove. So the wolf broke down the door, found all the children, and gobbled all of them up. But there was one child he couldn't find, the child who had crept behind the stove. The wolf then went out and fell asleep in front of the house.

When the old woman came back, the surviving child told her the whole story. The old woman then took a knife and cut open the wolf's belly, and all the children jumped out and they shouted:

Hey ho!

Hey ho!

The wolf

Is dead!

Sometimes a Curse Is a Blessing

*T*HERE WAS ONCE A COUPLE who lived in a village, and they had no children. One day a rabbi came and he wanted to spend the Sabbath there. The master of the house and the lady of the house showed him a great deal of respect, and they served him good food and drink. Then, on Sunday morning, the host gave the rabbi a generous donation. The rabbi blessed them, wishing them disturbed nights and disturbed meals. And then he set out again.

When he was gone, the hostess dashed after him. "Rabbi, were you dissatisfied with the alms? Is that why you cursed us?"

The rabbi laughed: "I gave you a blessing so that God would give you children. In a house with children, there are disturbed nights and disturbed meals. Sometimes a child cries at night, and his parents are disturbed. And sometimes a child throws down a glass, and so a meal is disturbed. And those are purely blessings when you have children."

A Letter to God

*O*NCE THERE WAS A POOR JEW named Fayshl. He had lots of children and a wife. Passover was coming, but Fayshl didn't have enough money to celebrate. So his wife said: "Listen, my husband. Sell our bedclothes, then we'll have enough to celebrate Passover."

Fayshl replied: "What should we cover the matzos with? I'll try something else. I'll write God a letter, telling Him that if the Lord God wants me to celebrate Passover, he should help me to do so."

Dear Fayshl wrote God a Yiddish letter and sent it floating through the air, and it wound up at the door of a Gentile judge. His servants brought him the letter. The judge opened the letter and he saw that it was a Yiddish letter. He couldn't read it, so he sent his servant over to summon the head of the Jewish community. The head of the community read to the judge the letter that Fayshl had written to God: "If the Lord God wants him to celebrate Passover, he should help him to do so."

The judge took ten ducats and told his servant to take the money to

Fayshl. Fayshl was beside himself with joy! Finally, when he calmed down, he said to his wife: "You know, Khayle, my child! Goodness only knows what the judge shaved off for himself—I'm sure that God sent me a lot more!"

The Count and the Jew

ONCE THERE WAS A POOR JEW, and there was a count who always helped him and gave him alms. But the Jew always said:

"God Blessed Be His Name has helped me—that's who."

One day, when Passover was approaching, the Jew believed that the count would again be giving alms for Passover. So the Jew went to see the count. The count was very friendly to him, but he didn't give him anything for Passover, because he was deeply offended that the Jew always said: "God Blessed Be His Name has helped me—that's who!"

When the Jew came home, his wife was expecting the money. But he had nothing. So she wept and wailed because she had nothing to celebrate Passover with.

Now the count had a monkey, whom he dearly loved. And the count always gave the monkey lots of gold pieces to play with, and the monkey always swallowed them. Now one night, after the monkey died, the count's servant threw the monkey's corpse into the Jew's house. The Jew saw that something was wrong. So he lifted up the monkey, and a gold piece fell out of the corpse. He lifted it up again, and another gold piece fell out. So the Jew said: "God has helped us!" And he became very rich.

The Grateful Corpse

ONCE, A RABBI WAS USHERING out the Sabbath with the traditional final meal, and they were singing "He Who separates between holy and profane." And they heard the Hebrew word "khol" (profane) in advance. They wondered where the word came from. So one boy offered to find out. He walked into the forest and shouted, "He Who separates between holy . . . !" And he kept hearing the word "profane" from inside the forest. So he kept walking for three days. All at once he came to a house and he shouted into it: "He Who separates between holy . . . !" Then, from inside, he heard the word "profane." So he went inside and he shouted again: "He Who separates between holy . . . !" And again he heard the word "profane." So he asked: "Who's inside here? Who's shouting the word 'profane'? Then he spotted a heap of bones, a corpse lying there, and the bones said: "I'm the one who's been shouting 'profane.' You have to bury me outside, and I'll reward you for that." And so the boy buried the corpse.

One day, the king's daughter was strolling, and an eagle came and carried her away. The king announced that whoever found his daughter would marry her and get half the kingdom. So the boy told the rabbi that he wanted to go and look for the king's daughter. And the rabbi replied that if the boy wasn't afraid, he could go.

The boy climbed up the mountain, there where the eagle lived, and the boy spotted the king's daughter and he went over to her and he said: "I'm going to marry you and I'll teach you Jewish prayers, and you are going to be my wife."

And that was what happened. The boy then gathered the skins of the various animals that the eagle had eaten and he tied them together like a rope and he lowered the king's daughter. However, there was a swineherd down below and he took the king's daughter and he went to the king and said that he had found her. Then the boy lowered himself, but as he was halfway down, the rope snapped, and when the boy was falling, a hand came out of the mountain and it grabbed him. And the boy was frightened and he shouted: "Let me go!" But the hand said: "I'm the person you buried." And the hand pulled him into the mountain and lowered him.

And when the boy came into the city, he saw that the king's daughter was about to get married. So the boy went to the wedding, and when the king's daughter saw the boy, she collapsed. So they asked her why she'd collapsed, and she said: "That boy saved me, so he should become my husband."

The swineherd was then beaten to death, and the boy married the king's daughter, and they live in great bliss and joy even today.

A Tale about a Little Boy and an Old Man

ONCE THERE WERE A MAMA AND A PAPA. They had an only child, a boy, and they were very poor. The papa was a woodchopper.

One day the boy went into the forest, and there he saw an old man carrying a huge load of wood. The little boy felt sorry for the old man and he took the wood from his back and carried it to the old man's cottage in the middle of the forest. The old man was very happy, and when the boy was leaving, the old man gave him something wrapped in paper and he said: "Open it up at home."

When the boy left the cottage and turned around, he couldn't see it anymore. So he instantly realized that the old man was the prophet Elijah. The boy went home and unwrapped the object that the old man had given him. Inside the paper he found a small menorah with a tiny chime, and the writing on the paper said: "So long as the boy grows, the menorah will also grow, and whenever the boy goes to town, the chime will ring."

One day, the papa went into the forest to chop some wood. And the mama gave the boy lunch to take to his papa. The boy started out but then he got lost in the forest. He kept walking and walking until nightfall and he kept crying. Now that it was night, he fell asleep. And in the morning, he kept walking, until he came to a huge desert. But he couldn't find his way out because the desert was so huge. The boy cried and he ate the fruit growing on trees. The wild beasts didn't touch him. And all day long, he studied a small Pentateuch that he had. And several years went by.

One Chanukah, the boy, who was now big, remembered his papa and his mama, and he was homesick and he cried. And when he started off again, the old man stood in front of him, the old man who had given him the menorah. And now, the old man took the boy's hand and said to him: "Because you were so good to me, I'll show you the way home." And the old man whistled, and the two of them rose into the air and quickly flew away.

Meanwhile, the boy's parents were still crying for their only child. They believed that he was no longer alive. And all at once, when the mama went to prepare the Chanukah candles, she heard something from the chest, she heard a big chime ringing. She was very frightened because she didn't know what it was. So she looked into the rags inside the chest, and there she found a big menorah with a big chime. She quickly called her husband, and they promptly remembered how their boy had gotten the menorah, which was standing on the paper, and the two of them quickly said: "Ah! Our boy is still alive and he's come into the town." That moment, someone knocked on the door, and then their son walked in, and they saw that he was a great scholar because he had kept studying the Pentateuch, and they promptly sat down and spun the *dreydl*, the Chanukah top.

And if they haven't passed away, then they are still alive today.

Dora Shulner
(1889-?)

Dora Shulner, born in the Kiev Province and immigrating to America after World War I, began publishing stories in Yiddish periodicals in 1940. Aside from several auto-biographical novels, she mostly wrote realistic stories about her native and her adopted lands. Like most Yiddish writers, no matter how realistic, Shulner penned several tales with folk motifs. The *shekhinah*, an ancient Jewish motif, is the visual manifestation of God's presence. For a detailed study of this concept, try "Shekhinah: the Feminine Element in Divinity" in: Gershom Scholem's *On The Mystical Shape of the Godhead* (New York, 1991 [translated by J.N.]). Shulner's two stories translated below are from her collection *Milthin* (1946). Their awkwardness in narrative and diction makes them sound like orally transmitted folktales.

THE SHEKHINAH

(in loving memory of H. L. Maytes)

ONCE A REBBE (A HASIDIC RABBI) was traveling through a forest. He was riding in an elegant carriage. His assistant was sitting at his side. The coachman was driving the horses slowly. It was in the month of May. A lovely spring evening was setting in. The birds were about to stop their wondrous singing. The sun was gathering its final rays in a huge fire in the sky. The road was flanked by lofty and fragrant evergreen trees. A cool breeze melted into the bodies of the travelers.

The rebbe sat comfortably in his seat, keeping his eyes closed and listening to the chirping of the birds, which darted from tree to tree, singing God's praises.

Now the rebbe opened his eyes, scanned the distance, and saw that God's creatures were joyful as they crooned their hymns. Amazed at this delight, the rebbe suddenly spotted a cottage on the very end of the woods, and he saw the shekhinah shining on the roof of the cottage. The roof was virtually wrapped in gold. The rebbe wondered who could be living in this cottage. So he ordered the coachman to drive there and he told his assistant to step inside the cottage and find out who lived there. The coachman halted at the cottage door. The assistant vanished inside, and the rebbe gazed at the shekhinah, which encircled the entire cottage like a crown. The rebbe's face was radiant; his snow-white beard, his intelligent eyes, and his entire stature added to his beauty. The coachman felt the rebbe's restlessness. He jumped down from the coach box and fed the horses. Now the assistant reappeared and he told the rebbe that the cottage was inhabited by two Jewish women, a mother and a daughter. They were spinners. They spun linen and sold it in the marketplace. That was their trade.

The rebbe was astonished. The travelers entered the cottage, which was very poor but clean. The loom was standing on the side. The table was covered with a white tablecloth, and there were lovely curtains on the window. The rebbe and his assistant now stood and recited their evening prayers. When they were done, the rebbe said to the mother:

"Tell me, my daughter, what kind of good deeds do you do?"

The mother smiled warmly and said: "Holy man, what sort of good deeds can I do in this out-of-the-way area? I do nothing but work with my child, and we maintain ourselves more or less."

The rebbe then asked her: "But do you keep the Sabbath?"

"No," was the answer. "My dear man, we don't even know when the Sabbath has come."

The rebbe was amazed and he said to the mother: "Listen, my daughter. Make a sign for yourself: the week has six days and the seventh is the Sabbath. And on the sixth day, Friday, you should work only half the day. You should then bless the Sabbath candles. Finally, on the Sabbath, you should do no work at all. You should observe the Sabbath because you are very deserving."

The woman promised that she would do so and with a cheerful face she served the travelers drinks, but no food since they didn't care to eat.

The travelers said good-bye to the two women and rode off, and the rebbe praised God for His gifts, which He distributed to everyone who deserved them.

Somewhat later, the rebbe again wished to see God's beauty in the shekhinah shining on that cottage roof. He told his coachman to harness the horses, and the rebbe and his assistant rode back to see how the two women were keeping the Sabbath and how the shekhinah would be shining there.

They drove to the end of the tiny shtetl, looking for that cottage, but it was nowhere in sight. In his sorrow, the rebbe imagined that the cottage had to be there. He thought he recognized it by the bench standing outside. The rebbe stepped inside: Yes, this was the cottage. The two women were delighted with their guests, but the rebbe was not delighted. He asked them:

"What have you done here?"

The mother said: "Holy rebbe, you told us to count six days and to put away our work on Friday, the sixth day. We blessed the Sabbath candles and we enjoyed the Sabbath. On the seventh day, we went out and sat on the bench. Neighbors came over and sat down on our bench, and we chatted with them. That's what we've been doing on the Sabbath."

The rebbe listened to the mother, then he sighed and said: "It's not your fault, it's mine. I should have told you that when the Sabbath comes, you should unite with God and serve him with love. But because of my silence and my failure to teach you, the shekhinah has vanished from your home."

The rabbi kept silent all the way back. The birds were still singing God's praises, but the rebbe was absorbed in his own thoughts.

THE MILLER AND THE SERPENT
A Folktale

In memory of Rive Gitl Veynshteyn

IN A VILLAGE IN THE PROVINCE OF VOLHYN, there lived a miller with his wife. He was a very honest man and very generous with alms. His wife helped him with his charity. Ten years after their wedding, they were still young, but they had no children as yet. In those days, a husband could divorce his wife if she bore him no children. But the miller loved his wife very deeply and he didn't want a divorce. So they went to ask their Hasidic rebbe for advice.

Back then, travelers rode wagons, and their rebbe lived forty-eight hours away. The wife prepared a lot of good things for the trip. As they rode, they talked about the rebbe, saying that he would, with God's help, give them his blessing, so that they would, God willing, have a son. They both agreed that they would do whatever the rebbe told them to do.

The drayman halted at two inns, and they gradually consumed their provisions. And the miller told everyone that God would help them, and when he and his wife had a child, they would reveal who they were.

They reached the rebbe Thursday morning. The couple was not well off. But they were both very pious. And that was why they were so warmly welcomed by the rebbe. All day Thursday, they had a good time with the rebbe's household, and on Friday morning, after prayers, the rebbe's assistant led the miller and his wife into the rebbe's study.

The rebbe, a wonderful and beautiful man with an intelligent face, a man who commanded respect, asked his guests to sit down and to tell him what they were after.

And so the couple told the rebbe that ten years had passed since their wedding but that they still had no children.

The rebbe smiled heartily and he asked the husband what kind of work he did. The miller replied that he drudged very hard but earned next to nothing. His wife was good to him, and they didn't want a divorce.

The rebbe smiled again and he said: "Why a divorce? Why should you get a divorce? You will, God willing, have a child this very year. The main thing is: have a good rest, don't work so hard, and spend the Sabbath with me." The rebbe then ordered his assistant to tell the rebbetsin, the rebbe's wife, that she should befriend the visiting wife, and the rebbe then told the young man to prepare himself in the bathhouse. And so the Sabbath was very beautiful and sacred.

The couple was in seventh heaven! And on Sunday morning, before saying good-bye to the rebbe, the miller asked him for advice:

"Rebbe, a small serpent has crawled into my porch. It doesn't bother anyone, but at times I'm scared of it, and so is my wife."

The rebbe calmed his fears: "Don't be afraid of any serpent. The serpent may be your luck, but beware of it."

And the couple joyfully said good-bye to the rebbe and they arrived home safe and sound, and the miracle occurred. A child was born to them that same year. And the child brought them lots of good luck. Business improved. A lot of farmers came to the mill from the surrounding villages, and the miller prospered. And the child grew, and the serpent on the porch also grew. And it was miraculous: the child and the serpent became friends. The serpent would coil around the child, and the child would laugh merrily, and his parents were no longer bothered.

But one day, the boy accidentally stepped on the serpent, and the serpent ferociously bit the child. And the child soon died.

And when the miller saw the horror, and his wife fainted in her misery, the miller grabbed an axe and chopped off the serpent's tail. The serpent vanished from the cottage, the child was laid to rest, and the miller and his wife were miserable once again.

Business went down, and the miller recalled the rebbe's warning that they should be wary of the serpent.

In deep sorrow, the miller went to see the rebbe. He arrived bitterly and told the rebbe about the misfortune that had struck the child.

The rebbe attentively heard him out and he gave the miller some advice:

"First of all, forget about the child, you have to forget about him. If you earn the privilege, you will have other children. But your business has to improve. The serpent, I told you, was your success, and you shouldn't have chopped off its tail. But so much for that. Still, I have some more advice," the rebbe went on. "You have to go into the forest, find the serpent, and take it back home with you."

The miller asked: "Holy rebbe, where can I find the serpent?"

The rebbe replied: "You'll find it—after all, it doesn't have a tail. That's how you'll recognize it. Go and look for it in the forest."

The miller promptly went into the forest. He walked through the dense woods, he looked and searched, and he was about to give up the idea of finding the serpent. All at once, he spotted the serpent in a lair. It was lying there, ashamed and gloomy, and the miller joyfully dashed over, bowed meekly, and using the words one uses with a serpent, the miller begged it to come back home with him. He told the serpent about his misery and bitterness. His business had come to a standstill, and the serpent just had to come back with him. "Come with me, come. I'll forgive you! I beg you!"

The serpent let him beg and beg, but finally, it yielded and it agreed to come. It crawled on its belly, and the happy miller walked at its side.

Halfway home, the serpent halted and said to the miller: "No, no, my friend, I can't go to your home. I can't see your sufferings, because you said yourself that I was your luck. And when I enter your home, your luck will start shining, and when you prosper, you will instantly remember your child. But I will never forget my tail. You've injured me forever. It would be best if you went home by yourself. That would be better than going with me."

And before the miller could answer, the serpent started back to its lair.

YITSIK-YOYL LINYETSKY
(1839-1915)

Coming from a Hasidic milieu, Linyetsky grew to hate Hasidism, as viciously shown in his semi-autobiographical novel *The Hasidic Boy* (1867), which, like many narratives of the Jewish Enlightenment, makes extensive use of folklore in order to debunk it and wield satire as the sharpest weapon. The anti-Hasidic humoresque included below is taken from a small collection of Linyetsky's writings, *Der Pritshepe* (*The Quibbler*, Odessa, 1876). Its language is raw, crude, clumsy, as are the overall narratives and characterizations, which, in confusedly groping for a literary diction, sound all the more like folklore. After all, like it or not, the Yiddish writers of the Jewish Enlightenment were seeking access to the "folk," the uneducated Yiddish-speaking masses who could barely read Hebrew.

The untranslatable alphabet song that closes the story is a device rooted in Psalms and also in "Virtuous Joseph" (1382), a verse narrative composed at the dawn of Yiddish literature.

THE HASIDIC STEAM ENGINE
(1876)

*E*VER SINCE I CAME TO MY SENSES—that is, ever since I became a Hasid—several years ago, twenty-five to be exact—I've never understood a certain pronouncement uttered by our Sages (long may they live!). It goes something like this: "Good is Torah with good manners." Well, we know for sure that the word "Torah" here means "Hasidism" (what else!?). Now, at first glance, it may seem like a wild miracle worked upon our Holy Sages. How can they claim that good is Hasidism with good manners? The very opposite is true! They should say: "Good is Torah (may the merciful God save Hasidism!) without good manners." What connection does Hasidism have with good manners? You can ask all our Hasids (according to any investigation), and they will reply that the whole of Hasidism is based on wildness, and the man who is preoccupied with worldly matters is a true atheist—that is, a heretic in regard to the faith of the Sages—who openly profanes Hasidism!

And so we are clearly led to believe that ever since the establishment of Hasidism all our Hasids have been nothing but idlers, loafers, fantasists, gossip-mongers, freeloaders, and wild men. And, so we hear, we know nothing about any worldly matter here and there—and do not want to know (may we pray!), and that is our glory! But quite the contrary! Let just one of the educated enlighteners produce even one fact that we are not what I say we are! Forget it! Not a chance in a million! The whole world knows that not even one of our Hasids wastes so much as a minute thinking about his family, his congregation's problems, or the community at large! Nor does any Hasid think about all the stupid philosophers in Berlin, the followers of that Enlightener, Moses Mendelsohn—not by a long shot! Aside from anything new they might offer in the world of action, they are opposed to Hasidism! Furthermore, we know plainly that all their ideas and devices are nothing but vanities upon vanities upon vanities as opposed to the least invention by the least wonderful Jew. And I don't even want to mention our rebbe—who starts preparing for the Sabbath as early as Wednesday! If I tell you a few surprising things about our Hasids, you'll be confused and astounded and you'll know on your own that your philosophical brains are totally incapable of grasping our wonders!

Imagine, say, the following:

A Jew is performing his ritual hand-washing, preparing for a meal, as he stands with a dipper full of water over a slop tub. He's already washed one hand and he still has to wash the other hand. But the dipper has only one handle. Now according to Jewish law, he can't hold the dipper with his washed hand, because the handle is unclean from the unwashed hand. Shouldn't he take the handle with his washed hand? After all, he is worried that a drop of water might drip down from the unwashed hand into the dipper, and the drop is already unclean. Now if the Jew washes his other hand, won't he be washing with unclean water? The Jew, poor man, is truly scared. He stands there, clutching his dipper, not knowing what to do. And meanwhile the poor man is starving to death!

Now tell me: what could all your crude and clumsy philosophers do to prevent the Jew from suffering that torment? What crap! They are expert morons! They send eighteen telegrams with forty locomotives—which are the same with or without them! And with such a crucial issue, such an important business as washing the hands with a blessing—their wisdom peters out! However, one of our Hasids invented a vessel with two handles! Now what do you say to that? You're amazed, aren't you? Just wait! Let me show you a stunning miracle!

Imagine, say, a Jew who drudges practically all year long in order to celebrate Passover. And then, on the eve of Passover, he labors with both the members of the household and the demons. When he finally comes home from synagogue, he slips into the traditional smock, settles on the traditional Passover couch, and he's thoroughly exhausted as well as shattered, hungry, and sleepy. He then hands out the Passover ware, hoping to have a bite that much sooner. In the midst of everything, stop! The poor man has been standing there for just about an hour, clutching the traditional shank bone and not knowing where to place it! On the right, as the Bible says, or on the left, as that one says.

Well, my dear engineers, think of some way that Jews can avoid a lot of torment. Believe me! It's no small matter deciding where to put the shank bone! Why, it affects the entire community! It's a lot more preferable to your thousand threshing machines and water pipes. A bunch of crap! There you have it—your stupid brain has dried up! The very opposite of our people! Even a Misnagid, an anti-Hasid, promptly hits on the solution! If you place the shank bone in the middle, you can satisfy both sides! So what do you say there? Do we need your stupidity since you won't measure up to even the slightest Misnagid, much less to a Hasid, much less to the rebbe himself?!

Now if I tell you something, you will become null and void, as worthless as a garlic skin with all your wisdom! Take, say, the following task. Imagine an awful situation. It's a winter night, the frost is raging, the snow is one ell deep, and the rebbe and a minyan (a quorum of ten) are standing outdoors, waiting for the new moon to emerge from the dark clouds so that they can bless it. They wait for a quarter of an hour, half an hour, three quarters of an hour, finally a whole hour. They have long since finished the meal that ushers out the Sabbath and they are wearing nothing but thin caftans. In short, they are freezing to death, and the moon still won't emerge. And it's already the last night that they can sanctify the new moon!

Now I ask you: what can you crude philosophers come up with to prevent those poor, naked Hasids from dying of cold? The rebbe isn't afraid of the cold, because for one thing he is always surrounded by the heat of a pillar of fire. For another thing, he is wearing a good fox fur coat and warm shoes. Aha! You're holding your tongues. Nobody stays home when such a crucial and profound ceremony as the blessing of the new moon takes place!

When the hour is up, the rebbe—long may he live!—stands there for another ten minutes, deeply absorbed—and suddenly, he emits a wild and joyful shout: "Haha! Haha! Miracles! Divine help! We've known for a long time that the moon is a haughty creature! But on the sixth day of Creation, the moon already lodged a complaint with God, stating that two monarchs cannot reign under one crown. Haha! Divine help! If the moon is truly so haughty, let's incite her by talking to her until she proves that she is older and stronger than we! Haha! Miracles of the Creator!

"Now, children, quote the following Hebrew sentence in unison: 'Just as we dance across from you, and we cannot touch you, so too you cannot touch us!'"

Imagine the achievement! The moon then really and truly shows up in her glory and splendor! Now is that only for your teensy brains? Wait a bit, and you'll enjoy an even greater surprise than our people!

Imagine: a rich man in Kodnye built a brick house. And when the house was completed, it was time to move in. But meanwhile, a gang of demons had settled there, and they spent every night dancing and prancing and throwing stones, which made it impossible for anyone to approach the house!

As is customary, the owner of the house asked the Preacher of Kodnye for help and he paid him 412 silver rubles. The preacher entered the house and tried exorcising the demons by using the Divine Name and tatters of books owned by his holy ancestors. "May the heretics rot! May they leave this house immediately and go back to the other side of the Sambatyon River!"

But the demons didn't hear him and they explicitly stated that they wouldn't leave this house because the owner, while building it, had failed to place talismans in the basement. The house was therefore unclean—which made it an ideal place for demons! So what kind of advice can you ardent philosophers provide in order to prevent rebuilding the entire house just because of the talismans? And how can you stop the demons from exercising their control? Huh? How can you? You do admit that all your stupid machines are worthless in regard to a matter serving the entire community.

In his divine wisdom, the Preacher of Kodnye (R.I.P.) told one of his escorts to bring him a pipe, tobacco, and a match. When these objects were brought to him, the preacher took the pipe and the match and said to the crowd:

"It is well-known that the demons have never broken their word. Haha! You living father! Now you will see wonders of Creation!"

And as he spoke, the preacher turned to the demons: "I implore you to leave and stay away until I finish smoking this pipe and, after that, I will let you revel here forever!"

The demons agreed and went away. Well, and what did the great preacher do? Instead of smoking the pipe, he stored it in a cupboard and said that as long as the house was to stand, no one was to move the pipe from where it was.

Do you crude minds understand such divine shrewdness? As long as the pipe was not smoked, the demons had no power over the house. So what do we need your stupidity, your worldliness, your crude devices against such heavenly things?! . . .

Now if I may ask: How come our sages (R.I.P.) say: "Good is Torah (Heaven forfend!) with good manners"? I've been torturing myself now for twenty-five years, trying to understand that unpleasant statement, according to Hasidic law—and it remained beyond my grasp until a few years ago.

You see, the rebbe (long may he live!) had to flee across the border, and our entire flock escorted him all the way. And that was the first time in our lives that we ever rode in a train. The rebbe (long may he live!) lay in a bunk, like a High Priest, in the innermost place—and I and Shmarye were deeply absorbed in the engine. A wild dispute arose between us.

"Well, Shmarye," I said. "Just tell me what that is!"

"Why don't you, Itsik, tell me what that is!"

"No, Shmarye, you tell me first! Then I'll tell you!"

"You tell me first, then I'll tell you!"

"What will you tell me?"

"What will you tell me, then?"

"I want to hear what you have to say! Then I'll know what to say!"

"And when I hear what you have to say, I'll know what to say!"

"What do you want to hear from me?"

"What do you want to hear from me?"

"What do you mean? I want to hear from you what that is!"

"And I want to hear from you what that is!"

And so our dispute raged on for some thirty minutes until our minds were upside down from all that investigating! . . . I now decided that I was truly dealing with an unclean force of the world of demons! And there wasn't much to think about! But Shmarye (R.I.P.) was delving deeply and he said to me:

"Listen, Itsik, all this monotonous blabbering and jabbering are only for form's sake—all talk and no action! And the whole force that pushes the monstrous machine is hidden by a great secret. You probably know the following story about the Baal-Shem-Tov, the beloved founder of our Hasidism —may he rest in peace!

"One day, while traveling, he spread his belt across a wide river and walked over the water. Well, now the legend is clearer! The fools, the philosophers, heard about this feat and so they disguised themselves as Hasids and came to visit the Baal-Shem-Tov one night—may he rest in peace! They pretended to come for prayers, but actually they stole the belt! That night, you, see, the Baal-Shem-Tov happened to be away. His mind was immersed in divine matters—like Joshua's mind when the sun had halted in the sky during his battle with the Gibeonites! . . . Well, what do you think? The thieves soon cut up the belt in a million bits and they placed a patch under every boat. And this drove the boats to the ends of the earth."

The story moved me deeply and I took it as the whole truth, beyond all doubt! However, on the way, we again had to board the train. And when I looked at the locomotive, I shouted for my Shmarye—may he rest in peace!—with a wild miracle:

"Well, Shmarye, what do you say now? The Baal-Shem-Tov's belt is able to push a boat only across water, and here we are moving across dry land!"

Shmarye pondered for a quarter hour. Then he swore on a stack of Bibles that when the rebbe was traveling, he was virtually wearing the seven-league boots and could cover long distances within moments at a time! But Gedalya took an oath and he explained to us that all the pushing was due to the fact that the entire rails had been deliberately laid at an angle, so that if you gave the carriages a single push, they would all dash with impetus! . . .

"How is that possible?" Shmarye broke in (may he rest in peace!)! "How do the carriages get back to their own line?"

"Listen," said Gedalya, waving his hand. "What don't you understand? There are probably a few quorums at both ends of the line, and they lift up or put down the lines for the comings and the goings."

"Hey, hey, hey!" said Paltyel, my uncle's son-in-law. "Gedalya is also absorbed in philosophy—God forbid! And in my opinion, there's no substance in regard to all that running!'

"Oh, c'mon!" exclaimed Nokhem. "We can clearly see that it does have a substance! Look for yourself. After all, the distance between Zadkivets and Konele comes to some hundred twenty miles, and we reached Konele within one hour!"

"Now, listen!" said Paltyel. "This too is purely visual evidence! So it has no substance!"

"You fool!" Gedalya hit the roof! "How is that possible? Why, I personally checked the rebbe's watch, and that's proof enough!"

"Listen!" said Paltyel, waving his hand. "A watch is no visual proof!" Upon saying those words, we were joined that very minute by our Sholem-Shakhne, who boomed like thunder:

"You miscreant! You heretic! According to you, our rebbe carries a lie in his breast pocket! Huh? Oh, fools, fools! Have you taken leave of your senses—arguing about such stupid matters!? A newborn child could grasp all this!"

We all gaped at our Sholem-Shakhne for we know that he is an ardent and fervent Hasid, and if he says something then he must know whereof he speaks.

Sholem-Shakhne gaped at us, furrowed his brow slightly, and then said: "Morons, morons! You can see for yourselves that all those engines run on the energy of pure smoke—on steam! Well, so why are you surprised? Why are you amazed that smoke has the strength to push millions of pounds?! Just where are your eyes? Huh? Figure it out! What is the source of all those engines? Where did the miscreants, the philosophers learn that smoke has the strength to push an enormous weight? Huh? Where? They must have learned it from our rebbe—long may he live! You see it every day and you don't even notice it! Oh, how shameful! You don't see the rebbe's pipe every day? Huh?! Well, you morons! Why, his pipe was the first steam engine in the world! And the rebbe uses it every day to transport the sinful souls as well as the prayers and requests to Heaven. And to carry the steam engine back down for blessings and successes! With that power, the rebbe can build new worlds and destroy them. With that power he can transform the whole of nature! The rebbe's pipe is a line of communication with the archangel Michael! It is a telegram linking the rebbe and the Good Lord! The rebbe's pipe is everything, and everything is in his pipe!

"So why are you morons so astonished that smoke can push millions of tons? You can see that smoke can push spirituality into the supreme elevation of the Cabbala! And the world is full of that power! Yes, yes, my brothers! The rebbe's pipe has produced all the thousands of steam engines! And it's stupid to be surprised at them!"

We were dumbstruck by Sholem-Shakhne's words and we tried to figure out where we might be. And now I finally understood the utterance: "Good is Torah (may the merciful God have mercy on Hasidism) with good manners." For without good manners—that is, if I hadn't accompanied the rebbe on his journey and seen all those worldly things—I would never ever have found out how deep and great an instrument the rebbe's pipe is!

And at this point, our entire flock gathered together in ecstatic rapture, and we crooned an acrostic alphabet song in honor of our rebbe and his divine pipe!

MENDELE MOYKHER SFORIM
(?1836–1917)

In his poker-faced, tongue-in-cheek "analysis" of a Biblical tale that has become a popular folk story, the "grandfather" of modern Yiddish and Hebrew literature draws on a gamut of pseudo-interpretations.

THE FISH THAT SWALLOWED THE PROPHET JONAH
(Late nineteenth century)

AMID ALL THE GREAT MARVELS and miracles that have occurred since the Creation of the world, there is a wonderful tale that took place three thousand years ago. Indeed, it was so sensational that ever since that time, countless scholars haven't stopped talking about it. And it is not for nothing that we deal with this story. For it is narrated by a divine man, to whom this actually happened. That divine man was the prophet Jonah.

In his holy book, Jonah tells of how God ordered him to go to the great city of Nineveh and shout in all the streets that the people should do penance immediately if they wished to save the city from destruction. But Jonah ignored God's order and in Joppa he tried to escape by boarding a ship bound for Tarshish. Suddenly, during the voyage, a great tempest arose, and it was obvious that the ship was about to shatter. All the people on the ship cast lots to determine whose sins had brought this misfortune. And when the lot fell to Jonah, he confessed his entire sin and told the others to toss him into the sea. Whereupon the tempest died down. Scarcely had they thrown Jonah into the waves when, at God's orders, a gigantic fish swallowed him. For three days and three nights, Jonah lay in the belly of the fish and prayed until God took pity on him, and the fish disgorged Jonah on dry land.

There are many different readings of this tale.

The holy Zohar (the masterpiece of the Cabbala) assumes that the story is simply true as written, and it offers the scholarly interpretation that this tale is a parable. According to this parable, a human soul is swallowed by the body when a person comes into the world just as Jonah was swallowed by the fish.

Our holy sages take the story at face value and even go into farther detail: "First of all, the fish that swallowed the prophet Jonah was a male; and when the fish disgorged Jonah on dry land, he was instantly swallowed by another fish, a female, who had lots of children inside her, and so forth."

On the other hand, there have always been people who consider themselves great "philosophers"; they regard the story of Jonah as untrue and they make fun of the words of our sages for believing it. "First of all," they ask: "How can it be that a fish can swallow a man without promptly boiling him? And secondly: When Jonah was swallowed by the fish, he passed right into the belly of the fish. Now how can there be children inside the belly of the fish? Which creature in all the world carries children in its belly?"

When, for instance, a Jew, even a very pious and very learned Jew, suddenly hears that sort of question from someone, he pauses and, alas, remains at a loss to reply. Meanwhile the other man thinks of himself as a fantastic sage, and ergo, he profanes the Good Lord. And why is that so? Because our people are virtually unfamiliar with the nature of all living things. Most of them don't even know whether creatures are still in this world. However, if the "philosopher" did know everything, his knowledge would be very useful, and he could answer lots of questions by himself.

Hence, it is both very useful and very proper to describe the genus of a fish for the following reasons. First of all, we will know that there truly exists a fish that can swallow a whole man. Secondly, we will know that the story of the prophet Jonah is the whole truth and nothing but the truth. And thirdly, we will know that the words of our holy sages are very profound. And it is only when we know the natural sciences that we can grasp their meaning, and we will know to what extent they knew the nature of God's creatures in that time.

Just as the lion and the leopard acquired a standing with their claws and their teeth, a reputation among all the creatures on dry land, they became known throughout the world as the most ruthless and most insolent killers, who attacked everyone and anyone, big and little, tearing them to shreds. By the same token, a dreadful family of fish likewise acquired a reputation in the sea, a family that made all the ocean creatures tremble in terror. This dreadful fish was known as the shark.

These fellows are voracious gluttons and anything but picky—they'll gobble up anything and everything even if their stomachs won't digest it. They'll eat dead or living creatures, no matter which, so long as they can stuff their guts to the gills. They swim in gangs, following ships and snatching whatever drops overboard—pouncing on everything as if it were the greatest delicacy. Sharks have such arch-chutzpah that they fearlessly assault people swimming in the sea and they can devour an entire horse at one gulp as if it were a dumpling. And it scarcely suffices for them. They don't hear the world, and they are very nimble. They wrestle with the strongest ocean creatures and they always come out on top.

This family of fish is to be found in all the seas in the world, and people everywhere have no end of trouble with them. Some sharks lay long, rectangular eggs while others bear live offspring.

The shark family subdivides into more than thirty genera, who are all interrelated by blood and with one and the same disposition. The difference between them is apparent only in the external signs—that is: Not all sharks have the same number of gills, nor are the gills located in the same place on every back; sharks also differ in their colors and in the number of their teeth, and so forth. In this lovely family, you will find all sorts of venom. And since we are talking about it, it might be good for us to get to know at least some of these family members.

The smallest of the sharks are the dogs and the cats, and they truly deserve these appellations, for they are as murderous at sea as they are on land: the lion and the leopard in the feline family, and the wolf and the hyena in the canine family. The instant a gang of sharks smells a school of fish swimming on their course, the sharks plunge into their midst like a starving wolf into a flock of sheep and the sharks literally wolf the fish down. The fish that suffer these gluttons the most are the herrings. The sharks devour countless herrings, and when their stomachs are full, they vomit and then resume their feeding frenzy. And so long as they keep vomiting, they can keep gobbling and gobbling with no end in sight.

While the sharks devour the little herrings, they catch a distant whiff of liver oil. The surface of the water starts to shine as if endless barrels of oil had been poured out upon it. The fishermen have enough trouble coping with the gluttons. Besides gulping down all the fish that the fishermen can catch for eating and/or selling, the sharks wreak enough damage when their sharp teeth rip through the fishing lines. But if one of them falls upon one of the little hooks, he can kiss his life good-bye. The fishermen kill him even though he's not fit for eating.

Autumn is the mating season for the sharks, when they are fruitful. Then, in early winter, the females lay their eggs in seaweed. There the babies hatch alone; and while they are crawling out of their eggs, a tiny pouch with a bit of leftover yolk sticks to the bottom of each tot. The baby shark feeds on this bit of yolk until his teeth are sharp enough for cutting. No sooner has he polished off his victuals than the pouch drops off the baby, and he can make it on his own; and he becomes as murderous as his father and mother.

The only edible part of the shark is its liver, which contains a lot of oil. However, Dr. Sauvage, a French physician, claims that their oil is very harmful. He tells about four people who ate a shark liver. Half an hour later, they fell ill and then slept for three days in a row. Upon awakening, they were very nauseated, and their faces were covered with red spots. They recovered from their sickness only after all the skin had peeled off their bodies and their heads.

The most terrible fish in the whole shark family is the man-eating shark—or, as he is generally known: the man eater. He is seventeen or eighteen ells long. His maw is enormous. Entire horses have been found in the bellies of man eaters. Such sharks can be found lying dead on a beach. Their maws are open, and huge dogs have climbed in all the way to the stomach; and as if they were in a cellar, the dogs remove whatever hasn't been digested.

Our hero lives in all the seas, and he is top banana everywhere. All the ocean creatures tremble before his vapor; he ruthlessly gobbles them down. And even man, the supreme ruler of the earth, is anything but haughty in front of the man eater. If our hero catches a man, living or dead, he gulps him down into his stomach. All the people on a beach or out at sea curse the man eater. He escorts a ship the way a cow follows a calf and he pursues the ship until it reaches the shore. Most of all, he sticks to the ships that carry the unhappy captured slaves from Africa to America. He evidently figures that he can drive a benefit from escorting these ships, for many of the Africans die during the passage and are buried at sea.

When a ship is stricken with yellow fever, and people start dying, and their corpses are thrown overboard, the ship is followed by whole packs of sharks. These sharks are so vehement and ferocious that hearts pound and hair stands on end in even the toughest sailors, who have been familiar with sharks since childhood.

In the year 1798, during the great and renowned sea battle off the Egyptian village of Aboukir, when Napoleon fought the British and men were dropping like flies, whole gangs of sharks were swimming to and fro between the British and the French vessels. Grabbing all the men who had tumbled into the sea, the sharks were undaunted by the thousands of cannon thundering on both sides. A shark delights so lusciously in human flesh that he leaps high up from the sea in order to snatch his food. It has been reported that a man eater once leaped ten ells high, seizing a dead African on deck.

Rondelet tells us that he saw with his own eyes an armed human corpse in a shark's stomach. The great naturalist Miller tells us about an event that took place in 1758:

"A ship was sailing across the Mediterranean. A tempest arose, and a sailor fell into the waves. He began swimming and yelling for help. A few crewmen descended in a small rowboat. But before they could save their comrade, a shark had swallowed him up. The skipper, who'd been watching, ordered his men to fire cannon. The cannonball struck the shark, the shark disgorged the sailor, who was still alive and not the least bit hurt."

Felie tells us that he saw with his own eyes a shark swallow a girl.

Today's greatest naturalist, Brehm, tells the following story:

"While I was visiting the city of Alexandria in Egypt, it was impossible to go swimming in the sea because a shark was in control of the water, and he grabbed people in their homes along the shore."

Describing all the cruelty of the sharks would take us forever. Many people have already breathed their last in bellies of sharks or have emerged as cripples, without hands or feet, which the killers have torn off. A shark's belly is simply a warehouse crammed with all sorts of items.

In America, near the city of Yackson, a dead shark's belly yielded a whole fore-quarter of an animal, lots of sheep bones, half a pig, the forepart of a huge dog, many pounds of horsemeat, a whole chunk of sackcloth, and a wire brush. Another shark belly contained pewter vessels, hardware, lumber, and leather, as in a regular household.

It is fine to see the way a man, who always avoids sharks and refuses to have anything to do with them, suddenly joins the fun as he goes whale hunting. When the hunter sticks iron hooks into the huge whale's back, the shark rips large hunks from underneath the whale's belly.

Man, who, with his rational mind, eternally rules over all creatures in the entire world—over creatures on land, over birds in the air, over fish in the sea—also teaches the skillful creature and shows him who is the elder. Moreover, travelers inform us that West Africans boldly jump into the sea, clutching a long knife, confronting the shark, and slashing his belly. Dickson, an Englishman, says that when he was in the Sandwich Islands, he personally saw the inhabitants fighting a shark for a pig's giblets, which British sailors had tossed overboard.

Only savages would risk fighting a shark in such a crude way. Civilized Europeans resort to other methods. They take a gigantic hook, attach it to a powerful iron chain, stick a lump of meat or fish on the hook, and lower it into the waves. No sooner does the shark catch a distant whiff of the bait than he comes racing over and swallows the hook, which gets stuck in his innards. And our hero is done for.

Henglin offers a quite detailed description of how fishermen catch this giant. As he was standing on the deck of his ship in the Red Sea, he shot down a large bird, which then fell into the water. One of the sailors descended into the waves in order to retrieve the dead bird. No sooner was he back on board than he saw a shark reaching the ship.

"Rashid, my sailor," Henglin continues, "was terror-stricken—speechless! He could barely point at the uninvited guest. A second shark came dashing over and a third—a huge, clumsy creature. We decided to catch the three man eaters.

"We seized a big, long iron hook that was attached to an iron chain. Next we put a dried fish on the hook, which we then lowered into the waves. The iron chain was tied fast to the ship with an extremely thick rope. No sooner was the smoked fish a fathom under the surface than the smallest of the three sharks swam over and tried to taste the bait. Once the shark was thoroughly hooked, we attached the thick rope to a wheel and had a torturous time dragging the creature on deck. There we welcomed our fine guest with sharp axes and iron rammers, and we slashed and banged him over and over, until he lay there.

"After dealing with him, we again lowered the hook. The second guest didn't keep us waiting for long, he passed judgment over himself just as the first shark had done.

"For the time being, the largest shark vanished and he didn't reappear until several hours later. We tried to deceive him with mutton, but he ignored it. Instead, he swam alongside the hook as if he didn't see it. We lowered the hook deeper, and the shark couldn't stand waiting any longer, he pounced on the mutton. Hauling up such a living giant was very risky, he could have destroyed all of us. So while he dangled in the air, we shot two bullets into his brain, then chopped away into the bullet holes with iron axes and lifted him into the ship. No matter how deeply injured they were, all three guests writhed and wriggled so violently that the entire vessel shook. We slashed and lanced them until they finally died.

"We pulled out their livers, which were each two ells long, and we packed them in their own stomachs. The livers yield the best oil. We also chopped off their gills, which are used in India to polish and sharpen knives. The meat, which is inedible, was thrown back into the water."

However, seamen can't always catch a shark in that way. Very often, the instant the shark feels the hook in his maw, he starts twisting so intensely that he manages to break even the toughest rope. That's why it's dangerous to approach the shark in a rowboat with a tiny number of men. When the shark sees that he can't get rid of the hook, he begins to disgorge violently until he disgorges his stomach with the hook.

The great shark, or man eater, sticks close to the shore. The males sometimes fight over a female. The female lays between thirty and fifty eggs, which she hatches in her belly and then bears live offspring. When a baby shark comes into the world, he doesn't depend on anybody else's favor, the newborn is immediately on his own. He is already provided with weapons and he can grab its piece of bread. Nevertheless, the baby remains with his apron strings tied to the mother for a long time, and she protects him against all woes. And in an emergency, the baby climbs into its mother's maw or deep down into her stomach. It has often happened that when a female shark was killed, live children were hauled from her stomach.

It therefore comes as a great surprise that the huge and dreadful shark, who makes the whole sea tremble, lives on friendly terms with a tiny fish. And this tiny fish follows the shark everywhere like a loyal puppy. It turns on the shark's sides, swims past his maw, and darts ahead to clear the way for him. Ages ago, this fish genus was called Pompilus, but now it is known as the Lotzee Fish. The famous Komerson writes the following about this little fish:

"I had hypothesized that the story told worldwide about the shark and the Lotzee is purely imaginary. But now I feel that the story is true because I witnessed it with my own two eyes. This tiny fish always devours the shark's leftovers, and, quite amazingly, the big glutton doesn't swallow the tiny creature that hovers constantly around his nose. I have often seen a sailor toss a piece of meat overboard, and the instant the Lotzee fish catches a whiff of the remnant, it dashes over to the shark, leading him to the meat.

"Whenever a shark is captured, the Lotzee fish refuse to leave him until they are pulled out. They have followed the shark for days and days, and now they have to find a new shark that they can escort.

"All scholars who go to sea tell the same story and agree with Komerson. But how does it happen that this tiny fish can be so buddy-buddy with the man-killing corsair? Researchers offer many different reasons.

"Some claim that this great friendship is based on the fact that the tiny fish with the fine sense of smell always leads the shark to food so that it can also feed on the scraps that drop from the shark. Its goal is, alas, pure subsistence.

"Other researchers think that the Lotzee hovers around the shark in order to fight off his nautical enemies. But it doesn't have to be afraid of the shark for it can always slip away from him."

Dzopre tells about an ocean voyage he took to Egypt. He saw a huge shark following two Lotzee fish. When the pair of vagabonds reached the ship, they sniffed it on all sides, but found nothing. So they swam back to their boss and led him elsewhere. Meanwhile a sailor put a piece of meat on a hook and lowered it into the waves. No sooner had the meat splashed than the Lotzee fish whirled around, raced back to the ship, and licked the meat. Next they dashed over to their boss, told him the good news, and brought him back to the ship. Our hero, of course, filled his face and was then pulled aboard. Two hours later, they captured one Lotzee fish, which refused to abandon the ship.

During the battle near Aboukir, which we have discussed earlier, the Lotzee fish scurried like military policemen, leading sharks to human corpses.

Well, gentlemen! Now that you have read all there is to know about sharks, you can surmise that the fish that swallowed the prophet Jonah must have been a shark. First of all, the man eater devours men, and his stomach is so enormous that anyone can hide in it. Secondly, the shark doesn't digest his food right away; and that's what the Biblical verse says: "The fish disgorged the prophet Jonah." Fourthly, the shark is the only creature that can keep its offspring in its stomach. Ergo, we can see how obvious it is that our holy sages barely knew anything about natural science. And judging by their words, they plainly felt that the fish that swallowed Jonah must have been a shark. And they were right to conclude from the Hebrew word "dogo" (fish, female fish, small fish) that Jonah was swallowed by a female fish. As is commonly the case, you see, the female was hiding her own children in her stomach, and it was truly a miracle that Jonah could lie there for three days and three nights and still maintain his reason and then come out alive.

All the scholars who currently deal with natural science are unanimous in their view that it could only have been the shark that devoured Jonah; and that is why science refers to him as the Jonah fish—that is, the fish that swallowed the prophet Jonah.

DER NISTER
(1884-1950)

Pinkhes Kahanovitsh, born in Ukraine, took on the nom de plume Der Nister, which means the Hidden Man, the Cabalist. Chiefly a mystic, he penned dense, lyrical allegories rooted in symbolism, in Jewish mysticism, and in a melodic prose that quivered with rhymes, rhythms, assonances, and alliteration. Most of his material came from various Jewish folk traditions, especially Cabala and Hasidism in their more popular enigmatic forms. His lyrical translations of stories by Hans Christian Andersen continued the debate of folktales vs. artificial fairy tales—especially non-Jewish material. In his versions of Andersen, Der Nister, unlike many Jewish adapters of non-Jewish literature, retained the Christian elements such as a Christmas tree—though he omitted "The Jewish Girl" because of its missionizing thrust.

After spending 1921–1926 in Germany, where Der Nister also published his now famous collections of tender, mystical Yiddish tales, *Gedakht* (Imagined, 1922–1923), he returned to the Soviet Union. Forced to abandon spirituality in favor of Socialist Realism, he produced, among other fiction, his two-volume masterpiece *The Mashber Family* (1939; 1948). Despite his loyalty to Soviet aesthetics, he was arrested in 1949 and he died one year later in a prison hospital.

The stories "Tsum Barg" (To the Mountain), "Rebure," and "In Vald" (In the Forest) were included in Vol. 1 of Der Nister's *Gedakht*.

TO THE MOUNTAIN (1922)

*T*HAT NIGHT, I WAS IN A CERTAIN LARGE and savage forest, a guest in my granny's cottage, and together we waited in the evening, in the stillness, for her husband.

And a wind was gusting. The forest was alive and astir, outside the door and at night by the door, and in the cottage a candle was guttering, weak and waning, and it reflected on the walls, silently and somberly lighting up my granny and her oldness.

We sat for a stretch, facing each other, I saying nothing to her and she saying nothing to me, we were just quietly eyeing each other, staring in stillness at each other. For a long, long stretch, until slowly my granny stood up from her seat and from her lengthy evening sitting and trudged over to the stove and took some chips and twigs and put them in the stove and lit a fire. And she stood for a stretch, then leaned over again, and from somewhere took out a vessel, washed it, rinsed it, poured herbs and balms upon it, filled it with water, then placed it on the fire. Twilit and wistful, bowed and elderly, my granny then added a twig to a twig and a chip to a chip, and the fuel burned up. Then my granny left the stove and came over to me and to where I was, and she spoke no word and she pointed to a bed of boards nearby: It was late. . . .

Agreeing and not responding, not pondering, I followed her finger, I rose from where I was, went over to the bed, put my bag at its head, lay down, and turned over, my face toward the wall.

From the forest and from trees in the forest, we could still hear the wind and its wailing, and the cottage grew silent. Flame became fire, and kindling kindled twigs, and my granny stood over the fire, wistful and worried, staring at the stove and at the blaze, feeding the flames, poking them and stoking them—until the vessel began to seethe. Hushed and heard were the bubbles, boiling and bursting the water in the vessel, and brim-full and, lit by the fire, a steam arose and it steamed round the brim.

My granny then came over to my bed, stopped by my head, and, thinking I had fallen asleep, she started staring at me, gazing at my face, shaking her head, shaking it and pitying me: "So young, so young, and already a Wanderer. . ." She stood and stood, then went back to the stove, to the finishing fire: she poured the water with the herbs into a bowl, which she placed on the table, then put something else by the bowl, then went to the door, faced the outdoors, and, as if softly summoning, she called:

"Oldster! Hey? Oldster?" No answer.

"Oldster! What is it, Oldster?" The same again.

And my granny called a third time: "Oldster, Oldster, Granny is calling you. . . ."

Now, from the door and from the other side, there came a seeking and a rustling, some hand was rubbing, looking for the door latch in the darkness, and, in the end, finding the latch, and the door opened, and, on the threshold, a tall, solid, gray-haired Oldster appeared—with a stick in his hand, with a belt round his loins, with forest clothing, with a beard, and with a face worn by the wind and the woods, and he stopped at the threshold.

"Why so late, Oldster?"

"Because of the wind," the Oldster answered.

"And what have you brought from the wind?"

"News."

"Namely?"

"He's started out toward the mountain."

"Who?"

"Who's sleeping here, old woman?"

"A Wanderer."

The Oldster now turned toward me, came over to me, stopped, stared at me, stared and smiled, and with joy, silent joy, then turned toward my granny and said to her:

"Old woman, that's him."

"Him? So young and not yet tested."

"He is worthy and he will be tested."

"And his first test will be?" ·

"He will know who he is and will know he's being tested."

"And so?"

"So it's bad: if he knows, then his sacred non-knowing has been taken. If one may live, then one lives earlier; if one may be, one is earlier—if it's a divine punishment, then this is the first test."

"And when will this be?"

"It already is."

"What do you mean?"

"He hears and doesn't sleep."

And the Oldster now turned toward my bed and he said: "Wanderer, get up. We must get going today, tonight. . . . And you, Granny"—he turned toward the old woman—"give me what you've prepared."

"It's prepared." And the old woman pointed at the bowl and at the table.

The three of us then sat down at the table, silent and self-absorbed, we ate the herbs, and we didn't speak, we didn't talk, we didn't exchange glances. The Oldster ate and then he got up from his seat and left the table and buttoned his overcoat and bound his belt better and anew and ordered me to prepare myself. Silent and expectant, the Oldster gazed at me as I prepared, till I tied up my sack, slung it over my shoulders and over my back and prepared it like that.

"And now, Wanderer, come."

"For how long, Oldster?" the old woman asked.

"For long."

"For going with him?"

"No, for showing him the way."

"Good-bye today."

And we left the cottage and we went outside into the darkness and into the forest, the deep forest, and into the night.

* * *

We walked and we walked, from midnight into later night, from deep forest into deeper forest—an hour or two, until day started dawning in the forest. And we saw how pale and quiet the forest stood in its density and ubiquity, wan and weak from evening and nightfall, from wind and hush, stood there and dawned, dawned and hushed, and with trees, and with feeble trees, paler and paler into the dawning. And we kept walking. And suddenly. . . . We saw far, far away, in the forest and between the trees, a long and lanky Hunter arose; walking between trees, walking out, and stopped in our way, far, far away. Upon our approaching and arriving, we reached the place, the Hunter; the Oldster then faced him face to face, his long frame covering him from my eyes, quiet and wordless, gazing at him, the Hunter at him, and as if old friends, knowing each other and silently, they eyed each other, eye to eye, and kept silent.

"Hunter, what do you need?" the Oldster asked after looking long.

"You know it yourself," the Hunter replied.

"What is it?"

"Food for me and for my hound."

"The forest is empty, the forest has been robbed. Big creatures have left, small creatures are hiding in holes."

"Order them out."

"I give nothing and I order nothing."

"You are rich, Oldster."

"I am old and with nothing left."

"'Nothing,' you say?" And the Hunter peered over the Oldster's shoulders and stood there and silently and stealthily, and scornfully pointing at me, he asked:

"And that, Oldster?"

"The last—I don't give."

"Don't you go?"

"Tell me, just what do you want?"

"The right to have a look."

Compelled and coerced, with no choice and no chance, the Oldster then stepped away and aside and left me alone, and, silent and seeing, stood aside, and eye to eye and face to face, I remained with the Hunter, and the Hunter looked into my eyes, earnestly and lengthily stared and stared, deftly and adeptly, and never stopping and penetrating, till he finally found something of himself, something he desired, in my stare, and, smiling and contented, he turned toward the Oldster, he stepped aside:

"And now, Oldster, go."

And the Hunter with his hound left the way, the silent way, after seeing and hushing, and he walked into the woods, into the opposite woods, accompanied by my stare and by the Oldster's stare, vanishing deeper and deeper into the forest.

And after the Hunter's vanishing, the Oldster walked toward me, silent and stealthy, with his lanky physique, and mutely pointed his finger far away and into the forest and the Hunter's vanishing, and the Oldster asked me a question:

"And who was that, do you know?"

"I know," I replied.

"For certain, Wanderer?"

"Be calm, Oldster."

"Fine." Right after my reply, the Oldster cheerfully turned toward the trail, joyfully and jovially struck the stick on the ground, and called me to go farther and into the forest and called me to go into the forest.

*   *   *

And we went with those woods—with dawn and day, with woods and daylight, with trees overhead and with silence in trees, chipper and cheerful, and free in the forest, till we finally reached the foot of a mountain. The mountain stood in the midst of the woods, crowded and covered with trees all around, sloping with trees and green with grasses, and the mountain held its head so high above the woods. For a stretch we stood and stared aloft, stood at the mountain and at its foot. Then we walked around the mountain, found a place where we could climb, up we scaled and from there we saw:

Small and forlorn, old and hard of hearing, a ramshackle shack stood at the top, the doors and the shutters seemed abandoned and deserted, and dark and empty the desolation crept through the cracks. And the Oldster walked over to the door of the ruin and stood there, silent and respectful, then held up his hand and knocked on the door: "Old man! Old man!" Footsteps were heard from inside the hovel; something old and moaning stirred inside, fussing and fumbling for the door, and finally—the door of the hovel opened up, and on the threshold a broken and shuddering old man appeared.

"Old man, old man, I've brought you someone," the Oldster yelled closely in the old man's ear.

"Huh? I can't hear!"

"I've brought him, old man."

"Where is he? Bring him to me."

And the Oldster brought me to him, to the shuddering old man, placed his hands on my head, to let him pat me, and again yelled closely in the old man's ear: "Bless him . . ."

The old man then took me into his hands, he was ancient and fading, and he put his hands over my head, stood over it, holding it long and longer, in the silence, whispering something with his lips, garbling in the silence, and whispering he blessed my head. After the blessing, the Oldster took the old man's hand, turned him toward the door, and, supporting him and together with him, he took him into the hovel.

They spent a long time in the hovel, and I heard them fussing and fumbling, something silent and secretive was happening in the hovel, and I was standing outside at the door, waiting at the threshold, waiting for the end. After a long stretch, the Oldster appeared at the threshold, death and deathliness peered from his face and his appearance, a corpse and a carcass emanated from his body and his clothes. He gestured at me, called me to the threshold, and quietly pointed inside the hovel:

"The old man is dead."

And he turned his back on me quietly and he stepped inside the hovel for the ritual cleansing of the corpse and he silently gestured for me to follow him. So I went inside and I saw: The old man was already stretched out and straight on the floor, brought down from the bed, covered with white, by his head, candlesticks standing by his head, and with death and with day, with tapers and with silence, the tapers were burning. And the Oldster stood at the corpse's side, the old man's side, pointing at his other side, peering and peering by his head, for a long time, silently for a longer time, then turned to me and said to me:

"Wanderer, look. You are now going away into the world, leaving this threshold, you step across it, across it and me and the old man. . . . But see and know: It's only your sun, your day of luck, it rises and shines in your heavens, and it will rise and will rise then—and our sun will have set. . . . There was a time that he went away, a time that I went away, now to rest a little bit, for younger men to act. . . . Now go, but watch out for the Hunter. . . ."

The Oldster said his say and turned away from gazing and from the corpse, he first and I after him, we left the hovel, we crossed the threshold, and stood still. And in the silence the Oldster took my hand and said nothing for a long time, then bent toward me, kissed my head, bade me farewell:

And I went away.

And from that day a long time went its way, and I was still walking through the woods, further in the forest, never reckoning days or weeks, losing the measure of months, woods in and woods out, further and further, and no end of the woods and no freedom from the forest, until I found myself in a density.

It happened one evening. Dense and dusky the trees stood straight and unstirring by the side paths, silent and twilit the tree trunks loomed out from the silence, and no breeze was wafting, no grass was swaying, no twig and no branch were swinging. I then slowly and calmly walked along a trail, peering into the woods and into the side woods. The forest was hushed, sun, a weak sun, was already flickering on the treetops and the forest floor. Lights and bright spots faded on the trunks and on the grasses, and quiet and goodness, slow and trodden, together with the day, moved from the forest, moved out, went out and went away.

And I saw in the forest, far, far in the forest, the Hunter walking with his hound and appearing from deep, deep in the forest, coming toward me along my trail from far away, and started waiting for me. I trudged toward him and I stopped before him, our eyes on the same level, and calmly and straight before me, I addressed him:

"What do you want, Hunter?"

"To get to know you."

"Well?"

"But to say something first."

"Namely?"

"The Hunter is no enemy."

"Who says he is?"

"Everyone."

"And what does the Hunter say?"

"He denies it. He says nobody understands him."

"Meaning?"

"Fear means awakening, nets for small creatures, Hunter loves one, lead astray means weak ones on the way. He says: 'Wealth for the wealthy, and small creatures whirl for no reason in front of eyes.'"

"Go on."

"And you of the ones."

"You flatter me, Hunter."

"No, it's the truth."

"And the proof?'

"Let me tell you a riddle."

"I'm listening."

And the Hunter began:

The Hunter's Tale

A man set out to reach and catch a beast, as always with his hound, and he lost his bounds in the woods within the woods. Suddenly a pious hind with quiet eyes leaped across the trail, properly scared, and then halted. And stood with little harts, seven, with offspring, small, with children, beautiful, and a question was asked: "Hunter, what are you dealing, what are you stealing? The mother from her child, or the children from their mother?"

"The mother later—a long life be hers, may she multiply before wolves and bears, before beasts in the woods and by wells in the fields, mount and source, hunting for those little harts of yours—you, mother, are mine until the end, but as a matter of course. . . ."

That's what the hind said, and the Hunter replied:

"What do you mean?"

"What I mean?"

"A little hart."

"What does that signify?"

"A sham after a sham, a scam after a scam, and slow and fleeced and meanwhile let it graze. . . ."

"For whom?"

"For you."

"Till when?"

"Till my old age—your laughter."

"Guessed it! Because you of the ones!"

"A flattering hart—I won't give one."

"No, I'm just saying."

"It's useless, Hunter."

* * *

Suddenly, the hound yanked at the Hunter's hand, nasty and with a howl, yanked aside the leash, hauled the Hunter and hauled him on, and the Hunter was tugged and was towed along, after his hound and on his leash, followed him willy-nilly into the woods, all the time, turning away from me every so often, wanted to say something, add something—wanted and pulled, pulled on and on, until he finally vanished, from my eyes and from the woods and the side of the woods.

And the Hunter disappeared a second time:

It happened after I finally left the forest, roving and roaming, for long and for a long time, across wastelands and empty steppes, all alone, with no guide and no leader, ambling and rambling, rambling and ambling—until one twilight I arrived in an open field. Lofty and starry the sky in the center, far and far afield its corners settled down, late and still, it was busy with the horizons, and at night, all night, with the sky and the heavens. Hushed and alone, I lay under a tree, staring through the branches, staring up at the sky and the stars, staring up at the field so far afield, and from the earth and from the distant earth I waited for someone's coming and certain coming. And as I lay on the earth, lost in thought, I felt the earth stirring slowly and silently under my head.

Finished my resting and for a minute—and finished waiting, and lying there on my back for a while, till my suspicion passed, and then I went on:

Digging and undermining, touching and exciting. . . . I sat up on my bed, took my Beggar's bag from under my head, peered at its place, peered and pondered its place, and at long last, and noticing nothing, I put the bag, put it back in its place, bent over it, and, like before, I wanted to keep the bag in its place. And suddenly. . . . The moment my head touched the bag, all at once and abruptly, the ground heaved, it strewed and scattered, and nocturnally, from under the ground, a tiny creature came forth. . . . Leaped and lunged, it heaved with the ground, and I saw:

Lithe and earthen, tiny and possessed, the teeny creature, swift, barely seen, dashed around the teensy hole, rushed and raced, around and around, in a round and a round, got up and was going, and didn't rest up, and kept sneezing and sneezing from the air and the free air. Sneezed its fill and rested its fill, the creature finally got up on its hind legs at the edge of the hole, and silently, as if nothing had happened, it calmly and foolishly, and with a monkey's front paw, it started working in its nostrils: slow and calm, at length and at ease, working slow and monkey-like and foolishly and peered with its eyes:

"Who are you, little creature?"

"The freak."

"What do you seek?"

"He sent me here."

"Who?"

"The Oldster."

"How come?"

"He's scared."

"Of whom?"

"The Blind Beggar."

"Where is he?"

The freak moved its teeny hand from its teensy nose, and, calm and collected, and it promptly pointed behind me: There he stands. And no sooner could I even turn my head around and twist it down, than behind me and near me and next to me, aligned with my face and with my shoulder, long and lank, stood a Blind Beggar and he blessed me:

"Good evening, Wanderer."

Startled and stepping away from the Beggar and his nearness, I saw his face and his blindness and, amazed and not answering him, I focused my eyes on him. . . .

Then the freak stealthily touched my garment below and tugged it, quickly warning me, pointed its finger at my lips, pointed and quietly warned me:

"Not a word from me!"

And now the Beggar addressed me again and said more loudly: "Good evening, Wanderer."

"Good evening, Beggar."

"Sit down and let yourself sit, Wanderer."

"I let myself sit, Beggar."

And the Beggar removed his sack from his back and slowly and blindly bent over the ground with his sack, found a spot for his sack, placed his sack on that spot, weary and groaning sat down by his sack, and I facing him. Silent for several minutes—and then the Beggar addressed me and questioned me:

"I've heard you've started out for the mountain?"

I answered him: "Yes."

"Have you run into anyone along the way?"

"Yes, the old man."

"Did he tell you about the mountain?"

"Not a word."

"And he doesn't know a thing so far?"

"What do you mean?"

"That there's no trace of the mountain; that winds have ground it down; that tempests have carried its dust all over; and times and generations have flattened its dust across the surface, across the earth."

"No, I don't know."

"Then you must hear the Beggar's tale."

"I'm listening."

And the Beggar began:

The Beggar's Tale

Beggars tell us a tale about a man who had big eyes. Born alone on the earth, the head was always turned toward the sky, not seeing the nose, keeping its eyes raised toward the mountains. Once, he was told about that mountain, so he started out. Went and went, his youth worn away, his strength torn away, and one day he was seen near a horizon. Suddenly a wind whipped up, suddenly from the mountain, from there. Two dots of dust bore small demons, they flew and they flew and they met the Wanderer in his walking. The dots of dust wafted into his eyes and settled in those human eyes.

"What happened then?"

"He became blind."

"Well?"

"The Blind Beggars sing it at all markets, and the seeing give warning."

"And the seeing?"

"Hear and keep walking."

"Fine, because the Beggars tell lies: poor are the Beggars and blind from birth."

"That's not true."

"And then?"

"I want to present you with something."

"What?"

"To be my guide and lead me round the markets."

"I won't go, Beggar, my Oldster is more trustworthy."

At those words of mine, the Beggar halted, he held his tongue, waited and waited and finally spoke:

"Your Oldster is a wizard."

"What if I don't believe you?"

"I'll go from there."

What happened to be?

I did see: the old man still lying on the ground, candles standing at his head, your Oldster staying over his body and speaking, he said: "You won't be buried by me, you lie in shame by me, until the young man grieves by me and is absorbed by the world for me, and comes old to me and shattered for me. . . . Let him go over hill and dale, wandering in time and at times, as you led my world astray, let him also go astray, lying, lying all the way, let him send out others along the way, and the demons' mountain should live eternally, in eternity."

"Here's your Oldster."

"Well?"

"Study yourself, Wanderer."

"I've already done so, Beggar."

"And what have you decided?"

"I'm going with you! . . ."

And up I suddenly jumped from my place, grabbed my bag, bowed to the Beggar, and held out a hand to help him up: "Come!"

But as the Beggar held out his hand, and as I was about to help him up, the forgotten freak suddenly and unexpectedly sprang up from his long sitting and silence, flew toward the Beggar, swift and skillful, to his lap and to his face, grabbed his beard with one tiny hand, struck his eyes with his other hand, and—started striking: one and two and swift and swifter, all that time in a single voice, shouting and spitting, ugh, ugh: "Reveal yourself, Beggar, ugh, ugh, it's bedazzlement . . ."

Promptly and suddenly, the Beggar got up from under his place, and got up with the bag from under his place, and a hound yanked, and with surging and scaring, and with howling and heaving, and with its leash it dashed across the field, and the Hunter jumped up and after his hound, and didn't look, and nimbly faced the field, and with shame and no eyes, and with bow and arrow in his guise, he turned around and raced after his hound.

*   *   *

And I met the Hunter a third time.

One afternoon, one summer day, I came to a river. Bright and summery the afternoon, the green-grown banks were mirrored in the water, calm and silent the trees on the sides peered into the river, and green and clean, the tops stood upside down in the sky river. Hushed was the afternoon. Wide and open between the shores, the river tore, silent and streaming, the waves all rolled in the sun's gold, and clear and high, summery and blue the sky was mirrored in the deep water. And so I arrived at the river, I halted on a shore, peering a while at the water and the river, then I spread out a cloak and settled upon it, and planned to stay and rest for the day and for the afternoon.

And as I lay on the shore, I spotted far, far away, by the water and by both shores, calm and collected as is their way—I spotted two Storks coming out, slowly carrying their white bodies on their long legs, their heads and their necks cast back, they strode along, one on one side and the other on the other side, stopping at times, dipping their beaks into the water, dipping, removing, and moving on, approaching me and my place, from afar, step by step.

And the Storks came closer to me after walking so long, then stopped at my place as if their stopping were settled and certain, facing each other across the river, stopping and standing face to face. They peered at each other, the Storks, in long silence, waiting—and then, the Stork that stood on my side of the river turned toward the Stork across the river and asked the Stork:

"Stork, while flying, didn't you witness the Wanderer?"

"I did witness," the other Stork replied. "What's wrong?"

"I was told he took off for the mountain."

"That's stupid and ludicrous!"

"So what's wrong?"

"Since the birds in the heavens gave him up for lost, have reptiles and tiny things started to creep and crawl?"

"But there are no reptiles, Stork."

"Wow!? . . . Eagles, ours, have flown across oceans and deserts, looking out for wastelands and dry lands and they found none at all—and so they will find."

"Why not?"

"Because the mountain has no substance, it's all in our minds."

"What are you talking about, Stork?"

"What you hear is truth and an ancient tale."

"Tell me the tale—please do."

"Now hear what Storks tell."

* * *

It occurred in the youth of our granny, the granny Stork, one evening in autumn, when she was flying to the warmer lands, across the ocean and through a tempest, and she lost her Stork, our granddad. When, arriving in a land there, on a lovely day there, she found herself in a place there. Lonely and with no nest, no match, no shield, she wheeled and wheeled in the air, drew circle after circle, flew around and around, worn and weary, craning her neck, stretching her legs, peering down and all the while howling and hollering: "Vra-vra! Vra-vra! I was widowed young, I lost my beloved in a tempest. Let me mate with the first single Stork to come along, and let him build a nest for us both."

A Stork somewhere or other heard her voice, and he flew toward her wailing and found her weeping. And he fell in love with her. Because our granny was young and beautiful. She kept her body dear, clean and clear and, still and silent, she thought about her earlier beloved and, proud and regal, she flew into her widowhood. . . . And she hated it, and, for days and whole days, she would stay away from the nest, far away, all alone, and astray in the vast fields, turn and turn, hours and silent hours and silence, and sad and strange she would turn back at dusk and return to the nest. And after a while, the Stork, watching her, felt sorrow, he loved her and suffered and in the end he asked her for love.

And so the female Stork said to him:

"What we don't have we can't give away, what you don't own don't ask for. I can't love you. But if you wish for love, there is only one place, there is a high mountain, it stands at the end of the earth, you can reach it only after flying for years. If you reach it and bring back some of its grass, I will taste it only once, I'll forget what was and I'll be able to love you. . . ."

The Stork heard each word, mulling and musing, a day waned and two, and in the end the female never saw him the length of her life, and that was what she wanted: to remain all alone in the nest, and undisturbed in the dawns and the dusks think about her lost beloved. And that is the tale.

* * *

"And you believe that?"

"Why not?"

"I heard a very different tale."

"What?"

"I heard that the mountain exists, that the mountain is far, and great the privilege and few can gain access. . . ."

"Shh, Stork."

"What is it?"

"The Wanderer is lying there." And the Stork from the other shore craned his neck toward my place and signaled my Stork to shh.

"And why did you tell your tale so loudly?"

"To let him hear."

"And then?"

The Hunter asked me:

"Not good, Stork."

"How come?"

"Because. . . ."

"I heard it! . . ." Suddenly and swiftly leaping up from my place, I shouted out to my Stork. And at that very moment and abruptly and not knowing from where, I heard a shot, and a bang and a bullet struck the Stork on the other side of the river, struck on the spot. . . . And the Stork on my side waved his wings, shocked and swift he heaved aloft, wiggled and wriggled, and mortally wounded, he left the other Stork on the shore.

And lifting my cloak from the shore, I quickly dusted it and donned it, took hold of my stick and stuck my bag on my back, and, calm and free, I left the Hunter and the Hunter's ordeal and I set right out that afternoon.

* * *

And I wandered and wandered all over the world. Alone and lonesome, across steppes and wastelands, meeting no one on my way, no settlement and no sign of a settlement, finding no rover and no roamer. But at night and in darkness and dawn and in wastelands, I strode along under the sky, wandering and wandering.

And years wore by. Far and forlorn, the steppes lay before me in the nights; gloomy and lonely, the old, deaf roads stretched across them; sad and absorbed, the sky and the earth met somewhere or other. And no creature was around, no hovel in sight, no village and no light, no life and no voices. . . .

And then one night: I was trudging through the night, across a sort of steppe; all alone, along a trail that was empty, a dirt road that was forgotten—forgotten by a wagon and by a bell, by a horse and by a traveler, I trudged, all engrossed, hoping for nothing, waiting for no one, forlorn and despondent. . . . All at once, I spotted, far, far away, by the side of the road, on the steppe and on the lowland there, some sort of shine did appear: a red shine, a weak shine, as if from the depth, as if from a pit, with reddish and nebulous streaks of light standing as if over a depth. . . . So I trudged and trudged, until I reached that place, till I came to a cave. And I saw him still and asleep, curled up and in a cloak, and with his face buried, a night guard sat on a rock at the mouth of that cave: a stick in his hand, and his head against the stick, and bent like that and with body and silence, and lit with a shine, a weak shine. Stopping and seeing, I watched the guard and his sleep, and after a while and two, I went over to him and placed my hand on his back and started waking him up:

"Guard, hey, guard. . . ."

"Huh, what is it?" And the guard suddenly sprang up, waking up from sleep, coming down from the rock and from sitting, ashamed, his eyes downcast, and as if from wrongful and sinful, talking all the time to himself and scolding himself.

"Sleepy and sluggish . . . almost overslept."

"Overslept what?"

"You and your arrival."

"What do you mean?"

"They're waiting for you, we were told to wait."

"Who told you?"

"You'll see soon." And at those words, the guard headed back to the cave, bent over the cave, propped his hands by the mouth of the cave, dropped his body into the cave, into it, and sticking his mouth over it, he shouted out, he sounded out: "Wanderer!" And I mimicked him. And just as we took several steps deeper into the front of the cave, the two of us, the guard first and I followed him—we halted on the threshold of a grand and glowing chamber and we saw:

Around a table that stood in the grand and the midst of the chamber, there sat a silent and nightly congregation, concealed, and clad in long and in black robes, and waiting and peering forth, a lone candle was burning on the table, and silently lighting up the young faces with their black and edged beards. The congregation was waiting for us, all faces were facing the door, head by head, and body by body, and all eyes were turned toward us. And at the head of the table, at the top of the table, an old man, excepted by all, a grey-haired man stood up, looked at me and my entrance, looked across the candle and at the door, and with authority for all and full permission on behalf of all, he said to me:

"Come here, Wanderer. We've been waiting for you."

And the guard made way and yielded the way, and let me go through the chamber, past the door, and I crossed the chamber, and I stood in front of the old man for a few minutes, and he stared at me and kept studying me and my appearance, then spoke to me and said:

"Wanderer, we've heard, and we've been told: You've set out for the mountain, the ancient mountain, which stands on the border between our being and the secret of our being. . . . And so we—this congregation here— have come together from all over the world, on paths and dirt roads, from all corners of the earth. We all hear your name everywhere. People say you are self-assured. . . . You don't query, you don't question other Wanderers who've been present, who've trodden trails all over the world—you tread alone. . . . So all of us have clustered in the cave today, and we wish to know: How does a young man like you, how does he get so much self-assurance? . . ."

And while the old man talked, the whole congregation, silently and honorably nodding, and peering now at him, now at me, asked the question together: "How does a young man like you, how does he get so much self-assurance?" Finishing the question, and all as if one stared at me.

"We're waiting," said the old man in front of the hushed congregation.

"For what?" I asked.

"For repentance," the old man replied.

"I have no repentance. My repentance is hidden. My response is my life and what will happen to me, and what—I can't say."

"And how did you let it start?"

"I wasn't thinking and I set out: for my will—my world; for my desire—I've gambled my life."

"You've sacrificed?"

"I've sacrificed."

"And who gave you the right?"

"I took the right."

"And how can one do so?"

"I figured as follows: Since everything exists, it is given to man to make his choice, his sacred choice, even his own life, and life with no choice, and I risked my life."

"And who vouches for you?"

"My angel and my self-assurance."

"And what does he do for you, your angel?"

"He shields me."

"Against what?"

"Against all doubts and against all evils."

And after a while, a long while, after my answer, when the waiting was done, the old man stared, still and silent, at my manner and at my appearance, from top to toe and toe to top, taking my measure, then turning away from me, turning toward the congregation and asking the congregants:

"Did you hear, did you hear?"

"Yes, we heard," the congregants replied, mumbling and muttering with one another.

And the old man stood up from his seat and from the head of the table, silent and engrossed, leaving the congregants and their whispers and unnoticed by them, and signaling me, calling me away from the table, leading me to a corner. Regal and royal, the old man stood at the corner, in front of me, exchanging glances with me, and then, silently and secretly, he asked me a question:

"And who is your angel, Wanderer?"

"My Oldster," I answered him.

"And when did you see him last?"

"Long ago."

"Would you recognize him now?"

"Certainly."

"He's in the cave now. . . ."

Quick and swift, I turned my head toward the table, nimble and in a minute, I scanned the company there, to and fro, back and again, I found no one, then I suddenly and as if reminded turned to the old man standing in front of me and. . . . Silent and powerless, I flung my arms about him, silent and sorrowing, and pressed by him, I lay in his arms, my head pressed by him, he petted by me, calmed me and comforted my world. After waiting and comforting, he let go of me:

"And now, Wanderer, go your way. Beasts, birds, and reptiles will guide you along, till you finally come to the Cloud-Man, and when he calls you to come up, you must come up. . . ." And the Oldster bade me good-bye. And before leaving, I turned and took my last look at the chamber and at my Oldster and at the silently sitting and seeing congregation, and before leaving, I nodded:

"Good night, holy congregation."

"Good-bye, Wanderer."

And I left the cave.

* * *

And after a while, my first encounter was with the Fox.

It was dusk in a vast steppe. Far-flung and faraway, silent and before the world, before the earth, the sun had already started to set. And huge and fiery, it stood on the edge of the sky, and its edge and its blazing edge touched the final earthly line. Bright and peaceful lay the infinite earth-and-sky circle, and my way, straightaway, led up to the sun and to the sunset.

And so I trudged and trudged along the trail, and I watched the sunset, and from time to time, once and again, the sun already settling then, and I found it settled and set. A minute and two, slow and more—and the sun had already and totally vanished from the horizon. And suddenly. . . . And I spotted, far and away, and facing me, and where the sun had set, a tiny creature, and bright and full of light, it surfaced and stood still.

Small, far, and bright, the creature stood on the skyline, as if it had never been there, never witnessed there, on the steppe, never featured its length, and with faith and faithlessness for the arrival, mulled over the place and its great distance. A while and two. . . . And the creature tore itself away from its place, and it had to and needed to leave the skyline, and it ran toward me and ran across the steppe toward me.

And so it ran from the skyline, the far horizon, and I saw that, as it ran, it kept twisting its head aside, and with doubt and with fear it turned around and turned back, and didn't believe, and so, in its fear, it ran deeper and deeper into the steppe and nearer and nearer to be seen by my eye. And at last the Fox arrived and faced me on my path, far and trodden, with fear and finding a place to flee from, and didn't rest and didn't stand still, and twisted and agitated in front of me and in front of my place it stood still after all. Stood there eyeing me, in front and below, didn't believe and didn't dare, and finally, as if having no choice, the creature cried out to me after all:

"Dear Wanderer, help me!"

"Where is the dear Fox hurrying to, and hastening to?"

"Into the world."

"For whom or for what?"

"For wisdom."

"What happened?"

"Wisdom shifted from my head to my tail. . . . I feel as if it's running and running after me."

"How did it happen to you?"

"I twisted around, I chased my own tail!"

"With what can you be helped?"

"With bread, Wanderer."

"The Fox is hungry?"

"Yes, Wanderer: The world is big, and brains are small, and the head will never reach the tail, and wisdom comes to help, and sages go begging: 'Give what you have.'"

I removed my bag from my back, pulled it aside then, and untied it then, sought and found something, took it over to the Fox and wanted to give it to him.

"No, throw it to me," shouted the frightened Fox, springing away from his place. "Throw it to me—I'm scared!"

"Of what or whom?"

"Of guards and helpers."

"What do you mean?"

"That is the punishment for wisdom!"

And I threw what I'd found.

And springing and jumping like a dog, the Fox grabbed what I'd thrown, and the Fox, broadly and greedily opening its maw and its eyes, grabbed what I'd thrown, he bit down and hard, thanked me and doubted me, and he was about to dash off to the side. . . .

"Wait!" I shouted.

"What is it?" the Fox asked me, standing aside.

"I have to ask you something."

"Just wait!"

And the Fox struck aside and slowly into the steppe, dropped the food betwixt and between on the ground and leaned over it, and hastily and hungrily divided it into pieces and wolfed them down and wolfed them down and divided it into pieces. And, after eating the food, the Fox, more silently and contentedly, turned toward the trail, toward its earlier place, and, calm and collected and sated, he said to me:

"And now, Wanderer, ask away!"

"While you were running, didn't you see, didn't you run into the Cloud-Man?"

"No, Wanderer."

"Did you at least hear of him?"

"I did hear—yes!"

"From whom?"

"From the Eagle. And I first saw the Cloud-Man today. I asked him for a bit and a bite. And so he sent me to you and told me to say: 'The Cloud-Man is asking now.'"

"Asking after whom?"

"After you!"

"And where does the Eagle live?"

"In the land of rocks and mountains."

"Thank you, dear Fox."

"Walk well, Wanderer." And we made our farewells: the Fox dashing off into the steppe, and I walking off into my way.

* * *

And I arrived in Eagle Land. And promptly on arriving, I climbed and clambered to the top of a lofty rock and I peered all around and around at the place and the land. Wild and waste was my chosen lank and lofty one, standing on the rocky mountain, with my head in the clouds and with my feet leaning against the chasm. And with peak and with height, with eyes and eyesight, they ruled over all the mountains in that entire area. And I made a place for myself on the mountain and I waited for the Eagle and its arrival. A day, and two days—and the Eagle didn't come. And on the third day, high, and under the small sky, I sat and sat on the rock. In the daylight and the distance, and from my height, I gazed at the far mountains along the horizon. And so, and from my rock, I could hear the hush of the mountains, the hush of the day. Bright and pure was the day that day. One by one and one after one, the faraway line of lofty mountains stood there in the day and the distance, and far and bright one atop the other they peered over the other heads, in rest and repose, absorbed in themselves and in their heights, and from behind and below, by foot, and they thought of no valleys and paid them no heed.

And as I sat there, high and small, on my rock, I noticed, still and sudden and far away, a shadow passing across all the mountains around, coming to all the brightness, and, across the area, the entire area, the sun and the shine of the sun darkened over.

And I stood up from my sitting. And from the mountain, from its height, first for me, then turning to my back and to my sides, I searched with my eyes and, finding nothing, I suddenly and unexpectedly raised my head and raised it to the sky and I saw:

High in the sky and from above by the sun, a vast and massive Eagle was flying, and in his mouth and his flying, a huge snowy-white and downy and disheveled goose was caught. And so flying, and flying from above, and from the sun and emerging, the Eagle finally came flying to my rock and landed with his prey. . . . The light turned around: mountains and area were farther away and, as is usual, in light, soft and silent, it overcame the anger, and peaceful it returned to the day and stood in the shine of the day.

So for a while the Eagle stood in his place, breathing and staying there without stirring, holding his prey at his feet. Then, having rested from high and from flying, with his eyes he peered at the mountain and around the mountain, and finally noticed me standing on the mountain, and the Eagle focused his eyes on me and, surprised, and severe, he peered at me:

"What do you need here?"

"I'm asking about the Cloud-Man."

"Who's sent you here?"

"The Fox."

"What did the Fox tell you?"

"You ran into him while flying."

"Yes, he still asks after you. And he said to tell you if I see you: You won't find him until you see the Mole."

"What does that mean?"

"Those are his words."

"The Mole and the Cloud-Man?"

"Yes: the Eagle flies high, and wide his eyesight, to discover prey, and prey is his from behind. . . . The Mole is cursed, the Mole has no eyes, yet he sees what isn't shown to him: the heavens from the depths. And now go!"

"And where will I find the Mole?"

"Here, behind." And the Eagle showed me, he saw the mountain and what lay around the mountain.

Upon hearing those words, I leaned over my place, took my bag and my baggage, took my leave of the Eagle, silently escorted him with his eye on one side, moved his eye, and climbed down the mountain and clambered down.

* * *

At the very foot of that mountain I looked and I settled and sat on my place, and I waited for the Mole and for his appearance. And then I spent some time in the valleys and then I wandered among the mountains, climbed among rocks and crags, searched the fissures, and dug into the caves, but I didn't find the Mole, until one evening. . . .

And I was lying at the foot of my mountain—in the evening, before falling asleep, with one hand holding up my head, the other hand tearing out the hard wild grass at my side, at random, no reason, and all that time and all the while, on the ground, peering out from my sleeping place. Silence reigned between my mountain and the neighboring mountains, rest and repose among the high, deaf stone walls, the final streaks of sunshine silently flickering on the mountain heads, and calm and more than calm, the night seeped into the valleys. So I lay in my place, with everything growing darker and darker, the light fading more and more, deafer and resounding the mountains gathered in the silent evening, and with no voices and no echoes the day faded away.

And lying there, I noticed that, dark and slow and silent, and also uncertain, a mound of soil was heaping up at my side, rising and resting, resting and rearing, with a little soil and with soft soil pouring at my sides, and pouring its fill something stuck out from the tip and the top of the mound—a small head, its nostrils slowly sniffing the air, blind and seeking, virtually peering around, and then its whole body was fully emerged from the mound. This was the Mole.

And for several minutes the Mole stood on the mound, blind and sniffing and seeking on all sides, and finally and suddenly he turned toward my place, toward me—and without any effort—he simply asked me:

"Wanderer, are you asking about the Cloud-Man?"

"Yes," I replied, standing up.

"The Cloud-Man also asks."

"And where did you see him?'

"In the heavens?"

"You?"

"Yes, I pleaded."

"Well?"

"Once, while digging in the ground, I reached a spring in the rock. Hard and bolted, the rock lay upon the spring, barring my way and keeping me from digging farther.

"So I knocked on the rock of the spirit of the spring: 'Spirit of the spring, spirit of the spring, open up for me!'

"'I can't,' he replied.

"'Why not?' I asked him.

"'Because heavens are in the spring and heaven's before the eyes—I can't!'

"I burst into tears and wept a long while and I gave my word: 'I won't walk away, I'll give no peace, I'll knock and I'll knock until I die. . . .'

"So he pitied me, and he moved the rock and he split my eyes and he showed me wonders upon wonders in the spring. . . . And deep and clear in the spring I saw a blue sky, and one by one, white and downy and clearly bedded cloudlets drifting from the horizon, and on one cloudlet, a laughing and luminous sky-face, the Cloud-Man was sitting, dangling his feet, and, with big and bright eyes, he was peering all around, from far behind and beyond, seeking something and searching for something.

"And suddenly, the Cloud-Man saw me peering into the well, and he peered over clouds and with heavenly laughter he shouted at me:

"'Mole, I think about you! Thanks from us, you dig for us. You'll dig so deep into the very depths. . . . And listen to me: In a while the Wanderer will come for you and ask about me. And you should say to him: 'I wait for him and seek him along the ways. . . .' And listen to me: Teach him and tell him about the depths, which for years are dug, and which you found while digging . . . all and all.'"

"Well?"

"And now Wanderer, wander. Three things you must seek, three things you will find, and at the third thing the Cloud-Man will call you. And remember: keep your head down, and focus your eyes on the ground."

Finishing, the Mole, with his little head on the mound and on the mouth of the mound, twisted around, and for a while his nostrils sniffed the air. Then he stuck his head into the mound, dug down, and disappeared.

And so, in that place, at the foot of the mountain, I spent the night, that night, and with the day and with the daylight I left the Mole-and-Eagle Land, and I crossed the mountains and I wandered along paths and places, and I walked and wandered across the world.

* * *

I walked and I walked, for a day, for two days, a week and a week, a month and more, keeping my head down and not peering aside, peering solely at my feet and my steps, seeking and searching and finding nothing—until one evening. . . .

It took place on a pale and pallid moonlit evening. High and wan and partly covered, no full moon shone in the sky, in half shine, and half consumed, in the moonlight, in front of a wild and distant evening steppe, and in its soil and distance, and its wild distance was shrouded by a white and faded and feeble mist.

And so that evening I stepped into the steppe, all alone, keeping to the center of the steppe, the step in its breadth, virtually sliced in half, and I walked on for an hour or two, from the start of the evening till the later evening, from the later evening to the deeper evening, until I reached midnight. And then—I suddenly and unexpectedly tripped over an old and white Skull.

The Skull lay in the moonlight, in the middle of the earth, with its eyes toward the ground and its neck toward the sky, as if ashamed and mortified, with no hands, and with no chance of any passerby coming or going, and waiting, and waiting its fill. And I slowly approached the Skull and its lying, and for a while I stood over the Skull, on the steppe and under the moon, watching the Skull's lying and clumsiness. Then I picked it up and I shook and dusted it, and in front of the shine and the moon, and with my hand I put it across from my eyes, and then I asked it a question:

"Skull, who are you?"

"The punished man," he answered me.

"And how did you sin, Skull?"

"I looked up."

"How were you punished?"

"With my eyes facing down."

"And who were you in life?"

"A stargazer."

"Well?"

"I turned away, I went away from the world and from people, I left settlements and towns, I wandered through deserted steppes and deserts, I climbed mountains in nights and late nights, and at times, in desert nights I peered up at the heavens, seeking my star for years and years. . . ."

"Well?"

"And then one night, after years of peering at the sky, when I was old and decrepit, when I'd lost my strength and my eyesight, and the world and life were under my shoulders—one night I saw in the faraway heavens: small and pale, barely visible to the naked eye, a tiny and distant star twinkling. . . . But the instant I noticed the tiny star in the sky, I felt a hand on my back and I heard a call. . . .

"I turned around and I saw Death: 'They are calling you, stargazer.'"

"'Me?' I was astonished.

"'You!' Death replied.

"'But I only just spotted my little star.'

"'You're mistaken, that star isn't yours.'

"'And mine?'

"'Here you are!' And Death raised a long, white, bony finger over me and over my head and pointed to the heavens, to a shiny and lively and shimmering star: 'This is your star!'

"I peered at Death and followed his finger toward the star and I stared and saw: Truth.

"But at that very moment, the star shifted from its spot, and it went and, long and silent, it left a long, white streak—and I fell facedown and I've never been buried.'"

"'Go on!'"

"After a while, the Mole made a home for itself in me, the Skull, and it settled there and lived there for a time."

"Before leaving me in a lurch, the Mole said to me: 'Skull, look. Tell your tale to the first person or creature to raise you from the ground.'

"Well?"

"So I've told you my tale."

"And what is the Skull teaching me?"

"It's teaching you that years are short and the mind follows them."

"And so?"

"Life is an account: if you don't reckon it, you'll live in mistakes, so beware of mistakes!"

"What do you mean?"

"'Don't crane your neck or strain your eyes. Look down and seek the egg."

"What is that?"

"The secret of everything and the start of everything."

"And where is it to be found?"

"On all paths."

"And how can I thank you, Skull?"

"Take me along, and then bury me in the place where you find the egg.'

"I promise you."

* * *

So from then on, I carried the Skull in my bag, on my back, on the road, walking and walking, keeping my eyes on the ground, on the road. And so, all the while peering down, I only mulled and mulled over the words of the Skull, and then one dawn, I entered another forest.

It was summertime. Pure and at daybreak, the vast field, the grassy mead, was misty with dew and day dew, and the trees and the shrubs were clad and clothed in the daylight. And in summery slumber, in woods and at dawn, they waited for sun and for sunup. And the forest was still hushed. Straight and not stirring were the trees, standing and sleeping and about to awaken. Silent at dawn, the trails were white and they vanished in the gloomy woods, and low and small, and dense and dark, only the boughs and their nests could rest.

And suddenly. . . . Some sort of playing came from the forest, from the depths and the woods, from faraway and somewhere, a playing, an announcing, for all and for rising, and for all the dawning. Now the first red and warm sunbeam already appeared.

So I went into the woods, silent and barefoot, walked along a path, calmly peering at either side, and I kept getting deeper and deeper in the woods and brighter and brighter with the rising sun.

I walked toward a place, and with my bag I settled on the ground and on the grass and I lay down and turned aside and leaned my hand on a cheek, and so, and at dawn, after wandering and weary wandering, I slept away all that day and in that place.

The day grew very bright. Woods and trees were already standing in the light, branches and bushes had already shed the night, birds and broods sent the mothers out for foods—and I slept on.

Noon came. Earth and paths lay in the sun, woods and trees stood without stirring, fledglings were chasing one another in the trees—so I turned over.

And when the afternoon wore away, when the sun was slipping away toward the west, and when shadows, and silent shadows, moved from the east and farther into the forest, and when they quietly pondered on the ground and the grass, I started to stir, slowly stretching and straightening limb after limb. And all at once, fresh and frisky, I opened my eyes.

I was awakened by a Cuckoo.

The forest was quiet and twilit, calm and with no creatures, hushed and snuffed the final sun spots were lying on the ground, dim and despairing the day still lay in the woods, and feeble and yielding, as if peering all around. And there, in the stillness, I suddenly heard a Cuckoo from somewhere in the depth and the trees, from the woods and from Cuckoo's hiding place. And over some water, some forest water, in the twilight, in the hush, in the distance and the silence, Cuckoo burst into song: "Cuckoo! Cuckoo!"

Heard and echoed, Cuckoo's counting, far in the forest, through the air and through the woods, through the twilight and through the trees—sad and long, gloomy and stopping, finished counting and now pausing, hushing, and then starting again, once and twice and thrice . . . and the woods grew still again, still in the air and in silence, still the trees and their trunks, no treading on grass, no rustling of branches, no swishing of wings from above and from the air. . . . And silent and swift and sudden, and as if stealing, something flew over the forest, and silent and concealing herself in a tree, some sort of bird flew into the leaves.

So Cuckoo came flying from far in the forest and she quietly perched next to me in a tree, rustling and struggling in the leaves for several minutes, and she found a place for herself in the branches, turning silent and holding her tongue. A while and two—and Cuckoo stuck her head out from amid the branches, and her eyes encountered mine. And after a long silence, trading glances with me, Cuckoo then said to me.

"Wanderer, I've heard and I've been told that you've set out for the mountain, and you've been walking for a long time, seeking for a long time, and a lot has happened. So I've been waiting. I was told you were coming to our area, and I've been watching for a long time, watching out for you and your good coming: I have to ask you for something."

"And what is it, Cuckoo?"

"Listen to me!" And Cuckoo began:

Cuckoo's Tale

A while back, in spring, early this year, a male was chasing me, asking for my love, he tracked me and traced me in all my places—gave me no peace, scarcely let me breathe. Then one evening I left this area, and quickly and quietly, with daunt and with dread, with a robber's dismay, I flew away, far away—I didn't know how far and how long, a day and a night, or two days and two nights, until I came to a wild and faraway forest, and I perched on the very first tree . . . I stood there a while with eyes shut, resting from my long journey, my long journey, my long flight, shaking wearily, shaking. And when I finished resting and I opened my eyes, I saw: the male perched on the same branch as I, he stood there, too, catching his breath from his flight. And at that same instant I saw on the ground behind us in the woods—I saw an elderly woman, a little old lady, carrying chips. . . . The old woman also saw me and she said to me:

"Listen, Cuckoo! The male has his worth, he loves Cuckoo, so yield to him, he's your true love for the length of your life. And see and hear: And turn around with the egg, with the fruit of love, turn around in that area from where you had come. And turn around: in a time a Wanderer will wander through, tell him and give him the egg of love. . . . Then tell him on my behalf, and also on behalf of the Oldster, he must guard the egg, carry the egg, until it is needed."

"This altogether!"

"And where is the egg, Cuckoo?"

"Just look!"

And Cuckoo sat up and got up, from my place and from my perch, and turned to where she faced and pointed, and she saw:

Small and silent, at my side, and at my head, in grass and in darkness, a white and clean egg lay there, without care or custody, alone and on its own, and hushed and silent, as if bedded in a nest, lined with little feathers, and a still and soundless and absorbed nest mother with little wings on her feather-bed. So I took the egg in my hand, playing with its smoothness and its cleanness, and I peered at the egg. Then I turned to Cuckoo and asked her a question:

"And Cuckoo, why can't you stand to be alone?"

"Cuckoo is cursed!" she replied.

"With what?"

"Her offspring will be hatched by someone else."

"How come?"

"Cuckoo has no nest."

"What does the Wanderer learn from that?"

"He learns that nest birds are well off."

"How come?"

"Because the children are holy, and holier the mothers: the wind carried, the wind will bear."

"And what about it?"

"Guard the egg."

"Be safe, Cuckoo."

"Thank you, Wanderer."

And again a rustling was heard from the tree and the leaves, Cuckoo flapped her wings, and quickly and quietly and unnoticed she vanished into the darkness of the forest.

And I then got up from my sleeping place, opened the bag from the ground, took out the Skull, and quietly, and in the forest evening, in that same place, I dug out a grave and buried the Skull, and then I took hold of the egg and trudged to my earlier trail and I wandered on that very same night.

* * *

One day I came to a place.

Before me lay, huge and isolated, a vast and distant stretch of a steppe. Ominous and sinister, a mountain loomed in the faraway midst, waste and wild, and watching on the side, the mountain faced me.

Hushed and there, waste and wild and twilight, the half-day stood in the steppe, indifferent and desolate the earth and the sky lay before the day, not waiting and not watching out for anything, simply at random and in tandem, they didn't look forward, they stepped alone into the steppe, waiting aside, and not waiting for a coming, not waiting for a newcomer.

And I peered at the mountain, which stood on the skyline, facing me, and I thought to myself that tall and stretched out, far and wide, a man stood on its peak, stood long, and staring at the steppe stretch, and staring at my standing, staring and not stirring from his place. And we finished waiting, and I from my side and he from his side, and hushed and wordless, and far from each other, and we finally came to a decision: I was to leave my place, step into the steppe and across its edge, and go on to the mountain and to the man's place: He was waiting for me and standing and waiting. . . .

I looked around for a small settlement emerging from the horizon, and I raised my eyes and no longer gazed at the ground, and I set out toward the mountain and in its direction across the steppe.

And as I drew close to the mountain, I saw how on its height and its length a strange, long rock goat was standing and stretching and, like a Golem, facing the steppe.

Silent was the steppe for now. Dismal and dreary, and also aimless and hopeless, lay the rock goat's vast and boundless earth, its distant and shifted horizon corners lay waste and wild, and high and long, calm and rock goat-like, and huge and dull and foolish the Golem peered at all that.

And I turned to the rock goat and I asked him:

"Golem, Golem, what are you waiting for, Golem?"

"For the Wanderer," he replied.

"And who told you about the Wanderer?"

"The Oldster."

"And what should he do here?"

"He should hand over an egg and take a scroll."

"What is the egg for?"

"For my nest."

"But you're dead for the rock goat, Golem!"

"Externally."

"And internally?"

"I live."

"I brought it for you."

"Walk behind."

So I turned away from the rock and the goat, and I walked around him, turned around his back and circled him from the side.

And I climbed upon his tombstone, the high tombstone, high in back, under the neck, and I peered into the nest. And then and in darkness, while entering, I saw the scroll. And I took it out, and in the light and on the smooth surface, I read these words:

"Place the egg in the nest, don't remove the scroll, go away and read the text on the way."

And again I leaned over the nest, peered inside, and then, deep and from behind, I saw a nest on the ground: round and twisted, motherly and bedded too, with feathers and a feather bed the nest lay on the ground and, hushed and silent, waited for the egg . And I put the egg in the nest; careful and cautious, I placed it on the soft and proper place, and before leaving, I peered again, and finding it there, I took my leave after saying:

"A good forever, egg." And I walked away.

* * *

And as I walked, I unwrapped and opened the scroll, and peered at it, and, peering and walking, I read the following words:

"The Wanderer doesn't stop for us, he doesn't stand, he's been walking and walking, he's seen a lot and sighted a lot. We wait for him and we trust in him and we keep looking at him, in the faraway—and so far away on the way, with the bag on my back. Do not think but that the Wanderer should look so calmly—look at high mountains, and in deep caverns, strain and sprain for him, we count the steps and measure the roads—and spread out and bed out for him, and put on prayer straps. We wait there for a great congregation, in places and concealed—first and foremost to learn above love from the Oldster.

"And the Oldster says: 'The Wanderer shouldn't ponder while wandering, he's walked into the way, provided with everything. . . . He's been tested so far and he'll be tested farther—and he should hear a faraway voice, he's being called again, he's being called.'"

And when I finished reading the scroll, a thought came to me from far away, from behind me, and from high up, some kind of voice called to me:

"Wanderer, Wanderer!"

And when I turned around toward the voice and the Cloud-Man, and I opened my eyes and I saw:

"Hushed and midnight, I was in Granny's forest cottage, lying on the bench bed, nightly and nocturnal, with the candle stub flickering and guttering, and lighting the cottage, and the forest was filled with whirling wind and turmoil, and they roared in the fireplace and in the window. And Granny was standing over my bed, folding her hands on her bosom; and mulling and musing, she stood there, shaking her head, shaking and pitying me:

"So young, so young! And already wandered as the Wanderer."

IN THE FOREST

WHAT DO THEY WANT FROM ME? What does the playing of my life have? After all, I swore to my soul that I would live with it in stillness. And I said to my soul: "Here you have woods, wild woods, with dawns and dusks, with silent awakenings and more silent sleepings, and with a cave and with a life, an isolated life, and you'll be friends only with young squirrels on trees, with blind moles in their burrows, and on radiant daybreaks you will draw water from the well, and on dark evenings your lips will whisper evening prayers, and you are related to no one, and you are obligated to see no one, and no one will disturb your rest, and no one will disrupt your forest life."

That was what I promised my soul, and it believed me and it agreed, and like a Daughter it put its head in my bosom, and I caressed it and calmed it: "Yes, Daughter, and yes, Daughter."

And we went into the woods and lived there for a while, and suddenly—an affliction: and when no one needs the player he will be here, and when no one summons him he will appear, and when there are no winds in the woods the player will make us hear winds, and when no rain is falling, he makes it rain in the woods, and in the quiet dawns he disturbs our rest, and in the dusks and in the sundowns he doesn't let us sleep; and the Daughter is already dominated by the player, and the Daughter, immersed, already goes about, and she has already forgotten her father and his promise, she peers into the trees—she wants to know and grasp the player, and so one must dig, one must delve, and determine who he is. . . .

And, in the ancient forest, the only Dweller spoke to himself, and he felt that an alien force, not his own and not his loyal power, had appeared here to cheat him of his place, disturb his way of life, and destroy his silently created world. So he mulled and mused and meditated, seeking advice and chiefly taking care of the Daughter.

And then one dawn, when he sent the Daughter to the well for water, while remaining in the cave, he extricated an intricate thing from his bosom, unwrapped it and mused upon it and rewrapped it and returned it to his bosom, and then, as if strengthened from the thing, he said already with greater strength:

"There is a solution, there is a resolution for the first trial-night."

And since the Daughter then returned from the well, clutching the pitchers, Forest Dweller turned to her and, still standing on the threshold, said to her:

"Daughter, I know you're nervous, and your thoughts are pondering the player, and you wish to see him, and you hunger and hanker for him, and you can't force yourself, and I don't have the strength to stop you, and keeping you against your will is not in my power, I've therefore decided to help you and decided to assist you, and with your strength and mine we'll struggle our way to what and whom we wish—come with me."

And Forest Dweller took his Daughter and led her into the woods, the deep and dense woods, and he didn't tell her where he was taking her and he didn't reveal his intention to her; but as they walked, they stumbled upon an animal hole in the ground, under an ancient tree, rotted out and hollowed out. The Dweller paused there and halted there and shouted there and yelled to the Dwellers there: "Who is there and who is at home now? I have to know and I am traveling through with my Daughter."

Someone cried out: "My husband's gone away, and I'm at home with the children today, and what's happened this way, and what can I do for you?"

And Forest Dweller replied: "Perhaps you recently emerged on moonlit nights and, among the trees and among light and dark, your children were playing with the player, who never appeared until now, no kith and no kin;

did you see him and can't you tell me what he looks like, who he is, and what he is doing here?"

"No!" The answer came from the hole. "Nothing of all that has happened to us, not recently and not earlier and we don't know, and our male doesn't know either, and this is the first time we've heard all that, and neither our neighbors nor our kith and kin have heard anyone talk about it."

Forest Dweller heard it all, and with his Daughter he went his way, and the forest was already filled with broad daylight, and everything was busy with work, and birds, big and small, were hunting for food, and worms and beetles stirred on the ground and under the leaves, and the sun warmed, and the woods fed, and light and dark played hide and seek, and swatches of light and freckles chased after them. So Forest Dweller peered around, he and his Daughter were already far from home, and they had walked a good stretch of the way, and they walked barefoot, for they hadn't brought along any shoes from home, nor did they have any food, for they had prepared nothing to eat on the road. So Forest Dweller paused and he peered all around, and then he turned toward his Daughter and to his Daughter he said:

"My girl, it's almost noon, and we left home without food, and you're already weary and hungry for sure. Just wait, my girl, and we'll see where we are."

And Forest Dweller peered every which way, and his forest sight, tried and tested and true, sent all the transparencies through, and his eyesight pointed to a place and they went off and walked a long while till they reached that place, and they found a beehive, a forest hive that bees kept on low branches. And the travelers paused by a silent mass of bees, and only a few bees were circling the living bee silence, flitting to and away and keeping very busy; and there was honey galore. And the queen bee, an acquaintance, turned to Forest Dweller and he asked her for her permission, and the queen bee permitted him, and he took honey for his Daughter and also for himself to refresh himself.

And they ate, and Forest Dweller and the queen bee talked and talked with each other, and she asked him why he was traveling so far from home, and what he was doing here with his Daughter in daylight. And he told the queen bee that in the forest an unseen player had appeared, disturbing the Dweller's and his Daughter's rest. And his Daughter was uneasy and her mind was scattered, and the Dweller had to see the player and show him to the Daughter, and if the queen bee had seen the player and heard about him, would she be so kind as to tell the Dweller.

"No!" the queen bee retorted.

And Forest Dweller said good-bye to the bee and thanked her for the food. And he busied himself with his Daughter, and he walked away into the day and into the woods and he reached the higher half, and the woods grew very silent, and the Dweller and his Daughter kept walking, not speaking to each other, and each was immersed in thoughts, and neither abrupted the other's thoughts, and on and on they went among the trees.

And it lasted a long, long while, and neither noticed what happened, but all at once Forest Dweller stopped in his tracks, and his Daughter bumped into his standing. And they saw that the evening was thickening in the forest, and a coolness was permeating everything, and the trees were standing straight and unscathed, and somewhere faraway in the forest the remains of the sun's reddishness flickered in the sky; but all around, everything was settling in for the night, and no sign of the day and no sign of the day's business were to be seen; so the travelers stood still.

And Forest Dweller peered all around and he looked at his Daughter and he noticed her day's fatigue, and since it was already time for her to rest, and since the evening was always asleep at this time, the Dweller peered into every nook and cranny, till something struck his eyes, and he pointed it out to his Daughter: "Look, Daughter, and see what's standing over there in the woods, and we're in luck and truly in luck!"

And Forest Dweller summoned his Daughter, and it took them quite a while to approach their goal, to get near their goal. And they finally spotted a guard's cottage made of poles and branches, and a sloping roof of mosses and grasses, sloping to help the rain pour down, and a hole served as a door, as an entrance, disguised as nothing and hung with nothing.

And so there they stopped, and Forest Dweller turned toward the entrance and said: "Good evening!" And from there and from the darkness of dusk first a head stuck out, and then a body with a guard's warm topmost for the night and for guarding against the cold, he covered up and thrust out and answered: "Good evening to you!" And he asked who had come.

"I," Forest Dweller replied, "I, Forest Dweller, to you, forever and for all time in the forest, and with my Daughter I went away the livelong day, and now I've come to your site to spend the night."

"And what happened?"

"This and that. Some player appeared in the woods, and he robbed me of my rest and my Daughter of her rest, and I'm seeking advice. . . . And please lend my Daughter your bed for this night."

And the forever-and-for-all-time man emerged from the guard's cottage, and he went over to Forest Dweller stranding there with the Daughter. And the man's lashes and eyebrows were thick and gray, and in the evening he himself looked like a plant that had climbed out from the earth, and he wasn't old, but covered with a colorlessness, and he smelled of dry leaves and last year's soil, and he came out and left his bed for Forest Dweller's Daughter, and the Dweller turned to his Daughter and pointed toward the cottage and told her to go inside.

And the Daughter went there and went in, and she lay down on the bed, and left her father and Forever Man outside. And both of them felt at home together, and both had known each other so long, and they had both been out of touch for so long, and now that they had run into one another they conversed and they questioned. And they chatted softly, and they stood at the entrance, and finally Forest Dweller removed from his chat and his bosom the thing he had held since dawn, and he showed it now to Forever Man, in the evening stillness. And Forever Man peered inside a long while, and nodded his head as if saying, "Good!" And then he said something to Forest Dweller, who then turned away and went over to the cottage and stuck in his head and called to the Daughter; and when she responded, he handed her the thing, a pouch that held a piece of parchment, and a string to carry it on. He gave it to her, and for the night and for her sleep, he told her to wear it around her neck. And the Daughter took it, and Forest Dweller turned away from the entrance and went back to his friend.

And then it was good night outside, and all the woods were already asleep, and from time to time they sighed, and there should have been a Moonlit night, but the Moon wouldn't rise till late at night and it wouldn't appear in the woods till very late. And the two friends went away from the cottage and settled down on a log that had dropped from a tree and was lying nearby, and Forest Dweller thought about sleeping and he told his friend, and his friend said, "It's not right!" And his advice was to keep seated, he wanted to hear, he wanted to be present, and then his friend would advise him what to do; but first and foremost, he kindled a fire.

And Forever Man walked back to his cottage, and there, from an ash pit, he plucked a snuffed and final coal, and he brought it together with slender twigs, and he fanned a fire, and he brought more twigs, an entire pile for the fire, and he slipped the twigs under the flames and he added them to the blaze, and the blaze grew bigger. And then it darkened in the forest, and shadows stuck around the fire and forest densities, and no voice and no step could be heard from the woods, not from a passing beast and not from a bird that was talking in its sleep; but every so often, some tree somewhere moaned; and by the fire, the two men saw nothing and could know nothing about where the moaning came from. So the two friends sat there silently, and the night wore by, and the Moon had not yet risen, and Forest Dweller's Daughter was sleeping in the back room of the cottage, and the father and his friend stayed by the fire, but conversed no longer, and still and silent they looked as if they had hushed and were waiting for something. . . .

Suddenly, from the depths of the forest a playing was heard, an instrument, a single one that could be heard far away, a whistle that someone plays to indicate presence, and since no one was there, you could go out, and the fife called, and you mustn't ignore it.

And the playing was heard and it seldom brought anything good—an announcement that the Moon was already below the forest, and now the forest would be lit from the side, and the hour was right, and the hour was hidden, and you now had to rise from your bed, and you were not to awake from your sleep, and also with shut eyes, and you could go outdoors, and the Moon and the moments before the Moon would take you to where you must go. . . .

And after the playing came around, and he promised the Moon and the stars, and now throngs of many people clustered on the peaks, with sacks and with aprons, with packs and with kerchiefs, large ones, and many men and women, a mass and endless, poppy and moths, spread over the mountains, and the sacks were stuffed with gold, and the aprons with fine gold. And the Moon lit them up and their mass, and the shining of the Moon gladdened their riches, and they accepted it, and they didn't stop accepting it, and when the sacks and the aprons were full, they gathered together with their riches, and men and women mated on the mountains, and they celebrated weddings, wealthy weddings. . . . And the instrument imagined the mountains, and pictured the gold pickers, and whoever heard the instrument also yearned and yearned, and whoever heard the playing wanted to be among those happy people. . . .

And Forest Dweller and Forever Man heard it all and they rose up from their places and pricked up their ears, and they heard the wondrous calling and the wealthy promising. And they could catch the Moon with singular concealment, shining from among the forest trees, shining from amidst the forest trees. And the two friends returned to the cottage, and they looked at it, and at the exit and entrance, they guided the sleeping Daughter out with her eyes shut, and she didn't stir, and she stretched out, facing the Moon, the rising Moon, and with her body, her whole body, she directed herself in that direction and peered at it. And lit up pale she stood there, and she was pure hearing, and she seemed about to leave her place and head toward where she was called. And great sorrow spread over Forest Dweller's face, and he looked at his friend, and his friend looked back at him, and calmed him with his look: and he told him to wait and keep still, because the danger was distant, and as for what now hung round the Daughter's neck, she would guard it and safeguard it from going to the Moon. . . .

And the Moon then rose a bit more, and the forest came toward the Moon—with concealment and with night, with tree fragrances and with a kind of hammered silver shine. And the little fire that was lit on the ground turned pale and lost its redness, and with ashes, glowing ashes, and it virtually listened to the distance and what was happening in the distance. . . .

And the playing called again and it talked to Forest Dweller's Daughter, and it promised: "A night, and it wasn't present, where young riders ride along field roads, on young steeds and on intensely proud steeds, and with high and prideful heads; and the riders are cheerful, and young women accompany the riders on their road; and soon they come riding to the fringes of the forest, and they dismount and they tie their mounts to trees, and the riders turn to the women, and each rider turns to and takes a woman for fun; but one rider, the handsomest of the riders, will remain alone and without a match; and he will be sad and take no part in the pleasures; and when his friends try to cheer him up, he will turn away, and he will emerge from the fringes of the forest into the enormous field; and he will stand alone, and he will stare from the side, and from the forest there will come yells and shouts of pleasure and merriment, and the rider won't budge from his place, and he will ask the sky and the Moon about his lady: 'Where is she and when will she come from the field?' And Forest Dweller's Daughter is the woman awaited by the rider, and the rider will watch for her: Why is she delaying and why won't she face him in the field?'"

And Forest Dweller watched his Daughter leave her place and try to walk toward the Moon, and the Dweller turned toward his friend and watched. And Forever Man calmed him down and looked at the Daughter again, and sent her back to her place, she was standing and stretching, listening but not leaving; and Forever Man suddenly grew serious, and the playing also prepared for more serious things. . . .

And suddenly Forest Dweller, virtually over the fire glowing on the ground, saw something flying and dizzy, something taken from the wings of a creature, a quick one. . . . And that was a bat and it flew obliquely across the fire, and it promptly vanished from the eyes and somewhere in the forest. And Forever Man's place was empty, and Forever Man left no sign in his place. . . . So the Dweller understood: his friend had headed toward the forest to find the place where the playing was heard and from where it came. And when he flew away, he would fly to his goal, and he would carry out what he undertook; so he waited and he stood and stood; and all alone, his Daughter stayed and waited, and she felt all alone; and she feared "perhaps something was happening." And the playing was heard again, and the instrument started calling.

Out into the world, and while it's still late at night, for soon the day will come, and whatever is possible at night will be impossible during the day; and a border at the fringes of the world was imagined, there where day encounters night, where it is waste and wild and silence, and a wind blows around, and whoever arrives there—the skirts of his coat fly apart; but no one comes there and no one deserves to come there; though at night and a few times, when they have loved one another so much and have spent the night together, and time has meant little to them, and they haven't given all they have, they haven't shared their goods, and they still need time and place, and they haven't lived out the night. If they should happen to wander that way, and he is wearing a long robe, and she is cool at the edge of the world, and he wraps her up, and he takes her under his robe, and she snuggles solidly against him, and with closed eyes and with her beloved, and her remaining nightly love now survives. . . . Let them hurry to the edge of the world, for every night, just one night, a couple arrives, and tonight the instruments call "them."

And Forest Dweller saw something like an icy cold permeating his Daughter's body, and she snuggled, and she looked for a second body next to her, to lean her head against it and take out from under his robe; but there was no one next to her. . . . Then another bat flew through the fire on the ground and got dizzy and floundered over the fire, and the bat didn't remain; and in the place where Forever Man had stood Forever Man stood again, and as if weary from wayfaring and worn out from flying; and his back was turned toward Forest Dweller, and he somewhat leaned his face and his upper body as if holding something there and bringing something back from flying, and fussed over something that couldn't be seen. Then Forever Man turned toward Forest Dweller, and faced him with his face, and Forest Dweller saw:

By his feet and before his knees, a creature, a small one, monkey-like, stood, wearing a cap and flattening with his little eyes, peering pitifully at the slave and the prisoner, who had placed himself in alien control and under alien command, and a terrible dread expressed that capture. And his little body was hairy, with a skin and with black hair, and he had calf-like feet with young hooves, cleft and cloven, like a calf, a young one. And his little hands concealed his little face. And Forever Man mistook it for an ear, stiff and not released, solid so it wouldn't try to escape.

And Forever Man, with his creature, turned to Forest Dweller and presented his creature, and then Forever Man told him to go to the fire, and with his creature Forest Dweller went to the fire, and Forest Dweller signaled that they should sit and settle down, and Forest Dweller himself sat down and kept the creature at his side and didn't let go of the ear. Forever Man waited a while, gaining time and getting rest, and also letting the creature rest, so that it might come to; and then Forever Man called and commanded:

"And now, you little demon, tell us!"

"About what, my lord?" the demon heaved in dread.

"Who are you, and what kind of nuisance for Forest Dweller?"

"We are demons, and I am ready, my lord!"

And the little demon told his tale.

The Demon's Tale

Quite a while ago, one of our demons, a large one, a well-known one, sprained his ankle. . . . He felt like dancing on our old drum. . . . The drum is our legacy, ancient and parchment, and its sides are still yellow and newish, but the middle is already black and worn—from being beaten at parties and demon weddings, cheerful ones, and so the center was weak as well. And one day the demon had an urge and he summoned us, a huge throng, instruments, and we were told to come prepared with all our instruments, and the demon alone would dance on the drum, and if the drum were needed, if necessary, he would bang his feet on the drum and keep the beat while dancing. . . .

So we gathered together in his huge hall, his rich hall, and its walls and its floors were covered with cloth. Then they placed the drum in the center, and the musicians lined up along the wall, and there was a big audience besides the musicians, and the demon turned up in the center, and he climbed up on the drum.

And he ordered the playing to start.

On a hot summer day, the demon is dismal, he doesn't know where to go in the middle of the day. . . . And the forest is crowded, and its core is cramped, because the heat beats in his head, and the light finds him even in the cave. . . . And he has no one to see, and he finds no one to meet, because the demons are still asleep from their night, demons are resting from their labors, and they are hidden in hollowed trees, and where is he received, he has slept his fill, while the other demons won't be awoken. . . . Then the demon remembers that a cloudlet is keeping on the edge of the sky, since dawn, on the blue celestial sea, a tiny isle somewhere, its shores are lit with snow light, all higher and higher, but at the very midpoint, a small black and ancient patch has darkened. . . . So it can bring hope from that place to the demon, bring something good and refreshing . . .

And we played it for him:

And we drove the heat into the forest, and in the forest we barely breathed. . . . And the demon, dejected, kept wandering. He couldn't find a place or a shady nook. So we sent out a breeze to the heavenly cloudlet, and the demon on the drum started stamping lightly on the drum, and running round and round on the edges of the drum, and lightly running, and carrying in a circle, and the breeze reached that cloudlet, and on that hot day it gathered more cloudlets into a single and colossal cloud, and a breeze messenger came into the forest, and a puff of air floated among the trees and their tops, and it announced: Something has started outside the forest, and soon it will reach this far in the forest. . . .

And it really began. From the sky and on the earth, a huge wind emerged, and high above it drove clouds, and down below it whirled up dust, and the wind blasted into the forest, and among the trees it caused a commotion, and trees swayed and rocked, and the demon in the forest breathed fast and fresh and he bared his chest to the wind, and the demon on the drum was delighted, and leaned his head behind his shoulders, and peered up at the ceiling, and smirked and opened his mouth, and ran around the edges of the drum. . . .And then in the forest a darkness spread, and the sky covered up, and the demon on the drum raised his eyes to the sky. . . .

And the glow grew dimmer, and the demon on the drum peered higher and higher, keeping his eyes hard on the ceiling, and he didn't stop smiling, and with an open mouth and with sheer delight; and the sun didn't stay, and the forest sank into the darkening dusk, and after the commotion the forest was quiet for a moment, and in the hush a pallid daytime flash then flashed, and the demon on the drum stood up, expecting and held up by the dazzling flash. . . . And suddenly, in the air and in the sky, in the forest and in the drum, there was a boom—a thunderbolt struck the earth and struck out-doors, and on the drum and in the center, burst, the demon, with a bolt and with a foot, stumbled into a hole. . . .

And the demon sprained his ankle, and the demon couldn't remove his foot, and we all dashed over to help him come out from there, and with great pains for him we freed him from the hole, and from then on the patient remained in bed, and from then on and since that day, a long time has waned away.

Lying in bed and being sick, the demon dreamed up many things, and during that time, various ideas came to him, and one of those things was the very last thing—he knows and he's learned that Forest Dweller has a single Daughter, a single child and a loyal one, and she lives with her father in isolation, and the forest is a home for them, and the silence is her mother, and we should go and mind their business, and we should disrupt their life and their silence. And the musicians should go: after all, they made him sick, and they are the cause of his sickness and his gloomy lying, and so they should try to cheer him up, and they should try to help him pass the time; and so we went: after all, we are under his jurisdiction. And that's what we did, for he is our lord, and we played and we planned to deceive the Daughter of Forest Dweller. . . .

And that was the end of the Demon's Tale.

"And how can we guard her against you?" Forever Man asked the demon, still mistaking all that for an ear.

"I don't know, my lord."

"You must know!"

"I was a dead man next. And after saying my say, my people won't be able to show themselves. I will be burned to ashes, and my ashes will be scattered every which way."

"I won't desert you!" Forever Man said.

"My lord!" the demon pleaded with him.

"No use!"

And Forever Man peered into the demon's eyes, and the demon cast his eyes toward the ground and he mulled silently while time waned on. And since nobody helped, and since Forever Man stayed calm, and didn't let go of the ear, the demon raised his eyes from the ground and he peered and pleaded, and he once again tried to plead with words and great pity:

"My lord! . . ."

"No use! And if you don't tell me, I'll hold on to you until dawn and then take you to the sun and to brightness."

"You shouldn't do that, my lord: I'll say and I'll tell you!"

And the demon said: "Let the lord shave a spot, the size of a coin, on the tip of my head. Then gather the shaved hair and take it to the fire and let the fire smell it, and the hair will smell singed and charred, and it should be held under the nose of the now sleeping Daughter, and she will feel the hair and wake up, and, as on the first night, she will safeguard what she wears around her neck and she will smell the hair on the second night too. . . . Do all that, my lord, and release me all the sooner. . . ."

"And on the second night?"

"That's beyond my control."

"And what should I do then?"

"The same as you've done today. And every night has its secret and has its special power, a power and an anti-power, and as for that power in control tomorrow and the day after tomorrow, it isn't revealed today to anyone. Tell me."

"Fine."

And Forever Man brought the demon to Forever Man's cottage and he entered the cottage, and then found his razor, and brought it outside, and led the demon to the fire, and bent the tip of the head, and he shaved a circular spot the size of a coin. And the demon held back, and he gave his shaved hair to Forest Dweller, and Forest Dweller took the hair to the fire, to be smelled by the fire; and it caught fire and shrank; and Forever Man signaled to Forest Dweller: he should enter the cottage, and give it to the fire, to be smelled by the fire, give it to the Daughter, who'd already gone back to her bed. And Forest Dweller obeyed Forever Man: And he entered the cottage, and he found the Daughter in her bed, all pale, and the night-seeing was still on her face, and the Moon-seduction was still roaming in her eyes and under her brows; and Forest Dweller brought her the hair to be smelled by her, and the Daughter breathed in her sleep, and the smell entered her nostrils. And she turned over toward the smell—and she started waking up. The third time— and she opened her eyes.

"What is it, Father?"

"Sleep, sleep, Daughter, it's nothing. . . ."

And Forest Dweller left his Daughter in her bed, and went out alone. Now he didn't find the demon at the side of Forever Man. And Forever Man was all alone, and in the forest and somewhere far away the very first awakening in the nightly nest, the very first chirping of the dawn bird began. The night would soon be gone, and the day would soon come. And Forever Man then advised Forest Dweller: He should lean under a tree on the ground, and lie down and catch forty winks in the daylight, and he too, he was weary from the night, and it was time to rest, and everyone should now relax.

And Forest Dweller lay down, and Forever Man went to a different place in the forest, and they both fell asleep and didn't see the dawn. And daybreak broke. And the sun ruled high in the sky, and the forest creatures were already sating their first daily hunger. And Forest Dweller's Daughter was long since up, and on the fire remaining from the night she cooked food and she used the cookware of Forever Man—for the elders, for when they got up, they should have enough and not have to cook for themselves. And the Daughter sat there and sustained the fire, and the food cooked, and the smoke smoked, and the forest was dense with its own doings, and with day and with din, daily din, and glad with its creatures; and the food was cooked, and Forest Dweller's Daughter took it off the fire.

Forest Dweller was the first to get up, and he got up from under the tree, and he still drowsily went to his Daughter, and then, and Forever Man, barely up, he came over, and Forest Dweller's Daughter gave them water after their slumber, and then she served them food and they all ate together.

And by then it was noon, and after the meal Forever Man separated from his friends, and went alone somewhere in the woods, and Forest Dweller remained alone with his Daughter, and cleared the utensils away, and helped her to wash them. And he didn't talk to her at all, and he didn't ask her about the night, and didn't ask if she'd slept well, and how she felt at dawn. They merely acted in silence, and put everything in order.

And then Forever Man returned from his departing; and he brought along fresh rods, just chopped off, bare and already leafless, smooth and with all twigs lopped off, and with a bundle of rods, a whole bundle, he approached the father and the Daughter, and he told them that they should deal only with barest necessities and that they should follow him, for today they'd spend the night in a different place. And father and Daughter obeyed him, and they dealt only with barest necessities: a pitcher for water, and a pot for cooking, and minor things, and cloths, their own, and soon they were ready to go with Forever Man. And he called to Forest Dweller, and the two of them started out, leading the way, with the Daughter behind them, and clutching utensils.

By then it was already late in the day, and the sun was lopsided in the sky, and leaning westward. And the travelers walked, and they kept silent in the day, and they went into the core of the forest, from place to place, and they came from one coming to the next coming. And when twilight came, and when the sun was at an angle to the earth, on the side of the forest, and the sun shone through the trees, and long shadows of trees were already resting on the ground, and everything was hushed, and everything prepared for the sunset, and the sunset hour was already beneath the forest, and the final rays and beams of sunset were gradually fading in the shine and the brightness, and the light came out, and the travelers came to some kind of place, a remote and isolated place, seldom reached by chance and seldom found by chance. . . .

And the place was a clearing in the forest, a large clearing, and a clear area, and aside from grasses no sapling and no bush could be seen. And the clearing was circled by huge evergreen trees and unusually high ones, and the trees had lofty trunks, and naked trunks with golden hues, and the trunks only greened at their tops and their tips, and the trees loomed alone in the entire forest, loomed in the sun and clad in its light, and in the twilight, in a rare remaining and sustaining; and no twig swayed above, and no trunk stirred the slightest stir, and only the high tips and tops stood and were standing in understanding: They, the highest, were the only ones to witness the sun's waning and the day's fading. . . .

And Forever Man now took the bundle of rods from his back, took the rods apart on the ground, and took out an ax. And he chopped the rods, honed them, sharpened them, and thrust them into the ground, and withdrew, and shifted them asunder. And the rods then turned into a guardian's booth with three walls, but no roof on the walls, and the booth wasn't covered. And Forever Man then went over to Forest Dweller's Daughter, and from her things, from the cloths she had brought along, he took some and threw them up to form the roof, and he covered the walls somehow or other.

And the newly built cottage was ready for night, for a person and for someone to spend the night. And the sun had long set, and it had also left the lofty treetops, and there, in that place, a rare silence emerged, a cleared and middle hush with no kind of trees, and bare, and the lofty trees stood guard only by the sides and in a circle. . . .

Then Forever Man turned to Forest Dweller's Daughter and pointed to the cottage: Let her go inside, for the evening was already filling the forest, and a dawn, a vast dawn, had already stood up, and after a day and a night of long wandering it was time for her to lie down.

So she obeyed Forever Man: And she went inside the cottage and she lay down, somewhere lay down, and she covered herself with the leftovers, covered herself. And the elders both remained outside the cottage, and silently listened to the Daughter's lying down, and also listened to evening, to that evening, which already ruled the forest and calmed everything around them; and for evening, that evening, the elders started no fire, and remained with no light whatsoever. And all around them the darkness set in, and the

Moon had to rise late tonight, and before its rising the coming of night grew more and more earnest. . . .

Suddenly they heard a flocking. And the flocking wasn't far away and it was under the concealment of trees; but on the place where the two friends stood there was no one to see. And the flocking was heard, as if a huge and hurried thronging were pouring into that place, and the flocking wasn't smooth, and wasn't random, it was hunting for someone, and it found the prey in that place. . . . And a squeal was heard, as if a small creature had been grabbed by lots of large hands, which couldn't grasp it, and only a squeal of doom and despair could do such a thing, and then it was hushed as if choked. . . .

And the friends understood, they realized that the demon, the shaved one, had been seized, and he wouldn't emerge alive, and no limb would survive the capture. . . . And they listened some more: And the flocking and the captured prey went passing by, in a throng, a crammed throng, and the captured prey was virtually held by all, and it managed to be grabbed, and they all were drawn to it and to its little body. . . .

For a brief stretch there was silence, and nothing could be seen or heard. But then suddenly a shine appeared, a red shine, and it struck away, somewhere not so far, and reaching from the forest, and the shine grew greater and greater, and more and more earth and air it covered. So the friends peered around and they saw: In the forest, a fire, a huge fire, appeared, a fire pile, giant, gigantic, and a mass and a mob of massive and more massive creatures, and also small creatures, spread the fire, in a ring and in a loop and in a circle, and on the fire and high above it, a little body, a black body, childlike, hung with its little face upward and with its little legs spread and splayed, and right on the vast burning and blazing. . . .

And the two friends turned away from looking, and both of them, the illuminated two, peered at each other. . . . And suddenly their faces faded, and the friends were confused from the earlier fire shine, and in the first few instants they stood as if lost to one another. And a while wore away, till the dizziness of light left their eyes, and till the shine of night, and till the possibility of peering returned to the friends. Next they saw: And the forest became a forest again, and the place became a place again. And it was already late in the evening, and the Moon and its start peeped through the trees, through the first signs and the first pallor. And the cottage divided for them, now dimly lit, and Forest Dweller's Daughter likewise felt as if she and her sleep had forestalled the Moon. . . .

And the forest friends stood in their places, and Forever Man was calm, but as if he'd shaken everything off, and as if he were dealing with distance and not nearness. And the Moon rose up, and its greater shine appeared on one side of the forest, and that shine already stood in illumination and in the

Moon's manner, and not yet the opposite side, and the Moon peered into the illumination. And from that night again a playing was heard, from the forest and from the Moon's concealment, and the playing said:

"In the first night they called, and in that night they didn't call their fill, and they requested—and no one heard the request; but he who had called didn't rest all that day, and he could barely wait for the second night, and now he's sad, and he's alone again. . . . And now high in the sky, under the Moon, the silent Moon, a cloud was standing, a dark and lonesome cloud, and the cloud is a cottage, a nightly cottage for the heavenly shepherd, who spent all day in the fields, and now he's come home, and his sheep sleep in folds, but he himself knows of no rest, and he sits and braids sandals now in sadness. . . . And if someone wished, and if someone only escaped the forest, then the shepherd pulled a rope aloft, in the night and to the heavenly cottage. . . . And what happened, and where was the promise given, and doesn't one forget by the river, when a lamb stood at his feet, and the lamb rubbed its face on his feet, and sheep drank then, and sheep, after drinking, stood along the shore, one by one, squeezing together, in a row. . . . And where is the promise, and where is the word, the word back then, and why isn't it remembered, and why does no one echo the call of the Moon? . . ."

And the playing started again, and the playing told its tale:

"The shepherd was so heartbroken that he went to the sky, so heartbroken that he roamed through the night. And he found a forest, a nightly one, and the forest was lofty and next to a river. . . . And in the forest there were high crags looming, and at their feet silent wellsprings gushing, and, from the forest tops and tips, rushing downward, down to the river. And near a crag and near a wellspring sat an old man, white and woodsy, and only near whatever appears on the water on Moonlit nights. And he was almost bare, and half-naked was his flesh, and on his head the hair was dried with grass and strewn with evergreen needles. And the old man spoke and he whispered on and on, and he told and talked and softened his mouth.

"And now the shepherd came down to him, and the shepherd brought him presents, a bunch of wool, and a small jug of sour milk to devour. And he gave the gifts to the old man, and he stood in front of him, and he stood with esteem for the old man's age; because the old man was the prophet for the shepherds, and in bad times the shepherds would come to him for his advice . . .

"And the old man peered at the shepherd and saw his sorrow, and told him to go home and stand at his gateway and stand there till dawn, and at daybreak pull his hair with him. And he mustn't leave all that time, and *she* will remember, and with the first kids, the first guests of the day, and *she* too will appear at the first gathering of the herd."

And Forest Dweller's Daughter heard the playing, and she rose from her bed and went over to the door, and then crossed the threshold, and with eyes shut, she set out, set off. And Forest Dweller watched all this, and he wanted to block her way, but Forever Man held him back: to let her go and not be bothered, it won't matter, and she wouldn't get very far anyhow. . . .

And the Daughter went across the square, the empty square, her eyes closed, her arms stretching out, as if seeking someone and seizing hold of something. And the elders peeped after her, keeping their eyes on her, and they didn't disturb her, and they let her be. And when she came across the width of the place and came to the first fringes of the forest trees, she stopped there and halted in front of a tree. . . .

And the playing was heard again, and Forest Dweller heeded it. And suddenly Forever Man didn't remain, and in Forest Dweller's eyes a shadowy spot was dizzied and, at that same time, somewhere high and on a treetop, the quivering of a night bird was heard. . . . And the playing resumed, and a shepherd appealed on his fife to the field:

"He is alone in the field and he sits under a rock now, because the field is cloudy, and sunshine is blocked; and winds are blasting, and no one knows what the winds will bring—rain, or hail, or a huge daytime storm. And shepherds are alone, and shepherds are unprotected, and shepherds have only a patched-up cloak for a cover, and only a rock to slip under. . . . And the prophet of the shepherds rides on a cloud, and also covers himself with a cloak, and with his beard disheveled on the wind, and with his head bare in the heavens, and he cautions and he calls out to the shepherds—to protect themselves under rocks and under crags. And shepherds emerge from under them, and shepherds begin to finish their fifes, peeled already and filled with small holes, and the fifes are new and ready, and shepherds are the first to try out the fifes. And the young shepherd says:

"'Her father turned my beloved away, her father led my beloved astray, and her father blocked the road to me, and he bewitched her in nights Moonlit; and she certainly can't live with him, because she's already lived with him, and she won't live with him, because time has worn him away; and I'm alone, and I've got no one, and shepherds know me, and shepherds should speak, and there's still room under a rock, and that room is ready for her, and if she comes into a storm, the cloak should cover them both, and cover my body and hers—and what is her father for her?'"

"Father!" cried Forest Dweller's Daughter, standing by a tree and embracing the tree. "Father!" And Forest Dweller tore himself away and he wanted to run over to her. But at that very instant, they heard the birds blowing in the treetops, and at that very instant for Forest Dweller Forever Man returned and reappeared. . . . And again he was not alone, and again he brought back a captive. And this time it wasn't a demon, he was holding a big fife in his hand; and Forever Man mistook it for a horn, for one of his two horns that grew on his forehead, above his temples. And small were the horns, and as with a bullock, a young one, but Forever Man held him fast, and he dug in, into his flesh and into the root of the horn. And the demon, abashed, with his head a bit bowed, stood there, discouraged for being in someone else's hands, and he was disheartened, and he peered askance, with the whites of his eyes, terrifying, and hairy and furry, and his feet were cloven and sharpened like the feet of all demons, and solidly, and as obstinate as a bullock, he leaned against the ground. Forever Man held him for a while, as if he'd replied and as if he'd rested to bring him over, and then, well rested, he turned to him and he said:

"Demon, listen. We've tided over two nights, and on the third we need your help."

"There's no help to give!" the demon said.

"What did you say?"

"Our lord didn't reveal his secret the day after."

"How come?"

"He had a bad time with the demon."

"And so?"

"I don't know."

"You're in our hands, and we know what to do with such captives."

And the demon silently mused for a while, and then added and said:

"You must take my word and take my advice. Tomorrow our lord, on his sickbed, will be carried out into the forest, and he will remain long with his playing, and lead the playing alone, you have to get him and strongly hold his hands."

"And who can get him out and free him?"

"Only the bewitched one, she to whom he turns with his playing."

"Ha!?" And Forever Man pulled the demon over by his horn and peered into his eyes, and the demon pulled his head away, and he didn't let himself be seen, but the eyes couldn't free themselves from Forever Man's peering, and Forever Man read the truth in those eyes. And Forever Man read them through: The demon didn't lie now. And he held the demon for a while, and held him silently for a second while, and then, and from his clenched fist Forever Man let go of the demon's horn, and let it loose, and said: "Now, go!"

And the demon freed his head, and, freed, he clicked his tongue, joyful and joyous, and cheerfully and with a demonesque din the demon turned his back to Forever Man and with his body bowed in half and with his hands held on the ground and with his feet slung the other half over the first half, and once and twice and several times he somersaulted; and somersaulting over and above, and with a fife and with a click he dashed into the forest and away, and nothing remained of the eye. . . .

And the demon didn't lie, and things were as the demon foretold. And in the coming night, after Forest Dweller's Daughter fell asleep, after the forest fell utterly silent, and the Moon arose, and its light shone on the concealed and tree-circled clearing. And everything was already ready, and the time of magic drew closer, and then Forever Man drew away and further from his friend, he said nothing and he went away, alone, and vanished for a while. . . . And this time Forest Dweller was very frightened, and he didn't leave the door to the guard's cottage, and he peered at it and he guarded it with his eyes. And so time waned for a while.

Suddenly the Moonlight was covered with darkness, and there was no telling where the darkness came from. Was the Moon cloaked by a cloud? Or had it slipped into the forest and behind the trees? And after the coming of the darkness a breeze arose in the forest and made the treetops rock and sway; and an earnest forest breeze wafted through the tops of the trees; and that earnest feeling was then also felt by the trunks, and they too were stirred by the heights and the hush; and they began to spread apart and bow to one another in full length and at first not in full swing. . . . And the Moon grew murkier still, and a half-darkness came into the forest, and a great gloom gnawed away in that darkness, and the wind announced that gnawing among the trees. . . . And Forest Dweller stood alone by the cottage, and he watched all this, and he got scared of the wind, and scared of the snuffed-out Moonlight, and of staying alone and only with his Daughter. . . .

And he heard this: He heard the playing resume in the forest, and it was suddenly abrupted and disrupted. And a turbulence emerged in the playing area, like an interruption, and some misfortune occurred, and what it was wasn't known, but it was felt that the playing was suddenly amazed and astounded. . . . Right after the shock they heard a distant sound, and they heard a nearby sound amid the trees, it sounded like a breaking of branches and like an arrival in the forest. And it wasn't long before a figure emerged from the trees, and not a tall and normal human figure, and it was the height of two men and higher, and the figure was virtually dressed for a festivity, in brand-new clothes and in pure black, and the figure also wore white gloves, and the figure bowed as it went, and its hand clutched a cane to lean on.

And the figure emerged from the forest, and with its head it went to the center of the clearing, and walking ahead of Forever Man it walked at his side, and a great earnestness was expressed by its face and by its overall behavior. And the figure was free and easy with Forever Man, it paid him little heed, and the figure felt solid and certain, and the only sign of control over the figure was the way it walked at Forever Man's side and needed to do so.

And they went out, and they neared Forest Dweller's area. And Forever Man then turned to his friend, and he pointed at the tall figure, and his eyes aimed and they said: He must know what to do and remember, and recall what the nightly demon had said. And Forest Dweller understood, and he grasped the night and today's earnestness, and he turned toward his Daughter's cottage and toward her slumber there, and he guarded his Daughter, and he indicated, weakly Moonlit, and he designated her face, and no stirring and no shifting escaped his face or him. And the figure meanwhile was soundless and wordless, but when it came toward the cottage and it felt close by, the figure peered with one eye and peered aside, and at the same time the other eye peered even further askance, at Forest Dweller.

And he pretended to know nothing and he pretended to have seen nothing, and he turned to Forever Man and peered at him, and his peering requested: Since he limped on one foot and he couldn't stand on it, would Forever Man allow him to sit on the ground? Forever Man allowed him, and the demon sank to the ground, wedged his cane between his legs, and he turned his face to where he had come from, and then he raised his face in that direction.

The wind was still wafting through the woods, and trees were swaying and sighing in their tops. And all at once, Forever Man spotted a demon sitting on a tree across from him, and right at that moment on the top of that tree; and he looked like yesterday's demon, like the one who'd been captured yesterday, and who'd been freed after being questioned. And now he'd been on the top of the tree, and he looked down, and he peered at his lord, who was sitting on the ground, and he waited until his lord, sitting below, on the ground, would order him to do something with his eyes.

So he felt him, and he raised his eyes, and, lordly, and in a demonesque way, they exchanged glances for a while, and then he who sat overhead got out what he'd been waiting for. Then he clicked his tongue—for himself and for his joy, great joy, and for merriment, and for readiness to serve his lord, and also for faraway demons, and for others of that ilk, who didn't see their lord, and were isolated from him, and they gave a sign, and they understood. And the playing then began, and when it was heard, an instrument drew out, and it pictured in its playing:

When the Moon appears on the sea in the evening, it encounters a fishing boat in the midst of the sea, and it gilds and silvers the calm of the sea and the fisherman's net, which is spread out. And the boat is already anchored, and the fisherman waits for his net and his luck. And he's got nothing to do because he has to wait a while. . . . He looks at the Moon and he looks at the sea, which is spread out, and he has no one at his side, and the Moon is his sole companion. And she tells him about the Merman, who has a lot of white brides on the floor of the sea, and with little white fish it commands them in the evening, and sends out another little fish for every bride, and the little fish circles and circles the bride, and it peers and it smells with its little face, and then it swims to the Merman and brings greetings from his bride. . . .

And the fisherman, holding his head up toward the Moon, halts; and the sea finds itself spread out; and in the bride, who recalls that she escorted him ashore, and then she went home, and as she went she certainly looked back, and she watched him swimming for a long time, and now he wanted to see her, and by the Moon show the figure its bed, and she shows her to him, and the cottage carries from the shore to the sky, and the bride peers out through the small window, and peers down to her beloved on the sea, and before going to bed she wishes him "good night," and a triumphant catch in his net. And then she takes her head out of the window, and goes to bed in the nightly cottage, and the fisherman stays alone on the sea, stays through the night, and to think all night about his bride in the cottage. . . .

Now Forest Dweller's Daughter heard all this in the forest, and she stood up from her bed, and she crossed the threshold, and she bumped into her father, who was standing there. And Forest Dweller held his hands splayed, and he blocked her way and wouldn't let her go away. And the Daughter held her head high toward the sky, and with her closed eyes and through her shut eyelashes she looked for the Moon and its light. But the Moon wasn't in front of her eyes, because her sight was blocked in the night by the trees, and the Moon was drawn out today, and only a feeble shimmer reached the Daughter's face. And the demon on the treetop was still sitting on his place as earlier, and peering at his lord, who was down below. And Forever Man kept his eye on both of them. And then something else was heard in the forest:

And if a tempest happens to brew on the sea, at night, and the Moon is in the sky, and the fisherman is in the midst, and billows burst, and winds bring swift clouds, and they carry them past the Moon and block its shine. And a darkness settles on the sea silver, and a gloominess on the sea gold, and the boat rocks, and the boat can't stay calm, and the fisherman has to weigh anchor, and quickly draw in the net, because billows burst in from all sides, and in all the corners of the sky danger mates with darkness. . . .

And the bride in the cottage under the Moon is awoken from her slumber, whether a wind or only the Moon has tapped on her window, and she leaves her bed and looks out through the window and watches what's happening on the sea. Then she turns toward the Moon, while her fisherman, who's stayed with his boat, and who now stands on his boat, and who rows in all sides with his rowing—he should now take in all the wickedness of the sea, and with its wildness he should pass through, and he should reach the shore in one piece, and come home safe and sound, and no billow should block his path, not from a side and not from below, and no pit ahead should devour him. That is the bride's prayer for the Moon. . . .

But when the sea dashes and crashes some more, and the Moon is busy with itself, because clouds have swelled and are swollen now, and the tempest at sea is already black, and clouds and waters are blacker still, and an enormous blasting rules the horizons, and a tumult and a turmoil are in the midst of the sea, and the boat is tiny in the sea, and what should be done, and what should be seen of the boat, where should it turn to, and what will happen and occur? . . .

And Forest Dweller's daughter then took a step toward her father, and pushed him from his place, and in the middle of the place, where the demon, the lord, was sitting, and Forever Man was standing, the daughter endured stress and strain, and unusual as if by strength, and not stopped by the father, and admired by those surrounding her. . . . And the daughter remained standing, and the father hurried over to her, and Forever Man now looked feeble and unable, and the demon, the lord, watched it all, and a deep satisfaction and a smiling self-assurance appeared in his eyes which were seeing sidelong. And the demon on his treetop kept looking at his lord, and continued finding the right time, and somewhere in the forest he gave his sign again. And it was then heard again, and the musical instrument drew out again:

And then, and when the tempest crashed over the sea, it was too late to do anything at all, and even big ships are lost in such moments, not to mention smaller ships, and from such small ships nothing is expected; and the boat is a chip in the sea, and the sea is terrifying, and the Moon can't be seen, and whatever is seen is likewise terrified, and the fisherman's terror is greater than ever; and his minutes are his last, and the boat isn't even flooded, and it's held from going under, and miracles have kept it afloat— and so, what remains for the bride? And her sorrow is huge, and her beloved is at his end, and she has nothing to help him with; and light is not light, and Moon is not Moon, and the world and the water are blocked from her prayer; and what good is her cottage if the fisherman's boat has already capsized, and the fisherman has fallen into the sea, and he clutches the end of the boat, and he won't be clutching for long, and until a huge billow comes and yanks the boat out of his clutching, and now the billow has smacked the boat, and the boat has plunged into a watery pit, and the fisherman has crawled out by himself, and struggles for several minutes, and next, he too will vanish.

And so what should she do if not stand at the cottage window, and watch the final struggle of her beloved, and then, in the final minute, from the height, from the window of the cottage, leap into the water . . . ? And now the minute, the final minute, has come, and the fisherman's hands have lost their hold, and his strength has waned, and a lightning bolt has cracked through the clouds, and in the sea a pit opened up, and the last and the lone man left in the sea hurtled into the depths. . . .

And the fisherman's bride plunged through the window and from the height, and—

At that very moment the playing broke off, and the Daughter of Forest Dweller broke away from her place, and the demon, the lord, who stood in his place, and the cane that he leaned against, and that was wedged between his legs, suddenly rose aloft with him. . . . And he approached the Forest Dweller's Daughter, and she was already stretching out her arms to him, and with great desire and great effort she was drawn to him, and Forest Dweller threw his arms around her, and Forest Dweller wanted to hold her back, but the Daughter tore away from him, and the demon gave her a hand, and she grabbed it, and she pulled herself up with the cane, and she mounted it for herself, and they all rose higher and higher toward the Moon, and they flew higher and higher, and the demon embraced her, holding and holding and not letting go.

And the father saw them riding to the sky, and Forest Dweller fell face-down on the ground, and Forever Man saw this, and Forever Man had no help and no comfort for his friend. . . .

And the next morning, when day came, the two friends brought their things together, and wordless and speechless they left that place, to return to Forever Man's cottage and to his home. When they reached it, and Forest Dweller settled in with his friend, and Forest Dweller from then on remained with Forever Man, and for a very long time, and he's still there today.

REBUKE

A PORCELAIN PUPPY is standing on the desk, a worried and anxious puppy: his teeth ache, and his cheeks are like human cheeks, and his face and his head are wrapped in a kerchief, and a pipe sticks out from a corner of his mouth. . . .

A writer is turned toward the puppy, a certain modern writer. He peers at the puppy and he asks the puppy:

"Why so worried?"

"You can see," the puppy replies. "My teeth ache."

"So what?" the writer asks.

"Have you ever had a toothache?" the puppy retorts.

"Yes."

"Did you look at yourself in a mirror?"

"I looked."

"And what did you look like?"

"Like you now."

"Then why do you ask?"

"No special reason. A subject struck me."

"You think you'll find the subject with a dog?

"I do indeed."

"Fine. But I can't guarantee the subject. It's going to be full of aching teeth. . . ."

"No matter."

"Do I have to give?"

"Give."

"I look at you all the time," the puppy says, "and I watch you at work. To tell you the truth: It's awful to look at you—at you and at everyone who comes in to you. Sometimes I hear your conversations. Moron! You want to work against your own fate. You don't want to work against the laws you've been given. You want to leap over yourselves. . . . You fools!

"So I ponder: The greatest achievement is in the great humiliation during the great surrender when the miracle occurs. And harness the head in the yoke—that is the vocation and elevation of creatures. And as for you: Before setting out on your road, you've got your goal, your already achieved and your springing goal. And as for your horses, which are allowed to leap over barriers: They have purchased from Gypsies and protracted diseases, and how do you wish to go, and where have you won world wagers? . . .

"And I ponder further: Here I stand, a puppy, before you, a small puppy and not a real one, a mere plaything, a foolish toy, and yet I know the tradition of the real puppies, and although a canine tradition a correct one— and we can learn even from dogs. . . ."

"Quite the contrary," the writer requests.

"It is told"—the dog won't wait to be asked—"that before the first wolf decided to become a dog, he already had a great village. He already went so hungry for a long time with his wife and his whelps. And they drew closer to the human habitation—closer and closer. The human had put a sort of fence and enclosure around him and around his estate. Nor did he resist with his bare hands, and he used poles and sticks and shafts. And somehow the wolf managed to make it through the summer, and somehow managed to drag something from the human.

"But then when the winter came, when the frosts dominated the forests, and mounds of snow piled up, and children whined in the caves, and from the humans' rooftop he saw a warm smoke rising and sometimes smelling of meat, and each time with something cooking—and then the wolf often came to the humans' home, a very long distance, and the wolf hunkered down on his hind legs, and he craned his head toward the roof, sitting and watching and watching the smoke. . . .

"He pondered: It's true that wolfish freedom comes from God, the commandments warn us not to be wolves, in winter nights, gathering in packs, and the forerunner running ahead, and strengthening one another, killing each other, to be strong, to occupy and acquire. . . . Well, and when you've acquired, and thanks to the teeth, and in the pedigree of strength and in strength of love, you've brought them into the cave. And soon enough, she made the wolf happy with several whelps, and she is exhausted by motherhood. And her whelps suck out the final drops. She lies there, and her eyes are full of pity, and you are poor and, and all she's wearing is a meager hide.

"And the winter is cruel, and at night the fronts are stronger, and the sky is strewn with poppy stars, and poppy doesn't make a meal, and the moon pours milk, and it supplies the children with nothing—and how should we recall wolfish commandments? And how should we hold an old legacy and proud beliefs? And all the wolves in the region have perished, and all the survivors migrated, and all that's remained of the entire tribe, the local tribe, are empty lairs.

"And the human grows stronger, and his cottage is secure, and his children grow up and his children help him, and his wealth increases and his prosperity expands, and you are as you were, and for long generations nothing has reached you—if it weren't for the surrender, if it weren't for the plan to put aside the gun and in weakness confess? . . .

"And the wolf mulled one night and came to no end, and a second night—everything facing the human's cottage, and he saw smoke rising, and the third night—he came home. And he met the she-wolf nearly half-dead, and the children, with no peep and no food, warmed themselves on their final bit of belly warmth. And when the wolf awoke the she-wolf and presented his plan and his thought, the she-wolf stayed silent, barely listening, barely grasping his words. And when the wolf awoke her and touched her and tried to hear a final word from her, she turned around and with her final nastiness and with her weakly carcass-like teeth she bit him—she retorted:

"'You can see!'

"And the wolf promptly left his lair, and he reached the human's home and he silently came to the cottage and shuffled over, and all night long he guarded the threshold of his cottage. And in the morning, when the human got up and went out and met the wolf at his door, he didn't understand at first, he thought that the wolf was frozen. . . . But when he saw that the wolf did stir, the human grabbed his thick stick, smashed it with all his might into the wolf's legs, beat the wolf and wouldn't stop—he assumed that the wolf would run away. And when the wolf didn't run away, when he meekly peered up at him all the while, from his paws, as if he'd put aside his pride and all that was wolfish, the human understood: The wolf was coming with thoughts of peace, and as of today the wolf stopped thinking about war.

"And so the human kept beating the wolf—this time to test him: And perhaps he would re-awaken within him, remind him of his habit and again resist him, resist. But the wolf endured this time, endured—and the human made peace with the wolf and brought him out food and drink.

"The next morning, the human met the wolf's wife and whelps at hi door. And he pitied them too, and he guarded them, and he invited the whole household to live with him, to serve the human in devotion.

"That was what happened to the wolf, and the human beat out his pride. And you too are a human and you have to beat your pride out of yourself. . . ."

"So what do you want?" the writer grumbled.

"Don't get angry. I didn't guarantee the theme. But it is my duty and my vocation. There was a good reason why our grandfather arranged his first banquet for your grandfather. . . . Peace is peace, and serving and devotion are doggish matters: I warn you."

"Words! What do you mean?"

"I see your sorrow but I can't watch it. You and yours have set out to leap over yourselves, and as you leap, you lose your final few coins from your pockets. More clearly: You convinced yourselves: limits are limited. The real powers that be are freedom in the void, a revolt against the wheel and its whirling! And you are lost in the void, and truth is given in limits, and true freedom is the wish to be free, and sometimes the taking on of the yoke is the greatest revolt. . . . And that's why I've told you the tale of the wolf."

"It's silly and it's a dubious story."

"You don't trust a tale but you do trust a dream. So here's a dream."

"A dream that you dreamed?"

"No, a dream that you dreamed but forgot."

"Remind me."

"Late one night I was standing on your table, the night lamp was burning, and you were sleeping in the bed across the room. All at once, you burst out crying. First softly, then stopping, then starting again, now loudly and horribly. And now the Lord of Dreams appeared in the room. You didn't see him, but I've known him for a long time, for many nights and many visits with you.

"He went over to your bed, leaned over you, and removed your hands from your heart. You calmed down. Then, like a doctor, with a bedside patient on a chair, descending, gazed at you for a while, peered with your eyes. Next he talked to me, talked a blue streak, questioned me: How were you, how was work, how were things? I told him everything I knew, and the changes I had noticed lately in you, and that you were suffering great anguish every week, and that you often cried at night, in your sleep. And the Lord of Dreams heard me out and kept still, kept still and shook his head: Yes, he cried. He had every reason to cry. . . . Every week, the people did not spend their last, they kept strong and sturdy. But in sleep they tore everything out from them.

"And why was he weeping now?

"He had seen, said the Lord of Dreams, how a town stays within walls. . . . Bricks and clay, dust and bars, and everything that's part of building. . . .

"And the building went swiftly and the working went quickly, and the bars were already taken apart, and the walls were complete, and the windows were grated as if in a prison. And all at once—the masons didn't remain on the outside, and every mason was inside, in a prison, peering through a grated window. And all at once: All walls became a single wall, and this single wall sat there alone. . . .

"And it wasn't long before it saw itself as a young eaglet with a small yellow beak and short wings, and its eyes yearn in the twilight, as in an old prisoner. . . . And all at once: and the eaglet remained an eaglet, and it alone sat on a chair at the table and with paper, and ready with ink and a quill, and the eaglet dictated a letter to its father, and it set it down on the paper.

"And this is what the eaglet dictated:

"'. . . And I write to you, Father: I've never been so miserable, I've never felt so miserable for a brother, as now, during these past few days. And I've been developing with him and eating from the same dish with him. . . . And, Father, no son has ever loved his father as much as I. . . . And when I shut my eyes, I visualize us sitting on the highest world rock, and the world around us is vast and not occupied, and you and I view the world from our rock, sitting and peering, and from time to time we pick at our feathers with our little beaks, and all at once, you say to me:

"'Son, we are flying!'"

"'And so we circle the earth, you first and I behind you, and you are I, and I teach you, and holy the traces of your following me, and with your advance breath—I breathe, and I hold for your drawn-out wheel. . . . And you show me your sovereignty, and what I will inherit from you, and I fly and follow you, and I learn to restrict my tears. . . .

"'Father, and I also cherish your prison (and I'm reliable in it), and in a slight dawn or in a dark dusk, a silent thought sneaked through the bars, and silent, and unnoticed by anyone, on the high and distant mountains, I set out to seek you. No one will block my way, no bars will build me a fence, and meanwhile I stay awake, and from time to time, I kneel and pray for your bars: Father, don't forget your son! . . .'

"And the letter was complete, and the eaglet silently fed his fancy. And suddenly he (that is, you) removed his head from the table and from the paper and from the writing and glanced at the window. And so the eaglet saw that the bars were broken. And the opening was large enough for the eaglet to slip through. And he awoke from his fancy, and he pointed a finger at the open window: 'Come on, it's open.'

"And the eaglet went first, and he was followed—a wing dragged along on the ground, and he was lame and he looked sickly, and he accompanied the eaglet from behind. And out they came upon the street. And when they had gone a stretch of the way, they encountered a cattle and poultry medico, and he was hung with instruments and laden with implements, and loaded with scalpels and medical devices, and also with his belt pocket, with various salves and ointments for smearing. . . .

"And the eaglet turned toward the medico and blocked his way and pointed at the wing. The wing dangled down and was very painful, the eaglet dragged himself along and couldn't fly. The medico then bent over the eaglet and felt his armpit and his joint, and then he stood up and he said:

"'No harm for the armpit, no hurt for the joint. It's been since my birth, and I think that it's doomed.'

"He burst into tears, and the eaglet looked dejected, and his wing was orphaned and it lay and lay on the ground and dragged along. So they had a wake for the wing, and the eaglet sat somewhere or other, and then he dragged the wing along. And the medico wanted to help him but didn't know how. So he too lowered himself to the ground, and for comfort they told him a tale of Job, a tale of woe.

"And this is how it began."

"I was on the way home from a fair. I had healed cows and horses there, and lame and blind creatures and even constipated cripples. In each case, I received my fee for the cure. Except from one person, a pauper, with a poor and pitiful horse-and-wagon, and the horse was sunken, and the man called to me, but I couldn't help him. And in the midst of the treatment, the horse stretched out its legs and gave up its soul to the fair. And the pauper didn't pay me my fee. Right after the horse's demise, a flayer showed up and he bought the carcass. And when the pauper received his cash, he beckoned to me: 'Come join me in the tavern for a final drink.'

"'And how will you get home?'

"'I'll tell you in the tavern.'

"When we arrived, and sat down, and had our first and second drinks, and my pauper warmed up, he told me:

"'Whether it's poor or drunk, or my sorrow and my poor horse-and-wagon, he started emitting steam. I can't guarantee it, but I said as follows:'

"'This is my last, and I don't have enough to get home with, and I probably don't have a home by now. And I'm beginning my second transmigration, and in my first transmigration I was rich and I had a lot of property. . . . And the more I had, the more I was given. . . . And I owned lots of land, and I had fields from horizon to horizon, and when the time for plowing came, and I rode my horses out into the fields, and I had the heavens overhead, and I saw oxen hitched to plows and trudging across the heavens. And the oxen trudged across the sky and whipped up dust across the sky, and from one horizon to the other, and to and fro, and with my plowshare I did my share, and by noon I had plowed up half my field, and in the evening, when the heavenly oxen trudged away toward the horizon in quest of a place to rest for the night, my field was now ready and black . . .

"'As with my plowshare, so with other chores. And during the time of harvest, reapers appeared in the sky, bowing all day and all bowed out, and sweat came pouring out of them, and they drank water from heavenly pitchers. And the heavenly grain was fully reaped, and my field here, down below, and huge stacks of sheaves of grain were set up. . . .

"'And by whose merit—I don't know, and for whose good deeds—I don't know either. But that was how things stood with the grain taken in, and with the threshing and grinding, and that was that year after year—and always with wonders. And my cottage was chockfull, and my barns were brimming toward their tops, and my cattle were healthy, and I was given their work and the fruits of their labors, and I lost nothing, and I lacked nothing, and the blessings crossed my threshold, and my lips never cursed at all.

"'But then one autumn evening, heaven sent me a guest, a sickly guest, a groaner, a wordless, an autumn guest. And that evening he crossed my threshold and put down his bag. He asked if he could spend the night, and I didn't say no. I pointed out a place, but I wasn't happy about him. He struck me as too alien, as if he were bringing something bad.

"'He spent the night and then got up. I blessed him with a "good morning." And he acted as if he hadn't heard me, he stood there facing the window, peering into the outside. It was raining outside. The autumn wetness was watering the windows, scrubbing them, and the heavens were washing them. And suddenly the guest turned around, and he noticed my dissatisfaction, and he told me to hitch some horses for him; he was sick, he said, and he couldn't walk. . . .

"'And I retorted, and I asked him to stay a while longer, though, for appearance's sake, for I really didn't want him to stay, and I didn't want to hitch horses for him, I wanted him to leave alone and leave my cottage as fast as possible.

"'And he caught my drift and he didn't say a word and he only leaned over his bag and lifted it up from the floor, and he didn't sling it over his shoulder, he clutched it in his hand and he carried it outside, and there someone was waiting for him.

"'And honestly, when he said good-bye and stepped out of my cottage, and I accompanied him across the threshold, and there at the door I saw a horse-and-wagon standing. And the guest climbed into the wagon and goaded the horse and he said:

"'And if ever you need it, the horse-and-wagon are ready for you. . . .'

"'And the guest rode away, and I crossed back across my threshold, but something remained of him, something that couldn't be named by its name, but it was certainly a curse. And he certainly left it in some nook or corner.

"'And from then on, the mornings were mournful, and the evenings weren't cheerful, and a sorrow hovered in the fireplace, and someone climbed my ladder at night, and the fire in the oven crackled strangely, and the evening lamp kept going out. And the autumn was autumn, and after the autumn winter came, and when the winter came, the guest still remained behind. And the cattle were under the weather, and no healer appeared, and the cows fell away, and I didn't sell their skins to a skinner, and by the end of winter I too fell ill, and I remained in bed for a while, and in the spring and at plowing time I went out to the field empty-handed. And one warm day, when I dragged myself across the threshold, certain fortune oxen appeared in the heavens. And again I hitched them and again I harnessed, and again I thought that *my* fields were ready, and I thought the oxen had come to till my soil. And I was delighted, and I blessed them in the morning and with hitched-and-yoke, and then I watched them, watched after them, as always, and suddenly—and the oxen turned around and deserted my supervision, and dragged along another man, a neighbor, to work with him all day. . . .

"'In the evening, when they turned away from my work, and when they rode past my fields, weary at sundown, and bidding good-bye, I turned to them and I asked them why they were avoiding me. Now on their way, they turned up and they answered me: 'We aren't avoiding you, we have nothing against you at all. If you like, you can come very early tomorrow, and we can go and work with your neighbor.'

"'And what about me?" I asked.

"'The road to your fields isn't ready as yet. . . .'

"I caught his drift: My time was gone, and my blessing had left me. I said goodbye with the setting sun, and my fields were blessed, and I reached up to the oxen, and I was taken up, and I endured—and in the morning, with them, I drove to other men's fields.

"'And so I left the world, and for many long years, I was driven and I drove under other men's heavens. And then, when I was fed up, I asked to be lowered and let down. . . .

"'And now my guest appeared again, and still a sickly man at that, and didn't let me my old remember, and he was some sort of supervisor, and he held the keys to stable gates. And when he heard my request, he led me to a stable, unlocked the gate, and opened the gate, and brought out my long-ago horse-and-wagon:

"'You can take this, but take care of the horse, the horse is weak. If it collapses, you'll have nothing to come home in, then you'll have to lie around.'

"'The horse-and-wagon pauper told me the tale, and I've retold the tale to you—' and that was how the healer finished.

"And why did I tell the tale?" he asked the eaglet.

"First of all, because there are transmigrations; and perhaps in the first transmigration you, in an autumnal and coughing fate, you trod on your foot.

"And secondly: As a healer I tell you: Turn around. . . . Bad, bad, but a home is a home, and sick people shouldn't drag themselves along. . . .

"And suddenly (and the Lord of Dreams continued his tale), and he and the eaglet saw themselves in prison again, and the grating fused back into one again, and no opening and no aperture were to be noticed again. And the eaglet was melancholy, and seeing this, he was very sad, and again, he found himself at the table again, with paper and a quill. And the eaglet dictated a letter, dictated, and *he* wrote down the letter:

"'And once, when I bowed my head down in the armpit, and silent and freezing, and I remained warm there all night, I saw the father in heaven, in his high domain, and as long as I was allowed to look. . . . And often, when we fly together, I cross his path ahead of him, and I feel his powerful wings: He follows me and he keeps me in sight and with his son he flies after me and delights in me. And sometimes, the greatest happiness is mine, when his voice reaches my ears. He yells at me and strikes me then: "Fine, son, fine, and as one needs, you fly. . . ." And I catch my breath in joy and flight. And if only I could keep my head in my armpit, and I would suffocate, and the father would receive a breathless legacy. . . .'

"'But recently, Father, when I reflected and deliberated with you, I suddenly sighted him on his high rock, and a wind came whirling. And the entire sky around the rock came clouding, and the wind around the rock grew powerful, and your lofty aerie, which stuck to the peak of the rock, was torn by the wind, and you could barely stay seated, and your feathers scattered every which way, and your eyes were bloodshot, and suddenly—and I saw you as an old man, as your years were fulfilled. And the storm spread over all the world, and blasted it apart. Very fearful and heaven grew more and more fearful. . . .

"'And in your fearfulness and in your clouded fear, I opened a place: Two eagles appeared with burning candles, emerged for you and on your rock, and underneath, from the place where they emerged, a vast circle of eagles appeared, and at the center of the circle there was a small bed, already made for you, a place from where they wanted to emerge along with them from the rock. . . . And they came to you, and they made their final confession in the storm, and they submitted in an eagle manner—and—alas! Before my very eyes, Father, they carried and bore, and I couldn't accompany you at all. . . . Make an effort for your son. . . .'

"And in the middle of his dictating his letter, the eaglet buried his face in the armpit and he burst into tears, and you, peering at the eaglet, burst out crying.

And the puppy added:

"You saw it in a dream. And it was pointed out to you in a dream, and you can weep and wail, but with shattered wings you are not dragged through a fair—that's what healers say! . . . Do you remember the dream?"

"Yes, you've reminded me."

"About what?"

"Thank you for reminding me."

"And so?"

"And you are owed a fee for your rebuke."

"And even more?"

"Why more?"

The writer smiled.

And he turned away from the puppy and from his toothaches and from the bandaged cheeks. And he sent for ink and a quill in order to set down everything.

SHOLEM ALEICHEM
(1859-1916)

In one of his few excursions into popular fantasy, the master humorist follows the Enlightenment practice of using folk material to debunk.

THE RED JEWS
(1900)

A Fictitious Account in Two Parts

PART ONE

CHAPTER ONE
(The Red Jews, their pedigrees, their manners and mores,
their lives, their professions, their Sabbath "strolls,"
their appearance, and their cuisine.)

*F*AR, FAR AWAY FROM OUR AREAS, somewhere beyond the Mountains of Darkness, on the other side of the Sambatyon River, which never flows on the Sabbath, there lives a nation known as the Red Jews (the Ten Lost Tribes of Israel).

The Red Jews are very remote and isolated from the rest of the world and they have little contact with any outsiders; hence, they've grown coarse, and in many ways downright savage. Worst of all, they've abandoned Jewish life, Jewish history and language, and to so great an extent that they seldom if ever understand a word or phrase in the Holy Tongue—aside from borrowings like "interest-free loan," "cash on the barrelhead," "charity," "alms," "le'khaim," "mealtime," "dinner," "meshugge," and other such Hebrew terms that have become part and parcel of their everyday vernacular, which goes by a bizarre name: "Jargon."

Nevertheless, if you converse with them, they are the greatest sages in the world. They know everything, they understand everything, they like to laugh at everyone, poke fun at everyone, ridicule everyone. A lot of Red Jews consider themselves great experts and grand philosophers as well as critics and mullers, and they can talk a blue streak. And along with all these other virtues, they are as stubborn as can be—Heaven help us! If you want to debate with them, you have to gird your loins thoroughly; indeed, contradicting them is out of the question. Moreover, their greatness, their haughtiness are indescribable. Each Red Jew regards himself as the finest and the best and regards everyone else as the smallest of the small.

When the time comes to marry off a child, it's sheer disaster! They can't make a match for the heart, they can't agree on the right pedigree. And that's why they mostly find a prospective spouse in other places; each parent seeks his equal in a different town. The groom may be a bathhouse attendant so long as he's not from here. This isn't such bad business for marriage brokers; they deal very nicely in live merchandise, which—knock on wood—does passably well, so that these Jews make a decent living. . . .

The life of a Red Jew is not as cheery and merry as it may seem at first glance. There are few rich Jews, and each has his Gentile landowner—that is, each landowner has his Jew, who makes his living thanks to the landowner. Most of the rich Jews are tradesmen—that is, they pull off the greatest deals in the world. And they keep pulling and pulling until they reel in both themselves and their customers, and they refuse to die until they've gone bankrupt at least once in a lifetime. Whenever they receive money, they live it up like there's no tomorrow, and when they die, they get buried in someone else's winding-sheet. The Red Jews who hate "swindle" focus on "free loans"—that is, they lend one another money, charging interest, as was permitted in a roundabout way by Rabbi Meir of Lublin in the seventeenth century (may he rest in peace). But because of the bankrupts, who are very numerous there, a lender rarely sees his money again. Indeed, he's glad just to get his interest; but the principle is doomed. . . .

The Jews who are better off are the "usurers"; these are young men, sons-in-law still living with a wife's parents or already out on their own. They wander about on weekdays in their Sabbath caftans, smelling and ransacking whomever they may and whomever they shouldn't. These are small leeches, and once they get going, it's hard to tear them away from their sucking until their bellies are stuffed. . . .

Nor do the holders of religious offices lead such bad lives: the rabbis, judges, kosher slaughterers, cantors, beadles, intercessors, thorough-going Jews, who deal with alms boxes and with charity and with other congregational matters. And those Jews who are utterly useless and have no occupation become educators; that is, they impersonate abecedarians; these poor men drudge in the sweat of their brows, they cram their pupils; that is, they sit in dark, cramped, smelly schoolrooms, yelling from dawn to dusk, hitting, flogging, maiming Jewish boys. . . .

A large number of Red Jews are poor artisans, who spend their entire lives working for a dry crust of bread, while the others have nothing to do but bang their heads against the wall and indulge in would-be brokering—they wander about, clutching a cane and mulling: "What are we gonna eat on the Sabbath? . . ." But once the Sabbath arrives, they are unrecognizable: they dress like noblemen, and their wives and daughters adorn themselves like aristocrats, in silk and satin, sporting little hats, gloves, parasols, garnishing themselves with the devil only knows what—and they go for a "stroll": the streets are flooded with all sorts of colored frocks and with red-yellow-dark-green-ash-gray feathers. If you look at these lethally colored "ladies" and "mamselles" taking their Sabbath strolls, you could mistake them for royal children, who've never been confronted with graters, stew-pots, Sabbath stew boards, kitchen knives, and kneading troughs. You are certain to assume that they have never seen anyone adding yeast to challah dough, peeling potatoes, salting meat, or pickling cucumbers. . . . After the Sabbath pudding, the street looks like a masquerade, a circus with disguised clowns, and everyone knows very well that when the game is over, the clowns will shed their baubles and trinkets, strip off their flesh-colored holiday garments, and climb back into their old, dowdy, patched-up, every-day clothes. . . .

The Red Jews almost never eat meat—not because they're vegetarians, i.e., people who won't devour flesh. No! They avoid meat because the government has inflicted a tax on anything that's kosher, and the Red Jews can't afford the kosher meat tax. Nevertheless, their dishes are quite varied, they could fill a book. Here's a list of their culinary delights: groats, Wallachian borsht, beans and dough balls, huge amounts of corn pudding, buckwheat in honey, fat-fried dumplings, (pampeshkes with garlic), cheese cake, honey cake with poppy seeds, plum dumplings, and so many similar delicacies that don't require meat—not to mention Sabbath goodies; you can understand that they've got a dozen different kinds of Sabbath pudding: noodle pudding, layered pudding, kneaded pudding, rice pudding, raisin pudding, dumpling pudding, strudel pudding, almond pudding, hazelnut pudding, innards pudding, and so many other varieties. And they've got all sorts of fruit and vegetable stews: plum stew, parsnip stew, carrot stew, pear stew, apple stew, raisin strew, apricot stew, a spicy bay-leaf stew.

More than anything else, the Red Jews love bitter herbs and bitter condiments—for instance: lots of pepper, good, sharp horseradish, black radishes. Also: onions prepared in any number of ways: onions with fat, onions with radishes, onions with eggs, onions with herring, onions with cracklings—

and just plain onions. . . . That's why their faces are so splendid. Indeed, they get sick quite often, they have stomach problems, and they keep treating themselves. If our doctors heeded my advice, they would resettle on the other side of the Sambatyon. My goodness, they'd have tons of work—a lot better than thronging to Yehupets and Kasrilevke, squeezing together there, fighting over a patient, clawing and scratching one another like cats. . . .

CHAPTER TWO
(The capital of the land of the Red Jews, their language,
their secretive speech, their exaggerations, their curses
and their vows, their names and their literature.)

The Red Jews are actually scattered among a great many towns and townlets, and the capital is known as Red City. Now just why is it named Red City? I haven't a clue. But it strikes me that given the mud puddles that are strewn there all year round and don't dry out until the height of summer, the capital should really be called Black City. However the Red Jews are in the habit of speaking in code, in euphemisms, calling a spade a non-spade. They have a nickname for everything, so that you have to learn the very opposite of what is meant. Thus, if you encounter a man who is dubbed a "sage," you can rest assured that he's a fool, no matter how you slice it. "A man of his word" is a liar, a "penitent" is a sneak, a "polite" man is a boor, a "philosopher" is an ignoramus, a "trustworthy" man is a bankrupt, a "rhetorician" is a stutterer, a "fire victim" is an arsonist, who burns once a month like a thatched roof, and so forth.

Furthermore, the Red Jews love to exaggerate ten times over. For example: when they want to describe someone as a "good person," they roll up their eyes and they say, "A kind-hearted man, a pearl, a diamond! A Jew without a drop of gall!" And they add in Russian: "An outstanding person!" On the other hand, if the man in question is not so virtuous, they take the opposite route: "A villain! A Haman! A murderer! May his name and all memory of him be blotted out!"

For them, an attractive girl is a raving beauty! A gem! A rare jewel! And they add in Russian: "A dazzling sight!" On the other hand, a not so attractive girl—God forbid!—is described as "Ugh! A nasty troll! So feeble that she's about to croak!" For the Red Jews, a rich man has stuffed pockets: "I should be so unlucky and have one one-thousandth of his money!" While an ordinary man is a Pauper, a beggar, a shnorrer, a parasite, who starves to death a hundred times a day except for supper! . . . However, their truly precious gift is their ability to grasp one another merely by winking. From a single word they can guess a dozen more, and they don't have to converse for long. If ever we happen to be standing on the side while two Red Jews are engaged in a dialogue, we won't catch a blessed—or not so blessed—thing.

As for their curses, their raving and ranting are compliments, a welcome wagon to vent their fury: "A stinging, a wringing, a slinging, a burning, a turning, a twisting, a wiggling, a wriggling, a sighing, a crying, a drying, a withering, a dithering, a shrinking, a blinking. . . ." Nor is their swearing normal. You can hear oaths that you've never heard in your entire lives—for instance: "If I tell you even the slightest white lie, let me be nabbed and grabbed—may I be led and led until I've been led in and led out and led astray, may I become a mountain, a rock, a bone, a broom, a piece of wood, a viper, forever and ever!"

Believe you me, it would be worthwhile for our wise linguists to also deal with the language of the Red Jews. Why, according to our speculative thinkers, they have so far beautified themselves with their great achievement—may they be fitting. I assume full responsibility—it won't do them any harm, God forbid!

And their names are as weird and clunky as could be! Since the Red Jews, the enlightened Jews, love to ape other nations, parroting them in every respect, they have also taken over their names, altering them in the process: Avrom becomes Ibrahim, Beryl becomes Benedictus, Yosl becomes Julius, Feifl becomes Petronius. And Moyshe has actually been transformed into Akhriman, Mendl into Tripon, Khaim into Epifanus, Hershl into Harbona, and Velvl into Vizte. Among the aristocrats of the Red Jews you will find such names as Haplap, Scurviatus, and Sniveler—any name goes so long as it's not Jewish.

And their wives, modern women usually, likewise change their names: from Hannah to Agripina, from Deborah to Glapira, from Rebecca to Cleopatra, from Sarah to Francisca, from Leah to Isabella, from Yente to Dulcinea, from Esther to Putrife, and so forth.

For the Red Jews, the aping of names, clothes, and customs is so fashionable, that if, say, a foreigner were to cut off his nose, these Jews would all cut off their noses that very same day, and the price would be a ducat a nose!

I'm obliged to say a few words about the "Literature" of the Red Jews, about their writers, their "authors," their holy books, their secular books, and their gazettes. They have an abundance of gazettes and newspapers, which focus chiefly on polemics or so-called "criticism." One paper criticizes another, one author polemicizes against another. Their critiques are crucial. The critics try to sniff out what the other paper has to say, so that they can say the very opposite. Let's assume there are two papers: one is called *The Rose*, the second one is called *The Thorn*. *The Rose* is as conservative as *The Thorn* is radical. When *The Rose* writes merely that yesterday was warm and lovely, bright and cheerful, the sun shone and the birds chirped, *The Thorn* writes the very contrary: Yesterday was the most horrible day since the beginning of the world, clammy and gloomy, damp and dirty, smooth and very slippery. Every Sunday, the conservative *Rose* prints a description of the rich man's Sabbath pudding, which was a rare success, as fluid as a nightingale, and it croons a Sabbath hymn.

The Thorn, which knows all about that first, starts off with an editorial against puddings in general and rich men's puddings in particular, and it blazes away like a fire, proclaiming that it's high time we exterminated that disgusting dish, which Gentiles deal with. "Pudding, Sabbath, oy veyz mir!" That is the "criticism." The polemics they carry on between one another are not meant to ruffle the other one's esteem—God forbid!—without touching their personalities.

For instance: *The Rose* writes:

"Yesterday *The Thorn* ran an article attacking us with, as usual, dirt and filth. We won't respond with even a single word. We will only ask him: 'You poor, dirty, filthy, slimy, naked thorn! How much longer to you intend to rule?'"

To which *The Thorn* replies: "As long as that servile lowlife, that bribed, hypocritical soul maintains its chutzpah, insolence, and arrogance toward us. We ignore *The Rose* and we have only two words to say: You impudent thing, hide your pages and hold your tongue forever!"

Literati in general cannot compromise their authority—especially among the Red Jews, who by no stretch of the imagination, can come to terms. That's why one journalist levels a "critique" at another. Anything an author says is instantly contradicted by another author! Then the first one "criticizes" him in return, often vilifying him. Next the second author gets even, as is his due! And so very frequently a war breaks out between the writers—God help us!—and rivers of ink go pouring and gushing.

CHAPTER THREE
(The mud of High-and-Dry Street, its history,
its buildings. The sense of smell among the Red Jews,
and the romances of their boys and girls.)

The streets of Red City are, by and large, muddy, filthy, and soiled. The mud is so deep and thick that, long, long ago, on the eve of Passover (this is what "old householders" tell us, and we have to trust their word of honor), a wagon went under in the middle of the market. The driver and his horse both drowned, and the load of matzos vanished in the mire. It was only later, in early summer, when Jews celebrate Shevuoth, that the mud dried a bit, and all four victims were found: the wagon, the load of matzos, the horse, and the driver. However, since the Red Jews love to overexaggerate, I believe that the whole story is . . . a fabrication.

So let's return to the streets of Red City.

One street is called High-and-Dry Street. It is the paragon, the boulevard of the city. Why is this street called High-and-Dry Street? After all, everyone knows that its mud is the same as the surrounding mud. Well, I've browsed through ancient tomes, interviewed locals, and wondered if the Red Jews had some hidden agenda—and I was made aware of the following story:

Long, long ago, the government issued a ukase ordering the cobbling of this street. Naturally, several bids were put in by contractors, who at first underbid one another like there was no tomorrow. Then they compromised, joined forces, took hush money. I don't know what happened next. Old householders claim that originally this was no street, it was an ornament, as smooth [they say] as a noodle board, as dry as pepper, as clean as a plate— it was like a mirror! That's what old householders tell us.

But for all my intellect, I can't grasp it. So I ask only one question. If this is different than when the street was once paved with cobblestones, how, I ask you, wouldn't even the tiniest stone, as they say, get mired in the mud? What then? We have to infer that High-and-Dry Street has never been paved with cobblestones. And so how do we deal with the old householders? Isn't it obvious and evident that the whole story about the ukase, the bids, the contractors, and the hush money is a big, fat lie? In short, what good are Jewish casuistry and Gentile philosophy? If the street goes by a name, let it be! I ask you: Who is obliged to battle with an entire city and contradict a stiff-necked people like the Red Jews?

At any rate, it—that is, High-and-Dry Street—is the most beautiful street in all of Red City. That's where the richest people live, the finest house-holders, and the best Red Jews. There you will also find two-story brick houses covered with tin, plus carved porches and balconies as well as red, green, and yellow shutters. However, the architecture is very bizarre. The buildings look as if they were constructed out of spite—one wall goes in, the other goes out, one is low, the other is high, and all of them are squeezed and squooshed together, while trying to shove one another away, jutting ahead of the others, as if saying: "Shush! Let me through!"

The windows and the balconies all face the mud, but it doesn't matter, the inhabitants find it utterly charming. And the stench, you ask? Well, a stench is a stench—what can you do? The Red Jews—God help us!—aren't the pampered kind, gasping for air. "Air-Shmair!" they say, half in Russian. Consequently, their sense of smell is very numb. And since their noses are generally stuffed—may you be spared!—they have a hard time pronouncing an *M* or an *N*. They often turn an *M* into a *B* and an *N* into a *D*. So "mother" becomes "bother" and "Nathan" becomes "Dathan"! Here, for instance, is a dialogue between a man and his wife:

"By gooddess, how butsh bust I tell you to take a deedle and thread and patch my trousers?"

"Stop dagging be. I've got eduff to do! I have to bilk the cow and begid our beal! I'll prick you with my deedle, God forbid!"

All week long, High-and-Dry Street is deliciously silent. In the summer, the windows are closed to keep out flies, and the shutters are closed to prevent any sunbeam from sneaking inside—God forbid! The inhabitants remain hidden indoors. Market vendors spend the entire day in their shops, watching for a customer. Not a living soul can be found on High-and-Dry Street! But after the Sabbath pudding, the street is unrecognizable! Red boys and girls go strolling on the boulevard—but not like us, not like a hodge-podge of borsht and porridge, not like a mingling of males and females. Not on your life! It just won't do among the Red Jews. There, the girls and boys each go their separate ways. Just as if they were dancing a lively dance! And if their paths happen to cross, they peep at one another, pretending that elbows and caftans graze accidentally. Faces blush, and soft titters can scarcely be heard.

And so hushed romances frequently develop. They begin with an intense stare, a grazing of the caftan or the elbows, and sometimes even with a deep sigh. Usually, however, in contrast to romances in Yehupets and Kasrilevke, nothing comes of all that.

CHAPTER FOUR
(The first encounter of the Red Jews with one of our
own people, the glad tidings that he announced for them,
and how they shouted Hooray for him!)

One Sabbath, during the hot summer, while pairs of Red boys and girls were strolling along High-and-Dry Street, something caused an uproar, a turmoil, a tumult among the Red Jews. It all began on High-and-Dry Street and then it spread over the entire town. What was wrong? The townsfolk saw a stranger, a bizarre outsider—not a Red Jew at all! Such a man had never been spotted here before. They couldn't even imagine a Jew with no red hair—what a freak! Everyone halted to view God's wonder. They pointed, they exchanged looks, and they asked one another:

"Who is that? What is that? Where is it from? And what is it doing here? A freak! Heeheehee!"

The "freak" looked like a true Jew, an elderly man, with a high, broad fore-head, long hair and a long beard, a clear, bright, beaming face, and kind, ever-smiling eyes. It turned out that he absolutely didn't notice the hubbub he was causing. He simply walked along like a householder, with his hands folded below and his head perked up. He gazed at High-and-Dry Street with its colored houses while softly humming a ditty to himself as if no one cared a hoot about him. And the street was seething and humming ever louder and louder.

"Zhhhhhhhhhhhhh! Buzzzzzzzzzzzzz! Who is that? What is that? Where is that from? And what is it doing here? A weird character! Heeheehee!"

It was now decided that they should go over to the "character" and ask *him* personally who he was, what he was, where he was from, and what he was doing here. But since no one wished to be the first to address him, each man tried to send another, and each man became an expert in regard to the stranger.

"Go and converse with him!"

"Who, me? Why don't you?"

"Follow him! Question him!"

"You question him! Why should I?"

"Just go over to him, and I'll do the talking!"

"You go over, and then I'll do the talking!"

The Red Jews stood there, arguing and arguing, until they finally besieged the stranger on all sides. He saw that they wouldn't let him go forward or go back. So he halted and cried out to the entire throng, while his eyes lit up and burned like two coal fires.

"Good Shabbes to you, my dear brothers and sisters! I see that you are surprised by my arrival. You would like to know who I am, what I am, where I am from, and what I am doing here. So I ought to introduce myself to you. I am your brother, your full brother, your own flesh and blood—one of your ten million brethren who live on the other side of the Sambatyon River. And it's quite possible that you don't have even the slightest inkling of us while we certainly know about you. I consider myself lucky because the lot has fallen to me to announce the glad tidings. People on our side of the river think very highly of you, they act on your behalf, they wish—please understand me!—they wish to take all the Red Jews from this alien country to which you were driven 2,500 years ago, and they wish to resettle you in your own land."

"Hahahaha! Truly the Land of Israel!" Several hundred people laughed as loud as the booming of ten cannon. "He's saying odd stuff! He's crossed the Sambatyon, he wants to take us to the Holy Land. A Jew from the Land of Israel! Hurray for the Jew from the Land of Israel!"

"Hurrrrray!" Several hundred more voices joined in, and the street was soon inundated with people. They all laughed, holding their sides and yelling in one breath: "Hurrrrrrray! For the Land of Israel!!"

The stranger, welcomed so delightfully for his glad tiding, was dumbfounded. He was totally at sea! Extricating his arms and legs, he turned back, and the whole company of boys and girls followed him, laughing, whistling, and shouting "Hurrrrrrrah!" They shouted to one another, urging everyone to hurry and see the surprises:

"Hurry! There he goes—the Jew from the Holy Land! Hurry, or you'll come too late—God forbid!"

Our visitor was staying at the Red Inn, and he barely managed to get back there by the skin of his teeth, whereupon he locked the door behind him. The Red Jews still kept besieging the inn, shrieking and screeching, hollering and bellowing, rolling with laughter and roaring: "Hurrrrrrrray for the Jew from the Holy Land!" Luckily, it was Sabbath. Otherwise they would have shattered the inn to bits! Nobody wanted to move and go home—until the innkeeper, a tough Red Jew, stuck his red-haired head through a window and screamed at the top of his lungs:

"You Red hoodlums! You nasty sluts! You lousy idlers and freeloaders! What the devil didn't you see here? A guest came here, a man like any man, but not a Red Jew! Why does he deserve a thrashing? I warn you: get out of here, this very minute, this very instant! Dissolve like salt in water! Otherwise I'll beat the crap out all of you!"

Only now did the crowd disperse, and each person went home to his or her rest.

The Red Jews like it when you tell them something and make it stick. . . .

CHAPTER FIVE
(The Red Jews gather for an assembly, the stranger delivers
a sermon, the Red Jews are in a hurry, so they interrupt him!)

Saturday evening, right after the ceremony ushering out the Sabbath, the guest summoned all the town worthies to the inn—the finest people, the sages, the rabbis, the scholars, the well-to-do, the enlightened Jews, and a few craftsmen and simple Jews. The stranger sent word that he had to discuss an important matter affecting the entire congregation, a crucial problem involving them to the core.

There was a wild hullabaloo. Some stranger, a guest, one of the Black Jews, had come here from the other side of the Sambatyon. He claimed to be a Jew from the Holy Land and he was bringing news. They had to go and hear what he had to say. The Red Jews certainly didn't wait to be asked twice and they attended the meeting: young and old, from any and all classes—not for the subject matter per se, but because everyone wanted to view the stranger, a Holy Land Jew, and hear him out. . . .

The Red Inn was quickly mobbed by Red Jews. The crush was awful— a deadly, dangerous pressing and pushing. Everyone wanted to be in front, as close as could be. The walls sweated, the crowd grew denser, more and more newcomers shoved their way through—until the Red Innkeeper had a brainstorm. He locked both the front door and the room door and he soundly cursed the living daylights out of the external crowd—as is his wont!

Only now did the guest stand up. There was a smacking and a shushing—it was ear-splitting!

"Silence! Shush! Shhhhhhhhhhhh! Shhhhhhhhhhhhhhh!!! Shut up! Shut up!" The Red Jews screamed in unison! Then they sniffled and sniveled and blew their noses—as loudly as if their noses hadn't been drained for three or four years! Next, once everybody had emptied his nose, a cough was heard, then another, then a third, and so forth and so on—until they were virtually trapped by a coughing epidemic!

"What's all this coughing about?" the wealthy Jews screeched. "Cough your lungs out! Couldn't you do all your coughing at home?! You had to save it till you got here! Cough your guts out! The nerve of these Paupers—coughing here!

That very instant, the crowd hushed up. There is nothing the Red Jews dread so much as a rich Jew! When a rich Jew says, "Don't cough!"—then you don't cough! . . .

"Listen to me, gentlemen! Hear me out, my dear, cherished brethren!" That was how the guest began his lovely sermon, as a fire started burning in his eyes. "Your local brothers, the Red Jews, didn't welcome me today in a friendly and hospitable manner. They gawked at me as if I were a lunatic, and they shouted 'Hurray!' They didn't grasp what I said. Please don't think that I'm nursing a grudge—God forbid!—or that I've lost heart—Heaven forfend! I simply feel sorry for you, my brothers, for I can see how crude you still are and how boorish the people! But as you are here now, the town worthies, you are the very cream of the crop. I see rabbis, sages, scholars, well-to-do Jews, enlightened Jews, and such fine and noble people. And so I surmise that *you* will understand me.

"You must know, my brothers, that I managed to make my way here only with a great effort, an enormous self-sacrifice, my dear Red Jews. For you are tucked away the devil knows where—if you can forgive my language. To reach you, a traveler must traverse many deserts and wastelands, many mountains and valleys, forests and woodlands. And as for crossing the Sambatyon, I can tell you a thing or two about that! The Sambatyon!

"I knew very well that the journey would be very, very harsh. I knew that I would lose a great deal of time, a great deal of health, a great deal of money, and a great deal of esteem. For if I had failed to undertake this journey, my brothers, I'd be a lot better off! A lot better off, and my children even more so! . . . But my heart drew me to you, to you, my brothers. So I renounced esteem, I bade farewell to my worldly pleasures, and I set out to my martyrdom. I wanted to see you, my dear Red Jews, bring you the best greetings from your ten million brethren on the other side of the Sambatyon—your dear brothers, who serve the same God as you, have the same roots as you, from Abraham, Isaac, and Jacob. I so much yearned to see what was happening with you, and I wanted to bring you the glad tiding that you are on our minds, that we are concerned about you. For your sake, we are doing something that will gladden your hearts—God willing! . . ."

"Namely? Let's hear it! Why does he keep us on tenterhooks?" Several Red Jews who were in a big hurry were suddenly yelling!

"You brethren, please understand me, I wish to extricate you from here. It's high time you stopped wallowing in the mud, shaming yourselves—the laughingstock of all nations! It's high time you stood up, washed yourselves, cleansed your hair, and became decent human beings. They want to get you out of here just as your forebears were gotten out of Egypt, and they want to resettle you in your own land, the land of your fathers, the land that God promised Abraham, Isaac, and Jacob, the land where we once had our own Temple, our priests and Levites, our own king and our prophets—the Land of Israel! That's the name of our land, the Land of Israel, the Holy Land, where our ancestors shed so much blood, where a divine radiance emerged—our Torah. And the Torah has illuminated the whole world, opened everyone's eyes, given all nations divine radiance, freedom, science. Why, we've given everyone brightness and scholarship; yet we ourselves have deviated far from those things. We've given everyone freedom, yet we have submitted to being lackeys, servants, slaves!

"Why are you gaping at me? Why are you holding your tongues? I call to you, to you, pious Red Jews, rabbis, scholars, Hasids, orthodox Jews in four-cornered undergarments, in long caftans, with beards and earlocks. You do know what the Holy Land is, the Land of Israel! Jerusalem! Why, when you say grace after a meal, you do talk about Jerusalem." And he proceded to quote fragments from a mishmash of prayers that mentioned Jerusalem—including the utterance closing the Passover banquet: "Next year in Jerusalem!"

"Well, of course we pray!" cried several pious Red Jews. "We *are* Jews, after all! We have to pray and serve God!"

"Pray and serve God?" the guest shouted. "That's just it! You pray, but you don't know what you're praying! You talk, but you don't know what you're saying! You're sick, but you don't know what's wrong with you! You wander about aimlessly, you lie in a daze, and you sleep badly!"

"Get to the point! Get to the point!" the hurried Red Jews hollered. "Enough moralizing! Get to the point!"

"You want me to get to the point? You hate moralizing? You hate being told the truth? I tell you: You sleep badly! So I've come to wake you up, yank you out of your sleep, and shout into your ear: 'Get up, brothers! It's time! You've been lying in the mud for two thousand years already, and you don't sense how miserable you are! The worm lying in horseradish feels that there is nothing sweeter in existence! . . .

"'Get up! Look around you! Think about your situation! Your situation is dangerous! You're in danger—terrible danger! You grow weaker by the day! You sink deeper and deeper in the darkness! You keep growing cruder and cruder! You suffocate in the crush! You eat one another alive!'"

"The upshot! The upshot!" cried the hurried Red Jews. "Tell us the upshot!"

"You want to know the upshot? You're in a hurry? The very same thing was true for us! The very same people with the very same character! It was the same for us, the ten million brothers, on the other side of the Sambatyon! But then we looked around in time, and we saw that we were a small nation and that people wanted to devour us. They dropped hints—that is, they beat and battered us. We understood that the world is an ocean, and people are fish. We came to realize that all the sweet ditties crooned to us in all times by our prophets and our choristers were certainly very beautiful. But they were in fact nothing but songs performed long ago or in the distant future, when the Messiah came!

"We now felt that help was purely in our own hands, and that no one would help us if we didn't help ourselves. We knew that if we wanted to live, we would have to be like other people—as we ourselves had been long, long ago. We got acquainted with our own wonderful history, our own beautiful language, and we saw that we had no reason to be ashamed of our name: Jew. We are a nation like any other nation, but we lack a land, a land of our own. So we shouted at the entire world: 'Land! Land! Give us a land!' We began all going to a single place, all talking about a single theme. We concluded that we first had to wash ourselves, cleanse our hair, and wash and cleanse our children. We had to educate ourselves, become decent, prepare ourselves and our whole nation for the immense task awaiting us. We started having meetings, congresses, collecting money, establishing a fund, teaching our children, building religious schools and secular schools—shkoles!"

Several hundred Red Jews suddenly yelled in Russian: "Shkoles? We don't want shkoles! We don't need to know! We don't want shkoles!" And the whole crowd began talking, yelling, screaming in all ways. One man shouted: "We don't want shkoles!" And another man screeched: "We *do* want shkoles! We *do*!" And a whole mishmash resulted, a wild concert! "We know enough! We don't want shkoles!" "We *do*!" "We don't want shkoles—the hell with shkoles!"

CHAPTER SIX
(The stranger gets up from the table, and the Red Jews
all talk at the same time. They argue, they quarrel, they outyell
one another, then they disperse and go home peacefully.)

When the Red Jews hold their tongues, they hold them. But when they talk, they talk a blue streak, they gesticulate—and all together! They howl, they holler, they bellow, they chatter like the magpies in the forest. Their mouths don't shut! Human strength isn't powerful enough to stop them! No matter how hard the guest begged them to let him talk, to finish what he had started, no matter how loudly the throng pounded on the tables and bawled: "Shushhhhhhhh! Shhhhhhhhhh! Shut up! Shut up!"—it didn't help in the least! And they paid as much heed even to the rich Jews! Our unfortunate visitor had to break off his sermon in midstream and shamefully step away from the table, while hearing the Red Jews chomp and chew his words up, each version according to his own mind and matter.

"He wants shkoles. . . . We don't want shkoles. . . . From the other side of the river. . . . Noodles. . . . Says something about the Holy Land. . . . We need associations. . . . We don't want associations. . . . What do you say to his gift of the gab? . . . I wish I were there. . . . Shush! Silence! . . . What kind of swindler are you? . . . The Holy Land—give me a break! . . . If you're told you're nuts, you'd better believe it! . . . Forgive me, but you're a moron! . . . You creep—I'll slap your face! . . . Associations—we need associations! . . . What an idea—and who's gonna pay? . . ."

"Did you hear? We're already talking money!" The wealthy Jews grabbed their pockets. "Do they mean us? Huh? C'mon! Let's go home!"

One of the associations—the Bread and Muzzle gang—called out to a rich man: "Are you hosting a card game tonight?"

"Of course. I wouldn't miss it for the world! Where were you all yesterday?"

"Visiting the sage till it was time to go to synagogue."

"Really? Who got buried? Who groped the Tartar? Tell me, tell me!"

"Oy! Don't ask! It was a regular conflagration! First the well-mannered man crooned a Sabbath hymn, as was customary. Then the victim of the fire sweated. Next the practical man's four kings topped the three aces.

"C'mon, let's go! Time's a-wasting! The night doesn't stand still for anyone!"

"Heretics! Hoodlums!" the rabbis screamed! And so did the other religious officials, who'd gathered in a corner. "Heathens want to take us to the Holy Land! Christian priests want to bring the Messiah! Jews! Why are you holding your tongues? Help us! Help us! Rescue us!"

The toughest resistance was put up by the sages and scholars among the Red Jews, the ponderers, the philosophers, the politicians. They demanded that they be given to understand by way of wisdom, scholarship, history, philosophy, politics, and humanity—to understand how it was possible and where it had ever been heard! How could anyone do this to a nation like the Red Jews, who have been residing calmly on this side of the Sambatyon for two thousand years now, who wouldn't harm a fly, and who never stick their noses into anyone else's business? How could anybody suddenly tell them: "Gather together, Red Jews, pack up, go across the Sambatyon, and settle there in some wild country among wild Turks!"? What will all the other nations say, especially the Turks? Who has ever heard of such a thing? We ask you: Prove to us that such a savage business has ever taken place in history! That's one thing. The second thing is: You're slapping civilization in the face—it's shameful and disgraceful! The whole world is looking forward to the sunshine—every nook and cranny will be lit up. All the countries will become a single country, all nations will become a single nation, all languages will become a single language, all human beings will become a single human being. . . ."

"Good morning to you and good luck! You've hidden well! What do you mean: All human beings will become a single human being?" A bespectacled youth jumped into the fray! It turned out that he too was a scholar. "Look, I can understand that all nations will become a single nation. But this?"

"Not so fast!" He was interrupted by a scholar with a huge bald spot on his head. "Let's review things from the speculation aspect. What do we mean by 'nation'? Where does the term come from?"

"A people is called a nation!" the bespectacled youth threw in. "The word 'nation' is spelled with a 'T' but pronounced 'nayshun.' Nation! Do you get it already?"

"It's crucial!" said yet another scholar, a man with bushy eyebrows. "It's crucial, it would take a whole book to describe it!"

"A paper!" This was said by yet another young scholar. He was delighted that he had managed to interject such a lofty word.

"What's all this chatter about a paper?" said the bespectacled scholar, who envied the other scholar for using the word "paper." "A book is one thing and a paper is another. A book is a treatise and a paper is a paper."

"It's all the same thing!" the scholar yelled angrily. "It makes absolutely no difference!"

"They're as different as night and day!" the other scholar shouted.

"I beg your pardon!" cried the first scholar. "But there's absolutely no difference at all!"

"I beg *your* pardon!" the other scholar yelled in lousy German. "But there is a wide-world differentshul!"

One of the Maskils (enlightened Jews) butted in: "Let it be already! Have you ever heard of scholarly men being totally unable to compromise? When one says 'day,' the other says 'night'! You'd be better off forming an association and bringing unity among the Red Jews so we can start to achieve something! That's a bit more necessary than all your scholarship and philosophy, all your treatises and scientific papers!"

It was already past midnight, and the Red Jews were still rattling and blabbering, shouting and screaming, all together and gesticulating wildly, as usual. The rabbis were hollering: "Heretics! Hooligans! Devils! Pork eaters! *They* want to bring the Messiah!"

The sages, the scholars, the philosophers kept arguing, squabbling, quarreling among themselves. They only wanted proof right away, on the spot—evidence of how it would be done. How would an entire nation be taken across the Sambatyon and resettled in the Holy Land? It just didn't stand to reason! Let's check out the histories of all the other countries. . . .

"All the other countries are simply different!" cried a scholar. "And the Red Jews are also very different!"

"It's all the same!" yelled another.

"Like day and night!" shouted the first scholar.

"I beg your pardon, but there's absolutely no difference!"

"I beg *your* pardon, but there is a wide-world diffrentshul!"

"Enough is enough!" the Maskils shouted. "We should try to do something that would benefit the people. Your speculation won't fill any bellies. Find some other solution if you don't like the idea of the Holy Land. The nation is waiting, the nation is looking at you. And all you care about is speculation, philosophy, and politics!"

"That's so true!" added the poor people. "Believe you me! You should also start thinking about us! Do something for our sake and for our children's sake!"

But no one heard them. Everyone wanted to talk, nobody wanted to listen. And they kept talking and talking until they gradually started dispersing. The first to leave were—slowly—the rich Jews. Then the Bread and Muzzle gang. And as the Jews went home, they poured out aphorisms and witticisms, they discussed and derided the stranger, who had crossed the Sambatyon, and they poked fun at the Red innkeeper and the rabbis and the scholars and the Maskils and the new Association of Jews from the Holy Land and all the Red Jews and the entire world.

CHAPTER SEVEN
(The blessing of the moon indicates the start of the late-summer
month of Elul, and a master remains a master.
The stranger leaves, and the Red Jews remain Red Jews.)

The next morning, when the Jews woke up, the guest, the stranger, seemed to have vanished. Meanwhile, the rabbis couldn't stand the stranger's heresy. Just imagine! The Red Jews had long been looking forward to the arrival of the Messiah, fervently reciting the Credo—Ani Maimin: I believe— and unanimously shouting: "Next year in Jerusalem!" And now suddenly, they were supposed to think about the Holy Land too!

Well, they weren't indolent. They headed straight to the authorities and they wrote and submitted a document that said as follows:

"See and know that a stranger, a devil, has come into our city and has incited the population. We have witnesses—the entire city will swear that it is true. We therefore beg you, for the country and for the Exchequer, to understand that this is no minor issue. Indeed we cherish the Exchequer more than anything else on earth. We must waste no time, we must look around and take measures to keep the Red Jews from leaving the straight and narrow path—God forbid! And since we do not know who the stranger is, where he is from, what he is, and what he is up to, we must search him to see if he has anything in black and white. We must determine whether he is a counterfeiter or a fugitive or a renegade or one of today's rogues, who inflame the populace, lead us from the path, lead us astray, to Gehenna! The whole business is definitely not kosher."

And so it was. The stranger was still asleep. Meanwhile, the Red innkeeper received a "drinker," a Gentile. And the drinker said to him as follows:

"Just listen, brother. We always figured you to be a man of few words, an honest Jew. You'd sooner take in a carcass than deal with illegal goods, with contraband."

The Red innkeeper was an experienced man and he was esteemed by all the drinkers. First he got a small flask with two glasses.

"Just listen to what they write about you," said his buddy, putting on his glasses to read the document. "And who do you think writes this stuff? Your God-damn Red Jews. How could we tell what's happening here if your people didn't write these denunciations?"

"And what does your lordship desire?" said the Red innkeeper, pouring refills for both of them. "But first, let's be healthy and let's drink le'khaim— to life! Le'khaim, your lordship! May God give you everything I wish for you! Now tell me, what is your desire?"

"Just tell me, old chum," said the drinker. "What sort of bizarre person did you put up on the Sabbath? Where's he from, and what's he doing here, and what kind of sermon did he deliver yesterday?"

"May you be strong and sound in all your limbs!" cried the innkeeper. "I don't understand a word of what you're saying, it's all Turkish to me! First of all: I don't know who he is! Secondly: He left here long ago! And thirdly: I've never put up such a traveler in my entire life! I haven't the foggiest idea what this is all about! L'khaim! L'khaim! Let's both of us be healthy! Your lordship—may at least half of what I wish for you come true for you!!"

"Oh, are you ever a shark!" the drinker laughed. "You really should've been strung up on a tree branch long ago! Luckily I like you—the devil only knows why! I know that you lie like a trooper! Listen to me and 'fess up and show me this character! I want to sound him out! . . ."

"Ah, with the greatest esteem! Is there anything I could be hiding from you?" The innkeeper then hurried into the visitor's room and woke him up.

"Yehudah Blau! Get up, get dressed, get packed, and get going—but fast! You're in serious trouble! I'll get the horses hitched for you! Don't delay! Have a good trip in the name of the God of Israel! You mustn't look back! And when God brings you home safe and sound, by the skin of your teeth, you should—God speed!—say the blessing for a person who's escaped a great danger! Don't ask any questions, pull yourself together, and get the hell out of here! You don't know the Red Jews and you don't know our clerics. . . ! Travel safe and sound and greet each person very amiably!"

From then on, the Red Jews have lived in peace and quiet—thank goodness!—in utter silence! Each Jew thinks only about himself, each is busy with his own concerns. The shopkeeper looks out for customers, the money lender writes IOUs "With permission to receive interest," the small leeches charge usury, the craftsmen drudge in bloody sweat, the butchers slaughter, the cantors sing, the abecedarians teach, the market vendors carry their sticks through the streets and ponder: "Where can we get our Sabbath food?"

Young Maskils publish their cumbersome articles in the gazettes; they gather every Sabbath eve, hold meetings, and they talk about where to obtain money for buying land in the Holy Land. No sooner do the rich Jews hear the word "money" than they exclaim: "How should I know? Paupers, beggars, shnorrers, abecedarians, adolescents want to buy the Holy Land! What a laugh!"

The "assocrats" or the members of the Bread and Muzzle Association chant in unison with the rich men and make fun of the new association, "Red Holy Land Jews." They play cards—various sorts of card games—including sixty-six. . . . The sages and scholars likewise get together every evening and never stop arguing about the question of the Holy Land: Can the problem interfere with progress, can it harm civilization? One line of reasoning leads to another, every question raises another question. They talk, they sharpen their tongues, they ventilate their speech, they quarrel and they squabble— they don't omit the slightest smidgen of material. They finally get to that age-old enigma: What came first? The chicken or the egg? The egg, from which the chick hatched? Or the chicken, which laid the egg in the first place? And how come the white and the yolk lie together but never get mixed?—And so many profound suppositions and so forth and so on!

And what about the poor? Not a word! The poor are the poor, they quietly starve to death—who can prohibit them, by God? Death is a divine issue. We all die eventually. And their children likewise go about as free as birds, naked and barefoot, unwashed and ill-kempt, and they wallow in mud with all the pigs and with—if you'll forgive me—the rabbis. And their other clerics? Let them be! They've got enough work dealing with the Sabbath laws, with Passover liquor, with closely supervising the production of matzos, and with all the other aspects of Jewish life. They also have to make sure the Red Jews have what they need on the Feast of Tabernacles: ethrogs—though not from the Holy Land, God forbid!

In short, that side of the Sambatyon is silent (knock on wood!): still and calm, a thick, dark, hushed night has been overtaking the Red Jews, and they want to sleep. . . . Shhhhh! You know what? Let's not disturb them. Let's disperse quietly, tiptoe away, and let's wish them a good night and pleasant dreams.

Good night, Red Jews, sleep soundly!

Part Two

Chapter Eight
(The rulers of the land, their hatred of the Red Jews—
the stroke that struck them abruptly and unexpectedly.
The stunning things they describe about that misfortune.)

The Red Jews are not the only people dwelling on that side of the Sambatyon. There are other nations there too: Arabs, Persians, Indians, Turks, Tartars, and so on and on. And they claim to be the top bananas, the rulers of the country, and they call the Red Jews merely a background, a leftover of troubles. And even though the Red Jews claim that they belong here too, and even though they provide historical evidence that they are ancient residents, equal to any and all other ancient inhabitants—nonetheless, the latter turn a deaf ear to the claims and the evidence of the Red Jews, who therefore regard themselves as aliens, foreigners, visitors, outsiders—the devil take them!

For many centuries, the other groups lived in peace and harmony with the Red Jews—that is: They allowed the Red Jews to live freely in the places where they had been living. And no sooner had they settled somewhere, than they were in great pain! In the towns, they were assigned special streets for their esteem—where they could do as they wished: open shops, run taverns, sell liquor, buy grain, act as brokers, agents, traffic, lend money, charge as much interest as possible. . . .

And that was what triggered the first dislike of the Red Jews, the first hatred. When their money was needed, they were treated with the greatest delight, the greatest tenderness. But then, when it came time to repay them, and no funds were available, the Red Jews started presenting IOUs, promissory notes, the responses were violent: "Leeches! Exploiters! Heirs to their fathers! Spongers! Parasites! Swindlers! Men who don't see and don't reap, but they do eat—how they eat! What do we need them for? What do we need the Red Jews for? Let them go back where they came from!"

The Red Jews heard all these things and they merely said: "They can bark and bark till they're all barked out! When they need us again, they'll come back to us."

They operated on the assumption that all their power lay in their cash, that a Jew should focus on earning a livelihood, that he should make money—and the more the merrier! The Red Jews, who made fun of everyone and laughed at the entire world, including themselves, uttered some very crude things about themselves: "All human beings are divided into two categories: scoundrels and scoundrels. If you have no money, you're simply a scoundrel; and if you do have money, then you are certainly a scoundrel! For if you weren't a scoundrel, you wouldn't have any money! A scoundrel with money is better than a scoundrel without money! If you're gonna eat pork, you might as well indulge like there's no tomorrow! If you've got money, you've got respect, you've got a pedigree, you've got the Torah, you've got wisdom. In a word: Money makes the world go round!

"The other nations ridicule us. They call us: 'Ragamuffins! Charlatans! Villains! Bloodsuckers! Exploiters!'" Let them rant and rave—who listens to them? We ourselves know who we are. We are the chosen ones, God's aristocrats. After all, we do pray to Him: 'Thou hast chosen us among all the nations. . . .' What good is all their blabber compared with—if you'll forgive my uttering them in the same breath—a single reading of the weekly Torah portion in synagogue? What value do they have compared with the honor of reciting Biblical verses in synagogue? Let them talk, let them write! We've suffered worse Hamans—and we'll survive again, God willing! We'll keep going to the rebbe again, grabbing sacred morsels from his table, celebrating the Sabbath. So once and for all: Don't worry! It's a great life:

"The rebbe told us to be glad,

"To be glad!

"And drink till dawn,

"And drink till dawn!"

That was how the Red Jews consoled themselves, and it went on for several years, until a short while ago, when suddenly a thick, dark cloud came drifting over them. There was thunder, and flashes of fiery lightning illuminated the terrible gloom. And a hailstorm, a dreadful hail of stones, erupted and dropped upon the heads of the Paupers huddling somewhere outside the town. The Red Jews awoke as if from a long, long sleep, wiping their eyes and asking each other: "Hey! What is it? What's happened?"

"What's happened?" cried one Red Jew. "I'll tell you what's happened! A fine thing's happened! Jewish employees of a Jewish shop got into a fight with the Persian clerks of a Persian shop over a Persian customer! A Jewish employee of the Jewish shop—his name was Itsik—deliberated and then called the Persian customer. The Persian clerk—his name was Ahaswerus (like Esther's husband)—deliberated and then said to the Jewish clerk, to Itsik: 'Yid!' The Jewish clerk—Itsik, that is—deliberated and then said to the Persian clerk: 'Oaf!' The Persian clerk deliberated and then said to the Jewish clerk—Itsik, that is—'You're all spongers, scroungers, garlic eaters!' The Jewish clerk—Itsik, that is—deliberated and then said to the Persian: 'And you're all pigs, drunkards, and morons!' So the Persian deliberated and then said to Itsik—"

"It's a shaggy-dog story!" the others interrupted. "He deliberates, then he deliberates! There's no rhyme or reason! It happened to a landowner, a country squire named Agg! He had put up his estate as collateral, with his forest, his mill, his coach and horses, and he had been paying interest on all his loans until even the principle was swallowed up! He lost his estate, his forest, his mill, his coach, and his horses—he was bankrupt! So the squire swore he'd have his revenge!"

"A fairy tale! That's not what happened at all!" a woman broke in. "*I'll* tell you what happened. There's a noblewoman, a very wealthy landowner—her name is Vashti (like Ahaswerus's first wife). And she's got a son around eighteen. He got tangled up in debts, signed IOUs. Boy, did they ever get a leg up from his loans!"

"There's no rhyme or reason!" a poor woman broke in shrilly. "That's why ducks go barefoot. Since Vashti's son signed IOUs, they had to smash my shop, rip my bedding, and scare my kids to death! Do you get it? It wasn't enough for them to wreck my shop and make me miserable, they had to invade my home and—"

The poor woman burst out shrilly and wanted to describe her misery, but they wouldn't let her! The men pushed her away.

"Go and bother the rabbi, bother him! Complain to him, not us!"

And the crowd kept dropping bombshells about what had happened. Everyone was ranting, everyone was raving, gesticulating wildly, hitting the roof, repeating everything as it had happened, as it had begun, and interrupting one another.

"What did they want from me?" a snub-nosed woman lamented. She dealt in eggs, thereby supporting a blind husband and seven children. "What did they want from me and my eggs? A full basket of eggs. Vey iz mir, vey iz mir! What am I gonna do now?—How awful, how awful!"

"I had only one dress—for the Sabbath!" sighed a young wife, raking the garbage for shards, tatters, feathers, and fragments of glass, hoping to find something. Her pillows were shredded, her dishes were shattered, and even the chipped soup tureen was—alas!—smashed to smithereens!

"We're all totally impoverished!" said a shopkeeper, a haberdasher—one of the Paupers! In the good years, his income had amounted to as much as a decent person can drink in a minute. Now his ribbons were drenched with olive oil, with kerosene, with tar, with matches—a hodgepodge! His hands demonstrated the hodgepodge.

"That's nothing!" a dry-goods dealer consoled him. "Grabbing whole pieces of material and cutting them into bits—that's a feat, that takes expertise!"

"I ask you—what am I gonna do now? What chance do I have without a workshop?" cried a poor cobbler with a waxen face.

"Where there's no flour, there's no learning!" This proverb from *Ethics of the Fathers* was quoted in Hebrew by a lame tailor with feathers in his earlocks. "What do you need a workshop for anyway? There's no work to be had. People are saying that the city fathers are thinking about doing something for us, but I don't much care for their line of thinking. They've been thinking too long. God only knows what they can think up!"

"What are you scared of? It can't possibly get any worse!" the cobbler replied, looking at a poor woman who was standing in the middle of the street, with her hands folded, her head twisting. She was talking to herself in a raspy voice: "Oh, God! Oh, God! Oh,God! God! God! God!" She'd lost a child in the panic, and her mind was gone. Children, urchins, kept running up, parroting her—pulling, yanking, snatching! When parents spotted them, they chewed them out: "Get the hell away, you scoundrels, you wranglers, you hooligans! The hell with you!"

The youngsters backed off, scattering like frightened magpies, and they headed for the synagogue. A cluster of Red Jews was standing there. A young man was describing miracles, telling how his grandfather, eighty-something years old (knock on wood!), had escaped misfortune purely because of his great virtue, his piety. The young man was gesticulating, and the entire crowd was listening to him.

"As soon as the whole business began," the young man went on, "I rushed over to my granddad—long may he live! When I got there, more dead than alive, I looked—and I saw my granddad—long may he live!—sitting calmly, wrapped in his prayer shawl, and poring over a holy tome, as if nothing were happening.

"'Grand-Papa,' I said. 'God is with you! Take off your prayer shawl, hurry up, and let's get out of here before they manage to arrive!'

"'Go, my child,' he said very calmly. 'Go, my child. Go! I'm remaining here.'

"'What are you saying, Grand-Papa? God is with you. But what if they get here—Heaven forbid? C'mon, Grand-Papa, hurry, hurry!'

"'There is no escape from God!' he replied. 'If my time has come, then the Angel of Death will find me no matter where. He can't be fooled! Go, my child, and good luck to you.'

"And imagine! Just as I was leaving my grandfather—long may he live!—who should I encounter but—"

At that instant, a mob of Red Jews came gushing out of the synagogue, the cluster outside came apart, and the young man broke off in the middle of his story. All of them went up a hill, to a graveyard. They trudged, speechless and wordless, bowing their heads. Old Jews murmured, weeping and weeping softly and reciting Biblical verses. . . . What was this? A funeral? A corpse? Who had died? No one had died. They were carrying the holy parchment shreds of the sacred tomes in order to bury them in the cemetery, as is the custom.

"See, dear God, and look," said the rabbi to himself, first in Hebrew, then in Yiddish. And two tears rolled down his sallow cheeks and vanished in his beard. "See, dear God, whom have you punished?—Heaven forbid! For whom have you displayed your great power?!?"

And from above them, the fiery sphere looked down at them, the sun, burning, baking, roasting, singing the huge, dark spot on the earth—the spot known as Paupersville.

CHAPTER NINE
(The great assembly in the studyhouse, the rich Jews don't wait
to help the young men talk about emigrating—the Jews decide
to form a committee—"We don't need a committee!")

It has been an ancient and unbreakable law for the Red Jews: Whenever they are victimized by a danger, a panic, an evil decree, a fire, an epidemic, they pull themselves together as one man, assemble in the synagogue, and deliberate. They deploy all methods, trying to annul the misfortune and get rid of the disaster. First they do penance; they figure that before anyone else, they are at fault. God doesn't punish for nothing, so you have to reconcile with the Good Lord—namely: pray, recite Psalms, order the whole congregation to fast, and so on. And God is a father, after all. If you call him, He responds.

However, this disaster, which hit the Red Jews so suddenly, was so new and unjust that they were confused, stupefied, dumbstruck. They were in a daze, they didn't know what to do, where to go, whom to shout at. The misfortune was so enormous that the town didn't wait to be summoned by the congregation. The rich men took the task upon themselves; lugging sacks, householders trudged from home to home, and each man gave whatever he could: a loaf of bread, a roll, a little flour, salt, pepper, onions. But on the third day, just as it's hard to stuff a live sack, the Red Jews among the Paupers began starving. And they were furious! Why were they holding their tongues? So they decided to call for a big assembly in the big studyhouse, and all the finest householders were to attend.

The poor Red Jews received a new skin; each one gained a new vital strength when they learned that the wealthy men had informed the rabbi that they, the wealthy men, would most certainly attend the assembly—God willing!—with no excuse for absence. And they, the wealthy men, would ponder the problem and figure out how to assist the Paupers. They, the wealthy men, said they clearly agreed to help as much as they could. And even if it cost them a bit of money, they didn't care—at least didn't care that much, of course. For nothing much that is pertinent to this problem can be quantified with a gauge, a measure—especially money, you do understand? . . .

However, by the time those words, going from mouth to mouth, reached the Paupers, they had rolled and grown like a rolling snowball, getting bigger and bigger. A rumor spread among the poor that the rich Jews were promising them the moon, no matter what it cost them—the rich were willing to give away their last shirts, do whatever it took to aid their poor brethren.

And the Paupers were delighted! And poor Jews started going to the town, lots of married couples with little children, and they lay siege to the great studyhouse and occupied it. That day, each poor Red Jew felt as if he were a precious stone, a trembling child, an only son, who was spoiled, fondled, pampered. You were so nervous about him that you never got a good night's sleep. Wow! To utter a mere word! Red Jews and Paupers in the bargain. Apparently, today is *their* seventh year! They're in seventh heaven— seeing how Paupers become great among themselves and inaccessible! A city father tried to converse with them, but was chased away as if the Red Jew had said: "Have respect, you scoundrel! Who are you and who are we? You're a simple householder, and we are poor people, from the Paupers! . . ."

Later on, when all the finest congregants gathered in the great study-house, the rabbis, the Jewish judges, and the rich Jews arrived, as did the remaining "Seven Better Householders of the City." The beadle then mounted the studyhouse platform and knocked three times: "Hush, be silent! Hush, be silent! Hush, be silent!" Next, a rabbi stood up and delivered a very long sermon, quoting the Bible endlessly, entangling the verses, demonstrating according to the Midrash (the body of post-Talmudic legends) and according to tradition that this was the true end of days—that is, the coming of the Messiah. He *had* to come, damn it! He *had* to! And now that the Red Jews were facing disaster—not to mention the Paupers, who were virtually at sea—the town saw that it had to help them as best it could: some with advice and some with money. . . .

"No, it's the other way round!" cried several wealthy men. "We will help you ourselves as much as we can. And even if it costs us a little money, it doesn't matter, of course. For nothing that is pertinent to this problem can be quantified with a gauge, a measure, especially money—you do understand?"

It was hard to understand why the rich men were now so good, so mellow, despite the scourge. Indeed, people could infer from their statements that they felt guilty about something, that they had sinned against the poor

Red Jews. The rich men were so cheerful, so hopeful, that they even allowed young men, Maskils (Enlightened Jews), to stick in their noses, offering advice that was written down.

"There's only one approach!" said the Maskils. "Only one single way to help the poor: emigration."

"What does 'grayshun' mean?" the rich men asked.

"Emigration," said the young men, "means 'emigrate, go away, travel, leave here, and resettle in other countries.'"

"Go where?" the rich men asked. "To what countries?"

"Where? Far, far from here," the Maskils said. "To India, to Ethiopia, to Babylon, and especially to Egypt. Because there's lots of land in Egypt, but few people. Everything there is dirt cheap. They're practically giving the soil away. That's what it says in the newspapers."

At some other time, the young men wouldn't have been tolerated, they would have been severely punished for daring to butt in among older men. However, the latter were deeply moved by the idea of emigration. It was a way to get rid of the poor. No laughing matter, huh?

"Wow! It's an interesting idea!" said the rich men. "Honestly, why shouldn't we try it out? Egypt is a possibility."

"What are you talking about?" the rabbi butted in. "Have you forgotten what we say at Passover every year? 'We were slaves to Pharaoh in Egypt.'"

"Never mind Passover!" the rich men replied in a peremptory tone. "How can you compare today's Egypt to the Egypt in the Hagada? Why, now it's the Holy Land and no longer Egypt!"

The young men were very glad that the rich men were siding with them. They moved closer to tell them what the newspapers were saying about emigration and committees. First of all, they had to form a committee.

"Welcome to a new idea!" A Red Jew attacked the young men. "We've already got committees galore! Who cares about committees—come with tees? You'd do better talking about money! Where do we get the money to help so many poor Jews—knock on wood—to move away?"

"Money?" said the rich men. "Money is crap! Each man will register a monthly donation, as much as he can. Not too much, of course, for too much is too much. For nothing that is pertinent to this problem can be gauged or measured, especially money—you do understand?"

"Emigration! Egypt! Committees! Monthly donations!" The Red Jews were all screaming together, each louder than the other—yelling, shouting, gesticulating, as is customary. And when the Red Jews who were outside the synagogue heard that the Jews inside were talking about emigration to Egypt, about forming committees, and about agreeing to monthly donations, all hell broke loose—all hell!

"What's that?" they shrieked. "This is why they brought us here? To form committees, toss balls, child's play! What good is fussing and fretting, talking about gray-shun, starting committees, making promises, building castles in the air? You give us today, and God will take care of tomorrow! You send us to Egypt! To Goshen! You send us to the devil! So long as it's right now, today! After all, we can't return to the Paupers. Our wives and kids wander over the bare earth under God's heaven, starving to death, and you wanna form committees for us? Never!" They then added in Russian: "We don't want committees! We don't want them!"

Shouting and shrieking, a whole lot of poor people burst into the study-house, and the hubbub and hullabaloo became earsplitting! At first, the rich men didn't know what the yelling was all about. But when they heard the words: "We don't want committees. We don't want them!" the rich men got agitated and they defended themselves:

"Have respect! Have some reverence! You beggars! The town is meeting here for your sake, we're thinking about you, we're racking our brains, trying to figure out how to help you, how to send you away from here. You've got some nerve, you beggars! Go home! There you can call the shots, you can boss around the Paupers!"

THE LAST CHAPTER
(Material for the historian in regard to the history
of the Red Jews. A letter from an émigré
who wound up in Egypt. The end of the Red Jews.)

Someday, in later generations, a historian will write the history of the Red Jews; and when he reaches this chapter, he will halt. He will not believe many of the stories and he will omit many other things. He will be ashamed to divulge things that can normally take place only among savages. Jews call themselves the merciful and the sons of the merciful; and the historian will not believe that some Jews could possibly benefit from the misery of the people, earning a livelihood from their misfortunes, embezzling a lot of community funds, stealing right and left, squeezing their purses, feeling no mercy for Jewish blood. . . .

"God help us!" That's what the historian of the Red Jews will say. What kinds of Jews were those who treated their own poor brethren worse than animals? What kinds of people were those who drove the poor émigrés the way you drive a flock of sheep to the market? What kinds of creatures were those who let their sick wives and their tiny tots wander across the bare earth under God's heaven, in rain and in frost? What kinds of companies were those who ran ads in all newspapers, claiming that for a small price they would take whole families of Red Jews across the ocean and resettle them in the free and happy land of Egypt; but then it turned out that they had deceived the Red Jews, pocketing the cash and haphazardly abandoning the poor travelers en route, somewhere in the desert. What kinds of dandies were those who spent money like water, tricking and enticing poor girls, promising them castles in the air and then selling them to the Turks for enormous sums?

"Oh, my brethren!" the historian will say, quoting the writer Mendele Moykher-Sforim (Mendele the Book Peddler), who has achieved an eternal name for himself among us, on our side of the Sambatyon. "Oh, my brethren! . . . I weep for other slaps and I say: 'Good people and sick people suffer often in this world. Perhaps they wish to repeat their remorse. But when slapped people slap themselves, when scratched people scratch one another, I weep—oy-vey!—and have nothing to say. When I remember—alas!—the people you yourselves have captured, have tortured, it breaks my heart! My heart weeps and shouts: 'Oh, my fiercely beaten, my savagely fallen nation of Israel!'"

When the historian comes to write the history of the Red Jews, he will keep tearing out his hair upon reading the correspondence printed in the newspapers of that era or described in the letters sent home by the Red Jews from the "free and happy" land of Egypt. Here we have one of those letters:

A Letter Sent Home by a Red Jew
My dear and faithful kith and kin,

I am writing you, not in ink but in bloody tears, from this happy land—may it burn to a crisp! If it had sunk into the ground like Corah, that wealthy man who defied Moses and Aaron in the desert, then I would have recognized it in time! If only I had broken a leg at home, before I was scheduled to leave. And since I did leave, I wish I had died on the way, before arriving here, in this wild Egypt. If I tried to depict all the misery we have endured from the very start until now, there would not be enough pens and paper in the entire world. Nor does the Sambatyon River contain as much water as the tears we and our wives have shed so far. The agents who brought us to the ship took away all our packages—including our prayer shawls and prayer straps—and that was the last we saw of them.

It was the eve of the Sabbath, and our wives wanted to bless the candles, but there were no candles to bless. Our wives moaned and mourned, and their curses were also aimed at the committees! Next, a tempest arose, and we barely escaped with our lives. The waves were as high as houses, as tall as brick buildings. We had already said our final prayers, we were sure that we were goners. We suffered three weeks of this torture. We didn't eat a crumb of food. All we saw around us was sky and water, until we just barely, barely managed to reach dry land. And upon staggering ashore—sick, broken, tormented, starving—we had to spend a day and a night out in the rain. And at this point, my wife, Esther-Rose, decided to give birth—to a boy. The boy died, and my wife—may we be spared!—remained deathly ill. We didn't have even a spoonful of soup or jam to refresh us.

It was only on the next day that they took pity on us. People came from a committee. They registered all our names, led us away, and put us up in a stable. There we were given rolls and oranges—one to each of us. We were then taken somewhere else, all our names were registered again, and we were put on another ship. And we traveled for a day and a half. And the sun baked and burned us like the fires of hell, until we were tossed ashore, in a place of sheer sand—no trees, no grass, no houses, only sand and sky, sky and sand. And that was where they wanted us to settle. We were given work: hauling driftwood from the sea and building houses, digging earth and planting trees. And we were assigned an angry, crazy foreman, who slapped and punched us. We yelled and screamed. So they tied up each one of us and whipped us mercilessly. We barely managed to survive.

Once we were untied, we scurried every which way, in all directions, as far as the eye could see. Eventually, several families gathered in one place, here in Egypt, where we might be all right, since you could make a living here. We were given jobs: standing at the machine, turning the wheel from the crack of dawn till the wee hours of night, for which we got a silver dollar every day per adult and half a dollar per child. In short: It wasn't so bad. Every man here is addressed as "Mister." Horses wear eyeglasses, and people wear paper chemisettes. But there's a shortcoming. They don't celebrate the Sabbath, they don't honor holy days, and we don't understand their language, for they stammer and stutter—goodness only knows what that language is!

They are pitiless. You could starve to death in the street, and no one will stop. Unless there's some kind of sensation! Everyone runs, everyone works! And if somebody can't work and wants to buy and sell, he can deal in whatever he likes—old clothes, matches, shoe polish, or buttons. And he can "make a living"—that's what they call it here. But I tell you: "It could be worse!" A lot of people earn less than me. The other day, I ran into Yankl (Mordkhe's uncle) and boy! Was I dumbfounded! He had changed so much that I barely recognized him. He was dressed like a crazy organ grinder, in a short jacket, a long robe, and a high fur hat like a stew pot.

"Yankl," I says, "is that you?"

"Who else?" he says. "Of course it's me! Except my name isn't Yankl now, it's Mister Jack."

"What are you doing, Mister Jack?" I says. "How are you faring in this country?"

"So-so!" he says. "At first, it wasn't much fun. But now, thank God, 'I'm making a living'!

"What kind of work do you do?" I says.

"I wash laundry!" he says.

"What do you mean: you wash laundry?" I says.

"I mean," he says, "that I've learned to wash and iron clothes."

"So that's what you call: 'Making a living?'" I says.

"Oy, veyz," I says, "mir! My uncle's son has to be a washerwoman, and in Egypt to boot!"

He then told me what had happened to our other friends, the Red Jews, who had managed to get here. All of them, thank God, were "making a living." Moyshe had learned how to seam holes in underpants, Beryl was hammering pegs into heels, Mendel was baking bagels, Mottl was selling brooms. Others were unemployed and begging for alms. As for the rest, Mister Jack didn't know what had become of them, perhaps they were gone.

The two of us had a good cry, consoling each other, and we swore that we would get together at least once a week. It would make things a bit easier, for we were so homesick that it was killing us. I felt I'd forgive them for all their happiness, hand them all my dollars just for a glance of the Paupers. Oh, if I had wings, I'd fly over to you, my dear and faithful kith and kin! We send you our friendliest greetings, and please tell them that we do not forget them for even a minute. And we beg you—that is, I and Esther-Rose, long may she live!—beg you to send each single one a friendly greeting. And be sure to greet Uncle Yossi and Aunt Sossi and each one of their children. And Uncle Shaye and Aunt Khaye and each one of their children. And greet my sister Beyle and Aunt Keyle from us and from our children, and tell them not to move from where they are; for they will regret it and they will curse themselves thoroughly, like Pessi the widow, who was punished along with her two daughters, alas, and lots of others like her. You see, she let herself be talked into believing that the two girls would be happy there; they'd marry very wealthy men with lovely presents. But in the end, they were fettered and sold as slaves to the Turks—supposedly for a whole lot of gold. . . .

For God's sake and for goodness' sake: Do not let yourself be talked into anything by any of those dandies with their white chemisettes and gold watches—those dandies who promise you the moon! Be especially careful with your daughters—guard them like the apple of your eye! If only I had turned a deaf ear to stupid assurances, committees, emigrations, if only I had been certain that I would die and be buried according to the Jewish tradition when my time came—among my dear and faithful Paupers.

And we ask you—that is, I and my Esther-Rose, long may she live!—we and our children ask you again to bring greetings to Uncle Yossi and Aunt Sossi, to Uncle Shaye and Aunt Khaye, and to my sister Beyle and my Aunt Keyle, and their children. Greet each single person very cheerfully, and for God's sake and for goodness' sake, do not leave where you are!

Such were the letters that the Red Jews received from their fathers and mothers, their sisters and brothers, their friends and relatives galore! And even though the news was generally dismal, each letter sadder and sadder, the recipients kept looking forward to better news. They didn't lose their faith, they kept hoping that the letters would grow more joyful and cheerful—God willing! Did their hopes come true? We'll find out later, when God will give us life, and we go sightseeing and find out how things stand with our brethren in Egypt—the Red Jews in their new Exile, their new Diaspora.

There is one thing I can tell you for sure: The Red Jews who remained in their homeland are not the same Red Jews as before. Ever since that clap of thunder, their lives were turned upside down. They virtually sobered up, awoke from a long, long sleep, and started grasping their situation, understanding that it couldn't go on, that they had to come up with something. And when they started mulling, they finally digested the words spoken by the stranger who had visited them from the other side of the Sambatyon and had told them a tale about a land, their own land: the Holy Land. And the Red Jews tackled this issue with ardor and fervor, as is customary for them.

But you want to know the outcome, don't you? The ultimate results? Did the Red Jews do anything? Did they right any wrongs? Or were they satisfied merely to talk and to talk and then talk some more? Or did they reach an agreement? Or did each man fend for himself? Or did they eventually talk themselves out? Or, as they reached a climax, did they hear a voice shouting in Russian: "We don't want it!"

But this is where the curtain drops, and we bid farewell to the Red Jews for a long, long time.

I. M. VAYSENBERG
(1882-1938)

Born into a poor family in Poland, Itsik Meyer Vaysenberg (also spelled Weissenberg), a worker in diverse trades, began publishing his Yiddish writings in 1904. A realist for most of his life, best known for his gritty novella about a workers' strike, *A Shtetl* (1909), he nevertheless penned a tiny number of folk-like stories early in his literary career. The Yiddish texts of the two stories presented below appeared originally in *Shriften* (*Writings*, Warsaw, 1911).

"The Penitent" offers a recurrent plot in Jewish literature—particularly when the Jewish man is seduced by a non-Jewish woman. The theme even went beyond the confines of Jewish literature when Adelbert von Chamisso, a French-German poet, titled a verse novella "Der Baal-Teshuvah." Incidentally Chamisso popularized the story of Peter Schlemihl, the man without a shadow, who eventually wound up in Jacques Offenbach's opera *The Tales of Hoffmann*.

Toward the end of his life, Vaysenberg, surprisingly or not, turned almost exclusively to mystical themes.

MAZEL-TOV
(p. 1911)

A SCENE

THE SHTETL WAS IN AN UPHEAVAL—the rebbe had suddenly fallen ill, and you could tell from the very first minute that the gates of heaven were waiting!

There were all sorts of mixed, heartrending shrieks. The women stood in the doorways of their shops, their faces pale and bleary as they gaped silently and curiously at the end of the street. Khaye-Gitl, who dealt in pottery, was scurrying about, flushed and deeply confused. When she ran into another woman, she raved and gestured wildly. And Hirshl the teacher dashed at the head of the group, his neck long and scrawny, his head poking out, his hands in his back pockets, his thin elbows thrust aside like the wings of a skeletal goose about to take off. And a schoolboy, with skinny legs and blazing cheeks, with shiny little eyes, dashed after the teacher.

"Come to the synagogue! Come to the synagogue!"

The synagogue was mobbed.

Teachers and pupils from all the surrounding Jewish elementary schools came pouring and fusing together.

A man draped in a red shawl stood at the lectern and, with hands stretched out and imploring, he recited the Ninetieth Psalm verse by verse, in a lamenting voice—the Prayer of Moses, the Man of God. And the worshippers echoed those words so sorrowfully, poignantly, and confusedly that the children stood there with gaping mouths and gawking eyes. . . . And at the wall, a bitterly groaning adult buried his face in a small Psalter, then raised his eyes to the ceiling and shut them again. He stood still with a craning neck, like Isaac about to be sacrificed by his father Abraham. . . . All the men kept praying and praying. And they tried all kinds of numerological approaches to the letters of the rebbe's name, the initial of each verse, and the crowd sighed and prayed some more and sighed some more.

The rebbe's courtyard was chockfull of worshippers. The simple craftsmen—cobblers, tailors—stood with gawping eyes. Young, silent Hasids trudged back and forth, each one on his own, tripping over the end of his belt. They didn't talk to each other. Teachers and pupils were coming back from the synagogue. The teachers stood in a special group, exchanging glances, conversing softly. Schoolboys, mischievous brats, and ordinary children clambered over the fence around the rebbe's orchard and across the roof of the icehouse, where they lay down lengthwise and crosswise. All their eyes were fixed on the rebbe's window. . . .

In their confusion, beadles and frequent visitors dashed in and out. Yeshiva boys, prize students, stumbled after them. And if you asked any one of them how things stood, he would throw out his hands, sigh, and hurry on.

And there, behind the porch, a whole flock of women stood in the corner, making faces and clutching their aprons, ready to weep into them. . . . Suddenly, a shouting came from the house, a yelling. The crowd stirred. Someone screamed through the window: "The doctor says we have to pray!" The crowd was petrified, and the women pushed through the horde of men, who made way for them. The shrieking women poured into the street. More women joined them. As they reached the marketplace, the women divided in two. One throng headed for the synagogue, the other for the graveyard.

The men in the marketplace roamed about like lost, silent sheep—until someone brought the worst news. The crowd froze, and trembling lips murmured the words that Jews recite upon hearing of a death:

"Blessed be the True Judge! Blessed be the True Judge!"

And now the crowd had nothing—no hope and no comfort. . . . All it could do was to pity the rebbe's widow and her fatherless children. The congregation had already moved aside, relying on God's mercy and putting up with His decree.

The beadles were dashing to the post office with lengthy telegrams. The window of the room where the rebbe was lying was blazing red. A cold drizzle was coming down from the leaden sky, and it dripped and dripped and it clung to your flesh, making it twist and bend. Craftsmen put up their collars and buried their heads in their arms. Teachers wrapped their necks in red shawls, and their faces grew darker and darker, shrinking in a deeper blue. Lips quivered and eyes half-closed.

That night, wagonloads of Hasids came rolling in from the poor shtetls; and by morning, the area was jammed, the streets were teeming with droshkies and coaches. By noon, all shops were locked up, and the entire populace gathered in the rebbe's courtyard. Suddenly, a shout came from the doorway: "Open up! Open up!" The stretcher carrying the corpse appeared, and the crowd stirred.

They entered the graveyard to hear the oration. The worshippers were packed in like sardines and they stood there cheek by jowl, men and women together. And over the tables and over the desk from which the Torah is read—it was dense and black everywhere. And the candles burning in the chandeliers added a terrible heat. All faces were red and drenched with sweat, and the hot, stale air was suffocating. The stretcher was put down in front of the Holy Ark, where the Torah scrolls are kept, and the Hasids lifted themselves on one another's shoulders, trying to catch a glimpse across the sea of heads. And all the Hasids hovered aloft, atop of each other, and all of them together. And all eyes silently focused on the very center. . . .

And then a shrill voice was heard: "God, You are taking too great a hostage for our sins. You have taken our crown—the crown on our Torah! And, for our many transgressions, You have taken the instrument without which we can do nothing!"

And again silence reigned. And then a muffled sniveling emerged from among the girls and the women, with kerchiefs on their heads half-revealing only their eyes.

The stretcher moved, and the crowd pushed its way out through the two doors and through the windows, which had been slammed open.

The street was already blocked. A chain of Hasids on both sides and a throng accompanying the stretcher pulled and pulled, like a long strap made up of thousands of faces. Biblical verses were recited all the way. And the rebbe's son, his heir, followed the stretcher, resting his forehead on it and burying his face in his hands. . . .

At the cemetery, the grave and the coffin were already waiting among the trees. During the burial, the worshippers said "Mazel tov!" And the entire crowd then turned to the son and said: "Mazel tov, rebbe! Mazel tov!"

The grave was full, and the new rebbe was reciting the Kaddish, the Jewish prayer for the dead.

And comfort and new hope began to blossom. Faces were purged, and a fresh spiritual love began to flower in the eyes. And the Hasids all gathered around the new rebbe and with glowing eyes they saw the Shekhinah, the Divine Radiance, resting on his pale face.

A hush settled in the cemetery, the trees swayed silently and whispered their prayers.

THE PENITENT

A TALE

ONCE THERE WAS A JEW, a peddler, and he trudged through the villages, with his pack of merchandise on his back: needles, ribbons, corals, and other little things. On this income, he barely managed to support himself, his wife, and his child.

Now one winter's day, the peddler was wearing only a light jacket with a thin belt and carrying his goods on his back. It was snowing heavily, and the wind was blasting so hard in his face that he could scarcely catch his breath. He was also dog-tired and barely able to drag his legs out of the fallen snow. The peddler therefore thanked the Good Lord upon reaching a small forest and sitting down to rest under a tree. As he sat there a bit screened against the wind, the peddler felt his exhaustion. His eyelids drooped and he dozed off, forgetting that it was extremely dangerous to sleep in a frost. You run the risk—Heaven forbid!—of freezing to death. Nevertheless, the peddler dozed off, with his goods on his back and his head against the tree, and he had wonderful dreams. He dreamed that he had found a treasure and was counting the ducats—and meanwhile he was freezing more and more. And he would have simply frozen to death, counting the ducats in his dream, and then leaving this world.

But then a peasant woman and her boy, the two of them wrapped in a fur and a kilim, came driving through. When they spotted the Jew lying there, they pitied him and they started reviving him. They rubbed him with snow until his complexion changed, and he emitted a soft sigh. Next, they put him into their sleigh and headed back to their village. Once there, they doused the coach with cold water from the village well, stripped the Jew buck-naked, and put him in the coach. They rubbed him all over with the cold water until he heated up, turned red, and started gradually coming to. Next they wrapped him in coarse cloth and laid him on the warm oven so he might catch up on his sleep.

The Jew awoke at dawn. The daylight had just begun seeping through the tiny window. The roosters were crowing in the garret. When the Jew found himself lying on an unfamiliar oven in a hot room, he was dumbfounded! Upon stepping into the room, he saw a holy icon with a flickering wick hanging in the corner. A bed stood by the wall, and a peasant woman was sleeping in it. Her hair was disheveled, and she wore a tiny cross on her throat. And a peasant boy was lying and snoring on a bench by the oven.

Unable to grasp all this, the Jew thought to himself: "A dream!" Relying on God's mercy, the Jew shut his eyes again and went back to sleep.

When the Jew awoke once more, he saw that the peasant woman had already gotten up. She slipped into a petticoat and went over to have a look at the oven where the peddler was lying. He shut his eyes yet again. He was still certain that it was all a dream. And when he reopened his eyes, he saw that the woman had washed and was now kneeling at the image in the corner, murmuring softly with raised eyes, and then crossing herself.

The Jew rubbed his eyes, he now sensed he wasn't sleeping and he tried to move a limb, but he couldn't. All his limbs were aching, but he understood that he wasn't dreaming, he had suffered some kind of accident and was now lying sick—may you be spared! But he couldn't recall when and where he had fallen ill or how he had gotten here.

Meanwhile, the woman had stood up and turned around. And when she saw that the peddler was awake, she amiably smiled up at him on the oven and said "Good morning" in Polish. But he was afraid to respond. Perhaps he had been kidnapped—God forbid! When she saw that he was scared, she calmed him in her language, and she told him everything that had happened to him and how he had gotten here. Upon hearing this, the Jew became miserable—poor man! When she saw his reaction, the peasant woman asked him why he felt so sad.

He said to her: "Why shouldn't I feel sad? I'm a long way from home and I'm sick. "

The peasant woman comforted him. Then she lit a fire, warmed up some milk in a glazed pot, and handed him a clean glass. He refused to take it, however. So she said that a sick man must drink. He mulled for a minute, then took the glass of milk. Next, she woke up the boy. She told him to go and water the cow, then she went back to the fire. She set two huge pots of water to boil bran for the cow and the pigs. The boy stood in the middle of the room and got dressed. He looked up at the Jew and he smiled. The Jew now realized that the boy enjoyed the fact that he and his mother were keeping the Jew alive. Tears started running down the Jew's cheeks. The peasant woman came over to him again and asked him once more whether the oven was too hot for him to lie there. She then brought him a bundle of straw and prepared a bed for him in front of the oven. The Jew lay there for a while, and she waited on him loyally, serving him all sorts of food and drink that a Jew can consume in a Gentile home.

Meanwhile, at home, the Jew's wife and child were waiting for him. And the people in the shtetl were already saying that he had frozen to death out in the fields or been devoured by hungry wolves. Supposedly, the snow had buried him, and his body or at least his bones wouldn't be found until Passover, in the springtime, after the snow had melted.

Day after day wore by, and the Jew was living in good health, in the home of the peasant woman. They had grown so used to each other that he was gradually forgetting all about his home and his family.

One night, when the small window was frosted over and the room was silent, the Jew was lying on his bed in front of the oven, and the peasant woman was sitting on the long wooden bench. Holding a spindle, she spun flax near a pine splinter that was burning in the fireplace. When the Jew looked at the frozen pane, he shuddered from top to bottom and he thought to himself: "Who knows where I'd be buried in snow now if they hadn't helped me!" His heart wept and he sighed.

The peasant woman heard him. Looking up from her spinning, she saw that his face was transformed. She felt very sorry for him and she asked: "What's wrong, my dear Jew? Why are you sighing so deeply, and why have your features changed so much?"

He replied: "I can't help sighing—my life is so full of misery!"

She comforted him: "Look, you're still very young. Why do you allow yourself to be so miserable? Tell me what you're missing, and how I can help you?"

"I'm not asking anything of you. I couldn't possibly repay you for everything you've done for me."

"No, my dear Jew!" she answered him. "I've done nothing at all for you. And since you live in such great poverty at home, why don't you stay with me? You'll lack for nothing. I've got a whole farm—a field, wheat in my stable, a garden, beehives, and some cattle. All I'm missing is a man to run the farm. . . . If you like, you can run the farm and you'll lack nothing."

When the Jew heard this, he flushed, cast down his eyes, and held his tongue. She gazed at him with loving warmth in her eyes, like a sister peering at her lone brother. Then she silently stood up, took his hand, and looked into his eyes. She wanted to ask him why he was so embarrassed, but she felt his hand trembling in hers, so she let go. Since she had a kind heart, she didn't wish to make him unhappy.

She snuffed the pine splinter in the fireplace and went to bed.

The Jew was unable to get a wink of sleep that night. He silently prayed to God, asking Him to stand by him in his temptation. But then he glanced in her direction and saw that she was sleeping in her bed. And the flickering of the wick under the icon cast light on her face and her exposed upper body. All at once, lust overcame him. And when she got up in the morning, she knew that the Jew would stay with her and be agreeable to everything. And at Easter, when the Catholic priest made the rounds of the villages to sanctify their bread, the Jew and the peasant woman went along with him. They stepped into a church, where the Jew converted to Catholicism and married her.

Years passed, and the baptized man forgot that he had once been a Jew. One day, a cow had wandered off into the forest, and he went looking for her. He trudged and trudged, wearing a sheepskin and a four-cornered hat, clutching a whip and whistling a ditty. As he trudged, he penetrated deeper and deeper into the forest, amid dense trees—and he still couldn't find the missing cow. Eventually, however, he spotted the tail end of a kaftan sticking out from under a pile of moss. Raking it with one foot, he discovered a corpse, a murdered Jew, whom the Jewish community was traditionally liable to bury. The man was terror-stricken. He covered the corpse and dashed away.

But after taking a few steps, he heard the corpse say: "Why are you deserting me? You're a Jew, aren't you?"

Thinking he was imagining it all, the convert hurried on. But he was haunted by that voice, which became all the louder and more tearful: "Please don't abandon me! My wife will remain a grass widow. According to Jewish custom, I ought to be buried by the Jewish community."

The convert shuddered and he turned back and sat down by the corpse. He sat there, all alone, in the depths of the forest, gazing at the corpse, despondent and wistful. His heart poured over and, out of dread or yearning, he remembered the melody of "The Thirteen Divine Attributes" [Exodus 34, 6–7], which include God's mercy, and he crooned the words to the melody of "Majesty, Dread and Terror"—a prayer sung around The Days of Awe.

But then the carpenter of the forest came driving by. He was going to celebrate a circumcision in his home and he was bringing the kosher butcher to perform the task. Now when they heard the sobbing voice, they went over to see what was wrong. First they put the corpse into their wagon, but they no longer recognized the convert. So they asked him how he knew that a Jew mustn't abandon a Jewish corpse. However, he didn't answer, he turned away with tears in his eyes. The two Jews then drove to the shtetl to bury the corpse, and the convert went his own way. While trudging home, he removed the cross from his throat and threw it into the grain field.

From then on, he felt a deep longing to usher in the Sabbath on Friday evening. He stopped going to the tavern with the crowd of peasants. Instead, he sat outside his door, peering across the field and yearning quietly. And at times, unbeknown to his wife, he stole out of his home and he hurried two miles to the carpenter's cottage. Before reaching it, he lay down in the grass and, from far away, silent and despondent, he gazed into the window, where the Sabbath candles were burning. The carpenter and his wife and children, with shiny faces and in their Sabbath garb, sat around the radiant table, joyfully singing hymns and praising God. The next day, on the Sabbath, the convert spent the entire day in his garden, lying all alone, under the beehives, and very fidgety.

Whenever he now drove into the forest to gather wood, he would be overcome with heartache. He then tossed away the ax, sat down under a tree, and began reciting psalms in a weeping voice. And he kept reciting until past nightfall. It was only when the stars appeared that he loaded up his wood and drove home so quietly that no one found out.

One day, after harvesting his grain, cutting his hay a second time, and attending to his beehives, the convert joined a few of his neighbors—all of them Gentiles. Together they loaded their hay into several wagons and drove off to sell it in the town. When they arrived, the convert saw that the marketplace and the surrounding streets were deserted. Not a living creature could be found. The doors of homes and stores were nailed shut, while the booth in the center of the market and the tables bearing pork and baked goods were empty. The whole shtetl was forsaken as if it had died.

However, a loud din came from the side where the synagogue was located. So the convert left the hay and dashed over to the synagogue. Through the open doors, he spotted burning candles, and Jews in smocks and prayer shawls were swaying to and fro, praying to God. A few women, who had come late after caring for a sick child or nursing a baby, hurried by in their stockings and white garments and, fearful and frightened, they dashed into the women's section. Then a greater clamor was heard—thousands and thousands of voices at the same time. And the convert shuddered like a tiny bird in a tempest, he was overcome with the terror of the Day of Atonement. Then he hurried back to his wagon and lay down underneath it. And his heart wept dreadfully and his entire body shook.

The peasants asked him whether they ought to go home, but he didn't reply. They figured he had gone crazy and they went off to the Christian baker, while the convert remained alone under his wagon. At the synagogue, the sobbing and the weeping grew louder and the clamor spread across the entire marketplace. And when it came time to recite the Prayer of Validation for the awesome Day of Judgment, the convert began shaking, and a deluge of tears came pouring from his eyes. He wept deplorably and he poignantly crooned the melody of that Prayer of Validation. And so the convert lay under his wagon the entire day, all alone, his face down. He was dressed in his sheepskin, his fur cap, and his dusty boots, and he lamented so powerfully that the very stones melted.

Toward evening, when the sun was setting and the day was fading, the worshippers in the synagogue began chanting "Ne'ilah," the final prayer on the Day of Atonement. The convert wept even more ardently—and suddenly he shrieked, stood up, and dashed to the synagogue. There he threw himself on the threshold and he shouted:

"Jews, sons of mercy, I want to repent, I want to become a Jew again!"

And before the worshippers could reach him, he gave up the ghost.

HERMANN GOLD
(1888-1953)

Arriving in America in 1905, Hillel Gurny wrote under the pseudonym Hermann Gold. His collection of *Mayselekh* (*Fairy Tales*, New York, 1928) for children contains a number of folklore themes, including the perennial motifs of sibling rivalry, mate hunting, etc.

THREE SISTERS
(1928)

Girls, you girls,
Stop your chatting,
And listen to me.
Listen to a tale,
Bright as a candle
And truly correct.

ONCE UPON A TIME there were three sisters and three brothers. The three sisters lived in one end of the world, in Egypt, and the three brothers lived at the other end of the world, in the land of Persia, by the Sambatyon River, which rests on the Sabbath. The three brothers didn't know about the three sisters, and the three sisters didn't know about the three brothers.

Now one day the first sister went to the marketplace to find a husband. And she spotted a Turk standing with a goat, and the Turk called her over. So she went over to him. And the Turk said to her:

"Come here, my girl. I've got a goat for you. Milk her every morning and every evening, and give the milk to your intended, so that he will love you."

The sister looked at the goat and she didn't know what to say. The Turk then said: "You don't have to mull it over, my girl, I don't want a lot of money. Give me a silver ducat, and I'll give you the goat."

So she took her hand out of her pocket, but she didn't know what she was doing. She gave the Turk a silver ducat and she took the goat back home.

When the other sisters saw the goat and heard the story about the Turk, they burst out laughing:

> When a Turk with a goat
> Spots a sage, he will gloat,
> And my oh my,
> The Turk will lie!

The first sister now realized she had done something stupid. So she joined in the laughter. They all loved her, so they didn't care.

One day, the second sister peered through a window and gazed at the marketplace to see if her intended was coming. The first sister said to her: "It would be better, my dear, if you went out to the marketplace. And after you find a husband, I'll find one too."

So the second sister went out to the marketplace. And there she saw a Tartar sitting on the ground and playing on a fife. The Tartar then said to her:

"Come here, my girl, and you'll see the fife that I made the first time I visited my intended. And when I played the fife, I knew she had captured my heart. Now we are old, and so I've brought my fife to the marketplace."

The second sister looked at the fife and she didn't know what to say. The Tartar then went on:

"You don't have to mull it over, I don't want a lot of money. Give me a silver ducat, and I'll give you the fife."

So she took her hand out of her pocket but she didn't know what she was doing. So she gave the Tartar a silver ducat and she took the fife back home.

When the other sisters saw the fife and heard the story about the Tartar, they burst out laughing:

> A Tartar with a fife,
> He's got black hair in life,
> His trousers are black,
> And he lies, alas, alack!

The second sister now realized she had done something stupid. So she joined in the laughter. They all loved one another, so none of them cared.

One day in early summer, the third sister picked a fresh flower in the garden and she twisted a new braid. Then she sat down by the door to see if her intended was coming to the marketplace. So the second sister said to her:

"It would be better, my dear, if you went out to the roads that run along the eastern fields, since the marketplace is filled with clever people who will cheat you. And after you find a husband, I'll go out and find one too."

So the third sister went out on the green roads. Then a horseman came riding toward her with two horses. And the horseman said to her:

"Come here, my girl. I've really feasted my eyes on you! Mount the second horse, and I'll ride into the king's residence with you. There you'll pick the finest husband in the world. I've lost my pouch of ducats, so I'll sell you a horse to buy food for them and also for me."

The sister looked at the horse but she didn't know what to say. The horseman went on:

"You don't have to mull it over, I don't want a lot of money. Give me a silver ducat and you'll mount my horse."

The third sister took her hand out of her pocket, but didn't know what she was doing. She gave the horseman a silver ducat and she mounted the second horse.

The two of them rode along. The third sister forgot all about everything in the world, and the image of her intended was reflected in front of her along all roads, in all colors. And she was truly bewitched.

So they rode for a long time until nightfall. All the stars were spread out. And the sister's eyes were already tired.

The horseman then said:

"Why don't we dismount and rest between two mountains, and the horses will rest too."

So they left the horses among the trees. And the sister and the horseman promptly fell asleep.

When they awoke, the day was ice-cold. Snow was cutting across the roads, and the horses were flying with the wind. And the third sister was tied to her horse, and her eyes questioned the horseman.

And the horseman said to her:

"You were sick, and the doctor said we should ride along the roads with you until you recover, because you keep talking about everything you see along the roads. The roads have bewitched you. It's been eight months since I started dashing with you, and now we've reached the ends of the earth!"

The horseman untied the third sister, and she began remembering what had happened to her. Now at the end of the road there was a tavern, and as they came closer, the horseman said:

"I'll leave you with your horse for a while and I'll ride into the tavern courtyard. I'll come back out very soon."

And he rode into the tavern courtyard.

Meanwhile the three brothers were sitting in their father's vineyard, which looked out at the Sambatyon River at the ends of the earth. The brothers were talking about sending out the oldest brother to the distant roads, which run into the far world. And when he found and brought back a bride, the second brother would go out to the distant roads.

All at once, they saw a wanderer coming in the distance, with his bag on his shoulders. And indeed, the wanderer was none other than our Turk with his goat.

When the Turk came closer, the brothers served him bread with salt and a pitcher of water from a wellspring that flowed between boulders out of the Sambatyon. And the Turk sat down next to the brothers and he said:

"Meanwhile I'll stay with you for a while, drinking your water and eating your bread, until the girl comes with my goat."

The oldest brother came alert as if waking up from a dream. And he asked:

"Can your goat be milked, and is the milk sweet?"

The Turk replied:

"You can milk her every morning and every evening, and the milk is sweet—as is the girl."

The oldest brother mulled for a while and calmed down. Then he said to his other two brothers:

"Well, I'll sit here now and wait."

One day, on the eve of a holiday, the Turk was fishing in the river that flows at the ends of the earth, right against the Sambatyon. And the three brothers sat in their father's vineyard, as snug as a bug in a rug, and they talked about sending the second brother into the distant roads that run out into the wide world. And the second would find a bride and bring her back. Then the third brother would take to the roads.

Suddenly they spotted a distant wanderer with his bag on his shoulders. And indeed, the wanderer was none other than our Tartar with his fife.

When the Tartar came closer, the brothers served him bread with salt and a pitcher of water from the wellspring that flows out of the Sambatyon. And the Tarter sat down next to the brothers and he said:

"Meanwhile I'll stay with you, drinking your water and eating your bread, until the girl comes with my fife."

The second brother came alert as if waking up from a dream, and he asked:

"Can she fife on the beautiful fife, and will she come alone?"

The Tartar replied:

"She fifes beautifully, like magic—you'll see! And she is beautiful too. And she'll come with her sister, and both sisters are beautiful!"

The second brother mulled and he soon came to. Then he said to his brothers:

"Well, I'll sit here and wait."

One winter's day, when the dear white snow was spread over the entire vineyard, and the Turk and the Tartar cleared away the snow from around the house, the three brothers were sitting and saying that when the snow had melted and the beautiful summer came, they would have to send out the third brother along the roads that lead into the wide world, and he was to find and bring back his bride. Next the other brothers would go out along his roads. Suddenly they saw far away a horseman riding all this way. And this was no other than our horseman, with his two horses and with the third sister!

The horseman came closer and he rode into the tavern courtyard.

And they served him bread with salt and water from a wellspring that came flowing out of the Sambatyon. And the horseman sat down and he said:

"Meanwhile I'll stay with you, drinking your water and eating your bread, until the other two sisters arrive."

Now the third brother came alert and woke up as if from a dream, and he asked:

"Where is the third sister, the youngest of the three, who should be coming along the white roads?"

The horseman replied:

"I'll come out of the snow and then she'll be here by the count of ten!"

The brother mulled for a while and then he came to. And he said to his brothers:

"Well, I'll stay here now and wait."

The other two brothers joyfully hugged him and kissed him, and they said:

"We'll all wait together! And all three sisters will come here soon!"

Now the horseman entered with the third sister. And the third brother and the third sister hugged and kissed one another as ardently as if they had known each other for a long, long time. And the Turk and the Tartar likewise came in. And they all formed a ring around the third sister and the third brother. And they danced around them in a circle.

Now let's go and see what's happening with the other two sisters.

Those two sisters saw that the marketplace was gone. All the wagons had driven away. It was getting close to midnight, the gates of the town would be locked, and the third sister still hadn't come back. So the first sister took the goat, and the second sister the fife, and they left the town and went out in search of the third sister.

As they were walking outside the town, they ran into a beggar with a bag, and the beggar said to them:

"Come here, girls, and I'll tell you where your sister is, since I'm actually coming from where she is."

The two sisters looked at him and didn't know what to say. For they didn't know where he knew their sister from. And the beggar went on:

"You shouldn't be so surprised, for there are only three of you, not a hundred, and I know the entire world! And if you like, I can even tell you where your intended are!"

The sisters were so surprised that they were at a total loss for words. And the beggar went on:

"You don't have to mull it over, I don't want a lot of money. Give me the milk from your goat, and that will be enough!"

So they gave him the milk from the goat, and he drank his fill, and he lay down in the field, under a tree. And he said:

"I'm tired. Play something on your fife, and I'll have a nap. After that, I'll stand up well-rested, and I'll tell you all the good news!"

So they played on the fife for him. And he fell asleep right away, his bag at his head, and the two sisters sat at his feet and waited.

They simply sat there and waited. And they felt sleepy. But they were afraid to shut an eye. And they mulled:

The beggar's a liar. The beggar's cheated them.

Then they heard the beggar talk in his sleep, and he sang:

> Sisters two,
> That's who!
> Soon the dew
> Will cover them too!
> Everything at dawn
> Will wait till morn.
> The beggar didn't lie,
> He says to wait
> And don't worry about fate.

And the sisters laughed:

"Tomorrow brings sorrow! The night is almost through, we've watched and waited too. Let's rest and have a nap and not be cheated."

So they had a nap and they dreamed that all of them were riding the goat. The beggar in front and the sisters in back. And the beggar fifed the fife so high. And he drove the goat so high, all the way to the clouds in the sky.

The sisters asked the beggar:

"Why are you fifing the fife so high, good beggar, driving the goat all the way to the clouds in the sky?"

The beggar laughed and he replied:

"I fife high. If you wake up, you'll see that this is no dream, it's reality. And I drive the goat so high, all the way to the clouds in the sky, because I fly with you across the biggest oceans in the world. And I'll fly to the ends of the earth with you."

They opened their eyes and they saw that this was true. They were flying across the entire world. And in broad daylight. And they were flying very swiftly, as swiftly as a day in a minute. And they flew across the days and the nights like birds, and they vanished with their black heads. They couldn't understand how you can see all that with your eyes!

It began to snow. So they knew that winter was here. And the beggar said to them:

"Now we're approaching the ends of the earth, where the three brothers live. For every sister a brother. Without the goat, you would never have managed to come to them. And without the fife, all this would be a dream."

They soon came down to the ends of the earth, where the Sambatyon flows, and they stood there with their goat and with their fife, and the beggar with his bag. The second sister took the fife, and she didn't know what she was doing, and she fifed on the fife. Now the second brother came running, and the other brothers after him, with the third sister, with the Turk, with the Tartar, with the horseman. And they danced in a circle.

The sister pounced on their sister, and the sister on the brothers, and the brothers on sisters, and they celebrated wildly! The four strangers sat down— Turk and Tartar, horseman and beggar—on the two horses, two on each horse, and they zoomed across the Sambatyon, where the rocks are thrown and fall on them, and a moment later the four strangers had vanished.

Cockadoodledoo!
The tale is through.

THE WISE FOOL

KING SOLOMON WAS SITTING at a window in his palace, thinking in his wisdom about the wide world and its wonders. For he was very wise and he knew everything. All at once, he saw a dove flying toward the palace; the dove, whose wings were covered with dust, tapped wearily on the pane. Solomon opened the window and let the dove come in.

The dove raised its right wing, releasing a letter consisting of seven lines, written in seven languages, in seven colored inks, and sealed with seven royal stamps.

King Solomon peered at the stamps, then peered into his books, which described all the states in the world—those that were under his rule and those that weren't. But he couldn't find out whose stamps they were.

So he tried to read the languages in the dove's letter. But they were foreign, alien to him!

The king was saddened because all his wisdom had made him a fool together with the foolish dove, even though he had mastered all the seventy languages of the world! So he said to the dove:

"You've brought me an enigma. Now give me the key to its solution. I won't rest until I know everything."

The dove replied:

"Your Majesty, I come from a distant land on the other side of the sun, and your greatness is known everywhere, and people talk about your marvelous wisdom. So I soared all over the land until I reached the vast forest where the world ends. There I selected a tree and I rested in its branches seven days and seven nights.

"By the eighth day I felt fresh and strong enough to begin a new journey. Then, I heard a bird pecking above me, in the tree. It told me to come up. I flew up to the bird, and the bird said to me:

"'Have you ever heard of King Solomon? He's a big fool!'

"'I said:

"'No, he's a great sage. And I've come from my land on the other side of the sun and I've been traveling all over the world. And I haven't found any spot under the sun where people don't know about King Solomon's great wisdom. Now I'll turn back to his country and bring greetings and tell him that his name is praised throughout the world!'

"The bird then said to me:

"'Please take him this letter. And if he can decipher it within eight summers, I'll bring him blood from Evereverland, which, if you just look at it, you will live forever!'

"That is all that I can tell the king."

King Solomon said:

"If I don't decipher the letter then my name isn't Solomon!"

The king summoned all the sages of Jerusalem and all the magicians of Egypt. But none of them could solve the enigma.

Solomon then called out over the entire lands of Judah and Israel and the surrounding countries: All the sages should come and demonstrate their wisdom, and all those who had traveled all over the world were to come and tell him about the wonders they had seen. And everyone who could satisfy the king would receive a large gift.

Men and women came, young and old, from far and near, some all the way from Ophir, the land from which Solomon got his gold. But none of these people satisfied the king, for he already knew everything they told him about—the crocodiles in India, the serpents in Ethiopia, the magicians in Egypt, the sages in Zur, and also the Queen of Sheba.

The eight years were soon over, and the king still didn't know a thing about what he wanted to know, and only eighteen days were left.

The king was sad, and the entire palace was shrouded in sadness. Music was no longer played, and the boys and girls of Jerusalem no longer danced in the palace gardens. The king no longer uttered wisdom in front of the guests that gathered here, coming to his table daily from the four corners of the world, and no one knew why the king was so sad.

Ten days wore by.

Then, on the eleventh day, before the dawn edged over the mountains of Harmon, an old beggar came along and he knocked on the palace gates:

"Open up the gates, so I can appear before King Solomon and tell him about my wonders, which I have seen all over the world!"

The gates were opened, and the beggar was taken to King Solomon. The king asked him:

"Where are you from, and what wonders do you want to tell me about?"

The beggar said:

"Your humble servant is 269 years old, and his name is Joseph. He comes from Damascus, and ever since his childhood he has loved wandering around the world and seeing its wonders. And he has wandered twenty times to the lands on the other side of the sea and he has spent the night in the forest at the end of the world!"

Upon hearing that the beggar came from where the dove came, King Solomon was delighted. And then the music resounded again throughout the palace, and boys and girls from all over Jerusalem came to dance in the king's gardens. And King Solomon said:

"Tell me, tell me about the forest at the end of the world. The lands on the other side of the sun are wondrous, and their birds are wondrous too!"

And the beggar said:

"I'll tell you the wonders of the wonder bird. One day, I came into the forest at the end of the world, and I had no bread left in my bag. So I wandered wearily until I collapsed by a tree and fell asleep. Next the bird came and it began pecking on my bag. I woke up, saw the bird, and I laughed: 'You silly bird! My bag is empty, and you can't peck for anything!' How surprised I was when the bird answered me in my own language!

"'You silly fool,
You foolish lad,
You have no brains
Inside your head!'

"The bird went on: 'If you do as I say, you'll have enough food for yourself and also for me. Take your sack and tear it into thirteen strips and then wrap the strips around the bottom of that tree. Next, dig up some fresh soil and put it around the bottom of that tree. After that, lie down and go to sleep. And when you wake up, you'll see that sprouts have come up. Pull out the sprouts, keep half for yourself and give me the other half. Just sniff the sprouts, and you'll be sated!'

"I did as the bird said. And I fed on the sprouts until I came to a settlement. A wind then blew and it tore all the sprouts from my hands and carried them off!"

King Solomon said:

"You've told me a lovely tale! That will be enough for today. And tomorrow, you'll tell me about more wonders."

On the second day, the beggar was greeted with joy and music, and he told his second tale.

"One day, I left the forest and I went astray in a desert. I didn't have even a drop of water in my skin pouch. Furthermore the sun was roasting, and not even the slightest shade could be found far and wide. So I sat down on the hot sand and I begged my soul to let me die. But then I heard a pecking under me in the sand. I peered down and I saw the wonder bird standing there and it said to me:

> "'You silly boy,
> You foolish lad,
> You have no brains
> Inside your head!

"'Come and help me dig, and it will be good for me and also for you.'

"So I went over and I did as the bird said. And soon I saw a wellspring with fresh, crystal-clear water. I drank my fill, and the bird also drank its fill. Next, I filled my pouch and I was about to go on. But the bird laughed:

"'You drink from the wellspring and you don't know what you're drinking! Take a drop of water, pour it into the desert sand, and avert your eyes. Within a single moment, a gigantic apple tree will shoot up, and its shadow will protect you and me.'

"I did as the bird said, and I was refreshed with the finest apples under a fresh and splendid apple tree. After eating my fill, I fell sound asleep. And I stayed and rested there three days and three nights, and I felt good and well."

And King Solomon said:

"The wonders of the wonder bird are wondrous, and your tales are beautiful! Today that will be enough, and tomorrow you'll tell me more."

On the third day, the king was already waiting for the beggar with seven of his most beautiful wives. And the beggar told his third tale:

"One day, I was sitting in the forest, eating my meal from my bag, and I deeply yearned to see the wonder bird and its wonders. The summer was almost over, and when the cold nights set in I would have to leave and migrate to the eastern lands on the other side of the sun. This made me feel sorry, so that my meal didn't taste so sweet. Suddenly I heard the wonder bird calling me from far away, and then it arrived:

"'You silly fool,
You foolish lad,
You have no brains
Inside your head!

"'You don't have to worry about me, you poor beggar! I'm waiting for a great king to worry about me. But since you helped me last time, when we met in the desert, I'll tell you where I've been. You must know that I'm the oldest bird in the world, and all the wisdom and all the magic of the magicians of Egypt and all the sages of Jerusalem and Zur are clearly before me because the wind brings them here with all its wings from the four corners of the world, brings them to me in the forest at the end of the world. And you should know that ten thousand years ago, there was a terrible desert here, and the desert where you met me by the wellspring was a part of that forest.'"

At this point, the beggar broke off.

King Solomon said:

"So far you've been telling me the loveliest tale, and if you continue, I'll have you dressed in purple, and you'll be like a courtier in the kin's palace."

The beggar replied:

"Your Majesty, I'll tell you the rest of the tale, and the rest is even lovelier, and its wonders are as big as the world. But I've forgotten the rest of the tale. Let the king give me time until tomorrow, and then I'll continue telling the tail."

The king said:

"Your wish is granted!"

It was the fourth day. The king and his wives were waiting impatiently for the beggar. The music was already playing, and the boys and girls were dancing when he arrived. And he continued telling the tale:

"'But I found that wellspring and turned its water into a forest with my own wisdom. All the winds were angry at me for running a border and forcing them to stop in my forest. But they could do me no harm. And when all the sages in the world found the forest with their wisdom, the forest to which all wisdom and all enigmas are brought, they, the sages, wanted to learn and know more wisdom. And my forest was open to them, for I also wanted that.

"'Once there were seven sages in seven lands, and each sage ruled over 127 lands; but no sage knew about the others sages. Now one day they came to me in the forest along seven different roads, and here they all met for the first time. They were overjoyed, and so was I. And they learned wisdom from one another, until they had learned all wisdom. Then they wanted to go home, along the seven roads on which they had come. And a king said—'"

Once again the beggar broke off and asked King Solomon to let him wait till morning so he could remember the rest of the tale, and the king replied:

"Since your tale is the loveliest of all the tales I've ever heard, and since your wonders are the greatest in the world, I will let you wait till tomorrow. But you have to get here earlier, together with the morning star. Then you can tell me more."

On the fifth day, the beggar came together with the morning star. And he was dressed all in purple, like a courtier in the palace. And the king and his wives didn't recognize him at all. And they were overjoyed when he continued his tale:

"'Now that we will go back along seven different roads, each one of us should write down the finest wisdom of his kingdom, in his language, in the ink of his land, and he should apply his seal as a memento. And each one of us should know where the other kingdoms are and we should have one another's seals.'

"'So each king took his paper and he wrote down his wisdom in his language and with his seal and he handed it over to the next king. In that way, seven different sheets of paper went from hand to hand. And the seven wise kings saw what big fools they were. For none of them could read the languages of the other six kings, and none of them had even heard about each other seal and each other kingdom. So they refused to go home, for they were embarrassed about their wisdom, which had made fools of them.

"'And they sat and wept for the years they had spent not knowing what they had wanted to know. Until the cold nights arrived. And when they saw that they had to die, they summoned me and they said:

"'You must know that seven roads lead to wisdom and all roads lead to the end, and a king is born each time, a great king who learns all the wisdoms of the world with all their languages and enigmas. We will leave you the seven sheets of paper. You will keep one under your wing and bury the others under that tree. And when the great sage is born, you will send him a letter, and he will see, this will open his eyes. You should do that seven times.'

"'Then they died one by one, in seven days. And when the wind heard the story, he was furious and he said—'"

The beggar couldn't continue his tale and he again asked if they would let him wait until tomorrow, and the king replied:

"This is a wonderful story, and I can barely wait until tomorrow, I won't get a wink of sleep! So I'm going to order my servants to give you a room in my palace. You can sleep there, and tomorrow you will continue the story even before the morning star appears."

The sixth day came. The king had spent all night writing his Book of Ecclesiastes, not sleeping for even a moment, until it was time for the beggar to come. And the beggar came and he went on with his tale:

"'I won't rest until I carry away the papers of the wonder bird and drive him from the world!'

"'I heard that and I wondered what would happen to me. A thousand summers passed, six sheets of papers were still buried, and I kept the seventh one under my wing. The dead sages had long since become dust, and the sage who should carry my letter hadn't been born yet. Until the name of King Solomon began to rise from the eastern sun to the western. I raised my wing and started preparing the letter that would soon reach the king. But then a huge windstorm blasted in from the north, it grabbed the letter and flew away. The letter was as valuable to me as my life, for I had been waiting for a thousand years, and I was all set to suffer a certain death if I couldn't grab the letter back.

"'The wind flew to the desert, and I chased it. There the wind blew into a crack in a rock, and I stood and waited. The sun burned like a hundred suns, and there was no shade anywhere, and I knew I had to wait by the crack in the rock until after the great heat. I would certainly have been burned to ashes, but then I saw you far away. So I flew over and started pecking, and then you came and helped me. Without you I couldn't have done a thing.

"'When the heat had waned, I snatched the wind coming out from the crack in the rock, and I grabbed the letter. All the winds blasted after me, and after thirteen years of struggle I came home, when you started worrying about me.'

"Upon hearing this story, I said to the bird:

"'I'm heading back soon to Jerusalem, and I will see King Solomon in ten summers. Now if the bird wishes, he can give me the letter, I'll carry it to the great king, and I'm sure he will give me a gift.'

"'The bird laughed:

"'When the winds find out what you are carrying in your bosom, they will hurl you into the seas, they will plunge your bones to the bottoms of abysses and then yank you back up to the sands of the beaches. I would rather confide the letter to the mute dove, who will bring it to King Solomon in just four summers. But if you like, you can tell him the story, and he'll give you a gift.'

"And that is the end of the tale, my dear king!"

And King Solomon said:

"You will remain in my palace and eat at the table for the rest of your days!"

The king now went to his room and wrote the rest of the Book of Ecclesiastes. Then he fell ill and he died on the third day.

He died like a fool.

LEYB KVITKO
(1890?-1952)

Born in Ukraine, Kvitko started writing in Yiddish at the age of twelve. Eventually he became one of the most popular and most prolific children's poets in the Soviet Union. His works were translated into many languages, and he in turn translated many foreign works into Yiddish—including a collection of Belorussian folktales (*Vaisrusishe Folkmayses*, U.S.S.R., 1923). This was at a time when Yiddish was one of the official languages of the Belorussian republic.

In his brief afterword, the poet explains that "for pedagogical reasons" he has avoided religious themes and unfriendly characterizations, while focusing on fantastic motifs. Still, there is a reminiscence of the Book of Jonah in the story translated here, while most of the material seems to derive from the international gamut of folklore.

Kvitko also lists the published origins of each tale; the following story was adapted from a Belorussian collection that came out in 1891.

In 1952, during the Soviet slaughter of Yiddish culture and Yiddish speakers, Kvitko was arrested and shot. He was rehabilitated several years later.

IVAN BELARUSKI
Ivan Expelled

IN SOME LAND, IN SOME COUNTRY or other, there lived a man who was called Ivan Belaruski. And his son was likewise named Ivan.

Now Ivan junior was a great hunter, he was always out hunting, but he never caught anything.

One day, the son went out and he spotted a poor peasant tilling the soil. His nag, all skin and bones, was accompanied by a colt, a precious creature.

Ivan liked the colt and he said:

"Sell me your colt, you poor peasant!'

"Ah, good sir! I've just barely gotten it."

"C'mon! Sell it, and that'll be that! I'll pay you a lot!"

"How much, for instance?"

"How much for instance? For instance a hundred rubles!"

The peasant mused and mulled. After all, it was a whole lot of money. And then he said:

"Oh, you can have it!"

Ivan promptly hitched up the colt and went away. The nag didn't neigh, and neither did the colt.

Upon arriving home, Ivan put the colt in the stable.

That night, Ivan senior had a dream:

"Your son has bought a colt. It will bring him joy and you sadness."

He mused and mulled deeply and he consulted a book of dream interpretations: What could that mean?

He saw that he was really in a very bad way, and he thought to himself: "We have to take the little thing and hide it, maybe drown it—as long as they could get rid of it!"

One day, he summoned his son:

"Come here, Ivan. I have to tell you something!"

"What do you want to tell me?"

"Come with me and I'll show you the seashore. I'm old already, and I'll die soon, and I want you to know everything."

"Very good, come, Papa!"

He didn't care so much about seeing the seashore, he enjoyed running around. They started out, and the father was very uneasy and filled with bad thoughts. Ivan junior sprang around, dashed this way and that, until he ran into an apple tree hung with apples. He knocked the tree with a stick, so the apples fell—they fell. Suddenly the apple tree said:

"Ivan dear, Ivan dear! Don't knock down my apples! I've got a dry gnarl. Why don't you knock it down? Make two bundles of wood. Put one under one armpit, the second one under your other armpit. It will definitely be useful for you tonight."

The son did as he was told, and with the two bundles of wood under his arms he hurried after his father.

The father was angry because his son kept vanishing.

"Why don't you stay at my side?"

"No special reason. I keep jumping to, then fro, then I do it again!"

And that was that!

Finally they arrived at the seashore, the blue sea, and the father said:

"Well, have a good look, and there you'll see a white rock."

"Where, where? I don't see it, I don't see a thing!"

"Oh, right there! Go near! Go nearer!"

Actually, there was no rock in the sea. But Ivan junior went all the way to the water and peered deep, deep into the sea. The father came over and shoved him into the sea and then hurried away. He didn't look back, he didn't listen, even though his son was yelling and begging, and the father should have felt some pity.

The father simply fled.

Meanwhile, a fish came and swallowed the son. The son looked around and he smoked a cigar. Then he laid out the two bundles of the apple tree's wood and built a large fire. He took out his knife, cut out pieces of the belly of the fish, which he roasted on the fire, then ate. And so the fish carried him around a day or two. But by then the fish could no longer endure the fire and the pain, and so it spewed out Ivan on the shore.

Ivan's clothes were rotted and falling to pieces—he was almost naked.

He couldn't go home, he was terrified of his father. It was better to take to the roads on which travelers walked or rode. Perhaps somebody might feel sorry for him.

So he sat there, he sat along the road, and no one was heard and no one was seen. Still, he kept waiting—perhaps something might occur after all.

Suddenly he heard a distant clatter. He had a good look, and yes! It was a carriage after all. So he thought to himself: "It's shameful to present myself so raggle-taggle! I have to hide somewhere. That might be a great lord." And Ivan hid beneath a tree.

A puppy was running alongside the carriage. The puppy caught a whiff of Ivan's trail and it started barking at him.

And there really was a great lord riding inside the carriage, and he said to his coachman:

"There must be someone hiding here, my puppy doesn't bark for no reason. Go and have a look."

The coachman went out and he spotted Ivan. And he shouted from there:

"Some naked boy is sitting there!"

"Bring him here!"

So the coachman brought him. And the great lord asked Ivan: "What do they call you?"

"Huh? What? What they call me? They call me and my father Ivan!"

The great lord then said to his coachmen:

"That is my son, truly! My son is just like that." Then he said to Ivan: "How did you get here?"

Ivan lied: "I don't know who brought me this way or led me astray!"

"Well, we'll figure it out. Get into the carriage!"

Ivan got in and the carriage rolled on. It rolled through a shtetl, the lord bought clothes, he decked Ivan out, and they came to the lord's home.

They arrived and oh! The lord found his son at home! Next, when the sons came together, people couldn't tell who was the home son and who was the stranger.

"Well, let it be!" said the lord. "Let both of them be my sons. One will be my home son and the other my found son."

Both sons turned out well, their hair, their voices like one person's. And they lived well, they played together, ate together, and never fought with one another.

And so they were raised, and meanwhile the lord grew old. Of course, actions speak louder than words.

When the lord was very old, he summoned his sons:

"Well, my dear children, one of you is a home son, the other a found son. But still, I'm leaving each of you half of my estate, so that you may be happy and remember me well!"

The two Ivans split his estate and lived happily.

Ivashke Gray Sermiashke

AFTER A WHILE, THE TWO BROTHERS felt they should marry.

Ivan, the real son, was to get hitched first, and Ivan, the found son, would act as marriage broker for now. The found son knew of a beautiful noblewoman somewhere in a land, in a country. But no one was allowed to ride there, you had to go and search on foot.

The found son ordered a simple, gray jacket to be made for him. He put it on as if it were a peasant's coat and he said to the home son:

"My clothes shouldn't bother you. After all, I'm your marriage broker. But you are the bridegroom, so deck yourself out. And don't call me Ivan or brother, call me one of your servants—Ivashke Gray Sermiashke."

And so they made ready and they started their trip, heading straight for the palace with the beautiful daughter.

As they drew near, they sent a letter:

"Blah-blah, my lord, you will be visited by potential bridegrooms, Belorussian lordlings!"

Meanwhile they walked and walked and they came to a wondrous forest that was hard to depict and hard to describe. And in the wondrous forest there lay a man, heavily clothed, in corduroy trousers, a warm lining, a cotton jacket, a fur cap with lappets, and he kept shouting:

"Oh, cool! Oh, cool!"

So Ivashke Gray Sermiashke went over to the man and said:

"Why are you shouting? It's warm out, after all! We're down to our shirtsleeves and we can't stand the heat! You're so heavily clothed, and yet it's summer!"

"And I'm very hot in the winter, very hot, and I can't stand the cold in the summer!"

"Well, come with us and we'll warm you up"

"Fine, I'll come!"

And the man stood up and went with them.

They walked and walked until they came to a field, a wondrous field, full of bugs and beetles and frogs and flies and gnats. And a man was crawling in the field, grabbing the creatures and eating them, and he kept shouting:

"Food! Food!"

Ivashke went over to him and he said:

"Listen, why are you crawling here and eating these disgusting things? You'd be better off going to the village and eating bread there. Then you'll be full!"

The man said:

"The villagers drove me out because no matter how much I eat, it's never enough! I need lots and lots of bread!"

"Come with us, and maybe we'll make you full!"

"Fine, I'll come!"

So they went in a foursome.

So they walked and walked—and actions speak louder than words—until they came to a forest and a river, and a man was up to his mouth in water and he was shouting:

"Oh, a drink! Oh, a drink!"

Ivashke went over and he said:

"You're standing in a river. Just bend a little and drink your fill!"

"Really?" replied the man. "Once I drink up the river, what else can I do? I'll die of thirst!"

"Don't worry, we'll give you your fill of water!"

"Fine!" said the man. He bent over and in one gulp he drank up the entire river!

But the crabs and the frogs and the fish remained on the bottom of the river. So the hungry man jumped in and ate them up.

The thirsty man began again:

"A drink! A drink!"

"Come with us."

And so they all went off together.

Meanwhile the lord found out that they were coming, and he sent them a message:

"Come, come, my in-laws with all your servants. I've been waiting and waiting for your arrival. I've prepared a good bath for you."

And indeed, even though they were miles away from the bath, they felt the heat because the bathtub was made of cast iron and it was red-hot!

The cold man shouted:

"Oh, I'll warm myself up!"

And Ivashke supported him: "Yes, yes! We won't stand the heat. Hurry up and warm yourself up!"

The cold man went to the bath. He let down his trousers and he took a deep breath. And soon the bath grew cold. And the marriage brokers and their servants tapped the kettles and said:

"Now there's a lord for you! He didn't have enough wood anywhere in this land to fuel the bath properly!"

And the lord said:

"Come here, marriage brokers!"

Marriage brokers or not, they wouldn't have come if not for the fee!

Next the lord asked:

"Would you like a drink?"

"Oh, oh, yes!"

"Well, if you drink up all the wine and whiskey and other liquor in my castle, I'll give you my daughter for your lordling."

"Well, thirsty man," said Ivashke, "what do you say?"

He bent over to him and whispered:

"I'll drink the good brandies, and you'll drink all the other drinks."

"It's a deal!"

All the other liquors were brought out, the drinker pounced on them, and within moments not a drop was left.

Then they called out:

"Oh, what a lord you are! You couldn't prepare enough liquor for even five people. We're still thirsty!"

The lord was surprised:

"Well, marriage brokers!"

Marriage brokers or not, they wouldn't have come if not for the fee.

"Well, maybe you'd like to munch on something?"

"Oh, what for?!"

"After a bath and a bit of liquor, it's good to munch on something."

And the lord ordered his men to slaughter all cows and bulls, hang up the kettles outdoors, and cook the carcasses.

Cooked up and sliced up, they ate up, ate up, but they weren't full.

Then they shouted:

"Now there's a palace for you! It can't even prepare food for a couple of guests!"

And the lord said:

"Well, marriage brokers!"

Marriage brokers or not, they wouldn't have come if not for the fee!

"Well," said the lord. "Hail and farewell. After such and such a time you can come to the wedding!"

They bid each other fond good-byes, and the marriage brokers started for home.

Now they came to the place where the thirsty man had stood: The river was full again!

The thirsty man thanked them:

"Thank you for having me drink my fill for once!"

And he stepped into the river and began shouting again:

"A drink! A drink!"

Then they came to the hungry man's place. They stopped, and the hungry man said:

"Thank you for having me stuff my guts for once!"

And he remained there.

Then they walked, and walked on, till they came to the place where they had met the cold man. And the cold man said:

"Thank you for warming me up at least once in my life!"

And he too remained and shouted, shouted out!

The two brothers walked on and came home, and the real Ivan said:

"Found brother, let me go to the wedding. But cast off the Sermiashke—it's a shame!"

"Ah! What sort of shame? I won't take it off!"

Footless and Handless

IVAN THE BRIDEGROOM'S FRIENDS gathered together, and great lords drove up to the wedding. And when they saw the bridegroom's friend, Ivashke Sermiaskhe, they said:

"No, this in-law won't travel with us in such a bare state!"

"What do you mean? He's my marriage broker!"

"Well, but it's a shame to show oneself in such a jacket! We can't travel with such a pauper!"

"You know what? We'll disguise him among us in the carriage. That way nobody will see him!"

So for now, each traveler sat down in his place, and the beautiful carriage started off again.

But on the way, the travelers began again:

"We can't travel with such a pauper!"

"Let's get rid of him!"

"Let's throw him out of the carriage!"

"Yes, yes!"

"But slowly, so he won't get hurt, God forbid!" said the bridegroom.

And Ivashke ignored them, he paid them no heed—but he was angry!

The carriage stopped, and they threw out Ivashke!

And Ivashke said to himself:

"Ah! If only I had a better horse than their horses!"

And just as he spoke those words, a horse suddenly appeared, a fervent horse! Ivashke mounted it, and soared away, and outdistanced the carriage. The travelers were upset—who would have thought? And they conferred.

One of them said:

"Let's take him back into the carriage and hitch up his horse with the other horses, and his horse will light up all our horses."

No sooner said than done, and then on they rode.

As they approached the town, they sent a courier to the lord, claiming that the horses were exhausted and requesting fresh horses.

Meanwhile they headed toward a nearby townlet. Here there was a blacksmith who could forge and reforge, fuse and fuse together. And Ivan ordered the carriage to stop at the smithy—he needed something there.

Ivan climbed down and said to the blacksmith:

"Good day!"

"A good day to you, Ivashke Gray Sermiaskhe!"

"I need something from you!"

"What can I do for you?"

"Make me a bridle weighing twelve poods [480 pounds]!"

"What do you mean? What do you need that for?"

"I need it! You mustn't know why, and I mustn't tell you!"

Well, the blacksmith made the bridle, and the travelers were all surprised. Maybe Ivashke knew something they didn't know—something trivial.

So they sat back down in the carriage and they drove on.

Meanwhile a jade, an ardent jade, came trudging from the lord! As if made by twenty demons, it moved on and never rested, and the rider, barely alive, hung from the jade, tormented and tortured. The jade was for the bridegroom, and he wanted to mount it, And Ivashke said:

"Let me be, I want to try it out a bit, it's very uneasy!"

And he unhitched his earlier mount, jumped on the new mount, and dashed away. The jade came in hot pursuit and soared and snorted, and it soon collapsed. Ivashke quickly caught it and mounted it. And it carried him off and it soared into the clouds. And he drove it, and he turned and twisted, and soared to and fro until his mount collapsed.

And the travelers sat back down in their carriages and they came to the palace.

"Thank you, my lord, you sent us a puppy and not a horse! It had to rest along the road. Couldn't you give us something better?"

"You have such strange in-laws!'

"In-laws or not, if there were no in-laws, we wouldn't have come!"

"Well, then we'll celebrate the wedding!"

So they celebrated the wedding, they partied and reveled.

After the feast, the bride said to the groom:

"Oh, Ivashke! Come up to the third floor! We can play there and toss a ball!"

And Ivashke said to the groom:

"Listen, don't go to the third floor. Don't forget, just remember: don't go!"

But Ivashke's mind wandered, and the bride said to the groom:

"Come up to the third floor, we'll play ball!"

So the groom went with her. When they reached the third floor, the bride tossed the ball to him and she said:

"Grab it!"

But the ball crashed into the wall and remained stuck there.

And the bride said:

"Well? Throw it to me!"

But he just sat there and didn't stir.

Meanwhile Ivashke looked around. But his brother wasn't there. So he went up to the third floor and found him. And so he said:

"Oh! My brother, my brother! Bride, he's still ashamed, and you got him to play ball with you! Is that how you people toss a ball?"

"And you people?"

"That's how!"

And he kicked the ball. And the ball crashed through the palace walls and fell in the town.

"That's how we people throw a ball!"

The celebration went on until it was over, and then they drove away with the bride.

When she came home, she thought to herself:

"I'm going to play a trick on Sermiaskhe!"

The bride had a sword weighing eight poods (320 pounds).

Sermiashke was exhausted and he went to bed and to sleep. In his sleep, he turned and twisted topsy-turvy—his feet at the head and his head at the foot of the bed! The bride stole over and brought down the sword. She thought she was chopping off his head, but she struck his feet instead! The bride dashed away, and the groom awoke, and silently and noiselessly he climbed out and on a path. There he bayed and barked. Then someone came along:

"Who weeps there and wept yesterday?"

"Who are you?" asked Sermiashke Footless.

"I'm Handless!"

"Oh! You poor man! You have no hands, too bad! But I'm worse off!"

"True. Well, let's get together then. I'll carry you on my back."

And he went over to Handless and bowed:

"Put your arms around my neck." And he took him on his back.

"So where should we unhappy people go?" Handless asked.

"It's so lucky I found you. I know where we should go. To the deepest and densest forest!"

"And what will we do there?" asked Handless.

"We'll attack people, those rolling or walking, and we'll grab their money!"

"Ah, how delightful! And I've been worrying and worrying where my next meal was coming from."

And so they went!

Anyone driving through, a lord or a Jew or a merchant—they would pounce on him and rob him. And so they collected a nice amount of money.

Meanwhile autumn was coming, and the air was growing cool. The two men tried to figure out what to do—they needed a cottage.

Along came a blacksmith, he was going to a tavern, he was carrying lots of axes. So they took little from him—just five apiece. Handless took Footless to a tree. Footless chopped down the tree. Handless went, and Footless hauled the tree. Then they chopped it up and built a cottage.

Once they were done, they went back to attacking passersby: Jews and merchants and lords and priests and anyone else who had money. On the other hand, they helped the poor. But things were in a bad way. When they came home, they had to heat, cook, bake—they had a lot of work.

Footless said:

"You know what, Handless?"

"What?"

"We need to get a housewife."

"Where can we find one? It's almost winter."

"Carry me, and I'll get you one."

"Where will you carry me to?"

"To the village. There people dance and sing in the tavern. And there are a lot of girls. We'll go at night and we'll stand in a corner. And when the girls come out to cool off, we'll grab one, and she'll be our housewife!"

And so that's what they did. The girls came out, one of them went a bit farther. And they grabbed her. In the darkness no one saw or heard anything.

The father was despondent, the mother worried and agonizing since they knew nothing about what had become of her. So the parents wept and lamented until they stopped.

The Granny in the Mortar

*F*OOTLESS AND HANDLESS brought the girl into the forest and calmed her down:

"Don't be scared, don't be afraid. You won't have a bad life with us. Jews travel through, they carry flour, groats. We'll take it all and bring it to you. You'll cook and you'll bake and you'll eat too, and you'll pour our drinks."

At first, she was very anxious and haggard. Then she peered around and calmed down, and she was again pure and beautiful.

After a while, an old granny started visiting them, and the girl got very close to her. The granny had an iron foot, she traveled in an iron vehicle, and ran it with iron rods. At night, when Handless and Footless were out attacking travelers, the old woman would knock at the door, and the girl would open.

"Oh, my child, seek in my mind!"

So the girl bent over to her and sought. And the granny placed a tube on the girl's heart and sucked out her blood. And she sucked it thoroughly. Then she sat down in her iron mortar and departed.

The highwaymen returned at dawn:

"Well, is our meal ready?"

"It's ready, my dear!"

The men ate their fill and drank their fill and then went to bed.

In the evening, they left again, and the granny came back:

"Oh, my child, seek in my mind."

The girl sought, and the granny sucked her blood.

After a second time, Handless and Footless noticed that the girl had become very pale and that she could barely keep on her legs.

They asked her:

"What's wrong with you, girl? Don't you have enough bread? Are you lacking something?"

"Oh, my dear! Not that! No!"

"What is it then?"

And the girl told about how the granny with the iron foot came with a crash and a smash, in an iron mortar and sucked her blood.

"Really? Well, we'll grab the granny. We won't leave today. We have to grab her!"

Night fell, and the girl went to bed, and the men guarded her. Around midnight— aha!—the granny came. The girl let her in, and the man grabbed the granny. They put her in her iron mortar and started pounding her!

"Wait! Footless and Handless! Stop pounding and crushing me! I want to tell you something very good! Let me go! Your hands and feet will be restored!"

"C'mon! C'mon! We won't let you go! Test what you want to say!"

"Come with me!"

They held her tight, and she led them to a well.

"Wash yourselves here and you'll get your hands and feet! "

Handless already wanted to bend over the well, but Footless grabbed him:

"Wait a while!"

And he took a small branch and dipped it in the well, and the branch burned up.

So they started to pound the granny again, and she asked again:

"Just wait, Footless and Handless, you'll be getting feet and hands!"

"Wonderful!"

"Follow me!"

Then they came to another well. Handless bent over it, but Footless held him back:

"Wait a while. You have to test it too!"

And he threw a rotten root into the well. And the root turned green and blossomed. So they washed themselves there. And soon their hands and feet grew back. And now they turned upon the granny and they pounded and clobbered her and threw her on the ground, barely alive.

Where did they put her? Huge oak trees stood there, hollowed out, and the granny had long braids. They tied the braids to a pole and they put the pole inside an oak and they chopped up the pole.

Once they were done, they left. But on the way, they changed their minds: They shouldn't have left the granny alive. And they turned back. But who? And what? The granny was gone, and so was the pole.

"Well, brother! We'll be damned if we don't finish her off!"

"Right! Come on! Let's go and find her!"

Now they came to a lovely cottage and they stepped inside and they found: a girl, such a dear girl! She was cooking soup and potato pancakes.

"Good morning, my girl!"

"Good morning to you! What do you have to say to me?"

"We're looking for something."

"I know! You're looking for my mother! You really pounded her ribs, she won't stop sneezing. You know what? If either of you takes me as his bride, I'll tell you where my mother is."

"Very good!"

"There and there in a cellar."

They promptly left. Suddenly they pounced on the granny and wiped her out.

The men returned to the lovely house and they decided that Handless would take the girl as his bride. They celebrated a lovely wedding, and Footless said:

"Since we have a housewife in our cottage, we have to let this girl go back to her parents. You'll give me a little money for the road, and I'll go home and see what my father's been doing—I'm homesick already."

And that's what they did. They gave the girl a lot of gifts and took the happy girl to her parents. They were delighted to see her. And Handless remained with his bride in the cottage in the forest.

A Bet

*I*VASHKE WENT TO SEE HIS FRIEND, the lord. He looked—and oh my! The boy was tending swine!

"Brother, what's happened to you?"

"This and that! My wife pesters me, she beats and scolds me and tells me to kiss hares under their cottontails. And where have you been all this time?"

"I've earned a pair of feet!"

"What do you mean? You already had feet!"

"Your wife chopped them off! She wanted to chop off my head, but she hit my feet instead. Give me your swineherd clothes, and I'll give you my clothes. I'm gonna teach your wife a good lesson or two! I'm tending the swine today, and you must wait for me on the top rung of the bath."

Later on, Ivashke drove the swine back into the courtyard with shouting and yelling. The wife came out and she saw him whipping and walloping the swine. And she screamed and she wanted to pounce on him.

And he begged her:

"How can you touch me? I'm so filthy and muddy. Let me go to the bath first and clean up a bit."

"Well, go, you dirty dog!"

She waited and waited, but he didn't come. The murderous anger grew in her. So she ran over to the bath. No sooner was she inside than—ah!—he grabbed her! He snatched a twisted rod and he lashed and lobbed her wherever he could. And she writhed and wriggled and she screamed and sprang. Then he grabbed a few wire rods and worked her again:

"That's what you get from a swineherd! And take that from a dirty dog!"

And she jumped and she begged him:

"Darling, stop! My dearest! My wonderful man!"

And he gave it to her good! She barely survived the beating!

She hurried home amid suffering and issued an order:

"Hitch up the horses tandem and drive to the lord in the bath."

The carriage drove over, and Ivashke took off his swineherd clothes and put them on his friend, who climbed down from the top rung.

"Drive home!" said Ivashke.

"I'm scared. Why don't you come with me?"

"Don't be scared, you'll be fine! I have to go home and see what my father's been doing!"

His friend left the bath and drove off, and his wife received him with respect and esteem, and from then on everybody treated him like a lord.

And Ivashke traveled through villages and tried to earn something. He knew how to bleed horses, but none of the horses in the villages were restive, they were all calm. So there was no work for him to do. However, the villagers told him that the lord had a horse that might need to be bled. Perhaps the wanderer should go to that lord. But no one could hold that horse—that was how ardent and fiery it was.

So Ivan started off to see the lord. And the peasants laughed:

"A fine worker! Better men than he have lost their lives—and he wants to give it a try!"

He reached the palace, and the lord was already very old and gray, and he said to Ivan:

"My good man, do you wish to bleed my horse? You should know that if you try and fail, you will lose your head, but if you succeed I'll give you my head!"

"Fine, my lord!"

Ivan went over to the stable. When the horse caught a whiff of him, it champed at the bit. It kicked the iron gates, it bent the steel walls, it dashed about for a long, long time!

Ivan walked over, calmly, calmly, and placed a hand on the horse:

"Stiller, stiller, my dear little horse!"

The horse recognized him and bowed its head, bowed its head and calmed down.

Ivan bled the horse, soft and still, and then he went over to the lord. The lord was terror-stricken:

"I've lost!"

"My lord, do you know who I am? I am your son!"

The lord was delighted, then he burst into tears:

"My son, take me, do what you wish to me. I'm guilty toward you in every way!"

"No, father! No one has ever seen or heard that a son should mistreat his own father!"

The father was delighted and he threw a great banquet, and the entire land was filled with glory and grandeur!

FISHL BIMKO
(1890-1965)

Born in Poland, Bimko prolifically wrote drama and fiction both there and in the United States, where he settled in 1921. His works run a vast gamut of serious and humorous writings, which included a sprinkling of folk-like stories. The two tales presented here deal with dreams—a frequent theme in folklore. The original Yiddish texts are included in *Helle Blikn* (*Bright Glances*, 1926).

THE DREAM
(p. 1926)

THE SKY TURNS DARKER, gloomier, the cloud cover thicker and heavier.

The trees are soughing quietly, preparing for a rainfall. Thunder rolls somewhere far away as if in a closed barrel. Lightning glitters like the red eyes of a wolf lifting its head and peering into the night. . . .

The forest is black, the pines stand motionless, not a single one stirring.

The road is white, milk-white the highway, like the outstretched arm of a woman who has stripped the black sleeve off her arm.

The old ruin is deserted, the walls of the crumbled buildings shiver, and they seem fairly unsafe, as if they could be blown down by any faint breeze, like the nests that birds have built in the holes.

A soft singing. . . .

Toads croak. . . . Tiny fish stick out their mouths from the small ponds, they draw some air and delight in the fresh raindrops that create rings—small rings amid large ones.

Fireflies glow, glisten, smolder as they flit through the grass, fading out as they fall to the earth.

A bat swishes. . . .

It is the deep, hushed, forceful night, filled with fragrances after a hot summer's day. Dismal clouds have gathered in the sky, moving atop one another, like chestnut horses. And dew falls on the ground, redolent of berries and wild mushrooms that grow in the full, dense rains.

Along the roads, the drivers seem to have sweetly dozed off on their coach boxes, leaving the horses to drag on as in the imagination.

On such an evening, a woman emerges from the ruin, a tall, slender woman, and she seems to move as if with blind eyes and outspread hands: transparent garb on white flesh, shining like a bright streak on the ocean surface. She starts toward the road, but instantly melts. And her head remains behind while her feet move away. Her arms spread over a vast distance and then withdraw, staying back, while her body has almost reached the road. . . .

And the girls who go home here—their faces are aflame, soft music rushes in their ears, and hearts beat joyfully. And eyes devour their shapes, and gaze themselves full. . . .

"Who are you?" the girls ask. "You wondrous woman, sprinkled with silvery stars and coming out to us every evening?"

The woman doesn't reply right away, but when they lay down their heads and blissfully fall asleep, she caresses them and she smiles with her silvery smile:

"I am your sweet dream. . . ."

THE SHEPHERD BOY
(p. 1926)

DAYBREAK. A BRIGHT, tender dawn. The sky was still fresh, the field was radiant and smelled of dew. The saplings crooned, the birds warbled. Now the shepherd drove out his flock of sheep to graze behind the hill.

The shepherd was tired, his eyes were still heavy from his night of sleep. So he trudged very slowly, wrapped in his cape, his bare feet moistened by the dew.

His sheep scattered behind the hill, feasting on the juicy grasses that grew from the earth, while the exhausted shepherd let his head droop. As he sat there, sleep weighed on his eyelids. Dozing off, he thought about his sheep, and his lids rose several times on their own, revealing his pupils, which peered through narrow slits, as he looked for his sheep and counted them again. Then his eyes shut soundly, and his head dropped heavily, remaining, as if decapitated, between his knees.

Sleeping into broad daylight, as the sun laughed at the vast fields, the shepherd dreamed about the red-haired girl who had come to the well yesterday, holding a pitcher and drawing water, and then helping him to water the sheep.

By now, he had often fifed his songs under her window, but she had never emerged at night. But then yesterday, watching him lug the heavy barrels of water from the well and empty them into his trough, she unexpectedly dashed over and seized his hand:

"Wait, shepherd boy, let me help you water your sheep."

When the wheel turned, he saw the thick flesh quivering above her elbows, and her cheeks were as red as the fur of a red fox. His heart was overjoyed and it thumped gloriously:

"Slowly, you lovely girl! Slowly, you lovely girl! . . ."

Next, after the sheep had drunk their fill, the shepherd drove them from the other side of the hill into the valley, where they could delight in the high, luscious grasses. There, he sat on the ground, his legs under him, and he gazed at the red-haired girl who stood before his eyes, while he fifed sweet tunes and sang for her, the red-haired forest girl, who hung before him on a cherry tree branch, turning wantonly like a red squirrel spinning on a wheel in a cage.

And while singing, the shepherd failed to notice a wolf cub poking out its head from among the frontmost trees, its green eyes terrifying the sheep. The poor sheep all looked over and shouted in unison:

"Shepherd boy, shepherd boy! Drive away the big bad wolf!"

But by the time the boy sprang to his feet, the wolf cub had a sheep in its maw and was racing off to its forest lair. . . .

The shepherd dashed after the cub, though empty-handed, to beat it. The cub was running slowly because the sheep in its maw was struggling wildly, banging against the wolf's front legs. So the shepherd soon caught up with the wolf and he threw it to the ground! He kicked it in the neck so it would release its prey and he started punching it with his bare fists:

"Wolf, you thief! You want to grab a sheep before my very eyes?"

And the wolf finally died.

The shepherd took the mangled sheep and, driving home the flock, he refused to drop the chewed and bitten sheep. Licking off the blood that dripped from its wounds, the shepherd washed them, cleaned them like a mother nursing her tiny baby.

By the time they reached the fold, the victim was doing a lot better. The sheep all clustered together, snuggled together, huddled together, pressing their heads together. And when the fold grew dark, their long, thick wool looked like downy snow that had fallen through holes in the roof.

The sheep all closed their eyes, not moving a single hair, but the scare they had suffered that day remained fresh on their faces.

The shepherd's eyelids hung over the injured sheep, which twisted in agony, while the shepherd kept stroking, petting, fondling the poor creature:

"Sleep, sleep, my young sheep! Your wounds will heal very soon. Sleep, sleep, my treasure!"

Suddenly, the sheep's eyes grew radiant, and the radiance filled the entire structure, as if the moon had risen outside and was peering into the fold. The sheep seemed to rear on its hind legs and straighten up, it sloughed off its pelt and appeared naked with silky skin like a newborn infant.

And the shepherd recognized his red-haired girl in the bare skin—and she petted his head and told him:

"Don't worry, my handsome shepherd boy, for not guarding your steps in the field. Let the sheep return to the fold on their own. Since you shielded me against the wolf's teeth today and tore me from its maw, I will never leave your side again or leave you all alone, my handsome shepherd boy. . . ."

And the shepherd woke up.

The sheep had already eaten, they were sated, and their udders were full and drooping heavily. So the shepherd drove them to the well, where the red-haired girl had already filled her trough and was now laughing at his loud voice:

"Why did you oversleep today, shepherd boy?"

And he told her his dream.

SHOLEM ASCH
(1880-1957)

Once again we find a Yiddish realist who, despite his enormous realistic output, nevertheless penned a fantasy—this time about Satan and Lilith.

THE BIRTH OF SATAN
(1920)

GOD HAD CREATED JUST ABOUT EVERYTHING, but He had not yet created the Will. He sat on the axis of the space of creation, where the suns, the stars, and the comets wandered, burning or extinct, and He saw the suns orbiting and revolving at enormous speeds to avoid spilling their oceans, casting their light or casting shadows on other suns, lights, and comets. And everything whirled for months, years, decades, centuries, and no heavenly body touched any other, and the minute arrived, the month and year, the point He had determined in His calculations. God was proud of His work and He sat down on His throne, which was suspended over the space of creation, and He accepted praise from the angels, who had come to laud Him for His labors.

And amid the singing and the playing of harps, hundreds and thousands of angelic hosts arrived, burning or extinct, some in black fire, some in white fire, some with wings and swords, some with lilies and harps—and they bowed to Him and knelt before Him and sang His praises.

And God glanced once more at the space of His creation and, in the enormous oceanic darkness, He saw the moving, burning lights that revolved around other lights at tremendous speeds and reached the point that he had determined. But He was slightly bored with their punctuality, for He, God the Creator, knew that His creations could not know that there is such a thing as the Will. The moons and stars, the suns and comets could not have a sense of the Will, because they were creations, made, set, and determined by someone else and they could do only what was determined for them to do.

And when the angels came to praise and laud Him, He gazed at them with His Godly eyes, and He saw that every last one of them was praising and lauding and singing because it was determined for them to do so, because there was no Will in their doings, and they were only doing what they must. God therefore grew bored with their singing and He turned away from them.

God turned toward His heavens and watched the dancing of the lights, which reached Him from the endless space, and He scornfully looked away. "This is no creation," He said to Himself, "for there is no Will here." And God searched for the Will.

As of those days, God was very sad.

One day, the Archangel Gabriel came hurrying over to Him (always the Archangel Gabriel) and he stretched his arms out to the heavens and cried out: "Our Creator: something has happened in Your heavens! One of Your angels, Queen Lilith, refused to sing Your praises, and when our hosts came to Your throne, she turned away from us. We don't know what that means."

The Creator was overjoyed. He felt something He had never felt in all His existence as God: another being's Will. And he joyfully called out: "Where is Queen Lilith. I want to see her."

"We sent her away to the limits of your creation because the queen's behavior was new and wild for us."

In the dark night, God wrapped Himself up in His dark mantel of clouds, and alone, unaccompanied, He went across the heavens, across His creation space, and emerged on the other side of His universe. And on the edges of endless black night oceans and night abysses there sat a woman braiding her hair.

"Was it you, Lilith, who refused to praise Me?"

"Yes, it was," she said into the night, without turning her face toward God.

"Don't you know that I am God, Who created the heavens and Who created the space where the millions of suns, worlds, and comets revolved?"

"So what!" said the woman into the night. "You created them to while away the time, so that they would do only what You order them to do. But just look at their doings: They don't realize they're moving, because there's no Will in what they do."

"And who are you?"

"I am my own god. I created myself, I created what You did not give me—what You could not give me."

"Just what did you give yourself?"

"I gave myself a Will. You cast me from a bit of light in Your angelic mold, and I emerged as one of the millions of angels that are cast from Your mold and can do nothing but follow the course determined by You and do only what You command them to do. They sing Your praises—You haven't taught them how to rebel. What good are the praises from angels whom You've taught nothing, what good is the creation of thousands of worlds? They revolve and receive light from one another because they have no choice—You haven't taught them anything else. But I created 'something'— something You didn't give me. I made myself godly. This is my will: not to praise You."

"Give me your 'will,'" said God.

"Take it if You can."

God tried to take it, He held out His hand—and the queen, the angel, began to burn.

"You're only taking back the fire You gave me in my form, but You cannot take my will!" she cried, burning.

God breathed on her, and again she stood before Him. And God said to her: "I want your will, I'm drawn to your will."

From that day on, God could no longer listen to the singing of the angels, could no longer look at His universe—for what good were all the Godly creations and the singing of the angels against one will?

And God stole away from the angels and every night He came to Lilith and He looked at her—and He was greatly drawn to her will, but He could do nothing to her.

One day God said to her: "Come, let's create a human being on the worlds that revolve in My universe. I will give him my Godliness, and you will give him a sense of will, for I am now repulsed by the paeans of the angels, who can't help singing paeans to Me. I want to hear the singing of human beings, who have the choice of praising or cursing Me. I want to have their will."

Our mother, Queen Lilith, replied: "I'd like to help You create a human being with a will. But since he'll be alone, with no one to protect him, You'll easily get the better of him, You'll kill him with Your thunder, You'll make him tremble with Your lightning, You'll send the seas across the shores at him, and the quivering of Your clouds will terrify his heart, and You will defeat him and subjugate him to Your power. That's not the way to go, God. If You want to create a man, then I want to have a son of will to help me protect the human, for I am a female and I am too weak to shield the human being's will, and You are a God, and Your power is great, and you've subjugated me with Your constant visits, and what good will it do if You present the will and it vanishes completely from the universe?"

"You're right," said God. "I want to have a fruit of the will with you, so that it will protect the human's humanness. Are you willing?"

"If You make him a god, if You let him rule the world. His strength should be equal to Yours, the strength to rule world and man—and then I'll have a son with You and from You."

"Our strength will be equal," God replied, "and I will make him ruler of the world, over every heart and every feeling. And he should persuade them to rebel against Me and to curse Me. From the enchantment of the power of his words I want his will, I want to have the man's heart from under his hands. Against himself and against his will, the man should come to Me. I want to break each will. And I will send your son to destroy and devastate, to bring corruption to men, and I want to have man's heart from under the ruins.

"And wherever he doesn't come," said Lilith, "there will be no destruction, there will be no darkness, because there is no light. There will be no life in their life, no desire in their deeds. They will be dead in their life. Like shadows they will spend their days, useless for themselves and for others. Their prayers and their paeans will never reach Your ears, will never touch Your heart, for there will be no desire in their singing. Their praises will be like threshed stalks that the wind blows away with the dust from the earth. But wherever man does come, his will will rule. Men will carry their days away in streaming desire. They will drink and get drunk in their living lives. With the counted minutes that You throw them with a chary hand, they will make eternities. They won't be bothered by being on the edge of the dark abyss, which You will always show them in order to break their will. My son, the king of will, will drown out the sound of their clocks with a roaring music. He will line the edge of the abyss with blossoming roses so that they won't see its darkness, and when they are drunk with happiness and their will, he will lead them to the edge of Your abyss."

And God spent that night with her, and they conceived a son, and he named him: Satan, the king of the will.

And ever since, there has been a constant war between God and the king of the will over the human heart.

Satan, the king of the will, stands like an armored prince and guards the human heart—guards the will.

ANONYMOUS

Bovo of Altona, a figure whose forebears go back to the tenth-century Danish invaders of England, entered Yiddish literature in 1541. That year, Eli Bokhur (1469?–1549), a Yiddish writer and Hebrew teacher residing in Italy, adapted the Italian version of the story. Penned in *ottava rima* (ababbcc) like the Italian original, the Yiddish text, a mock epic, was actually composed in 1507 but not printed until 1541.

Bovo's story became one of the most popular tales among Ashkenazi Jews, reappearing in verse and then prose. During the nineteenth century several anonymous prose versions were published in pamphlets.

Bovo became a true folk character, surfacing in messy, bewildering, and even self-contradictory prose with both serious and comical elements that sometimes made no sense, but still developed even in contemporary Yiddish literature—e.g., Y. Y. Trunk's highly sophisticated and richly spontaneous adaptation.

The prose rendering translated here was published in 1878 as a typical Yiddish "folk book."

THE STORY OF BOVO
A Lovely Tale about Bovo and Drezne
DRAWN FROM THE ARABIAN NIGHTS
PUBLISHED BY FEYVEL MOLODOVSKY
(WARSAW, 1878)

ONCE THERE WAS AN OLD KING, who took a young wife as his queen. The king's name was Guiden, and the queen was called Brandei. The queen bore a son, whom they named Bovo. Now the king had a captain named Sinbald, who lived in a castle named Shinshumin. And the castle stood in the midst of a forest. Nowhere in the world was there a more powerful fortress. The king kept his treasures and his royal possessions inside the castle, which was located one league from Antinne. The castle was built on a high mountaintop.

Now the king said to his captain: "Take my son to live with you, and your wife will suckle him. And you should raise him with everything he needs to be a prince."

The captain took the infant and brought him to his wife in Shinshumin. She suckled the boy very gladly, for she loved him and she enjoyed being with him.

By the time he reached the age of ten, he was able to fight and beat three men at once. And no one could outdo him. The captain taught him fencing and shooting, so that the boy grew very wild—he wanted to slash and kill everybody.

One day, Bovo, accompanied by five underlings, went to see his mother. But she showed him little love, she hated him because of his old father. And she said to herself: "You've caused me a lot of sorrow in my heart. What great sin have I committed to make me marry an old man? Soon, he won't be able to go anywhere, and I'll be all alone. I have to think of a way out even if it costs me my life."

Now the queen had a captain named Ritsard, who was very smart and evil. And she summoned him to her private chamber and said to him: "My dear captain, you are not to betray me. I want to reveal an important matter to you and I will pay you a thousand ducats. But if you fail me, I will have you killed. I'll shout that you tried to murder me."

The captain then replied: "My dear queen, you don't have to threaten me—there is nothing I wouldn't do for you."

The queen said: "You must prepare to set out and go to Frenchland. The young king of that country is named Dudin and he comes from the town of Mayence. My old husband killed Dudin's father with his sword. Dudin will avenge his father's blood. Give him this letter and tell him that I will help him. He is to come here as swiftly as possible and kill my old king. This is what my king normally does: He goes into the vineyard in the forest. And I will send him out hunting. The young king should be waiting there with his men, and he won't have to make much of an effort with my husband. Next, the young king should hurry into the town, and I will soon join with him and make the town surrender, and I will welcome him with open arms."

Captain Ritsard took his leave of the queen and rode to Frenchland. But during the trip, he moaned and groaned, he felt very sorry for the old king. Several times, he was about to head back. But much to his sorrow, he continued his journey. And so the captain reached Mayence and went straight to the royal palace, where he had the servants announce him. The king bid him enter and he asked the captain what he wished. The captain handed him the queen's letter, which the French king promptly read, and he was extremely astonished. He showed the letter to his advisors, who said:

"Dear king, perhaps there's something wrong here, perhaps they want us to get Bovo. Put Ritsard in prison and clap him in irons and tell him that we don't trust an untrustworthy man, just as King Solomon said (may he rest in peace): 'Never believe liars, for they will lead you astray.'"

Ritsard was terrified and he said to the advisors: "Dear burghers, as true as God lives (blessed be He), I am telling you the truth, and no one else knows about this. Only I, who carried this letter for my queen. If this matter turns out to be untrue, you can burn me at the stake."

The king said: "I understand, this must be true, for no young woman loves an old man. Ritsard, you can hurry back home and you can tell your dear queen that she should expect us, and I will quickly help her in her distress." And they set a time for the action to take place.

And Ritsard went back home. And he told the queen what had happened at the court of the king of Frenchland. And when the queen saw that the appointed time was drawing near, she pretended to be sick and she wept and wailed and said she was at death's door.

The old king instantly came to her and he said: "My darling, what's wrong?" And he summoned many doctors. He then said to the queen: "Do you want to eat something?"

And the queen said to the king: "If you go to the trouble, noble king, I do have a very tiny request. Tomorrow morning you should go hunting and bring back some venison and roast it for me and give me some to refresh me."

And the king lay down, and they chatted till daybreak. And when the dawn was setting in, the king got out of bed and called for his hunting gear and he ordered all his men to come to his court: "We are going hunting."

And the queen said to the king: "You shouldn't take along so many men. A small number is enough."

The king gave in, and that same morning he rode into the forest with only two men and a sparrow hawk on his wrist to help him catch prey.

Meanwhile, King Dudin of Frenchland rode out with four hundred strong heroes, and, as instructed by the queen's letter, they hid in the vineyard, waiting for the old king, who didn't have a clue as to what was happening. He rode along, looking for prey and not expecting any misfortune. Suddenly, young King Dudin came galloping over and jammed his spear into the old king, who fell to the ground and died.

Next, the young king and his four hundred men dashed into the town and started burning the houses and stabbing the burghers. Upon witnessing that, Queen Brandei ran out toward the French king and she grabbed his hands and led him into her private chamber with great delight.

Well, my dear friends, you can see what misfortunes can be inflicted by wicked women. The queen had her husband's corpse chopped to bits. As King

Solomon said (may he rest in peace): "Among a thousand women one cannot find even a single good woman."

Now the town was filled with great lamenting and weeping and shouting: "Oh, our dear king—we lost him so quickly!"

The burghers wanted to fight back against the young king and they seized their swords and lances, and the young king was about to kill them all. But the unlawful queen swiftly summoned the burghers and began cajoling them: "What good will it do to kill the young king? Will that bring the old king back from the dead? What's past is past. The old king was very loyal to you, and you will see how loyal the young king will be. He will give you fields and vineyards and interest. And so, my people, you should take my advice and let the past be the past, and you should swear your allegiance to the young king."

The burghers thought about her son. And they also agreed that the past was the past and they swore their allegiance to the young king, but not wholeheartedly. Well, let's leave them for now and let's write about Bovo.

The boy heard about all these events from afar, and he was well concealed, no one knew his whereabouts. Captain Sinbald was very worried about Bovo and he scoured the entire castle, probing every nook and cranny, till he finally found the boy. Bovo threw his arms around the captain and he said:

"My dear captain, please tell me what's been happening."

The captain described everything from start to finish. Then he said that all the sixty old burghers who had remained loyal to the old king had escaped into the forest and were seeking refuge in the Castle of Shenshumin. And Ritsard, who had brought the queen's letter to the young king, was among those sixty burghers, but they didn't know about his treachery. And the treacherous Ritsard thought to himself: "Why should I upset the young king? I'll go and advise him to hunt down the old burghers."

And Ritsard went to see the young king and he told him that the old burghers were heading toward the castle, where Bovo resided.

When the young king heard this, his anger flared up, and he said to himself: "When I lay my hands on them, I'll get even with them!" And he ordered his drummers to summon his men and he commanded them to chase the sixty old burghers. "And don't spare their horses. And to make sure those men don't escape, go after them right away and hunt them down."

Ritsard sped back to the old burghers and told them: "Ride slowly, you don't need to hurry, the enemy won't catch up with us." Ritsard lied to them in order to betray them.

So they slowed down. But when they got within just half a league of the castle, they spotted a huge army charging after them. Captain Sinbald said: "They are really trying to hunt us down, they are going to kill all of us. We have to hurry!"

But Ritsard the traitor said: "I'm going to go and see who they are and where they're heading." And Ritsard dashed over to the young king and said to him: "Hurry up and don't spare a horse and chase after them—otherwise they'll escape." Then Ritsard galloped back to the burghers.

Now Captain Sinbald had a son named Strong, who recognized Ritsard's treachery. And Strong said to his father and to the burghers: "Can't you see that Ritsard is a traitor? He wants to betray us. But I swear by God that I will strike him down." And Strong tore over to Ritsard and killed him, and Ritsard fell to the ground. Strong then flew back to the burghers and told them to hurry to the castle. And they started riding swiftly.

However, young Bovo couldn't keep up with the burghers. He was mounted on a high horse, and when he thrust out his lance, his horse heaved forward and backward, dumping Bovo on the ground. Bovo lay there on his back, the enemy army grabbed him and pulled him up. Meanwhile, Sinbald and his burghers reached Shinshumin Castle, rode inside, and yanked up all the drawbridges. When they saw that young Bovo was missing, they began to weep and wail.

The young king found poor Bovo, took him back, and brought him to his mother, Brandei. The queen welcomed him with open arms and inspected him on all sides to see if he had been injured. The young king then said to his army:

"Let's not stay here for long. The army has to collect at the castle and beleaguer it for a whole year, and there will be enough food for the men and endless quantities for me, and all sorts of delicious things." And there were cattle and salt and wine and oil and grain, and there were four hundred men inside. Why, the devil himself couldn't have taken the castle. King Dudin was furious. "I won't keep silent! I may lose all my men but I won't give in!"

The king had a brother named Alberig and he summoned him from Frenchland, and Alberig arrived with all his men, and they besieged the castle and won the war in days and years.

One night, the king was sleeping on his bed in the tent, and his army was also asleep. Suddenly the king began to holler, and all his men woke up, terrified.

The king's brother asked him: "Why are you hollering?"

The king said: "I have to laugh at myself! When I fell asleep, I dreamed that Bovo was standing over me with a naked sword and that he chopped my head off!"

The king's brother, Alberig, said to the king: "If you like, please take my advice, for your dream was not meaningless. Bovo will indeed kill you in several years. If you want to prevent him from killing you, don't ask for him now. Instead, tell his mother to have him murdered in secret."

The king then said to his brother: "Go home to my queen and describe my dream to her. I'm certain that she will banish him or slay him. That's how deeply she loves me."

Well, Alberig said: "I'll be glad to do it." And he rode into the town, went to the queen, and told her about the king's dream.

The queen was horrified, and she said to Alberig: "Tell your brother and my king that he needn't worry, I'll get rid of my son Bovo."

So Alberig went back to the king and brought him the queen's reply.

Meanwhile the queen pondered how she could prevent her child from reaching a ripe old age. She sent for her son, who came immediately, and he said:

"My dear mother, what can I do for you?"

And his mother said: "My dear child, I feel like taking a stroll."

So Bovo went strolling with her, and they strolled through one palace after another, through all the gates, until they reached the lowest palace of the royal court. And, as if she had forgotten him, she locked Bovo up in one of the chambers. Bovo started yelling and weeping, he felt awful and he said to himself: "When can I get out of here? This is terrible! How could my mother forget me?! I need to eat something!"

Well, Bovo wept and wailed for three days and three nights. His mother, that wicked lady, stayed far away to avoid hearing him. After mulling it over, she decided to put deadly poison in his food and send it to him so that he would die immediately. The mother then took a fresh chicken, had it roasted, and poured the deadly poison into it.

Next, she summoned her maid and she said: "I've forgotten all about my dear son for several days now, and he hasn't eaten a thing. Take this chicken to him, so he can eat and stay alive. And tell him to overlook my forgetfulness."

And the maid took the chicken to Bovo, who could barely crawl around. He grabbed it with both hands and was about to devour it. But the maid said: "My child, listen to me, don't eat a bite of that. Your mother wants to send you a misfortune. She has poisoned the chicken! If you don't believe me, test it and feed a piece to that dog." Bovo took a small morsel of the chicken, and when the dog gobbled it down, its throat swelled up, and it suffocated.

Upon witnessing this, Bovo beat his chest and he hollered in a lamenting voice: "Heaven help me! I'd sell myself into slavery if it would help me get out of here! My wicked mother won't see me anymore!" And the boy tried to think of some way of escaping. But he couldn't find one. Eventually, however, he managed to climb out a window and he landed in the garden, where he gorged himself on fruit. The garden was surrounded by a high wall, and Bovo kept looking for an escape route, until he found a wooden section of the wall. He broke through and found a swamp on the other side. He took a plank from the wall and laid it across the swamp like a bridge, and he walked across it. Next he took the second and the third till he reached the other side. He then jumped, landing with one foot in the mire. But he had escaped safe and sane!

> Well, let's leave Bovo and see
> What's happening to Her Majesty.

When the queen remembered Bovo, she went to seek him in the palace, but he was nowhere to be found. Bovo wasn't there. She then had her servants scour the garden, but she was told he wasn't there either. However, they said, one section of the wall was smashed, and so the queen went to see for herself. She spotted the hole and the swamp on the other side, and she was certain he had drowned. She then promptly wrote a letter to her young king, saying that she had taken her son's life.

> And so let's get back to writing
> About Bovo and his tale so exciting.

When Bovo climbed out of the swamp, he started bitterly crying and lamenting, and he said to himself: "What should I do today? My beautiful complexion is pale." And he began running so fast that not even a horse could have kept pace with him. His great terror gave him the strength of a giant. But then he weakened and grew very tired. He sat down to rest a bit. Then he broke into a run again, and he kept running till he reached the sea. Here he collapsed, and he was so hungry that he ate grass. Then he dozed off and he slept all night till three hours of the dawn.

Now a ship filled with merchants came sailing from Barbaria, and, from far away, one of the merchants spotted Bovo sleeping on the shore as if he were dead. The merchant said to the other merchants: "I can see a person lying dead on the ground."

Four of the merchants boarded a small boat, went ashore, hurried over to Bovo, and carried him to their large boat. He still looked like a corpse and he couldn't move. The merchants tried to revive the boy by feeding him sugar and rose oil and rubbing vinegar in all parts of his body, until he started regaining his memory. And when Bovo finally remembered who he was, he looked around. How had he wound up on this ship? He was quite astonished. And he said:

"Am I blind or didn't I see a path or did the river carry me here?"

The merchants told Bovo what had happened to him. And they liked him a lot and practically wanted to wait on him hand and foot. And whenever the merchants wanted him to do something, he quickly served them with a cheerful heart and with a dance.

Now as the merchants sailed on with Bovo, they kept fighting over him. One merchant said: "Bovo belongs to me because I was the first to sight him." Another merchant said: "Bovo belongs to me because I carried him on my back." A third merchant said: "Bovo belongs to me because I revived him." And the fourth merchant said: "I'll let him go over my dead body!" And the merchants all drew their swords and dueled with one another.

When Bovo saw this, he grabbed an oar and struck the hands of each merchant and said: "You don't have to fight over me. If you follow a word or two that I say, I will serve you until we reach dry land. You can then sell me, and you can divide the money among yourselves."

The merchants liked his idea and they shook hands by way of agreement.

Next they started asking Bovo about his father and his mother. And Bovo said: "God has made my parents suffer. They go begging for bread. My father was born in Hungary, and my mother is so stingy that she nearly let me starve to death. She was a wicked lady. And I was a wicked boy, and she made me suffer a little. So I wanted to shoot and kill her."

The merchants chuckled a bit at Bovo's words.

Now after sailing another two or three leagues, they were struck by a great catastrophe. There was horrible thunder and lightning and wind and rain, and the ship began sinking. The passengers started confessing their sins as is customary among Jews about to perish. The mast shattered into bits. But then God saved the day—they spotted an island in the middle of the sea. They managed to reach the island and they moored the ship until the wind died down. Then, in the distance, they sighted a lovely town named Armunio. Untying the ship, they went to that town, which was ruled by a wealthy king, who was also named Armunio. The town customarily shoots its cannons at any ship that it sees, and the king and his men go to view the ship. And so now the king and his men went to speak with the merchants.

And the merchants said to the king: "Why don't you buy our handsome slave!" And they showed Bovo to the king. Bovo was flawless from top to bottom, and the king inspected him front and back and on all sides, the way you examine a horse.

Now, you dear people, you can see what may happen to a person. Therefore no one should delight in his goods and his gold. For if misfortune strikes, he himself doesn't know how to treat the world properly. The world is like a ladder. One man goes up, and the other man goes down. We see how this happened to our handsome Bovo.

Well, now the king asked the merchants how much they wanted for the boy. The merchants said: "He is worth a thousand ducats."

The king said: "I'll pay you immediately, and you will bring me the boy." Now that the price was agreed on, they brought Bovo to the king, who then took Bovo.

The king asked the boy: "Who are your father and mother, and who are you?"

And the boy answered: "I am who I am."

The king took Bovo and handed him over to the marshal of the royal stable. The boy was to take care of the horses, and the king ordered the marshal not to spare the rod, for the boy was very spirited.

The marshal took Bovo to the stable, and Bovo spent two years there, feeding and watering the horses and cleaning the stable for the young king. Everyone liked Bovo. Whoever saw him riding a horse enjoyed the sight, for Bovo was very handsome and appealing. He had red cheeks and black eyes, his hair was golden. And whoever saw him riding a horse enjoyed the sight.

Now the king had a beautiful daughter, she was eighteen years old and her name was Beautiful Drezne. And there was no girl more beautiful in all the world. One day, Drezne was at her window and she saw Bovo riding a horse. And the horse sprang up an entire ell.

Drezne said to her young ladies-in-waiting: "I'll swear by my life that I'll fall out my window if I've ever since a more handsome man than that boy! I would pay a lot of money for him! His beauty has made me sick. If I don't see him again, something awful will happen to me."

One day, Bovo and his friends went riding, and Beautiful Drezne stood at her window and truly loved Bovo. And she signaled to him several times and she would have gladly leaped down to him. But her signals and laughter were useless—Bovo rode on by. The princess then sighed deeply and went to bed without eating supper. And she was very sick because of her yearning. And she couldn't wait to see the daylight.

The next morning, she ran over to see her father, who welcomed her with open arms, and he said: "Dear daughter, you are my comfort and my solace. Why have you come here so early in the morning?"

The princess said: "I'll tell you what I desire. This is what I wish. Please throw me a banquet today for my ladies-in-waiting and give me a waiter whom I'll like."

Well, the king said to her: "My dear daughter, you will have whatever you desire and any waiter you wish."

And she said: "I want to have Bovo and his companions."

And the king said: "Go and summon them."

Drezne quickly sent for Bovo, and he came to her, and she was refreshed, and she said to him: "You will wait on me."

And Bovo said: "Whatever the young queen orders me to do I will gladly do."

Now when the diners sat down at the table, the waiters served roast chicken and all kinds of fish and other delicacies. However, all day long, the young queen couldn't keep her eyes off Bovo, and her desire grew in her. And all the diners noticed her yearning and they said: "How can a queen yearn for a slave?"

Then Drezne dropped her knife with some meat on it. Bovo instantly started looking for the knife, and so did Drezne, under the table. And she said to him: "You must be blind, that's why you can't find the knife."

As she reached under the table, she gave him a kiss, and Bovo cast down his eyes and turned as red as tinder. He was scared: Diners sitting nearby might have seen him, and he couldn't get her out of his mind. When he went to the young queen to take his leave, he was too embarrassed to speak, but he managed to say: "God bless all women—I can't remain here any longer. I have to go to the horses and clear away their droppings." But he spoke without pleasure.

The young queen said: "Go then, my darling. You did a wonderful job of serving me. God should not forget you in case we don't see one another fairly soon."

Bovo was so embarrassed that he could barely lift up his eyes, and he hurried back to his work in the stable.

Soon after Bovo left, a horseman came riding from another country, named Armine. It was located a hundred leagues away and it was ruled by a king known as Mekabron. And there was no one else like him in the entire world. Mekabron had ridden here to get Drezne's hand in marriage. He brought along a thousand horses and a lot of money, and the king welcomed him with great esteem and let him make a beautiful castle of pure gold. However, the king was to set a time for having Mekabron joust on the square. For it was the king's custom that whoever came to ask for his daughter's hand must first joust on the square, to see if she liked him, and the whole town would witness the winner's victory.

Young Queen Drezne also went to watch the joust, and she wore a crown on her head. And one of her father's chamberlains stood by her and held a horn. As soon as Drezne told him to blow the horn, the joust had to end, for that was the king's order. Now the time came for Mekabron to joust with King Armunio's men, and his army came riding to the square, and so did Mekabron's army. Meanwhile, Bovo was cutting grass for his horses, and he made a wreath of grass and placed it on his head, and it looked good on him.

And so Bovo rode into the town to joust with his own strength. He was as strong as iron. When he reached the square, he heard an angry yelling, and he hurried over to see what it was all about. Upon arriving, he saw that Mekabron had been hit by a lot of the king's soldiers, but Mekabron made a strong effort to show Beautiful Drezne that he was a powerful knight. No one could resist him, and King Armunio's army was already exhausted. Bovo saw this and he laughed loudly. Then he said to his companions: "I'd like to join the tournament, but you have to give me a sword and a lance."

Bovo now rode into the stable in order to lay out the grass for the horses, and after doing so, he searched every nook and cranny until he found a sword under the gate, a thick and lame and crooked bolt. And when Bovo saw the sword, he was delighted—as if he'd struck it rich!

And he said: "How can you be useful to me now? You'd have to be somewhat straight, so that I could triumph over Mekabron, the strong hero!"

Bovo then mounted the horse and galloped to the square, and he hollered: "Step aside! King Mekabron has to fight me, and I will avenge every drop of blood, starting today."

Well, when Mekabron heard this, he wanted to plunge his lance into the boy. But our dear Bovo was more skillful, and he thrust his lance into Mekabron. The king's soul practically left him, and he toppled off his mount. His men instantly dashed over and put him back on his horse. All the onlookers started mocking and laughing at the king, who was so ashamed that he wished the earth would swallow him up. Furthermore, his arm had broken, but he was too embarrassed to say so.

Now upon seeing this, his men instantly charged Bovo, trying to spear him. But when Beautiful Drezne witnessed this, she ordered the horn blower to blow his horn and put an end to the joust. Then she ordered her retinue to escort her home, and the soldiers also went home, and Bovo likewise rode home, and he placed the thick bolt under the bridge. Next, he fell asleep on the grass and he slept till evening for he was exhausted. However, all the towns-folk in all the streets praised his strength and his beauty. And all the people said: "Long live the boy! He can conquer the entire world." And Beautiful Drezne wouldn't forget him.

While everyone went to dine, Drezne went to see Bovo in the stable and spend a little time with him, sitting on the grass. Bovo was lying on his back, fast asleep. And his cheeks were like two roses. Now when she saw that he was asleep, she sat there very properly, wondering in her heart of hearts how she could marry him. For she knew her background, and she had been miserable ever since Bovo's arrival. Her heart felt wretched, and she did her best to expunge the very thought of that sin. She wanted to avoid making her father unhappy.

As she pondered and was about to leave, Handsome Bovo woke up. Drezne was very embarrassed, and her legs buckled. So she sat down again for a while. Bovo was very surprised, and he asked her how she had managed to get here. And she replied: "I wanted to have a horse saddled so I could do some riding."

Both Bovo and Drezne then started talking together, and she said, greatly ashamed: "I'd like to know who your parents are and what their station is. For we can tell from your high station that your background is not a common one. Why can't you reveal who you are?—I'll make you happy. You yourself don't know how happy God will make you through me. I'm an only child, a daughter, and if we marry, the whole country will belong to you." That was what she said, for she wanted to touch his heart.

And Bovo said: "Since you ask me, I'll tell you. I drove them out of their home, and they go begging from house to house."

But Drezne said: "I don't want you to tell me lies. You don't look like a beggar, you look like a noble child."

But as they sat there, conversing, a misfortune struck the king and his men. The king of a foreign country arrived. His name was Suldan, and he was accompanied by his son, Lutsfer, and also by ten thousand men, who were all powerful heroes.

Now when King Armunio saw a strong king arriving with a huge army, he was terrified and he ran over to the wall, where he asked the foreign king what was going on and what he wanted.

And Suldan said: "Your daughter—you must give her to my son! And if you refuse, then I will take her with my sword. And you will die and so will your men. You promised, but you've broken your word. That's why you must hand her over!"

Suldan's son was so ugly, he looked like a bull. Anyone who saw him ran away. He was as black as a devil, and he had a beard like a ghost. He looked just like a devil and he came from a nation called Heathens. He was very big and tall, no one was his size, and he never stepped aside for even the noblest noble. And with his dreadful violence, he had overpowered lots of men. And nobody in the world was as strong as Lutsfer.

When King Armunio saw him, he said: "I should refuse both you and your father, for I never promised to give you my daughter. I would be ashamed to marry my daughter to a Heathen. Before handing her over to such a devil, I would stab her to death."

But Lutsfer said to the king: "Forget about your shame! You must hand over your daughter—or else it will cost you your life. Come to the square and let's fight."

The king then spoke to his men: "Take your guns, we're going to fight! Don't be scared—the noise will be heard everywhere!"

Mekabron likewise came with his men, and he said to the king: "You don't have to worry, we'll help you this morning!"

Several thousand men with swords and with bows and arrows left the wall and they found the army of Heathens, like sand on the sea. And they began to fight with one another joyfully, and very many soldiers were killed on both sides. And King Mekabron also came with his men and he fought very furiously. And each man fought and struck many of the Heathens, but Lutsfer fought on the other side and he killed many men, inflicting a bitter death on them, and he carried an iron pole that weighed fifty pounds. And young King Mekabron rode toward him and said:

"Now see me inflicting an awful misfortune on you! You wicked man—give up!"

But Lutsfer wasn't intimidated, and he galloped powerfully toward King Mekabron and thrust his spear into the king, who toppled to the ground. And Lutsfer grabbed him and bound him, till the prisoner was unable to move. Lutsfer took him to his father and then he plunged back into the fray.

Next, Lutsfer fought with the king himself and he said to him: "You are a decent man, I'll make you patient as I can."

Before the king could turn around, he was already on the ground, and he didn't even know how he got there. The king then said: "I want peace!"

But Lutsfer said: "No, you wicked man! You must remain a prisoner."

And they tied up the king and led him off.

> Well, let's leave them in the fray
> And let's talk about Bovo today.

Bovo was still in the stable with Beautiful Drezne, and they could hear loud weeping and clashing in the town. Drezne said: "What can that be?"

And Bovo said: "My queen, I'll go and see what that yelling and roaring are all about!"

And Drezne said: "I'm scared you'll join them. Swear that you'll come back to me."

Bovo swore and she let him go. And he dashed through the vineyard. There he found a lot of lords weeping and wailing. He asked them why, and they said: "Oh, oh! We've fallen into the hands of King Suldan, and King Mekabron has captured our king!"

Well, Bovo was very upset, and he raced back to the stable, and there he found Beautiful Drezne waiting for him. And Bovo gave her the bad news: "Oh, goodness! You've lost your dear father, he's been captured by Mekabron!"

Drezne started crying, but then she thought to herself that if an enemy heard her, both she and Bovo would be taken prisoner. So she held her tongue, and Bovo also said: "Don't cry. Maybe God will help us, and I'll redeem your father from King Suldan."

And Drezne said: "If you can go to him, you might pull it off! I'll give you a coat of armor and a sharp blade that belonged to my brother—he was killed in a battle. But there's one thing I have to ask you, and you must not lie! Tell me: Who is your father?"

Bovo said: "Since you've asked me, I will now tell you the truth. My father was King Guiden, and he ruled the land called Altinne."

Drezne was overjoyed to hear that and she hurried off to get the armor. She helped Bovo dress and, using both hands, she helped him mount his horse and she handed him a sword. She gave him the sword, which was named Pamele, and a horse named Rendzele. The sword was so sharp that it could slice a single hair. And the horse was enchanted by the devil—no musket or cannon could harm it, and it could fight a hundred other horses. And Bovo donned a suit of armor, and Drezne helped him mount and she wept terribly.

And Drezne said: "Ride, you dear companion. And may Almighty God accompany you and help you in your struggle!"

At this point, they were joined by Count Oyglin, the king's uncle, who was bringing the princess's beaker.

Upon seeing what was taking place, the uncle said: "Drezne, wicked men have captured your father, and you're not the least bit worried!"

When Bovo heard those words, he hit the ceiling! He stabbed the uncle with his sword, knocking him to the ground. Then he said good-bye to Beautiful Drezne and rode off to join the fray. Along the way, he encountered lots of men who had deserted the Heathens and were being hunted down by them.

Bovo said to them: "Dear lords, don't lose your faith in God! Come on, hitch up with me, and we'll defend ourselves. Haven't you heard the old saying: 'If you run away, you'll be followed that day! But if you fight, you'll be all right!'"

A lot of men took heed and turned back under Bovo, who received them with kind words and fresh hearts for the clash. Never had there been such a battle. There was a huge torrent of blood. Some men had their arms chopped off, some had their legs chopped off, and some had their heads chopped off, and some defended themselves. Bovo galloped along on his steed, Rendzele, angrily fighting everyone, and he went crazy. His horse helped him, it struck his legs both behind and in front! He took no prisoners, and with his sword, Pamele, he took many lives. He was the first in the fray, no Heathen would survive that day! And he saw Lutsfer, the young king, fighting behind him. Bovo saw many men die, the young king struck them down with his steel pole, which he always carried.

And Bovo was furious, his innards were ablaze, and he wheeled around on his steed Rendzele and swiftly raced over to Lutsfer and he said to him: "Tell me, sir! Have you come here to kill and to leave no one alive? If so, then I'll be a devil with my sword and I'll hack you to pieces! I won't endure your wickedness!"

Lutsfer peered into Bovo's eyes and he said to him: "You poor child! What are you doing here? You are beautiful. Come with me to my father's home and be a waiter. Why lose your life for nothing?"

And Bovo said to Lutsfer: "Fight me if you can!"

And Lutsfer saw that Bovo mustered his strength and dug his spurs into Lutsfer's horse. And the horse sprang, and Bovo thrust his sword into the horse, and Lutsfer tumbled to the ground, and Bovo's sword, three quarters of an ell in length, remained inside Lutsfer.

When the Heathens saw this, they wept and wailed, and they shouted: "There's no speaking or writing to tell, alas, how we've lost our young king!"

Bovo's men did not despair! They chased Lutsfer's army with great strength and no fear! King Suldan knew nothing about all this, for he hadn't joined the fight, he was tending the prisoners. But in the distance, King Suldan spotted a man going as swiftly as an arrow. The man had lost an arm, and so much blood that nobody recognized him.

He dismounted and fell to his knees in front of King Suldan, and he said: "Your dear son Lutsfer has been killed."

The king then said: "I've lost my dear son, Lutsfer, but I certainly won't forgive his killers! I'm going to avenge his blood!" Next, he said to the prisoners: "You have to come home with me! Your lives are at stake!"

Barely had he spoken, when another man came running up to King Suldan, and he also said: "You've lost your son, he was killed by a young man, eighteen years old. This man has killed many soldiers and he's coming here furiously. I left him and his men not far from here."

"Well, it would be better if you ran away!" The Suldan wept bitterly and he said: "I've lost my dear son, he's been killed. Pack up, all of you, and get ready to leave here!"

He wanted to tie up the prisoners and take them along. And when he saw Bovo and his army approaching, King Suldan said: "We can't stay here any longer!"

He left all his belongings and also the prisoners and he set out with only ten men and he reached the coast. Bovo and his men were chasing them when a wild tempest arose! But King Suldan had already leaped into a ship. Bovo would have liked to grab him, but he couldn't. All he could do was shout: "Don't think you've escaped me! I'll find you in your home!"

Next Bovo galloped back to the prisoners' tent, and there he found the king and Mekabron and many other lords tied up and lying on the ground. And Bovo jumped down from his steed and untied the king and Mekabron and then the other lords.

Bovo said: "Blessed is the hour when I can see you again."

The king said: "I never figured that Bovo would risk his neck for us." And the king was so happy that he burst into tears. And Mekabron joined with Bovo and they had no fears. And the king and Mekabron said: "If it hadn't been for what happened today, our lives would have been taken away!"

And Bovo said: "Listen, my dear friends. We can't stay on here for long. We have to beat the Heathens!"

Bovo gave each man a horse, and he gave the best horses to the king and Mekabron. And they charged out against the Heathens, and they killed each one they caught.

When the king saw Bovo fighting like that, he said to him: "My dear child, you are a cavalier worthy of our praises. You've served me today, so I'll never forget you in any way. You mustn't ride out on a horse anymore, you mustn't rinse a dish anymore. You must become my supreme captain! And I'll grant you any wish!"

And Bovo said: "I've already worked off the fee of the thousand ducats that you paid for me."

Now Bovo was riding home with the king and Mekabron, and when they reached the town, they saw Drezne coming towards them, and they caught the booming of cannon and the blaring of trumpets, and fifes and drums resounded, and everything could be heard from far away. And Beautiful Drezne joyfully welcomed them, and I'd better not say how she and Bovo carried on that day.

At nightfall, when everyone went to their respective homes to sleep, Bovo and Drezne remained with the king, and she sat down next to her father, and she said:

"Dear father, please thank me for the cavalier that I sent you and that saved you from King Suldan. I personally helped the cavalier put on his armor and I gave him a horse, Rendzele, and a sword, Pamele. And I swore to him that I would be his wife, and he would be my husband. That was why he risked his life. But now he's performed his task, and I'll likewise keep my end of the bargain. I have to marry him. However, it turns out that he is the son of a king. So I needn't be the least bit ashamed. His father was named Guiden. Therefore, my dear father, please give me your permission, for I don't want anyone else! He is worthy of being a king."

Her father said: "If that's what you want." And he stood up and sat down next to Handsome Bovo.

Now as they were all sitting together, they were summoned to the meal. Bovo and Drezne were so engrossed in their conversation that the king himself had to rebuke them. And when they were done eating, the king ordered them to retire to their individual quarters. Bovo was given a fine chamber with a lovely bed and many domestics to serve him. He then went to bed and slept till morning.

That morning, the news that Beautiful Drezne would be marrying Bovo was the talk of the town. "Well," everyone said, "that's wonderful! Now we don't have to be scared of the Heathens."

When the king awoke, he ordered a servant to bring him a gold chain and a black velvet robe for Bovo. And they shook hands and the engagement contract was written.

Now when the king's uncle, Count Oyglin, heard about the betrothal, he hit the roof! He then went to the king, who welcomed him very cordially, and his uncle said to the king: "Praise the Lord that you were saved from the clutches of the wicked King Suldan! Now I'd love to wish you mazel-tov, congratulate you, but I can't, because you're getting a wrong son-in-law. Where in the world have you ever heard of such a horrible disgrace—a king letting his daughter marry a servant!"

The king then said: "Listen, uncle! Stop carrying on that way! And please mind what you say! I've given this daughter of mine a bridegroom so fine! What good is a great pedigree if a man looks good to me! What good is a sacred grave if at home they rant and rave!" The king was furious at his uncle and he told him: "I repeat! Mind your own business!"

And his uncle left amid great shame and he said to himself: "I've got to use cunning and secrecy to kill Bovo! I'll have a key made for his bedroom while Bovo is asleep."

At nightfall, Bovo withdrew to his chamber, which the king had given him. And the king's uncle said to his men: "Grab your swords and go to Bovo's chamber, and we will kill him!"

They unlocked the door and they all stole inside, following the uncle. Upon entering, they saw a candle burning very brightly at the sleeper's head. And the sword named Pamele likewise lay by his head. The men were so terrified that they dashed out of the room.

One of them was an old soldier, and he said: "Milord, let's leave the chamber, for what can we gain if Bovo wakes up and sees us? He'll kill us all! Instead, let me give you some advice. Pretend to be sick and get into the king's bed at dawn when the king is gone. But cover your face too so Bovo won't recognize you, and send for him right away and you will say: "Bovo, my dear child, you have to take a letter from me to King Suldan, and the letter will say: 'The carrier of this letter is the man who killed your dear son Lutsfer. I'm turning him over to you so you can do for him whatever you care to do.'"

The uncle really liked this advice. So he pretended to be sick and he got into bed. And one of his men went to Bovo and he said: "The king is sick in bed and he needs you to go to him."

Bovo was terrified and he threw on his clothes and dashed over to the king's chamber. And the uncle, mimicking the voice of the king, asked: "Is Bovo here already?"

Bovo said: "Yes, I'm here." He thought he was speaking to the king.

And he gave him a kiss. And the uncle told him that Bovo was to take a secret letter to King Suldan.

Since Drezne might guess the secret if Bovo mounted Rendzele, he took another horse instead, one of the best, and off he sped, as swift as an arrow from its bow. He raced through many towns without stopping, and he finally reached the border of Heathenland just as the sun was setting. Now Bovo was exhausted, and he paused at the border to rest. He was also starving, but he had nothing to eat or drink. Then he found a German beggar sitting there, eating cheese and drinking fine wine from a bottle.

And Bovo said: "Dear friend, don't you have any food to refresh me?" And he dismounted.

And the beggar handed Bovo the bread. But Bovo couldn't eat it because it was very moldy, and the cheese was so hard that it would have broken his teeth. Next, the beggar handed Bovo the bottle of wine, which Bovo greatly enjoyed. And Bovo said: "Can you give me a little more wine? I'll pay you nicely."

And the beggar said: "I've got a flask of wine, but it's very expensive." The flask contained a sleeping potion. And the beggar handed Bovo the flask, and Bovo drank it up, and he collapsed on the ground and fell asleep.

The beggar lost no time. He emptied Bovo's money pouch of everything and he also took Bovo's ring. And he stripped him bare and grabbed his sword right there and he also took his horse that day and he tossed the letter away, and he dressed Bovo in beggar's clothes and let him doze with his beggar's bag, and let Bovo stay while the beggar rode away.

Now Bovo lay there with the beggar's things for twenty-four hours like a dead man. The next morning, he woke up, but he couldn't open his eyes, they were practically pasted together. He had to use spit to get them open. Then he looked for his money pouch and the sword and his horse and his clothes and his ring and everything, and he could find only the letter and nothing better than the beggar's clothes and the bread. And now he started to think that the beggar must have given him a sleeping potion to drink.

And Bovo said: "The beggar bamboozled me fine. I shouldn't have drunk that wine. What should I do now in my shame? I don't have a penny to my name to find food to ration and stave off starvation. I have to search the beggar's bag." He searched it and he did snag pieces of moldy bread. He ate some and he slipped the rest into his bosom.

Next, he put on the beggar's clothes and he continued on foot until he came to a town that King Suldan ruled. And Bovo asked some citizens the location of the palace, where the king held sway. And these citizens pointed the way. And Bovo went there and then he saw King Suldan sitting with all his lords.

Now when King Suldan saw Bovo, he felt he had already seen him before. Bovo bowed to the ground and handed him the letter and said: "This letter is from King Armanio."

As soon as King Suldan finished reading the letter, he fainted. The lords had to revive him. And when he came to, he shouted: "Oh, me! He killed my dear son! As you love God, you should grab the killer and string him up!"

And King Suldan's men did grab Bovo with both hands. Now Bovo had no weapons to fight them off. He had no sword, no musket, and no spear. Still, he wouldn't let the men catch him, he bit them and beat them and punched them. He killed some of them—but it was no use. They hurled him to the floor and tied him up hand and foot. There's an old saying: "With many a hound, the hare hits the ground." And they took Bovo out of the town to hang him. It mustn't take long, they had to hurry and scurry!

Now the king had a daughter, and she was known as Beautiful Marguerite. That day, she had gone hunting, accompanied by her servants. Upon approaching the town, she saw men dragging out a handsome youth, Bovo, accompanied by many people. Marguerite felt very sorry for the youth and she said: "It's awful hanging such a young and handsome person. I'm going to go to my dear father and get him to keep that youth alive."

She hurried to the palace, dismounted, and went to her father. She knelt at his feet.

Her father said: "Stand up, my dear daughter, tell me what you desire, and I'll carry it out for you."

The daughter then said: "My dear father, why must you order his death?"

King Suldan said: "He is the man who killed your brother."

The daughter said: "If he killed my dear brother, he must be very skillful. Who knows what happened to my brother? Maybe he started the fight, so the youth had to defend himself. If so, then he's not at fault. In that case, my father, you must take my advice and let him live and have him become a Heathen."

The king now said: "If he does that, I will grant him his life."

Next, Beautiful Marguerite galloped toward the execution site. There she saw that the hangman had already taken Bovo up to the gallows and had slipped the noose around his neck. Marguerite yelled at the hangman to wait for her.

And the hangman said to Bovo: "Lucky you. The king's daughter has gotten you a reprieve."

And Marguerite rode so hard that her horse practically got lame! She was scared she might arrive too late.

When she reached the gallows, she ordered the hangman to let Bovo down. Bovo was deathly pale, he didn't have even a drop of blood in his veins, and he could scarcely utter a word.

Marguerite said: "You mustn't despair, just do as I say. If you believe in our Mohammed, they will let you live."

But Bovo said to her: "No, I don't want to believe in him."

And she said: "I'll give you a gold chain and I'll make you a great lord and you'll be a supreme captain."

But Bovo didn't answer her with a single word. Marguerite quickly sat him on the horse and rode to see the king. And when Bovo appeared before King Suldan, the youth bowed down to the ground. And the king scrutinized him for a good while and he said to him:

"You're back again. Now if you agree to become a Heathen, your life will be spared, and I'll forget about what you did to me."

Bovo replied: "Even if you give me all your countries, I won't let myself waver. I believe in God, He is revered, and I won't disobey His commandments. I would rather be hanged or burned at the stake, for He is my Creator. Praised be He, He has never forsaken me. I will not despair in His Holy Name. So please let me be. I won't trade a living God for a dead deity."

King Suldan was furious, and he said: "Take this man out of my sight! He is not to see my face again! He must be hanged!"

But Beautiful Marguerite said: "My dear father, I won't let it happen!

Instead, you should clap him in irons and throw him into a pit. Then he'll have to accept our faith."

And the king said: "I'll do it for your sake, I'll keep him alive for a while."

Next, Bovo was taken away and put in heavy chains and thrown into a pit. The pit was ten fathoms deep and filled with lots of snakes and worms. Beautiful Marguerite came over to him and she said: "You'd do better to become a Heathen, then you won't have to endure these sufferings and you'll have great power."

And Bovo said: "You're wasting your breath, you noble, highborn girl. It's better to endure these sufferings. I won't abandon my living God."

The girl was very angry at Bovo, but she still sent him food every day. The king forgot all about him anyway, because he had sentenced him to twelve months' imprisonment. And Bovo endured great and bitter sufferings, and the girl visited him every day with kind words and she tried to coax him into accepting her faith, but he clung to his own faith.

Now when she saw that kind words were getting her nowhere, she grew angry and she said: "I swear by my honor that I won't be sending you any more food!"

And Bovo said: "I'm scared of death." But he had to suffer.

And as Marguerite went away, she thought to herself: "Let's see how he manages to get along without food!" And she refused to send him food for an entire day. She believed that hunger would bring him around. But then she saw that he was willing to starve to death. So she ordered her loyal servant to bring Bovo food and to pretend that she knew nothing about it. And the servant brought him the best food day after day.

Now as Bovo sat in the terrible dungeon, he said to himself: "Oh, my! Dear God, what else will I suffer in the dark pit in this terrible dungeon? I have to find a way out of this pit."

Bovo was so angry that he began digging in the ground. And a piece of sword he found. He was delighted! And he said to the piece of sword: "You're so big, you're worth a piece of gold! And how badly I need you now! I'm going to resist the Heathens!" And he placed the fragment next to himself.

Now when the twelve months were done, Marguerite went to her father and asked about Bovo. Had the youth changed his mind? And the king ordered his men to bring him Bovo and then take him out to the gallows. Twenty Heathens dashed over to the pit. Ten Heathens were lowered into the pit in order to tie Bovo up. Now Bovo was a fine youth and he grabbed his piece of sword and started fighting with the ten, and he killed them all then. Next another eight were lowered down while two remained above ground. As each Heathen dropped into the pit, Bovo killed him as he saw fit.

Bovo stripped naked and slipped into a Heathen's clothes and he grabbed a Heathen's good sword and he tied himself on the rope and he shouted in the Heathen language: "Pull him up—that murderer! We've tied him up, he won't escape!"

And the two remaining Heathens pulled him up. And there he fought and killed one Heathen and he slashed the other one, who could barely move. Then Bovo swiftly sped away like an arrow from a bow and he ran through the gates, and no one saw him. Meanwhile the slashed Heathen barely crawled to the king. He crept on all fours and he said: "I let the murderer go through the doors! He killed all the other men and he slashed me then. And away sped the foe like an arrow from a bow!"

When the king heard this, he was furious. But Beautiful Marguerite was delighted. Now King Suldan ordered his two hundred men to track Bovo swiftly then. One of these men was the powerful hero Iberey, accompanied by his powerful brother, a great man. They dashed after Bovo, but he was already three leagues away. He was so terrified that he sped forward, while Powerful Iberey ran ahead of his brother and the king's army. Iberey peered into the distance and spotted Bovo. The Heathen instantly aimed his spear and hurled it and he said: "You evil man, you must die today!"

Bovo dodged the blow, grabbed the spear, and thrust it into Iberey's body. Then Bovo took his sword and split the hero's head down to his palate as if he were already dead. Next, he started running again and he struck across fields and grain, across ears of corn. He ran until he was close to the sea. Meanwhile the army reached the hero's corpse, and all the soldiers and the hero's brother were grief-stricken and they wept and wailed. They lingered here for a brief while and they were in no hurry to catch Bovo.

At that moment, Bovo reached the sea, where he saw a lovely ship moored. The ship was filled with Heathens, and Bovo said to them: "Take me along, and I'll pay you nicely."

So they let him come aboard. They mistook him for a Heathen. Now as the ship was setting sail, the king's army arrived, and the soldiers saw Bovo in the ship and they yelled: "Hand over the murderer! He escaped from King Suldan!"

The steersman was about to turn back and hand Bovo over to the army. But Bovo begged the steersman for mercy and he said to him: "Sail and don't ask about the army!"

The Heathens in the ship then said to Bovo: "We'll all be hanged because of you!"

Bovo begged and begged, but he saw it was useless. He was furious and he grabbed the oar and smashed away at the Heathens. And he said: "You want to hand me over, but I'll kill all of you first!" And he began turning the ship around.

The Heathens on the ship saw that they were in a bad way. So they began to beg and they said to Bovo: "Dear Sir, please tell us our route and we'll take you wherever you need to go."

And Bovo said: "Take me wherever you wish."

So they turned the ship around. The Heathens on shore yelled and yelled themselves hoarse. But the ship was moving away on its course and ignoring the yelling. And when the Heathen army saw that the ship was heading out and ignoring their shouts, they returned to King Suldan in great shame and they said:

"The murderer escaped us. The Heathens on the ship took him in."

The king felt very bad, but Beautiful Marguerite was very glad.

> But let's let Bovo sail a few leagues away
> And let's see what Beautiful Drezne has to say.

No one knew that Bovo was gone then, except for Uncle Oyglin and his men. That same morning, they sat down to eat, but Bovo did not appear at his seat. So Drezne said: "Maybe he's not awake as yet." But then she was told that Bovo was gone.

The king said to her: "My dear daughter, I think he must be out hunting."

Now when night fell, and Bovo still didn't return, Drezne had a heavy heart, and she asked all the men if they had seen Bovo. But none of them had seen him.

Drezne could barely wait till the next day. She then went to the king and she said: "My dear father, please help me find Bovo. Something is wrong, I'm scared he might be abducted. So dear father, don't be still, let your voice be shrill. Make people shout, make them beat the drums out! If anyone has seen Bovo alive or, God forbid, dead, let that person come here instead."

The king said to her: "My dear daughter, you are right all the same! Go wherever you wish, and proclaim!"

So she went and had her servants proclaim seven or eight times in all the streets: Had anyone seen Bovo? If anyone could say he had seen him that day, alive or dead, that person would savor the king's favor and he would also get a reward of a hundred ducats.

Now Count Oyglin, the king's uncle, had a servant, a disloyal man, and he said to himself: "I won't hold my tongue, and I can use the money. I'll go to Drezne and tell her the truth." He then went to her and told her what had been done to Bovo, and how he had been sent away by the uncle.

Drezne hurried over to her father's chamber and she knelt down and she wept and wailed. And the king said: "Stand up, my dear daughter, and tell me what you wish."

She told him about what had happened to Bovo, about how the count had sent Bovo to deliver a letter to King Suldan, asking him to kill Bovo.

Drezne's father was dumbfounded and furious and he said: "I swear by my crown then, my uncle will die with all his men!"

Drezne ordered her servants to hunt for the count and all his men, to scour the streets until they caught him. And they did catch him in the streets, with all his men.

And the king said: "All his men will be hanged and the count himself will be drawn and quartered!"

The count begged for his life but it was no use. The king said: "You traitor—you must die today." The king then confiscated all the count's wealth.

Now Drezne really began to cry in dread. She sent messengers to see if Bovo was alive or dead. But she couldn't learn the exact truth. Some people said he would never come back again. Others said King Suldan had strung him up long since.

Drezne's father said to her: "My dear daughter, what are you after? Do you want to spend the rest of your life mourning Bovo? I tell you, he must be dead by now. You must stop waiting for him, you should stop crying. And you should never utter Bovo's name again. I will give you to young Mekabron. He's a great hero too and a handsome man."

When Drezne heard that, she burst into tears and she said: "My dear father, oh, me! You fill me with dread when you say Bovo is dead. Please let me wait a whole year. And if Bovo doesn't reappear at the end of the year, then I'll marry Mekabron rather than another man. So, dear father! Let's sign the engagement contract quickly, and the wedding will take place at the end of a year. Maybe Bovo will reappear."

The king sent for Mekabron, who came with two thousand men, and the king said to him: "You've looked forward to getting my daughter, and now I'll give her to you. But the wedding has to be postponed for a year. After that, she will be your wife so dear."

Well, we can see how Mekabron behaved. She was so dear to him, and he felt no woman was more beautiful than she. But Drezne didn't care, she longed for Bovo all that year, while Mekabron could barely wait. But Drezne scarcely laughed about her fate.

Then, when the year was at its end, Mekabron took Drezne back to his land. Many visitors came to attend the wedding, which people heard about far and wide.

> Now let's leave Drezne with the young king
> And we'll go back to telling
> What Bovo has been doing.

Bovo spent a whole month sailing on the ship with the Heathens. Then they saw a beautiful country far away, and Bovo told them to head that way. When they finally came near, they found a fisherman catching fish there. Upon spotting him, Bovo shouted at him and, as he boarded a small boat, he told the big ship's steersman to continue on his course.

Bovo then said to the fisherman: "My dear friend, please say: Whom does that city belong to today?"

The fisherman said: "I'll tell you. That city belongs to a great and noble ruler named King Mekabron. He is about to marry Beautiful Drezne, the daughter of King Armunio. Earlier, she was engaged to Bovo and she spent a whole year waiting for him."

Upon hearing those words, Bovo was overjoyed and he said to himself: "I'll waste no time, I'll arrive at the feast, and King Mekabron will rage like a beast. And I'll see Beautiful Drezne and take her away with me."

Now the fisherman hauled Bovo ashore, and Bovo thanked him. The fisherman bowed to Bovo, and he would have liked a reward; but Bovo didn't pay him a penny. Instead, Bovo headed off toward the town.

When Bovo reached the outskirts of the town, the beggar who'd given him the sleeping potion came toward him. And Bovo said to the beggar: "My dear friend, why don't we swap clothes? I'll give you my clothes, and you'll give me your rags."

But the beggar said: "I can't wear a good coat. If I do, I won't get a penny in alms or even a piece of bread. So I'd rather not trade clothes with you."

As they were talking, the beggar tucked in the skirts of his coat, and Bovo spotted his sword. He realized it was his own sword, Pamele, and he said to the beggar: "You awful man! You gave me the sleeping potion! I swear that you must die!"

The beggar was terror-stricken, he couldn't retort with a single word.

Bovo started beating the beggar mercilessly. And the beggar pleaded: "My good lord, spare me my life!"

And Bovo said: "No! You must suffer death!"

And the beggar said: "My good lord, I'll tell you where I left your belongings. I lost your horse playing cards, I gave away your ring. Now I plead before you: Spare me my life, and I'll teach you two things that will make you rich."

And Bovo said: "You just want to put one over on me again!"

The beggar swore it wasn't true, and he said: "I've got two vials, one contains a sleeping potion, and the other a different potion. If you smear the other potion on your skin, you get a different appearance."

The beggar smeared his face under his eyes, and his face changed. Bovo had to laugh his head off at the beggar. Now the beggar taught Bovo how to make the sleeping potion and also the other potion. And Bovo tested the second potion on his face, and it turned green and yellow. Next, Bovo took the beggar's rags and his hat and his bag and his sword Pamele. And he put on the rags and he gave his good clothes to the beggar. And then Bovo dashed into the town. He was in a terrible hurry, for he wanted to arrive on time for the banquet.

Upon entering the town, Bovo heard musicians playing joyfully. Indeed, the whole town was roaring. Bovo went to the main square, where he saw tables and benches, and people playing checkers. Bovo said:

"You good people! I've just arrived from Babylon and I'm a pauper. For Bovo's sake, give me food!"

And the townsfolk replied: "What are you saying? Our King Mekabron won't help you at all! He'll hang you! You see, he's issued a proclamation stating that anyone who so much as mentions Bovo's name will be hanged. For if anyone mentions his name in front of the queen, Beautiful Drezne, she instantly turns sad."

Bovo said: "If you don't wish to give me food, please tell me where the royal kitchen is located."

The townsfolk showed him the way to the royal kitchen, and Bovo said to the kitchen staff: "You good people, please give me something to eat for Bovo's sake!"

The kitchen people said: "You awful man, get away from here!" One of them grabbed a fire stick and hit Bovo on the head. But Bovo held his ground, he dug in his heels. He grabbed a cook and threw him into the fire and he burned another cook's eyes out.

The cooks said to Bovo: "Are you a devil? Do you want to kill everybody?" And they served him food and drink. And Bovo asked them not to tell the king that he, Bovo, had killed the cook. But they were already too scared to tell the king and spoil the wedding.

When Bovo had finished his meal, he went out to watch the people dancing, and among them he spotted Drezne. And she was dressed in gold and pearls and precious stones. And while she was dancing, Bovo managed to whisper to her that she ought to give him something for Bovo's sake.

Queen Drezne received him very graciously, and she said: "My dear friend, please tell me how you've gotten news about Bovo."

And Bovo said to her: "My dear queen, Bovo and I were prisoners of King Muldan, but the weight of the prison was too much for Bovo. His noble body couldn't endure it."

Upon hearing this, the queen was terror-stricken, and her face turned all sorts of colors. She left the ball and went into the next room and stood at the window and she burst into tears. She then said to her servant: "Hurry up and bring me the beggar here in this room! I want to give him some money!"

The beggar was brought in, and the queen ordered a meal for him. And a plate of fish was brought in, and Bovo sat down next to the queen. Now King Mekabron came into the same room and he found the queen sitting with a beggar, and the king said to her: "What are you doing—sitting here with a beggar?"

The queen replied: "For the sake of God, I gave him some food. But he has bad news, which has deeply saddened me. He's informed me that my father is very sick—may God grant him a speedy recovery."

But the king said to her: "Don't believe it! Your father would have written me if that were true! He would have sent me a letter! Get away from there and say farewell to the beggar!"

As they were conversing, some servants came hurrying in and they said: "You must know that the horse Rendzele has broken loose!" So everyone, including the king and the queen, dashed over to the stable to prevent the horse from running away.

The beggar likewise went to the stable and he said: "What kind of creature is so menacing that nobody can deal with it?"

Drezne replied: "This horse was hexed by the devil! No one can ride it except for Bovo! And since he's been gone, no one's been able to tend it or feed it but me. I alone can provide for it. And the moment the horse hears Bovo's name, it bolts from the stable and injures lots of people! The horse runs so wildly that you have to lock your doors and windows!"

The beggar then said: "Let me try to capture the horse. And if I fail, then it must be wild indeed!"

And Drezne said to the beggar: "Don't go to the horse—it will kill you!"

And the beggar said: "Show me the horse!"

Upon seeing Bovo, the horse began to circle him, and Bovo took the horse and mounted it. And Drezne was astounded that the beggar could ride the horse.

All at once, Bovo's cloak was uncovered, and Drezne saw the sword Pamele, and she hurried over and said: "Bovo possessed that sword! Can you tell me how you acquired it? And I see that the horse has recognized you. I realize that you must be Bovo himself! Please tell me the truth! For if you are Bovo, it can cost you your life!" Bovo's face was still smeared with the beggar's second potion. And Drezne said: "Wash your face so I can see your real countenance."

Bovo took some water and washed his face with his hands, and he thereby regained his earlier features.

When Drezne saw that the beggar was Bovo, she ran over to him and she said: "Tell me how to get rid of Mekabron! I'm doomed to share his bed tonight!"

Bovo said to her: "Follow my advice. You are to go to the bedroom and say to the king: 'My dear king, the beggar claims that he can teach you how to ride that horse within four weeks. But a bed for the beggar must be placed in the stable.'

"When that is done, I will give you a vial of sleeping potion to give him when you are led to the wedding bed. And you will say that it is very good."

"I will do so."

And Drezne took the vial from Bovo. The horse was then put back in the stable and tied up, and Drezne left the horse.

Next she showed Bovo an underground cave in the stable. The cave ran the length of a league. And Bovo said: "This is very good! Now as soon as you are led to the wedding bed, you are to slip him the sleeping potion and then escape through the back door of the chamber and come to me, and we'll flee through the cave."

Drezne then went to the king and she said: "I will tell you a wonderful thing. The beggar is riding Rendzele nicely, and he claims that he can train the horse within four weeks and teach it not to strike or bite. Anybody will be able to ride the horse."

The king said: "That's fine. Have the servants give the beggar food and drink, and if he manages to complete the training, I'll give him lots of money."

Drezne said: "We don't have to give the man money, all he wants is food and drink, plus a bed in the stable, so he can sleep there."

And the king issued orders accordingly. And they made a bed for Bovo in the stable. And Drezne took a fine rug and rolled up the good armor and sent it to Bovo, and she said: "Take this to the beggar in the stable so that he can bed down."

The servants did as the queen ordered them to do, and Bovo unrolled the rug and found his armor and his weapons. Meanwhile the young queen returned to the ball and acted as if she didn't have a care in the world. She danced up a storm and she was very merry all day long.

Now in the evening, everyone settled at the tables and they ate and drank, and they sang songs for the bridegroom and the bride. Next the couple was taken to a chamber. There Mekabron ordered everyone to leave and he locked the door.

When Drezne saw that, she said to him: "My dear king, why don't we first carouse a little and drink some fine liquors before we go to bed."

And the king said: "Good!"

The queen took the sleeping potion that Bovo had given her and she handed it to the king, and he drained the vial. And when he had drained it, his heart began to ache, and his mind was numb, and he collapsed and dozed off and he lay there dead to the world. And Drezne lost no time and she hurried through the back door and left the chamber and she dashed into the stable, where Bovo was waiting. And when she found him, he was already dressed in his armor with Pamele at his side, and he had already saddled Rendzele. And when Drezne arrived, they both mounted the horse and they galloped all night long, for they were riding through the cave. And they reached a forest. And on they galloped until they came to a well. Here they dismounted, and they sat by the well and they rested. And they ate and they refreshed themselves with the well water, and they were very cheery and their hearts were merry.

> Now let's keep them with their action,
> And write about the king's reaction.

When Drezne let the king sleep, and nobody knew about it, he slept until three hours of daylight, and since it was time for the queen to rise, all the courtiers were astonished that the king slept on with Drezne for such a long while.

The king's father said: "There's more here than meets the eye. We have to see if something's happened to them in their forgetfulness. That's why we shouldn't just sit there and calmly wait until noon." And the king's father refused to wait any longer—he started knocking on the chamber door and he kept knocking for a long time. But no one responded with even a single word. The father then said: "There's more here than meets the eye!" And he called for a hammer and broke open the door. Inside he saw Mekabron doubled up and facedown on the floor—dead to the world. And Beautiful Drezne was gone.

They started shaking and waking up the king, but it was useless. They tried to revive him with spices and vinegar, but nothing helped. He lay there like a corpse for twenty-four hours. Then he finally stood up on his own. And the courtiers asked him: "What's wrong? What happened to you?"

And Mekabron asked: "Where is Drezne?"

The courtiers said: "We don't know where she is!"

Now the king started yelling: "Damn it! I drank a sleeping potion! I'm afraid that Drezne has run away! I don't know what to think! I'm afraid that the beggar who was here yesterday is really Bovo! Check the stable immediately!"

But Bovo was gone, and so was his horse Rendzele. This proved that the beggar was truly Bovo. And Drezne had escaped with him. The king was miserable about Beautiful Drezne, and he started loudly weeping and wailing. Then he said to himself: "Drezne, I would never have imagined that you could be disloyal to me and abandon me! How horrible! How heart-wrenching! How awful! It's a wedding without a bride!"

The king then summoned all his men to court and ordered them to chase the runaways. But the king's father said to him: "My dear son, let me give you some advice. Stop wailing and tell your men to stay home. I've got someone who's half dog and half man. The likes of him have never been seen anywhere in the world. He can run many leagues in an hour, and he can kill a hundred men. And his name is Mighty Spotted Dog. He's chained up in my dungeon, and he's condemned to be hanged tomorrow! If you like, I'll send him out. And if we promise to spare his life, he'll definitely bring back the runaways. Just release him from the dungeon."

Young Mekabron said: "I don't need anything better. Just release him from the dungeon!"

So Spotted Dog was released. He came to the king and fell to his knees. And Mekabron said: "My good hero! I want to release you from the dungeon, but you have to do as I say. If you hunt down Bovo and Drezne and bring them back to me, I'll let you return to your country and also give you lots of money."

Spotted Dog said: "My good lord, I promise that you needn't worry. I swear that I'll bring them back by the day after tomorrow. But please give me my armor and my bow and arrow and my sword, which you took from me, and I will definitely catch up with the runaways!"

Mekabron ordered his men to bring Spotted Dog's battle gear to the court. Spotted Dog then powerfully scurried about on all fours, charging over hill and dale. He looked everywhere, sniffing like a dog and dashing furiously. And his barking could be heard far away and he kicked up as much dust as a huge army! And Bovo was fast asleep, and Drezne heard the barking from far away. She therefore awoke Bovo from his slumber and she said: "My dear Bovo, I'm afraid you'll have to defend yourself. Do you hear that loud barking in the forest?"

When Bovo heard it, he was terrified. He swiftly put on his armor and took hold of his sword and mounted his horse, and he was ready for the battle. Now he sighted someone dashing in the distance in a huge storm.

Whereupon Drezne said: "If that's only one person, he has to be Spotted Dog." And she was very frightened. Her face blanched.

And Bovo said to Drezne: "My beloved, you don't have to be scared! I'm not afraid of a hundred dogs, much less one single dog. And I can certainly fight someone who's half dog and half man!"

And as Bovo and Drezne were talking, Spotted Dog came running and he said to Bovo: "You wicked man! Go back with Drezne, otherwise you'll have to fight me!"

And Bovo said to Spotted Dog: "Keep quiet, hold your tongue! I want to show you a thing or two. You should know that I'm not afraid of your arrows and your blades."

Upon hearing those words, Spotted Dog took a one-league jump and started shooting arrows at Bovo. And Bovo grabbed the reins of his horse Rendzele and evaded the arrows. And Spotted Dog kept shooting until he had no arrows left. Next, he clutched his sword and jousted with Bovo. Each warrior wanted to kill the other. Spotted Dog fought like a huge storm, but Bovo fought back like a dragon. And his horse also helped Bovo. However, Spotted Dog was stronger than Bovo and he knocked him off his mount.

Now the moment the horse saw that Bovo was on the ground, he started fighting Spotted Dog with all his strength. Spotted Dog swiftly mounted the horse. And when the horse felt Spotted Dog on his back, he galloped into the forest and through the brambles. Spotted Dog's face was scratched and he would have liked to dismount, but he couldn't do it. The horse was very wild and he was still charging about with Spotted Dog on his back. Spotted Dog lost his sword and he grabbed hold of a tree. He tore the tree out by its very roots and he went back to Bovo and tried to kill him.

When Drezne saw this, she was horrified and she started yelling: "You Spotted Dog! You dear friend! What kind of calamity are you inflicting on me? Don't you remember how loyal I was to you when you were captured by Mekabron, and they kept wanting to hang you, and I managed to talk them out of it? Therefore, my dear friend, you should remember that and you should swear brotherhood with Bovo! Two heroes like yourselves can capture the entire world—and who can ever defeat you? Now if you listen to me, we can all benefit. But if you take us back to Mekabron, he'll hang you all the same, for he's a big liar."

When Spotted Dog heard that, he called to Drezne and he said: "I'll do what you say. Just tell Bovo to put his sword away, and we'll swear brotherhood to each other. If he likes, I'll join him and keep traveling with him, and we'll escape Mekabron together."

Drezne was delighted, and she hurried over to Bovo and she said to him: "My dear Bovo, I spoke with Spotted Dog, and he said he wants to make peace with you. But first, you have to put away your sword. Spotted Dog wants to wander with us until we come to our father in our own country."

And Bovo obeyed Drezne and he tossed away his sword and then ran over to Spotted Dog. The two warriors shook hands and swore brotherhood to each other. Next, they sat down to rest by a well and they stayed there all day. Then Bovo and Drezne mounted Bovo's horse, and Spotted Dog followed them like a hound, intent on getting away from Mekabron.

As they traveled, they saw a beautiful castle in the distance, and Spotted Dog said to Bovo: "My dear Bovo, I can tell you about that castle for I've spent a number of days there. The castle is called Kistel, and it is ruled by a great lord named Mighty Urian. He once battled with Mekabron and he stuck his spear in him. Mekabron has been avoiding him, but if he could he would have hanged Urian long ago! Lord Urian will welcome us with open arms!"

And Drezne said: "He's a good man. Let's go to his castle, I've known him for a long time, and I'm friends with his wife."

So they headed for the castle.

But when they arrived, and the gatekeeper sighted them, he blew his horn, and Lord Urian climbed to the top of the gate to find out who was coming. Upon seeing Spotted Dog, he was terrified and he said: "Mekabron has come to kill me." And Urian locked all the entrances to the castle and then climbed on top of the wall to gain a clear view of the travelers. He now saw Bovo and Drezne and heard them laughing and he was amazed to see Bovo and Spotted Dog together. After all, he was certain that Spotted Dog was in Mekabron's dungeon.

The lord of the castle said to his wife: "My dear wife, take a good look at these travelers."

His wife said: "Why, that's my friend Drezne. Let me go to her and welcome her in peace. I think they're escaping Makabron." The wife then shouted down from the wall: "Is that really you, Drezne? Should I believe it?"

And Drezne replied: "Yes! It's me. Open the gates, and we'll enter."

But the lord said to his wife: "First tell Drezne to drive away Spotted Dog, and then I'll let her in. I'm scared he might kill me!"

Drezne said: "I won't go in without him—even if you pay me a thousand ducats! You see, he and Bovo swore brotherhood together, so you have nothing to be scared of!"

So the gates were opened and the travelers were welcomed joyfully. Now Lord Urian asked Bovo and Drezne where they were coming from and where they were going. And Bovo told the lord everything that had happened to them.

The lord then had a lovely chamber prepared for them, and they were given a bed, and Spotted Dog was also given a bed. They were then served the finest food and drink. They had a wonderful time and they spent a few days in the castle. And King Mekabron didn't know where they were. He figured that since Spotted Dog had not found Bovo, he must have returned to his own country. So the king sent out other men to hunt Bovo down, and the king proclaimed that whoever found Bovo or Drezne would be rewarded with mercy as well as a lovely gift.

One day, Bovo went hunting in the forest with Spotted Dog, and they passed a peasant who was chopping wood. Upon sighting Bovo and Spotted Dog in the forest, the peasant went to Mekabron and told him that Bovo and Spotted Dog were in Lord Urian's castle. When Mekabron heard this, he was delighted and he said: "Today they won't be able to escape my clutches!" And his drummers summoned all his men, some twelve thousand, to his court.

They rode out and besieged the castle on all sides, and they beleaguered it for a long time, unable to do anything. Mekabron said: "I can't do anything, so I'll let them starve to death! Maybe that will make them surrender!" But it was no use his talking. The castle had enough provisions for many years to come.

Now after besieging the castle for many months without gaining ground, the king took one of his men, late at night, and reached the castle, where Urian was sleeping. The king shouted: "Lord Urian! Come on out! I want to discuss something with you in secret!"

Urian came out on the wall and he said: "Who is the person calling me?"

And Mekabron said: "I am King Mekabron. I have to talk with you in a place where no human can find us. If you obey me, I will make you very happy. You know very well that you rebelled against me when you took in the travelers. Hand them over to me, and I'll forget about your rebellion. I'll even give you an entire city."

But Lord Urian said: "My dear King Mekabron, I wouldn't hand them over to you, even if you gave me all your countries! For it would bring me everlasting shame and sin if I were to take their lives. So King Mekabron, please leave here immediately! If I shoot, I might kill you!"

And King Mekabron dashed back to his tent. And when he reached his tent, he scattered lots of money for surviving the arrows that Lord Urian had shot at him.

One day, Spotted Dog said to Bovo: "My dear brother, why should we keep sitting in this castle as if it were a dungeon? Let's fight King Mekabron! Why should we be scared?"

And Bovo said: "I like what you're saying! Let's leave the castle and fight King Mekabron!"

And Lord Urian said: "I'll take my men and fight the king too!"

And they strode out of the castle, and Spotted Dog led the way, followed by Bovo and Lord Urian with his forces.

Now when they left the castle, they found King Mekabron's gigantic army. Spotted Dog shot his arrows, and the king's army shot arrows back! And Bovo likewise shot countless arrows. And when King Mekabron saw that many of his men were being killed, he was furious, and he himself joined the fray with all his strength, and he was as hard as iron. And alas for Lord Urian, the king stuck his lance into him! And the lord fell off his mount. And he started to yell at Mekabron:

"Don't kill me! I surrender!"

And Mekabron ignored those words, and he said: "I'm taking you home with me, you evil man! You have to be hanged!"

When Bovo saw that Lord Urian had been captured, he fought harder than ever! Then Bovo and Spotted Dog realized things were going badly, so they turned around and headed back to the castle with part of Urian's army, and they drew the bridges. And when they entered the castle, a great clamor and lament and moaning were heard, for they thought that Lord Urian had been killed.

And when King Mekabron reached his home, he said: "You are a traitor, you evil man! You think I'll spare your life, but I won't! I'm going to hang you!"

And Lord Urian said: "No, my king, don't have me killed! I'm going to hand you your enemies!"

And King Mekabron said: "No, you evil man, I don't trust you!"

And Lord Urian said: "If you won't believe me, I'll give you both my children as hostages till I can hand over your enemies."

And King Mekabron said: "I'll go along with that!"

And Lord Urian wrote his wife a letter: "God bless you, my dear wife! You must follow my instructions. They plan to hang me tomorrow! So please send me my two dear little children. God will lengthen your life—I just want to see them one last time before my death. I want to hug and kiss them a little. Mekabron has sworn that he will send them back instantly."

The servant took the letter and rode away. And when he entered Urian's castle and delivered the letter to Urian's wife, she started weeping and wailing. Then she summoned Bovo and Drezne and she showed them the letter.

And Bovo said: "How can you refuse Urian? If Mekabron has given his word, he's sure to keep it."

But Urian's wife was furious! And her heart was bursting with all her sorrow! Her two sons then stepped into a carriage, and all the people in the castle were grieving and mourning. But the two children were laughing and singing, for they thought the journey was a major event. And the servant brought them to their father, and Urian threw his arms about them and he hugged and he kissed them.

Now when night fell, Urian turned in with his two children. And at the crack of dawn, he got up but he let his sons sleep on. He then fled to his castle and shouted: "Hurry up! Open the gates! I've escaped from King Mekabron!"

And Urian's wife opened the gates and welcomed him quite graciously. And then she asked him: "My dear lord, where are our two children, whom I sent out to you?"

And Urian said: "My dear wife, it's better for me to live than for our children to live. For if I live on, God can give me more children. But if I die, I can't father any new children."

Now Bovo and Drezne came over, and they were overjoyed that Urian was still alive. And they welcomed him quite graciously, for they didn't know about his evil thoughts and the treachery in his heart.

Urian then summoned all his men and told them that he had made an agreement with King Mekabron to send him Bovo and Drezne; otherwise he would kill them. Then the king would hand over the two children. And Urien said:

"And now, you dear men, please stand nearby, and if I call for you, you must be ready with your weapons. We are going to go into the chamber where Bovo is sleeping. We are going to kill Bovo and send Drezne alive to King Mekabron."

And Urian's men said: "We'll follow your orders. It's because of Bovo and Drezne that we've been besieged for such a long time, and we're bound to starve to death! King Mekabron is a powerful hero, and if he enters our castle, all of us will die! We'd do better to kill Bovo and Drezne and remain friends with Mekabron!"

Well, the men spent all night preparing, while Bovo and Drezne slept, completely unaware of what was happening. However, Spotted Dog sensed that Bovo and Drezne would be killed for he was very smart, and so he went to the door of Urian's chamber and he heard the lord arguing with his wife.

And she said: "I won't let you kill them in my home!"

And Urian said: "There's no other way!" And he started beating his wife.

And she yelled louder: "It would be better to kill me instead of them!"

Upon hearing those words, Spotted Dog dashed over to Bovo in his chamber and he said: "Get up fast! Urian and his men are planning to kill us!"

And Bovo got up fast! And he was furious. And Spotted Dog pulled out his sword and put it on, and then he went back to the door of the lord's chamber, and he could hear Urian still beating his wife, who wanted to rush out and warn Drezne.

At this point, Spotted Dog smashed his sword through the door and shattered it, and he dashed into the chamber and he said to Urian: "You must die today!" And Spotted Dog killed Urian, and he let his wife keep weeping and wailing. And then Spotted Dog dashed over to Bovo and told him that he had killed Urian. Next Bovo and Spotted Dog hurried to Urian's chamber, where they found some two hundred men wearing armor and raring to fight.

And Bovo said: "By my honor, we've come in the nick of time!"

And they fought and they killed lots of men, and other men fled. And Bovo found an old soldier, who'd been serving in the castle for forty years, and the soldier said: "Mercy, my Lord Bovo! Let me tell you how you can escape King Mekabron and keep him from following you!"

Bovo said: "Talk or I'll kill you!"

The soldier said: "I'll show you an underground cavern ten leagues long."

And Bovo said: "Show it to me!"

The old soldier showed him the cavern, and the entrance door was made of iron. Bovo thanked the soldier, and then he ran and he killed the remaining soldiers. And he also killed the old soldier so that nobody might know about the secret cavern. And some of the men leaped down from the wall and dashed over to King Mekabron and they said: "Bovo has killed Lord Urian and lots of soldiers too!"

Meanwhile, Bovo and Drezne and Spotted Dog mounted Bovo's horse Rendzele, and they fled through the cavern. By now, it was daytime, but Drezne was already in her ninth month, and she didn't have the strength to ride any further, for the cavern was very long. And she asked Bovo not to ride so hard. Next they galloped out of the cavern, and far, far away, they saw a vast forest, and they rode toward it. Upon reaching the forest, they dismounted, and Spotted Dog tore out branches and built a hut. And as they rested, Drezne burst into tears, and she said: "I'll be bearing a child soon, and where can I get a midwife? And I have no sort of refreshment."

And Spotted Dog said: "Stop crying! You've got Bovo and me! You have nothing to worry about!"

And now Drezne's labor began, and she bore a beautiful son!

But the moment the boy was born, Drezne started bawling something awful! "Oh, my goodness! I must have a second baby coming." And no sooner had she uttered those words than she gave birth to a second son. But upon bearing the two beautiful children, she had no sort of refreshment. She lay on the ground and she had nothing to eat.

And Spotted Dog said: "Beautiful Drezne, you have nothing to worry about. I'll find something for you soon."

Spotted Dog rushed out of the forest and he finally saw a beautiful palace surrounded by a large moat, and the drawbridge was down. Spotted Dog hurried over to the bridge, and when the people standing there saw him coming in the distance, they were terror-stricken by his frightening appearance, and they raised the bridge.

Spotted Dog yelled at them: "What are you doing? I'm coming to you as a friend to obtain a little bit of food for my lord and my lady, who have been ravenous for several days now! Why, they are of noble birth!"

However, the people at the bridge ignored him, and they stuck to whatever they were doing. Upon seeing this, Spotted Dog blew up and he yelled at them: "Damn you all! You haven't a smidgen of pity for other people! I've got to get back at you!"

But the people laughed their heads off at him and they said to him: "Well, you don't look like a human being! And we're sure your lord and lady don't look much better than you! Go to hell! You don't have any business here! You'd be better off among your peers!"

Spotted Dog again tried to speak to them in a friendly way: "You should know that my lord is Bovo the hero and his wife is Beautiful Drezne. She has just given birth to twin boys and she has no sort of refreshment. She is starving to death! I'm a human being too, by nature, and I've got a human mind. But I've been temporarily cursed by a witch!"

Still, the people at the bridge paid Spotted Dog no heed. So what did he do? He dove into the water with all his weapons and started across the moat. The people all hurled lots of rocks at him, but he shook them off and kept swimming.

The lord of the palace happened to be standing at a window and he witnessed the whole scene. He then rushed down to the bridge and he said: "Stop throwing rocks at him. Let him join us. Why should we be afraid of him? After all, there are scores of us, and only one of him!"

In short, Spotted Dog swam all the way across the water. The elderly lord, with his countless men and his weapons, went over to the moat. Spotted Dog immediately realized that this elderly man was the lord of the beautiful palace, and Spotted Dog fell to the lord's feet and said graciously: "My lord, you will save the lives of four people if you give me some food."

The lord of the palace asked him: "Who are you, and who are your lord and lady?"

Spotted Dog replied: "My lord is Bovo the hero, and my lady is Drezne."

The lord of the palace then said: "I've heard their story, and now I can believe it."

And the lord allowed Spotted Dog to enter his palace. However, the guest was followed by many armed men, for they were still afraid of him, afraid he might cause destruction. The lord of the palace ordered food and drink for Spotted Dog, who ate like ten men!

[Page missing in Yiddish text]

Spotted Dog went to bed. Then two lions emerged in the forest and they wanted to seize the humans, and the lions ran into the hut. As soon as Drezne saw them, she yelled loudly. But the one lion wagged his tail, protecting her from other wild beasts, and he wouldn't harm her, for she was of noble blood, and no lion can harm a person of noble blood, for the lion is the king of all the beasts!

Now when Drezne had yelled, Spotted Dog had heard her and he was aroused from his sleep. And he saw two lions in the hut, near Drezne, and he was furious, and he grabbed hold of his sword. Now when one lion saw Spotted Dog, he sprang out of the hut! But Spotted Dog whacked the lion's head with his sword, and the lion reared up on his hind legs and began grappling with Spotted Dog. Spotted Dog fought back, and the lion was in terrible danger. The lion then tore a chunk of flesh from Spotted Dog's cheek, and the earth was stained red with blood.

Spotted Dog was even more furious, and he thrust out his sword and he shoved it into the lion's belly. The lion collapsed and he stretched out his four legs and he died. Then the other lion emerged from the hut and sniffed the first lion and saw that he was dead. And Spotted Dog was exhausted and he lay down on the grass to rest a bit. And the lion roared very loudly and he furiously bounded over to Spotted Dog and he started beating him with his tail. Spotted Dog wanted to drive him away, but he was exhausted. The lion was vigorous and he tore and thrashed Spotted Dog, and then he ripped off Spotted Dog's nose and mouth and he dragged him across the ground. And Spotted Dog had no strength left and he couldn't stir. And the lion tore him apart and he didn't eat a bit of Spotted Dog's flesh, for he was sated with blood! And the lion went away.

Now when Drezne saw that Spotted Dog was dead, she wept and wailed and she was afraid that Bovo might likewise have been ripped apart by the lions. Why was he taking so long to return? And she said: "Poor me! What should I do? If I stay here, I'm scared I might get torn to bits by lions! With God's help, I'll wait for my pious Bovo one more day. And if he doesn't come back today, then I'll have to leave this place." And she started weeping and wailing bitterly, and she spent all day lying in the hut with her little babies.

The day waned, and Bovo still didn't return, for he was having massive struggles with wild beasts and dragons. And Beautiful Drezne couldn't catch a wink of sleep all that night, and she rose at the crack of dawn and she was almost crazy. For she saw that Bovo was still gone. So she took all her belongings to get to court, and she carried one baby on her back and the other baby in her arms, and she loudly wept and wailed, and she said: "May God take pity on us! If I had obeyed my parents, this wouldn't have happened to me!"

And Drezne hurried over hill and dale, and God worked a miracle with her, and she found her way out of the forest. And the babies started weeping and wailing, and all she could do was to cry.

Now as she hurried across the fields, she saw a shepherd far away, and she was overjoyed! And when she approached the shepherd, she said: "Please direct me to the nearest town."

And the shepherd told her where it was, and she thanked him and she entered the town to which he had directed her.

Now from that town she could see the ocean, and she went over to the shore and she found merchants standing there. And she walked further and she saw lots of ships moored there, and one ship bore her father's insignia. And the crewmen were preparing the vessel to continue sailing, and they were weighing anchor and hoisting the mast. But then Drezne called out to the skipper, and four sailors rowed to shore in a small boat, and there they saw a beautiful woman, and they said: "If you serve us, we'll take you along on our ship."

And Drezne said: "Dear friends, take me along, and I'll be your cook until you reach your country."

And the men said: "Come along, and you don't have to worry—you can have whatever you need and you don't have to be ashamed to ask, you can have it all!"

And Drezne climbed into the small rowboat, and they brought her to the big ship, and the sailors boasted to the skipper and they said: "We've gotten a beautiful cook!"

Now the instant the skipper saw her, he said: "This is God's will! It must be Drezne—we've been sailing around to find her! And her father is half impoverished because of her!"

And the skipper went over to her and he gave her his hand, and she was graciously welcomed aboard, and the skipper said to her: "Aren't you Beautiful Drezne? We'll take you with your lovely name! Your father's missed you terribly and he's sent me out to find you!"

Upon hearing that, Drezne started weeping and she started wailing in front of the skipper and she started telling him what had happened to her. And they sailed away from this place, and they came to the country of Barbarye, and they kept sailing until they came to the country of Armunio.

When they reached the harbor, the townsfolk came to view the ship, and

Beautiful Drezne was sitting there with her twins. The townsfolk then hurried over to the king's palace and they said: "Your daughter Drezne is here, and she's come with two babies!"

When the king heard this, he was delighted, and he swiftly mounted a horse and galloped toward the ship, and when he got to the square, Drezne, his daughter, came walking toward him. And upon seeing her and her two babies, the king dismounted and threw his arms around her, and he started kissing and hugging Drezne, and he started weeping for joy!

Then he saw a servant holding Drezne's two babies and the king said: "You have to tell me the truth! Who are these two babies?"

Now Drezne began to cry and she said: "Bovo fathered them, and I'm their mother. But I feel awful! I'm scared I might have lost Bovo. I don't know what to think! I'm afraid he may have been torn to bits by lions, for we were lying in a forest!"

And the king said: "My dear daughter, please listen to what I tell you. Forget about Bovo! And you should remain good and pious and you should remain decent, and you shouldn't do foolish things as you've done up till now! If you heed me, you'll definitely achieve great glory! Why, there are many women who never marry!"

Drezne now told him about all her misfortunes. Next, the king led her into the town, and then a servant carried Drezne's two babies, and she said: "My dear father, the two babies haven't yet been circumcised."

And the king said: "You needn't worry, tomorrow I'll have a big circumcision festivity—God willing!"

The next morning, the king carried the two boys to be circumcised, and he asked Drezne what to call them. And she said: "When Bovo was leaving, he said to me: 'One baby should be named after my father, Duke Guiden, and one baby Sinbald after my wet nurse's husband.' Sinbald was his father's captain."

And the king celebrated a wonderful circumcision, and he enjoyed the praises heaped upon the festivity, and Drezne finally felt truly cheerful, and servants attended her.

> And now let's leave Drezne with her dad
> And write about Bovo, that heroic lad.

Now on the day that Drezne went away, Bovo came riding back, and he saw a lot of blood on the grass and a dead lion off to the side, and he wondered what it could mean. And then Bovo dashed over to the hut, and next to it he found one half of Spotted Dog.

And he looked for Drezne and the two babies, but he couldn't find them and he said: "Oh, me! My heart is so heavy! Wild beasts have torn them apart—Beautiful Drezne and my two darling babies! Oh, me! My dear wife—

what's become of you? There's no woman with a lovelier complexion any-where in the world! And how swiftly I've lost you! What should I do now? Where should I turn? I scarcely had any joy with you! And when I figured I'd escape this misfortune, I suffered a worse misfortune!"

And Bovo knelt down by Spotted Dog and he mourned him and he said: "You dear Spotted Dog, how could you leave me! I never realized I'd lose you so soon—but you were torn to bits by wild beasts! And now today, I'm the most miserable Bovo! For God has afflicted me, and I must suffer it!"

Bovo then dug a grave with his sword and he put in the fragments of Spotted Dog and he covered them with soil and he said: "Since you can't have anything more from me, I have the honor of burying you."

And Bovo was convinced that Drezne was lost. And he said: "Cursed be the day on which I was born!"

Then Bovo saw the ocean far away and he said: "I won't travel across the ocean now for I'm suffering too many misfortunes. Who knows how long I'll have to be on the water? Instead, I'll keep galloping until I find my destiny. If ever I should achieve great honors, then I can properly lose my life on the ocean."

And now Bovo rode off on his horse Rendzele, and tears streamed down his face, and he rode without finding a path or a road, and he encountered all sorts of beasts and dragons, and he had to fight them, and he didn't have even a restful hour, until he reached a town with beautiful gates, and he drew up in front of a tavern.

And the innkeeper was standing in front and he said: "My dear guest! Why don't you ride into my courtyard?"

And Bovo replied: "I'd like to, but I don't have a penny to my name."

And the innkeeper said: "That's no problem! You needn't worry! I can tell that you're the kind of man who repays a loan. You can stay here until the day after tomorrow."

Bovo then rode on into the town and he came to a place where lots of horses were gathered on the sides, and Bovo asked: "What do all these horses mean?"

And the people answered: "A great lord has arrived and he wants to hire lots of soldiers."

And Bovo thought to himself: "That's wonderful. I'm not ashamed. I'll sign up too!"

And he guided Rendzele, his horse, into a stable, and he dismounted, and he ordered a measure of oats for his horse. And then Bovo stepped inside the inn, and he found it chock-full of guests, and they were eating and drinking their fill, and the captain of the guests welcomed Bovo very graciously, and he was surprised how handsome and beautiful Bovo was.

One of the men said: "In all my life I've never laid eyes on so fine and handsome a person! He must be a great swordsman and a great lord to fight with! I'm sure that one of the two great lords who were in the world long ago has stood up!"

And Bovo strutted to and fro in front of the captain. And the captain asked him who he was, and what his nation was, and what his religion was, and what his name was. And Bovo said his name was Agust. And the captain asked him what class he was, and did he want to be a soldier. "If so, I'll pay you a huge salary and I'll put you in charge of four hundred men!"

Bovo then said: "You noble captain, I don't want to turn down your offer. You see, I've come here lawfully to conclude such a deal. Wherever you go, I will go with you, and you should say the same to me."

Well, the captain said: "You have to come to Lepirten with me, to a castle named Shinshumin. There you'll find a wonderful captain named Sinbald, and I'm his son. Now there's a duke who wants to occupy the castle, he resides in Antinne and his name is Duke Doden. The castle is located four hundred leagues from here, and I've promised the populace that I would help my father!"

Now when Bovo heard all this, he realized that it was happening because of him, and he knew that the captain was called Trits; for as boys they had learned how to read and write together. But Bovo didn't let on who he was and he pretended to know nothing about all these things. Indeed, Bovo was delighted and he praised God for the things that had happened to him, Bovo!

Then the captain summoned the innkeeper and told him to prepare the meal and serve him food and drink—lots of courses and fine wines. Bovo sat at the table and gobbled down large bites that would have filled ten men, since he hadn't eaten for several days. And Trits was dumbfounded and he said to one of his men: "I think he's come here solely to stuff his belly, he's been starving ever since he left Poland. But he'd be useless in battle."

Bovo heard Trits's words, but he pretended not to notice them. However, when he finished eating, the men all went to bed, and Bovo shared quarters with Trits. At daybreak, Trits then had the drummers summon all his men, several hundred, to the courtyard. As they started out, some on foot, some on horseback, and Bovo and Trits were armored and saddled, they divided up the soldiers between them. And they galloped swiftly until they reached Shinshumin Castle. Once there, Trits was very warmly received by his father, Sinbald, welcomed with drums and trumpets.

And his father liked all the soldiers but he liked Captain Bovo even more, and Sinbald said to his son: "Dear son, tell me. Why have you been gone so long, and where did you find this handsome captain?"

And Trits said: "He may look fine and handsome, but I think he's a nasty sort! I haven't noticed any hint of manliness on him. I've only seen him eating enough for ten of my soldiers!"

And Bovo heard him a second time and he was furious at him and in his rage went over to Trits and said: "Prove what you've said about me! You wretch! If you're fresh and brisk, we should have a duel! Then I'll show you what I can do! After that, we can be friends! And you can truly love me for the rest of your days!"

And Trits said: "I want to do this!"

And so they rode out to fight on the square, and each of them had four hundred soldiers. And Trits's father reclined in the window to watch his son fight the captain.

And as they fought, Bovo shattered Trits's sword to bits and poked Trits and knocked him off his horse, and Trits fell into the sand. And his soldiers came dashing over and they picked him up to his shame, and he remounted his horse. But he was furious, and so he galloped away from the square, and he said: "I have to hack that wicked man with my own sword!"

And when Sinbald saw that, he acted quickly and summoned both warriors and he spoke amiably to them, and he had them back off from one another, and he said: "My dear friends, you'd do better to live in peace. Then you can occupy the whole world!"

And he told them to be friends again, and the two warriors shook hands and they kissed and swore brotherhood with one another.

And Bovo had changed his name to Agust so that nobody might recognize him, and people called him Handsome Agust.

And since the two warriors were friends again, Handsome Agust said to Trits: "Brother Trits, if you take my advice, we'll gallop out to see what our enemies are doing, and we'll decide whether we can defeat them."

And Trits said: "We'll go there tomorrow!"

Now at the crack of dawn, the drummers summoned all the soldiers to the courtyard; there were some eight hundred men. Bovo and Trits were clad in armor and they rode with the soldiers and they rode until they reached Antunni, when the herders were driving the herds into the fields. The soldiers snatched the herders and the herds and drove them to Shinshumin Castle, and then they informed the townsfolk of Antunni that they had driven away their livestock to Shinshumin. The townsfolk rang the storm bell and raised a hue and cry about the herds.

One man shouted: "My cows!" And another man shouted: "My calves and my sheep!"

The townsfolk all dashed out of town and they sped along like an arrow from its bow. And the men numbered two thousand, and the ruler, Duke Dodon, and his brother, Alberig, and also many powerful champions hurried out to battle, and they were only half a league behind Bovo. So Bovo told his men to drive the herds faster to Shinshumin, while he and Trits halted.

And Agust asked Trits: "Who are the two men who are leading the army?"

And Trits said: "God protect us from those two! The first one is Alberig! He's been helping his brother to fight and to battle! And the other man is my true enemy! He killed my lord!"

And Agust said: "Watch me kill his people clean away!" And clutching his lance, he galloped toward Alberig, and Alberig likewise galloped toward Agust with his lance, and each man wanted to kill the other! But Agust was strengthened by his rage and he shoved his lance into Alberig's belly, and Alberig fell off his horse.

Agust then quickly pulled out his lance and he fought Duke Dodon, who was the actual ruler of Antinne. And both men shattered their lances. And then they drew fine swords from their sides and they started dueling. Now Agost pierced Duke Dodon with his sword, and Dodon fell off his horse. And Agust would have liked to take the duke's life, but so very many of the duke's soldiers came rushing up, and when they saw that their ruler was thoroughly thrashed, they all ran over to Agost and they wanted to kill him. But Bovo was faster and killed lots of those men and fought his way through and rushed away to Shinshumin Castle. And some of the duke's men chased after Agost, and some helped the duke to stand up and they escorted him to Antunni.

And when Agust saw that the soldiers were chasing after him, he and Trits turned around and they fought their pursuers ferociously. But when Agust and Trits saw that they were overwhelmed, they dashed back to the castle. However, the duke's men didn't care to reach Shinshumin. And when Agust and Trits entered Shinshumin, they locked the gates. Their pursuers then turned around and lamented very loudly, but the people inside the castle were delighted.

And Trits said to his father: "My dear father, if you wish to know, Agust fought magnificently. He pierced Alberig mortally and he thrashed the duke and he inflicted so many wounds. What can I tell you? In all my born days, I've never seen such a fresh and strong man as Agost! Praised be God that I've found this hero!" Trits claimed that if Bovo himself had been here, he could have done no better! "Agost really fights like a dragon!"

And Sinbald said: "It consoles me deeply that he will avenge the blood of my ruler, Duke Guidon."

And Sinbald ordered a fine banquet. And many sheep and calves were slaughtered, and the diners ate and they drank good wine. And Sinbald's wife was also joyful. And she brought many girls to the table. And Sinbald told his wife to sit at his side. And Bovo sat opposite her, and she couldn't take her eyes from him, and she said to herself: "Upon my life, I swear that this must be Bovo! He looks just like him!"

And she could hardly wait until the banquet was done. Next she summoned Captain Sinbald to her chamber and she said to him: "I peered into Agust's face and I saw that he must be Bovo!"

And Sinbald said to her: "You're a big fool! Bovo's mother had him exe-cuted. And whenever I think of him, my heart breaks inside me! And that's why I'll fight with Duke Dodon forever!"

When night fell, everyone hurried off to bed. But Sinbald's wife couldn't sleep all that night, she couldn't get Bovo out of her mind.

Now the next morning, she wanted to sit at the table again, and the captain again had her sit opposite Bovo, and she studied him carefully. And she saw that he was indeed Bovo. And she could scarcely wait until the meal was done.

When it was done, she took her son, Trits, and she said to him: "My dear son, I must tell you that your friend Agust is actually Bovo."

And Trits said to her: "My dear mother! That can't be!"

And his mother said to him: "My dear son! Listen to me, and I'll give you some advice! Take Bovo to the bath and you'll learn the whole truth! You see, he's got a sign on his back, a red spot the size of a rose, plus two moles on his shoulder."

And Trits said: "I'll have a look!"

He then went to Agust and said to him: "My dear friend! Let's spend a little time in the bath. We'll drink sweet wine, and I'll have a servant bring us a roast capon."

And Agust said to Trits: "I'd like that!"

And so the two of them went to the bathhouse, and Trits surveyed Agust, and he saw a red spot, just as Trits's mother had described. And Trits said to Agust: "Tell me, my dear friend. Where does that red spot come from?"

And Agust said to him: "I can't tell you. I've had it all my life, ever since my childhood."

And Trits could hardly wait to leave the bathhouse and report back to his mother. And when Bovo and Trits came home, Trits rushed over to his mother, and he said to her: "My dear mother! All the signs you told me about were really there!"

And his mother said: "I swear by my words that I have to be alone with him in order to recognize him!"

Upon seeing Bovo, she hurried over to him joyfully and she hugged and kissed him, and she said to him: "You are really Bovo! I raised you in your childhood and I fed you from my breasts!"

And he said: "It's true! I'm Bovo!" And he laughed and laughed! And he then said to her: "Please keep it a secret! Nobody is to know except for your dear husband and your dear son!"

At this point, Sinbald joined them, and Trits told him the whole story, and they all hugged and kissed each other, and they asked Bovo where he had been till now, and he told them everything.

Now let's leave them in their joy and let's see
What Duke Dodin was doing currently.

The duke had issued an edict summoning all doctors to come and heal him
on pain of being drawn and quartered. Many doctors arrived, but none of
them could help the patient.

So Bovo said to Trits: "God will help me carry out my plan! I'll disguise
myself as a doctor!"

Trits said to Bovo: "It sounds wonderful, and I'll be your attendant!"

And Bovo said to Trits: "This is what I plan to do. I'll go to Duke Dodin
as a doctor and kill him in his bed. Next, you, Trits, will go to all the lords who
loved the old king and you will inform them that Duke Dodin is dead. Then
they will open the gates, and Captain Sinbald will come with his army and
occupy the town and they will shout: 'Long live King Bovo!'"

And Sinbald said: "I like your plan, it's wonderful. But I'm worried that
Trits will be recognized."

And Bovo said to Sinbald: "You have nothing to worry about. I can
prepare a magic powder that will make him as black as coal! And nobody will
recognize him!"

And Bovo prepared the powder with all the elements that the beggar had
taught him. And when the powder was ready, Bovo smeared it with his hands,
smeared Trits's face from neck to eyes.

Then Bovo himself donned a black jacket and a black cloak and a wide
belt with a gold buckle, and he hung his sword Pamele under his cloak, and
he clutched a dulcimer and played it. And Sinbald gave him his own donkey,
and he gave his son Trits a good horse to follow Bovo.

And they soon reached Antuna. And they lodged at the finest inn. And
Trits went to the old lords who had loved the old king, Bovo's father, and Trits
gathered the lords in the courtyard of the inn and he said: "Please observe
silence, and I'll tell you a glad tiding! Bovo, the old king's son, has come back.
And I am Trits, Captain Sinbald's son, and we want to get rid of Duke Dodin,
we want to kill him!" And Trits told them that Bovo was disguised as a doctor.
And Trits went on: "Now I ask you! Do you want to join us? If that's your
goal, then say nothing to anyone. As soon as you hear that the duke is dead,
hurry over and open the gates of the town. One man will then climb to the top
of the wall and blow a horn. And our army is outside the town, and the instant
the soldiers hear the horn, they'll enter the town."

And when the lords realized that this was an excellent plan, they said to
Trits: "We really like your plan. May God help you carry it out, and may you
succeed!"

Meanwhile the townsfolk said that a fine doctor, who could heal any
illness swiftly and quickly, had arrived. Now when Queen Brandei heard about

this doctor, she sent out two servants to him, and they told him that he was to visit the queen tomorrow; and if this doctor healed the king, he would never again have to worry about material concerns.

Bovo could hardly wait for the dawn. When daylight emerged, Bovo and Trits went over to the royal palace, where the king was lying. And when Queen Brandei saw Bovo in the distance, she hurried toward him and she received him tearfully and she said: "My dear doctor, if you cure my king, I'll share all my possessions with you, even my own person."

And she took Bovo's hand and led him into the palace. But Bovo turned away from the queen, for he had been nurturing his anger at her for a long time. She then took him to the king's chamber, where he was lying in bed.

Bovo then said to the king: "Your gracious majesty, please tell me why you are so ill. Show me your symptoms, and don't worry, I'll heal you in no time. But I want to see your wounds. You'll have to strip naked, so I can examine them. Please tell everyone to leave—I can't stand having others present."

So the queen and all the courtiers were to leave the chamber, and Bovo bolted the door, and the king wasted no time, he exposed his wounds, and he said: "My dear doctor, I'm so sick! Only the Good Lord knows if I'll recover!"

And Bovo said: "My dear king, tell me how it all began, tell me how the fighting ran."

And the king said: "It's an old fight, it's been dragging on for a long time. But if God helps me recover, I'll end the war. However, there's one man I can't endure! He inflicted these wounds on me and he also stole a lot of my livestock! He must be the devil himself!"

And Bovo said: "Maybe he's the old king's son and he's avenging his father's death!"

And the king said: "Nonsense! He lost his life a long time ago! His mother did away with him a long time ago!"

And Bovo said: "Look closely at me. I'm Bovo! It's not enough that you murdered my father, the old king! You also want to murder me! I won't spare you! I think I can pay you back—and right now!" And Bovo took his sword Pamele and chopped King Dodon to pieces!

Now Bovo had avenged his father's death, and when Trits found out, he dashed about and he killed the ten guards on duty. And Bovo took Dodon's head and slipped it under his jacket, and he and Trits then left the palace. And Trits hurried over to the old lords, who had reached an agreement with him, and he told them to climb up the walls, and the horn was blown, and meanwhile the gates were opened. And Captain Sinbald went into the town with a thousand armed men, and they all shouted together: "Long live King Bovo!" And they fought in the town for twenty-four hours, until they occupied the entire town, as was proper! Now when Bovo saw that the town was occupied, he proclaimed that every man should lay down his weapons, and that the fighting was over, and Bovo ordered the burial of Dodon's remains. Well, the townsfolk heeded Bovo in every respect, and they welcomed him with open arms and obeyed him with great honor.

Then his mother, Queen Brandei, came over, and she expected mercy, and she fell to his feet, and she wept and wailed, and she said: "My dear son, I'm in your hands! Do with me whatever you like! It's true that I committed injustice! But I beg you: Forgive me! I'm your mother after all! Please spare my life!"

Bovo was so furious that he was unable to reply! But her weeping penetrated his heart, for she was his mother after all!

And Sinbald said to her: "Remember what you did! You had your husband killed! Then you wanted to have your own son killed! You deserve to have your head chopped off and dragged through the streets by your hair! But because you're Bovo's mother, you'll be spared and locked up in a convent!"

And Bovo sat down on the royal throne, and Sinbald and his son, Trits, remained at his side.

Now one day, Bovo was playing checkers with Sinbald, when a letter from Babylon arrived, and the letter contained lots of news, including the news that King Suldan, the father of Beautiful Marguerite, had died, and that she was all alone. And, she went on, the king of Sealand was trying to drive her from her country because he wanted to marry her! "And since I've heard that you, the noble King Bovo, have attained great honor, I am writing to you to come and help me and to show your loyalty for helping you when you were my father's prisoner. And as soon as you've driven away the invader, I agree to become your wife!"

Well, Bovo was very frightened by what he read, and he then handed the letter to Sinbald. And Bovo said: "I mustn't desert her, I have to help her! For she stuck to me in my misery. If not for her, I would have died!"

And Sinbald said: "It's only fair, we have to help her!"

And Trits then joined them and he agreed with Bovo!

And Bovo said to Trits: "You have to go there with me, and I'll make you the captain there over all the possessions. And meanwhile, Captain Sinbald, I have to leave my kingship in your hands, you have to govern my land in my stead."

Sinbald said: "You needn't worry! I'll take care of everything!"

And King Bovo had the drummers summon his army, and then King Bovo and Trits mustered the men. And the army was divided in two parts: one half under King Bovo and one half under Trits. And off they galloped to Babylon, and they took along a lot of food for the entire route.

And when they came toward the town of Babylon, King Bovo sent out two messengers, who were to ride in and inform Beautiful Marguerite that Bovo was arriving with his army. She then gathered her two thousand men and they waited for Bovo to appear.

Now when Bovo reached the outskirts of Babylon, he found the huge army of Sealand besieging the town and he attacked them. And countless men died away on both sides of the fray, and the armies did fight all through the night, and the day was dawning.

And King Shishmonim said: "I'd love to know who these men are and where they're from!" And he rode at the head of his army. But then Trits came riding over, and both men lunged with their lances, and they fought for such a long time that their lances shattered. So they drew their swords, and each man refused to flee! And King Shishmonim struck harder, until Trits began to weaken. But then Bovo came charging on Rendzele and he thrust his lance into King Shishmonim, and the king fell from his horse, whose name was Tirkeles. And the horse dashed off and it galloped away from Bovo, and it galloped into Bovo's army, and Bovo caught the horse.

And when King Shishmonim's men saw that their king was dead, they retreated, and Bovo chased after them and he killed a lot of them, and many of them sprang into the ocean, hoping to swim away. But they failed and so they drowned.

Now when Bovo and his army had defeated the enemy army, they joyfully galloped into the town, and Marguerite and her lords came toward them and bowed and scraped to them, and she said to Bovo: "You have shown me great friendship today. And now, my dear Bovo, if you desire them, all my possessions and my entire treasury are yours!" And Marguerite ordered a banquet and she showed more gold than other kings and queens showed iron.

And when the meal was over, all the lords went to bed, and Marguerite sat next to Bovo, and she said to him: "Do you remember that my father tried to talk you into leaving your faith? And you refused to listen to him! But today, if you take me as your wife, I will accept your faith."

And Bovo said to her: "If you convert to my faith, then I will marry you. But we have to wait for four weeks. That will give me time to invite many rulers and also lords." And Bovo and Marguerite shook hands, and they kissed each other, and then each retired for the night.

The next morning, Bovo ordered his servants to proclaim and to blow trumpets, inviting all the lords and rulers, both local and foreign, to attend the wedding. And messengers went to foreign countries, seeking guests far away. And Babylon was filled with great joy, and people danced and pranced in the streets, and all the bells were rung.

> And now let's leave them in their joys
> And see about Drezne and her two boys.

Well, Drezne was living with her father, and she heard about the great honor bestowed on Bovo after he killed his stepfather and became king of his country. And Drezne also heard that Bovo was to marry Beautiful Marguerite,

King Suldan's daughter, and that many lords and kings were going to the wedding, and they were very merry!

And Drezne said: "I won't allow it and I won't keep silent! I've got to reach the celebration in time! But my father mustn't find out, he would never let me go there!"

Meanwhile Druzne had learned how to play the dulcimer. And Bovo had taught her how to make the magic powder that the beggar had taught him how to make. Druzne prepared some powder and rubbed it into her neck and her face and she put on beggar's clothing and she set out with her two children and with her dulcimer hanging at her side, and she mounted a mule and traveled for a long time, until she saw the town of Babylon in the distance.

She then said to her children: "You'll find your father in this town!"

And they rode into the town and they fetched up at the finest inn, and the innkeeper asked her where she was from, and Drezne said to him: "I can be found at the wedding if I can make some money. I can play the dulcimer and I can sing with my children."

And the innkeeper said: "That's very good! You can earn a lot of money here!" And he ordered food for her. Then the innkeeper said: "Please sing something!" And she sang him a ditty. And her children helped her, and she also played her dulcimer.

The next morning, Drezne stood under a window of the palace and played her dulcimer very sweetly. And she sang a song she had composed about Bovo and Drezne and King Mekabron and how Bovo and Drezne had camped in the forest, and how she had been separated from Spotted Dog, and how Bovo had dealt with her.

Now when she'd sung her song, Bovo lay in the window, and he said to his servants: "Take the woman upstairs and serve her food and drink! I want to ask her where she's from and where she learned that song!"

When the servants came for her, she hurried away and she did say: "He doesn't need to give me anything!"

And Bovo heaved a great sigh for her and he pondered: "Perhaps Drezne is alive and well! The song appears to say as much!" And his servants hurried out to find the beggar woman, but they returned empty-handed, and they told Bovo that they couldn't find her. Bovo was terrified, and his heart was very heavy. Bovo and his men sat down to eat, but he was very concerned.

The next morning, Drezne adorned herself beautifully in garments embroidered with gold threads and precious stones, and anyone who looked at her was astounded. And Drezne put red velvet jackets on her children and brushed their hair as if it were spun gold. And she said to her children: "Go to the king in the royal palace, and if he asks you who you are, tell him that you don't know either, and that you've never seen your father. You don't know whether he was devoured by wild beasts. And your mother has told you to give him this ring, so that he'd remember everything." And the children went over to Bovo and bowed to him.

And Bovo asked them: "Who are you and who are your father and mother?"

And the children answered him: "We've never seen our father, and we don't know whether he was torn to bits by wild animals, and our mother is at the inn. And she told us to give you the ring so that you'll remember everything."

And Bovo took the ring and he recognized it and he said: "Upon my word! I gave this ring to Drezne." Bovo took the two children by the hand and he said: "Show me your mother!"

The children were delighted and they said: "We'll show you our mother!" And the children returned with many servants.

Now when Bovo approached her, he saw that she was very elegant and he said: "Praised be to God, for I have seen my Drezne again and she's alive!"

And they hugged each other joyfully, and she kissed him in front of the others to see! And Bovo said: "I thought that you were dead! But now, with God's help, I can see you alive once more!"

And Drezne said: "Dear Bovo, you don't have to be ashamed of me! You can take me back, you see!"

And Bovo said to her: "Don't worry! I'm your husband certainly!"

Then he took his two children and he hugged and kissed them. And he told them he was their father and he took them for a stroll in the palace.

Now when Marguerite was told about this turn of events, she was horrified and she fainted dead away. And Bovo revived her and he said to her: "You must be patient, and I'll give you some good advice. I'll grant you my dear friend Trits for a husband. He's just as good as I am."

Marguerite said: "I'll be satisfied so long as he takes me."

And Bovo straightaway sent for Trits and had him sit next to Queen Marguerite, and he told them to join hands. Next, Bovo had Drezne don the finest garments, and they had a wonderful wedding, and it lasted several days. And Drezne enjoyed herself with Bovo, and Marguerite with Trits. After the wedding, Bovo helped Trits occupy many towns that had belonged to King Suldan. And Bovo and Druze asked Marguerite's permission to go home again.

And Trits and the queen said: "May God remain with you and may God prolong your lives, for you helped me out of my dreadful situation!"

And Bovo ordered the trumpets to be blown. And Trits and Marguerite escorted Bovo and Drezne for two leagues, and they then said farewell, and they hugged and kissed, and they wept and wailed very loudly. And Trits and Marguerite now turned back.

And Bovo and Drezne returned to Antune with great pomp and circumstance. And Lord Sinbald welcomed them and he asked Bovo about Trits,

Sinbald's son, and how he was faring. And Bovo told him about all the things that had happened to them, about how his wife and children found him. And Trits had taken Queen Marguerite, and had become a great king, and now they led a good life together.

And Sinbald said: "That's good for my old age, and I will lead a splendid life!" And Sinbald returned Bovo's kingdom to him. And Bovo sat on his royal throne.

Then he went to help his father-in-law. He was fighting a battle with Mekabron, who wanted to conquer the land belonging to Bovo's father-in-law. And Bovo killed Mekabron and conquered his lands. Some time later, Bovo's father-in-law passed away, and Bovo took over his father-in-law's possessions, which included three kingdoms. And he gave each of his sons a country with lots of money and treasures.

And Bovo and Drezne were very pious in serving God with all their hearts.

Well, you dear people, now you can see the difficulties endured by Bovo and Drezne, and God helped them. And nobody should despair of God's help. And God should also help us out of our difficulties. And we should look forward to the coming of Elijah the Prophet, and may Salvation come swiftly and in our time.

Amen and let that be God's Will.